EDEN CHRONICLES: BOOKS 1,2,3

2021 EDITION

JAMES ERITH

COPYRIGHT

For Charlie

Eden Chronicles started out as a story for my Godchildren:

Isabella, Daisy, Archie, Iso and Ernest.

EDEN CHRONICLES BOOK-SET 1; BOOKS 1-3

POWER and FURY

SPIDER WEB POWDER

BLABISTERBERRY JELLY

by

JAMES ERITH

CONTENTS

BOOK ONE - POWER & FURY

JAMES ERITH
EDEN CHRONICLES

POWER
AND FURY
BOOK ONE

ONE

THE ROUTE TO SCHOOL

Archie's cupped hands cascaded cold water onto his face, the shock waking him. Wincing, he touched the mark, the nerve endings raw and sharp. A quarter of an inch, perhaps, as neat as a red underline.

The blade!

Memories rushed in. Archie stared at the rouge on his fingers, mesmerised, and rubbed till the stain cleared.

It can't be. His initial reaction.

How come? His second.

Archie crashed into the wall, then righted himself and spewed into the toilet.

Why? Why me?

He heard the others, but their words died before his brain could register what they said. He tried to speak, but the sounds reverberated back, spiralling as if he were in a tunnel.

In the kitchen, the sink and table spun around the room, along with the outline of his sisters and Mrs Pye.

Tinkling glass? Raised voices?

Grabbing a jacket, he weaved to the door. He needed to breathe, clear his head. He needed to run.

Archie tore across the courtyard to the track and cut down towards the river. He hurtled along animal tracks, weaved through long grass, leapt over fallen branches, jumped foxholes, and untangled brambles from his clothes as he ducked, crashed, and sped through thickets and bushes.

In the semi-darkness beneath the rusty canopy, he approached a huge round boulder three times his height. In his mind's eye he measured the distance and set off at a sprint. At the last moment, he sprang up and grasped hold of a stony outcrop just high enough to haul him to the top. He sat down and reached into his bag, drank from his water bottle, and swirled the liquid around his mouth.

Breathing hard, his heart thumping in his chest, Archie watched the sun rise like red-hot coals burning under the base of the vast black cloud jettisoned above.

He'd dreamt repeatedly that he had to do something horrific, something beyond imagination.

But why him?

Then, last night, he'd met a ghost.

And it really had happened.

He fingered the nick on his chin. How else could he have received such a neat cut?

He stared out over the valley, his eyes drawn to the candy shapes in the village of Upsall, perched just above the floodplain at the foot of the Yorkshire moors. He noticed the rugged, menacing, dark forest and jagged rocks that jutted out of the steep slopes like gnarled, angry faces. In contrast, manicured, cartoon-coloured, stripes of light and dark green highlighted the school playing fields on the valley floor.

Man's doing down below, he thought. *God's above.*

More questions crowded his brain.

What if he didn't survive? What if he couldn't find the stupid cave? Who was this ancient woman?

The ghost said it would return. It didn't mention a time, or a place, only that it would be back. Soon.

Great.

Archie cast his eye over the large old oaks that marked the position of the meandering river. To him they guarded the village like sentries positioned at perfect intervals. Upsall looked stronger, and more important, than the old, monastic-looking school buildings whose distinctive, high, square tower rose up into the heavens. It felt like a perfect contrast to the river curving elegantly in front.

In the distance, the soaring cliffs protected the village like a shield. He saw how Upsall had fostered a sense of security with its toffee-coloured chunks of masonry and loophole arrow-slit holes. Balancing this were subtle lines of symmetry; the intricate round, rose window pixelated with stained glass resting above a meaty, carved oak door.

Right now, he needed a shield of his own. But where would that come from?

He looked to his right towards the sheer rock face that climbed high above him, dwarfing all things below.

No eagles. No hawks or harriers circling or soaring like model aircraft.

He listened.

Strange.

An almost intolerable silence.

He flicked his wrist, glanced at the dial and sighed. If he didn't get a move on, he'd be late again.

Standing up, he extended his arms wide before sliding down the stone curvature and tumbling over and over until he collided with the thick trunk of a larch.

Archie brushed himself down, feeling a multitude of soon-to-be bruises birthing in the tissue under his skin.

Then he heard the noise, a rustling of leaves close by. A mild thrashing sound followed by a soft thumping, just beneath him down the slope.

Archie readied himself to run when he heard a yelp.

He reached in to the brambles and looked over the bank into the bushes below.

'What are you doing here? You shouldn't be in the forest, not a little leveret like you,' Archie said, his eyes fixed on the scared animal. The baby hare thrashed harder, rearing up and trying to get away only tying itself up more.

Archie held onto a branch, lowering himself into the brambles.

He spoke evenly hoping it was soothing enough not to frighten the creature even more. 'If I don't get you out, you're going to be the easiest meal old Mr Fox ever had. You mustn't go crazy. Understand?'

Even if the leveret had no idea what he was talking about, speaking to it felt like the right thing to do and Archie watched calmly, never taking his eyes off it, as the leveret once again tried to break free.

Exhausted, the baby hare soon fell to the ground. Archie noticed how its chest pounded from the exertion.

Unpicking several brambles caught in his clothes, Archie sneaked closer, the leveret's large brown eyes studying his every move. Archie reached down. Both hind-legs, as he suspected, were bound by thorny tendrils, an ugly gaping gash prominent on its hind-leg.

'You poor thing,' he said. 'Here. I'll cut you out... if you'll let me.' He hoped the animal understood.

With great care, Archie reached down and stroked the leveret behind its ears which were tucked flat into the animals head.

Archie pulled out his penknife and, keeping the blade out of sight, moved it towards the leveret's snared legs knowing full well that a sharp kick might damage both of them.

When the barbs were free, Archie noticed the cut was deeper than he'd previously realised and, instead of dashing off at high speed the leveret lay still.

'You can't stay here, little hare. You and your family belong up on the ruin or on the playing fields. Get away. Run off to your nest or wherever you want.'

Archie sensed the hare was somehow waiting for him. He leaned down and petted it again. 'I think I'll call you Rocky, little hare. I might have to carry you.'

Archie gathered the leveret into his arms carefully tucking-in its legs but cradling the animal's body all the same.

Ripping his jumper and shirt on every conceivable variety of thorn, Archie fought his way onto the makeshift path and from here he weaved through the undergrowth towards the silver band of the river that cut through the red and yellow apron of autumn leaves towards school.

Archie walked as fast as he dared along the towpath, over the bridge, and onto the playing fields. As he neared the chapel steps, he caught his breath.

Isabella saw him coming and ran over to intercept.

'Where have you been?'

'In the forest.'

'That's an understatement. Most of it's on you.' Her face twisted. 'And what is that?'

'Oh. This is Rocky. Rocky's a leveret. I found him trapped in the bushes on the way down—'

'Archie! Not another animal. You've got to stop this insane wildlife rescue mission crusade. It's becoming a joke.' She looked at him. 'You look a wreck.'

Archie shrugged. 'It wasn't my fault. I fell over a couple of times and I couldn't leave Rocky. It's a baby—'

'I don't care,' she stormed. 'Put that fluffy thing down and get inside!' She stopped and crinkled her nose. 'Oh my Lord! You stink, and you're covered in blood,' she said. 'Actually, you can't go in there.'

Archie scratched Rocky's head, moved to the side and set the leveret down watching it limp away. Archie stared at it with a smile on his face. 'I hope he'll be all right.'

'It's a hare, Arch.'

'Actually, technically it's a leveret.'

'And the smell?'

'Big deal, Bells. It could be Rocky, or I might have landed in something.'

'Archie. Go home and change. You're so embarrassing.'

'No way,' he replied defiantly. 'I want to know if Daisy made the team. It's unmissable.'

He pulled a sock up for her benefit, wiped his brow with a cuff and lamely brushed himself down. Then he sprinted towards the chapel door, Isabella chasing behind, slipping in moments before the door boomed shut.

He ran, head down, almost bent over double, across the flagstones until he found his row, squeezed in to his class position, and sat, conscious that others were almost certainly staring at him.

Further along, he noticed his twin, Daisy, chatting animatedly to her friends, others turning off their phones. He caught her eye.

She frowned back, and mouthed something at him.

Was it about the team?

She jabbed a finger.

Or about him? Was she having a dig as well?

He smiled back, weakly, and put his head in his hands.

For a brief moment, he experienced the intrusion of being watched, similar to the sensation he'd felt the previous night with the ghost. His instinct was right. On the platform at the far end of the hall stood Mr Solomon, the headmaster, whose eyes bored into him like lasers.

Archie's heart sank. Those who had even the tiniest scuffs, or tears, or missing buttons, were being entered into his dreaded red book. Maybe Isabella's warning wasn't so petty after all.

He gave himself a quick once-over. Utterly appalling. He had about three-seconds to get up and sneak through the side entrance.

Instead, he grappled with his tie, drew up his socks, and dragged a hand roughly through his hair, removing the tendrils of a creeper, several strands of grass and a piece of bark. Then, before he could tidy himself further, a familiar voice boomed through the hall.

'Good morning, school,' it said. 'Please rise.'

TWO

THE FATE OF WORLDS

With a tiny flash, a dreamspinner, spider-like in form with a delicate, smoky textured outline that melted into the atmosphere around her, uncurled from a fiery, electric blue midriff known as an "maghole".

Genesis stood on six long, thread-like, spidery legs and looked out over a desolate landscape through ovate black eyes. A soft wind brushed through her.

She sniffed at the stale air and remembered how, long ago, grasses, trees, and beasts filled the pink, green, and ochre-coloured landscapes of the planet of the Garden of Eden.

Carpeted in spiders, this area of the Garden of Eden had been a vast area of mixed terrains filled with insects and spiders, known as the arachnid lands.

Dreamspinners had harvested spider webs in these lands and from these spider silks, they had fashioned dream powders, or dusts, and turned them into dreams of love, kindness, and inventiveness. Dreams crafted for all living things.

These lands, though hostile to most and rarely visited by other species, had been bountiful to dreamspinners and beneficial to all living creatures, notably humans.

On this exact spot, an area had once been cleared and a tall, open-roofed structure had been hastily constructed. Its outer perimeter was like a giant wooden palisade, and from afar it looked like a fortress with outer walls high enough and thick enough to shield it from the lurking eyes and ears of the tallest and craftiest of beasts.

Genesis remembered how the Council of One Hundred had debated the fate of the worlds around a huge circular table made from one slice of the trunk of a pink mammoth tree. Here, the humans and animals and trees had argued and raged before finally putting their differences to rest.

Nestled on the rim of her mother's electrical midriff, Genesis had sat in the sky above the Council, invisible to all except other dreamspinners, bathing in the warm blue energy currents that splayed over her, watching the drama unfold below.

She recalled the desperate faces of the Founders of the Garden of Eden as they listened the charges against them. These five, four men and a lady, moulded by the irresistible energies of the universe, forged in birth from the collisions of sand and water and gas at the very beginning, were found to be guilty of corrupting all life.

The Founders had yearned for forgiveness, demanding an end to magic, begging them to find a way of destroying their immortality. They did not seek pity, just atonement for their part in the destruction. Tears had rolled down their cheeks, Genesis remembered, as they accepted their punishment; all bar one.

That man was Cain, from the planet of Havilah. Cain, who threatened to freeze every human being on Havilah if he was burned. Cain, whose light blue eyes exuded a dark, menacing power, and who held a magic beyond that of others. Cain, who felt his fate did not justify his actions.

Genesis uncurled a long leg, turning the tip into a needle and then a pincer before dipping it into her fizzling maghole, feeling the soothing mass of energy swirling within. The old memories were returning.

Cain had delivered on his promise.

The moment flames had licked at his flesh, his spell cast all Havilarian people into domed, crystal-like puddles exactly where they stood.

And now, devoid of form and starved of magic, Cain—to this day—had never been able to turn the Havilarians back.

Genesis had often watched the Frozen Lord, as he was now known, roaming his palace as a burnt spirit. Always looking, never giving up his futile search to find and restore his power. A desperate hope burned from within his spirit-shell, although, as millennia after millennia wore on, she'd noted how his vibrations had moved to frustration, and then to anger.

Genesis glided like a ghost, her limbs floating on particles of air. At the top of the great stone she stared over the wastelands of the desolate planet.

Strange how events had turned out.

The world of the Garden of Eden in front of her devoid of life, while Havilah, not even visible as a pinprick in the sky, was starved of people. All the while, Earth had trudged on, oblivious to the planets they had yet to discover, oblivious to the wars which had destroyed so much and oblivious to the machinations of the other worlds.

For this reason, dreamspinners were deeply associated with Earth. Nothing thrilled Genesis more than to sneak away and watch a human dream. It thrilled her to see how they twisted and reacted, how the dusts filled them with hope and creativity and gave their world meaning.

And, now, as if out of the blue, the mysterious energies of the universe had reawakened.

The inscription on the huge rock beside her had the instructions.

Genesis held her old, wiry legs out into the sky, scanning for vibrations, for *answers*. There was no point in denying these forces, these changes.

The fate of dreamspinners, the destiny of animals, plant life, and every living being on Earth was about to rest in the hands and minds of three humans under the protection of Adam, the elder of the Founders.

When Genesis gave the final part of the Tripodean Dream known as the Gifts of Eden, these three humans would be named as the Heirs of Eden. They would have seven days to fulfil their tasks and demonstrate the success of the current human race.

Fail, and all life on Earth would perish.

A new epoch would begin.

Now, only two parts remained to be given.

THREE

GOOD AND BAD NEWS

Mr Solomon patted the breast pocket of his coarse tweed suit and raised his thick eyebrows. Twenty-five years he'd been at the school, almost to the day. Twenty years as headmaster, and his performance every morning was the same now as it was then.

'Quiet... please,' he said.

Wasn't it strange, he thought, how noise levels always seemed to rise as conversations rushed to a conclusion?

He removed his glasses from his round, ruddy nose and inspected the students.

'Thank you. Sit down.'

Two hundred and seventy-two pupils parked on the hard, wooden benches lined up row upon row, the noise whispering into the safety of the huge, vaulted ceiling above. From weighty cross-beams, large chandelier lights dangled from thick, black metal chains, illuminating those below with a dim, almost church-like glow.

From their tall portraits on the sides, former headmasters eyed this generation of children sternly. While etched onto dark wooden panels running around the perimeter of the hall, the names of former scholars, captains, and musicians reminded the children of past glories.

Solomon stared out over the throng and cleared his throat.

'School dress!'

Archie audibly groaned. He had a strong urge to disappear.

'I see some of you shaking,' Solomon said, smiling and staring around the room. 'And rightly so,' he continued. 'Standards have deteriorated since the beginning of the term. After leave, those who fail to comply with every part of the school uniform code will discover the joys of detention. Now, to show you what I'm talking about, no one is quivering more this morning than our school goal-keeper, Archie de Lowe.'

A cheer went up.

'de Lowe, please be upstanding.'

Archie sat stone-still in disbelief.

Not again.

He felt a jab in his back and another from the side.

'Come on, Archie. Up you get.'

Archie regarded his worn shoes, and, taking a deep breath, rose from behind the significant frame of his friend Gus Williams. Every single pair of eyes stared at him. Archie heard girls giggling nearby. His face reddened, the heat of his blush growing by the second. He didn't dare look up.

'Archie, I really do hate to make an example of you,' Solomon continued, 'but this morning you have beaten your spectacular record of being a total and utter shambles.'

Cautious laughter flittered around the hall.

'It is almost as if you fail to realise that a dress-code actually exists. In fact, you are almost the perfect example of how not to appear in school.'

The head addressed the assembly once more.

'Let us take a closer look at our specimen. His shoes are filthy; he has no belt and, as a result, we can see rather colourful underwear. His socks are around his ankles because there are no elastic garters holding them up, and even these are torn to bits—like everything else.'

Solomon paused as laughter pealed into the rafters. 'His shirt has a button missing, his tie is halfway across his chest and, I'm not sure how this happened, but he appears to be wearing the wrong coloured jersey! Please turn around, de Lowe.'

Archie shifted.

'Yes, just as I suspected,' Solomon continued. 'Blazer ripped and, of course, his hair is not only too long, but a decent imitation of a mop head.'

Archie feigned a smile while others pointed and grinned.

On Solomon's instruction, while hopelessly attempting to pull his attire together, Archie sat down and glanced up towards his sister, Isabella.

Her hard, cold stare drilled into him. He spotted her grinding her jaw.

Never a good sign.

Solomon's tone softened as he smiled, showing his small, tea-stained teeth.

'Is there a reason for this mornings astonishing mess, Archie?'

Archie ran a hand through his hair, removing a burr. 'I, er, well, yes, sir.'

'And?'

'I found an injured leveret, sir, in the forest. Its legs were trapped. I carried it down—'

'A baby hare, trapped in the woods? An unlikely tale, de Lowe, as hares live in open land. Furthermore, they are not creatures one ordinarily carries about.' He paused for effect. 'You do come up with the most hare-brained schemes.'

The other teachers laughed politely. Students groaned.

Archie bowed his head.

'Hare or no hare,' Solomon continued, 'let this be a lesson to you all, not just you, Archie. Today, and today only, and because you are a key part of our famous football team, you are excused. And this, of course, leads me on to the other main item on this morning's agenda.'

With these words, the mood in the hall lightened as if a gust of fresher, happier air had blown in. The noise level increased.

Along the row, nibbling her nails, Daisy stared at the floor.

The headmaster raised an arm for quiet.

'Most of you are aware of the situation. As a small school, our selection for teams is limited and I regrettably endorsed that a girl could play in our boys' team. As you know, this team has gone on to great things to the tremendous credit of our school. However, we… were found out.'

The headmaster pulled a letter from his breast pocket and waved it in the air.

'Let me interpret the relevant parts of this communication I received yesterday from the president of our Football Association.'

He nudged his glasses onto the bridge of his nose and thumbed his way down the page.

'What they are saying, is this: if Daisy de Lowe has played in ten matches in a row this season, they are willing to be lenient. Well, anyone, has she?'

He spied a hand from the back.

'Yes. Sue Lowden. Do you have the answer?'

'Daisy's played in twelve, sir. Thirteen if you add the German team.'

'Thank you, Miss Lowden.'

A buzz moved around the room.

'*It is our opinion,*' he read, '*that Upsall School has taken advantage of the goodwill of our league. However, until we received an anonymous letter highlighting the anomaly, not one opposition team reported or noticed Miss de Lowe's disguise.*'

A hissing noise developed and several heads turned to the right.

Mr Solomon continued, this time up a gear.

'*Our decision is this,*' he read. '*Should Upsall School win, then, with the full backing of the Football Association, Miss de Lowe will be allowed to continue playing for Upsall*

School boys and the regulations across the county will be changed with immediate effect—'

Cheers filled the air.

'However,' Solomon said, and he raised his hand for quiet, *'should Upsall lose,'* and here, his voice went so quiet, *'then it will be Miss de Lowe's last game for the Upsall School's boys eleven.'*

Solomon picked Daisy out of the assembly and spoke directly to her.

'So, there we have it, Daisy. I have spoken with the authorities to make sure we completely understand this ruling. You will play in tomorrow's boys final against Sutton. Lose, and it will be your last game for the school until we have enough girls willing to play in a girls team. I hope that moment will not be too far away.'

Daisy nodded back.

'Very good,' he said. 'Regardless of the outcome, this doesn't mean your sporting career is temporarily over here at Upsall,' the headmaster continued, as a smile slipped onto his face.

'No, no, no! Not by any means. It would appear that your exploits on the soccer field have been "talent-spotted".' Solomon's eyes sparkled. 'After half term,' and here he slowed, using every ounce of his experience to engage the assembly, 'you have been invited to join the England ladies national training squad.'

Gasps shot out from the assembly floor.

'Yes, yes, I'll repeat it again. The England squad. It is a terrific honour that you've been picked to train with your country, the youngest player ever to be invited. Daisy, we are extremely proud of you.'

Applause rallied and Solomon let it continue for its deserved time.

'There we have it, Daisy. There's plenty for you to look forward to after half term,' Solomon said. He crashed his hand down on the lectern, making the juniors in front of him jump.

'But let's make sure that we jolly well win, so we can change these silly rules forever!'

Kemp watched as Daisy headed down the assembly row. As she neared he thrust out a leg stopping her in her tracks. Shrugging, Daisy promptly kicked his shin hard enough to hear a whimper.

'I only wanted to say congratulations,' he said, rubbing his leg.

'Yeah, right.' Daisy sneered, looking up at him. 'You've never congratulated anyone on anything, have you Kemp?'

'I meant it,' he said, hurt.

'Sure. If you really meant it,' she whispered, leaning down, 'you'd give me a kiss.'

Kemp almost toppled over the back of his chair. 'Jeez Daisy, you're weirder than both of the other two—'

'You're referring to my brother and sister, Kemp?'

He flushed and blustered. 'Yeah. I mean, no. Oh heck—'

Daisy tousled her hair and pouted. 'Don't be a shy boy, Kemp. I'm waiting.'

Kemp tried to pull himself together. 'No way. I wouldn't kiss you if you paid me—'

She smiled at his deep discomfort and whispered. 'Know what, bad boy, I sooo think you're on to me.'

Kemp reddened and his nose expanded sideways, incredulity sketched on his face.

A bellow of laughter came from big Gus Williams listening to every word in row behind. 'Daisy,' he said. 'You are totally hilarious. Forget this loser, if it's any consolation, I fancy you!' he flashed his friendly, toothy smile at her. 'I'll give you a kiss!'

'Yes, I know you would, Gus,' she said, as an entourage of fans approached. 'Thing is, you like everyone. Hey girls,' Daisy said, pointing at Kemp's red face. 'Look! And all I wanted was a kiss!'

Daisy winked at both the boys before being whisked away by the giggling, chatty crowd.

Gus turned to Kemp, his large eyes bulging with excitement.

'Kicked by a girl, but not kissed by a girl, Kemp. That's not right for a tough boy like you?'

'You're asking for it, Williams,' Kemp spat.

'Anytime,' Gus replied, his voice levelling. 'Happy to oblige, whenever you've got a minute. Just you and me, Kemp.'

FOUR

ASGARD UNDERSTANDS

Asgard the dreamspinner sat alone, floating, watching planet Earth spinning, as it always did.

Every so often a tiny burst of light, invisible to other creatures, flashed for a nano-second. He mused that he was not the only dreamspinner taking time from dream-giving to reflect upon Genesis's extraordinary news.

Asgard noted Earth's moon rising in the near distance against the endless expanse of space.

Twisting, as if his legs were made of rubber, he dabbled several slender legs in his maghole, enjoying how the warmth from the blue electrical field bathed them.

Was there still a need for inspirational, magical dreams? Dreams that offered insight or inspired change or for dreams that prompted love and joy?

Asgard cranked his small, round head, and stared at a distant star, as he replaced one leg in his maghole with another.

Their purpose as dream-givers would not end simply because no *joyful* dreams remained. So long as *any dream* were given, he reasoned, from *any* powder blended from *any* spider's web, surely the dreamspinners would continue to have a purpose? If dreams were nightmares, at least the dreamspinners would exist to knit and spin them?

This, he realised was the choice.

He thought of the boy. The boy who knew nothing.

What had fate in mind for him, and his sisters? Immediate death?

It was clear that Adam had failed in his task to nurture and train the Heirs of Eden, if indeed these three children *were* the Heirs of Eden.

Even Genesis could tell Adam was no longer the man he once was. The old man's sharp mind was but a shadow. Earth had drowned him in a pool of denial and apathy.

Asgard had tried to explain to Genesis that it must be a mistake. But the elder dreamspinner would not listen. Genesis had swept aside the doubters and told them that the words on the great stone could not be twisted.

He'd visited the monolith to see them for himself. And it was exactly as Genesis said:

The three Heirs of Eden of the human race are those who live under the protection of Adam on Earth.

They alone must receive the Tripodean Dream.

But the Heirs of Eden were children!

If they didn't die at the very first hurdle it would take them seven years, not seven days. If these children were the measure of life on Earth, then perhaps the planet deserved its outcome.

Maybe Adam was in the wrong place, caring for the wrong people.

Asgard noticed a pinprick of yellow light coming from a spot on the Moon's dark surface. The birthing of dreamspinners, he realised, hatching from cocoons in caverns dotted around the universe. More dreamspinners, to nurture, guide, and instruct in the art of dream-giving for the booming populations on Earth.

Asgard reached into his maghole with one hand and weighed up his last dream dusts from the planet of the Garden of Eden. Forty dreams, he estimated; more if he thinned them out. But did he really want to dilute such precious cargo?

Asgard flashed out of his maghole, landing in a huge cavern. He hovered in mid-air, extended his legs wide and switched, by thought alone, out of his invisible mode.

Suddenly, a flurry of activity appeared, like magic, in front of him. Dreamspinners dashed here and there across the sky, blue flashes denoting the arrival of some, the departure of others.

He turned his wiry neck upward towards the roof of the cave, and found it packed with yellowy-brown cocoons stacked in layer upon layer like the neat chambers of a beehive.

Walking across the air, he passed younger dreamspinners, who turned or bowed their heads in a sign of respect for their Elders.

He noted a flash next to him and turned.

'Gaia,' Asgard said, her fingers vibrating together so fast as to form words. 'I see you.'

'And I you, Asgard,' she replied, her vibrations softer. 'You have come to see the birthing of young dreamspinners?'

'By their movement, the time is close,' he said, indicating lines of dreamspinners perched in the air. 'Many crowd the chamber.'

'It has always been so,' Gaia replied. 'They are our future. But what kind of future do we leave them?' her vibrations dimmed. 'Have you heard who the Heirs of Eden are?' she said.

'I am aware that they are young. But, of course, this is nature's will—'

'There!' cried a voice. 'See! The sun is nearly in line with the entrance.'

A sudden flurry of activity began, with blue lights flashing everywhere. Asgard and Gaia were almost blinded as dreamspinners flashed into the chamber, unfurling from their magholes and into their visible forms as they did so.

The entire cavern buzzed with excitement.

From the cocoons high above, one chamber wriggled and shook more violently than before. Then another, and, before long, multiple cocoons along the length of the huge ceiling rattled, cracked, and split, exposing tiny dreamspinners.

Then, the entire ceiling seemed to open up like popcorn and before long, the tiny, stick-like creatures flapped about like new-born chicks, clawing at the air as if swimming in a thick soup.

The onlookers, dreamspinners of all shapes and sizes, vibrated words of love and encouragement.

'Fall! Jump into the light!' said a youth nearby, as thousands of shells cracked apart, sections of their nests spiralling to the ground like loose strands of straw.

To the mock-horror of the crowd of dreamspinners, the tiny creatures began to fall, plummeting head over heels towards the rocky ground beneath them. A collective gasp shot out.

Asgard noticed how Gaia covered her black eyes.

As they fell from the dark roof into the bright sunlight, a sudden bolt of yellow light flashed in, enveloping the first hatchlings in circles of iridescent light, stopping them exactly where they were.

Then, as if a firework display had gone into overload, the remaining hatchlings tumbled through the air and into the light. As the energy bathed them these fledglings were now dreamspinners; borne of light and energy, ready for a life of giving dreams.

Asgard too, vibrated his feelings, offering the newcomers strength, love, and a long life.

The energies of creation, he mused, were always beautiful.

He was about to flip into his maghole when an idea of immense magnitude slipped neatly into his mind. Picking his way across the sky, he leaned into the jagged rock-edges of the huge cavern, out of sight.

This last Earth night, he'd taken Cain, the Frozen Lord, to see the boy. Initially, he'd gone to ask the spirit what he thought about having children as Heirs of

Eden. After all, if anyone could remember and comprehend the tasks ahead, it was, he suspected, Cain.

Asgard recalled how he had flipped out of his maghole into the main chamber of Cain's old sprawling palace that stretched above the face of the canyon. The way the building overlooked the ruddy, sandy-coloured rocks reminded him of a beast who had sucked the life out of the city below.

He'd looked over the once bustling rock city of Havilaria, capital of Havilah, and its renowned stone formations and, even for a dreamspinner, the dramatic cityscape, with its huge craggy buttes that soared into the air like icebergs, and the deep canyon that circumnavigated it, filled him with wonder. He remembered how the cacophony of noise had once risen up from the narrow streets, and how the rock faces above were perforated with neat, square holes of ancient dwellings that had once sparkled with a million candles in the moonlight.

Now, the only sounds were echoes of squawks from the large birds, redundant from their past lives of flying people from one great rock to the next, who now inhabited roof tops, their wide, messy nests formed from debris and branches plucked from the river. The city's once celebrated house-caves were overrun with creepers and the diamond, ruby and emerald stones—found naturally in the rock —was now covered over by dust, forgotten and unloved.

Asgard had picked out Cain's low vibrations and talked to the ghost who'd answered in a brusque, hostile, and bitter manner. Later, in return for information on the forthcoming trials of the Heirs of Eden, Asgard revealed the dreamspinner's secret of the maghole, and when Cain realised how the maghole might transport him, the former Founder's mood lifted.

Asgard told Cain that three children were the Heirs of Eden and the ghost had thundered that this was impossible. He demanded to go directly to the Heirs of Eden to see the boy for himself—through his maghole.

Not long after this, Cain, the blind spirit, had faced the Heirs of Eden and stood in front of the Heir the humans called Archie.

Asgard needed to think.

Turning invisible, he flashed his head through his maghole, sending him in an instant to his favourite place miles above the Earth.

As he hovered in space, he remembered how he'd watched the ghost, Cain, produce a knife and flick the boy's chin. Watched how the ghost had marvelled at the spot of blood.

And all the while, the boy's eyes bulged. Disbelieving.

Cain had a kind strength ordinary ghosts did not possess. The way he could carry objects for a certain length of time, pull things, lacerate with a small blade.

But an idea had nestled into his mind and it had refused to budge. And now, as he floated alone above the blue and white orb below him, he considered it deeply.

What if one of the Heirs of Eden might somehow ally with Cain? Perhaps with this boy Archie?

Why did this sound so right and yet feel so horribly wrong? The more he dwelled on this idea, the more excited and more fearful he became until he realised he knew exactly what he had to do.

Asgard sensed his maghole expanding as the enormity of his mission dawned upon him.

After eons, the dreamspinners, the most lasting species created at the dawn of time, would no longer be neutral in the ways of the universes.

But it must be done, for the benefit of all.

FIVE

KEMP'S STORY

Archie draped an arm around his twin Daisy. 'What was that about—with Kemp?'

Daisy ran her hands through her hair. 'Oh, nothing. Just teasing him about being a pillock.' She smiled cheekily at her brother and sighed. 'Why does Kemp hate me so much?'

Archie rubbed his freckled nose and laughed. 'Because he's jealous of you. And because you booted him off the team. And I don't think he knows how to talk to girls.' Archie pondered this for a second. 'Or boys either, for that matter.'

Daisy shook her head. 'He was always giving away fouls and kicking people... and that was last year—'

'He's like an elephant who never forgets—'

'Well, he's ridiculous,' she complained, 'elephant or not.'

Archie grabbed his sister playfully by the waist. 'Strange thing though, you know, the way he looks at you,' he said, smirking.

'Never! Although I did ask him for a kiss—as a joke! Gus thought it was hilarious.'

Archie grinned and glanced over to the far end of the hall, where Kemp was talking to his friends. They locked eyes for a moment, then Kemp reached into his pocket for his mobile.

Archie turned back to his sister, concerned. 'Big mistake to kick him. You know, other people do actually feel pain in their legs, even if you don't—'

'I wonder,' Daisy said, staring airily into the distance, 'would Kemp even know me if I didn't play football? I mean, is there another side to him? How did he end up being such a knob?'

Archie shrugged. 'Kemp's OK. He's got problems—'

'Yeah, right. Tell me about it.'

'I'm serious. He told me about it in a session of detention.'

'I don't believe you.'

'It's true. He made me swear never to tell anyone.'

'Well, go on, then,' Daisy urged, nudging him. 'Tell me.'

'I can't, Daisy, it's a secret.'

'Don't be silly,' she implored. 'Why do you always do exactly what you're told? He told me his friends are going to kick the life out of me.'

'It's still a no,' he said. 'Do you understand what having a 'secret' means?'

'Of course.'

'That's why I can't tell you.'

'*Yes*, you can,' Daisy insisted. 'For curiosity's sake, and because it's sometimes wiser to know your enemy better than you know your friends.'

Archie wavered for a second and shook his head, even if Daisy did have a point. 'Sorry.'

'*Pleeease*,' Daisy begged.

'No.'

'*Pleeease*, Winkle.'

'God. Okay,' he sighed. 'As long as you swear you absolutely won't tell anyone. And don't call me that name.'

Daisy wobbled her head inconclusively.

'I mean it,' Archie said, 'don't breathe a word.' He eyed her carefully. 'If he finds out he'll rip off my arms, suck my eyes out and give them to Isabella on a stick.'

'Yeah, yeah. All right. Not a soul. I promise.'

'Okay,' he began, reluctantly, wondering how he'd given in quite so easily. 'The thing is, Kemp's parents died very suddenly when he was little. He never talks about it. And now he lives with his aunt, who he can't stand. There—'

'That's awful,' Daisy said, her eyes wide. 'How?'

'What do you mean... how?'

'Did they die?'

'Oh, I see,' he said. 'One night, driving along in an open-top car way up on the edge of the moors, they hit something, a deer, a fox—no one really knows.' Archie's voice turned to a whisper. 'The rest is properly grim.'

'Go on,' Daisy said, her eyes bulging with excitement.

Archie looked over his shoulder, and noticed Kemp exiting at the far end of the hall. 'Apparently, the car skidded off the road, smashed into rocks and plummeted into a ravine where it blew up. Charred, disjointed remains were found scattered much later.'

Daisy whistled. 'Jeeeeez! I can see why he doesn't want anyone to know.'

'There's more.'

'Is it worse?'

'Yeah. I suppose,' Archie said. 'It took days before the car was found. And when they did, they discovered the bones of only one body. They reckoned the other one was eaten by something.'

'No! That's terrible,' Daisy said, staring at the floor. 'You like him a bit, don't you?'

'Yeah, apart from when he's a jerk to you two.'

'Well then, Archie, come on, tell me more, I mean he's probably organising my death right now.'

Archie ran a hand through his hair. 'Beneath all that macho stuff he's quite soft —it's a barrier he puts up to protect himself, well, that's what his shrink says—'

'*Shrink?*' Daisy blurted. 'He has a shrink?'

A few heads turned their way. 'Yes, shrink, psychiatrist, whatever—keep your voice down.'

'They're not doing a particularly good job.'

Archie shot his twin a look. 'Tell me about it. He seems to snap in and out. I mean, in detention, when he said all this, he cried buckets and went on and on about wanting a normal life with a normal family. And then he thumped me really hard on the shoulder and ordered me not to tell anyone. Remember that massive bruise I had when I said I'd fallen out of a tree?'

'Oh yeah, I thought that was a bit odd.'

'I couldn't move my arm for a week,' he said, rolling his shoulder in its socket. 'He's sad, bored, and to be honest, lonely. Everyone hates him, and he knows it.'

'Even his sidekicks Jackson and Pulse?'

'Those freaks pretend they're best mates, but it's fear that glues them together. Ever seen how they jump to attention when he's around or their heads get cracked? One moment he's charming and funny, the next he's pure evil. It's like a switch flicks in his head—and he's strong for his age—the only boy who can match him is Williams—'

'Yeah, I noticed sparks flying between them earlier,' she said. 'But, Arch, why does Kemp like you?'

'Because,' Archie said, raising his eyebrows, 'I'm probably not worth beating up. And because I don't deliberately *piss him off.*'

Daisy thumped him playfully on the arm. 'He's a loser, Arch. Why doesn't he try being nice for a change?'

'Apparently it's something to do with offloading emotional pain. That's why Solomon and the teachers leave him alone so he can do what he likes; they're terrified he'll go even further off the rails. I mean, think about it, if our parents got killed we'd probably go a bit nuts, although to be fair,' and he pinched Daisy on the cheek, 'you're almost there.'

She smiled, sarcastically. 'Our parents are never around, so it's almost the same thing,' she said, a frown slipping onto the corners of her mouth.

Archie was glad that he wasn't the only one who missed them. 'Are you sure you're all right, you know, about the match?'

'Yeah,' she said. 'Thanks, Arch.'

'It's great news about the England call up. Nothing less than you deserve,' he said, smiling earnestly at her. His voice croaked. 'There is another thing,' he said. 'Do you remember,' he began cautiously, sensing his moment, 'anything about your nightmare last night?'

'Which one?' she said too quickly.

'Put it this way, you woke me up.'

She looked confused. 'Did I? Was it loud?'

'Yeah! The entire Vale of York are probably queuing up outside ready to beat you up. You screamed your head off—I thought you might remember, that's all. Wondered if you were okay?'

She shook her head. 'Now you mention it, I did have a nightmare about being in the middle of a storm.'

'And that's it?'

'And finding three tablets in a cave lined with totally random pictures.' She pulled a face and laughed. 'Crazy, huh? If I'm honest, it's a bit of a blur.'

Archie reeled. His face dropped. Eventually, he spoke. 'But nothing about me and, perhaps, the small matter of a murder?'

'Seriously? A murder, Arch?'

'Sure?' Archie reddened.

'Nah, Don't think so. Why?' she thumped him playfully. 'Was that scene this morning something to do with this? Mrs Pye's furious with you. And as for Isabella... So, tell me, who've you been bumping off?'

'It's not like that,' he replied, struggling to explain it. 'You see, I've had this recurring nightmare...' Archie petered out as if was too painful to broach.

'Actually—' she started, tentatively.

But Daisy was interrupted by the figure of Mr Solomon blocking out the light. 'Daisy, Archie, there you are. Now, where is that sister of yours?'

'Over here,' Isabella said, rushing towards them. 'Been showing my project to Mrs Douglas. Tuns out she doesn't know the slightest thing about paleomagnatism.' Her eyes rolled up as if reaching for the correct term.

'Her grasp of the matter is remarkably *loose*, to say the least.'

SIX

ASGARD'S PLAN

Asgard flipped into his maghole, arriving in the next moment on the planet of Havilah.

Wasn't it strange how all the inhabited planets had once been so similar, but so utterly different? How Assyria and Cush had been vibrant places bathed in a richness of plants and sparkling seas, living mountains and animals, content both on land and in the seas' great depths. And how Earth had embodied a range of more static options. The trees whose roots remained fastened to the soil, the mountains who moved like sleepy tortoises, and sands which lay flat and lifeless on the ground.

Then there was Havilah. In every corner there were marvels of nature: towering rock formations in vivid blues, reds, and sparkly whites. Moving forests with colour-co-ordinated trees, and luminescent sea waters. Not to mention the rivers that defied gravity and ran, like snakes, above the land, or the snow and rain that covered the rock cities in multi-coloured droplets like confetti.

Asgard remembered the golden ceiling and the glittering chandeliers that sparkled so brightly that people dared not stare long at them. He remembered the windows cut from jewels and the polished floors made from intricate patterns of coloured gemstones and shaded timbers. The wall of rock that made up one entire length of the palace, with clear, sparkling waters washing down one side like a waterfall.

Now, a veil of grey dust and grime smothered it like a thick blanket.

The dreamspinner walked through the air feeling for Cain's vibration. Soon,

Asgard found himself facing a huge piece of furniture with hundreds upon hundreds of drawers lined up row after row in neat columns.

A drawer opened nearby, its contents spilling through the air and spreading over the ground.

It was Cain, searching through his vast stores of precious stones and jewellery, looking for his branchwand.

'Who's there?' Cain called out. 'Which rapscallion of a rascal is it? I'll have you. I'll have you right and proper when I find it.' Another drawer dived through the air, splintering on impact, diamonds splaying into the dust. 'Because, thief, when I get my branchwand back, I'll have just enough magic to turn you into a vile piece of slime.'

Asgard materialised above Cain's head, his opaque outline shimmering, his blue maghole spraying from his midriff.

Cain sensed it. 'Who are you and what do you want? I may be blind, but I see things. Do not underestimate me.'

'It is I, Asgard, the dreamspinner.'

'The dreamspinner, again?' Cain said at length. 'Well, well, well. You have returned. It is lucky I am blind so I cannot see your ugly body.' He floated a little further down. 'All this exertion exhausts me.'

'You talked with the Heir,' Asgard said. 'What do you think?'

Cain sniffed the air. 'I do not believe those weak humans on earth are the Heirs of Eden. They are children. They have no magic, nor do they possess a sense of nature. IT IS WRONG!' he yelled.

'It is true,' Asgard replied.

'You jest, dreamspinner! Tell me, foul sorcerer of dreams, who are the real Heirs? Where are these men who are blessed with power and incantations? Huh, tell me?'

Asgard plucked his way across the air in silence and then spoke. 'Those protected by Adam become the Heirs of Eden, even if the old wizard has forgotten it. It has always been so. I have seen the writing.'

'That's as may be,' Cain snorted. 'It was a foolish idea. You wish to tell me something else though, don't you?' he asked.

'On Earth, the clouds are building, Cain, the sky is darkening—'

Cain went quiet. 'Then you do not lie,' he said, his voice barely above a whisper. 'While I am stuck here alone in this empty, dying land, the planet of the Garden of Eden may be reborn and inflict more useless creations on the worlds. It is diabolical—'

'I come with a suggestion,' Asgard cut in. 'The final part of the Tripodean Dream will soon be given—'

Cain roared as two drawers flew out at the same time, sailed through the air and joined the heap of smashed wood on the floor. Cain peered through the debris in silence.

'They will not succeed,' he said, softly. 'They require wisdom, strength and cunning—decades of learning and years of understanding charms. The must have attained physical training to the highest degree. But these infants are less than twenty years old. They do not even understand what is shown to them in their dreams. Is that right, dreamspinner?'

'Yes.'

'Then they will never make it past the storm.'

'It is my conclusion, also,' Asgard said.

'And what of Adam?'

'He has grown old. He remembers nothing,' the dreamspinner said. 'Earth has mellowed him. He may be more of a hindrance to the Heirs, than a help.'

Cain groaned. 'So, ugly creature, why have you returned?'

'I can aid you,' Asgard answered, his fingers vibrating the sound. 'The time for change is now.'

'You have my ear, dreamspinner.'

Asgard took his time. 'The supply of dream-powders from the Garden of Eden stored in the great Atrium have ended. Now, we knit and spin from powders made from spider webs on Earth and Havilah.'

Cain sounded genuinely surprised. 'Dreamspinners have stored dream-powders from the Garden of Eden for all this time?'

'Yes,' Asgard replied. 'These are the dream-powders that nourish us and the creatures we give them to.'

'And so, by taking me to the boy, you gamble that they will fail?'

'I do,' Asgard replied. 'To me, their failure is as clear as air.'

Cain sighed. 'What can I do? I was cut down from being a warrior, an artist, a lover, and a ruler to a restless spirit with the strength of a faun,' Cain moaned. 'Yes, I have way more sway than those vile ghosts I see from time to time, but I have neither eyes for magic nor enough physical strength for a fight. You have a plan for that?'

Asgard paused. 'I will tell you more of dreamspinners—'

'Oh why not!' the ghost replied, his voice laced with sarcasm.

'If a solid being,' Asgard continued, 'of flesh and blood travels through our maghole we may suffer to the point of death.'

'What is your point?' Cain shot back.

'You are not a solid being,' Asgard responded. 'You are a spirit.'

'Yes, yes. Why repeat yourself? It is how you took me to the boy.'

Asgard paused and then signed again rapidly, his slender claws flashing in the air, humming.

'What if you were to absorb a human body?'

Cain paused for a beat. 'Ugly dreamspinner, how would this be in any way possible?'

'Dreamspinners know that if a human was to freely and willingly offer its body to a spirit, there is not a law in the universe that says they cannot both be connected.'

'Ha! You talk piffle of a bygone age.'

'I do not jest,' Asgard replied. 'A merger would give you substance. You would move with purpose. You would have strength. You would be able to see.'

'Intriguing,' Cain mused. 'Get a human to absorb into me? I have never considered it. Why have I not known about it?'

'Because, Cain, this feat is not easy to accomplish—'

'Why so?'

'For many humans, ghosts do not exist. Furthermore, apart from you, spirits are weak. They have no desire for life. They move quickly to the other places.'

Cain let out a frustrated groan. 'But, dreamspinner, in a physical sense, how might this actually happen?'

'A union cannot be forced,' Asgard said. 'It must be the true will of the person of flesh.'

'I see,' Cain said. 'It isn't exactly the most ideal of negotiating platforms, is it?'

Asgard dipped a long almost icicle-like leg into the blue, radiating hole of his abdomen.

'As the storm approaches, you might try and form an alliance with one who realises that there is no further hope. One who might dream of a future elsewhere.'

'That would be possible?'

'Yes. For humans, life on Earth is cherished,' Asgard said, his vibrations softening. 'Better still would be an alliance with a child.'

'A human child?' Cain spat.

'Indeed. But you would have to offer something great in return. Something almost greater than life.'

Cain circled the dreamspinner. 'Your words are clever, you strange, vile-looking, dream-giving creature,' Cain crowed. 'But if I was to merge with human flesh, wouldn't it curtail my movements to travel through a dreamspinner? And then what?'

'I am unsure. It has never been tried. Yoking with a large human may harm,' Asgard said. 'Though a child, perhaps, might only wear us down, over time.'

'You're thinking of the boy you took me to?'

'That boy, exactly.'

'An Heir of Eden?' Cain chuckled.

'He is one of the three.'

'Oh, but can you imagine it?' Cain said. 'Stuck on that dead-end planet of Earth, harnessed to a revolting child.' He sighed. 'But then again, an Heir with me... in harmony. Do other dreamspinners know?'

'I am alone, for now,' Asgard said. 'But dreamspinners will rally to me when they learn the path I have taken. Dreams must always be given.'

'Indeed, I imagine they will flock to you,' Cain said, clapping his hands together, although being a ghost it made absolutely no noise.

SEVEN

A WORD FROM THE HEADMASTER

'A quick word, if I may,' Mr Solomon said, his voice kind and his manner fatherly but firm. He looked them over sympathetically. 'It pains me to say this, but this morning I received a communiqué from your parents who are somewhere in the Middle East. They will not be back for the football or indeed for the whole of half term.' He scanned their sad faces. 'It appears they have discovered something of great interest.'

Archie and Daisy exchanged glances.

'What does it say—what are they doing?' Isabella asked, and she attempted to read the headmaster's notepad upside down.

The principal folded the pad into his midriff. 'Well, it's light on actual detail, which, given the circumstances is the very least you deserve. To be honest, I'm not at all happy about it—'

'But we have—' Isabella started.

'Yes, I know you're fortunate to have your caretakers at Eden Cottage,' the headmaster said, 'but this is the third time I've had to reprimand you in the last two terms. Your parents have an obligation to you and this school beyond the callings of their work, regardless of their fame and regardless of their accomplishments in archaeology. What if your caretakers should suffer a heart attack or a seizure or a fall?' he continued. 'Then what would you do?'

The children stared at the floor.

Isabella finally broke the silence. 'Sir, Mrs Lowden's brilliant at helping out; I'll ask her tonight.'

Mr Solomon nodded. 'Very well, but before you go, Isabella, I'm going to entrust you as the eldest to take a letter back to your parents. Collect it from my office before you go.'

He cleared his throat and turned to the twins. 'I have given you some simple homework over the break. Please, at least, give it some effort, especially you, Daisy. Your academic record is nigh on appalling, so I'd like you to do some reading on this topic and then reflect carefully on it—preferably before you dream up some hare-brained scheme,' he smiled badly at Archie, 'that gets our animal lover here battered into little pieces.

'In Chapter Four of your textbook there is a particularly valuable resource for your essay after half term entitled, *"Did God create the universe, or did the universe create God?"'*

Then, in one movement, as though suddenly aware of the time, Solomon straightened, and looked over the top of his half-moon spectacles. 'Now, for good-ness' sake, over this half term, behave yourselves, children; I cannot and will not have the police and Social Services chasing us around with your parents nowhere in sight. Please do not run into trouble. Understood?'

'Yes, sir,' the children said in unison.

'Excellent. Very best of luck with the football tomorrow morning. There will be a big crowd cheering you on and several members of the press. The circumstances surrounding this game, and the fact that the final involves our rivals has caught the imagination of the entire region.' He darted a look at Isabella. 'Best behaviour, please. Now run along.'

Archie and Daisy scampered off down the corridor, the noise of their footsteps echoing off the old sandstone walls. Mr Solomon mumbled something about the time and, as he turned, saw Isabella lingering.

'Excuse me, sir,' she said.

'Yes, Isabella,' the headmaster said, impatiently. 'What is it now?'

'Well, it's the weather, sir.'

Solomon sighed. 'Yes, what about it?'

Isabella hesitated. For the first time in her life, her brain had jammed. 'I've made a weather barometer,' she finally spat out.

'Yes, congratulations on your skilful endeavour,' he replied. 'Mrs Douglas noti-fied me. And, atmospheric pressure isn't even on your syllabus—'

'From my readings,' she began, 'there's going to be a simply massive—'

'Storm?' Solomon interrupted with a wry smile. He bent down a little. 'Well, I'm pleased that your readings match up with the area forecast, but I don't believe there's anything to fear. A bit of rain and some thunder perhaps. As a precaution, do remind your class to take their umbrellas and waterproofs as I mentioned in assembly.'

The headmaster scratched his chin and smiled at her. 'While you're here, let me remind you that it would be a terrible idea to race on to the pitch again. Please leave events on the pitch to the referee and other officials—whatever the circumstances.'

Solomon smiled in a false, head-masterly way and straightened.

'I expect nothing less than immaculate conduct, Isabella. There will be drastic repercussions if you brandish that temper of yours again.' He paused for effect. 'Do I make myself clear?'

Isabella nodded.

'Good. Now, I really must fly,' he said.

That girl was one of Upsall's finest ever pupils. Making barometers in her spare time, for fun. He'd never have dreamt of doing such a thing, nor would ninety-nine per cent of pupils they'd ever had at the school. He liked that. And he rather liked the fact that she wasn't afraid to confront anyone who laid a finger on her brother and sister. And now that he thought about it, there were a surprisingly large number of incidents.

Well, it was perfectly sweet of her to try and warn him, but he had a leaving party and other pressing matters to attend to. Nothing would stop his celebrations, certainly not a little storm and a warning from a pupil with a homemade air-pressure contraption.

Sue looked up as Isabella opened the door. She noted how, when her straight brown hair hung like a curtain over her forehead, it made her look slightly older. She was frequently told how similar they were and the joke went round that they were more twins than Archie and Daisy, who looked nothing like one another.

They were alike in so many ways: top of the academic pile, both enjoyed intellectual challenges rather than sporting endeavour and their features were remarkably similar: Isabella with straight mousy hair, Sue wavy mousy hair. Both had narrow faces, straight noses and brown eyes, although Sue's lips were fuller and her eyebrows finer.

But Sue's appearance turned heads—she exuded sex appeal—and she looked after herself, her clothes and hair had a sense of style, whereas Isabella had a nerdy more academic air and her clothes often sat on her like cloth sacks. Isabella regarded boy's general infatuation with Sue as a complete waste of time.

'What's up now?' Sue said.

Isabella's scowl had pulled her brow over her nose as though it were held by an invisible clip.

Isabella slumped into a chair. 'You won't believe what I did,' she began. 'I told Solomon there was going to be a massive storm.'

Sue gasped. 'You did what?'

'I told him about the barometer.'

'Are you insane?' Sue said, turning a little red. 'I hope you didn't tell him it stemmed from my dream?'

'Of course I didn't!' Isabella said, holding her head in her hands. 'It was so embarrassing—he said he'd seen news of the storm on the forecast. I mean, what was I thinking?'

'I can't believe you did that,' Sue said, draping an arm around her and trying hard not to smile. 'But at least you tried.' Sue ran her hand over the scientific instrument her friend had made. 'Maybe your barometer's faulty—perhaps the calibration's wrong?'

'It's not possible,' Isabella said, frowning. 'Every time I reset it, exactly the same thing happens.'

'Well, please don't spend too long fiddling with it,' Sue said. 'You've got to watch the football tomorrow. It might be Daisy's final game. In any case, I'm required to keep you under control after last week.'

Isabella felt a burning sensation filling her cheeks. 'I know, I know. Solomon reminded me. But I just don't seem able to help myself—'

'Well, you must. You can't verbally abuse the referee and then get yourself manhandled off the pitch, screaming like a loon. And you've done it twice.' Her eyes flashed at Isabella. 'You'll be expelled if you're stupid enough to do it again.'

'But Daisy gets kicked and flattened more than anyone—'

'I know,' Sue said, 'but she doesn't make a squeak. It's a mystery she makes it through week after week and continues to smile as if nothing happened. It's half the attraction—what makes her unique. And the fact that she's a footballing genius.

'You need to do the same and control that temper of yours.'

EIGHT

CAIN WONDERS

Cain realised the dreamspinner had disappeared by the instant lack of the strange, intense energy they emitted.

He made a mental note to remember how the buzz tickled his aura.

For the first time in an age, Cain had a sense of urgency and energy about him. But he worried that he had confused this sensation with frustration, or, perhaps, trepidation?

Did the dreamspinner not understand how incredibly difficult it would be to succour a child to become a part of him? To the common eye, he was nothing more than a sad old ghost. Would an Heir of Eden do such a thing? And, in any case, why would *any* human child willingly give themselves over to *him*?

Cain hovered to the floor and lay back. He marvelled at the idea of being a little bit whole, a fraction human. Even partially flesh and bone and blood so that he might walk, dance, and maybe even see?

Was it truly possible?

His thoughts returned to the boy.

What had made him nick his cheeks with the knife? Was it the thrill of leaving Havilah or the desire to see if he could use his sixth-sense with the human form? Or was it a tiny piece of revenge?

It was a stupid thing to do, though, and he knew it. How would the boy trust him again, willingly, when he'd already violated him?

Cain threw himself at the door, flying straight through. He arrived in the old walled courtyard, scanned the area and hovered through it, dust puffing meekly to the side as he went. Cain located his thin cane and tapped it over the ground. Moving in a straight line across the yard he touched on a lump, like a large, over-turned saucer stuck down with glue.

Cain sighed and knelt down.

'Hello, young one,' he said. 'One day soon, you, and all my people will once again see the beautiful world of Havilah all for yourselves. The moons, the sky, and the court of the castle. You will breathe the air and taste the honey of our bees. And, one day, when you are bigger, you'll drink the wines from our vines and press the flesh of others.' Cain grinned as his mood changed. 'And you will sing and dance and fight and love. Just as I once did.'

'But, alas, as I have told you a million times, you will never see me,' he sighed deeply. 'And I, regrettably, will never see your dear, sweet face, with eyes, unless I can fathom a way to join with a human.'

Cain allowed himself a smile.

'And, on this score, my dear little fellow,' he said, 'I have news.'

Cain had no idea if the boy stuck in the puddle beneath him could hear. But he liked to talk, nonetheless, for there was no one else; aside from his man-servant, Schmerger, and Schmerger's mysterious, elven-like kind.

'So, child, if I am not able to use force, how shall a union with a human be done?' he said. 'In another time, I would have snapped off a finger or two, or pressed hot oil into orifices, and, yes, they would beg to do my bidding. But, now, if I am to find a person to join me, they must wish to do it with their whole heart.'

Cain tapped his cane on a cobble, thinking out loud. 'If these children are indeed the Heirs of Eden as Asgard claims, then how must they feel? Afraid? Fearful? Confused?'

Cain jumped up.

'The prophecy! The Tripodean Dream! I must recall every detail,' he said. 'How did it go? If my memory still serves me, the Tripodean Dream states that they must solve three riddles in order to find three tablets. And these stones hold the clues to the one key of the Garden of Eden.' Cain floated onto his back. 'They have one chance and all must survive. If they fail, Earth is destroyed and,' Cain smiled, 'Havilah awakens.'

Cain shot into the air startling a bird which shrilled in annoyance.

'Infants such as these Heirs could never do it. Never!'

Cain clasped his hands and floated down to the ground.

I suspect that that boy has an overwhelming desire to put the images he's seen in his dreams as far out of his mind as he possibly can.

'It is simple,' he said out loud. 'To secure the boy, I must take away his greatest fear.'

Cain grinned.

Love and fear, he thought, as the idea formed. *The two greatest weapons of manipulation known to mankind. And the thing is, I do believe I know where his fears lie.*

NINE

STORM WARNING

Sue Lowden looked up as Isabella opened the door, glad to see her best friend. When Isabella's straight brown hair hung like a curtain over her forehead it made her appear older; more like a seventeen-year-old, perhaps, than her fifteen years.

'Hey, everything all right?' she said.

Isabella slumped into a chair. 'I told Solomon about my barometer.'

Sue gasped. 'You did *what*? Are you insane?' she said, turning pink.

'He said he'd seen the forecast. What was I thinking?'

Sue draped an arm around her and held back a smile. 'But at least you tried,' she said. 'Look, maybe the calibration's wrong?'

'No, not possible,' Isabella said, frowning deeper. 'Every time I reset it, the same thing happens.'

'Well, please don't spend too much time fiddling with it,' Sue said. 'You've got until the football match to sort it out.'

Isabella smiled. 'I'm not sure I can watch. I'll just lose control again and then I'll be looking at a red card from school.'

'Oh, come on!' Sue chided. 'It might be Daisy's last game. You can't miss it, and anyhow, this time I'm going to look after you.'

She looked straight into Isabella's eyes. 'All of this,' she waved a hand at the barometer, 'is great—it's amazing, but it was only a dream. Do you think you're—'

'I'm doing this because I believe you, Sue.'

'You do?'

Isabella drummed on the desk. 'Yes, of course,' she said, her breathing shallower. 'You see, I know it sounds crazy, but I think I had the same dream.'

Sue nearly fell off her chair. 'You... as well? Why didn't you say something? How similar?'

'Well, most of it was to do with extreme precipitation, but at the end, it goes a bit crazy. I just can't remember.'

'Didn't you write it down?' Sue said. 'If you don't scribble dreams the moment you wake up, there's no way—'

'Well, I never do,' Isabella replied. 'It's where we differ.'

Sue tapped the spreadsheet. 'But if your evidence stacks up, shouldn't we say something?'

Isabella shook her head. 'Forecasters screwed up years ago before they knew what they were doing, before satellites and computer modelling,' she said. 'All we have is a homemade, slightly random experiment and a couple of freaky dreams. No one will believe us, look how Solomon reacted.'

Sue nodded. 'We'll be laughed out of school—'

'Yes, yes. I know,' Isabella said, rubbing her brow. 'I'll keep my mouth zipped, for now.'

'Me, same,' Sue said. She paused. 'Isabella, I really need to talk to you about something else—'

'Aha!' boomed the voice they least wanted to hear.

Kemp strode in, turned a chair around and sat down slowly.

Isabella straightened. 'What can I do for you, Kemp, boys?' she said.

'Chief nerd, Mrs Douglas, wants to see you right away' he said. 'And seriously, it's a real request. I'm just being super-friendly.'

Isabella smiled, but her eyes were narrow and icy. 'Thank you, Kemp. You've delivered your message so now you can leave; we're busy.'

Kemp opened a book. 'I'm gonna stay here for a while,' he replied putting his feet up on the desk. 'I believe I'm allowed to and, furthermore, I'd like to see this experiment you're doing. What's it? A barometer—'

Sue's eyes flicked towards the desk.

Kemp's followed. Then, he smiled and ran a hand through his hair. 'You don't by any chance fancy a date, Sue—'

Sue stared back at his happy face open-mouthed. 'With a jerk like you?'

'There's no need to be like that,' Kemp said, standing up and grasping his heart. He turned to his mates and winked. 'One day, Sue, it'll be you and me? I can feel it in my bones.'

As he headed towards the door, he extended his arm and gave Sue's bottom a playful tap.

Quick as a flash, she rounded on him, slapping his face, the sound like a snapping twig.

'Don't you dare touch me, you animal.' Sue chided. 'You're fourteen, and your hormones are clearly entering ignition phases, Kemp. So, let's get this straight once and for all.'

She spoke slowly. 'I will never, ever go out with you, even if we're the last two people alive on this planet. Do you completely understand?'

TEN

SWEAR ON YOUR LIFE

'You'll have to promise me you won't tell anyone,' Kemp demanded.

'Give me a break,' Archie replied.

'Archie, promise, on your life, that you won't tell anyone, that's all I'm asking. I mean, you can keep your mouth shut, can't you?'

'If you didn't want anyone to know,' Archie replied, 'why did you do it in the first place?'

'To protect the excellent academic reputation of Upsall School,' he said. 'And, anyway, your sister hates me and she cannot be trusted. Prove you're different.'

'Bog off, Kemp. My sister doesn't like you because you do idiotic things like throw barometers out of windows and sneak dead rats into sports bags.'

Kemp chuckled. Two years ago, he'd found a dead rodent by the river and hid it in Isabella's games bag. He waited. And every day he waited, getting more and more excited about the slowly decomposing rat. For the best part of a week, while everyone wondered what the terrible smell was, he waited. Then, on the afternoon of the school cross-country run, as Isabella put on her tracksuit bottoms, out plopped the remains, maggots spraying over her things like discarded rice.

Dynamite.

Archie sighed. 'Look, Kemp, if it means that much to you, I'll do it, but only if *you* swear, on your life that you won't do any more harmful, stupid, bullying things to Isabella, Sue, or Daisy.'

Kemp stuck out his jaw and moved it from side to side contemplating Archie's request. At last, he nodded and said, 'Okay, I agree. But it ends when she gets me into detention again.'

Archie nodded.

'Come on then,' Kemp said. 'You say it first.'

'Do I have to? I'm not five.'

'Yeah, course you do—if you want me to do the same.'

Archie rolled his eyes. 'I swear, on my life, that I won't tell anyone that you dropped the stupid barometer out of the window. Satisfied.'

Kemp nodded. 'Easy, wasn't it?'

'Now you do it!'

Kemp looked him in the eye. 'I swear on my life not to harm your sisters, and not to play any more silly tricks on them. There, that good enough?'

'I suppose.'

Kemp's tone changed and he ushered Archie aside. 'Hey, sorry, Arch. You don't have to say it... I know, I know,' he said putting his hands in the air. 'I've been a massive arse.'

'You're telling me!' Archie replied. 'Why, Kemp? Why do you do it?'

Kemp shrugged. 'Dunno. Boredom. Can't seem to help myself when I see your sisters—'

'Look out!' Jackson said, as he ran back into the classroom. 'Steele's on his way.'

'Come on!' Kemp said. 'Out of the window!'

They ran to the window and pulled up the blind.

Isabella, Sue and Mrs Pike stared up at them.

'Drat,' Kemp said, under his breath. He smiled pleasantly back at them.

'Kemp and Archie de Lowe,' the old teacher hollered. 'Who would have guessed? What can you tell me about the mess down here?'

Kemp opened the window. 'Hello, Miss. Is there a problem?'

'You know perfectly well there is!'

'Sorry. I don't what you're talking about, Miss?'

'This debris, here,' Mrs Pike shrieked, pointing at the concrete.

Kemp peered like a sailor looking down from deck, a quizzical expression etched on his brow. 'I have no idea what you're talking about,' he replied. 'Window's been closed all along, hasn't it, boys?' He shrugged. 'What is it?'

Isabella shrieked. 'Kemp, you know what it is!'

'Glass?' he offered. 'A smashed Coke bottle perhaps?'

'No, Kemp, it was Isabella's barometer.'

'A bar-hom-tier,' Kemp repeated, thickly. 'What on earth is that?'

'Archie, did you see Kemp with it earlier?' the teacher hollered.

Archie stared at the floor.

'Tell me, what happened?'

'Dunno,' Archie said, running a hand through his hair.

'Archie, what do you mean, you "dunno"?'

'Dunno,' Archie said again, reddening.

Kemp looked straight into Mrs Pike's eyes. 'Honestly, there's been no one around. We've been chatting about animals, life, and situation comedy—'

'Great!' Isabella stormed, addressing Archie. 'Kemp's made you swear not to tell or something childish like that, hasn't he? You, Kemp,' she said pointing at him, 'you were the last person to have it. It must have been you.'

'Then prove it,' Kemp said, thrusting out his jaw.

'I shouldn't have to,' she pleaded. 'Archie, all you have to do is tell us what happened—'

Archie shook his head.

'Expel him!' Isabella shouted pointing at Kemp.

'But I haven't done anything—'

Isabella stamped her foot. 'Yes, you have!'

'Prove it!' he yelled back.

'You had it last! I saw it in your hands, admit it—'

'NO! Innocent until proven guilty—'

'You are guilty!'

'In whose court?'

'*I DID IT!*' Archie yelled, his voice cutting above theirs.

The school bell chimed, the echo circling around their heads.

'It was me.'

'*You*?' Isabella quizzed.

'*Archie*?' Mr Steele said.

'de Lowe?' said Mrs Pike.

'Yes,' Archie sighed. 'I was fed up with you two always getting at each other, so I thought I'd, you know…' He bowed his head.

Isabella looked from one to the other. 'Oh great! You two have done a deal or something, haven't you?'

ELEVEN

GUS TALKS TO SUE

'Are those real tears, or are you just pleased to see me,' Gus said on finding Sue later, as he pulled a folded red and white polka-dot handkerchief out of his pocket.

Sue shot him a look but her face broke into a smile. 'Oh! I don't know. It's that oaf, again. He's got hold of Isabella's experiment and she's gone nuts.' She dabbed her eyes and offered it back.

'Ah. No, keep it,' he said. 'I've got a drawer full. Dad has a thing about them—'

'Thanks, Gus.'

'Want to talk about it?'

She shook her head.

'You sure? I'm all ears, and teeth,' he said grinning. 'Don't worry about Kemp —I've got a plan where he's concerned. Right now, there are disturbing rumours leaking about these corridors concerning our headmaster.'

'Solomon?'

'Aye,' he said in mock way with an eyebrow raised. He paused.

'Well—'

He shook his head. 'Can't tell you,' he said.

'Why not?'

'It might cheer you up.'

The corners of her mouth turned up and she hit him playfully in the chest.

'Well, I just happened to be in the old school—'

'Just happened?'

'Yes. Taking an arbitrary stroll down the passageways leading to his study—'

'Gus!'

'Do you want me to tell you, or not?' he said, stealing a glance over her shoulder.

She nodded.

'As you probably know, Solomon's having a massive party tomorrow night after the football. I happened to be standing outside when I heard this extraordinary noise.'

'What noise?'

'Well, singing, I think. Terrible sort of opera, like baritone cat-wails.'

Sue tittered. 'So?'

'That's not it,' Gus said. 'You see, he then started talking but I'm sure there wasn't anyone in there.'

'How do you know?'

'He hadn't shut the door—'

'You didn't—?'

Gus pulled a face. 'Only quickly. I couldn't help it. Bet you'd have done the same?'

'No way!'

'Well, anyway, there he was, wearing a dress—'

'You're kidding!'

'Yeah. Okay, so it was a kilt, I hope. Green and blue criss-crosses, and, on his top, a white string vest.'

'A singlet? What was he doing?'

'Introducing himself.'

'What?'

'Practicing his how-do-you-doo's, his voice getting posher and posher. *"Oh, how do you do, Mayor, how do you do Your Eminence, that sort of thing".*'

Sue laughed as Gus raised his eyebrows.

'Then what?'

'I sneaked off. Told you it would cheer you up. Now, important stuff. I need some advice.

Sue cocked her head. 'Go on.'

Gus's face contorted. 'I need a date. Got a party on over half-term.'

'You're asking me for a date.'

Gus coughed and blushed. 'Er. No. Not really. Just advice, or a bit of guidance as to whom I might approach.'

'Oh,' she said. 'Right.'

Gus couldn't tell if her tone betrayed a hint of disappointment.

'Anyone spring to mind?'

'Annie?' he squeaked.

'Which one? Martin or de Lowe.'

'Either.'

She rolled her eyes. 'Really?'

Gus looked taken aback. 'Why not?'

'Annie Martin is pretty, but she's, you know, a bit soppy, forever sweeping back her hair and sighing. You'd be bored senseless. On the other hand, Daisy might tear the place up, and, if there's dancing, you'd better have your dancing shoes on.'

Gus's forehead rolled. 'I hate dancing.'

Footsteps made them turn.

Sue squeezed his arm. 'I've got to go. I'll come up with something, don't you worry. I'll let you know before half term, okay?' She looked him in the eye.

Gus smiled. 'Thanks, Sue. Discretion, please. Don't want it leaked around or everyone will think I'm desperate.'

'No problem. Hey, and thanks Gus. Love the hanky.'

TWELVE

STORM GLASS

'You must think I'm a fool, Arch. It's perfectly clear that Kemp put you up to this.' Her tone softened. 'Didn't he?'

Archie kept his eyes down.

She sighed. 'Have it your own way, Archie. I just don't understand how you can be friends with him. I just wish you'd been honest with me, Arch. That's what really hurts.'

'I'm sorry about your experiment,' he said, raising his eyes.

Isabella pressed her lips together. 'Don't be. It kept bottoming out. Actually, I've researched a better idea. I'm going to make a Fitzroy storm glass.'

'A Fitz glass?'

'No, a Fitz-ROY storm glass. It's a brilliant bit of kit, a kind of old-fashioned weather gauge, and, as a punishment for your behaviour, you can help me make it.'

Archie smiled. 'Why the craze about weather stuff?'

'Well, if you must know,' she said, 'there's a curious weather system developing.' She hesitated a little. 'This may sound a bit strange, but Sue and I have had a premonition; a dream about torrential rain, flooding, that kind of thing.'

Archie reeled, and put a hand out to steady himself. 'You're always saying how unscientific things like dreams are, and that therefore they're irrelevant—'

'Nevertheless,' she said, curtly, 'dreams are viable mechanisms of the brain, Archie.'

Archie cleared his throat. 'Bells, do you dream a lot?'

'No,' she said. 'I never dream, well, not until recently. But I've got an intensely strong feeling about this one. So, I reckon there's no harm in trying to find out if there's any scientific substance to it.'

Archie scratched his head and wondered if he should mention *his* appalling dreams, and Daisy's shouting in the middle of the night. Instead, he heard himself asking, 'How does this Fitzglass-thing work?'

'It shows what's going to happen to the weather through the liquid in the glass. A reflection of what's going on outside, I think. So, if the liquid is clear, the weather will be clear. If small crystals form, then snow is on its way—'

'And if there's a storm…?' Archie asked.

'When a thunderstorm is coming, the liquid should be cloudy with small star-like crystals in it, and so on.'

'Nice.'

'First, I'll need a few ingredients—and this, bro, is where you come in.'

Archie nodded.

'First, go and bat your eyelids at Mrs Culver. Ask for ten grams of camphor; she'll have some for food flavouring. Tell her you need some in Chemistry to show how a compound can burn without leaving an ash residue. If she starts asking questions, mention oxygen in a scientifically related question. For some reason, Mrs Culver can't bear the word "oxygen".

'Then, go and find Mr Pike in the Maintenance Department. Ask him for distilled water. Fill a large, plastic bottle if you can; he keeps some for his forklift batteries.'

Isabella scratched her forehead thoughtfully, making sure she hadn't forgotten anything. 'Have you got that? Camphor and distilled water. I'll find some ethanol and the other bits from Chemistry later on. Shouldn't be too difficult,' she added, almost as a reminder to herself.

'Where shall we meet?' he said.

Isabella smiled. 'The science labs are free straight after lunch. One-thirty. I'll see you there.'

'Gotta look like you mean it, Archie,' Sue said, as she threw a lab-coat at Archie.

Archie handed over the camphor and Sue filled a beaker with distilled water, which she began to heat.

In silence, as Archie and Sue looked on, Isabella added each component until the beaker was half full. The ethanol and camphor were poured in last. When these had dissolved, Isabella asked Archie to find a large test tube sealed with a stopper. She exchanged the liquid into the test tube and filled it almost to the top, and capped it off.

Archie put the experiment in a holding device on the desk.

'Archie,' Isabella said. 'Wash those beakers while we put everything away.'

He headed to the far corner of the laboratory, but, just as he was about to place the beaker in the sink, the door swung open.

Instinctively, Archie ducked under the table.

'Aha! *There* you are,' Kemp said, with big smile. 'Been looking all over for you girls.'

'GO AWAY!' they shouted.

'Whoa! Calm down. I've come to apologise.' He looked down at the desk. 'What's all this then? Doing some illegal experiments, are we? That's terribly exciting. Creating a bomb or some poisons or a wee bit of chemical warfare—'

'It's none of your business, Kemp. Leave us alone.'

'Biological warfare?'

'No, Kemp it's—'

'Mustard gas? Come on, I'm offering an olive branch. I'm sorry about earlier. Got a little out of hand, didn't it? Actually, have either of you seen Archie?'

Isabella caught Archie staring at her from behind one of the desks, out of Kemp's eye line, shaking his head vigorously.

'Er, no. Sorry. No idea,' she said, brushing an imaginary speck off her lab coat.

Kemp regarded her suspiciously before his eyes moved to the test tube on the desk.

'This is your experiment, is it? A test-tube full of cloudy potions. Cor. Brilliant.'

'Thanks for your interest, Kemp,' Sue said, in her most condescending manner. 'But, to be honest, this is a very dull investigation we're doing, dealing with the creation of crystals using camphor, ethanol, distilled water, and a couple of other things you probably wouldn't understand.'

But Kemp was like a dog chasing after a scent, and his tone changed. 'So, if it's so boring, why are you doing it in lunch break?'

'As I said, Kemp, it's a simple experiment—'

'I don't believe you.' He stepped closer. 'It doesn't add up.'

'Please, go away, and leave us alone,' Isabella said, as sweetly as she could, remembering Archie's advice.

Her words fell on deaf ears. 'Why don't you tell me what you're doing?' Kemp quizzed.

'Why should we?' Isabella snapped.

Kemp smiled back. 'Cos, otherwise I'll smash it—'

'You wouldn't dare.' Isabella lunged for the test tube, but Kemp was too quick.

'Give it back, immediately!'

'No way. Come on, what's in it?' he said, inspecting it. 'A lethal poison, a nerve agent, a deadly virus—'

'Don't be stupid.'

'From where I'm standing, I'm not the one being stupid,' he said.

Isabella huffed. 'If you must know, it's a Fitzroy storm glass—'

'Well, well, well,' Kemp said, slowly. 'You're not still going on about this bleeding storm? When will you two grow up and do what everyone else does?' He shook his head. 'Watch the weather forecast on this thing called the telly. Oh, hang on, don't tell me; you haven't got one!'

'Of course we do,' Isabella raged.

Kemp raised an eyebrow. 'I'm not sure I believe you. Thing is, you de Lowes are so backwards I wouldn't be surprised if your mum has to shave Neolithic hair off her body. We'd never know, though, because she seems to have disowned you.' He cocked an eye at Isabella's puce face. 'And that old woman who looks after you, with whiskers coming out of her face like a cat...' he opened his eyes wide theatrically. 'I know! What you should make,' he paused, holding the test-tube in front of his eyes, 'is a potion for hair removal! You've got customers in your very own home!'

Kemp brushed aside Isabella's howls. 'Now, clever clogs, let me fill you in. Last night the man on the TELLY,' he said in a deliberately loud voice. 'He said that there might be a storm over the next couple of days, but not a big one, and certainly not one with white water rafting.'

Kemp marched to the corner of the room, near to where Archie was hiding under the table.

Isabella gasped lightly.

'I tell you what,' Kemp continued, 'I'm going to do you a favour, and put you out of this ridiculous weather preoccupation once and for all. I'm going to spin this tube thing like a spinning top. You do know what that is, don't you? By the time you get over here, it'll either be in bits on the floor, or, by some miracle, you may have grabbed it. But, if and when this happens, I'll be long gone out of the door. Then you can go and do what everyone else does, and watch the weather forecast on the box.' He grinned. 'You'll find it comes directly after the news.'

Kemp, with the test-tube in the palms of his hands, drew them quickly apart. The tube spun fast and straight, and, while the girls fixated upon it, Kemp strode through the door, turning the lights off after him.

The sound of the latch clicking seemed to accentuate the wobbling of the glass. In an instant, the girls rushed over in near darkness, but, in their haste, they careered into the lab furniture. The noise of scraping chairs and upturned tables filled the room.

As the crashing sounds receded, the test tube wobbled to its conclusion, followed, moments later, by the tinkling sound of breaking glass.

THIRTEEN

GENESIS CONSIDERS THE TASK AHEAD

The large dreamspinner studied each of her delicate, long, slender legs one by one, as if paying homage to them for their service. For the first time she noted the wear and tear; the way so many had turned grey when once they were bright white and how her slender slithers of knuckles and joints were now worn thin.

As Genesis seamlessly morphed each leg from a pincer, to a needle, then back to a long leg again, a deep sense of foreboding filled her.

What if these Heirs of Eden do not understand?

She shivered at the possibility. Putting the thought aside, she sent vibrations from her rapidly moving legs to the waiting dreamspinners, the Elders of the dreamspinner population: Gaia, Juno, and Asgard.

'The Tripodean Dream comes with a gift for each Heirs of Eden,' Genesis said, as she dipped three long legs into her maghole and withdrew some microscopic granules, studying the ends. 'These gifts are physical talents designed to assist each one to whom the prophecy has been given. They are known as the Gifts of the Garden of Eden.'

'Then the stories are true,' Gaia vibrated.

'Yes. These crystals were passed to me by my mother, as once they were handed to her. If the Heirs of Eden succeed in the tasks set before them they will open the planet of the Garden of Eden to life once more,' she said. 'Dream powders will be replenished. Wondrous times may begin afresh for all life.'

A strong vibration cut through the air.

'Why do we meddle?' Asgard said, his fingers moving quickly. 'If you had not spun the Tripodean Dream, who is to say that life would not have continued just as before. Besides, the Tripodean Dream has been given to Heirs of Eden who are but *children* of man. They are not equipped to tackle what lies ahead; the storm alone will tear them to pieces—'

'The riddles and tests were prepared by Adam the Great when he was a wizard at the height of his powers in the Garden of Eden. It is ancient magic—'

'But these children do not seek it. They do not even know of the consequences—'

'It is not the time to argue the rights or wrongs. The sequence of the Tripodean Dream has begun. Only the Heirs of Eden can interpret because they represent the Soul, the Heart and the Ego of Earth—'

'Even though they have no training—'

'The time has come for change,' Genesis said, her vibrations overriding his. 'That is the lore of the universe. It is natures will.'

Asgard scoffed, his vibrations slowing. 'They are not equipped—'

'Enough!' Genesis said. 'They are the ones who are protected by Adam—'

'But Adam does not know it. He does not even know his name—'

'He will remember,' Genesis said, the vibrations from her fingers singing through the air. 'He must.'

The old dreamspinner slowly dipped her hands into the blue electrical hole that filled her midriff.

'Juno,' she said, addressing a younger dreamspinner. 'Have the last dream powders from the Garden of Eden been dispersed?'

'Yes, Mother. The Atrium is clear.'

'Good. Then the final part of the Tripodean Dream will be given to the Heirs of Eden this Earth night, as they sleep. Afterwards, I will give them the Gifts of the Garden of Eden. On the giving of the Gift of Strength they will have seven days to solve the riddles and unlock the key.'

'But they will die,' Asgard said. 'It is a waste. The suffering will be immense—'

'I will hear no more of your objections, Asgard,' Genesis snapped, as she lifted her wiry, opaque outline up.

'The journey for the Heirs of Eden to find the tablets and fulfil the prophecy is about to commence. Regardless of what you may think, these children of mankind are the Heirs of Eden. The universal energy that combines the living in all corners of the universes has reasons for these things. Nothing can change it. When the gifts are given, life on Earth will be in the Heirs of Eden's hands and theirs alone.'

FOURTEEN

A BROKEN PROMISE

'Now then, now then!' Kemp said, flicking on the light. 'What's going on here?' he said, in a mock, policeman-like voice. He looked around to see an empty room and then, slowly, Sue got up. Her hair covered her face like a veil.

Then Isabella rose, too, rubbing her head.

Kemp's eyes were on fire. 'Brilliant. Blooming gold.' He pulled his phone out. 'Smile at the budgie.' The camera clicked and flashed. Kemp inspected the image. 'Lovely. You two look gorgeous. I'm gonna post this everywhere.'

Archie stood up, brushing splinters from his jacket.

'Archie!' Kemp exclaimed, his expression changing. 'Shit! Where did you come from?'

'I've been here all the time, you idiot.'

Kemp's manner changed immediately. 'Are you all right?' He pointed at Archie's sleeve. 'Is that…?'

Archie looked down at his hand. Blood was oozing from a gash at the base of his thumb and running over his hand.

'Satisfied?' Isabella said, as she tiptoed through the glass fragments towards him. 'Happy now?' she held Archie's arm and inspected it. 'Kemp, get the first aid box; we need to stop the bleeding. And Kemp, be useful and find a dustpan and brush.'

Isabella led Archie to the tap.

'This might hurt, Archie.'

He winced.

'There's a fragment in here. Sue, I need a towel, tweezers, and then we'll need to compress the wound.'

Archie gritted his teeth as she plucked out the tiny slivers before applying pressure on the wound.

When they had finished, Archie turned to Kemp who stood frozen to the spot. Archie looked him hard in the eye.

'You SWORE, on your life, that you wouldn't do this kind of thing,' Archie said. '*You swore—on—your—life,*' he yelled. 'I held my side of the deal, but at the first opportunity you couldn't resist it, could you? It's now entirely clear to me that you value your life as pretty much worthless. What would your parents think? Do you reckon they'd be proud?'

Kemp's face fell, and the colour drained from his cheeks. 'Sorry, Archie,' he said. 'I... I didn't realise...'

With Archie's words ringing in his ears, Kemp fled for the door.

After a long silence, Sue turned to Archie. 'Right, Archie. Where is it?'

'Uh?' Archie cried, feigning shock.

'Where is... what?' Isabella said.

Sue tutted. 'Oh, come along, come along, Sherlock Isabella. The storm glass, silly.'

'In fragments in the bin?'

Sue bit her lip. 'That isn't test-tube glass. That's beaker glass fragments, isn't it, Archie?'

'Beaker?' Archie replied, the corners of his mouth turning up.

'You've got it, haven't you?'

Archie couldn't contain himself any longer and laughed. 'Indeed, I have!' He slowly moved his gaze towards his trousers and pointed at his crotch. He began to unzip his fly. 'It's right here.'

'No way!' Sue exclaimed. 'Oh... my... God!'

Archie reached in and teased it out. 'DA-NAH,' he said, his eyes sparkling.

He held the test tube up in the air. 'Sorry, couldn't think of anywhere else quick enough,' he said. 'Then, when I crouched down, I lost my balance, and knocked over the beaker.'

Sue clapped her hands at Archie's story but Isabella looked horrified.

'Well, well, Archie. A storm in your pants. First time for everything, eh?'

Archie slipped the tube neatly into the rack.

'One thing, Archie. Do everyone a favour. Please go and give it a proper clean.'

FIFTEEN

A POINTLESS EXPERIMENT

By the time the de Lowes returned to the stone courtyard of Eden Cottage, the charcoal colours of dusk lay sandwiched upon the buildings and the landscape. Archie and Daisy immediately set about kicking a football. The scuffing, sandpapery noises of their feet, and the ball doffing back off the grey stone walls, roused Mrs Pye. She waved enthusiastically from one of the two windows in her flat opposite the farmhouse.

Isabella's mind tracked back to the conversations with Solomon and Kemp, who had both been so rude about their house.

It wasn't that bad.

She studied the exterior. So, it was a bit of a mishmash of an ancient moors farmstead, but it wasn't too unusual, was it?

Constructed from irregular, Yorkshire-grey boulders, and old, thick timbers, its slate roof was covered in moss and lichen that hung over too far, as though badly in need of a trim. Looking at the blackened, slightly crooked chimneys, the higgledy-piggledy stone arrangements, and the odd sections of glass and brick intermittently nestled into the walls, Isabella was reminded of a bag of loose sweets squished together and charred until they were all the same colour.

As Isabella entered the kitchen, she realised that this was definitely the heart of the house, a place that oozed warmth, love, happiness, and appreciation of fine foods. Bunches of rosemary, lavender, thyme, and dried, cured hams and fruit dangled from a row of black hooks. The smell intoxicating.

Even the stone slabs, laid out in great squares, had a warm, glossy sheen from years of wear. As she looked up, grey, oak timbers fanned out in clean lines above their heads, protecting those within.

Down the middle of the kitchen ran a long, chunky, dark brown oak table fit for a banquet. Next to the table stood a pleasing, red-brick, inglenook fireplace where the old wood-fired cooker sat.

Kemp was wrong. Even if the kitchen was a bit of a curiosity, it wasn't entirely archaic. Two waggon wheels suspended by three heavy chains had spotlights beaming down from the rim and, on the far wall, was Mrs Pye's pride and joy; a fifty-inch flat-screen telly.

'Well, come on then,' Daisy said, slinging a bag on her bed. 'Show me this amazing thing that's been holidaying in Archie's pants.'

Isabella unwrapped the test tube from her scarf and leant the glass between two books on the table. Three pairs of eyes stared down at it.

'Bit foggy, isn't it?' Daisy said. 'So, does that mean it'll be foggy?'

Archie raised his eyebrows. 'Don't be silly, Daisy. This is serious science.'

Daisy giggled and elbowed Archie as they continued to stare.

'Ooh,' Daisy cooed. 'Look at those little stars. What does that mean?'

Isabella pulled out her crib sheet. 'Tiny stars means that it will be stormy,' she said, and then read from her crib sheet. '*A cloudy glass with small stars indicates thunderstorms.*'

'Wow,' Archie said, sarcastically. 'Impressive.'

Daisy spluttered. 'And... is that it?'

'What do you mean, *is that it*?'

'Well, it's very pretty, but you know, as an award-winning scientist, I thought it might be a bit... cooler,' Daisy said, glancing to Archie for support. 'I mean, if you wanted to know thunderstorms were coming all you had to do was watch the forecast on TV.'

Isabella shot up. 'That's what that moron Kemp said.'

'Well, maybe he's right? Have you gone to all this trouble to find out something we already know?'

'There's going to be a terrible deluge,' Isabella fumed. 'Sue and I both dreamt about it. All I'm trying to do is prove it scientifically.'

'Don't get me wrong,' Daisy said, picking it up and turning it round in her hands, 'but how will this crappy thing help?'

Isabella sat down slowly, took the storm glass off her sister, and twisted it through her fingers.

'To be honest, I had hoped for something a little more dramatic, like the crystals speeding up or something.'

'But how would that change anything?'

'I don't know,' Isabella shrugged. 'It might give us a warning, or...' she shrugged. 'Actually, Sis, I give in. I haven't a clue. But I had to try something.'

Daisy handed it over to Archie.

'This must be the worst scientific experiment ever,' he said. 'If Kemp realised how poor it really was, then he'd rip you to bits.'

'Then don't tell him.'

'I'll never say anything again after what he did today—'

'Children!' Mrs Pye's strange voice screamed up the stairs. 'Hurry! Tea's on the table.'

On the kitchen table sat four bowls, brimming with noodles in a thick, soupy broth. A Mrs Pye "Ramen" experiment. The children slipped into their chairs and began sniffing like curious cats.

'Have you heard?' Isabella said, taking a small taste. 'Mum and Dad aren't coming back for half term.'

'What!' she cried. 'No. Well, I'm blown apart—oh deary!'

'Can't you say something to them when they get back?' Archie asked. 'They're never here.'

'Don't eat with your mouth full, little Archie,' Mrs Pye said, before sighing. 'It isn't proper for me to tell your folks what they can or cannot do. If they choose to be away, then it is for good reason. I know you won't think it's true but I promise they miss you twice as much as you miss them.'

Mrs Pye said this with as much conviction as she could, but she read the disappointment in their eyes and wondered what on earth it was that so completely occupied their parents' time.

In any event, she wouldn't have a bad word said about them. She only had to raise her left arm above her head or try and touch her toes to remember.

Old Man Wood had found her in the woods, miles up in the depths of the forest, on the verge of death, so they said. Her face and shoulder smashed, her clothes ripped to bits. Hardly breathing. He'd carried her all the way home, singing and keeping her going. She still sang that funny song, especially when she was lonely or tired.

And over the years she'd picked it up:

O great Tripodean, a dream to awaken

The forces of nature, the birth of creation.
Three Heirs of Eden with all of their powers,
Must combat the rain, the lightning and showers.
In open land, on plain or on sea,
Survive 'till sunset—when their lives will be free.
But the Prophecy has started—it's just the beginning.
And it never seems to end, and it never seems to end.

For several months, Old Man Wood and the children's parents nursed her, built up her strength, and tried to help her recover... and remember. But her memory never returned. She had no name, no address, no family, no lovers, no pets; nothing and no-one she ever recalled laughing with, or crying to.

Instead, she had had to learn everything again; although some things came to her quite naturally, like, strangely, making puddings.

The first time she recalled laughing was when the babies crawled to her and gurgled in her ear, especially little Archie. Isabella, on the other hand, would scowl and point at her scars, and continued to do so until she saw past the damage on Mrs Pye's face and into her heart.

These were her first memories, and cherished ones too.

After a while she didn't want to go anywhere else. Why should she? She loved the children. She loved the quiet remoteness of Eden Cottage, with its ballooning views over the Vale of York towards the peaks in the far distance. She felt safe being close to Old Man Wood, who, although he came and went, seemed not to have a harmful bone in his body. It felt right that she should care for the children while their parents were away, for a nurturing instinct ran deep within her.

As far as her name went, Isabella called her, affectionately, "The famous Mrs Pye", and it caught on. She'd been Mrs Pye ever since, living in the apartment on the top half of the converted barn across the courtyard.

SIXTEEN

HEADMASTER VISITS

'Evening, All,' Old Man Wood said, popping his head around the door. 'Smells marvel-wondrous.'

Daisy got up and wrapped her arms around him.

Old Man Wood hugged her back, closing his eyes. 'Now then, littluns. I must say, I can't remember such strange weather. Feels like a storm is brewing right bang on top of us. An appley-big one at that. I can feel it in my old bones—'

Isabella slammed her fists on the table. 'That's what I've been trying to tell everyone. No one believes me; Solomon, Kemp, you two—'

'Whoa! Chill, Bells,' Archie chipped in. 'Your experimentation is a bit... bonkers.'

Mrs Pye piped up, 'That nice man the weather forecaster on my television said there might be a bit of a storm. Localised—'

'Arrggh!' Isabella cried. 'NO! NO! NO! Not you as well!'

Mrs Pye turned puce and looked as though she might burst into tears.

'That's enough of that, Isabella,' Old Man Wood said, firmly. For a moment there was quiet. He furrowed his brow, as though deep in thought. 'What's funny,' he began, 'is that I've been having real clear dreams about lots of rain, flooding and storms. Thing is, I'm so old it could mean anything.'

Isabella gasped. 'You... you've had dreams too?'

The children stopped eating and stared up at him.

'Oh, yes. More than ever. Shocking stuff too. I should check those apples—'

'There's nothing wrong with them, I'm telling you,' Mrs Pye fired back from the end of the table.

'Well then,' Old Man Wood said, 'I do believe there's going to be a storm and three-quarters.' He reached across, grabbed an apple, rubbed it on his patched-up jumper, and chomped. 'Now, you're old enough to know,' he continued, between mouthfuls, 'that once upon a time there was a story about a great storm and a flood that covered the world.'

Isabella groaned. 'You're not referencing the original flood story?' she said, her tone loaded with sarcasm.

Old Man Wood seemed surprised. 'Ooh. Yup. I think that's the one. You know about it, do you? With a man they called … now, what was his name?'

'Noah?' Isabella said.

'Ha!' Old Man Wood clapped his big hands. 'There. That goes ding-dong. Been muddling that one for a while. So, you do know about it. How marvel-tastic.'

The conversation was interrupted by a rapping sound at the front door.

The family stared at one another.

'Who on Earth?' Old Man Wood said.

Before anyone else could move, Daisy tore off to see who it was. Shortly, she returned.

'It's Solomon,' she gushed.

For a minute they looked at each other, not sure what to do.

'Well, don't you think you should let him in?' Old Man Wood said.

The children headed towards the door.

'Mr Solomon, Sir.'

'Hello, Archie, Daisy, Isabella. Please accept my apologies for the late hour, but I thought I may as well potter up. May I come in?'

They led him to the sitting room, where Old Man Wood was adding logs to the orange embers.

'Mr Woodwood, how nice to see you,' the headmaster said, as he eyed up the old man. Old Man Wood was just as tall and wrinkly as he remembered, and had the strangest little tufts of hair protruding from an otherwise bald and patchy scalp. In fact, the old man looked the same as he had when he met him twenty-five years ago.

He remembered thinking then what peculiar clothes old Woodwood wore. His trousers and shirt were made of fragments of cloth that made him look like a moving patchwork quilt. It reminded him of Archie and his curiously modified school uniform.

Their clothes must have been stitched together by the lady who was loitering in the doorway. He strode over and shook her hand. 'Isn't that road terribly narrow and steep?' he said as a way of breaking the ice. 'It must be devilishly tricky to navigate when the weather turns. Do those parcel couriers ever manage to find you?'

Mrs Pye froze, and turned as pink as a doll.

Old Man Wood rescued her by moving in and extending his hand. 'Now then, is everything in order? Perhaps I could offer you a glass of something: apple juice, cauliflower tea, my own marrow rum?'

'How very kind,' Mr Solomon said, 'apple juice will suffice. I shan't stay long.' The headmaster rubbed his hands; for a man his age, Old Man Wood's handshake crushed like iron. 'May we have a word in private?'

Isabella, Daisy, and Archie streamed out of the room while Old Man Wood poured the drinks.

'Mr Woodwood, I'll get straight to the point. Can you give the children the kind of assistance they need if—and I do hate to say this—if anything goes wrong?'

'Depends what kind of... wrong, Headmaster?'

'Well, say if Archie was to break his arm again. How would you get him to the hospital? And what if there's a house fire?'

Old Man Wood burst out laughing, his vibrant, joyful tones bouncing back off the walls. 'They are quite capable of looking after themselves, with or without me.'

His comments had the effect of making Solomon feel rather idiotic. 'With respect, Mr Woodwood,' he shot back. 'Even though Isabella has conducted herself outstandingly well in her academic studies, can we be sure she won't disgrace the school by violently interfering with the officials during our remaining football matches? And, while Daisy shows exceptional sporting ability, she is on course to fail her exams."

Old Man Wood didn't know what to say, so he simply smiled back.

'And then there's Archie,' Solomon continued. 'Lovely fellow that he may be, he has no redeeming features, aside from his wildlife obsession and his siblings to retain his place at school.'

Solomon wondered if the old man had listened to a single word.

'Mr Woodwood, I will be frank with you. I have no argument with your family in any way.' He removed his spectacles, rubbing them on a cloth before setting them back on his nose. 'But I must tell you that I am to retire at the end of the term, and I've heard through the grapevine that my successor—a modern, disciplinarian sort—is looking to shake up the school. 'I very much fear that the children's bursaries will almost certainly come to an end.'

Old Man Wood scratched an imaginary beard. 'I'll make sure the children's parents understand the situation entirely.'

'Good, thank you,' Mr Solomon replied. He cleared his throat. 'Are you fit and well enough to continue in the role as the children's caretaker? I worked out you must be nearing the heady heights of ninety years—'

'Oh, Headmaster,' Old Man Wood said, 'my body and mind are ticking along quite nicely, thank you.'

'I ask for the children's sake—'

'Mr Solomon,' Old Man Wood chuckled. 'When you are as old as I am, you will find that love and well-being are the things that matter. While it is hard to hold on to the memories from one's youth, we are lucky to be in possession of decent health, and blessed that Mrs Pye feeds and nurses us.' He flicked him a smile. 'But, you're right to be checking up. We don't have so many visitors up here in the hills. Have you made plans for your retirement?'

Solomon leaned back in the armchair.

'Yes,' he sighed, pleased to switch subject. 'As a matter of fact, I'm hoping to go to the Middle East to see some of the ancient tombs and archaeology for myself. It's a small passion of mine, if you will.' He exhaled loudly at the thought of the unknown life to come after he left his beloved school.

When the men stood up, scuffling noises scratched towards the kitchen. Old Man Wood and Solomon exchanged a smile.

'Children!' Solomon boomed. 'I have something to say to you, so you may as well come back here.'

The children emerged, sheepishly.

'I've decided the time has come to hang up my leather binder and my red marker-pen.'

'You're leaving?' Isabella said.

'Yes, my dear, I am. It is time for some fresh blood at Upsall School. Please promise to keep this information to yourselves until I have made the announcement official, after half term.'

He looked each of the children in the eye. 'I would be hugely disappointed if any of you were to exit the school before me, so I suggest you work together to improve those areas that need addressing. For example, Archie and Daisy, a mastery of the periodic table and basic algebra.' He gave them a knowing look over his half-moon glasses. 'I have a suspicion that these may feature heavily in your exams.'

'The other thing is that I would like you to win the football trophy tomorrow. I don't mean to put any additional pressure on you both, but it would be wonderful to finish my tenure here knowing that we had reached the pinnacle of both sporting and academic endeavours. So, Archie, please hold your concentration for the entire game.'

'We'll do our best,' Daisy said. 'I promise.'

He smiled and headed out of the oak door.

Isabella seized her chance. 'But what about the storm, sir?'

He turned. 'Isabella, this is Yorkshire, for goodness' sake.'

'But I've studied the charts and...'

The door closed in her face, as Solomon's footsteps tip-tapped across the flagstones.

Old Man Wood pushed the thick bolt into the wall. 'What a fine man,' he said. 'I wouldn't worry too much about what he said. You're doing well at school, you're fit and well, and you've got friends—what more could you want, eh? Now, off to bed, right now.'

A rumble of thunder boomed high up in the night sky. Old Man Wood sniffed the air.

'Something tells me tomorrow is going to be a big, big day.'

SEVENTEEN

THE DREAMSPINNERS

The grandfather clock in the hallway chimed twice, its ring echoing around the old farmhouse. Two in the morning of the next day and the children's sleep was long and deep: the night-hour of dreaming.

Four dreamspinners arrived in a flash.

Using their long, wiry legs, each dreamspinner flew across the air until they stood above the children.

'You are here to witness the final part of the Tripodean Dream, for there must be no doubting it,' Genesis said, through her vibrations. 'Their sleep pattern is flowing. It is time. Come.'

Genesis walked deftly through the air towards Isabella. Bending impossibly forward, as if made from soft rubber, she pushed her head and one arm into her own churning, electrically-active void.

Moments later she held out microscopic-sized granules of powder at the end of a long pincer.

Fragments that hold so much power, she thought, realising that power was the wrong word. *They were far more than that, these were the opportunity of life itself.*

Genesis positioned herself so that her two long legs anchored above Isabella's sleeping head, steadying her for the dream Genesis was about to deliver. She bent down, almost doubled-over, and soon her fingers moved freely by Isabella's lips, ready.

With her ovoid, jet-black eyes, Genesis studied the girl.

Instinctively, she tuned in to the rhythm of Isabella's breathing.

IN … OUT.

IN … OUT.

'*Heirs of Eden,*' she thought, '*interpret this dream as best you can.*'

Beneath her, Isabella inhaled. As she did so, Genesis's two fingers spun at an incredible speed, releasing a fine dust which was drawn deep into Isabella's lungs.

Without taking her eyes off the girl, Genesis plucked more dust from within her maghole and, at the optimum moment, lowered her fingers towards the child's mouth and repeated the process.

After every breath, Genesis stopped and gauged the girl's reaction, making tiny adjustments to the rate of powder in proportion to the volume of air drawn in.

So far, so good, Genesis thought. *Already she tosses and turns. Soon she will begin her lucid and vivid journey. Nothing will wake her.*

Genesis glided through the air, across the dark room, and settled above Daisy. She repeated the procedure, scrutinising every movement, looking for signals, and making sure her dream was perfect.

Only the boy, now.

She noted the strong, intense reactions of the male sibling. But his haunting, wailing cries were reminiscent of someone else. Someone with whom she hardly dared to compare: Cain.

Genesis studied the reaction of the children, noting that the noises they made were not just the anguished cries of their previous dreams. These were sounds that exuded certainty and confidence; Daisy laughing, Archie smiling, Isabella's face beaming with happiness.

Maybe the final part of the Tripodean Dream was a reassurance that it would be worth the trouble ahead.

She dipped a hand into her maghole. *After all, there is always balance,* she thought. *Where there is fear, there is hope. And where there is life, there is death.*

Genesis, tired and aching, addressed the others.

'Last of all, I will give them the Gifts of the Garden of Eden. And then their journey will commence.'

Genesis's silvery-grey, ghost-like body now sat directly above Isabella's sleeping face, her maghole emitting blue shards of light over the girl's peaceful, pale face.

Quietly, Genesis began.

'*For the eldest, yellow dust—for hands and feet. Hands that guide, heal and lead. Swift feet for running.*'

She transformed the end of one of her fingers into a needle so long that it was like a sliver of pure ice that melted into nothing. She injected a tiny yellow speck into the soft flesh between thumb and finger on each of Isabella's hands. Moving down Isabella's body, she repeated the action on her ankles, the needle entering the tender skin by her Achilles tendons.

As she withdrew the needle for the final time, Genesis noted a fizz of electric blue energy flowing through and over the girl's sleeping body.

The gifts are undamaged by time, she thought.

Without hesitating, Genesis walked across the night air to Daisy, moving directly over her face. As she extended her legs Genesis signed again, the vibrations clear to the onlookers.

'Blue dust, for eyes to see when blackness falls, and ears to hear the smallest of sounds. With eyes so sharp and ears so keen, she will understand what others do not hear or see.'

A minuscule blue crystal fragment sat at the tip of the needle. With astonishing precision Genesis injected the tiny particles through the delicate tissues of Daisy's closed eyelids and into her retinas. Carefully, she slid a needle down each of Daisy's ear canals, and injected the crystals directly into her eardrums. As she withdrew the needle, Genesis saw the same electrical effervescence momentarily splaying over Daisy's outer body.

So skilful was her technique that, apart from the gentle rise and fall of their chests, Isabella and Daisy did not flicker, nor spill one single drop of blood.

Now it was the boy's turn. Genesis sensed the other dreamspinners vibrating nervously nearby. She stretched out an arm and drew it slowly back in, twisting her slender hand from side to side.

'Dreamspinners,' she announced. 'His first gift is to the heart. When the needle leaves his body it will trigger a reaction that will herald the start of their quest to open the Garden of Eden, and to save the Earth from damnation.'

'From this moment forth,' she continued, her vibrations like a whisper, 'clouds will build. There is no turning back.'

Genesis stood above Archie's chest, legs astride his face.

A roll of thunder drummed high above them as she steadied herself.

'Yellow gifts for hands and feet,' she said. *'Blue to hear and see, but red is the one for heart and mind—for power—and understanding what may be.'*

⌐ With aching limbs, Genesis galvanised herself.

'Red Dust, a gift of power, when strength is needed.' And on the word "power" Genesis thrust her arm high into the air.

She paused and steadied herself, marking the exact spot on Archie's chest where she would thrust the needle.

Moments later, the needle swept down and pierced the boy's heart.

His body fizzed as his chest cavity rose. Genesis held it as long as she dared, making sure every last speck of dust was instilled into the boy.

As she withdrew, a terrific thunderbolt spat out, rattling every window of the farmhouse.

Even Genesis trembled. Nature had awakened.

A sign from one of the other dreamspinners confirmed her suspicions that Archie's sleep waves were already changing. A strange feeling filled her. A sense of exposure, a sense she had known only once before.

My invisibility!

She concentrated hard on the boy.

Finish this.

She dipped a leg into her maghole and withdrew her final gift. *'Red Dust,'* she vibrated quickly. *'One for strength—another for courage.'*

A minuscule red fragment flashed into the tender flesh beneath Archie's chin. But before she could fulfil the task, she heard a gasp and felt a movement.

She withdrew the needle as a pain seared into her, her face burning.

Genesis looked up.

In front of her, with a face contorted by fear, Archie's eyes were open. Staring right back at her.

Candlelight filtered in to the corridor, and a soft light spread under the door into the attic room. Mrs Pye rushed in, out of breath, her hair hanging down to her waist and her sharp eyes accentuated by the glow of the candle.

'Goodness me! Oh, my dear boy,' she said, rushing over to him. 'I never heard such a terrible scream in all me life. I thought you'd died.'

Nursing him, she dabbed the sweat from his brow.

'I... I had the strangest dream, Mrs P. I swear, I was about to be stabbed by... by a—'

'Is that right?' Mrs Pye cooed. 'Stabbed? Goodness graciousness me.'

'It had an electric hole in its middle—'

'Well, well, I'm sure it did. Now, I think you're old enough not to be getting all a-tizz with that kind of bunkum,' she continued, helping him back to bed.

'Come, now. Lie back and get yourself off to sleep.'

'Please, don't go.'

'I'm staying right here till you're back in the land of nod,' Mrs Pye said sweetly. 'Now, don't you worry about a thing.'

Mrs Pye sat on the edge of his bed for some time. When he yawned, she stroked his hair and laid him down under the duvet, his head nestling into the comfort of a pillow.

A gentle, faraway tune came to her. A song that had been sung to her by Old Man Wood, who had once sat by her bedside himself. She hummed it quietly, the music soft and soothing.

Before long, Archie's breathing slowed, and he slipped into a deep slumber.

Mrs Pye kissed the young boy on the forehead.

What was it, she thought, *about this scruffy young lad? Sensitive, but coated with a layer of steel, just like Old Man Wood.*

Watching from the ceiling, her invisible status functioning once more, Genesis was relieved that the final dream had run smoothly, even if the boy might have missed out on the final part of his Gift of Eden.

If the children failed, would the blame be levelled at her?

Only time would tell.

Genesis drew her legs together and took comfort in the warm glow of electrical current that sprayed over her abdomen and nursed her burns where the boy's eyes had seared into her.

She wondered about the Tripodean Dream. Maybe Asgard was right; maybe the whole thing was foolish. And although she dared not admit it openly, she knew perfectly well this undertaking had never been designed for the children of man.

Perhaps *she* was the fool. At least she was wise enough to know that nature's wishes cannot be resisted.

And what of the old man—there to guide and help? But he had forgotten everything. Time had taken its toll, but was he now—in a curious twist of fate—*a liability?*

She dipped her claws into her maghole. She would make sure he was given a dream every night that would somehow, *somehow*—however hard, however shocking, however desperate—stir him into action. Something had to click, it just had to.

EIGHTEEN

SUE MAKES A DECISION

Sleep, on this quiet, sultry night, hadn't come easily to Sue. She'd tossed and turned, but something was niggling her, preventing her from nodding off fully.

Now, as she lay in bed, she flicked through the family photo albums.

She was particularly drawn to the pictures of herself as a baby, the ones in which she lay in her cot alongside Isabella. Friends from the very beginning. Friends now, and friends until they passed away.

There were only four pictures before she graduated to a toddler. One of the pictures was cut in half, the others were of Sue staring upwards on her tummy, always next to Isabella. A warmth spread through her.

She wondered why she'd been visited by the dreams. Why had she been lumbered with nightmares concerning the de Lowes?

Someone had once quipped that she and Isabella might be twins, but it couldn't be possible, not here. There would have been an outcry. People would have noticed.

Why would either the de Lowe parents or her own mother give away a child? Besides, if that outside possibility was true, then one of their parents would have told them by now, surely?

She examined one picture which seemed a little more grainy than the others. She noticed, in the corner, a large, old hand. She squinted as she tried to make out the background.

She pulled out her phone and applied the magnifying glass.

The picture rushed out of focus before regaining its sharpness. The camera phone blinked and, moments later, a 'bing' on her laptop told her the image had saved itself on her computer.

A couple of clicks later, and Sue was staring at an enlarged digital version of the grainy picture.

Opening her image-editing programme, she added the picture and started playing around with the options.

Zooming in on the background, she noticed a strange brown vertical wiggle in the corner, as if it might be a wooden beam of some kind. She sharpened the image and played with the contrast.

Quizzically, she slanted her head first one way, then the other.

An upright post, on a bed?

She thought about it and realised it could be a four-poster bed.

As far as she'd ever known, they'd never had one of these. Their house was modern and full of contemporary furniture. Sue knew it was the only thing her father had left her mother when she was small.

She looked again. That hand in the corner. So old and leathery, the nails thick and hard.

An uncle or her grandfather, perhaps. But her grandpa lived in Australia. She first met him when she was four years old. Her first real memory. And her uncle had brown, slender hands. Fit for an accountant.

Could it be …

She frowned.

Zooming back out, she looked at the overall image again.

She and Isabella were staring up at the lens, looking remarkably similar, although her mother insisted she was the baby on the right.

But now, zooming in on the picture, she queried this information.

She examined it close up. Wasn't that the same flop, the same little tuft of hair that fell forward on Isabella's brow, on the child on the right?

She realised whose hands they were: Old Man Wood's. The bed had to be the old four-poster with carvings that she had seen in his room.

She noticed her pulse racing.

Twins? It was impossible.

A plan quickly formed in her head. During half-term, she'd ask for her birth certificate. If that wasn't forthcoming, she'd head to the Town Hall and ask to see the registrar for Births and Deaths. That would, at least, confirm where she was from. She would then start asking questions, targeting those who might have seen them all those years ago: Hospital workers, perhaps, or the local postman.

With this knowledge, she'd be able to knock her doubts on the head.

She'd need a diversion, so that Isabella and her mother wouldn't ask questions. She'd also need a companion.

Instantly, she thought of Gus. He'd been so kind to her earlier. He'd under-stand the situation and, moreover, he could be trusted. She was certain of it.

In return for finding him a partner for his 'doo', she'd ask him to join her on her investigations. He loved doing strange things like this, even if he was a bit of a dork.

And, if she couldn't find a girl to go with him to his party, she'd go herself — at least with Gus it was bound to be a laugh.

She climbed out of bed and made her way to the window. Opening the curtains, she pushed the windows open and looked out over the rooftops of Upsall.

Glancing up, the cloud loomed larger than ever. Its blackness filled her soul with dread.

In bed, she opened her notebook. She read over exactly what she'd written down moments after she'd woken up, stains of her sweat still marking the pages.

All she had to do was tell Isabella. At least, that would unburden her from the feeling that a heavy chain hung around her neck.

She lay back and closed the book. Yes. She'd tell Isabella before the game.

After that, in secrecy, she'd get to the root of the twin thing once and for all.

She returned her diary to the desk and made her way over to the window, peering out over the eerie night sky with pinpricks of light from the streetlights in the distance.

As she looked, she heard a piercing cry from somewhere outside, the haunting notes of a scream caught on the wind. It chilled her to her core.

Quickly, she shut the window and raced back to bed.

She lay panting.

If that wasn't a cry of intense pain, then it was the cry of someone wrestling with agony.

Noting the direction, she wondered if it hadn't come all the way from Eden Cottage.

NINETEEN

CAIN'S LUCK

Asgard shifted. 'Time is moving, Cain,' he said. 'On Earth, the storm spills its anger when the Earth's sun moves to the highest point in the sky. It is time to go to the boy. It is known that one of his Gifts of the Garden of Eden failed.' Asgard hesitated. 'His "courage" may not be with him.'

'Excellent, excellent!'

'Soon, the boy sleeps. He has seen the Prophecy in his dreams. One part of it he does not understand at all. Death confuses him for he is young. That part relates to your mother, the one female Founder of the Garden of Eden. To him, she is known as the Ancient Woman. He dreams of her murder but it frightens him.'

'Her death and her end,' Cain replied. 'The power of life. I will use her murder to manipulate him.'

'Indeed. Come with me.'

Cain guffawed. 'There is hardly a stone unturned in your scheme. But hear me out one more time. How will the boy trust a spirit?'

'It may not be enough to remain invisible,' Asgard said. 'Can you bear garments?'

The ghost scratched a non-existent chin. 'There is a long, light overcoat with which I use to visit my primitive subjects. I have the strength to wear it for a short time.'

'Then gather it,' Asgard said. 'Hurry. Bring anything else that you require.'

Cain drifted away, his invisible presence marked only by the swaying movement of dust and papers wafting off the floor.

Shortly, he returned wearing a rimmed hat, a scarf, and a long overcoat.

Asgard stretched out a spindly opaque leg. 'Hold me. You will feel the sensation of energy. It is my maghole pulling you in.'

'Yes. The force is strong.'

'Good. Now crouch down, and dive like a bird as you have done before. Do this quickly.'

A tingling, gassy fizz vibrated through his ghostly frame.

'When you are ready, Cain, go!'

Cain thrust forward, a mild burning sensation shuttling through him. A millisecond later, he found himself lying on a worn carpet in a dark, creaking house.

He scoured the room, vibrations from objects and walls filling his mind with a picture, a sense of the world around him.

'You have little time,' Asgard said. 'Do the rest alone. Return to the fireplace at the bottom of the house. When you are done, hide in the chimney. I will be back before the sun rises, before the old man stirs.'

Cain floated towards the stairs.

'Remember,' Asgard called after him, 'make an ally of the child.'

'If he fears the murder of the Ancient Woman,' Cain replied, 'I will play on it.'

'Good. Arrange a place and time to meet him before the storm breaks, when he sees the power and the fury that is to come. Go now, in haste, Cain. Do your bidding.'

TWENTY

ARCHIE MEETS CAIN

Archie woke, his brief sleep disturbed.

He exhaled loudly, opened his eyes, and looked out into the blackness of the room.

Was there someone at the foot of his bed?

'Daisy? What d'you want?'

A windy chuckle came back at him. It wasn't either of his sisters.

Archie shuffled into a sitting position, stretched his arms out, and searched the room. Before long, he was able to make out a figure. A human figure, wearing a long coat and a wide-brimmed, cowboy-like hat.

Archie slipped back under his duvet. 'Who is it?' he called out in a weak voice.

'Aha! Hello!' the voice said, huskily.

Shivers raced up Archie's back. 'What can I... er... help you with, Mister?' Archie eventually stammered.

'You are the boy, aren't you?'

This wasn't the kind of question a burglar would ask.

Archie couldn't think what to say, so he remained silent as his eyes adjusted to the light.

'Ah! Forgive me for another little intrusion,' a deep, crisp voice said, 'but I have something to share with you.'

The cloaked man approached. As he neared, he raised his head.

Archie's eyes bulged. Beneath the hat, he saw straight through to the curtain.

'Now, boy, I need to speak with you about a rather urgent matter. The thing is, this time I need a favour.'

'No!' Archie reeled. 'Not you, *again*?' he blurted.

'I tell you what,' the ghost said, moving closer, 'perhaps you need a reminder?' In a flash, Cain whipped out a knife.

Archie froze as the knife floated through the air towards him. Moments later, he felt a nick just under the left side of his jaw. A drop of blood ran down his chin. Archie sidled down his bed.

The ghost moved closer, inspecting the damage. 'Goodness, now it matches the other side,' Cain said, coldly. 'You do believe I exist, don't you?'

Archie's bones rattled. He nodded.

'Good,' the ghost said. 'Let's be quite clear about that straight away.' Moving a little further from the bed, he said, 'you might be aware that you are on the threshold of something rather extraordinary. There are mortal challenges you must face. I am sure you know of them...'

'The dreams?' he stuttered.

'Precisely,' said the ghost, chuckling. '*The dreams.*'

Archie shivered. 'I don't understand.'

The ghost sucked in a mouthful of air. 'You've heard about the Garden of Eden?'

Archie's brain fizzed. Why was this ghost so interested in a place that only figured as whispers in his mind?

Archie kept as still and as quiet as he could, hoping like mad that the ghost would say his piece, not mutilate him any further, and go away.

The ghost stared at Archie for a few moments. 'Well, the Garden of Eden is where life began, where all things were created. But more recently it's been, how should I say, put on... standby. The thing is,' the ghost continued, 'there's a slim chance it may operate again, which would mean terrible things must happen to my mother.' The ghost paused as though taking stock. 'Everything clear so far?'

Archie had no idea what the ghost was talking about, but nodded anyway.

'Good. Now this event is known as the Prophecy of the Garden of Eden, and it involves you, my boy,' the ghost said, leaning in. 'I would like to help you in your quest and, in return, you can give me a hand. How do you say it, a tit-for-tat arrangement?'

Archie tried to remember to breathe. His eyes strained in their sockets, forgetting to blink. He sensed that the ghost was smiling thinly at him.

'In due course, I need you to take good care of the Ancient Woman, see that no harm comes to her.' His voice trailed off as he searched Archie's face. 'You do know about the Ancient Woman?'

Archie stayed silent.

'Well, you see,' the ghost continued, 'she's my mother and a sad old woman who's been hanging on to a mere thread of life for an awfully long time. But she'll never see any of it again because, like me, she's blind. Eyes gauged out.' The ghost paused solemnly as if remembering her. 'One day, maybe, I'll tell you more about her, but, to cut a long story short, boy, she took the noble but worthless step of sacrificing herself to keep a spark alive.'

'A spark?' Archie said, barely able to squeeze the words out. 'Of what?'

'A spark of life, I suppose.'

Archie thought he'd better play along. 'If you save your mother, will it mean you stop being a ghost?'

The ghost was thankful Archie couldn't see his face. 'Of course not,' he sobbed trying to bury the amusement in his hurt voice. 'My body is gone, but my spirit is forever.'

'But will I stop having dreams about... about death.'

'If you help me, then I solemnly promise that from this moment forth, this is exactly what will happen. No more violent, murderous dreams, young man.'

Archie exhaled. 'What... what do I have to do?'

'In due course, you must protect her, that is all,' the ghost whispered. 'There are some people that would want her dead. These people may think they are right, but rest assured they are mistaken. Dreams often show what you fear; they indicate the opposite action to what you must do in reality. In this case, you must protect her from harm—do you understand? I'm really asking so little.'

Archie smiled. Looking after the Ancient Woman seemed entirely reasonable especially as she didn't exactly exist.

He nodded, hesitatingly.

'Splendid,' said the ghost, whose invisible gaze seemed to rest on Archie for rather too long.

TWENTY-ONE

SOLOMON'S DANCING

Dancing! That's what he'd forgotten, the blasted Scottish reels! What had made him agree to that?

Goodness me, he thought. *All that twirling, stamping and clapping. The sets and the do-si-do-ing. He'd be expected to lead from the front!*

Solomon shook his head and rubbed his eyes. Drat. He hadn't done any reeling for years. It wouldn't do to make a tit of himself in front of his esteemed guests.

He climbed out of bed and studied his watch. Very early, even by his standards.

Drawing the curtains, he levered the windows open. Fresh air shot in and he breathed deeply, the oxygen waking him, and a soft wind brushing through the room. He frowned at the big cloud above, hoping that it might have blown away overnight.

He hummed a tune while moving downstairs to his office. He flicked through his old vinyl records until he came to the 'Scottish Reeling Classics'. Blowing the dust off, he pulled out the black disk and placed it over the gramophone deck.

He'd start with the "Dashing White Sergeant".

The sound crackled as the reeds of the bagpipes filled with air.

Solomon, clad only in boxer shorts and string vest, made himself a bit of space by moving a couple of chairs and exercise books off the floor. Placing a hand behind his back, he began hopping up and down.

Imagining a circle of his guests, he 'set' to an imaginary lady, clapped and turned. Yes, that was it. Set, clap to your partner, turn, figure of eight, and bow.

Onto the next.

The music of the Highland Band filled the room. Solomon skipped through the song, growing in confidence as the memories came flooding back.

Hop, clap, and turn. Bow and twist.

After the third tune, he collapsed into his armchair, and sipped a glass of water.

He wondered about his guest list. *Pity,* he thought, *that the de Lowe parents couldn't make it.* He shook his head. *One minute they were here, the next they'd gone.* No wonder the faces of the children had dropped when he'd passed on the news. Such was the archaeologists' life, he supposed.

In the public eye of archaeology, they were very much seen as stars in their field, even if they didn't show it. They would have fitted in happily with the guest list of prominent men and women of the area.

His train of thought moved on to the children. He had to admit the set-up up there on the moors was more than decent. The old man had looked well, Mrs Pye obviously cared for the children splendidly, and the house was in good order. Solomon wondered if he shouldn't have talked to Isabella further. Oh, well, the deed was done.

A passing thought struck him. He wondered whether he should ask the de Lowe children to come along to the party. Make a bit of a fuss of them. Perhaps they could help the catering staff with their chores. He nodded at the thought. Isabella was his most gifted pupil, a prize-winning scholar, and Daisy their greatest athlete. He could make a show of them, and introduce them to his guests.

Archie could look after the coats. Then again, he'd probably lose them.

He walked over to the gramophone and turned over the record. It was a sterling idea. He'd ask the children after the football match, as a surprise. A consolation prize, or maybe even as a reward for Daisy? The gesture would also show Isabella that he took her seriously.

Solomon smiled as he bowed to the music, clapped his hands, and, with one arm in the air, spun and hopped his portly frame around the room until the music ran its course.

After dinner, there was a disco.

What better way to get everyone going, than by having a few of the youth around to start the dancing? Rumour had it that Daisy was a very energetic dancer, particularly, he'd heard, at a type of movement called "rave".

He pondered this thought as he selected another disc from his collection, 'Disco Hits of the Seventies'. A cracker, if he recalled.

The music came on. Solomon nodded his bald head in time with the beat.

Feeling his body come alive, Solomon thrust a hand high into the air, and gyrated his hips.

'Daisy de Lowe,' he said, as he jived with the music, 'will be second fiddle to these kinds of shapes!'

TWENTY-TWO

CAIN OFFERS A PLAN

The boy—this Heirs of Eden—has absolutely no idea what is going to happen, Cain thought, as he hovered into the middle of the room. *He has found no meaning in his dreams. Do these people now ignore visions? If so, these Heirs of Eden will never survive the storm, let alone find the cave of riddles, the one place they must reach that shows the secrets to gaining the tablets that lead to the Garden of Eden.*

It is time to execute the plan.

He floated back to Archie's bedside. 'There is another way,' he crowed.

Archie didn't move a muscle, the leadenness of sleep preventing him.

'I want you to consider joining me, physically, as my flesh and blood.'

Archie yawned. 'Join you?'

'Not right now of course,' Cain continued. 'I'd like you to think about it. But bonding with me will save your life.'

Archie stretched his arms out wide. 'Save my life,' he repeated, involuntarily closing his eyes. 'Sure it will.'

'Good-good. I'm thrilled... delighted,' Cain said, feeling the weight of his coat on his frame. 'About the knife,' he continued. 'I don't have time to explain things in depth, so occasionally it pays to use other means.'

'But, Mister... sir,' Archie said, summoning his energy and his courage. 'If I did this bonding thing, what's in it for me?'

'For you? Ah yes!' the ghost crowed. 'What's in it for you, aside from saving your existence on this planet?'

The spirit drew himself up as best he could.

'I hold the secrets of ages past, boy. I will give you strength and courage, so that you are feared and respected. You will have the power of a horse and the courage of a lion. I give you my word. All you have to do is meet me tomorrow morning. Somewhere safe. Then, I will show you what will happens and when you know the facts, you will choose to join me freely.'

His voice turned darker.

'A terrible time is coming, boy. You have seen the prophecy and, deep down, you know it is a hopeless situation. I offer you salvation.'

'The prophecy,' Archie stammered. 'That's the nightmare, isn't it?'

'Yes, indeed,' the ghost crowed. 'Meet with me in no more than nine of your hours, and no less than eight, before the sun rises to its highest point. Tell me a place where no one will see us.'

Archie tried to think. 'Er... there's a back alleyway above the bank above the football field by the school,' he said, trying to swallow a yawn. 'You'll know you've found it when you see two houses leaning in on each other, sort of head-butting each other. It's usually pretty quiet.'

'Excellent,' the ghost gushed. 'Wear a long overcoat, like mine, and a scarf. Do you have a scarf?'

Archie didn't, but he lied and said he did.

'And do you like sweet treats, boy?'

'A bit, I suppose,' Archie replied, thinking what a strange question it was. 'Old Man Wood's the sucker for sweet things in our house. He's always dipping his fingers in the sugar bowl, and getting told off by Mrs Pye.'

The ghost chuckled. 'Is that so?'

A groan from the bed nearby signalled that Daisy was stirring.

'I must leave. We meet before noon in the alleyway,' the ghost whispered, drifting to the door. 'Tonight's chat, young man, is our own little secret. Any tongue-wagging and our deal is off.'

Cain stopped, as if an idea had popped into his head. 'Tell me your name, boy?'

'Archie de Lowe.'

'I will save you, Archie de Lowe.'

Archie caught a glimpse of the knife.

As the ghost reached the door, he turned. 'Be in no doubt that your life will change forever in a few hours from now. The strength of a horse and the courage of a lion! You will never regret it.'

Archie nodded. 'What... what's your name?' he asked.

'Ah, yes. The finer details.' His eye sockets bored into Archie, who felt as though his heart was briefly being sucked out. 'I am the ghost of Cain, Frozen Lord of Havilah, Son of the Ancient Woman. Do you have a cup of water, boy?'

Archie pointed to the table just behind him.

Cain hovered to it and dropped something in the cup. 'You will need this. Drink. It may give you strength.'

And with those words, Cain slipped quietly out of the door.

Archie fell back on his pillows, rubbing his eyes. *What the heck was that about?*

He didn't know what was real and what wasn't anymore. He knew, though, that there was no way he was going to turn up at this meeting with the ghost, whatever powers had been offered to him in return.

Lions and horses! Twaddle.

He studied the clock. Three-thirty-five.

He did a quick calculation. Eight hours from now and it would be… bang in the middle of the football match. Nine hours and the game would just be finishing.

Another classic Archie timetable cock-up.

He breathed a sigh of relief. Problem sorted; he wasn't missing the game, certainly not for a knife-wielding ghost, whatever the cost.

Relieved, Archie closed his eyes and drifted back to sleep.

Gaia raced across the air to the boy.

Cain, forever banned from leaving Havilah, had discovered a way to the Heirs of Eden only hours after the last part of the Tripodean Dream had been given! This was beyond comprehension.

Gaia anchored her legs either side of Archie's head, and spun a hazy-styled dream.

With any luck, as the sun rose and humans readied themselves for a new day, the meeting with Cain might feel as if it had never happened.

TWENTY-THREE

HAVILARIAN TOADSTOOL POWDER

Talking to Archie, an idea so simple, and yet so brilliant, had popped into Cain's head.

Cain pulled a small jar out of his pocket and examined it, smiling.

Havilarian toadstool powder; a lethal poison, with the power to kill those who came from the Garden of Eden. In one stroke, he'd reduce the old man to a spirit. Just like him.

Adam's value would be nullified, not that he had much worth anyway. *But why not take the chance, while he had it?*

Cain reached the hallway. *No signs of Asgard. Good,* he thought, *better the dream-spinner doesn't know.*

The ghost cursed. Wearing a coat for such a long time had drained his strength. He let the garment cascade to the floor as he searched the room, sensing vibrations. In no time he had created a map in his mind's eye.

He headed down a corridor, and came to an open door. He slipped through and instantly sized up the energy in the room. Before long, the outlines of a table and chairs, and the vibrations of plants and foodstuffs came to him, hanging off the easy-to-identify metal hooks clasped onto the beams of the ceiling.

Turning to his left, he discovered the strong vibrations of a smouldering fire— a cooker. Good.

He thought about sweet foods, like honey or, how did the boy say it, *sugary-things*?

Yes! There, near the cooker, in a small container. Sweet granules, exactly as he hoped.

It's easy to see, he thought, *when one has aeons of time. It's easy to understand how energy spins, fires and vibrates around every single thing.*

Cain cursed. His strength sapped by the coat, he found that pouring the Havilarian toadstool powder into the bowl was more of an effort than he'd bargained for. As he did, tiny squeals emanated.

Perfect. The fungi are alive.

Cain drifted out of the room, along the corridor, into the living room, and back to the fireplace.

He felt for the aura of the dreamspinner.

Nothing.

Above him, he could hear yawns. The old man stirring. Feet padding on the ceiling above.

Come on, Asgard, where are you?

A moment later, the stairs groaned with a heavy footstep.

Cain didn't want to hang about. Even though he knew he couldn't be seen, he certainly didn't want to be found in the house of his father, the home of his greatest enemy.

As the footsteps neared, a small vibration squeaked out. 'Master, it is Asgard. Dive straight ahead. Do nothing else.'

'About time,' Cain snapped.

Without waiting to be prompted, Cain knelt down and sprang towards the dreamspinner, hoping like mad it was the right place. As he left, he heard a small cough as Old Man Wood entered the room.

TWENTY-FOUR

SIMILAR DREAMS

Archie stretched his arms and thrust out his chin. As he did so, he felt the sting of a fresh cut. He froze. Cloudy images of the previous night rushed in. He dashed into the bathroom and stared back at his reflection.

A small incision, just as he expected, mirroring the cut from the night before.

Archie couldn't believe it.

And why were the words "horse" and "lion" swimming in his head?

'The weight of a horse and the looks of a lion? Nah,' he said aloud to his reflection, shaking his head. *The head of a horse and the body of a lion*?

Archie sprayed water on his face. *The bite of a lion and the kick of a horse? No, no.* Deep in thought, he headed towards the kitchen, letting the water spill onto the floor as he went.

Mrs Pye looked up as Archie came sloping in. 'You taking an elephant for a walk?' she said.

'Elephant?' he repeated, before realising what she meant. He tried not to break into a smile.

'What is the matter with you lot?' Mrs Pye complained. 'Slumping and skulking and screaming in the night.'

Archie coughed. 'Oh. Isabella and Daisy had a bad night again. I think they're talking about some, er..., girlie things. You know...' Archie mumbled.

'Periods?' Mrs Pye squealed. 'Daisy's becoming a woman now, is she? About time, I suppose.'

Girlie things? Archie went bright red. Oh dear. This was absolutely the last thing on his mind.

He changed the subject, fast. 'My throat's sore, Mrs P, and my head hurts. It's like someone's tightened a clip around my neck.'

'Come here and I'll take a look.'

Archie sidled over to the sink, and Mrs Pye took his head gently in her hands. 'What are these cuts on your chin? Have you been playing with your knives again?'

'Of course, I haven't,' Archie said, weakly. 'Caught my face on something.'

Mrs Pye looked at Archie suspiciously. 'I won't tell anyone about your knife throwing, you know that. I know you like to sneak off to that old potting shed and practice, though heavens only knows why.'

She took his hand, before feeling his forehead and the back of his neck. 'It's your big sister who doesn't approve.'

Mrs Pye finished her medical. 'Well, you is a bit sweaty, young man. Could be a fever coming on.'

She rubbed her chin, thinking about what might be the best cure. 'I reckon you need a couple of...'

'Apples?' Archie suggested.

Mrs Pye raised her eyebrows. 'How did you know?'

Archie smiled. Mrs Pye's medical knowledge was virtually non-existent and Old Man Wood's extraordinary variety of apples in the orchard just happened to be her number one cure for everything.

After an unexpectedly large breakfast they returned to their room. Archie felt it was time to question his sister. 'Daisy,' he began quietly, 'last night you called out, "Tripodean Dream" several times. Why?'

A shadow fell over her face. 'Another nightmare,' she began. 'I've had three, each one utterly disturbing, but this dream was the best... and the worst... and the weirdest.'

She turned to her sister for support. 'They've been so real. I could smell things, and understand everything. Birds, trees, and plants talked to me. *Talked, Archie!* It's so... so complicated and bonkers and confusing. I don't know where to begin.'

Daisy scrunched her face up and ran a hand through her hair, trapping a finger on a knot. 'One minute, there's this knackered old woman telling me about a wonderful, beautiful place. The next minute I'm in a terrifying storm, like an endless hurricane, and the storm is chasing me. Lightning, mudslides, and tonnes of water coming after me, beating me to death...' She tailed off, scratching the back of her neck.

'What is it, Daisy?' Isabella asked.

'I dreamt I reached a sanctuary. It was only then that I was safe from the storm. Kind of like heaven, but with pictures on the walls.'

She shook her head. 'I still don't know what it's supposed to mean.'

Isabella set her books down on the table and pulled up a chair.

'Daisy, in your nightmare, what happened to this Ancient Woman?'

'Well, I'm pretty confident this haggard old woman kept trying to tell us something,' Daisy said. 'But each time she did, she died.'

'Are you sure?'

'Yeah,' Daisy said, her eyes wide. 'A violent, horrible death, different every time. And it was like being there, standing next to her. I could feel myself screaming.'

She took the stunned silence from the others as a green light to continue. 'Look, I know it sounds nuts, but this Ancient Woman knew about us... she knew *everything* about us, even though I think we were on an entirely different planet.'

Her eyes searched her elder sister's face, urging her to believe. Daisy's bottom lip began to tremble, and tears moistened in her eyes. 'I've tried to blot it out, but I think I'm going crazy.'

Without warning, a teardrop spilled from Isabella's eye.

'Oh, no. Not you as well!' Archie said.

'Yes. Me, too!' Isabella cried, lines of water now streaming down her cheeks. 'Same, exactly.'

Archie's eyes nearly popped out of his head. 'But this is madness—'

'I know.'

Archie was confused. 'You're sure it was just like Daisy's dream? You're not making it up?'

'Yes! I'm positive. It's the truth,' Isabella insisted. 'I swear. Three intense, clear dreams like Daisy described, except I was in a hall of mirrors. I've never been so amazed or happy or terrified, and, just as Daisy said, the dreams ended the same. In death.'

She clenched her hand. 'I kept seeing lightning and rain. Torrential, terrible rain. You know how I've been going on about this deluge, it's terrifying me. It's as if this stupid storm wants to target us, alone, until we make it to this weird cave, just as you said.'

They both nodded.

'And, Bells, you saw this Ancient Woman?' Daisy asked. 'What did you think?'

Isabella thought for a moment. 'She'd been stuck. Abandoned someplace, I think. She's pathetic, desperate, waiting. Waiting for...'

'For what?'

Isabella shrugged. 'I don't know. Us, perhaps?'

'But her eyes had been gouged out, so she didn't know where she was,' Daisy said.

'Exactly! You're right.'

'No eyes, but she had a gentleness; an aura of kindness and love,' Daisy continued. 'She was disgusting to look at, though. All shrivelled up, like one of Old Man Wood's prunes.'

'Probably even more withered,' Isabella added with a thin smile. 'I don't know how she's still alive. It was as if she held the key to something...'

Archie had become noticeably quiet over the past few minutes. As if by instinct, the girls noticed.

'What about you, Archie?' they said.

Archie swivelled and faced the girls, his face ashen.

'Yeah,' he said, shakily. 'I've dreamt of this storm and this Ancient Woman on three occasions—just like you.'

The girls gasped.

Archie stared at them, his eyes red and brimming with tears.

He dropped his head.

'The thing is, in each of my dreams, it's me who kills her.'

TWENTY-FIVE

OVERCOAT

Eventually, Isabella spoke. 'Look. I know it's odd, but these are only dreams, you know. They're just our minds worrying about things. Dreams aren't real, however much they appear to be.'

'If you don't think there's any truth in them,' Archie said, 'why did you go to such lengths to make a barometer and a storm glass? You must have thought there was something to it.'

Isabella thought for a moment. 'Sue had had a similar dream, too. I suppose I wanted to try something—anything—to prove or disprove the dreams, scientifically.'

'So, four of us have had the same dream,' Archie said. 'Perhaps there's some kind of storm demon out there, hurling dreams at us, and we just happened to catch them?'

'But Sue had the dreams, and she lives miles away,' Daisy added.

Archie guffawed. 'She does sleep over a lot.'

'Don't be silly, Archie,' Isabella sneered. 'Of course sleep demons don't exist.'

Daisy suddenly piped up. 'The Fitzroy storm glass! Where is it?'

Isabella stood up, plucked the glass out of the fire grate, and placed it on top of the mantelpiece.

The children stared at it, as though it held the answers to all their problems. 'It's still cloudy with little stars,' Archie said, mischievously.

Daisy focused more intently. 'Actually,' she whispered, entranced, 'those little stars are belting around? What does it mean?'

Isabella sighed, 'I don't know what it means or what it's supposed to show. It's not my finest work.'

Daisy wasn't convinced. 'Just out of interest,' she said, 'for simple-minded people like me, who never saw it before, what was the glass like when you began this mad project?'

'Cloudy,' Archie said, 'just like it is now.'

'Thanks, Archie, very helpful,' Daisy said. 'Well, it's like a game of pinball in there,' she said. 'There's way more going on than simply cloudy little particles shooting all over the place.'

Isabella strode over and squinted. 'There's nothing here but a foggy substrate,' she announced. 'You're wasting your time, Daisy. Come on you two, get your things. You've got this big match to play today, or had you forgotten?'

Daisy frowned. 'You think we should just ignore it all; the dreams, the cave, the Ancient Woman, everything?'

'Yes, I do,' she replied.

'Really?'

'Absolutely. One hundred percent. I believe it's purely a coincidence, that's all. These dreams are parasites of fear.'

The twins grabbed their sports bags, Daisy stealing a last glance at the storm glass before Isabella popped it into her bag.

'We need to get a move on,' Isabella said. 'My guess is that, somehow, this big cloud sitting above us has made our brain patterns react oddly in advance of a storm breaking. With my scientific hat on, I'd say we ignore the whole thing. Yorkshire storms are never that bad.'

The twins shrugged. Isabella was the school boffin and, much as they hated to admit it, she was generally correct.

'I realise I'm pretty rubbish in Chemistry, or whatever science category the glass belongs in,' Daisy said, earnestly. 'But I'd keep a really close eye on that Fitzroy storm thing-a-me-thing if I were you.'

The children had barely stepped out of the door when Old Man Wood's deep voice stopped them short.

'*Wait!*' he yelled from the doorway. 'Did any of you leave this coat? I found it in the corridor.' A large overcoat dangled over his arm. 'Nice one too, with an unusual pattern on the lining. Sure I've seen it somewhere before.'

Archie missed a step and stumbled, righting himself before his nose split the floor.

Old Man Wood noticed. 'Yours, is it, Archie? Looks a touch big for you, mind.'

Archie doubled back, his body trembling. Without looking at Old Man Wood, he inspected the coat and shoved a hand inside one of the pockets. The hairs on his back shot up.

'Back in a second,' he yelled, as he flew up the stairs.

Archie sprinted into the attic room where he spied the cup of water, tinged slightly blue, exactly as he'd left it. In one movement, he drained the glass.

'Everything all right, Archie?' Old Man Wood asked.

'Fine,' Archie answered.

'Right-oh,' Old Man Wood said. 'Your coat?'

'Oh, yeah, it's a friend's. Must have grabbed it by mistake, in a rush.'

'Big fella, is he?'

'Yeah. I suppose,' Archie said, as casually as he could.

Old Man Wood handed him the coat. But as he did so a knife slipped out of the pocket and tinkled onto the paving slabs.

'A knife, Archie? You know you shouldn't carry one of those at school.'

Archie's heart skipped a beat. 'It's only plastic. A stage knife, you know... drama stuff.' He smiled, bending down to pick up the knife, just beating Old Man Wood to it. 'The bloke who owns the coat is the lead part in the play.'

'He certainly has an interesting taste in knives,' Old Man Wood commented, raising an eyebrow. 'Well, on you go, young Archie, and remember to save those footballs.'

Archie set off to catch up with the girls. As he ran, his heart was thumping like a huge bass drum, and his head buzzed with a mixture of dread and excitement.

Old Man Wood knew it was a beauty; a knife worthy of a powerful man. From the clinking noise it made when it dropped on the floor, he would have bet a coin or two that it was made from silver and steel. From the way the light reflected through the stones on the handle, he'd have taken another wager that its jewels were unique; most likely rubies and pink diamonds.

It wasn't a plastic knife. Not in a million years.

He couldn't remember how he could tell a cheap knife from a proper knife, but he had been the one to show Archie how to master a knife all those years ago: how to test the balance and weight that would determine the revolutions and power of the throw.

Old Man Wood mulled this over, wondering what light his brain might shed on the subject. No, nothing there, just a deep penetrating pain in his mind, like toothache.

And why did that funny old coat stir his curiosity? The lining had taken his breath away. Was it the pattern?

He'd seen thousands of patterns of snakes and trees, or snakes slithering around poles, all the way through his long life.

Why did this one make him feel nervous and thrilled at the same time?

He replayed the moment he glimpsed the lining for the first time. That odd feeling again, as if the snake had actually moved, as if it had slithered up into the tree right there on the fabric itself.

Old Man Wood paced around the room.

He'd noted the buttons too. A matching crest of a snake winding through branches.

Nothing I can do about it now, he told himself, *whatever it might mean.*

Suddenly, a thought smashed into his head, electrifying his entire body.

He sat down in his large, worn armchair, cupping his face in his big, leathery, old hands.

What if the material of that jacket wasn't from Earth?

He'd never seen a fabric that had the ability to change shape here on Earth before, but, if he remembered correctly, the marks of the snake and the tree were from... the Garden of Eden?

A surge of energy rushed through his body, making him feel strong for a second or two.

Time to research those old carvings, he thought, *and shed light on that overcoat's true home.*

TWENTY-SIX

THE JOURNEY TO SCHOOL

Assured by Isabella's dream diagnosis, the girls had a spring in their step as they headed down the track. From the top of the hill, the banks on either side of the road gradually increased in height, as if a giant digger had gouged the lane out of the hillside. The lane acted as a drain taking the water off the hill, and even in the driest summer a constant trickle dribbled from the moors to the river below.

Branches of oak, ash, maple, wild cherry, crab-apple, blackthorn and hawthorn made a thick canopy high above the road and today, it was coloured in a mat of rust, red and gold autumnal colours.

On a clear day it looked as if glitter had been sprinkled on the track as the sunlight flickered through the trees. Today it was almost pitch black, and the tree roots supporting the bank twisted through the rock and soil, reaching out like the arms and legs of decaying corpses. Sue still called it 'the big graveyard ditch', but the children were used to it; it was their daily walk to school. The idea of it being scary had long gone.

Nonchalantly, Archie told the girls that the coat was Kemp's dad's, and they must have got muddled up in the cloakroom. But although he slumped along quietly, his heart was thudding in his chest, and his brain worked overtime as he tried desperately to remember what had happened during the night.

The girls didn't bother to question him further.

For someone as disorganised as Archie, mistaking a coat was as common as being late for a lesson.

Half way down, they stopped by a large oak with a huge bough that leaned over the road. Daisy climbed nimbly up the steep, tall bank, using the roots as handgrips. At the top, she uncoiled a rope wrapped around the branch and tossed down the slack end.

Archie went first. He took off, climbing the rope until his feet settled on a large knot at the bottom. Swinging backwards and forwards, the warm wind rushed through his hair.

As the line slowed, he jumped down, running to a stop.

'Pathetic, Arch,' Daisy said. 'What's up with you?'

'Nerves,' he replied. 'Not really in the mood.'

Isabella went next. She sat on the knot and swung backwards and forwards at a leisurely speed, as she always did. Finally, Daisy mounted the rope and asked Archie to pull her up the hill as far as he could.

'Watch this,' she said, her eyes glimmering.

Archie let go, and Daisy soared forwards, hair flying, until she was horizontal with the bank, touching the canopy. She swung back, screaming in delight, and bashed into the bank on the other side.

'Daisy! Enough. We've got to go to school,' Isabella said, trying to catch the rope. 'Kill yourself on the way back, but we're running late as it is.'

'Oh sure,' Daisy said, coming to a stop and tucking the rope around a protruding root system. 'I bet we'll be too tired, or it'll be too dark, or some other rubbish excuse as always.'

'Daisy,' Isabella replied, 'after today, you have all of half term to swing yourself into hospital.'

At last the steep track levelled out and the height of the bank lowered, like the end of a playground slide. At the old wooden bridge, the children peered over the handrail at the water running beneath and looked for fish gliding in the pools next to the chunky oak uprights.

Isabella noted how, in the strange light, the school tower to their left looked enormous compared to the tiny boathouse by the river. She wondered if the old rowing boat they'd once played around in was still fit for purpose.

The children arrived at the lush, velvety green football pitch. White posts all the way round balanced safety ropes to keep the spectators at bay. Set back from each corner, the moveable floodlight towers dominated the pitch like metallic giants standing guard.

Daisy ran across the bold, alternating stripes with its tattoo-like, fresh white markings. She practised kicks, flicks, and tricks and commentated loudly on the goals she was going to score later.

Before long, they were across the playing field, and heading up the steps to their form rooms.

TWENTY-SEVEN

GENESIS CONSIDERS

Genesis drew her legs together, taking comfort from the warm glow of her electrical current.

She soothed the burns from where the boy's eyes had scalded her, and wondered whether Asgard was right.

Had nature, the universe, got it wrong?

Could the Heirs of Eden, mere children, survive nature's fury, and nature's power, and go on to find the tablet of creation?

This undertaking had never been designed for children of mankind. But nature's wishes cannot be resisted. Not at any cost.

What about the old man, too? Time had taken its toll. He was old, but was he now, in a curious twist of fate, a *liability*?

One by one, she dipped her slender legs into her maghole.

She would make sure a dream was given to Old Man Wood every night that would somehow, *somehow*, stir him into action.

Genesis stretched out another leg, dipped it in her maghole and watched as the blue light swirled in and around it like threads spinning on a stick.

With these thoughts, she dipped her head, and inverted through her maghole, vanishing into thin air.

TWENTY-EIGHT

KEMP TRIES TO MAKE UP

Archie noticed Kemp sitting quietly at his desk, reading a book.

Let sleeping dogs lie, he thought, *especially unpredictable dogs.*

Without any fuss, Archie made his way to the other side of the room, draped the coat over the back of his chair, sat down, and put his head in his hands. He desperately tried to remember what the ghost had said. A meeting, something about a lion and a horse? After writing down a couple of variations, Archie realised that it might be something to do with strength and courage.

He remembered that he would be saved, *but from what exactly?*

Hadn't he agreed on something as well, such as joining the ghost in some form of partnership? It didn't make any sense but, and it was a huge BUT, the ghost's coat and dagger were right here in this room. So it couldn't be a false memory, regardless of Isabella's certainty that their recent experiences were figments of their imaginations.

Archie teased the nicks on each side of his chin. Another reminder.

He pulled out a piece of paper, and nibbled the end of a pencil.

"*Possible meeting place*", he wrote.

He racked his brain. Was it down by the boatyard, or up by one of the big willow trees? He wrote both down, but shook his head. No. Neither option rang true. He wondered if it was the alley above the football pitch, and he wrote that down as well.

He underlined it twice and leaned back in his chair. Yes, that one rang a bell.

His thoughts were interrupted by a friendly, slightly painful, wallop on his shoulders. It was Gus Williams who had bounced into the room. 'Morning Archie. You're not by any chance writing a "to-do" list, are you?' he said sarcastically.

Archie smiled. If Kemp was an otter with big lips, Gus was a laughing donkey. 'No, don't be ridiculous,' he said.

Gus read the list. 'Lost something?'

'Nah. Just trying to remember a dream.'

'Oh, well that's okay,' Williams said, cheerily. 'So long as it wasn't a big and complicated one?'

'Well, as a matter of fact, it was.' Archie smiled. 'Now, go away and leave me to think.'

'News alert!' Williams announced to the room, his grin almost completely covering his face. 'Archie de Lowe is thinking! Give him plenty of room, oxygen at the ready.' Gus leant down again. 'Next, you'll be telling me Daisy's caught the same bug,' he whispered. 'Good luck!'

He smiled and sprang off like a big, energetic puppy to his desk at the back of the room.

Kemp had listened in to Archie's conversation with Gus. He'd bet money Archie had forgotten something again and by the looks of it this time the object was more important than usual.

Kemp stood up quietly. 'Morning, Archie, everything cool?'

Archie groaned. First Gus, now Kemp.

'Not really, Kemp,' he replied.

'Lost something?'

'No,' he started. 'Well, kind of.' Archie groaned. 'Actually, I had another dreadful nightmare. I'm trying to remember it.'

'Oh, yeah?' Kemp replied.

'Yeah,' Archie said. 'A couple of really strange experiences, but, poof, gone for ever.'

Kemp laughed. 'Want to talk about it?'

Archie stared at Kemp. 'I told you, I'm not talking to you after what you did yesterday.'

'Really?' Kemp sighed. 'Look, I had a think and last night I decided that I'm going to change. No more jokes, no more pranks. I promise—'

'You said that before, and let me down. In fact, you lied to me. Christ! Kemp, I had to own up for your stupidity, and you made me feel like an idiot. Luckily Isabella didn't believe me.'

Kemp sucked in his cheeks. 'I've told Jackson and Pulse that I don't want to be part of the gang. When I'm with them, I act like a... well, like a total dickhead. I don't know what comes over me. The bottom line is I'm actually sick of it, too.'

Kemp noted Archie's look of disgust. 'Arch, if you don't believe me, go and ask them,' he continued. 'They're over there in the corner playing on their phones like happy little freaks. Seriously, I don't want to hurt anyone anymore. I really don't.' He dropped his voice and briefly stole a look over his shoulder. 'I want to be your friend.'

'Blimey, Kemp, this isn't the time. Right now, I've literally got a nightmare on my hands. I'm not going to trust you until I know you mean what you say.'

'What do you want me to do? I've promised I won't be nasty to either of your sisters. I'm going to put all that anger behind me. I won't even speak to your sisters if you don't want.'

'I bet you've already arranged with your Sutton mates that Daisy's going to get a kicking though, haven't you?'

Kemp winced. 'There's not much I can do about that now, is there?'

'The only reason you're being 'Mr Nice' is because if they kick her out of the game we'll lose and she won't play in the team after half term. That would leave room for someone else, wouldn't it. And that person will probably be you.'

Kemp's expression had changed. 'You know what, Archie,' he spat. 'I meant what I just said. Throw it back in my face, why don't you.'

'Well, that's rich, coming from you,' Archie said, standing up. He looked him in the eye. 'I swore on my life that I wouldn't tell anyone about the glass and I kept my word. You, Kemp... well, you're a lying, deceitful disgrace to your dead parents, your aunt, your school and, more importantly, to yourself.'

TWENTY-NINE

AN ABUSE OF POWER

The dreamspinner was astonished to learn a couple of things. First, that it was Cain who knew about the children's dreams and their gifts. Second, that Archie had no idea about his own gifts; but Cain knew enough about them to exploit him.

Gaia thought it through, reaching the same conclusion. One of *them* must have gone to Cain. But dreamspinners were neutral in all things. They did not meddle, and they never had.

Only four dreamspinner Elders had seen the gift ceremony: Genesis, Asgard, Juno and herself.

Was Genesis bitter about appearing in front of the boy? No, it didn't add up.

What about Asgard? He was the one who had objected to the Gifts of the Garden of Eden being given to children, but he was also the most passionate about giving dreams.

Or Juno, the quiet one?

Yes, Gaia thought, maybe it was her. Why? What was her motive?

Another thought whistled into Gaia's mind. Cain was a spirit, so what if he had travelled through one of their magholes, or perhaps the maghole of another dreamspinner, to escape Havilah?

It was the only possible explanation she could think of.

She searched her vibrations.

Nothing close by.

This dreamspinner would have to be caught in the act. But dreamspinners moved so fast through the universes, it was as if they were a multi-dimensional fluid.

Catching one would not be easy.

THIRTY

ARCHIE TELLS KEMP

The incredible silence hovering over the room was broken by the bell.

'By my watch,' Mr Steele said, hitching up his sleeve and twisting his arm as though showing off a priceless treasure, 'the time is approaching half past nine. After I have dismissed you, you have an extended free period. Please use this for last minute drama rehearsals; like learning your lines, Mr Ford; or practising your clarinet, Miss Buxton; or for recital practice before the programme this afternoon, Mr Anderson.'

Mr Steele stuck his nose in the air and twitched his moustache. It was a signal that he was going to say something profound. 'Now, about the weather. There is a rather large cloud b*rrr*ewing right above us.' He rolled the 'r' rather dramatically.

'To put your minds at rest, our headmaster has been in touch with the Met Bureau to find out if this might be a cause for concern. I am happy to report that, as far as they know, there are none. This morning and this afternoon, there is a high chance that we may get a little wet; indeed there may even be a possibility of a heavy downpour. But all school activities are scheduled to go on as usual.

'Daisy de Lowe, please remove that lipstick from your desk. Now, remember, class, just in case lightning strikes, what would be the best course of action to take? Anyone? Ah, yes, Alexander?'

'Put up your umbrella, sir.'

'No, you do not, Alexander. And stop laughing. Allen, will you desist from flicking paper balls at Daisy please?' He glared at the boys, 'Umbrellas, as you know perfectly well, are for repelling water. I'm talking about lightning strikes.'

Steele raised his eyebrows in anticipation. 'Kemp, what would you do?'

'I'd get the hell out of there before I was shrivelled to a crisp.'

The class laughed.

'Well, it's better than holding up an umbrella, but where would you go?'

Little Jimmy Nugent put up his hand.

'Yes, Nugent.'

'I've been told that, if you get in a car, the rubber tyres would earth the strike, wouldn't they, Sir?'

Mr Steele clasped his hands together. 'Very good, Nugent, and you're absolutely correct. Either get indoors, or hop in a car—'

'My granddad,' Nugent continued, 'got killed by a bolt of lightning in 1983, while walking his bull terrier called Plank—'

'Did he, Nugent?' Mr Steele sensed one of Nugent's stories coming on. 'How fascinating. Perhaps you might fill me in another time.'

Steele turned back to the pupils. 'Now, Class, do your best today and make us all proud. Afterwards, have a safe and relaxing break. You are dismissed.'

The pupils instantly divided into several small groups. Archie remained in his chair, twiddling his pencil.

Kemp quietly made his way over. 'Come on, Archie, it can't be that bad. You look terrible. I can help if you want... if we're still friends?'

Archie shrugged. 'Sure. Sorry about the outburst. Been a bad morning, that's all.'

'Sounds terrible—'

'You have no idea,' Archie replied. 'Really, if I told you, you would never, ever believe me.'

'Try me.'

Archie sighed. 'Nah. You'll only laugh.'

'Go on. I promise I won't tell a soul.'

'Look, Kemp, we've been there.'

'If you don't talk to someone, it just gets bottled up. My shrink told me that.'

Archie fingered his pen. What did he have to lose? 'You won't believe me,' he heard himself say.

'I promise you I won't judge. I'll just listen. That's what friends are for, right?'

Archie exhaled. 'Okay,' he began. 'If you really want to know, last night I was visited by something that, as far as I could tell, was a ghost.'

'A ghost?' Kemp coughed. 'Really?'

'Yes. Really.' Archie fired back. 'I told you that you wouldn't believe me.'

Kemp eyed him suspiciously and raised his hands. 'Cool. A ghost... carry on.'

Archie rubbed his forehead. 'Well, this ghost promised me stuff if I met up with him.'

'Yeah? What did you say?'

'I think I kind of agreed. I was half asleep. What would you do?'

'I'd probably agree too,' Kemp said. 'Was it a nice ghost or a nasty ghost?'

'Bit of both, I think. It was wielding a knife, but at the same time I'm pretty sure it wanted to help.'

'Well that's all right,' Kemp said, sounding like an authority on the subject. 'The ghost had a knife and it didn't kill you. That's a start.'

Archie hadn't thought of this.

'Any idea where you're hooking up?'

'That's the problem,' Archie replied. 'I can't remember. I thought it was a dream, so I agreed to everything and said the first thing that came into my head.'

'What makes you think it wasn't a dream?'

Archie pointed at the coat. 'This.'

Kemp looked at it. 'An overcoat! Bleeding heck, Archie.' Kemp wondered if Archie hadn't entirely lost his marbles.

'I know,' Archie said, quickly realising it must sound idiotic, 'but I swear it's the same coat the ghost was wearing. I remember those buttons with the snake up a tree.'

Kemp thrust out his jaw and furrowed his brow. 'How do you know it isn't Old Whatsisface's?'

'Old Man Wood,' Archie said. 'His name is "Old Man Wood".'

'Yeah right, chill your boots,' Kemp said, holding the coat up. 'I mean it's pretty big—about his size—are you sure he wasn't... giving it to you? You know, offloading it before he took it to the charity shop.'

Archie shook his head. 'No, definitely not. Old Man Wood only has patched up clothes, certainly not an overcoat like this one. Anyway, there's more.'

'More?' Kemp raised his eyebrows. 'Blimey. I mean, great.'

Archie turned his head up. 'Look at these. Cuts from the blade of the knife I was telling you about—'

'From the ghost?'

Archie nodded.

Kemp inspected Archie's face. 'Nah, I don't believe you. You could have got those from a bramble or that hare when you ran to school yesterday.'

Archie shook his head. 'No, honest to God, look how neat they are. And a ghost definitely visited in the middle of the night.'

'You're one hundred percent sure?'

'Yes.'

Kemp guffawed. 'Look, Archie, everyone knows ghosts don't carry things like knives or hit people.'

'This one did.'

Kemp struggled to contain his laughter. 'Don't get me wrong, Archie, but it doesn't stack up. Why would a ghost want to harm you?'

Archie thought for a second. 'To prove it was real.' Archie felt in the coat pocket and slowly withdrew the knife, shielding it from prying eyes.

'Here. Look.'

Kemp's eyes fell to the gap under the desk where Archie held the knife. He swore under his breath.

'Blimey, Archie, that's a beauty,' he said. He could hardly prise his eyes away. 'So, what did this ghost say?'

'That's where it gets blurry,' Archie began. 'He said he was on a mission to save his mother. He said that she was going to die, and that I had to help protect her at any cost.'

'Epic. He sounds all right to me,' Kemp said. 'I'd do anything to protect *my* mother.'

Archie realised he'd hit a nerve. 'Sorry, Kemp. I didn't mean—'

'Chill, Archie, I know you didn't mean anything by it.' Kemp was fully intrigued. 'Was there anything in it for you?'

'Well, as I said, I think he talked about a partnership of some sort. That's the part I can't remember. I would find out at this meeting, I suppose, not that I can go.' Archie laughed and turned a little red. 'I think I agreed to meet it bang in the middle of the football match.'

Kemp chuckled. 'Blimey. Even with the dead, your planning skills are rubbish.'

Archie screwed up his face. 'Somewhere along the line, he went on about power and strength, or something,' he said, scratching the desk. 'Maybe it's in my head from a general lack of sleep?'

Kemp was intrigued, but also concerned about his friend. If Archie's story was completely made up, this was nigh on madness. You had to hand it to them, though; these de Lowe kids were damn interesting.

Archie studied Kemp's face, and quickly reached a conclusion. 'You think it's bollocks, don't you?' He put his head in his hands. 'I've been sucked in, haven't I?'

Kemp shrugged. 'Probably your old Old Man Woody friend playing a joke or something—'

'Or I've been hallucinating from one of his bitter apples?' Archie added.

'Yeah,' Kemp said, as though this would have been perfectly normal. He'd heard about the old man's curious apple collection. 'Probably one of those apples. I can't believe you didn't see it all along.' He slapped Archie on the back. 'You ought to be getting along, don't want to miss your warm-up.'

Archie cocked his head and looked at his watch. 'Rats! Is that the time?' He gathered his things together. 'Hey, Kemp, thanks for the chat. Please don't think I've turned into a nutter.' He slung the bag strap over his shoulder. 'Promise me you won't tell anyone about this.'

'You lot are all nutters,' Kemp said. 'But you, Archie, are the only one worth your salt.'

Archie noted that the look in Kemp's eyes had turned harder. Maybe his thoughts had moved on to his sisters.

Archie ran to the door. 'See you later.'

'Sure.'

Kemp shook his head.

If it wasn't strange scientific experiments, or an infatuation with ghosts, or girls being brilliant at games designed for men, then it was some other random thing in the de Lowe family. Extraordinary disorganisation, say, or manic reckless-ness, or unbelievably old helpers and missing parents.

Mr Steele reappeared. 'Time to lock up,' he said. 'Please grab your things as the school won't re-open until after half term. Take everything you need.'

Chairs scraped against the floor as the remaining students stood up. Kemp slipped into his overcoat and gathered the contents of his desk, dropping them haphazardly into his bag. He tucked in his chair and headed towards the door.

'Kemp,' Mr Steele called out, 'haven't you forgotten something?'

Kemp looked puzzled.

'Your coat?'

'That? It's Archie's,' he said quickly. 'But, er, don't worry, I'm seeing him later. I'll take it for him.'

At that moment, he saw the slip of paper covered with Archie's scrawny hand-writing.

Kemp scanned it for a second, and noticed the underlined location. It must be where he was meeting this so-called ghost.

He folded it and crammed it into his pocket.

'Jolly good,' Mr Steele said running his hand over his chin. 'Have a nice break, Kemp. It's good to see you've decided to watch the game after all. That's the spirit we like to see in you.'

THIRTY-ONE

STORM GLASS SHATTERS

Archie tore down the corridor, almost colliding with a bevy of girls.

Daisy stood in the middle of the pack, holding centre stage.

He reddened. 'Daisy, shouldn't we be getting ready?'

'We've got plenty of time,' she said, studying her watch. 'It's only just gone ten. At least half an hour before we need to change.'

Archie blushed even more and shook his wrist. Stupid watch. 'Yes. Sure. Right.' It wasn't going well. Individually the girls were fine, but as a group they scared him to death.

'I'm going to see if I can find Isabella. Want to join me?' Archie said.

'No. Not really.'

Archie's face went purple. 'Please,' he squeaked.

Daisy caught his eye. 'Okay, Ladies,' she said, 'I'm off to do battle with those big, bad, beastly boys, and kick the damn house down.' They shrieked their approval. 'Wish me luck.'

Each of the girls made a big play of kissing her on her cheek, before breaking into a chant.

'*GO, GO Daisy de Lowe! GO, GO Daisy de Lowe! GO, GO Daisy de Lowe! Go Daisy! Go Daisy! GO Daisy...*'

Daisy put one hand in the air as she waltzed away, wiggling her hips and fluffing up her wavy blonde hair.

As the twins turned the corner the chanting changed to the old *Queen* anthem: '*A-D-L, A-D-L, A-D-L—SHE WILL, SHE WILL, ROCK YOU!*'

'You're awfully glum-faced, what have you done now?'

Archie groaned. 'Oh, Daisy, I think I've done something insanely foolish. I told Kemp about my nightmare. I don't know why I did it. He'll probably tell everyone, like he usually does.' Archie caressed his temples with his fingers. 'It's social suicide.'

'Yup, it most certainly is,' Daisy replied as she pinched him playfully on the cheek. 'When will you ever learn? He's a moron. You're best off keeping well away from him.'

They found Isabella in the physics lab with Sue. They were running over an experiment, their heads buried in calculations while an assortment of rubbery tubes and glass devices lay strewn over the counter.

Daisy was full of bounce. 'Ready to go, girls?' she said.

Her jollity didn't really have the same effect on the science students.

'Daisy,' Isabella said, in her most serious tone. 'I want you to wear these, in your boots.'

Daisy looked at her in amazement. 'On my boobs?'

'Don't be stupid. In your football boots.'

She fingered the rubbery, gooey material that Isabella handed to her. 'What is it?'

Isabella peeled off her lab glasses. 'In short, it's a de-energising unit that we've created.'

'A what-erising-unit?' Daisy said. 'Why?'

'Just in case, that's why.'

'I don't understand.'

'Just do it, will you,' Isabella demanded. 'One for each boot.' She handed her a second one. 'You too, Archie.'

Archie studied it. 'What's it for?'

Isabella squealed. 'In case either of you gets struck by lightning. It might help you not fry, that's all.'

Archie stuck the strips to the insoles in his boots. 'Aren't you're taking this a bit far—'

A huge roll of thunder shook the building rattling the windows. They looked at each other.

Isabella raised her eyebrows. 'No, we're not. These could save your life.'

'Where's your Fitz-storm glass-thing?' Daisy cut in, her tone serious. 'I need to see what it's doing.'

'Next to Isabella's desk,' Sue said, wafting a hand.

Daisy picked the storm glass up before quickly putting it down again. 'I don't mean to be rude, science-y nerd folk, but have you analysed this lately?'

Isabella marched over as though it was a complete waste of time. 'What?' she snapped.

'This storm test tube thing,' Daisy began in an unusually serious voice. 'Have any of you noticed a) how hot it is, and b) that it's literally crammed full of crystals moving incredibly fast.'

Isabella stared at it for a moment or two. 'I have no idea what you're talking about, Daisy. Yes, it might be a little warm, but so what? As I told you earlier, I'm not sure how it works.' She dismissed it with a wave. 'We've moved on.'

Daisy shrugged. 'Well, you're supposed to know what you're doing but I'd keep an eye on it, if I were you.' She stretched out the gooey strip. 'Can I put this in my hair?'

'Please, Daisy,' Isabella said. 'It must be on the bottom of your shoe. Attach it to the underside of your boot using the sticky Velcro patch or in the insole.' Isabella sounded irritated by the intrusion. 'Now, run and get changed or you'll be late.'

Daisy skipped off, singing to herself and punching the air.

As her footsteps receded down the corridor, Archie picked up the storm glass. Immediately, he put it down again.

'Whoa! It's boiling, seriously. Try it.'

'I've just done that,' Isabella said.

Sue put her finger to the glass. 'OW! Scorching!' she sucked her fingers. 'Isabella, look! It's steaming.'

'A mild expulsion of water vapour, that's all,' Isabella said nervously.

'You think so?' They all started to back away.

'No, not necessarily,' Isabella admitted.

The test tube was beginning to glow, steam seeping out of the top.

'Has anyone added anything to it?' Isabella asked.

Archie and Sue shook their heads.

The activity in the test tube increased. They could hear crystals popping against the glass.

'Get out!' Isabella yelled. 'It's going to blow!'

They ran for the door, shutting it firmly behind themselves before diving to the floor. Seconds later, the storm glass blew into Smithereens.

Sue shivered. 'What does it mean?' she asked.

'I think it means that we were right all along.' Isabella's voice quaked. 'Here, above us, lies the storm from hell.'

THIRTY-TWO

SUE AND ISABELLA

'Sue, it's time for direct action,' Isabella said. 'Solomon clearly doesn't want to know about the storm, so we're going to have to either disrupt the match, or figure out an exit strategy—'

Sue couldn't face direct action. 'A leaving strategy gets my vote—'

'Good. If I can get Arch and Daisy over the bridge, then I think we'll be fine. When we get to the lane, the canopy of the tunnel should protect us. It's you that I'm worried about.'

'*Me?*'

'Yes. You.' Isabella confirmed. 'How are you going to get out of here? You'll need to get home fast, or get to high ground. Have you ever driven a car?'

'Of course not. Stop being ridiculous—'

'I'm not. You could steal one.'

Sue glared at Isabella, who shrugged back. 'I'll think of something, but you're getting weird.'

'That's not good enough,' Isabella snapped back. 'You need a plan. Come home with us.'

'I can't. Mum wants me back.'

'In that case, start engaging that brain of yours.'

As the two girls trudged slowly back from the science laboratories in silence, they could feel the buzz of the crowd making its way down towards the football pitch.

'I feel so edgy about this match,' Isabella said, as a couple of boys ran past nearly knocking her over. 'What if Daisy gets a kicking and can't run? Then they lose, the storm breaks, and she can't get home?'

'Isabella, that's not going to happen—'

'And what about Archie? He's all over the place, have you seen him? He looks ill, the poor boy. I'm worried he won't save a thing. He's even more scatter-brained than usual.'

'Well, it is the final—'

'I know that,' Isabella said. 'It's just that I've got a hollow feeling deep inside me.' Isabella closed her eyes and shook her head. 'You know, I'm not sure I even like football—'

'What tosh! You love it,' Sue replied, 'you're jealous of Daisy, just like everyone else.'

'That still doesn't mean I like it—'

'You're her sister and you're as sporty as a mole yourself, so it's natural for you to want her to do well.' Sue looked up at the sky. Her heart seemed to skip a beat. She whistled.

'Blimey. Solomon's floodlights are on,' Isabella said, her tone betraying her nerves.

'Every time I look up, my body starts shaking like a jelly,' Sue said, inspecting her watch. 'We've got five minutes.'

Sue slowed down and grasped Isabella's arm, as if setting herself up to say something important. 'Listen, Isabella,' she began, 'I've been meaning to tell you something important—'

'Important?' Isabella noticed that her friend had gone a little pale. 'You put the wrong mix in the storm glass—?'

'No. It's not about that... it's about—'

'You did add something to it, didn't you—'

'Isabella, I haven't touched it. I'm quite sure it did what it did perfectly naturally.' Sue added. '*It's about you*. It's personal.'

'Me?' Isabella's mind whirled. 'What? You've got a boyfriend and you haven't told me—'

'For goodness' sake, you know full well I haven't—'

'Okay, someone out there fancies *me*—'

'NO. Of course not. Listen, Isabella—it's got absolutely nothing to do with boys—'

'Sure?'

'YES.'

'Good,' Isabella said, 'they're such a waste of—'

'It's *about* you,' Sue said.

'Me?' Isabella said. 'OMG. You... and... me?'

Sue shrieked. 'For crying out loud, Isabella. NO! *Will you please let me speak*?' She took a deep breath. 'It concerns YOU, in fact it concerns all of you de Lowes. You, Archie and Daisy. All those things I told you about? Well, there's more.'

'More?'

'Yes! I wrote a whole lot of stuff down the moment I woke up. I'm pretty sure it's about you, and that in some way you're linked—'

'Linked? With what?'

'SHUT UP! Listen to me for just a minute.' Sue said, trying to compose herself. 'What I'm trying to say is that—'

The long shrill of a whistle and the roar of the crowd swept over them. Sue followed Isabella's eyes towards the floodlit football pitch.

'We're late!' Isabella cried. 'Your watch is slow.'

Sue tapped the face of the dial and compared it to the clock on her mobile. 'Oh no!' But when she looked up, her friend had already gone.

Isabella tore off down the track. *What was I thinking? I bet someone's scored.*

'Come on, keep up!' Isabella yelled over her shoulder, as she took off down the shingle path. 'You'll have to tell me later! I mean, it's not like it's life or death, is it?' she yelled.

'There are things you absolutely... must... know,' Sue said, her voice trailing off as she watched Isabella zoom away with extraordinary speed. In fact, she couldn't remember seeing Isabella run as fast in her whole life.

Sue felt empty, the moment lost. Everything that had happened in the last hour had started to confirm that what she had seen, heard—and felt—was going to come true. If there was even the tiniest chance of this happening, she needed to tell Isabella everything.

Because, increasingly, it really was about life or death.

THIRTY-THREE

KEMP FINDS SOMEONE

Kemp reached into his pocket, pulling out Archie's scrap of paper.

He leaned against the stone wall outside the school hall and held it up. If that Old Man Wood had played a prank on Archie and given him the coat to wear, then what were the others capable of? Perhaps this was an elaborate set-up, dreamed up by Isabella in order to get him to fight with Gus Williams.

Kemp could smell Isabella's cheap perfume all over this.

He glanced up. The sky was ridiculously dark and ridiculously huge. What if Isabella's experimental madness had some foundation?

Kemp's eyes returned to the paper. He read the middle, double-underlined, option.

'*Alleyway behind kissing houses.*'

Kemp thought about it. If he was going to meet a knife-wielding ghost in a quiet spot, it was a pretty good choice. It had the advantage that you could get out at both ends, and it was close enough to the playing fields for a quick getaway.

Clever Archie. Not just a scruffy boy.

The alleyway was also the perfect place for a fight. He clenched his fist. He remembered the look on Williams' face, the glimmer of madness in his eyes. Kemp twisted the fabric on Archie's coat. It was nice and strong, and light, too. A layer of protection if Williams came at him.

Kemp sucked in his breath. It was a set-up for sure. It had to be. After yesterday's performance, Archie had been duped by his sisters.

Oh, well.

Kemp tapped his pocket, feeling the metal object within.

If he was right, and Williams was coming after him, Gus Williams was in for a mighty big surprise.

From the road above the football field, Kemp scanned the crowd lining the perimeter of the pitch. They stood four deep behind the barrier rope at times, with smaller kids kneeling at the front. Kemp ached to be part of it, to have them cheer *him* on.

He'd never play alongside Daisy de Lowe, though. Never. Just the thought of her running beside him made his stomach heave.

He kicked a loose stone on the ground, which skipped across the raised pebbles and smacked a small boy in the knee with a dull crack.

The boy collapsed on the path as Kemp clenched his fist. *Nice one*, he thought, wishing it had been Daisy de Lowe's knee.

Kemp climbed further up the slope, towards the houses above the playing fields. He kept going until he was on his own, high above the pitch. As he walked, he thought about how he could occupy himself over the break with his dreary aunt. Last time, he'd nearly died of boredom, being dragged around endless museums, antiques shops, and flea markets. Sure, his aunt was pleasant and she tried hard, but her never-ending jollity and the way she talked to everyone about the same things over and over again drove him mad.

She was too nice, too wet and too dull.

His mind turned to his lost parents. They would have done awesome, cool, outdoor stuff, and they'd all get stuck in together, like sailing, or mountaineering, or holidaying abroad.

He imagined a trip by the side of the river next to a large campfire. Looking at the stars, his mother by his side playing guitar and singing, and his father smiling at him proudly, sharpening a blade.

It was a fantasy, of course. It was the idyllic family life he'd never have. Every time he thought of it, it brought an overwhelming sadness into his soul. He couldn't remember if his mother used to sing to him and he had no idea what his parents even looked like; but to him, the fantasy felt right.

A long rumble boomed in the sky above. Kemp spied another round pebble, and took a mighty swipe with his heavy, black boot. The stone connected sweetly, skipped a couple of times and then, on the last bounce, lifted quickly and seemed to whistle past the head of someone lurking by a lamppost near to the alleyway.

What was an old bloke doing standing over there in the first place? He didn't even flinch! Bloody weirdo. The stone must have missed him or else he'd have been knocked out cold.

Kemp put his head down and sauntered on as if nothing had happened. A few paces on, Kemp noticed a man just inside the entrance to the alleyway. He was sure no one had been there a moment earlier.

His heartbeat quickened.

Kemp pretended to read Archie's bit of paper while he studied the man.

It was a hunched over old man, he thought, shrouded in a long, dark cloak, with a thick scarf wrapped round his chin and nose. He had a kind of wide-brimmed hat pulled down over his head in such a way that Kemp couldn't identify a face. The figure leaned on a stick like a blind man.

Maybe, Kemp thought, *this* is Archie's ghost.

THIRTY-FOUR

SOLOMON'S PARTY PLANS

Solomon leant on the oak door, and listened as their footsteps receded down the corridor. He let out a sigh. Had she believed him? It was hard to read her expression.

Returning to the soft leather armchair, he picked up his schedule. Isabella's persistence was admirable, if misplaced. No, no. Nothing was going to stop today going ahead, neither a big storm nor a few drops of rain.

Goodness me, he thought, *this is Yorkshire, the finest county in all of England, God's Own Country! Thunder and lightning go hand in hand with the rough landscapes of the moors and the dales.*

Kids these days were getting soft.

He chuckled to himself. Met Bureau? What nonsense. He simply knew that the only way he'd be able to stop her in her tracks was to throw something scientific back at her.

But why Mr Fish? It was an implausibly good name for a weatherman.

In any case, he had a busy morning ahead. Press were turning up, and there were place names to sort out for the banquet in the school chamber. It was an evening he'd anticipated for years. How much sweeter still if they won the cup?

He hoped that sister of Isabella's, Daisy, would play her heart out again. What a player! He'd never seen the like. She was George Best, Pele, Messi, and Ronaldo, all blended into one slender slip of a girl. Brave as a mercenary, tough as leather, quick as a pike and slippery as ice.

He sighed before returning to the matter of wondering who he should sit next to tonight. Geraldine Forbes, perhaps. The star of Summerdale, the TV soap. Yes, perfect. Famed for her gritty Yorkshire one-liners, in reality she was a delightful, attractive lady, with beautiful green eyes and lips as full as cushions.

He pictured the scene in his mind; the hall decorated to the nines in the school's scarlet and green colours, candles accentuating the Gothic arched windows, and trophies and cups sparkling in the atmospheric light. Magnificent!

It would be a banquet that the governors, his friends, and their exclusive guests, would never forget.

Afterwards, he'd make his retirement speech and receive warm, generous, and heartfelt thanks from those whose lives he had touched. Yes, he mused. It was to be a glorious swan song.

Nobody, certainly not Isabella de Lowe, was going to stop it.

His mood turned from happy to jovial. Mr Fish. Ah yes! The forecaster who in 1987 told the whole nation there was no need to worry, shortly before a devastating hurricane ripped across England.

Solomon laughed out loud and dabbed his brow. What if Isabella rang up the Met Bureau and asked to speak to Mr Fish?

Whatever will they think?

THIRTY-FIVE

KEMP'S FIGHT

A roar rang out from below. Kemp spun back to the game. He picked out the chant of *"Daisy de Lowe, GO, GO, GO"* and smacked his fist into his hand. Dammit. She must have scored.

Kemp reached into his pocket and his hand touched a waxy piece of paper. It was a sweet wrapper. With a frown on his face, he tried to work out how it had got there. Of course, it was from a pack of Haribo he'd stolen from one of Daisy's girlie friends at break. He'd stuffed the sweet in his mouth and nonchalantly tossed one of the wrappers into the headmaster's rose garden, where it stuck comically on a thorn and flapped in the breeze.

So, how come this one was folded, and in his pocket?

He pulled the wrapper out, opened it up and stared at it. Strangely, the sweet paper not only looked larger than he remembered, but scribbled all over it were random lines like spaghetti plonked on a plate.

Just as he was about to trash it, a few of the lines started to look familiar. *Faces?* he thought. Kemp scanned it, turning it sideways and then round again. Three figures came out at him, like a "magic eye" puzzle revealing itself on the wrapper.

There were three clear faces staring back at him.

Then it struck him. It was the de Lowes! Absolutely, definitely, them, all smug and cheerful and ghastly. As he studied it, their faces seemed to melt away into the paper, like slush dripping through a gutter.

The next time he blinked, he was staring at nothing. Not a damn thing.

He turned the sweet paper over.

Blank.

Kemp felt a surge of excitement run through him. Was this some kind of joke?

He slapped his cheeks and rubbed his eyes. He looked at the wrapper again. Its colour was changing gradually from white through grey to almost black, like the vast cloud above them. The words "HELP ME" started to form in tiny molten streaks of lightning on the paper, as if the words were being burned into it.

Kemp crumpled the paper up and tossed it in the gutter.

His heart raced. For a moment, sickness overwhelmed him.

Instinctively, he started walking faster and faster, as if walking might make what he had just seen go away.

Kemp bounded up a series of wide stone steps back to street level, and tentatively made his way towards the street's beamed dwellings. He peered down the dark alleyway but it was empty, save for the black wheelie bins guarding it like mini soldiers.

As he took his first step under the buildings, he noted how the houses on either side weren't leaning over the street as if they were kissing, more leaning towards each other like fighters braced for combat.

He heard a groan from the crowd below, and moved to the roadside to figure out what was happening.

Bodies lay all over the pitch. Had Newton won a penalty?

Was that Archie staring up at him?

He waved back, before turning and walking into the alleyway.

Halfway down, he slowed. He sensed something behind him. Who? A teacher? Nah, unlikely. They'd be watching the game, or making last minute plans for the performances later on. In any case, by now they'd have said something.

Gus Williams. He almost spat his name out. Williams was coming after all. It was exactly his style to creep up on people.

Kemp curled his fist into a ball. 'Williams,' he said, 'I'm warning you. Stop, and walk away, NOW.'

There was no reply.

He could feel the presence edging closer.

Kemp bent down, pretending to tie his boots. His pulse raced. He readied himself. He sensed the person behind him was now only a couple of paces away.

'I've been waiting for this,' Kemp said, and in one movement swung around and threw his biggest punch. His momentum carried him forward, his fist unstoppable.

But it wasn't Williams. It was the old man.

Instead of connecting, his arm careered straight through the man, propelling Kemp onto the grey stone. His head cracked on the paving as he went down.

'You don't have to do that, Archie,' said a gravelly voice from behind the scarf. 'We're on the same team now.'

Kemp was struggling to get to grips with what had happened.

'Believe me, it is excellent news that you have arrived on time.'

The old man moved almost directly above him, his face covered by the scarf and hat. 'And I sense that you have brought my coat. Very well done; did the old man find it?'

Kemp was horrified and for a moment simply didn't know what to say. 'Yes, he gave it to me,' he lied.

'Are you ready to join with me, Archie de Lowe?'

Kemp's skin crawled. Everything Archie had told him was completely true. He needed more time. 'Join you?' Kemp said, scuffling backwards, trying hard to keep his face hidden. 'Er, can you remind me again? I was very tired last night.'

The ghost hesitated. 'Well, let me put it this way. I've got what you want.'

'What I want?' Kemp repeated. No wonder Archie was freaked out. 'What do you mean?'

The old man moved to one side and appeared to look up towards the sky. 'Why me, of course.'

'You?'

'Yes, me,' said the ghost. 'You see I'm the only one here who can help you escape from this place. And you have only about fifteen minutes in your time to decide.'

Kemp's brain went a little fuzzy. Fifteen minutes? In *your* time? Decide what? Kemp stole a look down the alley.

He needed to get away, fast.

The old man sensed his unease. 'You see, in a very short time the skies will open and it will rain for forty days and nights in a way you cannot even begin to imagine—'

Kemp looked confused. 'What... forty days and nights?'

'Yes. That's what I said, forty days and nights—'

'Forty days and nights—?'

'Yes!'

'What ... like Noah's Ark—?'

'STOP repeating what I say and listen!' the old man spat.

The words seemed to smack Kemp around the face. He lost his footing and slipped.

'If you think what I'm saying is any way over the top,' he said, bearing down on him, 'I can assure you that in a short while, all of this—everything here, everything—will be destroyed.'

The ghost gestured, almost triumphantly, Kemp thought, towards the playing field.

'Archie,' he continued, his voice mellow once more, 'there is a shift happening, a shift in time, a shift in the way of the universe and it is happening right here, right now. You are part of this, Archie. The wheels are turning and they cannot be reversed.'

Kemp reeled, wondering if he should play dead.

The ghost moved above him, his face covered by the scarf and hat. 'You have brought my coat. Well done. Did the old man recognise it?'

Kemp simply didn't know what to say. His voice stammered as a chill swept through him.

'Are you ready to join me, Archie de Lowe?'

Kemp's skin crawled.

'Now, look here,' Kemp said, 'you need help.' He felt a slither of confidence returning.

'Look at me, Archie,' the ghost said. 'You see that thing there—'

'Yeah, right,' Kemp said. 'A large, dark cloud. Big deal. Excuse me, freak, but I'm outta here—'

'No—you—are—not,' the old man said, spitting each word out so severely that Kemp slipped to the ground.

'Out of all the people on this puny planet, I've selected you. So be grateful, boy, because I'm giving you the chance to save your life. There is no other way for you.'

Kemp squealed, and looked down the passage. What was holding him back? Why didn't he go for it? Why didn't he say that he wasn't Archie? He felt oddly dizzy, as if a force was holding him against his will.

'I see you need convincing,' the old man said, his voice as smooth as honey once more. 'I'm going to show you something to... reassure you. All I'm asking for is a little co-operation.'

The old man took a step back.

Kemp stood up, his knees barely able to hold him.

'You see, I'm going to tell you the story of what has happened so far, and then I'm going to tell you what happens next. Do you understand?'

Kemp nodded.

'Good. Let me tell you about that piece of paper in your pocket, and how I generated your image in the lightning,' the ghost said, this time softer. 'Then, Archie de Lowe, I'm going to show you who you are and how we are going to help one another.'

THIRTY-SIX

THE GAME

Isabella dashed down the touchline. 'Sue, thank God I've found you,' she said. 'What's up with you? We're on drinks duty!'

'Hell,' she said. 'You're right. My watch...'

They rushed over to the old Volkswagen Combi ice cream van, known as the 'catering-cart', which acted as refreshment centre and mobile sweet shop.

Isabella and Sue pulled out a few tables, and lined out paper cups ready for jugs of orange squash. A steady stream began queuing for drinks, chocolate bars, and crisps.

Sue took the money while Isabella handed out cups, but Sue could barely keep up.

Isabella was working at an astonishing speed, darting here and there, handing out confectionery and drinks. She talked to everyone about the current score, or Daisy's brilliant goals, or the curious weather.

'How did you manage to serve all that in ten minutes?' Sue said, as she squeezed a few more cups into the overflowing bin bag. 'We've made a killing.'

Isabella breathed a sigh of relief. With no rain appearing so far, perhaps Solomon was right. Maybe the cloud would break later that afternoon. From inside the van, she looked out over the scene. The crowd was still three or four deep the entire way around the pitch, and she could just make out the steep rise of the bank on the far side that led up to the village.

The floodlights shone down, giving the players a strange, quadruple shadow. If it hadn't been nearly midday, there would have been no reason to suspect that they weren't playing a night match.

'Isabella,' she called out. 'Get a place left of the halfway line. I'll join you in a minute. I'm going to cash up.'

The feeling of dread that Sue had experienced before was building again. The vast black cloud seemed to be growing even thicker, and sinking even lower in the sky.

She knew she should get out of there and run to higher ground, but she was too swallowed up by the drama, and swept away by the skill of Daisy de Lowe.

A heavy challenge sent Daisy flying. The crowd swayed, and spilled onto the pitch.

The noise levels increased.

'That was late. Too damn late,' Isabella shouted, peeling off her scarf.

'Careful, Isabella. Watch it,' Sue said, firmly. 'You mustn't. You'll get expelled. I promised—'

'It was deliberate and dirty—'

'NO, Isabella!' Sue snapped. 'Bite your tongue.'

'But they're targeting Daisy exactly as Kemp said they would. They're going to kick her out of the game!'

Sue closed her eyes. Great, just what she needed! Still ten minutes to go, and Isabella sizzling like a firework.

'What was that noise?' Isabella said.

'That gargantuan thing up there?'

'Th... thunder?' Isabella said, momentarily removing her eyes from the action. Sue nodded.

Several members of the crowd started to leave, while others gestured upwards.

This is it, Sue thought. *This is where it starts, exactly as I saw in my nightmare. It even feels the same too. I've got to tell Isabella. I've got to tell her NOW.*

A ghastly feeling of panic swept over her.

They should stop the game. Get everyone away.

Sue's thoughts were interrupted as Daisy stole the ball and sprinted down the field.

Daisy skipped inside one tackle, then dummied inside looking for support.

The crowd roared, but, from nowhere, a couple of Newton boys smashed into her from opposite angles. All three lay on the ground as the ball was kicked away by another Newton player.

Play continued, but it was a poor decision.

'Yellow card,' yelled a senior boy. 'C'mon ref!'

The atmosphere flipped. Suddenly, late tackles flew in and players were being kicked indiscriminately out of eyeshot of the referee.

One of the Newton strikers stole into the penalty area, as a massive crash of thunder reverberated around them. At that exact moment, little Jimmy Nugent, running back, tapped the forward's foot and the player fell face-first onto the turf.

The whistle shrilled and the ball was placed on the spot.

'I don't believe it!' Sue said, quietly, 'the end of Daisy's dream.' She turned. 'Isabella, what on earth are you doing?'

Isabella was scribbling furiously in her notebook. 'Just watch for me a minute. You know, commentate, like on telly.'

She didn't need to. The groan told her everything.

'What happened?'

'The ball trickled past Archie. All he had to do was put his foot out. Two-all.'

'He is absolutely useless sometimes,' she said.

'Well, he's only in the team because no-one else would do it.'

'And to keep Daisy company, though, to be fair, he has improved, ' Isabella said as she thrust the paper into Sue's overcoat pocket. 'Ye of little faith, Sue Lowden,' she said. 'You'll see, she'll score again.'

Another roll of thunder boomed and cracked. More spectators started running away.

Sue's stomach lurched. It was now or never.

'Isabella, we've got to get out of here, now. I mean it. But listen to me first. There's something important I've got to share—'

'Please, Sue. Just shut up!' Isabella snapped. 'Get the ball to Daisy de Lowe,' she screamed. 'Give it to Daisy!' Isabella turned to Sue. 'Listen, hun, tell me whatever is so damn important at the end, okay. There's less than five minutes to go and it's two-all in the most important match of my brother and sister's life. Can you please just give it a break for five minutes? Five minutes. That's all I'm asking.'

With that, Isabella sidled out onto the pitch, ran down the touchline, and dived in among the spectators further down.

Archie stomped around the penalty area, his face burning with shame at the unsaved goal.

For some reason, just before the Newton player stepped up to hit the penalty, it had come to him. The person he'd seen way up on the steps heading into the alley was Kemp. It could only have been Kemp. For a start, his hair was a complete giveaway, and he was wearing the ghost's long coat, which made him look like a monk.

All he could think of was running up there to find out what the hell Kemp was up to.

If Cain *was* there, and Kemp had gone to find him, would Cain know the difference between them? Would he care?

Then, in the next instance, the ball had trickled past him into the goal.

Archie kicked the base of the post. The more he thought about Kemp and the ghost, the more certain he became that he was right.

All I ever do is look on hopelessly, he thought. *When will I stop being so pathetic?*

A slow-burning fury moved through his body, an anger borne of frustration and annoyance. It began to build up in him like a glowing light, as if he were being charged up like a battery.

Archie was about to kick short from the goal kick, but, from out of the corner of his eye, he saw Daisy in yards of space on the halfway line, catching her breath after the last attack. It was worth a try. He pushed the ball ahead, ran up, and thumped it hard. The ball rose high into the air.

Daisy saw it, her eyes never leaving the ball. She took it down in her stride and, with a burst of speed, tore past one player then another. She then stopped so suddenly that another player over-ran, and she side-stepped one more player who fell over. The crowd roared.

'… *She will, she will—ROCK YOU!'*

Daisy side-stepped again and, with an injection of pace, flew towards the penalty area with real menace. Four Newton players lay sprawled on the floor, leaving only one more to beat.

'Go on Daisy, you can do it,' Archie screamed.

Archie watched as the remaining defender was sold a beautiful dummy, which Daisy seemed to do with such ease that it was laughable. As she pushed the ball past him and effortlessly made her way around, he slid out a leg and tripped her up quite deliberately. Daisy stumbled and fell but she wasn't giving up. She crawled towards the ball and then, even as she lay on the ground with the ball wedged between her knees, she managed to keep moving.

But a warning cry went up as three Newton players and the goalkeeper converged on Daisy. It felt as if Daisy had fallen into a trap as the Newton boys cocked their legs and kicked out, striking more of Daisy than the ball, kicking her again and again in a kind of frenzy.

Still, she refused to give the ball up.

The crowd swayed and screamed before falling silent.

They could quite clearly see Daisy's face contorting in pain as the assault rained down on her.

THIRTY-SEVEN

SUE TELLS OF HER DREAM

For the first time in her life, Sue could feel a sensation of utter panic building up in her veins like one of her bubbling chemistry experiments. A series of flashes filled the sky, mirroring the extraordinary scenes on the pitch. Lightning fizzed then crackled. For a brief moment, the light formed a picture of a boy in the sky.

Sue gasped. *A boy?*

A thunderclap smashed overhead so loudly that the crowd cried out. Shrieks and screams filled the football field.

Sue fell to her knees, barely able to think, her body shaking. *No! It can't be! It's not possible. It's... it's... Kemp's face!* The lightning was Kemp's face super-imposed in the cloud. How was it possible?

She looked around. Where was Isabella? She couldn't have gone already. Sue followed the eyes of the crowd.

Isabella was striding towards the pitch.

'No! Isabella, stop!'

There was no reaction from Isabella.

Without thinking, Sue took off after her. 'Isabella, LISTEN!' she yelled as she ran. 'It's you!'

She ran on further.

'The dream is about your family, the de Lowes.' She sensed Isabella slowing down.

'You must ALL survive until sunset and find a cave. Do you understand?' She took a deep breath.

'Survive till sunset. You must all stay alive!'

Her voice was petering out as she realised she was screaming herself hoarse. She sucked her breath in again.

'Find clues in your house, Eden Cottage,' she hollered. 'You must find the clues.'

Sue coughed and then repeated the last part, adding,

'Get home. All three of you!'

She noted some of the crowd staring at her as if she was a madwoman. But she didn't care, not one little bit.

Archie couldn't believe it.

First Sue screaming nonsense at Isabella, and now this!

Where was the referee?

He thumped the goalpost, shook his head, and looked up. The giant, angry bruise of a cloud stretched above him like a monstrous airship. It sagged so low in the sky that he felt he could jump up and burst it as easily as pricking a balloon.

The heady smell of damp filled his nostrils as another crack of thunder escaped. Archie felt his blood boiling inside him. Five Newton players surrounded Daisy.

She managed to stand, but one of them pushed her over.

That was the final straw. Anger flooded through him. *No one*, Archie seethed, *does that to my sister.*

He tore down the pitch, the crowd baying and shouting as the referee desperately tried to separate the fighting players.

'NO! Don't retaliate, Archie—' he could hear someone yelling. It was too late, though. Hell had broken loose.

One of the Newton boys was holding Daisy's hair and leering at her, screaming in her face. Archie grabbed him by the collar and threw him away, the boy sailing through the air and landing in a heap on the ground. Archie punched another boy hard on the nose. He thought he heard crunching sounds, then found himself receiving blows although he couldn't feel them.

Blood coursed through his body. He felt strong and powerful. Invincible.

A couple of Newton boys jumped him but he picked one up with one hand and tossed him over his shoulder. The other boy he wrestled to the ground until the boy under him squirrelled away. Then he found another hitting Jimmy Nugent. He smashed the boy hard in the stomach and tossed him to the side like a piece of litter.

The whistle shrilled again and again.

Finally, a sharp, stern voice rose up out of the melee. It was Isabella. Archie could see her marching towards them. *Oh no!*

Archie looked around. Three Newton boys and the referee stared at him with their eyes wide open. *Was it in fear?*

This was a sensation he'd never experienced before.

Archie wiped his brow and allowed himself a smile.

Yup. It felt strangely good.

THIRTY-EIGHT

SOLOMON'S PENNY DROPS

'Sir,' a small boy said, running up to him. 'Sir. What shall we do?'

Solomon smiled, badly. 'I've been assured that there won't be any rainfall until this afternoon,' he said. 'I'm sure we'll be fine.'

'But, Sir. Look. I don't think it's safe.'

Solomon stared up at the throbbing deep bruise that filled the sky to the horizon. His heartbeat quickened.

'If you're worried, make your way indoors. Are your parents around?'

'No, Sir. They're coming to the music concert this afternoon.'

'Then I suggest you go to the library and find a good book. How does that sound?'

The boy ran back to his friends, and together they scampered over to the old buildings with the tower.

Solomon's knees were shaking. In fact, now that he noticed, his entire body shook, as if he'd been swimming in a cold sea. Nerves about the match, probably.

At the back of his mind he wondered about Isabella. I mean, *really*? Bah! It wasn't going to happen.

This was a small lightning storm with a bit of thunder. It would probably pass them by, or they'd have some heavy rain, but nothing like the deluge she was suggesting. That sort of thing never happened here in good old North Yorkshire.

A crack of lightning fizzed above. He noticed how the crowd were dispersing. How students flicked their eyes towards him.

'Come on Upsall!' he yelled. 'Jolly good play, Allen. Give it to Daisy.' He clapped his hands as the play moved from one end of the pitch to the other, Daisy narrowly missing to the right of the goal.

BOOM!

Solomon felt the ground shake.

'Sir—'

'The team need your support,' the headmaster said, loudly.

Suddenly he noticed how the players were almost attacking each other.

Oh Lord.

Moving quickly, he headed down the touchline.

'Coach,' he shouted.

The coach swivelled on his heels and ran towards him. 'For goodness' sake, watch out for Isabella de Lowe. If anything happens to Daisy—'

They watched as the Newton boys set upon her.

'Goodness. I'm quite tempted to get stuck in myself,' the headmaster said.

'Best you don't, Headmaster,' Coach said.

They both stared at the scene, their mouths open.

'Should we call it off?' Coach asked.

'No, no. It's nearly over—'

'Who's that, yelling?' Coach said.

'Well I never. That's Sue, isn't it? Whatever is she going on about?' Solomon said.

'No idea. Something about it being their fault?'

'Whose fault?' the headmaster queried.

'The de Lowe's. If you ask me, I think they've all gone mad. Oh no, is that Archie? It's not poss—'

'Lord above. He's beating them up! What has the world come to,' the headmaster said. 'Steel, Coach. Look! There! Isabella's on the march. Be good fellows and grab her before this melee gets completely out of hand!'

THIRTY-NINE

DIRECT ACTION

'Stop it! All of you.' Isabella screamed as she strode towards the players with a formidable sense of purpose.

The teams almost instantly ceased brawling. Isabella's direct approach had that effect on people.

'Pathetic, all of you,' she shouted, pointing at various individuals. 'It's like a wrestling match for the Under 5s. Newton, you three especially, should be deeply ashamed of yourselves.'

Isabella scooped up the ball. 'As for the refereeing. Twelve deliberate fouls totally unaccounted for and you haven't even got the balls to book them, let alone send them off for repeated violent conduct.'

The football smacked into the referee's hands. 'You should be struck off—?'

Before she had a chance to finish, she was grabbed by Coach and Mr Steele. They hauled her off her feet and away to the side line.

The referee responded by pointing belatedly at Isabella.

'You'll be dealt with later by the authorities,' he roared, blinking, trying hard to pull himself together.

Why couldn't he remember the procedure for dealing with a brawl?

It felt as if his brain had emptied.

'And along with that madwoman,' he continued, 'Upsall goalkeeper and number eight, and Sutton players five, seven and four,' he said pointing at the players, 'Get off this playing field!'

He waved his red card at Archie and the other players and scribbled in his book.

Another huge slap of thunder exploded almost directly overhead. The ground shook. A terrible feeling tiptoed up his spine, sending his hairs erect.

'Direct free kick to red,' he said, pointing to a spot just outside the penalty area. 'And the quicker we're out of here, the better.'

The ref studied his watch. 'Last couple of minutes,' he announced.

The girl was right, though. His had been a truly woeful performance.

Daisy dragged herself up and flicked a fleck of mud off her shorts.

What a crazy match! Her being kicked to bits, Sue screaming at Isabella, and Isabella going mad again and screaming at everyone else. Archie missed a total sitter and then beat up the opposition like a prize-fighter before getting sent off, while thunder crashed overhead, lightning fizzed, and everything was deafening.

Now, with the last kick of the game, Daisy had a chance to win the match. *Boy, pressure kicks don't come much bigger than this*, she thought. *Better make it a good one.*

'Come on, Upsall. Come on, Daisy de Lowe, you can do it,' roared the small section of crowd still remaining. They continued their chant.

"Oh, Daisy, Daisy. Daisy, Daisy, Daisy—A-A-Daisy-iii".

Daisy rubbed her tired, bruised legs, and drew her hands through her muddy blonde hair. She fixed her boots and selected a slightly raised patch of turf on which she carefully placed the ball.

She stood back and studied her route to goal. Twenty, twenty-three yards perhaps? Perfect. Just as she'd practised time and again with Archie.

She rubbed her eyes and concentrated hard. It was now or never. Everything she'd ever played for came down to this one shot.

She sucked in a large mouthful of air, her eyes focusing on the ball so intently that she felt she could see its entire trajectory and the precise spot on the leather where she aim her boot.

The whole atmosphere of the crowd, and the rumbling sky seemed to disappear for a moment, leaving behind a strange hush.

The referee blew.

Daisy exhaled. It was time to step up.

FORTY

SUE DISCOVERS A NOTE

There was more, Sue thought, but she'd finally said what needed to be said. Thank goodness she'd had the presence of mind to scribble down her dreams the moment she'd woken up.

'*GO! Run! Run… all of you,*' she screamed at the spectators. '*It's going to break. The storm's going to break.*'

Thunder rolled.

She sprinted up the slope towards the buildings.

As she passed the top end she spied Gus leaning on the lamppost, near to the leaning houses. She headed directly towards him. 'Gus. What are you doing?'

'Following Kemp. He's been acting weird all afternoon. Are we winning?'

'Listen, Gus,' she said as she caught her breath. 'Rain,' she panted, 'like you've never seen… get out of here… fast. You've got to believe me.' Her hand touched some paper in her pocket and she pulled it out. She remembered; it was Isabella's note.

Gus rolled his eyes.

She read it out loud.

'*Sue, there's a boat in the old shed. Key under a pot by door, oars on the side. Think there's a canopy in cupboard… just in case. Love you. Be safe, Isabella.*'

Sue kissed it in relief. Clever, brilliant Isabella.

Gus grabbed the note. 'What is it with you two?'

'Look at the sky, Gus. When that "thing" bursts it will rain harder than you can possibly imagine. In minutes, the water will flash flood. I've had a premonition. I'll tell you about it'

'A premonition? Blimey. Cool. You sure?'

'Absolutely. No one has a chance. Can you drive? Do you have access to a car?'

'Of course not!'

'Me neither,' she fired back. 'Some of the kids have gone but I'm being picked up later, after the music concert.'

'Same,' Gus said, trying to keep pace with her.

'Then we're stuck, Gus. Properly screwed. There's no way out.'

'Screwed? What are you talking about, Sue? Why should we be stuck?'

'Look up, Gus,' she said. 'That massive black thing up there. I promise you I'm not crazy. I'm being absolutely deadly serious. That cloud isn't holding an ordinary storm and when it lets go the result will be catastrophic. Come on, keep up.'

Gus frowned. 'You're really serious, aren't you?' he said, the smile slipping off his face.

'Never more so.' She stopped to catch her breath. 'Please, Gus, I need your help. Will you help me? Please?'

Gus scratched his nose. He liked Sue, and he'd certainly never seen her quite so animated. 'Okay. I'm going to have to trust you on this one. Where do we start?'

'Oh, great! Thanks, Gus,' Sue said, moving in and bear-hugging him. If she was going to do this, better to do it with big, strong Gus Williams than by herself.

'First off, provisions. Food: high-energy snack bars; chocolates; lemons; dried fruit; tinned food like tuna and baked beans; sweetcorn; a couple of lighters and firelighters; bottled water,' Sue rattled off, 'and blankets—'

'Blankets?'

'Anything you can get hold of.' She urged him to keep up. 'You're a Scout leader, aren't you? Grab stuff we can survive on.'

'To the shop, then,' Gus said, smiling his keen smile and feeling rather important.

'I've got about twenty pounds from the footie snacks and drinks. I'll pay it back later.' Sue did some calculations in her head. 'Actually, that's probably not enough. Have you got anything?'

Gus shoved his hands in his pockets and pulled out some change. 'Just short of four quid.'

Sue grimaced. 'In that case, Gus, I hope you don't mind but you're going to have to steal. Come on, there's not a second to lose. When we get in there, grab some bags and start filling them. Don't hesitate or stop, understand? When it's done, I'll drop the money on the counter and we run. Got it?'

'Blimey, Sue. What if we get stopped?'

'We won't. Oh, and if necessary, use force.'

Gus nodded, and handed over his money. His eyes were bulging with surprise. 'Where are we going afterwards?'

'The boat shed.'

'Boat shed? What boat shed?'

'By the river.' She waved her hand in its rough direction. 'We should have time to sort out some kind of cover and find survival things, then we're going to have to hope for the best. I don't know what we'll find when we get there, but, right now, it's our only chance.'

Gus smiled. He loved a girl who meant business. If there was to be some weird catastrophe, at least this girl had the whole thing planned.

FORTY-ONE

ARCHIE FINDS KEMP

Archie ran.

He had to find out what Kemp was up to, and fast. If he was right, there wasn't much more time left.

His stomach churned, and darkness seeped into his bones.

Thunder crashed and boomed as spectators began to flee to their cars and the school buildings.

Archie sprinted and scampered up the steep bank, pulling himself up on the longer tufts with his hands and using his studs to give him grip. At the top of the bank he caught his breath.

Another dramatic roll of thunder rattled the ground as Archie watched Isabella being marched off the football pitch. People were streaming away, pointing skywards.

Wow. What a mental couple of minutes. He couldn't believe his strength.

He shook his head and smiled. *Was it from the strange glass of water left by the ghost?*

He spied the alleyway and ran over, the studs of his boots clacking on the stone beneath him. He thought for a minute about taking them off but really, was there any point? *This ghost,* he thought, *couldn't really exist, could it?*

He peered down the alleyway and saw two shapes.

A sudden burst of lightning brought the pair to light and he could make out Kemp's hair, as well as another figure beside him wearing a long coat and a kind of wide brim hat. Archie's heart pounded. They were moving towards him.

OMG. Wrongo. So, the ghost *did* exist and Kemp had got there first.

Archie shrank down, wiping rivulets of sweat off his forehead.

Cain was blind, wasn't he? He'd gone on about the fact that he didn't have any eyes, like the Ancient Woman, so perhaps the ghost couldn't see Kemp.

So, what if the ghost thought Kemp was him?

Archie stood up from behind the wheelie bin so that only his head might be seen. Kemp was about ten paces away and Archie could definitely make out that the figure next to him was a ghost by the simple fact that he didn't have any feet and his face was mostly covered by a scarf.

A crackle of lightning fizzed above them and, from the light it momentarily threw out, Archie saw Kemp's face.

And his expression was one he'd never seen before on his friend.

One of pure terror.

Archie gasped.

Kemp's eyes widened as their eyes met.

Now, he could discern the ghost's words, like 'power' and 'magic' and 'strength'.

Archie was stunned. *This spook, Cain, really did think Kemp was him!*

The ghost held Kemp around his left arm. So was Kemp moving them closer, or was it the other way around?

He listened harder as they came to a stop just on the other side of the wheelie bin.

He heard Kemp's quivering voice. 'Tell me again about the Prophecy. I need to be absolutely certain before I make my final decision.'

'Did you not listen, Archie?' the ghost complained.

Archie reeled. *What was Kemp playing at?*

Why was he asking Cain to tell him about this Prophecy one more time? It seemed a pretty odd thing to do.

Was it for his benefit?

'I need to be sure,' Kemp croaked.

'Very well.' Cain tipped his head to the sky as though sniffing it. 'But we are running out of time.'

Archie stole another look at Kemp from around the corner of the wheelie bin. When he caught sight of Kemp's face, tears were streaming down his cheeks.

Why was Kemp crying?

He crouched down and listened to Cain's deep, powerful voice. 'There is a great shift that occurs every now and then in the way of the universe, Archie,' the ghost began.

'When this happens, the world changes. There is a change in the world's relationship to its surroundings, the infinite and beyond. The process of these movements have been given to you in the form of dreams. These dreams are the

Prophecy of the Garden of Eden and they are given to three people who are known as Heirs of Eden,' the ghost paused. 'You and your sisters are the Heirs of Eden. You are the anointed ones, charged with undertaking the tasks that have been shown to you.'

Archie's gut turned. *WOAH! Anointed ones! Blimey. The strange creature above Daisy had been feeding her dreams.*

The ghost coughed and carried on. 'It is complex. This is not the time to tell you the ways of the universe. All you need know is that the Heirs of Eden face fearsome challenges. The first of which begins with a terrible storm aimed entirely at you. If any of you do not survive the storm, it will rage for forty days and forty nights. It will wash away the world, bit by bit.' Cain paused. 'When the waters recede, there will be a different world and a new beginning.

'I tell you now. You children stand little chance. There is no ark to save you, nor any place you can go where you will not find yourselves shot at by lightning or washed out by torrents of rain. The earth will slip down hillsides, the rivers will swell, and trees will crash down. There is nowhere you can hide. I do not tell you this with any joy, but the storm was designed when men were strong, lived long, and knew how to fight with nature through other means such as magic. You are about to enter a time you are not equipped to cope with. Do you understand?'

Kemp nodded and his eyes bulged. 'Why?' he croaked.

'Young man, the Prophecy is a measure; a test, if you like, to see if the people on this planet are equipped to move into a new age. It was designed to test the strength, courage, intelligence and skill of mankind.'

Cain stopped for a moment and chuckled.

'You and your sisters, the Heirs of Eden, are now the measure of human life on Earth. Together you must survive until sundown and locate the cave of riddles.'

'Then what?' Kemp stammered.

'Then, the destructive force of the storm will cease and the Heirs of Eden must look for the clues that will open the Garden of Eden and save Earth, as you know it today.'

Cain sniffed the air. 'There is no more time,' he barked. 'It will break in a few moments.' The ghost faced him. 'Now boy, you must willingly make a choice.'

FORTY-TWO

GUS IN THE SHOP

Gus hurried after Sue, his arms nearly dropping off with the weight of the shopping bags.

In the shop, he'd rushed round and shovelled everything he could find into three carrier bags, much to the proprietor Mr Ranji's increasing curiosity. Sue was on the other side doing the same, before she ran up to the counter and literally threw money at the shopkeeper. Notes fluttered through the air like leaves and coins sprayed the counter. Sue spun on her heel and fled out of the door with Gus right behind her, burning with shame.

'Come back here!' Ranji shouted. 'Stop! Stop them! Thieves!'

Gus bit his lips and shrugged his shoulders, as a sort of apology, then ran off as fast as his legs could carry him. He headed down the hill, hoping like mad that a thunderbolt wouldn't get him.

When he took a little breather, he spotted Kemp in the alley looking nothing less than utterly terrified.

What the hell was he up to?

There wasn't time. He ran to the boat shed following Sue.

Sue' fingers shook so much that she couldn't lift the plant pot under which the key sat. Eventually Gus put his bags down and calmly tried it for her. The old and rusty key stuck in the lock, turning only fractionally. Gus forced it first one way and then the other, loosening it gradually until it clicked and let them through.

If that was the condition of the lock, he thought, *then what sort of state will this boat be in?*

The door whined open, as another crash of thunder and lightning crackled in the sky overhead. Gus shivered and brushed away a few old cobwebs.

'When was the last time this was used?' he asked.

'No idea,' Sue replied, searching for a light. She flicked the switch and a solitary light bulb sparked into life.

In the middle of the boat house, covered by a large tarpaulin, an old rowing boat rested on two large pieces of wood. It had three bench seats, and Gus reckoned it was probably twelve feet in length by four feet wide. He laughed. 'This is it? This piece of junk is going to save us? It should be in a museum!'

He dragged off the tarp, shook away the dust, and whistled as he inspected the vessel. Layers of peeling varnish and thick dust covered the wood.

'We need to build a canopy,' Sue said.

'Why?' Gus quizzed.

'So we don't spend the entire time bailing water out, that's why.'

Gus pulled the oars off the wall and nestled them in the rowlocks before searching the boathouse for wood. He found several lengths of two by four inch cut timber, as well as planks intended, he supposed, for repairs.

'How long did you say we would be stuck in this?'

Sue shrugged. 'How should I know? A day, a week'

'A week?'

'Maybe a month?'

'Jeez. A month.' Gus sprang into overdrive. He ran around the room finding things that might be useful and tossing them into the boat: rope; wood; a couple of buckets; a crabbing line, and a fishing net. He found a handy-looking wooden box and a sealed plastic container, which he told Sue to clean before putting in the matches and anything else that needed to be kept dry.

How would they anchor down the canopy? What would they sleep on? What would they drink?

He yelled over to Sue, who was still busy cramming the tarpaulin under a seat.

'A month? Really, a month! You think so?'

A huge crack of thunder smashed overhead.

They cowered.

She stretched her arms out. 'How long is a piece of string?'

Gus spied four, fifty-litre plastic containers. He ran over and smelled them. No foul odours. Good. He took two to the tap, then rinsed and filled them before heaving them up onto the boat. It creaked ominously under their weight.

'Make room for these,' he instructed Sue, 'one at each end.'

Gus tied the two empty ones to either side to act as bumpers or emergency buoys.

With this task complete, Gus spotted more loose planks on the far wall. He marched over and, without hesitating, levered the first plank off. As the nails bowed to the pressure and the length came away, he pulled two more weatherboards away and slipped them into the boat. 'Hammer and nails,' he yelled out. 'Have you seen any?'

Sue pointed in the direction of an old workbench.

It was a long shot, but if there were any tools it might make all the difference. He flew through the drawers and cupboards, finding paint and rags, paintbrushes and sandpaper. He dragged out a thick canopy and laid it aside. How would he attach it? To the right, another pile of workman's bits was covered by two large, crumpled dust sheets.

He handed the dust sheets to Sue, indicating that she needed to shake them out and fold them away.

Underneath all this he discovered a selection of woodworking tools hidden in an old, blue canvas bag.

Gus thumped the air. Clearly, someone had set out to repair the building and left everything behind.

Right, Gus thought. *I reckon I've got approximately twenty minutes to build a world class, life-saving canopy.*

FORTY-THREE

KEMP AND ARCHIE

Archie trembled. Everything Cain said rang true.

Archie heard Kemp's voice, strangely muffled. 'So, there's little hope for me and my sisters.'

'There is always hope, young man,' the ghost replied. 'But in comparison to the thickness of a rainbow, the chances that the three of you will survive this storm are but an atom wide. You are a child. You have neither the strength, nor the skills, to combat what lies ahead. You have no magic, and you do not understand nature. What chance do you have?'

He paused for effect. 'None. That is why you must join me now, Archie. While the world is washed away, I alone offer you the chance to escape through me. You have the opportunity to start again. All I need is the use of your body.'

'Will this help save your mother?' Kemp said.

The ghost seemed a little surprised. 'Yes. You have seen her and you know that she holds a great secret within her that others seek to destroy. By joining me, Archie, she will be saved. I guarantee it.'

Cain was laying on the charm. His persuasion was intoxicating. 'Here, on earth, the suffering will be great. Together, Archie, we can build a new future. I am nearly useless without you, and you are helpless without me.'

Kemp looked over at Archie whose terrified face had risen from the other side of the wheelie bin. 'But, I still don't understand,' Kemp whimpered.

Cain growled. 'These things are beyond your understanding. Open your mind. Give me your body.'

Kemp tried to make a run for it. He attempted to loosen the grip on his arm by suddenly charging at the bin. 'GO!' he screamed at Archie. 'RUN!' But the ghost held him tight and forced him to the floor. Kemp whimpered at the stabbing pain in his hand.

The ghost moved into Archie's path and began to unfurl the scarf wrapped around his face. 'I see,' he said. 'There is another.' His head moved. 'Only one of you is Archie. You have deceived me,' the ghost said.

'It is your choice, Archie. If you choose to come with me, you will be saved,' the ghost continued. 'My mother will be saved. Run, and you die.'

He released Kemp, who stumbled to the floor. 'Which is it going to be?'

Kemp's cheeks were streaked with tears. He caught Archie's eye, and stared at him. Imploring him, begging him to understand.

Kemp began to speak to his friend. 'Kemp, you are my only friend,' he said, 'and, not long ago, I swore on my life that I would never hurt you or your family. I failed.'

Archie frowned. *What? What was Kemp talking about? Had Kemp figured that the ghost was blind?*

Kemp began again, 'Run, Kemp, save yourself. GO!'

'Uh?' Archie said, confused.

'Yes, Kemp, you moron, get out of here! Flee to safety.'

Archie stared at Kemp.

And then Kemp said it again. 'Look, Kemp, you great big oaf. Go now while there's still a chance. Leave this to me, but promise me one thing.'

'What?'

'Look after that fishing rod.'

'Fishing rod?'

'Blimey Kemp, how dim are you?' he said. 'Go! Now. Run you idiot—GO!'

Archie stared deep into Kemp's tear-stained eyes and could see a spark of light.

Archie curled his fist into a ball and punched his friend lightly on the shoulder. He winked and mouthed the words, 'Thank you'.

'So long, Archie de Lowe,' Archie said. 'See you in the next place.'

Taking a deep breath, Archie turned and ran for his life.

FORTY-FOUR

ARCHIE RUNS

'It has started,' the ghost cried, his hat angled upwards towards the sky. 'Something more powerful than you can possibly imagine has begun.' He raised an arm towards the lightning and thunder.

'If you want to see your friend for the last time, follow his path. I doubt he will last long. You too may run now, but you would be a fool, Archie de Lowe.'

Kemp moved towards the end of the alleyway.

People were scattering even though the players were still on the pitch.

Kemp watched Archie hare towards the steep bank and out of view. Then he reappeared, running flat out, waving his hands in the air, sprinting onto the football field.

Kemp shifted his gaze.

Daisy struck the ball...

CRACK!

With a deafening roar, a massive thunderbolt flashed out of the sky right on top of Archie.

Kemp's heart missed a beat as he watched Archie collapse to the floor like a rag-doll, his body spasming one moment, then still the next.

Smoke drifted out from his friend's body.

Sounds of screaming filled the air.

Kemp recoiled. Everything the ghost had said had happened; the sweet paper, the lightning in his own image, and now the thunderbolt aimed at Archie who lay dead on the ground.

Laid back Archie, with his scruffy hair, who was always late for everything.

His fishing pal, the only person to whom he'd ever told the whole story about his parents.

He'd sent him to his death.

Cain hovered behind him. 'I am nothing more than a sad ghost,' he said, almost forlornly. 'I was stripped of my flesh and bones, but not my spirit. It means that I cannot move or touch anything with any great purpose, so I require flesh and blood to partially restore me. This is where you come in. I cannot do it alone.'

The ghost removed his scarf and sniffed the air around Kemp, who felt a chill on his neck.

'Rest assured, boy,' the ghost said softly, 'I have no intention of taking your life, only *borrowing* it for a little while. When my work is done and my mother is safe from harm, I will put you back near this spot. That is my solemn promise. But nature's curse is now upon us. A decision needs to be made.'

Kemp remained frozen to the spot.

'You must freely decide,' the ghost continued. 'The window is closing so you must decide now. I very much doubt you will get such an offer from the storm.'

FORTY-FIVE

THE STORM BEGINS

Confusion reigned as players and spectators ran hard towards the cars and houses above the football field. Screams filled the air.

Archie prised his eyes open and attempted to focus. His head! It pounded as if a road roller was travelling backwards and forwards in his brain.

He caught the sharp, acrid smell of burning hair.

When his eyes finally hooked up with his brain, he could make out a burning net and a smouldering goalpost.

'Archie!' Daisy cried as she rushed over. 'Please...'

Several inaudible words mumbled out of his mouth.

'Archie!' Isabella screamed as she tore across the pitch.

She placed her hand on Archie's forehead then felt for his temperature, checked his pulse and inspected his tongue.

'Thank God!' she said, cradling him. 'I thought you were toast. Say something —can you move?'

Very slowly he lifted an arm, his fingernails black and his charred clothes singed.

He smiled weakly.

'At least he's showing signs of mental stability,' Isabella said. 'Daisy, grab the tracksuits! I'll make sure his internal organs are functioning.'

Shortly, Isabella declared that Archie was well enough to try a couple of little sips of water.

Archie shut his eyes then opened them. Then he slurred some words.

'My strips must have saved you!'

'Urgh?'

'The strips you stuck on the bottom of your boots.'

Daisy returned with their tracksuits, slipping into hers before helping Archie into his.

'We won!' Isabella said. 'You did it!'

'Don't be ridiculous,' Daisy scoffed as she pulled Archie's top over his stiff hair.

'I'm not,' Isabella replied. 'The ball's in the net. It was blown into the goal. You actually scored!'

Daisy didn't know whether to hit her sister or cry. 'No,' she said furiously. 'I missed and Archie got fried. Look at him, it's a miracle he survived—'

'But you're fine now, aren't you, Archie?' Isabella said. 'Anyway, you're wrong. Your free kick was heading towards the corner flag but the lightning bolt deflected the ball into the goal. I swear it. The charge of particles must have gener-ated a force to deflect it without blowing the ball up. It is therefore, the most extraordinary goal of the millennium—'

'Shut up! Please,' Daisy snapped. 'Stop it.'

Coach was running over towards them. He went straight to Archie and checked him over.

'WOW-ee,' he whistled. 'That is one lucky escape, young man. I thought you were brown bread. It looks like the Gods spared you. You may feel a little groggy for a while, but, amazingly, I think you're gonna be all right. Try standing if you can.'

Archie, with the support of a person on each side, stood up.

'How do you feel?'

He couldn't quite hear or see them. He tried smiling.

'That's the match ball in the net, isn't it, Coach?' Isabella asked. 'I've taken a picture of it on my phone, for safekeeping.'

Coach clapped his hands. 'You know what, Isabella, you're right! Looks like we ruddy well won. We're only the bleedin' champions!' He slapped Daisy on the back, almost knocking her over. 'Quite amazing...' He stopped mid-sentence and looked up, his tone serious once again. 'Listen, if you think you can make it, Arch, you'd better get off now, up that funny track to your cottage. Otherwise, I'll give you a lift back, via the school.'

'Thanks, but don't worry, Coach,' Isabella said. 'It's not so far. We'll get him back in one piece, I promise. Anyway, you're not *that* poorly, are you, Archie?'

Coach eyed them. 'You sure? Well then, you'd better get going then. Best scarper before another of them thunderbolts zaps us.' He patted them on their backs. 'As fast as you can! I reckon it's going to bloody piss down.'

Coach skipped off towards the car park singing loudly. Then he yelled back at them. 'Great goals, Daisy, and bloody brilliant hairdo, Arch. You're all legends!'

Archie wavered a little and Daisy caught him. 'You really think we can get back home?'

Archie was trying to say something. But it came out slightly askew.

'What is it?' Isabella said softly.

'Storm!' he said, his words slurred. 'Go.'

Angry rolls of thunder boomed around them.

'Is anyone else finding this very loud?' Daisy asked. 'I've had to put tissue in my ears. Look!' And she pulled out the paper. Suddenly Daisy's face went pale.

Isabella spotted it. 'What is it?'

'I think there's another in-coming thunderbolt.'

'*What!*' Isabella said.

'RUN! NOW!'

They hooked Archie's arms around their shoulders and set off.

'I can hear the particles gathering in the cloud, I think,' Daisy said nervously. 'Sounds like a build-up of collisions.' She stopped. 'DIVE!'

A moment later, a massive crack tore across the sky and unleashed a lightning bolt that smashed into the exact spot where, moments earlier, they had been huddled together. The ground smouldered.

'Bloody hell,' Isabella whispered, her knees buckling, her heart thumping. 'That was close. It's like it's after us.'

'It is,' Archie mumbled. He closed his eyes and tried to work more saliva into his mouth. 'We have to survive... until dusk.'

'That's exactly what Sue was yelling about,' Isabella said. 'Survive till sunset.'

'Where do you get that nonsense from?' Daisy said. And then she twitched.

Isabella noticed. 'What is it, Daisy?'

'Another one—I think I can hear it!'

They reached the tree and slipped under the branches.

'We should be safer here.'

Daisy held her hands over her ears as a couple of tears rolled down her cheeks. 'My God. Here it comes!'

A lightning bolt crackled and smashed into the branches. The children screamed as a huge branch sheared off and crashed a couple of metres away.

They ran out hugging each other.

'**OH, NO!**' Daisy cried, her ears screaming in pain.

'What is it now?'

'It's like... like a power shower has just been switched on.'

A warm wind swirled and nearly blew them off their feet. Then the first few large rain drops like mini water balloons began to plummet out of the cloud.

'We need to move, NOW!' Isabella cried. 'This is the storm from hell we predicted—'

'*Predicted?*' Daisy yelled.

'Yeah, Sue and I ...' Isabella's voice trailed off. 'We've got about five minutes before this playing field becomes a river.'

'Oh, well that is simply marvellous,' Daisy yelled.

Isabella and Daisy folded his arms across their shoulders so he was properly supported.

'You've got to move your legs, Arch,' Isabella implored. 'HURRY!' she screamed, forcing the pace. The rain intensified as the wind blew in several directions at once. In no time, in front of them, on top of them, and behind them, a wall of water sluiced out of the heavens, pounding them, beating them hard on their heads and shoulders and backs. Isabella removed her coat and draped it over their heads. For the moment at least, it acted like a shelter.

'Where's the bridge?' Daisy shouted above the din of the rain. 'I can't see ANYTHING!'

Isabella slowed and stared at the ground. Water heads downhill, so it's got to be this way. If we get to the path, we'll find it. Without knowing why, she pointed her free arm ahead of her, closed her eyes and allowed it to guide her.

Soon the feel underfoot of soft wet turf made way for hard gravel. They followed it, but every step was tricky and they couldn't be sure exactly where they were going. Isabella rubbed the ground every so often with her foot to feel the hard path underneath. By the time they reached the bridge, the children were cold, soaked through and exhausted. And, more worryingly, water was spilling out of the river at an alarming rate—up to their ankles and rising fast.

'Bind—tighter—scrum!' Isabella yelled, 'We've got to move together, rhythmically, in time. I'll count.' She realised they couldn't hear her so she signed with her fingers: ONE, TWO... THREE and then she flicked out her thumb.

'Where's the bridge?' Daisy screamed, before suddenly losing her footing. They hauled her to her feet.

Isabella shook her head, imploring her to keep going. 'DON'T FALL.' She turned to Archie to see if he understood. He nodded.

Isabella counted each agonising step, the force of the water gaining by the second, pushing hard at their legs. Every breath was a struggle and their heads were bowed from the pressure of water crashing down upon them.

Isabella had no idea where she was headed. She simply trusted her hands and, as if by a miracle, they guided her to the rail. She breathed a deep sigh of relief.

They shuffled onto the bridge, still huddled together, their feet searching for the wooden boards.

Daisy suddenly went stiff, holding the others back. She turned to the others, her eyes bulging.

Collectively they realised what she meant.

'RUN!'

They scampered up to the brow of the bridge, Daisy leading the way holding Archie's hand on one side, when suddenly she dived, hauling Archie forward with all her might.

Bits of wood splintered around them, the noise deafening. Daisy picked herself out of the water, her feet grateful for the feeling of land, and discovered Archie next to her. He was fine; but where was Isabella?

She scanned the area as best she could but even as she called out Daisy knew it was hopeless; she wouldn't be heard over the din. The only thing she could hear was the roar of the rain and rushing water flushing everything downstream. And Isabella, she feared, was now a part of it.

FORTY-SIX

OLD MAN WOOD'S WORRY

As the morning wore on, Old Man Wood had been consumed by a feeling of utter dread, as if a toxic stew brewed in his stomach and a splinter had played darts in his heart.

Whatever he did, his anxiety would not go away. He marched around the house looking for something—anything - to alleviate this terrible feeling.

He studied the wooden carvings, tracing his fingers over the rich detailing on the panelling in his room. He inspected the old pictures for a clue, anything that might shed some light on the nightmares he'd had and help temper the worry that filled him from the top of his head to the tips of his toes.

Did the carvings and paintings mean something? If so, *what*?

Was a vital clue staring him in the face?

The more he played with this notion, the greater and deeper his feeling of despair grew, like a festering skin boil.

He wondered if he shouldn't go down to the school and watch the football match, but it didn't seem right.

Instead, he headed up to the ruin to check on the sheep and cattle.

The herd appeared quiet but jumpy. The same as him, he thought, as if the animals sensed something unusual. He made sure that the shelter was sound, before counting them: eleven sheep, three cows, six bullocks, and Himsworth the bull.

Old Man Wood sat down on a grey boulder at the head of the ruin and looked out across the vale. In front of him a sheer drop of solid rock disappeared into thick forest seventy metres or so below, before levelling up near the valley floor.

He could just make out the river curving around the rock face and, from there, it slipped around the corner.

Old Man Wood shuffled his boot in the dirt. He was too old for this, too old for riddles and memories.

Why the dreams every night, what were they trying to tell him? Why did he have that aching feeling in his bones which he hadn't had for ages?

He stood up as a deep roll of thunder boomed and crackled through the valley. He kicked a stone, which flew off the ledge and sailed through the air before crashing into the canopy of the trees below.

Looking out at the school buildings in the distance, lost in his thoughts, Old Man Wood saw a lightning bolt shoot out of the sky right into the heart of the village. This was followed by another, and then another. Each one came with a blast of light so bright and a crack so loud that Old Man Wood shielded his eyes and his ears.

A searing pain walloped into his chest. He bent over and cried out. The sky fizzed as another huge bolt crashed out of the sky directly onto the playing field.

This time the pain was unbearable and Old Man Wood crouched low, clutching his chest, struggling for breath.

Was this pain linked to the storm? He needed to lie down.

Old Man Wood straightened up as best he could and stumbled back down the pathway, stopping occasionally to view the tempest playing out over the school.

Wasn't it funny, he pondered, *how the storm seemed to focus only on the school?*

As he concentrated on this thought, his feeling that the children were in terrible danger accelerated. He hurried back, lay on his bed, and massaged his heart, as another thought crossed his mind.

If the storm broke, how would the children get back? The river would swell, and the track to Eden Cottage would act like a storm drain. What if they were trying to get home and were swept away?

He dabbed his handkerchief on his forehead. He had to *do* something.

But as he was preparing to get up, an instant tiredness washed over him, and a powerful urge to close his eyes enveloped him like a drug.

His head fell back onto his large pillows and a moment later the old man was snoring like the throbbing of an old tractor engine.

FORTY-SEVEN

KEMP JOINS

Kemp stumbled, dizzy and sick with fear. He faced Cain head-on for the first time.

All Kemp could see was a transparent gap between the hat and the overcoat. His teeth were chattering. 'If I don't—?'

'You'll almost certainly die, or be drowned in the rains. Or in the landslides, or the tsunamis which will sweep the land…'

'Will you kill me?'

'Me? Kill you?' the ghost chuckled. 'No. As I said, I'm just going to *borrow* you for a while. Why would I kill you when my purpose is to save so many? You must *trust* me.'

Kemp looked up at the sky. It was fizzing with electricity like an angry nest. A terrible boom rattled every bone in his body as a thunderbolt walloped into a nearby chimney pot.

He ducked and his head vibrated like a jack-hammer mashing up a road.

Kemp stared down the path, preparing to run. As his eyes focused on the dark shadows between the buildings, he found himself looking at a familiar face: Gus Williams laden with shopping bags. They locked eyes for several seconds before Williams simply ran off, as though someone had called him away in a hurry.

'Dreamspinner!' the ghost barked, impatiently. 'Open up. It is time to go! This boy is not the Heirs of Eden.'

'Wait,' Kemp croaked. 'Please! What do I have to do?'

'You must want to survive and you must absolutely desire to go with me.'

Kemp looked about. His mind was made up.

'Put on the coat and hat. Do it quickly.'

In a flash, he threw both of his overcoats to the ground and moved in close. As he did, he felt a strange coolness wash over him.

'Ignore that I am here,' the ghost said, as Kemp fumbled with the cloth. 'Put the coat on, as you would any other.'

Kemp grabbed the collar and pushed his arm into the sleeve, amazed by the sudden freeze that enveloped it. Then his other arm slid in. Kemp had a wonderful feeling of deep strength building up in him, as though a syringe was powering him with a thick energy juice.

The feeling started in his fingers, moved up to his wrists, through his elbows and on to his shoulders. All too soon, it was spreading down through his loins and into his legs and feet. Syrupy liquid, like freezing treacle, coursed through every vein and into every muscle and sinew of his body.

Kemp drew the coat across his chest as the curious feeling crept towards his heart and lungs.

He cried out and stretched his arms wide, as the ice-like goo rushed into his vital organs and washed through his body. He let out a cry of pure ecstasy, his shouts bouncing back off the old houses.

Kemp only had one more thing to do. He lifted up the hat and pulled it down over his head. Suddenly, he could feel the cold charge oozing up his neck and through his mouth.

He shut his eyes, enjoying the extraordinary tingling sensations of the liquid ice entering his brain and slowly dispersing through the back of his skull, tickling parts he never knew existed.

The surge of power moved around the skull and headed towards his eyes.

As it flowed into his eyes, everything changed. With a rapidity that took him completely by surprise, Kemp felt a searing, burning pain scream into his head, expanding like a balloon filling with air.

'What's happening?' he screamed. 'MY GOD, *my eyes!*'

He desperately tried to rip off the hat and wrestle out of the coat.

'My head! MY EYES! What have you done to me? Help me! *HELP! I'm burning!*'

As Kemp carried on screaming, the ghost chuckled.

'Welcome to me,' Cain said, his voice laced with triumph. 'Welcome to the burnt-out body of Cain, Frozen Lord of Havilah.'

FORTY-EIGHT

SOLOMON ROUNDS UP

Solomon felt a sharp pain in his chest. He looked at the schoolchildren and the adults streaming away from the pitch.

In an instant, he knew what to do.

He ran to the Newton coach. 'Go, directly,' he ordered. 'Please don't argue, get in your bus and drive as fast as you can away from this place. I believe this fearsome cloud is about to break.'

He didn't wait around. He ran on, sweat breaking out.

'Children,' he boomed. 'All those staying till later, do not go back to your classrooms. Go directly to the library in the tower. Hurry, there's not a moment to lose. Grab anyone you see on the way.'

Solomon rushed towards the buildings and ran, panting, into the classrooms.

'Get to the tower, now,' he roared, rushing in. 'Leave your things, just go there this second!'

A terrible realisation filled him. Children were scattered around the school. The noise overhead, like heavy artillery fire, made his eyes water.

He bumbled into the gymnasium, where a last rehearsal was underway.

'Stop what you're doing,' he ordered, climbing on to the stage while trying to catch his breath. 'Get to the library, immediately.' He hoped his firm tone would not go unnoticed.

Children poured out of the entrance. 'Good. Hurry,' he called out after them. 'You too, Mrs. Rose.'

He rushed back into the yard and shot into the canteen.

He gasped for breath. 'Chef!' he said, as an idea popped into his head. 'Take as many provisions as you can to the library, this instant. Bread, milk, anything.'

'Are you all right, boss?'

'Pile the contents of the fridge, the store cupboards, the larder into containers this very instant and head directly to the tower.'

The chef stared at him in disbelief and stole a glance towards his assistants.

'Do it NOW!'

'Everything?'

'Yes, chef, as much as you possibly can. Just trust me. There's not a moment to lose. And remember milk and orange juice. Do it now—all of you,' he roared.

They hesitated.

'Now! GO! There's no time!'

Solomon sped out of the kitchen then, as fast as he could, outside across the yard and into the art department. He struggled to breathe. 'Skinner, Moloney, run to the tower this instant,' he gasped, falling into a chair.

He wiped his specs. Who else?

The building splintered, the sound rattling the windows.

Good Lord. The changing rooms!

Then he heard the whooshes of wind, no doubt whipped up by oncoming rain. *No time!*

Out he shuttled, his body screaming at him to stop.

Three boys sat on the benches, staring out of the window.

'Don't just sit there,' he cried. 'Come with me.'

'Where to?'

'Safety,' he gasped, collapsing onto the wood.

'Sir, are you all right?'

Solomon clenched his eyes. 'Yes, yes. Now run along! Go to the library. I'll follow.'

'But, Sir?'

'NOW!'

The headmaster took several deep breaths. He'd rounded up as many as he could.

Where were the de Lowes? Then it struck him. They would be heading home across the playing fields. A twenty-minute walk at the very least.

He summoned his energy and threw himself through the door, rushing out into the corridor and then down the stairs.

As he ran outside, he saw far off in the distance three figures huddling together, heading slowly towards the bridge.

Oh my God, he thought, a feeling of utter despair gripping him. *They haven't got a chance.*

But as he sucked in a lungful of air to call out to them, the first drops of rain smashed into him, and soon the noise was deafening.

FORTY-NINE

GUS AND THE CANOPY

Within moments, water edged through the cracks of the boat house and stole down the sides, drumming like a carnival on the barn's tin roof.

Gus stared in disbelief at the rain. *Holy moly,* he thought, *she's right.*

Quickly, Gus stretched the canopy, which in truth was a thick, heavy-duty plastic sheet covering the length of the vessel from bow to stern. It would fit perfectly. Then, he formed a tent frame over the boat, hammering in nails as fast as he could go.

He stepped back. *Uneven,* Gus thought, *but it would do, so long as the nails held.*

Gus listened. It needed to be super-strong. He'd take more wood and prop up the mid-section if he had time later, once they were underway.

Next, he nailed two rough planks on both the port and starboard sides, leaving a gap in the middle for the oars. As fast as he could, he nailed batons over the canopy on the outside, repeating his action on the other side. In no time, the boat was covered in a tight tent. Better still, if it worked, water would run off the canopy into the river and not inside.

Sue looked on in awe. She tried where she could to help, amazed at his dexterity and speed. Gus didn't come across as the brightest spark in school, but my goodness he was practical.

She ran around the boat pulling bits of the canopy tight while Gus hammered, sawed and stretched the plastic sheeting. So immersed in their project were they, that they hardly noticed water seeping in, up and over the floor.

'Almost time to batten down the hatches,' Gus yelled, smiling.

Sue ran up and hugged him. 'I couldn't have done this w
and she genuinely meant it. Sue climbed in and sat under
sense of foreboding filled her. She desperately hoped they were ɯ
thing. She hoped like anything that Isabella and the twins had got away saiɯ.

Gus slipped in a few remaining planks and a couple more of the two by four
inch sections. He grabbed the remaining nails, the hammer, a saw, a small axe, a
hand-drill and a chisel, and threw them all in the box. Just before the water
covered the whole floor, he scanned the shed looking for anything else. Sue's
umbrella, for starters, and a couple of old empty paint pots with lids. More rope,
string, a whole reel of strimmer cord, and another large dust sheet, this one
already neatly folded. He rummaged through the cupboards like a man
possessed, and found an untouched bag of barbecue briquettes. He threw them in;
maybe they'd need fire.

Sue packed them away. Then with a few last-minute alterations, as the water
reached the upper limits of his boots, Gus clambered in to the boat. He hoped like
mad that, with the weight of the fresh water and timber and the two of them, they
wouldn't all simply disappear through the bottom.

The vessel creaked as it rose. No holes nor rotten timbers so far.

Sue shook, holding her hands against her ears as thunder and lightning blazed
outside. It felt as if they were waiting in the depths of the Colosseum before being
fed to the lions in front of an angry, baying crowd. The boat continued to rise,
finding its buoyancy. Then it started to drift.

'Here we go,' Gus yelled. 'Hold on tight.'

A moment later, the wood clunked into something.

Gus squeezed past Sue to the bow. He looked out and muttered something
under his breath.

'What is it?' Sue cried. 'Is there a problem?'

'Technical difficulty,' he said, scratching his chin. 'Pass me that hand axe.'

Sue scrabbled around in the box and handed it over.

Gus disappeared, and set about trying to smash the weatherboards. A short
while later, his banging stopped. 'It appears,' Gus said, popping his head back
under the canopy, 'that the water has risen higher than the gap the boat was
meant to go through.'

'What does that mean?'

'It means we're stuck!' he said, smiling his huge grin again.

'For crying out loud,' Sue howled. 'Can't you get the boards off?'

'What do you think I've been doing? Knitting?'

'So how are we going to get out? I was hoping we might be able to save Archie
and the others.'

us raised his eyebrows. 'There's a window directly above, so panic ye not. ⌐ got an idea,' he said. 'Pass me the saw, and move to the other end, please.'

Gus took the saw and stood on the seat right at the prow of the boat. He began sawing as fast as he could through the timbers surrounding the window. The boat sloshing from side to side.

After several minutes of sawing and hacking, Gus put his drenched head back under the canopy. 'Don't think that's going to work, either.' He smiled again. 'Rain's quite warm.'

Sue looked appalled. 'What are we going to do?'

Gus stretched out his legs, closed his eyes and took a deep breath. 'We wait.'

'Wait!' Sue roared. 'You must be joking. We'll drown if we stay in here. Can't you see that?'

Gus ignored her and smiled toothily again. It seemed to act as an anger-deflecting shield. 'You know what we haven't done?' he said, his large eyes sparkling.

'What?' Sue snapped.

'Named our vessel.'

Sue eyed him warily. 'Seriously, Gus, before we start thinking up names, do you actually think we'll get out of here?'

He raised his eyebrows.

'How?' Sue said, raising her eyebrows back at him. Getting a straight answer out of Gus was proving to be a bit of a nightmare.

Gus jabbed a finger upwards.

'God?' she yelled, sarcastically.

Gus's whole body galloped up and down with laughter.

He moved close to her so they could hear each other without yelling. 'No, you banana-cake, through the roof. So long as the water continues to rise,' he peered out of the end of the boat, '—and it is rising, just as you said it would, then up we go.'

Sue grimaced. 'Really? You sure it'll work?'

'Oh yeah. Far easier this way. There's corrugated iron sheeting up there, they'll lift off and then, whoosh, into the river.'

Sue couldn't help but admire his confidence, although she wasn't convinced. Wasn't corrugated sheeting heavy, especially with water beating onto it? 'So, what do we do now?'

'Well, let's see. We could start by naming our boat. It's definitely good luck before a maiden voyage. You got any ideas?'

'Not really. You?'

'Yeah,' and he smiled his big smile again.

'Well, what is it?'

Gus opened his eyes wide. 'I think we should call it the 'The Joan of'.'

'That's it?' Sue said. She looked mystified. 'The Joan of... what? What does that mean? It doesn't make any sense. That's not a name for a boat.'

Gus feigned a look of shock. 'Now, come along, brain-box. This little teaser shouldn't be difficult for super-smart Sue Lowden.'

FIFTY

OLD MAN WOOD'S DREAM

Old Man Wood hadn't reacted to any of the dreams given to him. The dream-spinner worried that if Old Man Wood could not understand his dreams, what chance would the children have with theirs?

Were the dreams proving to be too complex, too terrifying? Were the dreams suited to a different time? Perhaps their dreams needed a different blending of powders to aid interpretation?

Gaia dipped a hand in her maghole, removed the dream powder and rubbed a couple of fingers together. This wasn't the time for reflection, that would come later. While the children were still alive, for the time being at least, she needed haste.

She would give Old Man Wood a dream that would stimulate action and, at the end of the sequence, she would add a powder that would stimulate a shock. Yes, that was it. He needed something to get his brain working, to unlock his memory, so that he might help the Heirs of Eden as he'd been entrusted to do.

Gaia worked fast, her slender fingers moving like a blur in her maghole. In a flash, she was plucking tiny specks of dream powder out of her maghole and feeding them to the old man as he inhaled. Gaia took her time, and, digging deep into her memory of powders, knitted a dream ending with a reminder of a potion that Old Man Wood had stored away a long, long time ago.

Gaia stared down at the old man. *Maybe this time,* she thought, before inverting into her maghole and vanishing.

❄

Old Man Wood tossed and turned as the dream filled his head. He looked down and found himself wearing a pair of shorts. He was running. He felt young again, the same age as the twins. His skin was smooth and his mind was alert. He had hair! He dragged his hands through it. What a lovely feeling. As he ran, air filled his lungs.

On his feet, he wore a pair of football boots. Red ones, just like Archie's. He looked up. A football was flying towards him, and his immediate reaction was to duck out of the way. But out of the corner of his eye he spotted Daisy yelling at him. What was she saying? Pass it? He went towards the ball but it was too fast and it bounced off him straight to an opponent.

This wasn't as easy as it looked.

Daisy swore and chivvied him to chase the player.

He took off and was moving at speed. Much to his delight, Old Man Wood found himself gaining. He lunged for the ball but tripped the player.

The whistle blew. 'Do that once more and you'll be booked,' the referee said.

Old Man Wood caught his breath and brushed the mud off his knees.

Daisy was there in an instant. 'What do you think you're playing at?' she said. 'There's hardly any time to go. Don't make stupid fouls like that. We've got to win or we're never playing again.'

The other team lined up a shot and the ball was cruising towards the goal. But Archie danced into the path of the ball and caught it smartly. In a flash, he punted the ball wide.

One of his players passed the ball to him. This time he managed to control it and he slipped a neat pass through to Daisy. Daisy, now on the halfway line, jinked past one player, and then sped past another, her blonde hair bobbing up and down as she went. Boy, she was quick. He found himself sprinting just to keep up.

A defender forced her wide and she played the ball inside to him. Looking up, he passed it to Isabella on the other flank. He couldn't remember Isabella ever liking football, but she neatly passed it back to him just as she was clattered by an opposition player. He couldn't help laughing at the horrified expression on her face.

Now Daisy was screaming for the ball.

Old Man Wood found himself running with the ball and it felt brilliant. He did a dummy, just like Daisy had, slipping past the player in front of him. He knocked the ball forwards, finding Daisy, who held off a challenge and stood with the ball under her foot.

In a flash, she turned on a sixpence, the ball rolling under her other foot. Totally foxing the defender, she headed towards the goal. Old Man Wood felt himself sprinting into the area as Daisy smashed a shot at the goal.

He held his breath as the ball sped toward the goal. It whacked against the post and rebounded directly into his running path. Out of the corner of his eye, a defender hared towards the ball. He had to get there first, so he sprinted harder, cocked his leg back, and kicked the ball as hard as he could a fraction before the defender got there.

The ball screamed into the roof of the net, tearing a hole, and was still rising just as the defender crunched into his foot.

A heartbeat later, and a lightning bolt smashed out of the sky directly into him. A surge of energy fizzed through his entire body, through every sinew and fibre and particle of his being.

It took his breath away.

When at last the sensation wore off, he peered down to find a bottle of gold liquid on his lap.

Then he woke up, with a start.

FIFTY-ONE

KEMP'S PAIN

After the euphoric sensation of the icy power sluicing through his every sinew, Kemp experienced a pain like he had never felt before. His whole body raged with fire, the burning excruciating but, as he dissolved into Cain, Kemp kept repeating his name and his birthday, and his mother's and father's names and his school and his favourite colours and everything happy that he could ever remember.

The last thing he remembered was diving head-first towards the electric body of a weird spidery creature and then being sucked into a void. He must have passed out.

When he opened his eyes it was as though he was seeing through a grey filter. He could see grey shapes and objects, but nothing clearly; no detail.

He sensed he was lying on a bed. He shut his eyes, and tried to see if he could lose the pain—a constant, driving, nagging ache. He could sense that he was in a body that was gently rising and falling—his body—but it was surrounded by something else. Ash? Soot?

Kemp felt woozy and weak, and utterly helpless. Nothing he did seemed to make any difference. He had no control, but maybe he could use this time to think.

Cain stirred. The feeling like painful pins and needles in every orifice of his being.

Suddenly Kemp felt his entire body taken over and his brain and eyes and everything seemed to be fading away, like a gas lamp being extinguished.

FIFTY-TWO

ISABELLA DISAPPEARS

Isabella's world went blank. When she came to, her body tingled all over and every nerve and sinew sizzled like a spectacular case of pins and needles.

She coughed, spluttered, and violently ejected water trapped in her lungs. She gasped as her hands and feet instantly kicked into action, her arms and legs moving faster than she could ever have imagined just to keep her head above water.

She breathed, luxuriating in the intake of air.

Her hand grappled with a shrub branch. She tried to hoist herself up, but it fell away plunging her back underwater. When she surfaced, visibility zero, she knew she needed to touch down on the cottage side of the river.

Treading water, she did a quick calculation. If the river ran from the moors down into the valley, she had to land on the left bank as it went with the flow. Isabella kicked until she could feel the water pushing against her before twisting with all her strength and swimming at an angle into the current.

Moments later, she touched on something spindly and woody. She pushed her legs down and was relieved to find the water was up to her waist. With her feet on firm ground, she clambered across the bush and kept going until her knees hit on solid ground the other side.

Isabella coughed, spluttered, and retched, as though her insides were coming out. Without hesitating, she continued uphill, searching for the cover of a tree. She found one, leaned in and put her head in her hands.

Tears built up and for a moment they rolled freely down her cheeks. *Daisy! Archie! They'll think I'm dead.*

She imagined them waiting for her.

Please, please keep going! Every minute spent waiting is a minute wasted.

She wondered what had happened to Sue. Did she find the boat? In any case, that little boat would fill with water and sink in minutes. The whole thing was hopeless.

Isabella felt herself welling up, but a ripple of water washed against her shins. She had to move. Finding the others was futile now. She'd head uphill from tree to tree and find cover wherever she could.

She had to survive.

FIFTY-THREE

CAIN'S ADMIRATION

'Look at us, boy,' Cain whispered. 'Well, look at me. Aren't I *magnificent!*'

Cain studied his body in a tall mirror ringed with dull gemstones. Morning light seeped through a vast window. 'You're here, boy,' he said, as his voice echoed off the walls. 'Right here inside me. That's right; half ash, half man... or boy. Only a fraction ghost.'

Cain examined his reflection.

His borrowed eyes weren't anything like the proper article, his vision was filtered by a grainy film. But, what a sensation to see anything at all when, for thousands of years, he had tuned into the vibrations and presence of things using his highly developed sixth sense.

He studied his hands and turned them over. He clapped, the noise a muted thud. Ash puffed up and floated quietly through the air.

Oh, the joys of having a body, he thought, *whatever form it took*.

Cain removed his overcoat, took off his hat, and returned, naked, to stand in front of the mirror. His figure was the same size as the boy and his torso was covered in layers of flaky ash in every conceivable hue of grey. *How utterly remark-able*, he thought, as he rotated his hips from side to side.

His chest was a boyish replica of the one he remembered. His pectorals and abdomen were not so hard and toned as perhaps they once were, but the sinews and muscles on his thighs, calves and buttocks were pleasingly accentuated by the light.

His feet, he noted, were unusually large. He sprang up on his toes, only to find that a couple of digits simply dropped off. Cain stared, fascinated, as they instantly regrew.

In the reflection of the mirror, Cain moved close. His face appeared sallow and partially skeletal, with a flaky grey chin that jutted out more than he cared to see.

He nudged his thick plump lips, prodded his flat nose, and admired his eyebrows. He touched his hair, a mass of ash swept back off his forehead, and admired his eyes that sparkled like polished coals.

Then he noticed a strange cluster at the top of his legs. Wasn't this awfully important? Instinctively, he reached for it, but to his horror—and just as he remembered its purpose—the appendage severed, slipped through his fingers and careered to the ground.

Cain squealed.

His concerns were short-lived. Moments later it reappeared and he and his organ were reacquainted.

Cain's mood brightened.

'Thousands of years without one,' he roared, 'and instantly it falls to pieces!'

Cain realised his new body was a by-product of his incineration all those years ago.

His eyes narrowed.

How could he forget the burning and the eye gouging when his powers were taken away from him?

The verdict from The Council of One Hundred in the Garden of Eden, he remembered. *Oh yes, the very bad deal. Part of his original punishment.*

Cain flexed up and down on his knees. He had movement; real, gravity-based movement, and physical presence. None of this 'floating around' nonsense, none of this walking through walls and doors and people, although this skill did, from time to time, have its advantages.

Cain, Frozen Lord of Havilah, is back! He could almost taste the fear of the strange creatures that now populated Havilah. Trolls had moved into the forests close to the silvery sea, a tribe of Neanderthals had swept over the pink mountains that surrounded Havilaria and some marsh-men had dammed the planet's great river at its mouth. The dragons, snakes, lizards, and reptiles, once controlled by his undefeatable reptilian beast called Gorialla Yingarna, had risen in numbers, with many now living on the outskirts of the city of Havilaria.

Cain would return from the ashes to free his frozen people, so the rumours said, and bring the frozen domed puddles back to life. Cain knew that he needed to make the most of his new form, and fast, which was exactly what he intended to do even if it meant that he had to forcibly drag the boy along with him.

First, he would check up on the Heirs of Eden's progress towards their demise, now that their journey through the storm was underway. Perhaps he still had a chance of blending with an Heirs of Eden, instead of this rather cumbersome boy.

Asgard's dream-spinners were watching the Heirs of Eden. When they were close to deaths door, they would let him know.

Cain smiled. Everything was slotting into place.

And when that time came, in an instant, he would be there.

FIFTY-FOUR

DAISY GETS ARCHIE BACK

Daisy shivered, grateful that the rain was not particularly cold. Daisy knew, though, that even warm rain quickly chills, and there was just so much of it. She ventured from one side of the path to the other, as far as she dared and screamed once more for Isabella, but she knew it was hopeless; she couldn't see and she could hardly hear her own voice.

With every movement, her bones ached and her joints screamed out, as if her energy reserves were on empty. If only she hadn't just played a game of football.

She stamped her feet and jogged up and down. She concentrated hard on the water further down. For a moment, she was sure that she could see, much further down on the river bank, a body climbing out of the water. She shook her head. She must be imagining things, like a mirage in a desert.

She put a hand around Archie and hugged him close. His body warmth was like a hot water bottle. He seemed better, his eyes clearer, and he smiled when she touched his odd hair.

But the shock had rendered him dumb, as though his tongue had been cut out.

What had Archie said earlier? That the storm would follow them until sunset. How did he know? She didn't need him like this, she needed him on full alert, thinking and helping.

Perhaps, she thought, *he needs another shock.*

She slapped him on the cheek as hard as she could.

'Blimey, Daisy!' he yelled, rubbing his cheek. 'What did you do that for?'

'Got you back,' she mouthed, kissing his forehead. 'Sorry—necessary.'

'There's no need to hit me,' he yelled.

Daisy hugged him tight, and spoke into his ear. 'Aw, but it did the trick. Come on, Arch, we've got to go.'

'What about Isabella?' he cried, waving his arm downstream.

'She's a strong swimmer,' she said. 'She'll be fine. Come on!'

He looked at his watch and shuddered. Only two-forty-five. Sunset at what, five-fifteen, five-thirty? He wished he knew.

Every second of every minute would matter.

FIFTY-FIVE

MRS PYE WORRIES

Mrs Pye sat in the kitchen, fretting and fiddling with a bunch of herbs, her hands shaking.

She heard noises in the courtyard. The sounds weren't the sounds of a soccer ball scuffing over the paving slabs, which she associated with Daisy and Archie. Nor was it Old Man Wood returning from the cattle. He'd been back a while.

This was more like something being torn in two, and then crashing sounds audible even over the beating rain.

Must be my imagination playing tricks, she thought, as she returned to her task of flavouring a large beef casserole.

She concentrated on lighting the fire, before her ears instinctively pricked up. Those sounds, again.

Opening the front door, she reeled as a wall of water poured like a waterfall over the low, extended roof. Seeing a branch jumping about in the water nearby, she realised that the sounds she'd heard must have been trees crashing down around the house.

A pain, like a stubborn splinter, pierced her. For the first time in years, the long, thick scar beneath the mop of bright orange hair on her forehead throbbed, giving her a pressing headache.

She'd never seen or heard anything like it. Instantly, she recognised the gravity of the children's situation.

The longer it went on, the more she pined, as though the cord that tied her to her children was being ripped apart and pins pressed slowly into her heart. She tried to soldier on and put these feelings behind her. She had to. They would return, she was sure of it. Old Man Wood would find them.

But what if they didn't? What if her children were stuck out there?

Tears swam down her cheeks, falling in drops on the wooden surface. Her head pulsed with doubt and sorrow as she cradled it in her hands and wept.

Realisation dawned on her that if this storm continued, and if Old Man Wood was to go after them, she might be alone in the world for the very first time.

FIFTY-SIX

GUS' QUIZ

'Oh, *ARK*!' Sue exclaimed. 'As in, *"Joan of Arc".*'

Gus clapped slowly. 'Blimey. At long last. Remind me never to partner you in a pub quiz. Ever.'

'You mean,' Sue said, 'you've actually been to a pub quiz?'

'Of course, every Friday night with my dad.'

'Really? My parents never do that kind of thing. What's it like?'

Gus wondered if he should make it sound exciting. 'Well, it's OKAY. Actually, it's quite nerdy, so you'd probably like it.'

Sue's eyes sparkled. Gus was full of surprises. *Just goes to show*, she thought, *you really can't tell a book by its cover.* 'So, what subjects are you good at?'

Gus made his brainiest face, which made him look pretty stupid. 'Particle physics, geography, English history from 1066, current world affairs and, yeah, modern American history.'

'You're joking me!'

'Try me. Go on,' Gus said, moving even closer.

Sue didn't know what to think. She screwed up her face as though deep in thought and asked: 'Which President of the United States of America wrote the Declaration of Independence?'

Gus scratched his chin and made lots of quite odd-looking faces. 'Abraham Lincoln—'

'Ha, wrong—'

'Won the Civil War,' Gus continued, ignoring her. 'Thomas Jefferson was the main author of the Declaration of Independence.' He tried hard not to smile. But he did raise his eyebrows. And they were huge eyebrows.

Sue couldn't believe it. 'Correct,' she said, trying to think of another question. 'Name the English monarch who came after William Rufus.'

'You can do better than that, sexy Sue.' He pulled a serious face. 'William Rufus, heir to William the Conqueror. Shot by an arrow by a noble who thought he was a knob-end. Succeeded by Henry, as in Henry the first, also a son of the Conqueror, who sat on the throne for a middle-age marathon of thirty-five years.'

Sue shrieked. She couldn't believe it. 'Gus, you're brilliant at this. Why are you such an idiot in class?'

Gus shrugged. 'Low tolerance to teachers.'

A clunking noise stopped them in their tracks. Gus raced up to the bow step. ''The Joan of' has hit the roof,' he yelled. 'Here we go.' Gus ducked his head inside the canopy. 'I hope you're ready for this. Pass me that long bit of wood and sit at the end. And Sue...'

'Yes?'

'Whatever you do, don't scream. It won't help.'

Gus had never really expected the water to rise quite so high, nor so fast. In fact, he was pretty sure they'd remain in the boathouse, quite safe from the tempest outside. Now, it was different.

He grappled with the piece of wood, eventually holding its base, and thrust it up towards the corrugated sheeting directly above. *Come on, you little beauty. Move.* Nothing happened. He changed his tack, trying to lever the roofing off. *Move, you little tick,* he murmured, as he pushed the wood with all his might.

As he pushed, he became aware that the entire building had begun to move. Gus stopped hammering on the roof and watched as the shed began to drift off all on its own. He couldn't believe it.

He wondered if, incredibly, the buoyancy of their boat had given buoyancy to the entire building, and now it had gone adrift with them inside it. That, or he was suddenly immensely strong.

The only thing he knew for sure was that the whole unit was moving quickly into the swollen floodwaters. As far as he could tell, they were safe. In fact, he rather suspected they were safer than any place they could otherwise have expected to end up in, so long as 'The Joan of' didn't fall apart.

He ducked down under the canopy to find Sue crying hysterically.

'Everything ship-shape and dandy, Captain,' he said, saluting.

Sue looked confused. 'What's happening, Gus? I'm scared.'

Gus shrugged. 'I pushed the roof and the entire shed came away. Funny thing is, I always suspected I had superpowers.'

'Is it safe?'

Gus looked at her blankly. 'Truthfully?' He shrugged. 'I've no idea, but, so far, so good. Now, how about another brainteaser.' He sat down and put his legs up. 'Can't wait all day.'

Sue peered up at him. She simply couldn't believe his brazen attitude to the disaster unfolding around them. The boat lurched and her eyes widened. But Gus rubbed his eyes and yawned.

'Gus Williams,' she said. 'I don't know how you do it.' She took a couple of deep breaths to settle her nerves. 'We're on the verge of plunging into Armageddon and you want another teaser?'

Gus nodded. 'Yeah. Absolutely.'

'Good Lord. Okay. Physics question—you said you were good at physics, right?' He nodded. A question popped into her head. 'Where does bad light end up?'

Gus confidently put his feet on the seat. He was grinning like mad, which Sue later discovered was a sign that his brain was working. 'Okay,' he began cagily, 'either it's in an ohm?' Sue giggled but shook her head. 'OR,' and there was quite a long pause. He clicked his fingers, 'In a prism?'

Sue clapped her hands. 'Brilliant! You're a big, bloody genius, aren't you?'

Gus was bursting with pride. Big and genius—in the same sentence—from delicious, sexy Sue. He hardly dared tell her he'd read the answers in a magazine at the dentist. 'One for you,' he said. 'What did the male magnet say to the female magnet?'

Sue burst out laughing. 'I'm seriously attracted to you?' She turned purple on the spot.

Gus caught her eye. 'Not bad. Want another try?'

Sue shook her head. 'Tell me.'

Gus looked quite serious. 'From your backside,' he began, 'I thought you were repulsive. However, from the front I find you rather attractive.'

Sue clapped her hands and laughed as Gus punched the air.

Suddenly, a terrible noise, like the body of a car scraping along a road, stopped both of them in their tracks.

Gus slipped out the front. Then he dived back in, and dashed toward Sue at the rear. 'Move up front,' he ordered.

Sue shuffled up as Gus headed out of the canopy at the bow.

Seconds later, he reappeared. Without hesitating, he sat in the middle of the boat and grabbed the oars. He started to row, pushing the oars in the water to go backwards, as fast as he could.

'What's going on?' Sue cried.

'Our time has come. 'The Joan of's' moment has arrived.'

With a terrible crunching noise, the back end of the shed levered high into the air, as if the nose had dived headlong into the water. Gus took a deep breath and, praying 'The Joan of' held together, he rowed with all his might. The little boat plunged backwards, creeping under the raised end, out into the river.

Now, for the first time, rain whammed into the canopy and the boat rocked in the water the sound like a relentless pounding of drums.

After a couple of minutes, Sue put her head out as far as she dared, and tried to survey the scene. The only things she could see were the faint outlines of cars, wood, and sections of plastic, bobbing along beside them.

She ducked under the canopy, her face ashen.

'Everything all right?' Gus yelled, noting the distress in her face.

'Isabella, Daisy, and Archie are in this, with no protection,' she yelled back. 'They haven't got a hope.'

'They'll be fine,' he yelled back. He looked down. 'Sue,' he hollered. 'Get a bucket NOW and start bailing!'

FIFTY-SEVEN

OLD MAN WOOD FINDS A CLUE

Old Man Wood stared around his room and thumped the air.

'What a marvel-blister of a goal!' he roared.

He stared at the ceiling, a big smile on his face, his head sizzling as though a rocket had detonated gone off. His entire body tingled.

'What a wonder-apple-tastic dream,' he said to the empty room.

His foot throbbed. 'Ouch!'

He discovered he'd walloped the end of his bed and, looking closer, noticed a hole in the wooden board that covered the bed-end. He studied it, pulling a few wooden splinters away, chuckling at the absurdity of it all.

Old Man Wood wiggled his toes, grateful that he'd lain on his bed with his shoes on. Leaning forward, he heard the rain pounding down and his heart sank. His earlier worries flew back to him. He kicked at the broken piece of wood, as though recreating the goal might lift his spirits. It wasn't the same.

He climbed off his bed and peered out of the window, but the rain was so heavy he saw only grey lines.

His heart filled with heaviness.

Were the children safely tucked away in the school? What if they were outside trying to get home. What could he do?

If something happened, he was responsible.

Old Man Wood lay down.

He looked at the hole in the wooden panel. A tiny flicker of light, like a dim torch whose batteries were running low, leeched out from behind it.

Now, wasn't that strange, he thought. *A trick of the light?*

He tried the light switches. None of the house lights were working.

Maybe he should crank up the generator. At least it would give him something to do. He swung his feet off the bed and, as he did so, the flicker from behind the wooden panel intensified for a second or two.

He inspected the hole a little closer and found that there was indeed a faint glow emanating from behind it. He prised it open with his fingers and, feeling more than a little intrigued, began to wrestle with the wooden surround that covered the bed-end.

Old Man Wood found a torch, and went to his tool cupboard under the stairs. He selected a crowbar and returned his room.

Old Man Wood wedged the metal in behind the panel. He attempted to lever the wood away by leaning on it gently but firmly, as he thought necessary. But whatever angle he tried, the panel would not budge.

He scratched his head and slipped out of the room, returning moments later with a flat head screwdriver and a hammer. Old Man Wood thrust the flat head into the tiniest of gaps and gave the end a smart whack with the hammer. The nails securing the panel lifted a fraction.

Placing the crowbar in the newly created gap, he levered it once more. After a few more hits, the panel popped off.

He rubbed his chin. 'Well, I'll be blowed,' he said, as he ran his fingers over the three panels that now stared back at him. 'What in the apples do we have here?'

In front of him were three beautifully inlaid panels that seemed to glow like three small monitors, rather like the children's computers. The difference was that these were part of the bed, and were surrounded by similar, matching carvings.

He stared at them for a while, his face a picture of confusion and the wrinkles on his forehead deeply etched. Every now and then, images in the panels moved, causing Old Man Wood's heart to race.

Was he seeing things?

Overlying the images he noticed a blurry, streaky haze, as if, somehow, he were looking through water.

Maybe, it was mirroring the weather right now.

As he became more accustomed to the movements, the images on them became a little clearer, until he realised each panel focused on a figure.

'Three panels, three figures,' he said out loud. 'And why do they look so familiar?'

He studied the carvings to the sides of the screens.

He touched an ornate arrow icon that faced away from the first panel. To his astonishment, the image moved out, exactly like a zoom on a camera.

He did the same with the next panel pressing on the arrow that turned in. The picture zoomed closer.

The blurry image showed a person in the panel who appeared to be walking, and tripping, as though trying to negotiate a pathway.

He rubbed his hand over another carved icon adjacent to the arrow, which he thought looked rather like a cloud. He pressed it and magically the picture transformed, the layer of rain disappearing altogether from the image.

Old Man Wood gasped as he stared at the new image. That balance and gait could only belong to one person, and that person was Daisy. He pressed the inward arrow a couple of times and saw her in detail.

He was viewing the children, right now, in real time. He realised that if he could determine which buttons to press, he'd be able to see exactly where they were. He did the same to the panel on the right, pressing the cloud and zooming out.

He clapped his hands. Archie! It was definitely Archie, with a kind of spiky hat on his head, sitting next to Daisy. But where were they?

He zoomed out. They were by a large tree with a rope, or a creeper that hung down from a branch.

The oak tree with the swing, it had to be.

He pressed the away arrow and the image zoomed out even further. Apples alive! Look at the water gushing down the track.

He clenched his fists. Oh deary! No, no!

His heart sank. At least the twins were together. What about Isabella?

He scoured the left panel and picked out her outline. He honed in on the image, pressing first the cloud icon, and then the outward arrow, in order to try and figure out her position.

She was heading towards a large rock-like object with a sheer face, pushing past bushes and through trees. The only sheer rock he could think of was the cliff underneath the ruin. The question was, how come she'd separated from the others?

Old Man Wood breathed a sigh of relief. At least they were alive. He looked at his clock. How long was it since he'd been out for a walk? Two hours? He trembled.

That long?

His heart thumped as he spurred himself into action. He needed to find them, and fast.

FIFTY-EIGHT

DAISY AND ARCHIE FIND SHELTER

At long last, Daisy recognised a boulder at the bottom of the covered tree track.

A mini triumph, Daisy thought, as a long booming thunder roll drummed gruesomely overhead. She covered her ears, wincing, but after only a few paces she realised there was a far bigger problem. She kept close to Archie. 'Mud!' she yelled at Archie. 'Look! Mud and stone, rushing down.'

The lane was so knitted with branches, brambles, and rocks that every step forward was like walking through barbed wire.

Worse still, the canopy of branches, bushes, and creepers above the lane was bowing to the pressure of rain. Branches were falling in. Not just dead twigs, but stems as thick as a man's wrist. Even though they'd only stepped a few metres in, the canopy was clearly close to breaking point.

Archie slipped as a branch whacked into him, the muddy water dragging him down the hill. He dug his fingers into the bank, grabbed a root, and pulled himself to safety.

Daisy climbed up onto a large stump on the bank and waited. She looked down the track to see Archie struggling. For every two steps forward, he slipped one back.

'COME ON!' she screamed.

Every time Archie tried to grapple with the side of the track, it collapsed in on him. Not only that, but his ankles were being stripped bare by the mud, stones, and wood.

At last, he made it to Daisy's position and climbed up next to her. Gasping for breath, he rubbed his scratched, blood-covered ankles. 'We'll never make it. Not like this.'

'We have to!' Daisy yelled into his ear. 'Do you think it'll be any easier out there?'

'But it's a massive ditch,' Archie complained. 'It's become a gigantic storm drain. All the water's cascading down here. It's about as dangerous a place as you could wish.'

'What's your suggestion?' Daisy fired back.

'Up the bank and crawl along the top,' he yelled.

'But it's a mile of crawling—'

'I know. One mile of not being swept away. And we can use the shelter of the trees. There's no other choice.'

Using the roots of the big oak they were sitting beneath, they climbed up the bank. On hands and knees, they made their way uphill, brushing aside the branches and thorns which willingly tore into them. After several minutes, Daisy collapsed under the thicker branches of the next large tree.

She rubbed her legs, pierced by blackthorn and dog rose. 'Great idea, Archie!'

'Look!' he replied.

Through the veil of rain, she could just see a moving torrent of mud and branches halfway up the bank. It was flushing downhill at great speed.

'Okay, Okay. Good decision.' Daisy drew in her breath. 'How far up are we?'

'Soon, we'll come to the big oak with the swing rope. We can rest there.' Archie had no idea whether this was true. But he noticed how Daisy's eyes kept closing. Giving her a target was probably a good idea.

Another huge boom clapped overhead, followed by a lightning bolt that smashed into the sluicing lane.

They crawled on, Archie leading, with Daisy closely behind. But, after a short while, when he turned, Daisy wasn't there.

He backtracked fast. Hanging halfway down the bank, dangling above the rushing waters, and held only by the thick tendrils of a rose, he found Daisy screaming at him.

He grabbed the base of the rose and tried to swing it towards him. But the huge old rose was near to breaking point and sank further, its thorns digging into his hands. He swore.

There had to be a better way. He shuffled to a nearby hedge and noted a small ash tree. He bent down, put his hands around the trunk, and tugged with all his might. The roots slipped their anchors and, with one last effort, it broke free.

In a flash, Archie turned the tree round, ripped off some branches, and lowered it to Daisy. She grabbed hold of it and, as the rose tore into her, Archie heaved her out.

They moved under the relative shelter of a nearby oak tree and gasped for breath.

'So,' Daisy yelled between gasps, 'we've learnt three things from that. The first is that the bank is collapsing. The second is that I'll be plucking out thorns from my skin for the next decade, and the third is that you've been working out without anyone knowing.'

Taking a wider berth away from the track, they continued on all fours, rain pummelling their backs, necks and heads until they were numb.

Eventually, they reached the large oak tree with the rope, which now dangled down from its branch into the running water.

Archie pushed Daisy ahead and upwards, her hands gripping the nodules and hand-holds of slippery bark as though her life depended on it.

Where the branch with the rope met the trunk, a huge bough curved over like a mini cave. For the first time in ages, it offered them almost complete protection from the downpour. Archie sat with his back against the trunk and Daisy sat in front of him, leaning into him.

They shut their eyes and in no time, Daisy fell asleep through sheer exhaustion.

Archie didn't mind. He checked his watch. At least an hour until sundown.

The problem with being stationary was the cold, for now the wet had soaked, sponge-like, into the marrow of their bones. Body warmth was crucial.

Archie wrapped his arms around his frozen sister, her body rattling like an old engine. A rest was a good idea, but Archie knew they weren't safe. At some point, they were going to have to keep going.

As Daisy dozed, her head resting on Archie's chest, her mind swam. She dreamt fleetingly of the cottage, of Old Man Wood and their parents. She dreamt of scoring a goal with a sensational bicycle kick and Archie making a flying, fingertip save. The storm could have been a million miles away.

A noise clicked in her brain. It was that same crackling sound, like sizzling bacon. She studied the noise, her eyes shut tight. Then she realised what it was.

'MOVE!' she screamed. 'NOW!'

Archie opened his eyes. 'Eh? What?'

'Incoming. I can hear it. MOVE!'

'Where to?' Archie yelled. 'We're on a branch!'

The sizzling increased, the noise building miles above them.

'To the end, Arch. GO!'

Archie did what he was told, and shuffled his bottom as fast as he could down the branch, the rain smashing down once more.

'Further,' she screamed. 'As far as you can.' She was skimming along, almost bouncing, when she stopped and wrapped her arms and legs around the thick branch. She hugged her body into the wood and hoped for the best.

Archie continued on his path, oblivious to Daisy's action. From out of nowhere, a terrific surge of power smashed into the tree. The branch severed like a beheading and crashed down, bridging the track just above the flowing mud.

Daisy convulsed with electricity and her ears smashed with pain. She uncurled her body from the branch as rain crashed over her back and head.

Archie?

'Archie!' She called out, barely a croak coming from her. Even if she could scream for help, he'd never hear.

Suddenly, a hand flapped out of the water, and momentarily it gripped the end of the branch. Then it fell away, caught in the torrent.

She shrieked and fished pathetically into the water feeling nothing but twigs, leaves, and debris flashing beneath her.

Daisy thumped the branch, tears streaming from her eyes, rain biting into her back. How much more could she take?

Not much, she realised, especially now she was on her own.

FIFTY-NINE

OLD MAN WOOD'S PANEL FALTERS

Old Man Wood hadn't taken his eyes off the panels. It was impossible. How could children so young survive the tumult out there? *They're only little,* he kept thinking, tears forming again in his eyes. Now the panels changed as a huge flash burst onto the screen.

Old Man Wood fell back. *Lightning, again? Sweet apples!* His skin prickled.

Daisy lay on the tree branch as it crashed into the bank, but where was Archie? Daisy was hanging on for dear life—so Archie must have been swept away. What was she doing? Screaming?

He couldn't take his eyes off the scene. Another flash struck directly at Daisy. Old Man Wood shrieked and felt for his heart. He could hardly bear it. He watched as the entire branch of the tree hurtled down the makeshift drain towards the swollen river, Archie dragging behind, under the water.

Old Man Wood yelped and clasped his head in his hands. How did the boy have the strength? Daisy lay there, just as she had before. She hadn't moved. The screen flickered, as though faulty.

Old Man Wood leaned forward, and gave it a tap in the hope that that might restore it, but it flickered again. Lines cut through the clear picture as if there was poor reception.

All of a sudden, he figured what this meant.

The colour drained from his face.

'NO, NO, NO!' he yelled out. 'Don't give up, Daisy. Whatever you do, littlun, DO NOT *EVER* GIVE UP!'

SIXTY

ISABELLA GETS TRAPPED

For every step Isabella took forward, she seemed to slide back two more. When she was out in the open, she found herself pushing blindly through sheets of water with no idea where she was heading.

She extended her hands out in front of her and felt a gentle pull, first one way and then the other. With each step, her feet touched on harder ground. Sometimes, her hands swung her around at right angles, and every so often she had to back-track. She trusted in it, though, for it was the only hope she had.

The one thing that terrified her was the thunderbolts.

Daisy seemed to be able to hear the thunderbolts forming. Every time Daisy screamed, they'd run away and a thunderbolt crashed into the spot where, only moments ago, they had been. Now there was no Daisy, and Isabella sensed that it was only a matter of time before another thunderbolt would come. She had a deathly feeling in her gut that it would come directly at her out of the blue.

She moved forward, all the while waiting for the crack or the blast. As fast as she went, the trickle of water around her ankles kept swelling. For every surge she made forward out of the water, in no time the level had caught up with her, some-times to as high as her knees.

A stomach-wrenching fear filled her.

Isabella redoubled her efforts, crawling and scampering over fallen branches and brambles until she bumped into the base of a tree that would offer her decent protection from the rain.

Isabella leaned back and, instinctively, pushed her hands into the air above her head. She forced her palms outwards, her fingers touching.

She channelled every thought, every single ounce of energy she had into protecting herself. She didn't know why, but her hands and her spirit were her last hope.

She closed her eyes and waited.

Just as Isabella thought of putting them down, a thunderbolt sliced out of the sky. A fraction after she heard the distinct crack, Isabella slammed herself towards the space in front of her with everything she had.

An intense burst of heat thumped into her hands, her flesh instantly burning, her body pushed into the ground.

She gritted her teeth and pressed against it harder and harder. The stink of burning skin invaded her, as if rods of molten iron were being welded in the place of her fingers.

As suddenly as it had arrived, it was over.

Isabella slumped to the ground, her hands smoking and her eyes closed, a look of peace fixed on her face.

Splashing water woke her up. Isabella opened her eyes, aware that her body was shivering like it did after a swim in the cold North Sea.

The thunderbolt! She'd survived! How long had she been out? Five minutes, or half an hour.

She sat up and inspected her hands. Even in the dim light, she could see that large, black, circular burn marks radiated on her palms. Her body tingled, the electrical charge still fizzing through her like gas in a soda.

How? She thought. *How had she done it?* It didn't make any sense. By rights, she should be frazzled.

She checked her limbs one by one. They worked, even if her body ached like crazy, and her head sizzled as if someone had opened up her skull and given her brain a scrub with wire wool.

'Keep going,' she thought she heard from somewhere. 'Move! Now!'

She looked around.

She heard it again, as if someone was with her, egging her on, boosting her and begging her not to give in.

She forced herself forward and, instantly, fell flat on her face.

Again, she heard the voice, encouraging her on.

She crawled, finding a steady rhythm with her knees, elbows, and hands. Soon she was above the waterline, and she kept on going until she doffed her head on a large, sheer rock.

'BLOODY HELL!' she cried, rubbing her forehead, conscious that the rain had now ceased pummelling her.

She must have arrived under a rock shelf, she thought, and, for the first time in ages she felt a thimbleful of comfort.

She sat back, stretched her legs, and cradled her head in her hands. Damn, she was hungry.

But where would the next meal come from, if she remained alive long enough to eat again.

Isabella pulled herself together and tried to find her bearings.

She inspected a split rock. She wondered if she could narrow down where she was by working out where this type of stone might typically be found on the river bank.

Moments later, there was a terrible explosion of noise, as though two trains were colliding, crunching and scraping right above and all around her.

The sound grew closer and closer, and, for a ghastly moment, the noise went right through her.

She curled into a ball, shut her eyes, and covered her head.

Out of the sky, a deadly cascade washed past, careering onto the area from which she had crawled.

Isabella shook uncontrollably. Even above the noise of the water, the cracking, crushing, and splintering sounds told her that everything in its path had been obliterated.

For several seconds, the cascade rattled on until the landslip had done its bidding and the cacophony ceased. Isabella's heart thumped wildly. She wouldn't have stood a chance.

At length, she ventured out into the rain. Only a couple of metres forward and through the veil of water, she encountered a vast pile of boulders, rocks, mud, and splintered wood, that rose up like a slag heap in front of her.

She slunk back to her sheltered position as a terrible thought began to wash over her.

If she'd found refuge underneath a cliff face, the likelihood was that it was either a landslip off the top of a hill, or—and she thought this to be more likely—a section of the cliff face had simply collapsed. That would explain the boulders.

In her mind, she pictured the geography of the area and, especially, the position of the cliffs. She knew that behind her probable position was a ledge. Above this, a sheer wall of rock rose up vertically for seventy metres or thereabouts.

Then, like a thought one doesn't want to think about but cannot avoid, she had a terrible realisation that if Archie and Daisy had come after her, they would not be alive right now.

The other thing she realised, much to her shock, was that she was completely and utterly trapped.

SIXTY-ONE

ARCHIE IN THE RIVER

Archie flew into the air and landed in the middle of the torrent, his body shipped away by the water. He swam with all his might. When he surfaced, a huge branch straddling the track lay directly in front of him.

His lungs burned.

He reached up, but however hard he tried he couldn't get a hand-hold on the bark. After several attempts, he felt his nails starting to detach.

Before long, Archie let go.

The water took him. He needed to keep his head up, but every time he did the rain battered it down. While he searched for buoyancy—a branch or a tree he could grab hold of that might keep him afloat—he thrashed out like a madman, kicking the water beneath him in a last, massive effort to survive.

Something caught around his left leg, rendering him helpless. A root?

He succumbed, shattered and beaten and smiled as he let himself go, Cain's words coming to him as he floated away: *If it wasn't the thunderbolts and it wasn't the rain, it was the landslides.*

But, to his surprise, he remained bound by the snare around his leg and found the water pushing him towards the bank. He made a grab for a protruding root, twisting his body round while keeping his head up.

He sucked in a mouthful of air and gave his foot a yank. It did not yield.

He tried again, this time while holding the root on the bank with his other hand. It moved! He did it again, and then again. Now there was enough slack to allow him to bend forward and feel his ankle. He pulled his left leg towards him and touched something coarse and thick. Archie's mind worked overtime. Then it struck him. The swinging rope!

He pulled harder and the rope came away a little more with just enough give for him to try and untie the knot.

It wasn't the trickiest knot he'd ever come across, but the rope was thick and the water pulled him away from his task. The rain beat down, and every time he thought he had untied the knot, the slack tightened and he was back to where he started. He gave the rope an even bigger tug. The whole branch jerked. This time, the rope slipped off his foot and, while holding on to the end, he tied the rope around his waist.

He heard a scream. Even above the roar of the rain and the torrent, it couldn't be mistaken.

It was Daisy, screaming:

'INCOMING!'

She's still on the branch!

Archie pulled with all his might and felt the wood slip. He tugged harder, nudging the branch towards him. He gritted his teeth and jogged it, pulling in rhythm.

Suddenly, the branch twisted off the bank and slid just enough to give him encouragement.

There couldn't be much more time. One huge yank was all it needed.

He harnessed the rope around his shoulders and hollered.

The branch broke free and sped forward, just as a thunderbolt crashed into the bank almost exactly where the bough had sat moments before.

Archie wondered if Daisy had managed to get out of the way. But, he had no time to think, for now the branch began slipping down the slope, joining the torrent, washing everything down the lane.

Archie felt the rope go tense and found himself dragged behind it. Trying to keep himself above the water but gaining speed, he hung on for dear life as the branch hurtled into the main body of the river. As the river levelled out, he pulled himself along the rope, closer to the tree-trunk, and gritted his teeth as he dragged himself up and onto the end of the branch.

He dropped his left leg out, using it as a rudder, and the great branch pitched towards what he hoped was the bank on the left-hand side.

Exhausted, Archie collapsed, his head face down on the wood, water bucketing over him.

Hearing a noise, Archie lifted his head. Was someone sitting near him on the branch?

'Daisy—Daisy' he groaned.

'Come with me, Archie de Lowe,' the voice said. 'Only I can save you now.'

'Save me,' Archie repeated.

'Say yes, and it will be done.'

Archie's eyelids closed. 'Cain?'

'Archie, just say the word.'

What did he have to lose, why didn't he just agree?

'Do the easy thing, boy,' Cain continued. 'Your life is not over by any means.'

Archie's brain swam but all he could think of was his sisters.

Nothing else. Only Isabella and Daisy.

The branch jolted.

Right then, he knew there was no other way. Archie had to move Daisy to safety and then find Isabella. Better to die together trying to save the world, than not trying at all.

'I'd rather die with my sisters than join with you,' he called out, weakly.

The voice laughed back, 'I will return, Archie, one more time. You may need me yet. Your dear sister is so very close to her death and, when that happens, you will all have failed.'

SIXTY-TWO

CAIN AND KEMP

Back in Havilah, Cain wondered how his relationship with Kemp would work in their combined state should his alliance with Archie not happen. Right now, the boy was slowing him down and there was so much to do.

Would the boy continue to do as he commanded?

Cain threw his arms up in the air and clapped his hands as a shower of ash fell over his head.

All of a sudden, a feeling of heaviness overcame him.

Sleep again? Really!

Cain clenched his fist and found that when his concentration focused on that movement alone, the fingers came together whether the boy liked it or not.

Cain pressed one foot down, followed by the other. He felt a modicum of resistance, like a badly-fitting drawer that needed to be forced shut.

He willed his leg to move, but the movement felt sluggish and sleepy. Instead, he pulled his leg back and thrust it forward in a loose kicking motion, ash spraying everywhere.

He flailed his arms about, moving them faster and faster until the boy trapped inside him did exactly as he wished.

'We've places to go, my little friend, and there's not a moment to lose.' Cain said out loud. He couldn't tell if the boy inside him could hear, though the odd cries he heard told him that the boy wasn't entirely deaf.

'Do my bidding, little friend of Archie de Lowe,' he said, 'and everything will work out just fine. We may even get to like one another. But until then, I am going to make you do as I wish.'

But as hard as Cain pushed and cajoled, the boy inside him soon slowed to a standstill.

Where was this child's energy? Wasn't that the point? Or was the boy being deliberately difficult?

A few minutes of rest should do the trick, and then he'd be off. What was it called, *sleep?*

Perhaps he also needed food and water. He'd try Schmerger and see what the elf might come up with. Anything to get the damn boy moving properly.

'In due course, there will be sustenance and rest for you,' he spoke out. 'But for now, boy, I need your energy. Resist, and I will hurt you.'

If the boy was going to be a nuisance, then he could play at that game too.

SIXTY-THREE

'THE JOAN OF' MOVES

Gus tried to row with the flow of the water but the current was too strong and, besides, he had no idea where he was going. When he stole a look from under the canopy, he was met by a wall of water sluicing from the sky.

He pulled in the oars, inspected the canopy, and drove a couple of nails into the areas where he sniffed a weakness.

Then he returned to the bench to help Sue bail out water. With the amount coming in, it needed both of them to work flat out. Sue felt like she'd scooped out enough water to fill an Olympic-sized swimming pool three times over. Her arms ached so much she thought they might simply drop off.

As 'The Joan of' pitched through the waters, and as the storm smashed down upon their tiny vessel, Sue thought of Isabella, Archie and Daisy.

They wouldn't stand a chance out there in this weather, and every time she imagined them trying to soldier on or getting swept away, her spirits sank. Her previous thoughts of rescuing them could never happen.

Every so often, 'The Joan of' would bash into something hard and solid, like a wall or a car, and they would be thrown forward. It was at these moments that both of them knew the strength of the boat would be tested.

All it took was a crack or a small hole, and that would be the end of it.

At other times, "The Joan of" ground against something, or span around as it diverted off an object, the water pitching the boat one way and then the other.

Several times, Gus levered the boat away with an oar, lurching back into the swell.

Sue kept her head down, sobbing as he went outside. On returning, Gus would hold her, and stare reassuringly into eyes which betrayed nothing less than abject terror.

His eyes, she noticed, were wide. Not so much in fear, she thought, but with excitement. To her, Gus was having the time of his life.

She heard him singing a hearty sea shanty as he tossed the water out with his bucket, his singing grew louder and louder with each movement until it was in direct competition with the rain.

Sue didn't know whether to laugh, cry, or hit him.

For a while, at least, the singing stopped her wallowing about the disaster and about her friends.

After what felt like hours, Gus pointed upwards. 'I think we've moved away from the main rain belt.' She nodded in agreement. 'Problem is—how far do you reckon we've gone?'

'No idea,' she said. And it was impossible to tell.

SIXTY-FOUR

OLD MAN WOOD TO THE RESCUE

Seeing Isabella's monitor struck by lightning followed by Daisy's monitor crackle spurred the old man into immediate action. What should he take with him?

He turned on the torch and shot off towards the shed. His heart and mind racing, he grabbed a section of rope, a small axe and his hard helmet with a built-in torch on the front. He dashed into his cold room where he stored his huge variety of apples. He selected eight rather small ones from the special box he kept near the door.

In the cloakroom, he found his long, waterproof coat and his walking boots, which he slipped on as fast as he could.

He returned to the bedroom and stared at the screens.

Archie was cradling Daisy, he could see that. Tears streamed down the boy's face.

'Oh, you poor things,' Old Man Wood cried. 'Keep her warm. Speak to her, little Archie. Don't let her drift away.'

At least they had found somewhere to disembark. It was by a huge pile of rocks, which didn't feel in any way familiar.

Now, where was Isabella?

He furrowed his brow. Blimey, she's in a funny place. Bang next to a rock face and surrounded by a heap of boulders. She's shivering. No wonder. How did she get there? He zoomed out and pressed the cloud button, which cleared away the rain.

'Apples alive!' he exclaimed, bashing his head with his hands. 'They're on opposite sides of the same pile of rocks, and they don't even know it!'

He zoomed out further on Isabella's monitor. 'I know where it is!' he exclaimed, his eyes almost bulging out of his head in excitement. He checked his watch. It was ten minutes before four o'clock or thereabouts. Just over an hour before nightfall. He'd have to hurry.

He darted out of his room, bursting with an energy and purpose he hadn't felt in years, when an idea shot into his head. He turned on his helmet light, and skipped down the cellar stairs.

Now, which door was it? He headed along a musty brick corridor that smelled of old wet rags. He stopped outside a low, thick wooden door laced with metal studs right at the end. Cut into it were the markings "II". Roman numerals for cellar number two.

Now, he thought, *how did the door open?* There wasn't a key, he was sure of that. It was something smarter; keys could be lost or discovered by nosey children or unwanted guests.

He strained his brain trying to work out what it might be. 'Oh, come on!' he cried out. 'Why does my brain always go blank at times like this?'

He thumped his fist on the wall. One of the bricks shifted. His eyes darted up and he groped about, pushing the bricks to see if anything would happen.

Nothing.

He screwed his eyes up. He couldn't even remember the last time he'd been down here. From the corner of his eye he spotted a piece of stone protruding from the wall. *Maybe that was it.* He pushed it.

Again, nothing.

He left his hand there as his head tilted forward, and he tapped the wall with his forehead in frustration. The stone moved! He doffed it further and heard a neat 'click'.

'Ah-ha!'

He twisted the metal ring on the door and the latch clicked open. He was in.

Inside, a smell of moss and dust and linseed oil surprised his senses and, as he brushed past the cobwebs that drooped from the ceiling, he shone his helmet torch to see what he could find.

He smiled. Neatly stacked on slate shelves running around the walls were hundreds of small bottles obscured by layers of dust.

Starting at one end, he picked each bottle up and blew the dust off to reveal the writing which was neatly etched into the glass. Names like Spindle Old Man Wood, Ogre Blood, Wood Ox, Willow Potion, and Oak Spit. He hurried on, hoping like mad that when he saw it, he'd know.

A flood of memories rushed in, almost overwhelming him.

These were his bottles. HIS potions! From a time... well, from a lost time, a time he'd forgotten.

He continued along the row, reading out the names as he went until he spied three bottles with the words 'Resplendix Mix' in bold writing scratched on each.

He pulled one off the shelf and brushed it down. In the torchlight, the colour was like liquid gold, and, as it moved, little diamonds of light danced within it.

Resplendix Mix. This brilliant stuff would help them, he was sure of it.

He shoved a bottle into his pocket and tore out of the room.

Closing the back door, he was instantly set upon by the water, the weight on his hard hat pushing his head into his body.

What was the best way to the bottom of the cliff?

The lane was acting like a drain, so the road was impassable.

Maybe he could lower a rope from the ruin and let himself down? He fingered the coils strapped around his torso. But he knew the rope wasn't long enough, and what if he was swept off the top?

No, he would have to go across country, through the woods and then somehow up, along and onto the ledge.

He'd need a lot of luck and most of all, he needed to hurry.

SIXTY-FIVE

CAIN'S HUNGER

What a wonder, Cain thought, rubbing his new eyes. *Sleep. How invigorating - if only for a few moments! But I have a strange feeling of emptiness inside me.*

'Food!' he yelled out. 'Schmerger, I think I require food. Where is my food?'

Lying down, Cain saw the black pointy beard of his servant stopping at a respectable distance. The little creature bowed. 'Your Lordship?' the bent figure of Schmerger said. 'With respect, Sire, you haven't eaten for a thousand years. Are you yourself today?'

Cain rose and marched up to the servant. 'I require food, immediately. A feast.'

The servant recoiled. 'You have become... ASH, Sire.'

'Marvellous, isn't it. I have a human child within me and it requires feeding. Understand?'

'But there is no kitchen,' he replied.

'NO KITCHEN! What kind of palace is this?'

Schmerger shook his head. 'May I be bold, Sire, and say that ever since I was assigned to your Lordship, there has never been a kitchen. Your Lordship banned them.'

Cain thrust out his arm, picked the man up by the throat and threw him at a table which splintered over the floor. 'Is that so?'

The servant rubbed his neck.

Cain walked over and pulled the little man up. 'How and where do you eat, Schmerger? Show me.'

The servant bowed and led the ghost down the wide main staircase, down a corridor and through several doors, before entering a small room.

Cain followed, delighted that for once he could actually see the outline of rooms and his grand bed. Even his dim profile in the mirror was now visible. It was a shame he couldn't see with any detail, but it was a great deal better than nothing at all.

Schmerger picked up a wicker basket. 'From Mrs Schmerger, Sire.'

'Tell me,' Cain quizzed, 'what is in it?'

'It was lunch, Sire,' he said. 'Little remains.'

'Give it to me!' Cain said, thrusting his hand into the basket. He pulled out something black and stodgy and, without hesitation, stuffed it in his mouth. For the first time in ages he chewed. Aside from a tingle, it tasted like soot. But he hoped the boy inside found it favourable.

Schmerger backed out of the room, trembling, leaving the food for Cain.

Cain pulled out another piece and popped it in. This time, it crunched and splintered. Cain spat it out. 'Schmerger,' he yelled, 'what is it?'

'It is the leg of a bird,' the servant said from outside the door. 'One does not ordinarily eat the bones.'

Cain crashed a fist down on the table. 'I need more food. What is there to drink?'

'Nothing but water, Sire,' Schmerger said, bowing. 'Your Majesty has never had a requirement for any.'

'Well, I do now. Bring me some this instant. We have a great thirst and there may be little time.' Cain marched out of the room a trail of dust behind him.

Cain knelt down and brushed a glass-like puddle, seeing a face smile up at him. 'Let me reacquaint myself with my poor frozen people.' He stood up. 'In time, let us banquet. Let there be a glorious feast with wine and song.'

Cain marched through the doors and found himself at the foot of the grand staircase, his mood bordering on euphoric. He wanted to know the situation with the heirs.

'Dreamspinner, dreamspinner, dreamspinner,' he called out.

Moments later Asgard appeared, his maghole tingling with electrical current. 'You called?'

Cain smiled. 'Now, my dear ugly dreamspinner, why don't we pay another short visit to find out how the Heirs of Eden are dying? Earlier I sensed Archie was close. Perhaps this time I can persuade the boy to join willingly with me, before his poor soul is cast into the wild expanses of space.'

Asgard's maghole opened wide and Cain, seeing it's outline for the first time so clearly, forced the boy within him to bend down. And in one motion, they dived through.

Instantly, they arrived by the big log that straddled the track. He surveyed the scene and was frankly amazed that the Heirs of Eden were still hanging on to life.

They looked pathetic, their struggle nearly over. Surely their bodies could not take much more of a pounding. And where was the old man? Ha! He didn't even know what was going on. Sad. Truly.

If he could just get Archie, an Heir, to join him, then in one easy step this theatre, this charade that held on to the idea that these puny Heirs of Eden might survive, would cease, and everything would be resolved as he had originally imagined.

SIXTY-SIX

SOLOMON IN THE TOWER

Fifty-seven! Solomon scrolled down the page of names. He rather hoped that perhaps one hundred people had fled by car, and others had gone when the lightning started.

Still, that left an awful lot unaccounted for. He hadn't factored in the opposition players, parents, and supporters.

Half the football team were missing; no Sue Lowden, no Williams, Kemp or Allen. The list went on… five of his teachers out there, somewhere, too.

He only had to look at himself to shake with shame.

He'd found the doorway to the tower as much by luck as by design, and was dragged in by Mrs. Rose who'd reached out into the curtain of water and swept him in. Exhausted, he sat on the step catching his breath and waiting anxiously to see if anyone was close by.

Only one other person came in after him. It was a small girl who had felt her way around the exterior walls, inch by inch. Solomon cried as he helped her up the stairs.

It had made him hope there were more, but no matter how long he stayed, no one else came by. Looking into the sheet of water flashing from the sky, it was no surprise.

In no time, the water level forced him to move up the stairs, as a pool of water quickly formed beneath the first landing. He insisted the door should be left open, just in case.

The children spread themselves out over the two floors of the library in the tower, cowering together. As the storm smashed overhead, the children sobbed, despite teachers doing their best to keep spirits up. Even the teachers, Solomon noticed, had anxious eyes as they flicked nervous glances towards one another.

The chef, along with his assistant, fed the group bread buns from a huge sack they'd pulled across the yard moments before it all happened.

Only when the water reached three quarters of the way up the front door did they shut the door. A realisation that the level might get higher and higher dawned on Solomon and this time he wasn't taking any chances.

Solomon excused himself and headed up to the old library right at the top of the tower, accessible only by ladder. Up there, he removed his jacket and trousers and sank into an old chair.

Placing his hands over his eyes, he sobbed openly.

He couldn't remember the last time he'd cried. When his father died many years ago, he'd shed a small tear, alone.

Now, tears flowed.

When his grief had subsided, he tried to reflect. Of course, with the benefit of hindsight, he realised that he had been nothing short of a fool. No more, and no less. A stubborn fool at that. He hadn't listened.

His brightest pupil had demanded his attention, and he'd refused her.

Worse still, he'd lied to her!

Lied! Dammit!

Solomon felt his stomach knot. He'd lied to a student who had gone out of her way to prove that something major and remarkable was about to happen.

And he'd pushed her warnings straight back in her face.

He banged his fist down on a dusty table. Wasn't that what headmasters were supposed to be good at, listening, giving people the benefit of the doubt. Encouraging students in their academic and recreational activities?

All he'd been interested in, he realised now, was his banquet, the glory of his school and his moment in the limelight. And now…

Three times Isabella had tried to tell him. Three times he'd denied her.

All along, it was as if she knew, and Sue knew. He recalled her crazy screaming. Was that part of these strange happenings? Perhaps even Archie knew, the way he let the penalty slide past his foot into the goal.

Solomon stood up and moved over to the window. On a good day, the view expanded way across the Vale of York in one direction, marked by a green patchwork quilt of fields and woods. In the other direction, the tree line of the Hambleton Hills wiggled around the North York Moors, intersected by cliff faces and shadows.

This was the exact spot, twenty-five years ago—almost to the day—where he'd fallen in love with the glorious scenery, the light, and the big skies. He remembered how he'd accept the job at Upsall school on the spot.

Now, he stared at death, destruction, and chaos.

He knew that, if and when this rain ceased, the scenery would be a different hue, the land would have a new orientation. A vale filled entirely with water.

'Isabella,' he said. 'Will you ever forgive me for ignoring you? For being such a toady old idiot.'

He sighed and brushed another tear from his eye, knowing that it would be a miracle if the de Lowe trio ever made it home.

All that talent, he thought, *gone to waste. And I could have prevented it.*

'I am so terribly sorry.'

SIXTY-SEVEN

ARCHIE HOLDS ON

Archie stared at his watch. It had gone four. When was sunset; five, half five?

He'd hauled himself onto the log and found his twin. Now he cradled her in his arms.

'Hey, Daisy,' he said, sheltering her face. 'Don't give up on me. There's only a little while to go, you know. And I'm going to keep you alive, if it's the last thing I do.'

He ran his cold hands over her face.

If he was cold, then she was icy.

Softly, he massaged her heart. He didn't know why, but it just seemed the right thing to do. 'Please, Daisy, you've got to come back. Don't you dare back out now. I don't know what I'd do without you. If you go, we've all had it. Everyone, not just us.'

Her eyes flickered and the corners of her lips turned up.

Thank goodness, he thought. A spark.

He'd keep talking, and, somehow, he had to keep her listening.

'Right, here's what we're going to do,' he said. 'I'm going to pick you up and start carrying you over these rocks and stuff, okay?'

Very gently, he picked her up and negotiated footholds in the debris. One step followed another, each one swaying, each a desperate act of concentration.

Every so often he studied her face to make sure she was still with him before carrying on. He leapt from one rock to the next, disregarding the rain, disregarding his burden, worrying only about the next step.

As he climbed, he carried on talking. He spoke about what was going to happen and how safe they were going to be in only a little while. He chattered about anything else he could think of.

When he ran out of things to say, he started singing.

The first song that came into his head was a song their mother had taught them when they were young. With chattering teeth, he sang it as best as he could. When he forgot the words, he hummed it, his voice shaking with cold.

After a few minutes, Daisy's eyes flashed open. He looked down at her and smiled, trying to hold back his tears while he continued humming.

He felt her tensing. Her eyes opened wide, telling him something.

What was it?

Her eyes rolled back.

Archie tensed.

NO! NOT ANOTHER ONE!

Instantly, Archie tossed Daisy over his shoulder in a fireman's lift. He reached the top of a boulder and tried to see beyond it, but saw only the steady veil of rain.

'Daisy!' he cried out, 'I've got to jump and I don't know where we'll end up. If this goes badly, just remember that I love you. You're a cool girl, sis.'

He had no more time.

Archie sucked in as much air as he could. He closed his eyes, bent his knees, and jumped as high and as far as he possibly could into the dark unknown.

Archie had no idea where he might end up, but a broken leg was preferable to being flash-fried to death.

They splashed in a pool and sank down to the bottom, at the exact moment two lightning bolts smashed into their previous position. Their brutal force displaced shards, pebbles, and larger stones. Everything shook. Water fizzed, the currents jabbing at every nerve-ending in their bodies.

Archie stayed down, holding Daisy and cradling her head for as long as he dared. Suddenly her eyes opened wide.

Archie thrashed to the surface and winced as a stone hit him on his shoulder. Another whacked him on the head. He let go of Daisy and felt his mind begin to drift away.

The pool and the torrential rain were blurring together.

He saw stars spinning.

Daisy was accelerating away from him.

With one last effort, he pulled himself up but his head spun so fast that in no time he felt himself go, his body slipping away to a place of softness and light.

A feeling of warmth enveloped him, like a comfort blanket brimming with love, holding him tight.

With his last breath of consciousness, Archie had the wherewithal to reach up and grasp a hand-hold. And then his mind slid into the darkness of a black and deep abyss.

SIXTY-EIGHT

A LEAP OF FAITH

Shivering, Isabella remembered their last holiday as a family, skiing, high up in the Alps.

Beautifully hot with a bright blue sky, at lunch she had stripped off her jacket, thrown off her hat, and ditched her long johns, giving them all to her mother who crammed them into a rucksack.

They'd jumped on a chairlift and headed up to the top of the mountain. Halfway up, the chair had stopped and swayed in the air. They stayed like that for ages. An hour, maybe more.

Then, the weather had changed.

First, the clouds blew in, followed by an icy, biting wind and horizontal snow.

She sat there, freezing, with nothing but her father's arm around her to protect her. In the seat behind, her mother was holding the bag with her clothes. An hour later, every bone in her body ached, from the top of her head to the tip of her toes.

She remembered how it took two hot chocolates before she could move her jaw open enough to say anything.

What she would give for that hot chocolate now.

What had her father said?

Keep moving, girl. That was it. *And if you can't keep moving, hug someone. Hug them nice and tight.*

A warm feeling filled her as she remembered how Archie thought this was the perfect excuse to go around hugging people. Everyone had thought him rather cute; even, momentarily, Daisy.

Isabella tried to smile. Now out of the rain, the cold had begun to creep into her like roots of frost knitting into soil.

She needed to move. Using her hands as a guide, she felt for a jagged, protruding rock so that she might get a decent foothold. She found one, lifted herself up on it and then fingered another further up. She'd done enough climbing to know that planning a route up and making sure one's feet were stable were the keys to success.

The problem was visibility. Combined with the numbness in her fingers, it meant that she couldn't determine if her grip was true. She slipped back and landed with a wet thud on the ground. Isabella shook her hands vigorously out in front of her, and slowly the blood began to return. She jogged on the spot, the wet remains of her trousers sticking to her legs, and rolled her head on her shoulders.

She needed to search further along.

Once again, she followed the face of the rock, guided by her hands, her legs now knee-deep in the water. A little further on, she found the perfect spot; an outcrop of stone concealed by bushes.

Moving them aside, she found two easy steps. She pulled herself up, placing one foot carefully on the first step, then, hugging the rock, she tested her weight slowly on the next. It felt solid, as if purposely carved out of the rocks.

Her arms searched around trying to find another foothold. She levered herself up and did the same again, noting that the steps curved around. She climbed until she realised she was on a flat ledge.

With the rain driving at her, she had lost her sense of direction. She sat on the ledge trying to fathom the angle of the steps in relation to the rock face. She crawled on her hands and knees in the direction of the cliff face, scanning for any sudden gaps or boulders. Aside from pebbles, it felt smooth.

She edged on further before she realised the rain was subsiding, then it ceased altogether. She wiped water from her face and leaned into a big, round rock. Isabella felt strangely elated, as if she'd solved a tricky equation.

She examined the boulder, and figured that it sat directly under the cliff face, with the incline protecting her from the rain.

But how would she get out? The logical answer was to head high up to the right, towards Eden Cottage. The light was failing fast, though, and the rain still wasn't letting up. Maybe she'd have to stay put until the morning. At least, she'd be out of the rain.

Anyway, hadn't Archie told them the storm would continue until sunset, or some nonsense like that?

Two lightning bolts suddenly blasted out of the sky. They were directed just beyond the landslide, where she'd come from.

She hardly had a chance to react, only to duck down.

What if those were for...?

In a heartbeat, she threw herself off the ledge, just before a huge charge spat out and smashed into the exact spot she'd been standing.

Isabella tumbled into the water.

She sank as low as she could go, amazed at how much the water had risen in such a short time. She stayed underneath as long as her lungs could hold her, hugging the cliff face, as splinters of rock and stone punched the pool like deadly shrapnel.

When Isabella surfaced, she noticed a big difference in her surroundings. The water level had edged close to the surface of the ledge, so that instead of climbing the stairs, she simply pulled herself out and sat down with her feet dangling in the pool.

She shivered in the near-darkness, her heart thumping wildly.

She realised what the difference was. Drizzle! The torrents of rain, the endless pounding, had almost gone.

With the quiet came an enormous sense of relief.

She smiled through her chattering teeth.

The remains of her clothes stuck to her like cold, soggy slime, but she still had to survive through the night. The temperature would drop, as it always did at about this time of year, and there was no hope of a warming fire.

In the next breath, her thoughts turned to Daisy and Archie. There had been three huge thunderbolts; one for each of them. Why—she had no idea, but it felt right—even if it was absurdly illogical and absolutely terrifying.

She shuffled along looking out in the darkness.

'Archie. Daisy!' she yelled *'Are you there?'*

She listened, but heard only the swishing sounds of the running water beyond.

Again and again she called out, trying to hear a response.

No reply was forthcoming.

Deep within her, Isabella sensed they were near, but it was so hard and she was so tired, so cold, so hungry.

Come on, she told herself, no time to be lazy; look for them. A thought kept returning: what if they were a few feet away and died in the night because she couldn't be bothered?

Isabella crawled along the ledge as far as she dared, all the while making sure she kept a firm grip of the surface, calling out for them in turn *'Daisy! Archie!'*.

She shivered, her lips quivering involuntarily as she stared out into the darkness. Occasionally she heard a groan, but it was hard to tell if it was the crunching of metal on metal, like cars or sheds being swept down the river and colliding with each other, or whether it was the desperate cry of people or animals.

Tears built as an overwhelming sense of sadness flowed over her. Her feeling of helplessness was almost complete.

As if in response to her cries, a tiny sliver of light appeared on the lip of the horizon and threw a grey light over the water. Isabella peered at it and, for a short while, thought that she must be dreaming. It looked so beautiful, a gentle sparkle of light catching the rim of a silver bracelet. She blinked and shook her head.

The moon? *Moonlight.*

Now, she could distinguish the outlines of boulders and a flat ledge. Looking up, the sheer face of the cliff carved above her like a prison wall. She scoured the valley, observing a dull, ever-changing watery mirror that gently lapped in front of her.

As the moon rose, its brightness lifted her spirits further.

She noticed how the round boulder she had hidden underneath before the lightning struck had been reduced to rubble. Where it once stood, an unnaturally dark hole beckoned her in.

Isabella approached. With every footstep, she grew more curious.

She edged closer, testing the cracked sections that might be unstable, until she found herself peering up at a perfectly symmetrical entrance of a dark cave.

Without hesitating, she placed one foot ahead of the other and, leaning against the side, she made her way in.

She caught warmth on her face.

Hot air, here?

She took another step, hoping that her eyes would adjust.

It's like a warm hairdryer.

Thermal rocks, here, in Yorkshire? Never!

Isabella was about to take a further step in when she heard a strange cry coming from behind her. Her heart skipped a beat.

Daisy? Archie?

She scanned the area but found that the ledge was now only fractionally higher than the river, and it was hard to tell where one stopped and the other started. She heard it again, a groan followed by a cry and a tiny cough.

Her heart raced as she studied the ledge again. She concentrated and pushed her hands out, trusting them.

She ran to the right, urging her eyes to peer deeper into the night.

Nothing.

She walked cautiously to the left.

Nothing.

She repeated her movements.

To her right, all she could discern was a long shape, like a fat, black branch typical of the debris. She walked straight past it but turned when there was a tiny noise.

Isabella was there in a flash.

A body! Face down. Bending down she noticed dirt intermingled with bloody cuts, angry bruises, and tattered clothing.

They never made it, she thought.

Isabella's hopes sank.

As she turned the frame over, the white arms folded limply and splashed helplessly in a puddle.

The eyes were closed.

Isabella screamed as though someone had ripped her heart out.

In front of her lay Daisy.

SIXTY-NINE

KEMP CONTEMPLATES HIS SITUATION

Kemp felt another long burst of heat on his leg. He grimaced. Reluctantly, he moved his limb and the pain faded.

The de Lowes had had to save the world? But they were crazy, nutty kids. Never super-heroes.

Even now, the thought would have made him chuckle, if only he wasn't so filled with pain.

Why wouldn't the ghost leave him alone for just one minute?

When he yelled, Cain didn't hear him and didn't react. He needed food, water, and rest. How long had it been? Five or six hours constantly moving, constantly burned in little patches from head to toe.

It felt like a week, or a month even. He yawned, and felt his body moving off, his legs clumpy as if made with wet sand. Every time he stopped a surge of intense heat smashed into him and he had no choice but to keep going.

He could see, although not well. The sickly vapours of singed hair and fried flesh caught at the back of his throat.

Every sound was muted, like being underwater. Soon, his thoughts turned to death. If he refused to go on, would he burn to death within Cain?

SEVENTY

STUCK ON THE CLIFF

Old Man Wood was at the point where he needed to start making his way along the steeper, sharper cliff face. He faced the rock and shuffled along, happier in his step where the mud gave way to stone. As he angled across the cliff face, overhangs gave him welcome relief from the downpour, while other parts showered him with mud and loose rock. He dug his fingers into every tight crevice and small hole. Moving along as quickly and carefully as he dared, he hoped he hadn't started too high.

Presently, he was able to take stock of his position. He rested under a deep overhang where he found a decent foothold. He gulped in huge mouthfuls of air as he leant into the stone.

Should he drive a bolt in to the rock so that he could attach the rope, just in case?

He found a hole, delved into his pocket, and found a quick release bolt. He thrust it in and the metal fastened. He put his weight on it, and the bolt held. Good. He tied the rope to the metal loop, and attached the rest around his body.

As he turned to inspect his next footholds, a huge electrical pulse flashed out of the sky to his left. He looked on in shock. A second bright charge rocketed out of the sky from the same place a millisecond later, almost blinding him. His eardrums seared with pain.

The valley lit up, and he saw everything move like a huge grey beast filled with water. 'Apples-alive,' he muttered under his breath as his heart raced.

He was too high above the ledge.

He felt for a footing, making sure his hold was solid. He tested his grip and bent down, but, in the next moment, a huge thunderbolt smashed out of the sky directly into the cliff face beneath him.

For a second Old Man Wood held on for dear life.

There they were!

He could see them all, as clear as day for just one second.

His heart whooped in his chest. He had to get down there fast.

Old Man Wood picked his way along as fast as he could, letting the rope out behind him. After several metres, he tightened the rope and started to descend.

He sucked in his cheeks and braced himself. Pushing out with his feet, he flew through the air, rain smashing into his face as he readied himself to land.

It was going to hurt, he thought. Rather a lot.

The rope swung out again, this time gaining speed, and all too soon he was back to his starting position like a pendulum. He kicked out, and as he reached the limit of his arc, he suddenly noted that the rain had stopped.

The shock forced him to hold on, the moonlight offering a shadow of vision over the ledge below.

He swung out one more time.

As he looked down, he swore he saw Isabella walking away towards a rock.

He swung back, grasping onto the rope for dear life. He was wondering how much lower he ought to be when the bolt disengaged from the rock, and Old Man Wood and the rope plummeted down.

Old Man Wood lay in a heap, his breath knocked clean out of him, pain searing into his ankle and back.

He gritted his teeth and watched Isabella. Then he heard her scream followed by muffled cries.

Had she found one of the others?

Oh! apples alive, he cursed, *how could he be so hopeless?*

He summoned his strength, trying to ignore the pain screaming through his legs.

He urged himself on, but each time he slumped back down.

His eyes watered. He probed the swollen flesh, now juicy like a purple summer-pudding. Was it a tear or a break? He turned his head and his back screamed out as if a knife was stabbing at his vertebrae. Even his hands were hurting, blood pouring from a cut in the middle of his left palm.

What had he been thinking, swinging on ropes at his great age?

His body was beginning to shut down. Shock; Old Man Wood knew the feeling well. Then it struck him. The Resplendix Mix he'd found in the cellar! Of course, he'd self-medicate!

With his swollen hand, he reached into his pocket. He transferred the bottle to his bleeding left hand and attempted to remove the lid.

Did it twist, did he have to pull out a cork, or was there some kind of stopper?

Nothing happened, apart from his hand slipping around the rim.

He inspected the bottle.

But there was no lid, or stopper.

Maybe it needed a sharp pull. He tried, but there was nothing to pull on.

Old Man Wood shook his head in frustration. No shaking, twisting, pulling, or yelling would make it open.

He felt his eyelids grow heavy. He thought of smashing the top on a rock, but even this idea slipped away as he fell into unconsciousness.

SEVENTY-ONE

GUS WONDERS WHAT WILL HAPPEN

Gus put his head out of the canopy. 'Still can't see a thing,' he reported back, 'apart from muddy water. Fancy some grub?'

Sue was starving. Gus opened a tin of tuna and a bag of salt and vinegar crisps and took a swig of water. When they'd finished, he had an idea.

'Look, Sue,' he began, 'one of us had better have a kip—we're going to need to sleep at some point and there's not much room. If we do it this way, the other can keep look-out.'

Sue hadn't thought of this. 'Good idea, brain-box. On sailing boats, I think they do four hours on and four hours off. Want to give it a try?'

'Sure,' Gus said. 'It's five-fifty now. Have a sleep till half nine—if you can. Then I'll look out till one and do the early morning shift at four or five. Sound OK?'

With a bit of a shuffle, Gus pulled the planks he'd stowed from the bottom of the boat and made up a bed—of sorts—where at least one of them could lie down. Gus unfolded a plastic sheet and laid it on top of the boards so they wouldn't lie in the wet. Sue lay down and he spread the dust sheets over her. It wasn't great, but it would have to do.

Sue closed her eyes. She didn't really feel like sleeping, but having a rest now after all that bailing out was welcome. And Gus was right, one of them needed to be on look-out—especially if there was a place they could land—and it would be a disaster if they were to miss out while they slept.

❄

Gus moved out to the bow of the boat and breathed a sigh of relief.

Quite amazingly, it seemed that for the time being they had got over the worst and his makeshift canopy had saved their lives. He laughed. He'd have won the DT prize for that; just goes to show what you can do when the pressure's on.

He wondered if Sue had any idea how close it had been, and then he thought of his mum and dad. Mum would be worried sick, but he reckoned his dad would be chuffed to bits. He hoped they hadn't gone looking for him—there was nothing he could do about it if they had. Anyway, what a surprise it would be when he got home.

At least they had food and water and could keep dry. And so long as the boat held together they had every chance. Plus they made a good team. He took a deep breath as the last gasps of daylight started to eke away. Yeah, they made a very good team.

If only they had some way of telling where they were. He thought for a minute if it wouldn't be worth dropping the oars and trying to make it to land by rowing hard to one side. Or maybe he could drop an oar at the back and use it as a rudder. But, then again, what if he didn't have the strength to handle it and spilled an oar into the water. It wasn't worth the risk. He wiped the rain, which was now bearable for more than a minute, off his face. Best keep on and hope the boat might bank somewhere they could make off to safety.

He ducked inside and, as Sue dozed, he slipped past her, grabbed a bucket and started the process of bailing the water out all over again. How long would the rain continue? Perhaps they were over the worst, but what if the deluge came back? He shivered. They had been lucky—astonishingly lucky; he'd never seen anything like it—but he didn't fancy their chances if it happened again.

Staring at her peaceful face, he moved in and planted a small kiss on her cheek. What a curious stroke of luck, he thought, that they'd run into each other.

SEVENTY-TWO

GAIA'S DREAM

Asgard had betrayed the dreamspinners; Asgard had sided with Cain!

It was common knowledge and already many dreamspinners flocked to him.

Gaia poked a leg in her maghole.

In which case, she thought, *it was the time to add balance to the drama.*

Instantly, Gaia spun a dream into Old Man Wood's mouth, the minuscule, fine powders sucked deep into the old man's lungs.

Let the powders work fast on the old man, for the effect must be sharp and quick.

The dreamspinner hovered, waiting. She needed Old Man Wood to wake up.

Shortly, the old man yawned and stretched his arms out wide, then howled in pain.

Gaia watched as the old man's face contorted in agony then moved to an expression of surprise as he found the Resplendix Mix in his lap. He studied the bottle.

Let us see how he does it this time.

Gaia saw the old man place the top of the bottle to his lips and watched as he closed his eyes. The seal opened.

Excellent, Gaia thought. *It worked. And though the old man will feel great pain as he heals, there is a chance this drama will play out to the bitter end.*

SEVENTY-THREE

A CRY FOR HELP

Old Man Wood gritted his teeth as the Resplendix Mix set to work mending damaged parts. The liquid burned like the white heat of a soldering iron welding him back together.

Shortly, he rolled his head, blinked his eyes, and breathed deeply, the air filling his lungs like bellows. Invigorated, though tingling with shooting heat, he coiled up the rope and scoured the moonlit ledge.

Now, where were they?

He'd seen Isabella below him from the rope, but the other two? Old Man Wood headed out onto the ledge. There she was, kneeling over something. A body?

Old Man Wood hurried over.

As he neared, he heard a terrible wailing noise. He prepared himself for the worst and coughed as he approached.

'Looks like you could do with a hand,' he said, solemnly.

'Old Man Wood!' she said, flinging her arms around him. 'Look! Daisy! I think she's, she's...'

Old Man Wood bent down and ran a hand over Daisy's brow. He felt only coldness. He searched for signs of breathing.

'My goodness,' he said softly, 'you've taken a horrible beating, sweet Daisy.'

He withdrew the Resplendix Mix from his pocket noting how her lips were a pale crimson against her white skin.

He felt for a pulse and his heart nearly stopped. He couldn't feel one.

He could sense Isabella staring at him, searching for answers in his face.

'Now, Isabella, there is only one thing I can do,' he said, showing her the bottle. 'She only needs a couple of drops—'

'Anything, Old Man Wood!'

'It's an old remedy of mine for healing—I'll tell you about it another time. Thing is, Bells,' he continued, a deep frown filling his forehead, 'the bottle will only open if the potion within can heal the person whose lips it touches.'

Isabella frowned. 'Do it, please—hurry!'

Old Man Wood lowered the bottle to Daisy's mouth and pressed the top against her lips.

'Why don't you just open it?' Isabella growled, mostly in frustration.

'As I said, I can't. The bottle will open itself if it can heal, otherwise I am afraid we have lost her.'

He shook his head.

'What is it?' Isabella cried.

Old Man Wood's lips trembled. 'I'm so sorry.' A tear rolled out of his eye and landed on Daisy's cheek. He wiped it off and inspected the top of the bottle, which remained closed. 'I fear I am too late,' he said, his eyes glistening. 'I am so sorry, dear little Daisy. So terribly sorry.'

Old Man Wood bent over, his body shaking, tears falling.

Isabella stared numbly at her lifeless sister. An intensity of energy she'd never experienced before rushed into her. She demanded action.

Directing her hands towards her sister, she closed her eyes and screamed.

'Don't be stupid, Daisy de Lowe. You are not going to die. Understand! I will not allow it!'

A strange, pink glow emanated from her hands, cocooning Daisy's body like strands of candy floss.

'Do not give up,' she roared. 'Not yet.'

Daisy's eye's flickered.

It worked! What had she done?

Isabella held the glow as long as she could, then reeled, stumbling and falling, exhausted. The pink cocoon floating away like vapour.

Old Man Wood, reacted fast. Placing the bottle to Daisy's lips the spout opened.

'Come on, Daisy, one drop is all you need.'

Moments later, he noticed a blush of pink in Daisy's cheeks and felt the trace of a heartbeat.

The old man carefully scooped up her limp and cold body, and carried her into the darkness of a cave he'd noticed.

Inside, Old Man Wood switched on his torch and found a circular pit, like an empty, buried hot tub. It looked as good place as any to rest. More importantly, as he stepped inside, he felt a soft, sandy, talc-like substance which, to the touch, was smooth as tissue and as soft as thick fur.

He lowered Daisy in, making sure her head was propped up. Clambering outside again, he rushed to Isabella's side and placed the Resplendix Mix to her lips. In no time, he'd done the same to Isabella, placing her sleeping body next to her sister.

Two down, he thought, *one to go.*

At least the girls would be warm and out of danger while he set about finding Archie.

SEVENTY-FOUR

ARCHIE FLIES

Archie's mind was a blur, his head whirling. Before long, he found that his body was turning and heading into a spin too.

He steadied and, as he levelled out, he realised he was flying. He soared like a bird, swooping first one way then another before shooting high into the air, twisting as he went, enjoying the sensation of weightlessness. Each gust of wind caressed his body and he cried out at the freedom of flight and the thrill of speed.

Now he was diving, flying fast as an arrow. He screwed left and found himself heading, at breakneck speed, towards a rock face as if he himself was a bolt of lightning.

Maybe he was.

He couldn't stop, he couldn't turn fast enough and there wasn't enough room for him to manoeuvre. But he wasn't afraid. He would wallop it with his head and it wouldn't hurt, it couldn't hurt him.

BANG!

The rock shattered into several pieces.

In place of the boulder was the entrance to a cave. He looked inside. Isabella and Daisy were there with Old Man Wood. They were beckoning, teasing him to come in and join them, laughing and smiling. They wanted to tell him something.

He raised his foot and carried on through the entrance. But as he did he felt the anger of Cain smash into him and he fell, Cain kicking him, first in the ribs, then chest, and finally, his face.

Why would Cain want to hurt him? They were on the same side, right?

He felt air leaking out of him like a balloon with a small hole, shrivelling quickly.

He gasped, struggling to breath.

He gulped, realising he needed air so badly; so badly that it hurt...

Archie surfaced and thrashed the water, desperate to find a hand-hold. His fingers touched on a rock. He pulled himself up and vomited, expelling water from his lungs and gut, retching and hacking until his internal organs threatened to come out as well.

He lay on a flat stone and shivered.

Daisy? Isabella? He couldn't see anyone close by. In fact, he couldn't see anything at all.

He crawled further on and curled up like a baby, shaking uncontrollably.

Cold, so cold.

'Help,' he called out, his voice squeaking like a shrew. 'Help me.'

But with Isabella gone, and Daisy gone, who was left?

He wanted to yell for his parents, for Old Man Wood, for Mrs Pye. But in this cold and inhospitable, broken place, however, he knew there was only one person who could help him.

Cain.

'*Cain!*' he yelled. 'Cain, HELP ME!'

Through the cracks in his eyes, he swore he could see a figure appearing.

'Cain,' he cried. 'You've got to save me.'

SEVENTY-FIVE

SUE ON WATCH

The boat continued to float freely, bumping into driftwood and other debris washed out into the river and then into the North Sea. Occasionally, the vessel spun and pitched from side to side, but not with the same force as earlier.

Gus wondered what they were going to eat for supper, before resisting the temptation to wolf down a chocolate bar. He squeezed past Sue to the front of the boat where, through the drizzle, he imagined he could see a spark of light way off in the distance.

When Sue woke, they tucked into a cold pork pie and shared a few pieces of chocolate. Gus stated that until they had some idea where they were they needed to conserve every single morsel. Sue complained bitterly, but Gus made it quite clear that this was non-negotiable.

By the time they had given each other a few more brain teasers, and told stories about their childhoods, it was midnight. Gus reluctantly lay down on the planks while Sue kept look-out at the front of the boat.

For a while she hummed sad melodies, her thoughts turning to Archie, Daisy and Isabella.

Had they made it? Had any of their friends survived?

Once again, Sue wondered why she—like the de Lowes—had had the premonition of the storm. Gus's comment about her being a twin with Isabella endorsed her earlier observations about the baby photograph of the two of them.

As she thought the situation through, she noted how inseparable and similar they were, in so many ways. *But best friends do that, don't they?*

And anyway, wouldn't one of the parents have said something?

She'd told Gus she would investigate further and that when this was all over she'd begin by checking with the Registrars at the Town Hall. To her delight, Gus said he'd accompany her. He told her he liked that kind of thing.

An ache in her body made her wonder if Isabella had understood her mad shouting at the football, and she wondered if earlier, when the torrential rain gave way to spitting, that this 'event' was also something to do with them. Deep sadness filled her that she might never see them again.

At one o'clock, her jaw trembled of its own accord and her fingers reminded her of icicles. Staring out into the dark night, spat on by the rain as 'The Joan of' bobbed along, her eyelids drooped.

Sometime later, her chattering teeth woke her up. She knew that trying to stay awake was a hopeless task.

She climbed under the canopy and instinctively lay down next to Gus; nestling up to his warm body, rearranging the dust covers, and inhaling the boyish smell of his clothes.

'Thanks, Gus,' she said sleepily while staring at his sleeping face. She let her head fall down next his and wrapped an arm around him.

In no time, the gentle rocking of the boat sent her fast asleep.

SEVENTY-SIX

MRS PYE FINDS SOME RUGS

When she'd seen Old Man Wood slipping out of the door, his hard hat on his head and ropes wrapped around his torso, she'd been topped-up with confidence about seeing her children again. After all, Old Man Wood had once rescued her, so why wouldn't he rescue them?

Energised, Mrs Pye set about keeping busy. She waddled round as fast as her legs would carry her, placing buckets in every grate and under every chimney flue, mopping water out of each fireplace, rolling up the hearthrugs and adjacent carpets and then emptying buckets of water down the sink.

Round and round the house she went, from the children's bedroom in the attic, to Old Man Wood's room, to the parents' room. Downstairs to the kitchen, sitting room and study, then across the courtyard through sheets of rain to her apartment. She repeated this circuit many times, drenched to the bone.

In Old Man Wood's room, she noticed five filthy rectangular rugs that sat on the wet floor, each the size of a hearthrug. She folded them up and took them to the back door, giving them a bit of shake under the wide roof trusses. As she did so, flecks of mud and dust flew in every direction.

How revolting, she thought wondering if they'd ever been cleaned.

Though she never, as a rule, ventured into the old man's room, she'd give the old man a good talking to when he returned.

If he returned.

As the rain belted down upon them, a black sludge dribbled from the fabric, like slurry. Immediately, Mrs Pye worried the rugs might get washed away, so instead, she draped them over a wooden clothes-horse under the wide porch.

Then, covering herself in a blanket, quite overwhelmed with tiredness and worry, she nodded off in the rocking chair in the kitchen, next to the warm metal range beneath the thick oak beams.

Later, she woke suddenly wondering where she was.

She yawned and for a brief moment her excitement level rocketed as she thought she could hear tiny, shrill voices like the noises of children playing in the courtyard. She looked around searching in all the obvious spots but there was nothing. Just her imagination wanting them to appear.

In the kitchen, she added a handful of kindling and two dry logs to the range then struck a match, the bright light extending into the large kitchen before dying back. A hot fire just in case they returned.

She felt the familiar stabbing pain in her shoulder.

Where were her little angels? Where were the adorable children she'd grown up loving.

Maybe they were safe at school, playing with their friends.

She'd get Archie a whole new uniform when their parents returned. She'd insist on it. No more patched up clothes for Arch.

Then she thought of Isabella and Daisy. Funny, pretty Daisy with her wavy hair and red cheeks, her keen eyes and her warm smile.

Why, they all had warm smiles, she thought, as a tear rolled down her cheek.

Imagine being stuck out in that tempest all alone. The mere thought made her tremble.

She pulled her woollen blanket tight as she noticed the flames taking.

What would happen to her if no one returned?

SEVENTY-SEVEN

OLD MAN WOOD FINDS A BODY

At first glance, as Old Man Wood hurried towards the body, he could have sworn it was Archie's friend, the one who was always so deeply unpleasant to the girls, the boy Archie liked to go fishing with.

As he approached, Old Man Wood remembered the name. Kemp. That was it. The large boy with thick ginger hair, like dear Mrs Pye.

He wondered if the child was alive and just before he made to check, his attention was taken away by a strange groaning noise, followed by a high-pitched screech coming from the flood waters. Old Man Wood gazed over the water, squinting, wondering who, or what, it might be.

When his focus returned to the boy in front of him, he looked down upon the curled up shivering figure of Archie.

Old Man Wood rubbed his chin. Was he seeing things?

Kneeling down, the old man's heart sank. Archie's mouth foamed, and his eyes flickered in different directions. His body was battered and torn.

Then, to his surprise, Archie called out a name, 'Cain!' Then he said it again, his voice urgent, but slurring. 'Cain, Cain,' over and over, as if he was delirious.

Who on earth was Cain? he wondered. And why did this name strike a chord deep within him that made his hairs prickle?

Old Man Wood searched his memory. That name, Cain, seemed to dredge up a confusing mix of love and anger, hope and despair.

Later, Old Man Wood sat on the edge of the pit and studied the three children who lay sleeping in the strange soft substance in the base of the pit. The sound of their gentle breathing was the sweetest music he had ever heard.

He reflected on his fortune; the curious bed panels and the timely rediscovery of his Resplendix Mix potion.

Old Man Wood shook his head and whistled a note of relief. How had they survived the torrential rain, the lightning, the mud-slides and the cold? How, in all the apples in the world, were they alive?

He lowered himself down and examined them in more detail. The sheer volume of bruises and cuts on their bodies was remarkable. Daisy's legs were black and blue, criss-crossed with cuts. Some of these were deep and sharp, like punctures. Other lacerations were longer, where she must have been raked by rocks and thorns. Her fingernails were black, and on her fingers entire nails had become detached leaving red, raw skin. Her shoes had gone and her feet looked as though they had been 'worked on' by a garden strimmer. Her tracksuit bottoms were tattered, and one of her football socks was attached by threads that flapped against her raw shin.

Old Man Wood wondered if he should give her some more Resplendix Mix. But this was powerful stuff; and powerful potions, he suspected, needed careful portioning.

His attention moved to Archie. Like Daisy, the boy had been battered, beaten, and pulped to within a millimetre of death. But there was one significant alteration to his appearance; Archie's hair, though softer than when he'd found him, the follicles were gelled together, hard and spiky like brushed strands of metal glued together. He remembered that when he'd seen him on the panels he'd presumed Archie had put on a hat.

He inspected Archie's hands, which, like Daisy's bore terrible lacerations and bruises. He suspected a broken finger or two by the way his digits were angled. His head and body was marked with blows, as if he'd been sprayed by a rock gun. Some of his cuts seeped, others had already congealed.

Most extraordinary of all, and perhaps even odder than Archie's hair, were Isabella's hands. The markings on her palms looked symmetrical, as if they had been painted on using a circular template and black paint.

Now that he looked carefully, the flesh inside had been burnt through, as though punctured by a red-hot poker. He could see right through them as though they'd been drilled through.

Old Man Wood sucked in a deep breath and, shaking his head, he started to consider how he would get them home. He wouldn't attempt anything now, not while they needed to sleep. And they'd be safe enough where they were for a while.

In the fresh light of morning, he'd address their wounds and give them another drop of his healing mix, but sleep was their best method of recovery while the potion set to work.

Looking about, he noticed higher ledges; berths he could pop the children on if the waters continued to rise further.

He climbed out of the pit and headed towards the cave entrance, grateful for the moonlight reflecting off the water just below the stone ledge in front of him.

He pulled himself up onto a higher rock, stretched his arms out, and lay back, trying to envisage how far the water must extend. Two hundred, three hundred metres, or perhaps even a mile towards the Dales? It could be further.

And everything in its path destroyed in the space of a few hours.

SEVENTY-EIGHT

SUE WAKES

'The Joan of' felt, to Gus, as if it were climbing up a small hill before skidding down the other side. And the process repeated the rising and falling sensations. Up and down. Up and down.

For a second, Gus dreamt he might be at a funfair. He yawned, and found himself looking into Sue's sleeping face.

What an utterly beautiful way to wake up.

Then he wondered what his breath must be like. Probably gross. *Heck.*

Trying not to disturb her, he shuffled to the end of the boat and pushed his head out of the canopy.

He yawned, closed his eyes, stretched out his arms, and inhaled a lungful of fresh air.

He opened one eye, swiftly followed by the other.

After a few seconds, he whistled.

Okay, interesting.

He could hear Sue stirring.

'Morning, first mate,' he quipped, dipping his head under the canopy.

'Oh! Morning, Gus,' she said, rubbing the sleep out of her eyes. 'Still afloat, still alive?'

'Yep, think so,' he said. 'How was lookout?'

She cringed. 'Thought you needed company. And bodily warmth is very important,' she said, a flicker of naughtiness in the corner of her lips. 'Everything all right out there. Seen any landmarks?'

He ducked inside and sat down. 'Well, it's fine and dandy-ish.'

'Dandy-ish,' she repeated. 'Then I take it you have no idea where we are?'

'Ab-so-lute-ly none,' he said, smiling. 'Take a look for yourself.'

'What's for breakfast?' she yawned, as she crept down to the other end. 'I'm starving.'

She put her head out.

Gus waited, his expectation of a verbal explosion reasonably high.

'Oh!' she said, popping her back down. Her eyes were wide open.

'Oh?' Gus said. 'Is that it?'

'Yes,' she replied, curtly. 'Oh!'

Gus smiled his biggest smile to date. 'We've drifted possibly miles out to sea with no way of knowing where on earth we are and all you can say is "Oh".'

'Yes,' Sue began, her face pale. 'Oh.'

She took a deep breath. 'Right, Gus. Now the thing is, I've never sworn at anything or anyone before in my life. But I've heard my mum do it quite a bit and from looking out there after all we've been through, I think it's the perfect time to finally give it a proper go.'

Gus looked confused. 'Oh?' he said.

'You see, every time she properly swears, she actually begins it with "Oh".'

Gus raised his bushy eyebrows. 'Really?'

And with that, Sue slipped out from under the canopy, took a deep breath and screamed over the wide expanse of sea at the top of her voice:

'Oh — $*%@!' &^%*W$!'

SEVENTY-NINE

KEMP'S PAIN

Kemp groaned in agony.

He'd had a chance to say no, and he blew it.

For a brief moment, he'd been peeled out of their union and found himself lying naked on the ledge and set upon by rain that pummelled his skin. What a feeling to feel his skin again.

In front of him lay Archie, battered and broken, his body marked by cuts and bruises, his head bloodied. His body was motionless, pale, and deathly.

He'd looked at Archie's strange hair and managed a wry smile. A classic bad hair moment only Archie could pull-off. Thinking of hair, he wasn't sure that he had any left. All singed. Burnt down to his scalp.

Cain had tried to force Archie to go with him but Archie was too far gone to make a choice willingly, and Cain knew it. Cain had miscalculated badly.

And then the old man had appeared.

Kemp had given himself back to Cain freely. At the time it didn't feel as if he had an option. But now, he regretted it. He should have refused. If he had the chance again, he'd rather subject himself to the violence of the tempest than the burning hell he was now trapped within.

Cain burned him badly after he went back.

And now, here he was, living in the darkness of a body with no food, no water, and no sleep. Where Cain's energy fried his flesh like hot oil. Kemp imagined it had been less than one whole day. But even now he wondered how long he could survive.

It was like being trapped in space, he thought, with no one there to hear his cries.

EIGHTY

IN THE PIT

Old Man Wood slept fitfully. His mind raced from Archie's shouts about Cain, to the boy with the matted ginger hair, to the terrible injuries of the children. Then his dream flashed to the strange bed panels, his old cellar, the pictures on the cave walls, and scoring goals.

A fizzing, gurgling noise woke him.

Had he been asleep for hours?

The moon had slipped behind a high cloud and rain was falling as a light spray. The old man jumped down, his feet splashing into water over his ankles.

His heart missed a beat. *Water?*

Apples alive! The children!

He sloshed round to the entrance and heard a gurgling sound coming from a strange, billowing steamy cloud.

Cautiously, he peered in, his eyes wide.

Inside, the cave floor was dry, and water flowed along a neat, straight channel that he presumed led directly into the pit.

Old Man Wood's pulse raced and, crouching down, he followed the channel through the mist. As he crept closer, the colour of the water changed from blue to pink and he could tell it was gently bubbling. He put his damaged hand in. The water tingled on his cut and a warm buzz ran up his arm.

He leant over the edge of the pit, his heart thumping. Were the children alive?

He pulled his hand out and inspected it: the wound was healing in front of his eyes.

Then he heard a voice. Or was it laughter?

'Old Man Wood, what are you doing?' Daisy said, her face appearing like a ghost in front of him briefly before sinking back into the steam.

Old Man Wood reeled.

Daisy giggled. 'Hey, why don't you get in?'

Old Man Wood felt himself choking up. 'Goodness me!' he cried. 'Daisy! Is that you? Is that really you? I can't see you.'

'Yeah, it's me all right. Come on in. It's gorgeous and warm and fantastic,' she replied. 'And it smells delicious, like an ace blend of lavender, pine needles and lemon.'

'But are you all in there?'

'Yes! And we're absolutely fine,' she said. 'Come on in—see for yourself.'

Old Man Wood was confused. 'Are ALL of you fine, I mean Isabella and Archie?'

Old Man Wood heard a splashing noise. Archie's head popped out. 'Yeah. Not bad,' he said.

'Apples almighty! It IS you.'

Archie smiled. 'Well, it's good to see you too. How long have you been here?'

'Your head?' Old Man Wood exclaimed.

'Yeah, I know. I think it was a lightning bolt.' He patted his hard hair before drifting back into the steamy water.

Old Man Wood didn't know what to think. Perhaps he was dreaming. 'Isabella?' he called out.

'Uh-huh,' she responded lazily.

Old Man Wood's heart leapt for joy. It was impossible, a miracle. 'Right then, you lot. Watch out, I'm coming in.'

He could hear them laughing.

'There's bags of room,' Daisy said. 'Though watch yourself. Archie might puncture you with his hairdo.'

Old Man Wood removed his coat, socks, and boots, and dipped his foot in the water. Then, ever so slowly, he lowered himself into the hot pool.

The water, like a winning combination of champagne and cream, bubbled up and sparkled around him. He closed his eyes and let himself drift under. Almost immediately, he felt the bubbles caress his aches and pains, targeting each one like mini lasers.

When he resurfaced and opened his eyes, the children were beaming at him.

Old Man Wood laughed out loud. 'You did it! You made it! How in apples' name...? Are you better, truly recovered?'

The twins floated over and hugged him.

Old Man Wood inspected Archie, looking for the cuts and bruises on his head, hands, and ankles. He did the same with Daisy, but the procedure was quick and easy as their skin was smooth and clear, as though the battle through the storm had never happened.

'I can't believe it. I simply can't believe it,' Old Man Wood repeated. 'I thought you were, you know, not alive, you twins! Battered to bits you were, and now look at you...'

Old Man Wood listened attentively to their stories, noting that each one had survived an almost direct strike from a lightning bolt.

But there was an awkwardness in Archie's face, the same expression he'd seen when he'd handed over the strange overcoat? And he was keen to find out more about "Cain" that Archie had called out for?

'You lot must be starving,' he said.

As one they nodded back.

'I took the liberty of bringing you something special. Afterwards, it'd be a good idea to grab some rest. After all, we've still got to find a way out of here.'

'Mmm. A chocolate brownie,' Archie began, 'with a spoonful of ice cream!'

'Or a plate full of Peking duck pancakes with plum sauce, cucumber, and spring onions,' Daisy said.

'Or a huge slice of banoffee pie, with thick cream,' Isabella added, licking her lips.

Old Man Wood got out, made his way over to his coat and found the apples.

'Now, before you start complaining,' he said, 'these are my special ones, so make sure you eat the whole thing, understand? Pips and all. They'll fill you right up. Trust me. I don't know how, but they will.'

He tossed an apple at each one, and ravenously the children bit in. They were rewarded with tastes of golden syrup, honey, apple pie, and sweet raspberries.

Before long, the children pulled themselves out of the pit. Their bodies, now devoid of cuts and bruises, dried in the warm air. Old Man Wood pointed them towards the four protruding shelves, like stone benches, built into the walls high above the floor.

Daisy climbed up into the one nearest her and wearily tested it, scrunching her hand in the soft velvety texture, before she lay down.

'This is lovely,' she purred as she sank into it. 'Like amazing memory foam, really comfy…'

Before long, her soft snores filled the void above.

The others followed, and they too experienced the extraordinary sensation of the warm silky powder, softer than feathers, which seemed to mould perfectly around their bodies.

EIGHTY-ONE

WAS ANYONE LEFT?

From his bunk high up on the cave wall, Archie peered through bleary eyes into the night sky overlooking the expanse of the Vale of York. Rippling waves caught flecks of light that flickered over the moving floodwaters which already seemed to have risen higher than the floor of the cave.

A moonbeam radiated soft light over the walls, highlighting the lines of curious pictures sketched all around. He smiled. Strange how there was so much beauty and yet so much destruction in the world.

The thought that someone had been here long ago gave him a fresh sense of comfort.

He wondered about Kemp and the ghost. His memory was just a blur, an outline, but he still couldn't work out whether Kemp had sent him on his way to save him, or if he'd done it to deliberately to take his place at Cain's side?

They'd passed the first test. And he remembered how Cain had told him they didn't have a chance. His lips turned up at the thought.

His dreams had been right all along. And wasn't it funny how Sue had known, and tried to tell them.

But tell them what, exactly?

What had she yelled on the pitch when he ran over? Something about finding clues, something about Eden Cottage. And there was something else about the Ancient Woman perhaps from visions he'd seen in his dreams and a murder he's seen over and over again?

Perhaps Cain was right about her. Perhaps saving her was the future?

Isabella, he thought, as he breathed in deeply, must have known too. Her frantic efforts to persuade Solomon to abandon the game now looked like sage advice. What would Solomon make of them now… if he was still alive?

And poor Mrs Pye, sitting at home worrying. He could imagine her pacing around, mumbling to herself. Tears running down her cheeks.

And what of their friends? Had they made it? Would there be anyone left? Probably not—unless they'd escaped into the tower at Upsall.

There was nothing he could do about it now. When they'd discovered a way out of the cave and climbed up through the forest and back home, then they might find out.

He touched his hard hair and wondered if they'd been blessed. Strange how it was them, of all people.

He yawned, his mouth stretching to its widest point. And what of that strange spidery-creature he'd seen over Daisy? Was that also a part of this adventure?

Unwittingly, his eyes closed.

Just so long as he didn't get any more murderous nightmares… Cain said they'd end. And what if he really did have the courage of a horse and the strength of a lion…?

The mists of tiredness swept over every part of his tired body.

He could think no more.

In moments, the Heirs of Eden and Old Man Wood were all sound asleep.

Read Book Two, Spider Web Powder.

BOOK TWO - SPIDER WEB POWER

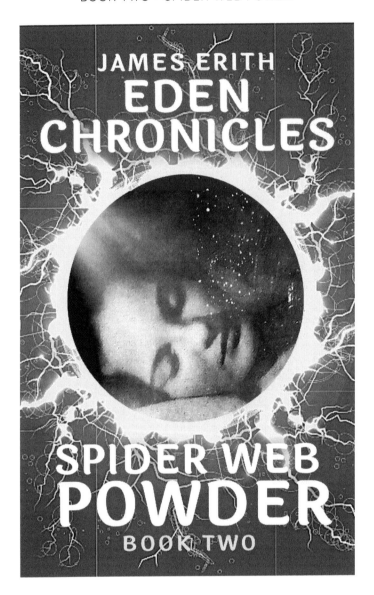

EIGHTY-TWO

DAISY'S EYES

Archie extended his arms and pushed out a sleepy yawn. Where were the purple curtains at the end of his bed? Where were the thick oak beams supporting the roof of the attic room that he shared with his sisters, Isabella and Daisy? What about the red drape that hung down like a Bedouin tent?

As his eyes adjusted to the gloom, he noted the grey, jagged rocks curving above him like a bad set of teeth, and was instantly reminded of the previous day's horrors.

Archie lay quite still, filtering the curious sand he was lying on through his fingers. Was this part of a dream? Was he even alive?

He moved his head to investigate.

Nestled into the walls were three ledges, like shallow troughs. These were the stone beds Archie and his sisters had sought refuge in last night to escape the storm. Now, they, like him, were stirring.

Moments later, a burst of steam erupted from the circular pool in the middle of the cave where hot water bubbled gently. As he stared, the surface glimmered from what he suspected were a multitude of fluorescent minerals.

Archie hazily remembered how their beaten and cut bodies were soothed and healed by this small pool. But even now his memories of last night were vague. Archie could only recall fragmented scenes, like pieces of a jigsaw puzzle.

His curiosity aroused, Archie moved his eyes around the cave, increasingly astonished by what he saw. He stumbled off his bed, rubbed his face, and attempted to smooth down his hair.

His baffled expression made his older sister Isabella chuckle from her bed along the wall.

'Your hair took on a new form, remember? It is now irretrievably spiky,' she said, the words echoing more dramatically than either had expected. 'The result of being hit by a lightning bolt. Remember?'

Trust Isabella to remember more than he could. He grunted a response and headed to the bubbling pool, wafting his hand at a cloud of steam that billowed into the high roof.

Archie dangled his feet and ankles in the bubbles. Soon, a sparkly feeling fizzled up his torso. He cupped his hands and drank a draught of the water, washed his face and splashed his strange, hard hair.

'I don't suppose there's anything for breakfast?' he said, more in hope than expectation.

'There's another apple each,' Old Man Wood said. The old man was like a grandfather to the three siblings, and Archie remembered how he'd come to their rescue last night.

Archie picked his way over the rocky, undulating grey floor and sat down next to him. Old Man Wood had found each one of them at deaths door after the violent storm and carried each one from the ledge into a sandy pit in this cave. Overnight, the pit had filled with water as the floodwaters had risen over the height of the ledge outside.

The cave entrance opposite filtered-in a hazy morning light, which appeared to ripple as he stared at it. For a brief moment, he wondered if a kind of see-through crystal-like substance had miraculously grown up in front of the cave's mouth, holding up a body of moving water behind it.

Old Man Wood handed Archie a small, perfectly formed apple from his large, weathered, and leathery hands.

Archie chomped hungrily and began to take in the caveman art that stretched all the way around the stony walls. He spotted three distinct human figures drawn with firm strokes, but others, he reckoned, looked more like stick men or animals. Some images were upright, others were lying down as if the figures were dead.

'Do you guys remember these pictures from last night?' he asked.

Daisy and Isabella were stretching their arms wide and yawning and didn't answer.

Archie searched further into the cave. 'Bit of a classic,' he murmured. 'This could be interesting.'

'What's up, Archie?' Daisy said, sleepily.

'We have a problem,' he said. 'In fact, we have quite a few.'

His twin, Daisy, yawned. 'Expand, bro.'

'Well, yeah,' he started, not quite knowing what to say. 'Let's start with how we get out of this cave.'

Daisy tittered. 'Seriously?'

Archie raised his eyebrows. 'Yeah. It's sealed itself off… I think.'

Daisy ambled over to the pool and splashed her face. 'Rubbish—'

'No,' he said. 'Look at the entrance, I think it's blocked.'

Daisy repeated the action this time dunking her entire head in the pool. 'Of course there's a way out. No way can we be stuck.'

Archie wondered if she knew something he didn't. 'Have you seen the paintings?' he said, changing the subject.

'Cool, aren't they,' Daisy said. 'Quite like Picasso.'

'What are you talking about?'

'The artist, Picasso. I'm sure I've seen stuff of his just like this.'

Archie's eyes bulged. 'Really, Daisy?'

'Yup. Simple, abstract lines. That kind of thing,' she replied.

'Oh,' he said, wondering when Daisy had become so knowledgeable about modern art. 'I thought they might be a kind of guide?' he said. 'What do you think?' He continued to study the outlines. He noticed oblong-shaped objects and lines of repetitive strokes like shadows.

Soon, Daisy and their older sister Isabella joined him. After a short while, Isabella's continual glancing towards her younger sister finally made Daisy snap.

'What!' she cried.

'Nothing!' Isabella replied.

'Well, stop doing that.'

'Doing what?'

'Looking at me. Weirdly.'

Isabella moved closer and shuffled from one foot to the other. 'Actually, Daisy,' she said, as she examined her sister's pretty face, 'Your eyes are—'

'What about them?'

'Well. I mean… I think—'

Daisy turned away, her face reddening.

'No, seriously, Daisy. Look at me.'

'Why?' she said, her tone betraying her concern. She looked up.

Isabella leaned in. 'You've done something to your eyes—'

'No, I haven't. They're absolutely fine,' she said rubbing them and blinking rapidly as if to prove it. 'What's the big deal?'

Archie joined in and whistled. 'Bells is right, Daisy.'

'Maybe it's a just a trick of the light,' Isabella said, as if Daisy couldn't hear. 'Hey, Old Man Wood. Come and check this out.'

'Seriously?' Daisy cried, flummoxed by all the attention. 'Stop it, both of you.'

Old Man Wood shuffled closer and gazed at her too. The three of them leaned over her.

'Thing is, Daisy,' Archie said, 'your eyes really are... different.'

'Different?'

'Yeah, very.'

'I need a mirror,' Daisy said, looking around.

'You won't find one here, sis,' Archie said. 'It's hardly the place—'

'Listen dudes. I really don't care. But please, stop looking at me—'

Archie's eyes narrowed. 'I can't help it—they're red.'

Isabella agreed. 'Ruby red.'

'Red?' Daisy queried.

Archie nodded.

'Don't be silly. My eyes are perfectly fine. There's nothing wrong—'

'Actually,' Isabella said, 'it's more cerise—'

'Or scarlet blending into burgundy?' Archie added.

'They're a red-apple-colour in my opinion,' Old Man Wood said, thoughtfully.

'Chilli-red, possibly,' Isabella added. 'Like a vampire.'

This time they all nodded.

'Tip of my tongue,' Archie said. 'But I'd run with Old Man Wood's description. It's definitely more of a red-apple-colour.'

'Look,' Daisy said, flustered. 'Maybe it's from the chemicals in the healing water in the pool...'

Archie squinted at her. 'Sorry, Daisy. Thing is, the white bit around them is still white,' he said. 'It's the middle bit that's changed—'

'It's known as the iris, Arch,' Isabella whispered.

'Yeah, I knew that,' he said, before addressing his twin. 'Basically, Daisy, your nice blue eyes have turned a rather fetching chilli-plum-apple-red-colour. Pretty cool, I reckon.'

'Cool?' Daisy replied. 'You're kidding. You're saying I've turned into a freak!'

Archie flicked his steely hair. 'Like me?' he grinned.

Isabella reluctantly held up a hand, where the outline of a neat hole punched through the middle of her palm. 'Like me too,' she said.

It was the wound she'd received yesterday as she protected herself against a lightning bolt. She stared at the circular cavities in awe, fully aware that somehow, however inexplicable, and incalculable, her hand-holes had saved her life.

'If there's a school left to go back to, we're going to stand-out big time—'

'The de Lowe super-weirdos,' Archie chipped in.

'Hang on! What about me?' Old Man Wood said, his deep voice filled with gentleness and soft humour.

Daisy leaned into the old man and looked up at his worn and lined face. 'Dear, lovely Old Man Wood, you're already a wonderful freak. We're just catching you up a little.'

Old Man Wood, couldn't help but smile back with affection. His wise, kind, dark brown eyes moved from child to child as he pondered their next move.

As Archie had just touched on, he had the not-so-small task of guiding them out of this sanctuary—or prison—back to Eden Cottage.

EIGHTY-THREE

ISABELLA'S CONFUSION

Daisy returned to her stone bed and lay back on the soft, sandy surface. She studied her siblings. Isabella was sieving bubbling water through the new holes in her hands, while Archie was still wandering around the cave engrossed in the curious artwork.

Daisy had briefly scanned the murals, noticing raised etchings and basic figures and recognisable shapes, but she hadn't given them too much attention. But when Archie reached the far side of the cave, deeper into the shadows, and stumbled, she decided to investigate further.

She made her way over to Old Man Wood, who had remained rooted to the spot, staring at the pictures as if he were looking right through them to another place and time entirely.

Daisy leant on him as if he were a lamppost, sneaked a hand into his pocket, picked out an apple, and then moved around the room following Archie.

'Right, guys,' Daisy announced after a circuit of the chamber. 'This art is like an instruction manual.'

'For what?' Archie asked.

'Primarily for getting out of here—'

'Why?' Isabella said.

'If you hadn't noticed we're trapped, just as Archie said. The entire valley is underwater. There is no way we can physically get out.'

'I'm not listening if we've got to do anything dangerous,' Isabella said from the pool. 'I've done enough surviving for an entire lifetime.'

'Well, I think you should listen, oh brainy-one!' Daisy fired back. 'Seriously, you need to know what's going on and, oddly, these knobbly walls have the answers.'

Isabella groaned. 'Please, Daisy. Can't we just go home?'

'Bells, if only it were that easy. If we could simply walk out of here, then yes, I'd be well on the way to a hot bath, a massive hot chocolate, and my own bed. But we can't because we're stuck.' Daisy flicked a strand of hair off her face. 'These pictures, I think, are the clues to our next meal with Mrs Pye at home.'

While the murals might not make sense to her siblings, to her they were as clear as day.

'Now, pay attention,' she said as she marched over to the far side. 'Once upon a time,' she began, relishing her moment in the spotlight, 'there were three brave knights. Here, here and here,' she said, pointing at three human outlines. 'They lived in a land where there were nice things to eat, like, um, apples,' she turned and winked at Old Man Wood, 'but there were also bad things, like nasty snakes. One day the knights were lying in bed,' she pointed at a gnarly squiggle on the wall, 'when they were given some cool gifts, or something.' She raised her eyebrows. 'Let's study these pictures in a more detail, shall we?'

Isabella splashed a foot in the pool. 'Daisy, this is ridiculous—'

'One of them,' Daisy continued, 'had extremely large eyes and sticky-out ears, another had big hands and fat feet, and the last knight rode horses and, um, lions.' Daisy chortled, briefly, surprised at her own explanation.

'Still with me? Isabella? Archie? Old Man Wood? Excellent!'

She dragged Old Man Wood to the next section. Archie followed and Isabella, defeated, stood up, shook out her feet, and following on behind.

Daisy indicated another faded mark on the wall. 'One day, loads of arrows shot out of the sky like you can't believe, with some fiery ones, like this lot... here. When the sun went down—here—our three knights had either died and gone to hell—where they kept on getting shot at—or, if they'd survived, as shown in this squiggle, their prize was to sit in a mega jacuzzi. After that, they climbed up to heaven. End of chapter one!' Daisy clapped her hands and did a small celebration dance.

'Oh, bravo!' Isabella said, her voice smeared with sarcasm. 'How enlightening. Are you done now?'

'Not even close, Isabella,' Daisy replied. 'Now, onto the next section.' Daisy dragged Old Man Wood by the arm to the next patch of drawings. 'Here,' she continued, 'five pictures show how to find three books or stones or tablets. If our heroes find the first one, it means they've passed the first stage and they move on to try for the second. But, if, at any point they fail,' and now her voice went quieter, 'then, they are going to... DIE.' She said 'die' in a slightly deeper and louder voice, which echoed back eerily, much to her satisfaction.

Daisy hopped up onto a rocky ledge and pointed towards the next section.

'In this bit, they've found the second stone and dumped it on top of the first one— and look, it's grows into a ginormous book, or stone, or whatever it is! Clever, huh?!'

'Why would it do that?' Archie blurted out.

'How should I know?' she replied from her lofty standpoint, before turning back to the images. 'Here, our three heroes must find a third stone and do exactly the same thing all over again... ooh,' she said, moving into and brushing the wall with her fingertips. 'A-ha. I see,' she said, as much to herself as the others who gazed up at her as if she might very well be making the whole thing up.

'Now, pay attention,' she continued. 'If our heroes are successful, they add the third stone to the ginormous book and, BOOM!'

Daisy's impression of an explosion made Archie laugh. She spun a little further round and theatrically pointed to the wall. 'And the blast leads to this.'

'What' Isabella said, 'are you going on about—?'

'A whole other place,' Daisy interrupted. 'A place like the surface of the moon with a single great tree bang in the middle.' She shifted her gaze further around the wall. 'And, behind this tree they find... they find a—a...'

'Yes,' Isabella said, 'what do they find?'

'They find a...' Daisy stared hard at the picture, her eyes glowing.

'A what, Daisy?'

'A woman.'

'A woman?'

'Yes.'

'What are you talking about?'

Daisy's face drained. 'O-M-G,' she said, pulling her hands to her face.

'Daisy, what is it?' Archie asked. 'What are you looking at?'

Daisy shook her head. 'Cool. No, nothing really. Thought it was something I'd seen somewhere before.' She regained her composure, turned to the others, and curtsied. 'There you have it,' she said. 'The story of the wall art.'

Isabella broke the silence with a slow hand-clap. 'Daisy,' she said. 'Nice story, but just for the record diagonal lines in ancient drawings generally indicate rain, not arrows—'

'Yeah, I know,' Daisy replied, rolling her eyes. 'It's called artistic licence.'

'And Daisy,' she continued, 'where are we?'

'In a cave, duh?'

'And what kind of thing is in the middle of our cave?'

'A hot tub-pit, jacuzzi thing-a-me.'

'It's not a hot tub, Daisy, it's a thermal spring that bubbles up due to naturally occurring heat generated by the Earth's core. And anyway, what do you think we battled through yesterday—'

'Stop being so damn patronising, Livi. I know, OK. I do realise. The cave is about us— I knew that all along—the rain, the sunset, the bubbling pool over there. The fact that I can see and hear stuff you guys can't. That you, Isabella, can repel lightning with your hands, like you did yesterday as we escaped from the storm. And Archie has weird strength, pulling trees up like a horse and stuff, like he did yesterday to get us here safely. You must think I'm completely stupid or something.'

'Actually, I do,' Isabella said, bluntly. 'And, to be honest, I'm hardly surprised you've jumped to these ludicrous conclusions.'

'Conclusions?'

'Yes. Because now you think the walls are telling us we're special, huh, with magical powers like wizards and witches. Come on, Daisy! The sooner you get this nonsense out of your head the better.'

'You're kidding—'

'No, of course I'm not. This cave here is quite obviously some form of prehistoric temple, left over from pre-Neolithic times. In my opinion, these cave paintings simply copy what is all around us in this chamber. Ancient tribal stuff. They probably sacrificed humans here—if, of course, the water couldn't heal them.'

'Please tell me you're joking.'

Isabella laughed. 'The fact that we survived is down to luck,' she continued. 'Pure and simple L— U—C— K,' which she spat out, letter by letter.

Daisy glanced towards Archie for support. 'Luck? What about my hearing?'

'The fact that you can hear stuff like lightning forming is possibly a freak acoustic accident with your eardrum that belongs to you and you alone, Daisy. My initial thoughts are that it comes from heading a football too much—'

'Heading? I don't really do heading—'

'Yes, you do! Of course, you do! You're a soccer player.'

Daisy reeled. 'What about your hands?'

Isabella looked affronted. 'The fact that the lightning hit my hands must be an oddity of particle dynamics which can, and will, be explained. I'm quite sure it has something to do with not only the mineral content in the soil the huge quantity caked over them just prior to the strike.'

Daisy stared at her sister with her mouth open. 'I don't believe it,' she spat. Her eyes lit up. 'Then how come, Einstein, Archie managed to pull out a tree yesterday and dangled it over the bank of the track?'

Isabella didn't even flinch. 'Archie's strength was obviously from sheer determination at helping out his dear twin sister,' she smiled, her eyes narrow. 'And, of course this was greatly facilitated by the fact that the tree roots were entirely saturated—so it came away with ease. I'm sure I could have done exactly the same in his circumstances.'

'But you didn't see the size of it!' Daisy roared.

'I know I didn't but face it, kids, you both have a bit of a reputation for these kinds of stories—'

A snort shot out of Daisy's nostrils. 'But you admit the storm and all those things you've just mentioned were true!'

'A-ha!' Isabella said. 'As far as this goes, we have only your word. There are no other witnesses are there,' she looked around, 'apart from you two, and Old Man Wood.'

Daisy gasped, her red eyes blazing with fury.

Archie stepped in. 'Don't be ridiculous, Isabella,' he said. 'What about the healing water?'

'Easy, Archie. We're in a hillside rich with complex blends of minerals and ancient volcanic dusts with, as yet, unknown healing properties that must have percolated up through core heat activity to make the pool.'

'And Archie's hair?' Daisy added.

Isabella hesitated. 'Science can almost certainly answer that too. Probably something to do with the molecular properties of his follicles, the chemicals in his hair and the amount of product he uses in relation to the electrical charge from the lightning bolt which struck him.'

'But I don't use hair stuff—'

'Yes, you do!' Isabella stormed.

'Actually,' he said, 'Daisy stole it ages ago, didn't you?'

Daisy nodded.

'Everything must be explained rationally!' Isabella yelled. 'The kind of things we experienced do not happen by chance!'

A rather awkward silence ensued, while Isabella's voice echo faded away until only the gently bubbling of the pool returned to earshot.

Archie took a deep breath.

'Thing is, Isabella, none of us know what's going on,' he said, as sweetly as he could.

Isabella squatted on to the floor and burst into tears. 'I will not believe any of this has happened! None of it can be true, even though you make it sound like it has.'

Daisy knelt down and draped a comforting arm around Isabella's shoulder. 'If it's any consolation, sis, a scientific explanation probably does exist for all these things. But science measures things that are known. If they're unknown, science attempts to understand, or prove, how the mysterious things in the world are known, in order to rationally configure how they exist. Therefore, it can't prove things that aren't understood or unknown yet, can it?'

Everyone stared at her.

Archie's eyes zig-zagged as he tried to figure out what she'd said. 'Jeez. When did you turn into a geek?'

'Shut up, Archie,' the girls said in unison.

'Look, Bells,' Daisy said, 'one way or another, we're going to have to figure out what's going on. Coincidence or not, science or not, magic or not. Whatever it takes, okay?' she gave her sister a kiss on the cheek. 'My guess, from looking at these wall pictures, is that we've got to find a giant stone book or tablet somewhere. So, when we get out of here, all we have to do is find a supersized book.'

'And you know what they say about giant books?' Archie said.

The girls looked at him blankly.

'Masses of words!' he replied.

Isabella tried incredibly hard not to smile but eventually she wiped her nose and gave Archie a playful shove, before hugging her sister. 'I never thought you could be so smart, Daisy. I'm sorry about calling you stupid.'

'Don't be silly,' Daisy replied. 'Made it all up to make you feel better.'

Isabella stared at her sister, not entirely sure whether to bash her or not.

While Isabella and Archie teased each other about Archie's book joke, Daisy ran to one of the pictures, studied it for a short while and quietly slipped to the far end of the cavern.

'I've found something,' she yelled over, excitement in her voice.

The others looked up.

'It better be good,' Archie replied, nonchalantly.

'It is. It's this invention commonly known as "stairs",' she said.

'I've looked already,' he said, 'and there aren't any.'

But when they looked in her direction again, she wasn't there.

EIGHTY-FOUR

CAIN WONDERS

Never in his wildest dreams had Cain's black-bearded elfin servant, Schmerger, imagined that Cain would come alive. For the few hours that Cain had been back in the palace, his servant sensed the power of the man, the presence and the fabled aura of Cain's imperious majesty and power.

In no time, news was spreading across Cain's planet of Havilah that their leader had returned and already, there was hope that this strange ruler, dormant as a helpless spirit for thousands of years, might finally be able to restore the planet to greatness once more.

Schmerger wondered if it was fate.

Havilaria City, the capital of Havilah, once the melting pot of all the worlds, once a bustling and lively place where vices were ignored, ruthlessness admired, and riches abounded. In all the worlds, this great city—one of excitement and opportunity—was enjoyed by all but the most pious of individuals. Even under Cains careful rule, fun and pleasure epitomised living here, hand in hand with the dangers it invariably bred.

After Cain's capture, after his trial by the council of One Hundred, and after his sentence to death by burning, his spirit had remained here in exile forever on this planet. Helpless, as nothing more than a ghost, Cain watched as the city deteriorated until it groaned in decay. His once vibrant world had slipped, over millennia, into ruin.

The new Cain, Schmerger thought, had reappeared as a half-ghost with the outline of a human boy, a teenager he supposed, with fat lips and a head of thick human hair and crammed full of vigour. Cain had combined with this youth to form a body that was made up entirely of re-generating black and grey ash leaving a mess behind him at his every turn which made the old servant wince. At first, he wondered if this really was Havilah's estranged, master? But, as Schmerger came to terms with the dynamism and fervour of his revived master, there was little doubting it.

Cain had returned, albeit without his magic or without his legendary power but with a sharpness, a brilliance and an edge of a man who meant to restore his land to splendour once more.

For the first time in aeons, Cain had the ability to rule and his demands were ceaseless. The messages he gave endless. Dictates to all the tribes and the species of Havilah ran through so many scrolls that Schmerger ordered his scribes to break into the archives and white-wash old scrolls from the vast storage caverns within the hillside so they could be re-used.

Cain had demanded immediate allegiance from the ancient human tribes, the elves, the ogres and the giants. His method was clear. He was back and he demanded nothing less than loyalty, or death.

Schmerger knew this action was borne on a wave of fanatical hope and fear rather than any real physical threat. Speed was of the essence.

Schmerger was an old elfin type, with a neat, long black beard, thick greying eyebrows and a nose that stretched pointedly outwards. He needed a break. After years of inactivity, the sudden demands for action had caught him, like everyone else, unawares.

Schmerger, elated by the sudden rush of work, felt invigorated; the new Master had requirements no-one could have foreseen; a kitchen; cooks; a well for fresh human water; flushing latrines; a soft bed.

Once, long ago, all of these had existed. Now Schmerger summoned the old maps and instructions for human inhabitation. And he had called upon the elven community to attend, to serve. Without hesitation and to his relief, they came from every nook and cranny of Havilaria, elves, desperate for change, attended his hourly meeting points. Under Schmerger's watchful eye, they studied the old scrolls and set about reconstructing the palace for their new Master. Teams of workers began what he called the 'Great Cleansing' of the palace.

Already, Schmerger's bandy legs ached from marching after this strange ashen creature and his scrawny fingers throbbed from making endless notes, and his brain verged on overload. For the first time in years, Cain had the energy to rule Havilah as the great nation it once was. He demanded writing paper and had set about dictating edicts and demands of loyalty from the distant tribes, dotted throughout the lands.

The servant closed the huge door to the great chamber where Cain, in this new ashen form, lay resting atop a soft, giant bed that stretched for twenty paces in each direction. Schmerger bowed low as he entered, noting how his master's body lay collapsed, he thought, with tiredness.

Schmerger, took in the mess where ash had freely fallen off the new Cain, even as he slept. The amount of cleaning up after his master, he sensed, was going to multiply hugely. Already, he didn't have the staff. And the sheets on this bed in particular were notoriously difficult to wash and iron at the best of times.

Cain felt an arm stretch out wide and bend briefly before flexing at the elbow and relaxing. Cain realised the boy within him was directing their limb without him and the feeling was thrilling, intoxicating even.

This blending or, he supposed, fusing of spirit, blood, and flesh, had happened so fast that he hadn't known if the boy would survive. Nothing like the gelling of a spirit and a boy had ever happened before. Now he had, once again, an extraordinary feeling of being. Was this sensation the same for the boy? Did the boy realise he might control both of them without his interference?

Up until this moment, Cain had purposefully forced every movement upon the boy because he needed to be in command. The spirit knew full well that time had taken its toll on every area of his planet and, up until a short while ago, Cain had been unable to do anything about it. That was going to change, and fast.

Their hand moved—without his aiding—to their face where it made to scratch their nose. Ash crumpled off and drifted to the floor, more ash growing back in its place. Cain couldn't have imagined how wonderful it was to have a nose again, even if looked like rather a big, fat nose, and even if his sense of smell was tainted by the constant tang of soot.

Better still was actually seeing again, even if his distorted vision was like looking through opaque glass.

Admiring his hazy outline in a mirror, he'd seen the ashen outline of both the boy and himself. Thick, swept back hair, larger lips than he remembered and, curiously, empty, ashen eye sockets, which lacked eyeballs. Nevertheless, he had a form of vision and he'd been nothing short of astonished to gaze upon his shapely, strong legs, large biceps, and his thick neck.

Seeing, was so much better than relying on his sixth sense; this understanding of energy that he had, over millennia, come to rely upon.

Cain waited as the arm fell back to its place beside their new body. As it did, he reached in with his energy and manipulated the boy's fingers. He chuckled. They moved—at his bidding!

The ghost allowed himself to smile, noticing how he could feel the corners of his mouth curling up ever so slightly. He marvelled at his huge stroke of fortune but also wondered, quietly, if he would ever quite get used to this curious union.

Cain's thoughts turned to the three children. These three children were the Heirs of Eden, meaning that they would be the ones who represented all human life on Earth to prove that humankind's evolution over time had worked.

Cain could still not believe that such a momentous task had been given to children. When men lived to be a thousand years, he thought, children of this age would be considered little more than babes. Cain smirked. Maybe, in this eon, humans simply grew up and developed faster. If Earth's fate rested in the hands of youth, he mused, then it would not be long before he himself might rule over the whole universe. Had the energies of the universe gone awry? Was humanity on Earth so desperate?

He had the strange creature called Asgard to thank for alerting him to this predicament. Asgard was a dreamspinners, one of the elders of an ancient, mysterious species that spun dreams to all living things. Dreamspinners lived suspended in the universe, watching over Earth, Havilah and the other planets from any point in the vast wilderness of space.

Asgard's elongated alien-like spider-like form was marked by long, wiry, arms and six legs. He had a bulbous head with cavernous oval black eyes, and a churning hole of electric light where an abdomen would otherwise be. Asgard called this light his 'maghole.'

This magical creature had approached Cain out of his own disbelief over the choice of Heirs of Eden. Cain smiled at this huge stroke of fortune. He had used Asgard's maghole to travel to all corners of the universe, bringing an end to his exile on Havilah after thousands of years. Who would have thought it possible?

What a remarkable turn of events. After so long stuck on crumbling Havilah, Cain realised he might now call the shots and exercise his authority on Earth.

Things hadn't gone entirely to plan. The laughably simple, yet brilliant idea of joining his body together with the boy Heirs of Eden, Archie, had, to his astonishment, come within a fraction of this reality. How close to universal domination he had been? But Cain knew that so long as he had the ability to travel anywhere he wanted through Asgard's maghole, and with Earth's demise almost inevitable, there would be other opportunities.

Cain stretched an arm out on the bed, noticing how a finger fell away and crumpled onto the sheets. The digit re-grew in an instant. He mulled over the sequence of yesterday's events.

Archie de Lowe, that scrawny boy, one of the three Heirs of Eden with a power the child did not even recognise had deceived him as the storm broke. He had swapped with his friend, Kemp, who was the boy residing inside Cain now, and run off, cheating death. But he knew that fusing with any human was better than having no human at all.

Even so, these three young Heirs of Eden were hard to fathom. While the surrounding area on Earth where they lived had been ravaged by rain and mudslides, these young Heirs of Eden had survived.

Cain's mood turned darker, a rage building.

The boy part of him shifted deep in his core.

How had the old man arrived at the cave just as he was about to join with the Heirs of Eden, Archie, all for himself? What did they call the old fool now? Was it Old Man Wood, or something equally absurd? And how had Old Man Wood recovered his wits to find and drag the young Heirs of Eden to the safety of the healing waters in the cave of secrets?

Cain gritted his teeth, noting how they disintegrated in a puff of grey dust, regenerating moments later. Did these children, these supposed Heirs of Eden, have the faintest idea what they were doing or what awaited them? Did they understand anything?

Cain guffawed. How could they? The riddles for the finding the sacred tablet-stones were designed for grown men. Men versed in magic, educated in battle, long in wisdom, and learned in the ways of nature.

In any case, he thought, what came next for those on Earth? Cain tried to remember the old prophecy. First flooding, then disease. Cain chuckled. Yes, of course. Disease came next.

The pathetic Heirs of Eden, these three de Lowe children, may have overcome the trials of the storm but that really was only the beginning. From the moment the storm broke, they had seven Earth days to unearth and understand the riddles that would lead them to three stone tablets.

Cain listened for the boy inside him and heard, faintly, the sleepy growls of a snore. It had a strangely calming effect. Even if these young Heirs of Eden had been visited by the vagaries of fortune, fortune, he knew, never hung around for long.

EIGHTY-FIVE

GUS AND SUE

Sue scanned the endless horizon and whistled. 'Sublime and ridiculous,' she said.

'What do you mean?' Gus said as he wrestled with his penknife and a can of tuna.

'OK. So, we survive a monsoon in a geriatric rowing boat with a ridiculous name, which could sink at any moment—'

'There's nothing wrong with calling a boat 'The Joan of,' Gus said, smiling.

Sue raised her eyebrows. 'Anyway, thanks to your sublime wood-working skills we're still alive, but like fools we wake up in a piddly vessel on the sea miles from anywhere in another perilous situation. Therefore, ridiculous.'

Gus flashed a toothy smile and poured the brine off into a cup. 'Well, if you hadn't fallen asleep at your post, none of this would have happened.'

'Gus, are you blaming me?'

'Absolutely,' he mocked. 'I entirely blame you. You should have woken me up rather than snuggle up.'

'But you looked so sweet,' Sue said, her face flushing. She turned away.

Gus didn't know if he should read anything into her comment. He'd never had a girlfriend. He'd never given girls any serious thought before, but here he was, fourteen years old and mature for his age. Most of his friends had dallied in some form of relationship. He thought about his interaction with girls and found that, although he was friendly with many, like Daisy de Lowe and Poppy in his class, Sue was the first girl he'd ever really talked to about stuff. Stuff like life and parents and feelings. Up till now, girls could have been aliens; they did things differently and they talked in a strange way.

Gus offered Sue first go at the brine that sat on top of the tuna.

'Oh really, do I have to?'

'Yes. Everything that can be eaten must be eaten and that's an order. No wastage allowed.'

She rolled her eyes and pinched her nose, swallowing the tangy bitter juice. It stuck to her gums and her face contorted in disgust.

She handed the rest over to Gus.

'I've never had a proper boyfriend,' she said, moving next to him and leaning on his shoulder.

'And I've never had a girlfriend,' Gus said, cringing. He felt his muscles tense. She smelt wonderful, like a juicy peach. Seated so close to one another there was no way of denying it; she was fabulous, even if her breath smelled a bit... fishy.

He sipped on the brine and spluttered.

She laughed and when he'd stopped coughing, she stared into his eyes. Gus was the most amazing person she'd ever come across. He'd saved her life. If they didn't make it, he'd smile right to the bitter end, she thought. Wasn't that amazing?

For some reason, she felt safer being with him than anyone else knew.

EIGHTY-SIX

MRS PYE

Mrs Pye had no idea how long she'd been asleep, but she woke suddenly to find a dim light filtering in through the windows and the fire smouldering in front of her.

Eden Cottage was as quiet as she could remember. She wore this sense of loss like a ball and chain. She missed the de Lowe children who she had looked after their whole lives, stepping in with Old Man Wood as surrogate parents whenever the children's real parents had to leave the farm on business matters.

In the kitchen, she put the kettle on the stove and stared out of the windows as morning light rose over the vale below her. She gasped. A lake—or was it the sea —filled the valley below?

Nearer the farm, trees lay in a wretched jumble. Her heart sank.

She hobbled about, wondering if she should go outside and look for the children. But what if they returned only to find an empty home? That wouldn't be right and, in any case, the old man would bring them back, wouldn't he? He had a knack of doing that.

After all, Old Man Wood had found her all those years ago. She was barely alive, so they said, deep in the forest at the bottom of a gorge. He'd carried her home for many miles. Old Man Wood would do the same with the children. She felt it in the marrow of her bones. There was something right about this feeling, a special quality the old man had that she couldn't quite lay a finger on.

If he couldn't do it, who else could?

She made bread, washed up, and when all was done, shuffled out of the back door to gather up the five filthy rugs she had found on Old Man Wood's bedroom floor.

Strange little things, she thought. Like hearth rugs but lighter and, as she realised when she gripped the fabric, stronger.

A cloud of dust fell blew out of one when she gave it a small whack, even though it was slightly damp. She knew Old Man Wood didn't like her in his room, and duly stayed away, but why oh why hadn't these little rugs been washed before?

For a brief moment, she had a good mind to toss them in the rubbish bin. Then again, she thought, trying to make out if there was a pattern on them, she might as well let them finish drying and slip them back in Old Man Wood's room, disgusting though they still were. He'd never know they'd gone.

She'd pop them in the washing machine when the power returned, if and when the electricity came back.

EIGHTY-SEVEN

CAIN'S PLAN

Cain watched his chest rise and his thoughts moved back to the strange dream-spinners. They were like peculiar wispy elfin ghosts, who darted invisibly around the universe. It was strange how they operated in such deep secrecy, providing a service that was taken for granted by every single living thing in the universe.

Dreamspinners were wisps of particles and matter, dedicated to their job of making and giving out dreams, but they did not concern themselves too closely with other life forms. Asgard, the dreamspinner who had come to him, had quickly realised that these young Heirs of Eden were not up to the task of finding the three tablets. Asgard knew that if the Heirs of Eden failed, there would be no more dream spinning for the dreamspinners. And Asgard knew that the only way to keep dream powders coming meant seeking his help.

But why him? Did Asgard know more than he'd let on? Was there really no one else?

Cain noticed, for the very first time, a gentle, rhythmical beat within his chest cavity.

A heart.

Cain coughed, momentarily forgetting to breathe at the same time as the boy inside him. My goodness, he thought. Beneath this strange exterior, he had a beating heart. He placed an ashen hand up to their chest and pressed gently. The hand slipped beneath folds of soft dust before he felt the warm, soft core of the body within him. He noted the steady patter of his heart's rhythm and sat in silence for a while, the gentle thump ricocheting around his entire frame.

What next? Cain thought, as he removed his hand from his chest and shook off the dust. He wondered what the Heirs of Eden were doing right now. Stuck, no doubt, arguing about their petty lives and their adolescent troubles.

To succeed, Cain remembered, they would require skills of observation to find the clues were painted on the cave walls. And if by a miracle they discovered those, they would need cunning and speed and immense strength to get out.

He laughed, his chest vibrating, ash spilling over the bedclothes. And yet they were weak, foolish children who had from the moment the storm started, seven days to save the planet. Even if they did escape the cave, they would still have to find the three deeply hidden tablets in, what, five days?

Cain allowed himself to smile, catching his bottom lip. Oh, happy, happy Earth days! With any luck the little Heirs of Eden would end up buried in the cave with dear, forgetful Old Man Wood. At least then they would be spared having to witness the rapid destruction of Earth, first from the storm, then disease followed by a break up of the entire planet; an outcome they were supposed to prevent.

Maybe he should pay them a visit and see how they were getting along.

He felt a long breath of air fill his new lungs, as the spark of an idea gathered in a dark corner of his mind. If the disease begins to spread from where the storm began, then maybe with his new friend Asgard, he could help speed things up.

He listened as the silence of the night was interrupted by the blissful sound of breathing.

What if he was able to add the disease particles—the lethal pathogen—into human dreams? And what if the dream-giving dreamspinners were to spread it that way? In a couple of nights, Asgard's dreamspinners would accelerate humankind's demise on Earth almost instantaneously.

A numbness, like a freezing chill, rushed through him. A sense of utter brilliance filled him entirely. He'd put humanity out of its misery—as they were doomed anyway.

Cain stroked his chin. Was this the greatest idea of all time? To make the plan work for the dreamspinners, they could manufacture the dream powders here in Havilah. By the time most of the world had received dreams from his new dream powders made from the spider webs of Havilah, Earth wouldn't be worth saving.

Furthermore, if the boy Heirs of Eden, Archie, knew of this, he might come willingly into his body to ensure himself lasting life on Havilah. The lone survivor of the human race.

Cain opened his eyes. Through the boy's clouded vision he stared out of the large window that overlooked the city of Havilaria. Where thousands of years ago lights filled the view, now only a couple of distant fires flickered. His mind crackled with a sense of excitement.

He felt a renewed sense of optimism that his dream of seeing the city of Havilaria lively and bustling once again might very soon come true.

His spirit soared as he realised that this was the way his people might be resurrected. They had been frozen and trapped in domed puddles for millennia, the result of a magical spell that had backfired; a gamble he had made and an error all of his own making. He had been unable to release his human citizens back. Now, the road would finally be clear. After the longest time imaginable, Cain thought, his frozen people would awaken from their glass prisons and breathe life into this land once more.

Cain urged the boy to wake up. He needed to sit. Actually, he needed to run. With his people back, he might lay claim to the one thing he had longed for, the greatest prize of all which had always been just out of reach. The planet where every living thing was originally formed, the same planet which had shut itself down thousands of years ago in order to end a mighty war.

This was the place the Heirs of Eden had to find, yet it would take a miracle for them to open this desolate land. They would not survive the task ahead of them, and there would be nothing left to stop him.

Cain stood up and spread his arms out wide. He roared, his voice echoing into the huge grimy ceiling. 'My time has come at last! The lost planet, the birthplace of all creation, the Garden of Eden, will finally be mine!'

EIGHTY-EIGHT

THE STAIRS

'The stairs are over here,' Daisy yelled. It isn't hard to find—'

'We don't have weird super-eyes like you, Daisy, remember,' Archie replied.

Daisy beckoned them to a tiny, almost invisible gap that opened up when viewed from a certain angle but otherwise looked identical to the cave wall. 'Clever, huh?' she said. 'When you squeeze through, you've got to turn sharply, like this.' She disappeared again.

Archie's fingers found the entrance and he eased himself in. 'It's a bit tight isn't it—'

'Just mind your head,' Daisy quipped, 'or you'll damage the walls.'

He touched his hair and threw her a fake smile.

Daisy moved up a couple of steps out of the way. 'Oh, and the stairwell goes miles up. Isabella won't know what's hit her. She's going to feel it in her legs.'

Old Man Wood's frown grew. 'How am I supposed to get in there?' he complained. 'And what about my things?'

They could see his point. The opening was wide enough for them, but not for a large man like Old Man Wood. Isabella barged past him and through the gap.

'Crawl—on your side—you should be able to make it,' Daisy said, trying to be helpful.

Old Man Wood continued to stare at the gap. He was an old man, not a bendy child.

Isabella held out a hand. 'Your hard hat,' she said. 'Archie, as you're the smallest, you bring his rucksack.' She sniffed the air and pulled a face. 'Come on. Can't wait all day.'

She turned to Old Man Wood. 'We'll go on ahead. See what's at the top. Come at your own pace.'

The children wound their way up the narrow, dark stairwell, each foot feeling for the risers while their feet scuffed the floor like sandpaper. Soon a rhythm built up, their feet trusting that the next riser was roughly equal to the one before, the stairs twisting up and up like a never-ending corkscrew.

After several minutes, Isabella stopped and held her sides. Her heart thumped. 'This is exhausting,' she said as the echoes died down.

'You're seriously unfit,' Daisy said.

'Actually, I'm hungry and freaked out, OK? And I just want to get out of here,' she said. 'It's like we're stuck in a weird, stupid dream playing a game where we have to stay alive.'

'Yeah, I get that,' Daisy said. 'But we survived the first bit, so what makes you think we can't do the rest?'

Isabella reached out into the dark and rested her hand on what she hoped was Daisy's shoulder. 'You sort of died, Daisy. Did you know that? I saved you, although it doesn't make much sense now...'

Daisy leant into the curving wall. 'I don't remember.'

'Well, lucky you,' Isabella said.

'I thought it was Old Man Wood's medicine, Repulsive Mix—'

'He calls it Resplendix Mix,' Isabella said, remembering the two drops on her tongue last night. 'Powerful stuff,' she said. 'Like rolling naked in stinging nettles and eating burning hot coals.'

'For some reason it didn't work on you at the time, Daisy,' Isabella said, remembering how she'd sent a pulse of energy over her. She couldn't bear to think about it. 'How about you, Archie? Remember anything?'

Archie thought for a minute. 'I got fried—'

Daisy laughed, the sound echoing up the stairs and back again. 'Yup. And landed your weird hair—'

'Archie's steely hair isn't funny,' Isabella snapped. 'Nor are your red eyes, or my stupid holey-hands.'

Daisy scowled back. 'Who said it was funny? I just said it was weird.'

'Well, yes—it is very odd, highly illogical' Isabella agreed. 'Nothing makes sense.' She needed to change the subject. 'Anyway, just imagine the devastation out there after the storm.'

Archie rolled his eyes. 'You really think so?'

'Let's say the river is fifteen metres above sea level, and there were approximately five hours of water at a couple of inches of rain per minute. That's more than ten metres of water, Archie. Now augment that with the water pouring off the hills and the spring tide and lunar situation...' Isabella frowned and her voice dropped to a whisper. 'The Vale of York will be underwater. Everything submerged. Only the top of York Minister—' And, although she didn't say it out loud, she hoped like mad that her best friend Sue, and all their other friends were okay, too.

'I know this is awfully fascinating, Bells,' Daisy interrupted, 'but can we please get a move on? I really want to go home and lie in my bed at home.'

'You think the farm will still be there?' Archie asked.

'Of course it will, you numpty. It's on top of a hill overlooking the vale. If our cottage is underwater, then so is most of England.'

The children shuffled upwards regaining the rhythm of the tight stairwell and the steep risers, climbing with both hands and feet. 'You know,' Isabella continued, stopping for a breather, 'these stairs go on and on.'

'Like someone else round here.' Daisy said under her breath.

'But you two are fit—'

Archie chuckled. 'Fitter than you, Isabella. But that's not exactly difficult.'

'Stop it, you two. I was only trying to give you a logical insight into what happened in the storm and a sense of the predicament we might find ourselves in when we get out of here.'

'Isabella, you never make any sense,' Daisy said, pushing her sister ahead. 'I hate to tell you guys, but I have a very strong feeling this is just the start.'

When they emerged at the top of the narrow stairwell, they found themselves in another cave. Beams of light filtered through tiny holes in a large, circular pattern at the far end, around twenty paces away, giving the space the appearance of a sacred chapel.

The children caught their breath, as their eyes became accustomed to the light. Beneath them lay a smooth, undulating rock surface that gave way every now and then to a patch of mud or a puddle of water. Water dripped from the ceiling, and each drip echoed in the quiet.

From the roof of the cavern, which was as high as a small house, jagged edges forced their way out of the stone like giant, misshapen crystals. Along the sides, dripping water had shaped the sides into small alcoves.

'See the problem?' Daisy said, almost in a whisper so that the words didn't crash back over them.

'That's a rock, isn't it, blocking the way out?' Archie said, his voice betraying his disappointment. 'It's stuck in like an egg in an egg cup'.

They stared at a vast boulder whose massive, rotund base sat in the ground as chinks of light illuminated the edges. The problem was obvious; to get out, they would need to roll away the gigantic boulder.

A deep muffled boom echoed up the stairwell.

Archie raised his brows. 'Fifty pounds he's wedged in.'

'You don't even have fifty quid,' Daisy said.

They hurried back to the stairwell.

'Are... you... all right?' Archie yelled.

A few moments later an echo returned, the sounds crashing into one another making them incomprehensible.

'I'll go down,' Archie said. 'There's no way he'll hear us from here.' After a couple of minutes, encased in the musty darkness of the stairwell, he slowed and tried again. 'Where... are... you?'

'Still... at... the... bottom,' the old man replied, taking in to account the reverberating noise. 'Jammed... in... good... and... proper.'

Sweet apples alive, Old Man Wood thought as he ran his leathery hands over the walls, trying to find a nodule to grip onto. He groaned. The problem was that the more he struggled, the more stuck he became.

If he could get back down—and it was a big "if"— he would have no choice but to head back out into the swirling waters thick with flotsam and jetsam. He would have to swim for his life, and he hated swimming.

He wriggled, twisting one way then the other, and managed to slip down a step. His outstretched foot touched a protruding stone and, using it to lever his body round, he pressed down hard; only to feel the stone retract into the step.

Before he had time to gather himself, a clunking noise filled the stairwell, followed by grinding and crunching and crushing sounds. Old Man Wood covered his head with his free arm, waiting for rocks to come crashing down upon him.

None came and, much to his astonishment, the stairwell walls began to pull back until a crashing boom sounded and the noise echoed eerily until eventually it ceased. The stairwell, much to his astonishment, was now at least a foot wider.

'Well, apples alive,' he mumbled, as he sat down and mopped his brow. 'Just in the nick of time. What sort of person would design something like this? And why?'

Old Man Wood dusted himself down, pulled himself together and stood up.

'What's... going... on... down... there?' he heard.

'Don't... you... worry,' Old Man Wood said, as he began his ascent. 'I'm... coming... up... littluns!'

He trundled on, finding a rhythm, stopping on three occasions to catch his breath. At the summit he sat down, taking in large gulps of air as the others gathered around.

'Apples alive! Two hundred and twenty-two steps,' he said. 'High ones and all.'

'What happened?' Archie asked. 'How did it widen?'

Old Man Wood wiped his brow. 'Must've touched a lucky stone, that's all.'

'A lucky stone?' Isabella repeated.

'Oh yes,' Old Man Wood replied. 'Extremely lucky.'

EIGHTY-NINE

KEMP'S PAIN

Trapped inside Cain's ashen body, Kemp twisted in pain.

He should have run off like his friend, Archie, rather than bend to the crackpot will and desires of a deranged ghost. He would have been better off dead, rather than being left alive and having to endure this persistent torture.

So, Kemp thought bitterly, why didn't Cain damn well look after him? The ghost had no understanding of real rest, or other requirements of human beings. Every action forced upon him felt as if rods of red-hot iron had permeated every nerve, muscle, and sinew in his body.

He'd given himself over. He'd put the ghost's coat on and became a body of ash. Right now, it looked like a terrible decision. Perhaps he should have run away, or stolen a car and driven off, or tried to escape the storm a different way. He had thought that Cain was his only option if he wanted to survive the storm. Another jolt of pain shot up his side. Reluctantly, he moved forward, placing one tired leg in front of the other as the ghost demanded.

Cain roared often and punched his subordinates freely. His fists hurt. His head hurt. His brain whirred.

On top of this, Cain was constantly rushing from one strange place to the next without a proper rest, without food and without water. Dizziness had become his constant companion. Soon, he suspected, it would kill him. But would the spirit care? The spirit didn't appear to care about anything.

Worse still, he couldn't even complain.

NINETY

THE BOULDER

Isabella leant on the six-foot-high and eight-foot-wide boulder and groaned. It was all that stood between them and the fresh air outside. Stains marked the boulder's surface with streaky patterns where the rainwater had leached down, the light grey stone now lined with blue and black veiny hues.

Maybe, she thought, it was one of those things that only needed a push. Isabella stepped back a couple of paces and charged at the boulder with her shoulder.

A moment later she shrieked and fell to the floor.

Daisy laughed.

'Oh! shut up, Daisy,' Isabella barked. She got up, turned, gritted her teeth and tried to push the boulder again.

Archie could hardly believe it. 'What are you doing? That's up there with the stupidest thing I've ever seen. Not even Daisy would try something as moronic as that.'

Daisy nodded.

Isabella thumped the floor. 'It's just that... just that I'm hungry and I want to go home and I want to know if Sue and Gus survived and... this is so preposterous and unfair and infuriating after everything we've been through.'

Best friends since birth, this was the longest time Isabella had spent without speaking to Sue and she didn't like it. She missed her friend more than she ever thought she would.

'But pushing it isn't going to help,' Archie said. 'That boulder must weigh more than ten tonnes. You're a fraction of that weight in comparison. You're the scientist, do the maths.'

Isabella frowned, sat down and let her straight brown hair fall over her face, hiding her tears. Aside from the gentle trickle of water cascading through the chamber, silence filled the cavern as the four of them sat and racked their brains.

A short while later, Archie jumped up as an idea formed in his mind. He turned to Old Man Wood. 'You said you touched a lucky stone? Was it like a lever or a knob? Did you push it in, pull it, or did it fall to the side?'

Old Man Wood thought for a second. 'Pushed it with my foot—'

'Well then, if this lump opened up the stairs, why not another to detach the boulder?'

Isabella studied him curiously. 'You think so?'

Archie shrugged. 'We haven't got much else to work with, unless you've got a better idea? Whatever this place is, it has been designed by someone pretty smart —so chances are that he built more than one escape route. What do you think?'

The others shrugged.

'I suggest we start hunting for odd pieces of stone that stick out, you know, secret devices like you see in the movies.'

'Cool,' Daisy said, twiddling a blond curl of hair with her finger. 'Let's scour— I'll start over there.'

They went to different parts of the cave and twisted, pushed, and poked every little cavity. Nothing worked. Not a wobble, a flicker, or a nudge.

The big boulder remained exactly where it was.

NINETY-ONE

SOLOMON GETS ORGANISED

'Chef!' The headmaster called out.

'Yes, Boss,' the portly figure replied.

'How much food did you bring?'

'Thanks to you, Boss, we should have enough for the next three meals.'

'Make it stretch to six.'

'Six! But without a cooker, a significant amount of it is inedible.'

'You need a fire?' Solomon said. 'Then I suggest you start dismantling some of the furniture. The tables and chairs stacked in here will do nicely. We have plenty of books you can use as tinder. Headmaster for twenty years, Solomon didn't relish the prospect of dismantling his beloved life's work, but stranded here with the surviving pupils after the storm he felt he had no choice.

'But there's nothing to cook on, Boss.'

Solomon looked around. 'What sort of thing do you need?'

'Saucepans, frying pans. You know, usual kitchen kilter.'

The headmaster spotted a suit of armour in the corner beside a large stone fireplace. 'Would the armour of Sir Guilleme of Aquataine be suitable? You could adapt the helmet as a saucepan and the breastplate as a frying pan? The leg armour, arm bracers and gauntlets might also come in handy. I imagine the steel is of a decent quality.'

Chef looked at him astonished. 'Isn't that a rather rare antique?'

Solomon looked out of the window and surveyed the devastation around. Nothing but water for miles around. 'The students in the room are a thousand times more valuable than this metal hulk. I imagine the armour is more than happy to be used for some good purpose rather than rusting away in a corner.'

For the first time after a cold, sleepless night, the headmaster felt confident of keeping the fifty-seven children and the seven adults in the tower alive for the next few days. By now, the adults had gathered around him.

'We need to ration,' Solomon continued. 'One meal in the morning; one in the evening. Let's try to catch rainwater for drinking. For sanitation, we are indeed lucky that the tower was built when going to the toilet meant plopping out of hole in the overhang of the tower. That overhang still exists, but we'll need to dislodge a few stones and have a few paperbacks on hand for the obvious. For starters, I'd leave a supply of books from the literary fiction section to wipe with first. Action and adventure—and, dare I say it, survival tomes—at this point might be unwise. Gather several containers of floodwater from the floor below for hand-washing purposes.'

'What shall we do with the children?' Mrs. Rose asked.

'We need structure. We need to set some general rules, and we need a timetable for how our day might pan out,' Solomon smiled. 'We might as well have some fun, though. You two can devise some games.'

'Games?'

'Yes. Low energy but intellectually challenging pastimes to take everyone's mind off things.'

Mr Steele frowned. 'There's nothing in here to play with.'

Solomon turned to him. 'My dear old thing,' he began. 'This is a library, with over a thousand books. Not only can we read, but we can act out numerous plays, and dramas, and then, perhaps, we can use our imaginations.'

Solomon beamed at them. 'If you cannot come up with decent entertainment in these circumstances, my dear fellows, then you should probably consider your positions as teachers.'

NINETY-TWO

DAISY EXPLAINS

'Anyone want to try pushing it?' Archie said hopefully. They shook their heads, a feeling of deflation sweeping over them.

Suddenly, Daisy sprang up.

'Daisy? What is it?'

'I've got an idea,' she said. 'Back in a mo.' She ran the length of the cavern and disappeared down the dark stairwell, her footsteps echoing behind her.

Archie stood up, as though he had instinctively understood her. 'Old Man Wood, exactly where were you when you touched this "lucky stone"?'

'Now, then,' the old man began. 'I hadn't got very far. First step—'

'That's it!' Archie cried. 'We're looking in the wrong place! The clue must be on the walls in the chamber, down there—not up here.'

Without hesitation he shot off after his twin sister leaving Isabella and Old Man Wood looking at one another with an expression of admiration that they could manage this physical feat without a second thought, given their struggle to get up which had left them puffing and panting.

When Archie appeared in the chamber below, Daisy was already studying the paintings on the walls again. Her lips moved as if she could read the story like a book, her eyes fixed in concentration. Occasionally, she moved close to the wall to brush dust off an image or icon, before stepping back to take in the whole scene. Archie was fascinated by the intensity of her stare. Her eyes shone as though a bright red light had been switched on inside her skull and directed out through each iris.

Daisy stared at one particular section for some time. She stood captivated, her mouth open, a frown creasing her forehead. Archie followed suit and looked harder until he noticed the faint image of a cross-legged woman with a crown of leaves resting upon her head, sitting just behind a tree. Her eyes were dark patches, as if someone had coloured them in. Resting on a cushion in her lap, in the shape of a heart, was a locket.

Archie's mind raced and his heartbeat quickened.

Archie thought he recognised this image. Before the storm, he, and the others, had had some troubling and strange dreams significantly about the storm. But now that he looked carefully he was sure that this woman, or a version of her, had featured in them heavily. And there were other things too. He realised he simply couldn't remember and now he slightly regretted not writing them down the moment he'd woken up.

The ghost Cain had appeared to him in the middle of the night, in fact, and had begged him to protect this woman. Although a lot of his memory was hazy, he remembered Cain well, for who could have forgotten such a cold, unsettling presence? According to Cain, this woman was his mother, called the Ancient Woman.

Archie rubbed his front hair spike and noted how his follicles had hardened like steel. Why would the image he had dreamed about be on the wall of this cave?

Were these images their destiny? Daisy certainly seemed to think so.

Archie felt weak. The last time he had seen Kemp, Kemp had given himself to Cain so that Archie could escape. He hoped his friend was okay, wherever he was now.

'You done?' Daisy said, waving her hands in front of his face. 'Woo-hoo! Anyone there?'

'Sorry, miles away,' Archie replied.

'Have you taken all of this in, absorbed as much as you can?'

Archie was a little confused. He looked around. 'Er... yeah. Suppose so.'

'Good,' she said, rubbing her eyes. 'As you are fully aware, my brain is completely rubbish, so from now on, I'm relying on you.' Daisy ran her hands through her curls and noted Archie's blank expression. 'Want me to explain?'

'Explain what?' Archie looked confused.

'What's going to happen, you numpty.'

Archie smiled and nodded.

'Right, you see that little picture at the base of the stairwell?' Daisy pointed at it.

'Uh?' Archie squinted. 'Oh, didn't see that.'

'Well, that shows us how we get out of here. Stroke of luck Old Man Wood pushed the other one, hey!'

Archie stared at the wall. He couldn't see anything. 'Sure,' he said dumbly.

Daisy eyed him. 'You have no idea, do you?'

'Nah. Looks like whitewashed rock to me.'

Daisy sighed. 'Look again at the cave entrance, Archie?'

Archie reddened. He turned and his eyes led him from the steaming, bubbling pool, along the path of the stream, to the entrance.

'Come on, Archie. There's some kind of plastic film or glass blockade or weirdo trick holding the water back. We're underwater!' She marched over to the entrance, put her hands on the material and smacked it with her fist. A hollow, thick ring like a church bell replied.

'Yeah, resin or glass or something,' she said nonchalantly, as though this kind of thing happened every day.

Now that she had reminded him, Archie saw the murky, swirling body of water behind it. He felt sick. 'How did the screen even get there?' he asked.

Daisy shot him a look. 'How should I know?'

'What's it doing?' Archie said nervously. 'Looks like it's wedged in, like a thick sheet of ice.'

'What do you think it's doing?' She hit it again, this time harder. A louder "dong" rang out.

'Daisy! Don't do that!'

'Why not?'

'You'll break it.'

Daisy smiled. 'It won't break, Archie.'

'How do you know? It might.'

'Look,' she said. 'If and when it breaks, we're in serious trouble. Actually, more like very, very, dead. But it's not going to break—quite yet.'

'Really?' Archie croaked.

She paced back to the wall. 'These marks,' she continued pointing to a very faint blur on the wall, 'tell us that there are two levers. One to widen the stairwell, and the other to release the boulder—'

'Of course,' he said rubbing his chin.

She moved in closer and pointed at them. 'These marks... over here.'

'Yeah,' Archie said moving in too high.

'No,' she said, 'these two.'

Archie shook his head.

'Whatever,' Daisy said. 'Thing is, there's one slight problem.'

Archie nodded dumbly.

'Well, you see these funny looking icons next to them?'

Archie bent down. 'Actually, no, not really.'

Daisy tutted. 'Well, they seem to indicate that the moment the lever is pushed the staircase begins to retract.'

'Cool.'

'No, Archie! Seriously uncool.'

He frowned. 'Why?'

'Because when that happens that barrier over there cracks, and water starts pouring in.'

Archie grimaced. 'OK. Yup, not so cool.' He turned to the entrance. 'So that thing—'

'Collapses, or dissolves, or something, while the person who pressed it has to rush up the stairs before it crushes them.'

'Jeez.'

'Your brain is finally stirring,' Daisy said, rather triumphantly. 'It's all written here.'

Silence filled the cavern as they thought through their situation.

'If you're right,' Archie said at length, 'we're dead, whatever we do.'

'I'm right, bro,' she said. 'That barrier is protecting a pretty big hole and as brain-box Isabella kept on telling us, there's one hell of a lot of water out there. The cave entrance is now several metres below the water line of the river and the water level is higher than entrance to the cave. This means that water must stretch for miles above entire Vale of York like a vast lake. And water, as you know, always finds the easiest route—'

'You seriously think that water stretches the whole way across the vale?'

Daisy shot him a look as if his brain had a leak. 'Of course it does,' she said. She pointed at the covered entrance. 'When it goes—'

'The pressure of water flooding in would be like firing a tsunami up the stairs,' Archie concluded.

'Correct-a-mundo,' Daisy said, punching him lightly on the shoulder. 'Now you're getting the picture.'

They stared at each other.

'The longer we wait here,' Archie whispered, 'the higher the water rises and the greater the pressure.' It was beginning to sink in.

'Yeah, something like that.'

'God almighty. Even deader,' Archie said. 'Have you got a plan?'

'Me? Nope. But if there was ever a time for Isabella's brains to come up with something, it's right now.'

NINETY-THREE

GOOD NEWS, BAD NEWS

The twins held their sides, doubled over, catching their breath. Climbing the stairs again had not been easy.

'There's good news,' Archie panted, 'and there's bad news. Which do you want first?'

'The good news.'

'OK,' Daisy said. 'Give me a sec.' She extended a leg and stretched her hamstring. 'OK. So, the good news is, I've found the lever to move the boulder.'

Isabella clapped her hands. 'Brilliant!' She noted her enthusiasm wasn't shared. 'And the bad news?'

'Basically, we die if we activate it.'

'Die—really? That's pretty drastic.' Isabella eyed both of them. 'It's another of your silly little jokes, right?'

Daisy raised an eyebrow as Archie folded his arms across the chest.

'You're... you are kidding, aren't you?'

Their serious expressions said otherwise.

'But I never saw any of this,' Isabella countered. 'Why didn't I see it?'

'I did though, Isabella,' Daisy said. 'I'm not really sure how these eyes work, but it's on those walls, I promise. On my life.'

Isabella listened as Archie and Daisy explained. Then she repeated it, just to be sure. 'What you're saying is that one of us has to press this lever and run like mad up two hundred and twenty-two stairs while the whole thing starts closing in and falling apart and water starts crashing through the cave opening. And then, and only then, will the boulder up here open.'

'Yup,' Daisy said blankly. 'And then we have to move on to the next part of the puzzle, finding three eggs, if I'm not mistaken. Anyway, if we fail, it screws the world. Apparently.'

Isabella wrinkled her nose and played with her straight brown hair and then stamped her foot hard down on the ground. 'Ridiculous.'

'Well, yes, it is,' Daisy agreed, 'but the longer we wait, the greater the water pressure, the harder it gets. Anyone want to volunteer?'

Old Man Wood put his hand up. 'I'll do it.'

Daisy smiled sweetly at the old man. 'No, you're far too old, big, and much too slow. Sorry. Anyone else?' she looked at the receding faces of the others.

Isabella cut in. 'Daisy you're nimble, quick... super-fit. It's got to be you—'

'Why don't I do everything?' Daisy replied, crossly. 'Look, my legs are pretty stiff after yesterday's football match.' Star player for her school, Daisy had been left battered and bruised by the opposition even before yesterday's storm. It had taken all the potency of Old Man Wood's Resplendix Mix to revive her. 'Besides,' she continued, 'I've just climbed up here for the third time. That's six hundred and... er—'

'Sixty-six.'

'I knew that!' Daisy fumed. 'You do it? You're two years older and you've only done it once.'

Isabella was running out of excuses. 'Archie. Come on—this is just up your street.'

Archie shook his head. 'I'm way slower than Daisy and I've done it twice.'

Isabella smiled—her lips wavering. 'Oh... oh, hell! All right. As usual it's going to have to be me.' Her lips quivered and then she burst into tears. 'I hate this,' she sobbed and wiped her eyes. 'You're right; you've done it twice. It's only proper that it's... me. I hate this stupid, nonsensical stuff. It's... it's—'

Old Man Wood moved in and enveloped her with a hug like a comfort blanket. 'Now then, young Isabella. I'm not sure we have a choice, do we? You're a strong runner so you'll be just fine. I can feel it in my bones.'

Daisy smiled. 'I don't mean to be pushy,' she said, 'but the longer we wait—'

'Yes, yes I know. You've already told me,' Isabella said. 'Oh, Daisy, you're finally finding some brains!' She gave her sister a big hug, took a deep breath and steadied herself.

'Old Man Wood, you stay here with Archie. Daisy, you'd better come with me and show me how these lever things work. When I've got it, get back up the stairs, and when you're at the top, shout down. Everyone got that? I'll push the lever, scream, and run for it. OK?'

They nodded.

Archie's face had turned as pale as snow and his hair stood rigid. His dark eyes watered. 'You'd better make it, sis,' he said. 'Go like the wind.'

Old Man Wood furrowed his brow. 'Good luck, young 'un,' he said, as she folded into him again. 'Believe in yourself, little Isabella, and you'll be just fine.'

Quietly, Isabella turned and began the long walk down the steep, winding stairs with Daisy following on behind.

NINETY-FOUR

KINGSFORD'S DILEMMA

Prime Minister Kingsford was basking in the last of the season's sun on his lounger by the pool of a villa on the Amalfi coast in Italy when the news broke. Three days into his break and the phones were going crazy. Typical, he thought. Of all the weeks! Here he was with his family, unwinding from the rigours of government, when an emergency of simply epic proportions springs out of nowhere.

It was true; you never got time out in this job he mused, and with an election looming, he had needed just one week to recharge his batteries. And now this. Oh well, what did he expect?

Running the country, he thought, was like looking after thousands of plates spinning on sticks and making sure that each person twiddling a stick kept it moving, If one plate fell, it became an event or an outcry or a scandal. When a whole pile of them crashed, the pointing finger of the media spotlight inevitably turned on him.

He caught a helicopter back to the United Kingdom the following day to see it for himself. By the time he arrived, England's heart lay in ruins. As the chopper flew north from London, he saw at first hand the extraordinary scenes beneath him. From as far south as Lincolnshire, through the Midlands, into South York-shire then on and up through the Vale of York between the Moors and Dales, he found a country underwater. Entire towns submerged, fields transformed into huge, muddy lakes, only occasionally interspersed by protruding islands of high ground.

His leadership hung by a thread. Those damn media people. What on earth could he do about a biblical-style freak flood? Furthermore, the damage had been so sudden, so brutal and so unexpected. The meteorologists hadn't picked out the storm as any huge matter for concern. No one foresaw the impending disaster.

Coordinating a rescue effort in these conditions and setting up COBRA, the emergency government council, took time. Time which he realised they didn't have. To the rest of the country, their efforts appeared disorganised and uncoordinated. 'Too little action, too late' the newspaper headlines screamed.

It must look he thought, like utter shambles

But they were doing everything they could.

Victims of the storm were being found every hour, bloated and floating in the waters, thousands of people displaced, homes ruined, infrastructure wrecked, businesses destroyed and lives shattered. The difficulty was that the rains hadn't let up enough to enable the waters to recede, while high tides meant the water had nowhere to go.

From his vantage point in the chopper, the Prime Minister now understood how desperate the situation truly was. The military faced an uphill battle to coordinate a salvage operation in such adverse conditions. But, as the hours went by, fingers pointed accusingly at the Prime Minister.

Worse still was the latest development. Word had reached the medical centres that a virus was spreading. The media had already latched on to it and world governments were clamouring for updates. Yet there was very little he could tell them. The only option was to meet the experts in North Yorkshire and find out what they knew first hand, so he might gauge what they were up against.

Kingsford knew his way around a dilemma. Be seen and reach out to as many people he could. Make sure there were endless pictures and footage of himself offering to help. Make the right noises, be actively involved. With any luck, this virus would go away as medical centres were set up and he could return to London.

The helicopter descended towards the peaks of the Yorkshire Dales. Kingsford gritted his teeth and readied himself for touchdown and the blaze of cameras.

NINETY-FIVE

ISABELLA'S CHALLENGE

'Right, Isabella,' Daisy began, pointing at the stairs. 'Here are the levers. That's the higher protrusion Old Man Wood knocked with his foot. The bottom one—here— is the dude you need to worry about.'

Isabella shook like a rattle.

Daisy noticed and reached out for her hand. 'Then run, Isabella.,' she said, earnestly. 'Run like you've got a seriously massive great monster after you. Got it?'

Isabella's eyes were wide open, her skin a sickly pale colour.

'Don't stop till you reach the top,' Daisy continued. 'Understand?'

Her sister nodded.

'Look, are you sure you can do this? I mean, I'll do it... if you can't.'

'No, no, Daisy,' she said pulling herself together. 'You must be shattered. Call down when you're ready. Gives me plenty of time to compose myself.'

Daisy smiled, trying hard not to betray her nerves, and moved in close to give her sister a hug. 'You can do it. Easily,' she said, her voice croaking. 'Piece of Mrs Pye's cake, sis. Easy-peasy lemon-squeazy.'

Soon, Isabella heard a croaky, eerie voice echoing down, which sounded nothing like her sister's voice.

Time to push the stone.

She ran her fingers through her hair, conscious that she was shaking almost uncontrollably. She inhaled deeply and tried to remember her relaxation classes. *Centre yourself, be calm,* she thought.

Breathe.

She moved out into the cave once more for a last look at the quiet, gentle steaming pool and the curious murals and the extraordinary seal covering the entrance. The stillness made her reflect on what had gone before and what was to come. When she was home, in her confines of her comfy room, she'd think it through, work out the events logically, like a scientist. Perhaps then the madness of their situation would be explained and vanish like a bad dream.

She stretched her legs and moved in front of the protruding knob.

Here goes, time to do it.

She put her hand on the stone and leant on it with all her weight, waiting for something to give, something to click—anything.

But, however hard she pushed, nothing happened.

Isabella stepped back into the cavern and took in a lungful of air. *Why wouldn't the damn lever move? What if it's stuck, jammed in some way? Perhaps she wasn't strong enough?*

She gathered her strength and slammed her foot down on it. Still, it would not yield.

'Right, you evil, stubborn, stupid thing,' she roared. 'I know what you need: a bloody great whack.' She marched into the cave and scoured the ground.

With considerable effort she rolled a boulder across the floor and squeezed it through the narrow entrance.

On her knees, she manoeuvred it up to the first step and, wary that it might topple off, quickly heaved it up to the second step, followed by the third. On the fourth it wobbled and she caught it, pushing it back on the ledge.

She breathed deeply.

Four more steps to go and, with the correct aim and allowance for the curvature of the stairs, she'd roll it off and nail the lever.

Her mood lifted.

At the sixth step, she wondered whether it would be enough. Quickly she did another mass and velocity sum in her head and tried to work out if there might be enough momentum and downward force to utterly pulverise it.

She cursed.

Up to the seventh step. Now the eighth.

'Right. Here you go—you horrible little, annoying, stubborn, nasty knob.'

Her fingers slid underneath the overhanging stone.

'Time to smash you into tiny little bits!'

❉

Archie and Daisy listened, their ears straining, the silence unbearable. Archie nibbled his fingernails until he'd run through both hands. Occasionally, he'd wonder if he'd heard a sound, like a click or thud, and he'd peer nervously down the stairwell.

Daisy shook her legs out, shut her eyes and imagined Isabella readying herself to push the stone lever, urging her to do so. She found that when she focused, she heard, quite clearly, Isabella's gasps and groans and mutterings, but the words bounced off the walls, reaching her ears as garbled sequences of noise.

The minutes passed. Daisy slumped down the wall. 'What if she can't do it?' she whispered.

Archie shrugged. 'What if she's not doing it right?'

'There's nothing to do wrong,' Daisy replied.

'Maybe it's stuck—you know, jammed,' Archie said. 'It must be pretty old—'

'Nah, I reckon her brain's stopped... or she's had a nervous breakdown...'

They leaned back on the hard stone and closed their eyes.

'Old Man Wood,' Archie asked, 'what do you think?'

The old man stared at the wall as though completely lost, miles away, and shook his head. 'Don't know, littlun,' he said.

The twins shook their heads.

'It must be at least ten minutes,' Daisy said, nudging him.

'I'm sure she's fine,' Old Man Wood lied. 'Just preparing herself, like she does.'

Daisy stood up and walked over to the stairwell. 'She's down there all right—I can hear grunts and scrapes. It's as if she's moving a stone, or a rock, or something.'

'I can't hear anything at all,' Archie said, leaning over. 'Are you sure?'

'Yep. Quite sure,' Daisy replied, her voice quivering. 'It's not right, Archie. Something has gone terribly wrong.'

Archie didn't know what to say. He watched as Daisy drew a picture in the sand.

She stared at it for some time. 'Archie,' she said, excitement in her voice, 'I think I know why Isabella's struggling.'

He shrugged. 'What is it?'

'She needs to hit it with a pebble—a stone—something hard. I've got to tell her —all it needs is a tap, a tiny little tap.'

NINETY-SIX

KEMP, IN CAIN

Kemp woke as a surge of Cain's energy tugged on his tendons and yanked at his muscles, threading into the fibres of his body. Heat radiated from the nerve endings of his fingers down to the tips of his toenails.

Kemp shrieked as the burning sensation hit him as if he'd been tossed into a bath of scalding water which forced him up and off the bed.

Why wouldn't Cain let him be? Did he have any idea of the damage he was doing?

Putting one leg ahead of the other was like wading through treacle, and the treacle was filled with electrical current. Kemp found himself almost unable to move. He was in agony, famished and desperate to sleep.

He found himself being forced to move through a huge room, in which he could discern the outline of just about the largest fireplace he'd ever seen. His head swam and he became aware of a door opening and then a hard table. His posture sat down on what he presumed was a chair.

A platter arrived in front of him containing tiny foodstuffs like nothing he'd ever seen before. Slug-like creatures that wriggled, foul stinking jelly, and cakes consisting of insects and flies. Breakfast?

His hand burned and he followed its directional path. Now his fingers burned. He picked up a gooey, snail-like object.

Cain was encouraging him to eat.

By the time the slimy snail arrived in their combined mouth, it was covered by a thick layer of ash. As the food morsel found its way into his body, he gagged. A burning pain shot up through his stomach and the snail flew across the room.

No water had passed into his stomach the entire time he'd been within Cain. It was little more than a day but it felt like a month. He'd been offered a liquid but it was nothing like water, more like slime. Worse still, even though everything had an overbearing odour of ash, he caught its sulphuric stink, like rotten eggs.

Every time he ate, and he'd tried every item laid before him, he spewed it back out. By now he was desperate for something. The bearded elf-like servant set another plateful in front of him. This time it was a slippery purple ball, the size of a ping-pong ball, with black and yellow pustules on it.

Kemp could hardly bear to think about trying it, but a sharp ache shot into his head. He shut his eyes and he stretched out an arm. As he attempted to pick it up, Schmerger, the servant, appeared with what looked like a pair of large tweezers and carefully aimed it in the general direction of their mouth.

It tasted like tapioca eggs with an outer shell of bark and sand. His stomach heaved. Schmerger fed him another foodstuff, a thin hard-backed slice of cake with a soft gooey centre that smelt of oil. He put it towards his mouth. The odour was too awful. He tried to chew with his half teeth.

...why... eat... slowly?

Kemp thought he could hear every second or third word, muffled, but he had no way of responding.

Come... much...... little time... world...... useless... to sort... hurry...

Was Cain talking to him again?

Kemp chewed as best as he could and as he ground the cake between his constantly re-growing teeth, a liquid suddenly burst out flooding his mouth. He involuntarily vomited.

Kemp's swollen stomach felt as if the tip of a wooden stake jabbed within his gut. His legs felt like lead weights. His head throbbed.

Kemp knew that his body was failing. It was as if his body wasn't even there. The pain of the burning seared him as if being sizzled in a frying pan and now his strength had gone. Poisoned, every last bit of it.

He stumbled and fell.

The last thing Kemp saw was a plume of ash bursting in front of his eyes.

And then blackness and relief of feeling nothing at all.

NINETY-SEVEN

THE PROTRUDING STONE

Isabella stared in disbelief, helpless to do anything as the square lump slipped through her fingers. The stone spun, touched the corner of the next step and launched into the air. Isabella gasped. She hadn't figured that it would bounce.

Clipping the protruding lever, the boulder smashed into the wall and shattered over the floor.

Isabella groaned, put her head in her hands and sank to the floor, defeated.

Idiot! Fool! What would the others say?

And then it happened. Everything shook. Chunks of stone sprayed from the ceiling and Isabella wrapped her arms over her head.

Then she heard a grinding noise; the gear mechanisms whirling, groaning, and crunching all around her.

The next rumble threw her off the step and she crashed down to the foot of the stairwell. She poked her head into the chamber and gasped. Cracks had appeared all over the barrier. Water dripped down until the drip became leaks, flowing like thick tears.

Her heart thumped wildly.

She'd done it!

More debris flew.

Isabella swore and started up the stairs, one at a time, then two. Onwards, upwards.

Then a boom, like a giant wave crashing into the chamber, filled her with a dread she had never believed possible.

The panel.

Isabella screamed and urged herself on, faster and faster. The sound of water was gaining on her, the crushing noises of the stairwell narrowing.

She focused and before she knew it her hands and feet sprang off each step like a tiger. She was bounding, round and round the stairwell, faster and faster, up and up, like a blur.

The walls on either side were so tight her sides were being scraped like cheese in a grater. A blast of wind caught her now, water rushing alongside, overtaking her, carrying her up to the peak.

She took a last gasp of air, stretched her arms out in front, and pointed her toes like a ballerina.

When she smashed into the ceiling, her hands padded her impact but she felt herself crumple in a heap.

Then a black veil swept over her and she felt no more.

Daisy knew what was coming. The moment she heard the wave of water rushing up the stairwell she was hit by a massive gust of air that propelled her on and, using its momentum, she threw herself out of its path and into the cave.

She stood up and gasped.

Suddenly, from out of the top of the stairwell water burst out and rebounded from the ceiling, dousing the cavern like a fire-fighter's hose.

Almost immediately, a large object splattered into the ceiling like a rubber ball, before clattering into her.

To her horror, a millisecond before she was knocked out cold, she realised it was Isabella.

NINETY-EIGHT

THE BOULDER

Archie thumped the air. 'Keep going, keep going!' he yelled, as the boulder at the front of the cave began to rise.

But as quickly as his euphoria started, it ceased, for the boulder sat in the entrance, the same size, the same width, but with no part nestled under the ground.

Why didn't it roll away?

A ghostly whistle spiralled out of the stairwell.

The girls!

A jet of wind shot out followed by a roaring, tsunami-like noise growing louder and louder and just as Daisy threw herself out of the stairwell a powerful jet of water followed and smashed into the ceiling.

The next thing he knew, both of his sisters lay on the ground, motionless.

Already the chamber was filling with water, the boulder acting like a seal.

Archie ran to Isabella and found her grated in gashes; some deep and dark red, others pink where skin had been chiselled away by the sides. Blood ran through her hair and streaked across her face, her arms, and her legs. Her body was limp, her arms bent over like towels over a washing line.

Archie moved fast. 'Old Man Wood!' he screamed. 'Get over here!'

Together, they waded through the water, moving the girls high up onto a ledge.

Old Man Wood pulled out the bottle of Resplendix Mix and placed the seal to Daisy's lips. Almost immediately, she opened her eyes, spluttered, and winced.

Now, it was Isabella's turn. She gasped as the first drop hit her tongue, coughed on the second, and screamed as the third drop set to work.

Old Man Wood kissed her forehead. 'Be brave, young Isabella,' he said soothingly. 'Healing, littlun, is a painful business.'

And this, he thought, as he studied her ripped torso, was really going to hurt.

Archie swam to the huge boulder. He weighed up his options as Isabella screamed in agony.

It spurred him on.

If he could somehow roll the stone, jog it a couple of millimetres, then at least some of the water would rush out. He had to try, even if it looked impossibly absurd.

Archie touched on a little ridge. The cave was now filling with water fast. Standing up, he took a breath and dived down under the surface. He bent his knees and, with every ounce of strength he had, heaved.

Archie resurfaced, drew in a lungful, and dived again. This time, as he pushed, he felt the grey mass slip on its axis—he was sure of it.

Standing on tiptoes he glanced over towards Old Man Wood who held the girls as high to the roof as he could beneath the rising water level.

One more go. It had to be this time.

He ducked under. His fingers grasped the stone finger-hold and he crouched low, bending on his haunches. Then, gritting his teeth and using every muscle in his body, he pushed.

It shifted, fractionally.

Archie resurfaced, treading water, gasping for oxygen.

It wasn't working fast enough. He had to do something else. Perhaps he could rock it from the top, and create a gap for the water to slip out and away.

He swam to the side and climbed. At the top, he pawed the ceiling with his hands while his feet gripped the boulder.

Archie bent his knees and pressed.

Nothing. He felt hopeless. He had no more than a couple of minutes.

Archie shut his eyes as an image of him trying to push a giant boulder rushed into his head.

He grinned and the grin turned into a chuckle.

And the more he saw himself, in his mind's eye, doing something so dumb, so stupid, so ridiculously impossible, the louder he laughed.

A boy trying to move a boulder?

He smacked and kicked the boulder and, using the ceiling as a prop, he pushed and pulled in a rocking motion, hooting like a maniac bending his knees to try and gain traction.

'What a stupid, stupid mug you are, Archie de Lowe,' he sang, between howls.

He was still laughing when he felt the extraordinary sensation of movement, as if he was slipping on ice.

A wobble, then water flashing on either side of him.

Archie held on.

'Oh no!' he screamed. 'HEEELP–!'

And in the nick of time, as the boulder started to rotate, he hurled himself to safety.

As the roar of water rushed by, the huge boulder thundered down the hillside smashing everything in its path.

With his chest heaving, Archie looked up towards the girls.

Daisy grinned back, from ear to ear. 'Jeez, Archie,' she said. 'You are one seriously crazy individual.'

NINETY-NINE

SUE AND GUS KISS

Gus took a sharp intake of breath. Oh, my goodness. Her eyes shone like jewels. His heart raced and his blood pumped fiercely through his veins. A strange kind of electrical current passed through him.

What the hell was going on?

She leaned in and kissed him; just a peck on his lips. She held her mouth close. He felt her breath on his cheek. It felt so perfect, so timely. Gus felt his head swim, stood up, and cracked his head on the wooden frame of the canopy above them.

Sue grinned. 'You've never kissed anyone before?'

Gus rubbed his head. 'Yeah, of course I have,' he lied, badly.

The corners of Sas's mouth turned up mischievously. 'Who?'

Gus couldn't think fast enough. His head was in a muddle. 'Seriously? Do you really have to know?'

'Yeah! Absolutely! No secrets out here. Come on!'

Gus played for time and rubbed his head. 'Er, no... I can't—'

'Go on!' Sue demanded. 'I insist! I promise I won't tell.'

'OK. It was, um, Daisy,' he blurted out.

Sue reeled. 'Daisy de Lowe, Annie Chubb or Anna Martin,' she fired back.

'Oh, ah, the first one,' he mumbled.

'Well now, you sneaky devil,' she said. 'Daisy de Lowe, huh?'

Gus reddened. 'Er, yeah. Didn't last for long,' he said, trying to sound casual while busying himself in the food box.

Sue frowned. Boys loved Daisy because she was beautiful and cool. But she was aloof, off in her own little world half the time. And anyway, she knew the de

Lowes better than she knew her own family and the whole thing seemed... unlikely. He was lying through his teeth. Maybe he had a crush on her.

'Now,' she said. 'Let's be honest, that wasn't a great start. We could give it another go if you'd like?'

Gus drooled. His speech deserted him. He nodded like a puppy dog.

Very gently they leaned in.

The moment their lips came together, Gus tried very hard not to snicker. He lurched forward and bashed his teeth on hers. There was a clank, which sounded a great deal louder to both of them than it really was.

He pulled away. 'Blimey, sorry. That was totally rubbish, wasn't it?'

Sue smiled. But before he could move again, she looked deeply into his eyes, put a finger over his lips and slowly replaced it with her own.

CAIN SUMMONS HELP

Cain's ashen exterior struck the floor and ash soared into the air.

'What is it now?' Cain screamed. 'Something's wrong, I cannot feel the boy,' he yelled. 'Schmerger, Schmerger—where are you?'

Cain's elfin manservant with his long black beard instantly arrived. 'You called, Master?'

'This damnable boy is not working,' Cain said, from his position within the ashen body lying on the floor. 'Do you think he does it purposefully? Does he do it to spite me?'

Schmerger made his way over to the pile of ash, grabbed what he hoped was an arm and manoeuvred, with great difficulty, the ashen bundle into a chair. Stepping back, the servant coughed and dusted himself down. 'I am unsure as to how you mean to continue your relations with this being.'

'What are you talking about, Schmerger?'

'It appears the creature may have requirements of which, sire, we are unaware. Is it alive within you?'

'I will check his heart,' Cain replied. He went silent and listened within their combined body using his senses to pick out life. 'Inside, there is a murmur.'

Schmerger rubbed his long black beard. 'It has come to my attention that he has barely ingested any of the food I laid out for him. Maybe these beings do not eat what we eat. Or it might be that he requires another source of energy? All living things must feed correctly to create energy, sire.'

In his excitement, Cain hadn't stopped to think through the boy's needs. 'Then we must find out what they are—and soon. Having this child within me is an absolute wonder, Schmerger. You have no idea—I must make it work. Do you have any idea how invigorating it is to be alive again after so long?'

Schmerger moved closer, and prodded the pile of ash with a long finger.

'What is wrong?' Cain asked. 'Now that I have substance, I find Havilah in ruins. My human people rest in their millions in frozen domes upon the ground, the other elves and trolls and primitive beings are hopeless creations. Havilaria is a deserted, empty city. And now the boy fails.'

Schmerger kept his counsel. 'Sire, this is a most unusual situation.'

'Of course it is an unusual situation, you fool!' Cain snapped. 'You are here to look after my "unusual situations". How can I restore Havilah if the boy is faulty?'

'Master, it is hard for me to know what species of being you have merged with. Tell me, is it one of the ancient breed of humans, or, perhaps a barbarian from the mountains of Havilah?' Schmerger knew to tread carefully. 'Invertebrate and fungus foods are not suitable, that is plain to see, so I have ruled out that it is of the humano-ape tribes who live in our great southern forests.'

'Clearly not,' Cain replied. 'The boy is made of flesh and blood from a planet called Earth. He is a human being, much like our own humankind who live in these domes upon the floors—'

'Of course,' Schmerger said, bowing. 'Then perhaps he requires a diet to fit humankind?'

'Well, of course he does!' Cain roared. 'The boy needs earthly foods and he needs them now! Tell me, do you know what the diet of man is, Schmerger?'

'There are many scrolls on the subject. I will pull them from the great library.'

'Does the library still exist?' Cain heard himself say.

'My great, great, great, great grandfather,' Schmerger replied, 'locked the library in case the knowledge of this land was to end up in the wrong hands. I have the key.'

Cain remained quiet trying to detect the life within him. 'Excellent, Schmerger,' he said. 'I fear the child is weak. I hear almost nothing.' A terrible feeling washed over him. 'If the boy dies...'

'I take it you can remove yourself, Sire?' Schmerger asked.

'I do not know. I don't see why not, If I leave, though, Schmerger, I will end up how I was. That is not good enough. No! I need a body that will willingly be a part of me. Understand this, this miracle may not happen again. If I were to release the boy and he recovers, would he give himself to me again freely?'

Cain listened for the heartbeat again.

Schmerger looked on anxiously. 'Is there anyone we can contact as to the boy's health?'

Cain thought for a minute. 'Are there any humans left alive here in Havilah at all?'

'Only in the caves, but they are the ancient type, unaffected by the magic,' Schmerger replied. 'They are troublesome and cruel; they would not help.'

Cain groaned. 'Who else?'

Schmerger stroked his long beard, contemplating the situation. Suddenly a light sparked in his eyes. 'As a spirit, sire, a ghost, you are part of another world. You might summon a human spirit to advise you.'

'Yes,' Cain said, as the idea sunk in. 'Brilliant, Schmerger. Of course. But who?'

'A spirit that is connected with him, one of his ancestors. Humans die so young, there will be many.'

Cain sat and thought. 'You're right, humans have a bond like no other. I will call for them, Schmerger. You should not be here when they arrive.' Then Cain added, as he often did, 'Good work, servant of mine, you will live to see another day.'

Even as a ghost, Cain often threatened to kill him. Part of the job, Schmerger suspected. The servant heeded his master's advice, turned, and walked to the door where he waited.

The room fell into silence. Cain began chanting, his voice calling out into the universe.

Spirits awaken, spirits come near.
Spirits come close you have nothing to fear.
I call to those who connect with this boy.

He stopped and waited.

O spirits from the reaches of time and space,
Come hither to connect with me here in this place.

Schmerger trembled as a wind enveloped him.

A host of ghostly presences whooshed into the building.

'Spirits of this boy,' Cain called out, 'I call upon you as a spirit myself. I cannot ascend into the sky, or plant my feet upon land, but I will always live. This child of man, your relative on Earth, willingly joined with me and in return I have saved him from a great tempest on that planet.'

What an ugly bunch, Cain thought, with matted hair, thrusting chins and thick red lips.

'The boy is failing fast,' Cain said. 'I have fed and watered him, but I do not understand his needs. The child requires your help. I call on the newest of you to reveal yourselves now.'

In an instant, a silvery, opaque-looking man appeared, kneeling in front of them.

Cain sensed the spirit's sadness, and saw a youthful, bent head and mournful face. 'Thank you. And you are...'

'I am the spirit of the boy's father,' he said in a deep voice.

The boy lost his father young, Cain thought.

'Thank you,' Cain said. 'There is no one better suited to help, other than the child's mother.'

'Indeed,' said the ghost. 'His mother lives and she knows not of her child. I was taken when our son was an infant. We were together...' the voice tapered off, sadness spilling out.

Suddenly things made sense to Cain. In his efforts to persuade the boy, he had told Kemp that joining forces would not only save his own life from the flood, but would save Cain and Cain's mother. Now, he realised why that had been so important to the boy.

Kemp had never known his own mother.

In the next second, Kemp's father reached into Cain's ashen body, his body following.

Moments later, the ghost re-emerged and settled over the ash. 'What have you done to him?' he roared. 'He is a child whose body is poisoned and burned almost to death.'

Cain hadn't expected the ghost to reach through him and into their combined body. He kept calm. 'Be assured, I did not mean any harm. We joined together in a union. I have been like you for a long, long time, but I am of the old type and my spirit is strong. In order to survive the destruction on Earth the boy came freely to me. He means more to me than you know.'

The ghost snivelled. 'It is fortunate that he is strong. If you do not wish to lose him, you have one option. Return him to Earth where they can nurse and nourish him. Can you do this?'

'I will try,' Cain said.

'There is little time,' the ghost said. 'The alternative is that he comes with us.'

'Should he go to his mother's side?'

The ghost shot into the air and swirled around before floating down. 'No. She may reject him. She does not recall ever having a son. Her mind was damaged. And he is too sick.'

'Then where shall I leave him?'

'Somewhere he will be found and helped.'

'And there is no one else who can help?' Cain asked.

Kemp's father swayed one way and then the other, testing the vibrations. 'His friends will have the answers,' Kemp's father said, as he drifted away as though on a breeze. 'His friends will know,' he repeated as he spiralled higher and higher and eventually away through the ceiling.

Cain felt him go. Spirits were a curious lot, but they did generally have their bloodline's best interests at the top of their limited agenda.

Cain mulled over the ghost's words. Was he referring to that confounded Archie de Lowe as the boy's best friend?

FISHING

Gus was so shocked that it took him a while before he joined in. Was it revolting or nice? It *was most definitely slippery and a bit fishy*. His tongue appeared to be battling like a mini eel, almost of its own accord. Either way, he couldn't decide. All of a sudden, a strange shot of energy passed straight through him, like a stab of electricity.

An electric eel, he thought.

He'd broken it off—a smile fixed on his face. 'Tuna?' he said.

Sue looked confused. 'Tuna?'

'Er. Yup.' Gus couldn't think why he'd said it. 'I'm totally starving.'

Truthfully, he felt a little out of control. Kissing could wait.

He noted her disappointed face. 'I ruined it, didn't I?'

'No,' she said, looking a bit embarrassed. 'Well, yes, you did a bit.'

'Sorry. It's just... you, er, surprised me and... I'd just opened—'

'Don't say a word,' she said. 'I'm starving too. Let's eat.' She prodded him gently on the arm. 'There's plenty of time for practicing!'

Gus divided the tuna onto the two paint-pot lids they used for plates and handed out two biscuits and half an apple. It wasn't really enough, but it was better than nothing. Gus had realised that running out of food was a real possibility, so he'd divided their foodstuff into meals that might last for two weeks. Realistically, he doubted they could hold out that long. However, in the back of his mind, if they could catch fish, it would be a "game-changer".

So long as the three big water containers were topped up, using his upside-down umbrella water-catching device, they would survive. If it stopped raining for more than three days, then they were in trouble.

After their meal, Gus tried not to think about kissing, and the buzz that tingled all the way through him. He set about thinking how they could get 'The Joan of' back to land. His first task was to make a sail.

Occasionally, he'd ask Sue to hold things or to pass him a nail or a piece of wood. Then, he gave her a length of string and Sue threaded it down a section of the tarpaulin which he'd cut with his penknife. As she did this, he wrapped the line around a long length of wood, which was to be the mast. When this was done, he wedged the upright in between the seat and the prow of the rowing boat so that it stuck up in front of 'The Joan of'. For good measure, he nailed the timber into the prow and bound it with rope.

The course they sailed, he realised, would be the direction the wind blew. He hoped like crazy they'd be fortunate enough to pick up an easterly which would blow them back to the English coast.

Wherever they were going, perhaps now they would get there a little faster.

While Gus moved up and down the boat, making adjustments and checking his ropes and trying to get wind in his sail, Sue reached into the wooden box stowed under the main seat and fetched out a fishing line.

She remembered a conversation between Archie and Kemp when they'd been discussing their fishing tackle. Something to do with sweet corn as bait and shiny objects that looked like large earrings, called Lures.

She inspected the nylon line. Then, she found a double hook that looked like a tiny anchor, which curved back on itself. Surrounding it were some faded feathers with a hint of metallic sparkle. She opened a tin, popped two corns onto the spikes and a couple in her mouth.

Carefully she removed one of her own earrings and, using the fishing line, tied it close to the hook below the feathers. Very slowly, she let the line out, further and further until the lure disappeared behind a roll of water.

Gus spoke to her from the other end. 'Mind if I squeeze in? I've just got to tension the mast and then, hopefully, we're done.'

Sue shuffled out of the way as Gus threw the rope above the canopy to the other end, ducked into the boat, and joined her.

The moment he pulled the rope, the wind caught in the tarpaulin and the boat lurched forward.

'Wa-hey!' he yelled.

He reached down and squeezed her shoulder. 'We'll get somewhere in no time,' he joked.

'Or is that nowhere in some time?' she threw back at him.

Gus beamed. The sea was calm and the waves lapped around the bow of the boat as it moved ahead.

'Now, how about we go back to just before "tuna"?'

She giggled, turned, and they kissed.

But now Sue broke away, a look of panic on her face.

'Man. What is it now?' Gus said.

'Fish!'

'What? Again?'

'FISH!' she repeated, pushing him away. Her arm was outstretched at a ninety-degree angle.

Gus stared at her with a puzzled look on his face.

She stared back. 'Stop gawping. Help me!'

'Uh?'

'Look.' She pointed to her other arm. 'I think I've caught something!'

Gus's face lit up, as he understood. Gently, with his hands on hers, keeping a steady rhythm, they wound in the line.

'You've got to keep it moving. Not too fast—'

'It massive,' she said, turning pink.

Gus didn't notice. 'Let the line slack a bit and then pull it again,' he encouraged. 'Don't lose the tension!'

She did as he said and slowly started to bring it home.

'You can do it!' he said. 'Go on, land it yourself!'

Sue shot him a look of panic. 'I can't. It's way too heavy!'

Gus's hand came back on top of hers. 'OK. When it's close, pull—in one sharp movement—into the boat.'

Sue could see the fish thrashing in the water.

'Nearly there,' he said. 'It won't bite!'

Sue could see the dark silvery coils, and black eyes staring back at her. Two more twists. Her hand felt as if it might detach.

'One more,' he said, calmly. 'Are you ready to finish it off?'

She started to heave, wondering if her muscles could take it.

The fish slipped out of the water and thudded into the boat, thrashing. Its tail flapped and slid and thudded against the wooden planks, until Gus grabbed the hammer and bashed the priest on its head.

The fish lay still, its battle lost.

'You did it, Sas!' he cried, his eyes sparkling. 'First go!'

He had no idea what kind of fish it was, but it meant that, if they were heading out to sea, they wouldn't starve quite yet. Brilliant, brilliant Sas!

'Sushi for tea?' he said.

'Oh, yes,' she said, her eyes fixing his. 'I adore sushi.'

KEMP'S DESIRE

A tiny pinprick of light flashed into the middle of the vast blackness of space. Then another, followed by two more.

'I feel you,' Gaia said, the fast vibrations of her long, slender hands making the noises of dreamspinners communication. Asgard had called a meeting of the dreamspinners to discuss their progress. The dreamspinners, the ancient dream-givers of the universe had found themselves in a tricky position following Genesis's giving of the most important dream of all, the Tripodean Dream. The Tripodean Dream had been given to the Heirs of Eden in order to test if human life on Earth merited its status and position on Earth. The dreamspinners knew that should the Heirs of Eden fail, their days of spinning dreams were numbered.

Gaia flashed into view, having inverted, like the other dreamspinners through their electric blue middles, their magholes.

'And I feel you,' the elder dreamspinners replied as the slender, bony, almost see-through humanoid forms of the dreamspinners silently, respectfully, acknowledged one another.

'Is Genesis not joining us?' Asgard vibrated with his opaque slender fingers.

'Genesis has gone to a place of rest in a distant star, to recover from her ordeal.'

'She has fled?' Asgard replied. 'I am not surprised to hear such a thing.'

'She suffered burns when the boy looked upon her, whilst she was giving the Heirs of Eden their special powers following the Tripodean Dream. She wonders if her time draws to a close,' Gaia said.

Dreamspinners prided themselves on delivering dreams uninterrupted. When Archie's eyes had opened during his dream, Genesis had taken it hard. She knew how important the Tripodean Dream were. They were the dreams that would help the children, these precious Heirs of Eden, in their task of representing life on Earth.

Asgard remained quiet. He stared out over the black universe, the uninhabited red planet of Mars spinning nearby in the great vastness of space.

'In her absence,' Gaia said, 'there must be a plan.'

'There can be no plan until the process of the Tripodean Dream, the prophecy, has reached its natural conclusion,' Gaia said. 'They have overcome the challenge of the storm, now we must await how they deal with what is left. That is the way.'

'I disagree,' Asgard said. 'If the outcome is not favourable to the Heirs of Eden, then what? There will be no dreamers on Earth, so we will have no reason for being. Dreamspinners will have no worth. What will become of us? What of our hatchlings? Dreamspinners have a right to know what will happen should the Heirs of Eden fail. They have a right to know what purpose they may have to look forward to if there are no dreams to knit and spin on Earth'.

'Were you not there, Asgard? The Heirs of Eden survived the storm,' Gaia vibrated. 'They are more than worthy of their title.'

'We all know this is not so,' Asgard said. He pressed on with a new angle. 'You forget. It is written that if the Heirs of Eden fail on Earth, there is still one last opportunity. The humans on the planet of Havilah will be freed from their frozen prisons. They will arise, live their lives again and they will dream, just as they did long ago. We must move our attention towards Havilah. Dreamspinners will have the opportunity to serve dreams to them, after all.'

'Your vibrations tell me you have already given up on the Heirs of Eden, Asgard. You give in too easily,' Gaia vibrated, her movements softer. 'Besides, do you think the other dreamspinners know the dream powders of the Havilah are tainted?'

Asgard slipped a finger into his maghole. 'They are still dreams—'

'I now understand why you have acquainted yourself with Cain, Asgard,' Gaia said. 'Cain has been seen on Earth, I am told, and others say that together you have devised a great plan. It is noble that you wish to keep the dreams of dreamspinners alive.'

Asgard hadn't expected to be caught out. 'Dreamspinners have a right to know,' he replied. 'The likelihood of the Heirs of Eden failing is high. They are children. The Tripodean Dream should never have been given to them. Now, it is Cain who represents the best chance for dreamspinners.'

'You have broken the trust, Asgard,' Gaia vibrated. 'You have risked the confidence we had with humankind on Earth, Asgard. You have drawn a line in the sand. You are upsetting the balance of life. Tipping it into an unknown place.'

Asgard's deep black eyes bore into Gaia. 'I have done what I have done for the good of dreamspinners, Gaia. Because I care about our future—'

'And in so doing,' Gaia responded, her vibrations gaining in strength, 'you have declared that you do not trust the universe. You have not let things run as they were intended. You have abandoned our main principle of never interfering with the natural energy of the universe. It is due to this one simple rule that dreamspinners have outlasted every other species ever created. Now, you threaten us all.'

Asgard's many legs twitched. 'What I do, I do for the process of giving dreams. I cannot sit by and wait till there is no use for us, until there are simply no more dreams to give. Dreamspinners are spirits of the energy of the ether. Do not forget it.'

And, with a tiny flash, Asgard's head contorted down and into his maghole and he disappeared into the atmosphere.

'Dreamspinner, dreamspinner, dreamspinner!' Cain shouted.

A second later, Asgard unfurled out of the air next to him.

'Aha! My ugly dreamspinners friend,' Cain began. 'It appears I am stuck within a dying body.'

Asgard walked across the air as if treading on invisible steps. 'Then you must return him.'

'Yes,' Cain said, 'but how can our plan work if there is no flesh on me?'

Asgard dipped two legs into his electric blue maghole. 'The boy may recover. He will go back to you if he has access to the one thing he desires most in the world.'

'And, pray, tell,' Cain replied, intrigued. 'What is that?'

'This is for you to puzzle over,' Asgard said. 'There is no time to lose. The boy tires me and I, too, must be sure of survival. I am unable to transport you both at will any more. There have been too many journeys. When the boy lands on Earth, extract yourself and return through me to Havilah immediately.'

Cain's good mood evaporated. 'Then find dreamspinners who will sacrifice themselves for the cause,' he demanded.

Asgard stared at Cain. He did not like taking orders, especially from a spirit. Maybe he had to get used to it. 'The consequences are difficult for dreamspinners,' Asgard said. 'We are not familiar with other species, other worlds—'

'If you are unable to transport us, Asgard,' Cain snapped, 'then find others who will. If you want the Garden of Eden to open, if you want to keep making your dreams, I suggest you give me your wholehearted support. Find other dreamspinners.'

The ultimate sacrifice? Asgard thought.

Asgard knew dreamspinners would have to change, but he didn't realise how drastically. Dreamspinners, the oldest curators of life, now faced a stark choice. Back the Heirs of Eden, or line up behind Cain. His meeting with Gaia and Gaia had made this perfectly clear.

Havilah was the only place that offered spider web powders of any note. And even if dream powders could only be spun into dark dreams, or nightmares, they were nevertheless just as effective as dreams from the the Garden of Eden. Although these dreams were not as wholesome, at least dreamspinners would continue to exist.

'Perhaps,' Asgard signed with his long, slender, opaque fingers. 'Perhaps it can be done, for the greater cause.'

'Indeed,' Cain crowed. 'If you are to change, dreamspinner, then you must accept choices you do not like.'

Asgard knew it was so, but right now he needed to get Cain and the boy inside him back to Earth. 'Master. Awaken the boy. There is one last thing to do. Dive through me once again. This time, save your strength, for you shall bear the boy's weight and steer him through my maghole.'

Cain reached inside and, for the very first time, did not force the boy awake. He talked to him gently, as if to a child. A glow—which wasn't particularly nice, nor unpleasant, just unusual—ran through him. He had to work with the boy, not force him, he reminded himself.

Cain's thoughts turned to the puzzle. *What was the one thing that would make this human come back to him? What was the one thing the boy desired most?*

Cain thought of the conversation with the boy's father, who died when Kemp was an infant, his wife by his side. *All this time his mother is alive, and the boy doesn't know it!*

It made perfect sense. Cain chuckled. *It is the answer. When the boy is fit and strong he will come back to me, because I will give him his mother. He will come willingly, and I will look after him.*

Cain's plan was building in his mind, and already it pleased him greatly.

The boy woke and started to move as Cain gently coaxed him on. 'Together, little Earth human, we will start afresh. Together, we will rule the universe!'

'Where shall I take him?' Asgard asked.

'Back to where he came from, dreamspinners. Place him somewhere where they will not fail to find him.'

'Let us go with haste. I am ready.'

With the boy stirring, Cain summoned every ounce of his ghostly strength and threw himself and Kemp through the dreamspinners' middle.

RETURN TO EDEN COTTAGE

Heavy drizzle from low, grey clouds in the failing light matched the de Lowe's sombre mood as they exited the cave and surveyed the scene around them. They hoped they would be able to find their way back to Eden Cottage. Looking around, it was hard to imagine the place they knew so well could look so smashed, so horribly pulped to bits. It had all happened in a few wretched, brutal hours, almost exactly one day ago.

Boulders, rocks, sand, mud, trees, bushes, and branches lay scattered and splintered randomly, with no care or enterprise. When the valley opened up beneath them, even in the dank gloom, they gasped.

Beneath them, a moving body of water stretched as far as the eye could see like a big, flat, silvery-grey monster. In the distance, where the tops of the gentle valleys of the Vale of York lay, small hillocks had emerged like little islands, stretching out like the backs of crocodiles basking in a river.

When they turned to look at the school in the distance, only the reflective grey of the water and the chapel roof beneath the school tower reached up into the sky.

For some time, the four of them stared, utterly agog. From this vantage point it felt that only they could have possibly survived.

Archie looked across the valley tops, realising how lucky they were that they could follow the high ground all the way back to Eden Cottage, if they picked their route carefully. He took Daisy's hand and led the way. Old Man Wood picked Isabella up and carried her over his shoulder.

'It's so quiet,' Daisy whispered. 'So, sort of... dead.' Her strange red eyes bulged, full of tears. 'It's like we've emerged on a different planet.'

'No birds, not a twitter,' Archie said. 'Everything churned up as though it's been in a gigantic cement mixer and spewed out.'

Isabella woke, and moaned.

Old Man Wood set her down, and for a while the four of them sat on the fallen bough of an old oak and viewed the landscape, a gentle wind brushing their faces.

'I hope the house is still in one piece,' Daisy said at length. 'And Mrs Pye's not been flushed out.'

Old Man Wood groaned. 'There's only one way to find out. Ready to go?'

Collectively, they turned and limped on, their feet squelching in the mud. Old Man Wood hoisted Isabella back over his shoulder and picked out a path, mindful of larger puddles and steep banks of slippery mud.

Before long, they came over the brow of the hill and looked out over where the cottage should have been.

'It's gone,' Old Man Wood said.

'Don't be daft.' Daisy said.

'Daisy, it isn't there anymore,' Archie said.

'Trust me, please,' Daisy said. 'It is. You're all being very dramatic.'

As they approached, camouflaged by the fallen trees at the top of the hillside, they saw their stone farmhouse, its roof covered by moss and lichen, blending seamlessly with the greens and browns of the forest. A large oak tree now leaned into the courtyard in such a way that the crown of the tree enveloped the house, making the buildings all but indistinguishable from the carnage around.

When Daisy spotted a thin plume of smoke curling out of the chimney the de Lowes exchanged glances and smiles, their eyes sparking into life. They knew that Mrs Pye was safe, and that comfort and food and warmth and sleep were not far away.

Never had the rough, misshapen, stone farmhouse in the middle of the forest on the edge of the Yorkshire moors been a more welcome sight.

With her jobs done and the house as spick and span as she could make it, Mrs Pye sat down in her rocking chair. The sweet aroma of fresh bread filled the kitchen and the dry, though still filthy rugs had been replaced on the floor of Old Man Wood's room. She swayed backwards and forwards for a minute or two, lost in her own world as she hummed Old Man Wood's peculiar song. Then her eyes shut, and she slept.

For some strange reason, she thought she heard someone at the door.

By the time she drew back the large, black iron bolt, and yanked on the brass knob, her pulse was racing.

The door yawned open. There, in front of her, stood the old man with the three children. One was draped over his shoulder, covered in blood and littered with an assortment of cuts and bruises. The others were hanging on to his coat, shivering, almost naked. Their remaining clothes hung off them, torn to shreds. One had strange, erect hair, and the other's hair was matted to its face.

Mrs Pye fell to her knees. 'It's a miracle, it's a damned, ruddy miracle!' she cried as she opened her arms, her voice cracking with emotion. Daisy and Archie folded into her as tears fell freely down their cheeks. 'Oh, my poor, dear children!' she cried. 'You're safe. Safe now.'

Mrs Pye sat them down in front of the fire and produced a basket crammed with soft, downy blankets and pillows. Shortly, a saucepan full of thick, milky hot chocolate appeared. She returned with homemade flapjacks and sandwiches bulging with raspberry jam.

Mrs Pye talked and cried in equal measure as she went. 'Do you have any ideas what a terrible, terrible time I've had?' she said repeatedly. 'Do you have any ideas how it's been for me, huh? Watching the storm out there and worrying meself sick,' she complained. 'And do you have any ideas how difficult it is being alone in the house with no one here?' At this point, she turned on Old Man Wood. 'What were you playing at—leaving without telling me? Left me on my own to worry—and worry I did, every minute of every night and every second of the day!'

She exploded into tears and told them all how much she loved them, and how she would never—over her dead body—let it happen again. She told them that she knew they'd be all right, and that she knew they'd come back.

It was a tirade borne out of complete and utter love, and the children knew it.

Archie and Daisy exchanged smiles as if to say, "If she knew what had really happened... then what?"

SUE REMEMBERS HER PHONE

Gutting the fish and cutting the flesh off the bones was another matter altogether.

The meat came away only after a lot of fiddling and considerable stink and mess. It was poor—too salty and slimy—and they joked that had it been deep fried in batter with a portion of chips, it would have been fantastic. They washed down what they could manage with an additional ration of water using one of the empty baked bean tins as a cup.

As night fell over the grey North Sea, the rain beat down a little heavier. Gus set up his upside down umbrella-rain-catcher and when this was secure, he laid the wooden planks down the middle of the boat and they clambered on top, the rain pitter-pattering gently on the canopy above.

'Pity we haven't got a camera,' Sue said. 'This should be recorded for historical purposes.'

'The intrepid adventures of Gus and Sue,' he replied. 'Survivors of the Great Yorkshire Storm.'

Sue laughed, before sitting bolt upright, her head missing the crossbeam by millimetres. Then she slapped her hands together. 'Of course! I've been incredibly dumb—I do have one. On my phone!'

'Phone! You forgot you had a phone,' Gus said incredulously. 'How?'

She shrugged, 'I only use it in emergencies.' She rummaged in her coat pockets, pulled it out, kissed the device and held it in the air as if she'd won the World Cup.

'I'll let everyone know we're here, wherever here is,' she said.

She pressed the power button. The lights flashed and the start-up mechanism buzzed into action. They stared at it for a while. 'Oh. No reception,' she said, her mood deflating.

She groaned and laid back, the presence of the phone a stark reality check. 'I wonder if Isabella made it home? They were still playing when we went past with the shopping. Fighting on the pitch, Archie slugging away—can you believe it?'

'Archie?'

'Yeah. And Isabella did her mad referee-bashing thing.'

Gus laughed.

'Do you think they had time to get over the bridge and up the lane?' she asked. For the first time, Sue's heart filled with a sense of loss. Before she knew it, tears were rolling down her cheeks. 'I'm sorry,' she cried, wiping them away.

Gus put a reassuring arm around her. 'Don't be. I'm sure loads of people are fine,' he lied. 'Isabella's probably tucked up in bed with a steaming hot chocolate having mad stories told to her by that very old man.'

Sue smiled and leant into him. She knew he was being nice. As she searched the depths of her soul, it didn't feel as if she had lost her friend. 'How bad do you think it was?'

'We'll only know if we get home, I suppose.' Then he had an idea. 'Sue, can I have a look at your phone.' She handed it to him. He stared at the screen for a while. 'Actually,' he said, 'better if you do it.'

'Do what?'

'Find an app with a compass, so we can start figuring out which way we're going.'

'You don't know how to use a phone?'

Gus raised his eyebrows. 'I'm more of a practical person. Old school, you know.'

'Here, is this what you're after?' She handed him the device.

Gus stared at it as if it were gold. His big smile radiated back at her. He twisted the phone in his hands and the compass point moved.

'What does it say?'

Gus beamed back. 'We're heading south.'

'Is that good or bad?'

He shrugged. 'Good, I suppose, better than heading north or east towards Denmark. Ideally, we want to head west.'

'How do we do that?' Sue said.

Gus grinned. 'A rudder for steering would help and we need to change the position of the sail.' He shifted his position and untied the sail rope before moving it into a new position on the other side of the boat. 'The Joan of' altered course.

'Turn your phone off for now, we may need it later.' He clapped his hands together. 'I'm going to make a rudder.'

Sue looked confused.

Gus smiled back. 'Just pass me things and tell me about this scary dream you had while I attempt to figure it out.'

As Gus set to work, Sue told him about her premonition: how she'd woken up sweating and instantly written down as much as she could remember.

And although it made little sense, the nightmare scared her so much that she confided to Isabella. And then Isabella went berserk trying to prove it was, actually, going to happen. Which it did.

'And the odd thing is,' she said, 'Isabella had a dream about the storm, too.' She strummed her fingers on the seat. 'Isn't that freaky?'

She paused as Gus bashed in a couple of nails, and then continued. 'Most of this nightmare centred on the de Lowes but what really got me most was just how incredibly real the images appeared. It was like watching TV.'

'Give me an example,' Gus said.

'OK, the violence of the storm, the lightning almost fizzling through my whole body. Then there was the weight of the rain and a deep sense that they had to stay alive till sunset.'

Gus looked up. 'Well, the storm certainly happened,' he said. 'Did you tell them about the sunset? Pass me the saw.'

Sue reached into the box and handed it over. 'Yeah, while they were fighting on the pitch and only moments before the whole thing kicked off. Then, I scooted off and found you. I don't know why I put it off for so long. I suppose I didn't think the nightmare would come true. And there was also another part...'

'Go on,' Gus encouraged. 'I'm all ears.'

'They had to find some clues to find three stone tablets, or something like that, in that old house of theirs.'

Gus began sawing the plank, the noise drowning out the conversation. It gave Sue time to think. 'Thing is, by the time I told them, the de Lowes were either fighting, being kicked, or being hauled off the pitch, so I don't know if my ranting got through to them.'

Sue ducked as Gus moved the rudder around in the small space. 'Do you think I'm crazy?'

Gus studied his handiwork and then lifted his eyes to meet hers. 'Who knows? There might be something in it. I mean, you were spectacularly right about the storm, and, if you remember, when nightfall came, the deluge gave way to spitting. Therefore, if they did survive, maybe what you saw really was a premonition. Spooky, huh?'

Sue looked at Gus quizzically. For a boy he was an amazingly good listener. She needed to get one more thing off her chest. 'Thing is, Gus, what bothers me, is why did I have a dream about another family? Why did it feel so heart-wrenchingly like I belonged?'

Gus relaxed, put his tools down, and faced her. 'Maybe you're related to them,' he said.

Sue guffawed.

'No, listen,' Gus continued. 'Don't get me wrong but you're incredibly similar to Isabella. You're the same height, you have the same hair, the same nose, a similar forehead. You both like the same stuff. You're as clever as each other and just as terrible at sport. You're just far more gorgeous.' The moment he said it, he blushed.

'Oh, that's so sweet,' she said, noting Gus' discomfort. 'But I don't know. Isabella's way smarter, but with a vicious temper.'

Gus smiled broadly. He'd been on the receiving end of Isabella's sharp tongue a couple of times. 'You know, twins aren't always exactly the same—'

'Twins?'

'Yes. Maybe you and Isabella are secret twins, separated at birth. Stranger things have happened.'

Sue kneaded her temples. 'I don't think so. Loads of people look the same, and best friends often act the same way too.'

'No one looks like me,' Gus said.

'You really are one of a kind, Gus,' she said, punching him playfully.

He raised his bushy eyebrows. 'Why don't you text Isabella. Remind her of all those things you've told me. If we get in range and they're alive, then it might help. There's nothing to lose apart from a bit of battery power. More than anything, she'll be overjoyed to hear from you.'

'For a boy,' Sue began, 'you're quite clever and absurdly sensible. When this is over, will you help me get to the bottom of this twin thing once and for all?'

'It would be my pleasure.'

Sue held up her phone. 'I'll tell you what. I'll send three texts. The first to Mum to say that we're alive, the second to Isabella with the things I've just told you, and a third to the coastguard. Can't be any harm in letting them know we're stuck out here.'

WHO IS CAIN?

Isabella's hands touched the soft cotton bed sheet. She allowed herself a smile as her head turned over on her plump, downy pillow.

Then, it started coming back to her: the match, the lightning, the ordeal in the cave, waking up and looking over the broken Vale of York. The excruciating pain.

She clenched her fist, amazed to find feeling in her fingers, although a strange, electrical current tingled through the palms of each hand and through each digit. Hadn't she smashed her wrists?

She opened her eyes and saw the familiar sight of her section of the attic room. Home! With a cry of joy, she sat up.

She examined her hands and a chill ran through her.

The holes!

The circular, see-through holes where the lightning bolt had smashed into her! She sank back into the soft pillows. She needed to think it through and work out what had happened, just as she'd told herself in the cave.

She made her way over to the desk, and wrote in big, bold letters on a piece of A4 paper:

'DO NOT DISTURB ME.

DO NOT TALK TO ME

DO NOT FEED ME.'

She pinned the paper to the outside of the closed, thick, velvet curtain that set her area apart from the rest of the attic room and shuffled back to bed where she slept, sometimes deeply, mostly fitfully, until midday.

❋

Everything that the eyeless ghost Cain had told Archie had come true.

But who was this Cain and how did he fit in? Archie couldn't figure out if the ghost meant well, or if his words fitted another agenda altogether. And why did Cain want him to protect the Ancient Woman? And how could he protect her if he didn't know where she was? After all, there was a pretty big chance she was a product of his imagination.

When he thought of the ghost, he thought about Kemp. Had Kemp merged with Cain as Cain had demanded? Had Kemp been dazzled by Cain's promise of power and strength, or had Kemp nobly sacrificed himself?

That was the problem with Kemp, Archie thought. He simply couldn't be trusted.

What about the huge spider who had hovered over Daisy, and then vanished into thin air? His mind replayed the images of the opaque figure that appeared to be feeding his sister with a dust from its long legs. Why did it have an electric pulsing blue middle? He felt a headache coming on.

He shut his eyes tight, trying to erase the memory, but it persisted like a stubborn head cold. Was it giving them dreams? Was that possible?

Archie slept and mooched about the house, avoiding everyone where possible. He was desperate to talk to Daisy about Cain, but in the back of his mind was his sworn promise to the ghost that he wouldn't tell a soul. And, deep down, he worried that Cain might resurface at any time. The mere thought made his stomach churn.

Archie ran a hand over his head and shuddered. He didn't like his ridiculous new hairstyle, or wire-style as Daisy called it. When he relaxed, he noticed that the fibres softened, but when he felt threatened or angry, the follicles tightened hard like steel. They seemed to act like antennae for his mood.

He noticed another thing. When his hair hardened, blood coursed through his sinews and fibres and gave him a feeling of power, of being indestructible.

Though he dared not admit it, this strange new sensation felt wonderfully good.

ISABELLA'S CONFUSION

'Come on, Isabella,' Daisy said from the other side of the curtain, as she read Isabella's notice. 'You need food. Lunch is on the table.'

Isabella groaned. She didn't want to see anyone, and she certainly didn't want to talk to anyone. *Couldn't Daisy read?*

'You missed breakfast and you didn't eat anything last night.'

Still there was no response.

'It's one of your favourites,' Daisy persevered. 'You can't hide away in your bed all day.'

I can, Isabella thought. *And I will.*

Daisy pull the fabric aside and strode in.

'Go away! Can't you read?'

Her sister ignored her and sat down on the side of the bed. 'How are your arms?'

Isabella rolled over.

Daisy sighed. 'Look, Einstein, you can't stay here all day, you'll get bed bugs and—'

'Daisy. Go away. Just leave me, please.'

But Daisy was in a stubborn mood, and she was bored. 'Make me.'

Isabella growled and pulled the duvet over her head.

Daisy stood up, fluffed up her hair, puckered her lips and made her way to the mirror. She stared at her red eyes. 'Freaky, but kind of cool, huh? What do you think?'

Isabella remained silent.

Daisy turned her attention to Isabella's neat bookshelves. 'Got any books on the universe? I might do that homework, the assignment from Solomon on whether "God created the Universe, or the Universe created God".'

'Please, Daisy—'

'No. You and Archie are so boring, feeling so incredibly sorry for yourselves,' she said and she flicked through a volume of Shakespeare's plays, read aloud two passages, folded it and tucked the book under her jumper.

'Old Man Wood's disappeared again. Gone to check his cattle. How about a game of something?' She sat down heavily on the bed and traced a finger up Isabella's body.

Isabella popped her head out. 'If I give you a book will you go away!'

Daisy cocked her head to one side. 'Might,' she said, pouting. 'On the condition that you come down for tea; Mrs P's knocking up a stonking curry. Helped her put the ingredients in—eleven in all—and I slipped in an extra chilli. Gonna be a corker. *And*, big sis, Banoffee pie for pudding. Your total favourite!'

'Anyway', Daisy continued, 'Mrs P's been droning on and on about my eyes, it's sending me nuts. She's talked more in the last few hours than the last year put together. Hey, look at these!' Daisy popped on a thin pair of metal rimmed, pink tinted glasses. 'Lush, eh? Found them in Mum's drawer.'

Isabella's head popped out. She pointed at the bookcase. 'Second row. Says "Mysteries of the Universe" on it. Please, grab it and go!' Her head flew back under the duvet.

Daisy stood up. 'Sure, you boring boffin. If you want to talk, chat about anything, I'm, you know, around. Not too busy today. Diary pretty much empty.'

Under the duvet, Isabella cringed. Daisy was only trying to help. She popped her head out again. 'Look, I'm sorry, Daisy. I know you're trying... it's just... I'm not ready.'

Daisy smiled. 'Yeah, cool,' she said. She turned to leave. 'You know, Isabella, whatever happened, happened. We can't change it and we don't know what's coming. That's it, really. Sometimes you just have to go with the flow.' Daisy opened the curtain. 'See you at lunch, right?' she said, drawing it behind her.

Isabella gripped her duvet in her fist. *Why couldn't she go with the flow like Daisy, rather than be tormented by questions and riddles?* She was always trying to make sense of things that didn't make any sense. *"Go with the flow!" If only it were that simple.*

Isabella closed her eyes and thought of Sue, her best friend in the whole world. Tears streamed down her cheeks. She had sent Sue to a certain death by slipping her a bit of paper with details of a rickety old boat in a rundown boathouse. A stupid little old boat no one had even looked at for years.

She pictured it in her mind. Sas; alone, cold, wet, begging for help, and drowning. She wouldn't have stood a chance, not three minutes against that storm. Not a chance in hell.

She'd only tried to help. If only she'd known, she could have done something else.

Isabella cried until her tears ran dry as she mourned for her dear friend.

Thanks to the strange sparkly potion called Resplendix Mix, which Old Man Wood had found in the cellars beneath Eden Cottage, Isabella's injuries had almost completely healed up.

Isabella, though delighted with her progress, was confused and concerned as to how Resplendix Mix worked. In all the science and medical journals that she'd ever read, she'd never heard of anything similar. She wondered if the potion had manipulated the cells in her body to recreate bone and tissue fibres. Was it a form of genetic science working at a hitherto unknown level, or was this a reversing potion of some sort? And were there short or even long-term side-effects? More importantly, what was Old Man Wood doing with it in the first place? Had Old Man Wood been a scientist like her when he was young?

When they'd quizzed Old Man Wood about how Resplendix Mix worked, or what its properties were, he replied that he had no idea, and this was the truth. And when asked where he had got it from, he took a deep breath and told them that it had been given to him a long, long time ago, most probably by an apothecary. And this was also true.

Daisy accepted Old Man Wood's explanation as perfectly normal, but Isabella's suspicions grew, namely because apothecaries didn't exist anymore. They were now called pharmacists or chemists.

Whatever her suspicions, the potion was like magic. The faster an injury was acted upon, the quicker it healed, although the pain was excruciating.

As they sat down at the kitchen table for Mrs Pye's curry, Isabella moved her forearms and cocked her wrists, testing her limbs, 'I have a question for you, Old Man Wood,' she said. 'Why isn't Resplendix Mix prescribed in hospitals or at doctors' surgeries?'

Old Man Wood raised his head for a minute and shrugged before cramming a forkful it in his mouth.

'I mean, look at me,' she continued. 'Almost fully healed apart from these stupid holes. If it was readily available to everyone, just think of the enormous benefits—benefits that could be used right now—out there,' she said, waving towards the window. 'And its properties could probably be transferred to other schools of medicine too. Think of it. No hospital waiting lists, no injuries that couldn't be dealt with. No nasty scars.'

Daisy groaned. 'I preferred you when you were asleep.'

Isabella shot her a look. She nudged Old Man Wood. 'Do you know what's in it?'

Old Man Wood shook his head.

'I'm going to analyse it,' Isabella said. 'Then I'll manufacture it and sell it worldwide. I'll make a fortune.'

'I'm not sure Mum and Dad would be too happy with that,' Daisy said.

'Why not? They're never around, so they wouldn't know.'

'They'll be back,' Mrs Pye said. 'I'm quite sure they'll be safe and sound.'

'Yeah, but they don't know *we're* safe, do they?' Daisy said.

Isabella ignored all of them. 'I'll go to America. They'd all bend over backwards for this kind of thing. In one go, I'd save all suffering on the planet—'

'Isabella, you haven't thought this through,' Archie said. 'If you made this stuff on an industrial scale, in one go you're wiping out all the hospitals and doctors and nurses and physios and first aiders and pharmacists and drug makers and more—'

'And the media would brand you as a witch,' Daisy said, mischievously. 'You'd be burnt alive.'

Old Man Wood hummed. 'Thing is,' he deep voice boomed, 'I'm not sure Resplendix Mix works with everyone. I've a feeling that, in the wrong hands, it's downright lethal.'

'Ha! So you do know what it is,' Isabella said.

Old Man Wood furrowed his brow. 'Nope. Not really littlun. Just a feeling.'

Mrs Pye beamed at him. 'Your Old Man Wood has a ton of remarkable strings to his arrows.'

Daisy coughed. 'Isn't it, strings to his bow?'

'Or, even, arrows to a quiver?' Archie added.

Mrs Pye shot the twins a beady look. 'Bloomers. You twins getting all clever on me, are you? You know exactly what I means. Now pipe down, and eat up.'

CAIN'S PLAN

With his mouth and nose enclosed by a clear plastic breathing device, Kemp sucked in a large mouthful of oxygen and opened his eyes. Slowly, he began to wonder where he was.

He listened. He could hear a gentle churning noise, like the dull throb of an engine, or of machinery gently running through its processes, followed by regular blips.

His body felt lighter and, as he ran a check over his anatomy, he noticed the burning didn't hurt so much. Perhaps he'd died after all.

Kemp searched for signs of Cain.

None.

For a moment his mind and body leapt for joy. Then, he remembered that Cain might be resting. And Cain never rested for long. His eyes felt heavy again.

His ears picked out noises nearby.

He listened. Voices, deep voices, whispering, occasionally louder. Concerned, anxious tones. One higher pitched than the others. A female? He tried to move his hands, but they felt leaden, as though fixed down by heavy weights.

A terrible sadness sank over him, and a tear rolled down his cheek. He yearned for someone to hold him and love him, for the comfort of a hug, of gentle words, or soothing kisses. He pined for the mother he never knew.

So tired.

He needed sleep.

Kemp drifted off once more.

❄

'You miss the child?' Asgard asked.

'Indeed,' Cain replied. 'I have been a terrible fool. My excitement of being partially alive got the better of me. Do you have any idea how wonderful it feels to dance with elves and confront Neanderthals?' Cain recalled their brief foray, via the dreamspinners's maghole, in the Neanderthal area in the southern mountains of Havilah where they had engaged a surprised group of ancient man, untouched by Cains spell. 'Ah, yes. It reminded me of the good old days.'

Cain floated up into the air. 'You see, dreamspinners, I haven't had a requirement for food, rest, nor bodily function for so long that I forgot there was another being inside me that needed these things. And now here I am; trapped here once more and reduced to less than an outline.'

He plummeted to the ground and hovered by one of the glass-like domes covered by a thin film of dust, the trace of a human face looking up.

'What good am I, if I am made of air? I did not realise how remarkable the status of actually *being* is, dreamspinner.'

Asgard had news. 'That child is in the care of humans. I spun a dream that will make him sleep for a long time to aid his healing. His burns are not as bad as you feared. He will survive.'

'That is a great relief. If you can collect a certain sap from the trees in the forests to the South of Havilah. They have great healing properties. Then, dear creature, you must take me to Earth so I might find out what the boy eats. Would you guide me to a place where I might learn such things? Schmerger!'

The little elf instantly opened the door at the far end of the hallway as if he knew he was about to be called. 'Sire.'

'You have two days to build a kitchen...' Then, an even better idea struck him. 'Schmerger. You will travel though a dreamspinners to Earth and find out what exactly Earth's humans eat and drink.' Cain spoke into the air. 'Asgard, would one of your kind be able to transport Schmerger?'

Asgard remained silent, as if in shock.

'Well? I take the silence is a 'Yes'?'

Asgard vibrated an affirmative response.

The elven manservant, whose face rarely registered a change of expression, raised an eyebrow. 'Sire. If I may. I have uncovered ancient scripts that tell of the human people's diet here on Havilah. It may help us identify the necessary requirements.'

'Very good, Schmerger. Excellent.' Cain said. 'Do plans—diagrams and descriptions—of the original palace kitchen exist? Because...' his voice trailed off as the reality hit him. 'We may have our own human population to feed in five days' time.'

Schmerger seemed remarkably cool. 'The kitchens were well documented.'

Cain suddenly realised they were woefully underprepared. 'Do you have sufficient help?'

'Since your return,' Schmerger said, diplomatically, 'Elves have returned from distant mountains where they have sought refuge all these years. Goblins too and some of the ancient types of humans. They are weary of life and many are sick. They anticipate something different is happening here.'

'Get them to work and get yourself to Earth via the dreamspinners, Schmerger,' Cain ordered. 'With only five Earth days remaining, I need that boy with me and when those Heirs of Eden fail, my people will awaken. If I am with the boy, they will know I survived. They will see that I did not altogether die. Without him I will exist only as a voice in their heads and they will shun that voice, knowing what I did to them. They will know that my gamble failed.'

'Have you thought about the one thing the boy desires more than anything else?' Asgard said, his fingers vibrating the words.

'Indeed,' Cain replied, an invisible grin on his face. 'His mother lives. Do you know which she is.'

'Indeed,' Asgard replied. 'But first, news on the new dream powders.'

Cain had almost forgotten.

Asgard's fingers moved rapidly. 'Pathogen particles have been mixed into the new stocks of spider web dream powders, deep in the caves of Havilah.'

'Excellent!' Cain said. 'What will these dreams be like?'

'Havilarian dreams from the spider webs here are different to those of the Garden of Eden and Earth. They produce troubling, manipulative, and angry dreams.'

'Nightmares?' Cain queried.

'Adverse dreams are as rewarding and enriching as they are pleasant,' Asgard said, bending a thin leg into his maghole. 'After all, they are only dreams. Remember, creativity and enlightenment come from the darker side of life too.'

Cain was intrigued. 'And what are the dream powders from Earth like?'

'Earth spiders are bland and lifeless. Their spider webs make powders that do not nourish dreamspinners as deeply. These dreams are not so interesting.'

'Why is that so?'

'To us dream powders are like food to mankind and water to creatures of the sea. Dreamspinners will spin more dreams from Havilah from now on. I guarantee it.'

Cain was genuinely fascinated. 'Has your band of dreamspinners grown?'

'There are many,' the dreamspinners said. 'Each day, as the sun sets, more join. Dreamspinners cannot resist a dream.'

'Especially bad ones, eh?' Cain said. 'You are most enlightening, and wise,' he added. He lowered his voice. 'Tell me, dreamspinner, how long before the plague particles in your dream powders are ready to be delivered?'

'The new spider web dream powders will be free to use once the sun sinks over the western horizon.'

Cain gasped. 'This very night? Already?'

The ghost danced an invisible jig. *What a turnaround! Nightmares stuffed full of plague, and a few days early at that.*

'Poor, dear, little Earthlings!' he crowed. 'They have no idea what is about to hit them, and not a helping hand in sight.'

'In the event of the boy returning to you,' Asgard continued, 'I have found a way of transporting you from place to place.'

'A better way than through you?'

'Indeed. Elderly dreamspinners who are too old to knit and spin dreams, do not wish to see the world shaping as it is. Many believe a new time is coming.'

'Are you suggesting some would sacrifice themselves?' he asked.

'The burning sensation of a smaller human through the maghole will not end their life, but it may speed up their end.'

Cain invisibly punched the air. 'Phenomenal news! Truly, Asgard, this is wonderful!'

Cain ran through the sequence of events on Earth. By the time the Heirs of Eden failed at the end of the seven days, as they were bound to, every living thing would have succumbed to the plague and died. He laughed. It was so easy: just let the world continue on exactly as it had for centuries.

Damn the wretched Prophecy, Cain thought, *damn the old man and damn the Heirs of Eden. Very soon they won't have a world worth saving.*

With the Heirs of Eden dead, Cain's human population in Havilah would rise and the prophecy would, in time, come to Havilah.

Now Cain had a different thought. If he had access to any point in any universe through the dreamspinners, why didn't he get the dreamspinners to take him directly to the Ancient Woman, his dear mother? She was the woman who held the key to life within her frame, the key that would reopen the creation planet of the Garden of Eden.

The Ancient Woman waited in solitude for the Heirs of Eden to come to her and find the key. What if he went instead of them?

Cain hummed quietly to himself. Could he really open up the Garden of Eden, all for himself? Did the rules of the universe allow him to go directly to her? He was, after all, only a spirit and weren't spirits beyond the universal laws? He'd check. Maybe Asgard would know.

Cain grabbed a stick and made his way to one of the strange domed circles, the puddles of his lost human population on the ground. He traced a hand over the glass surface, wondering who lay trapped underneath. A lady of his court, a son, a dancer, or a warrior?

Cain was enjoying where his thoughts were taking him. He reasoned that if he could go directly to the Ancient Woman, he'd open up the Garden of Eden himself and would soon have control of every cell of every single living thing. He'd nurture the creatures and beasts he chose and would shape a new Earth. He'd revitalise Havilah with an array of fresh, new creatures of his own making, just the way he liked and as the old man used to do. And would the old man stop him?

No, because he wouldn't know how.

The one thing he was missing was a pair of eyeballs, the source of all true magic. Using the boy's vision had reminded him of the great power of eyes. But how would this mystery come to him?

ISABELLA DOES NOT BELIEVE

'You know when we talked before about our dreams?' Archie began, now that they'd all finished their platefuls. 'And we realised we'd literally shared the same ones.' He searched the table to see if anyone was listening. 'Well, I think they might be coming true.'

Mrs Pye broke in. 'Now you're talking about dreams, that means bed for me, and I is pooped. So, I leaves you and loves you, and I'll be getting some sweet shut-eye in for myself.'

Old Man Wood stretched his arms wide. 'And I'm going to sit next door— softer, there.'

The children thanked Mrs Pye for the meal, hugged her goodnight, and shut the door.

They sat down again.

Daisy leaned across the table. 'I still don't get what that old woman you killed in your dreams, Archie, has got to do with it. Maybe the dream has an opposite meaning. Maybe we've got to protect her, or something, so that she won't die?' She flashed Archie a look. 'What do you think?'

He shrugged. 'Dunno. Sounds better than murdering her,' he said, as his thoughts returned to his crazy conversation with Cain. The last thing he wanted was a death on his hands. 'What if there's a deeper meaning?' he added. 'Something else?'

'Like what?' Daisy said, wiping the side of her mouth.

Archie shook his head. 'I don't really know,' he said. 'I was kind of hoping we could talk about it—'

Isabella leaned back in her chair and flexed her hands. 'Kids, this is ridiculous—'

'Archie's right,' Daisy said. 'Come on. Let's discuss this, if you're up to it, your brainy-ness—'

'Frankly,' Isabella sighed, 'it's too much for me to deal with right now so I'd rather we didn't.'

Daisy shot her sister a look. 'Actually, boffin brains, I think we should. We're in this together and dreaming of this Ancient Woman is our only common denominator.'

'No. I'm sorry,' Isabella said, amazed that Daisy knew what a "denominator" was. 'It's not going to happen.' With a loud scraping sound, Isabella slid her chair back and stood up. 'You two, by all means discuss it to your heart's content. Do whatever you feel you've got to do. Me? I think I can find better things to get on with, like study.' She grabbed her plate and marched over to the sink.

'What about Sue–?' Archie said.

'And the fact that I sent her to her death!' Isabella snapped.

'You don't know that—'

'There's no way she survived—'

'We did—'

'That was luck, Archie, as I told you in the cave,' Isabella said. 'Pure luck.'

'No, it wasn't—'

Isabella shook her head. 'Yes, it was. I don't understand which bit you think wasn't fortunate.'

'That's ridiculous,' Archie fumed. 'You know what happened—you were there!'

'Yes, of course I was. But there's no reasonable, logical explanation for it, is there? No truth.' She washed her dish, placed it in the rack to the side, and dried her hands on a tea towel. 'To be honest, I'm not even sure it happened.'

'What?'

'More and more, Archie, I'm thinking that we were part of some illusion or hallucination,' she said staring at their shocked faces. 'Hasn't it crossed either of your tiny minds that what happened might be nothing more than a figment of our imaginations.'

'Rubbish—'

'I'm serious.' Isabella smiled. 'Why not? There's every chance we accidentally took a drug, or, maybe the vapours from the storm glass may have contained a mind-altering cocktail and led us, unwittingly, to imagine it all.'

Isabella had made a Fitzroy storm glass with her friend Sue when she was worried that the storm to come was going to be bigger that anyone in her school could have realised. It had spectacularly blown up, and made Isabella realise that the events ahead of them had every likelihood of coming true.

'But I wasn't even there when the storm glass exploded,' Daisy said, quietly. 'It was just you, Sue, and Archie'.

Archie could feel his hair turning steely. 'OK. Let's talk about the storm glass, Isabella. When it blew up, you thought it was important enough to tell the headmaster, didn't you? And blocking a lightning bolt and getting holes in your hands isn't simply a matter of luck. Look at my ridiculous hair, and Daisy's red eyes!' He swivelled to his twin. 'Was interpreting the cave imaginary simply luck for you, Daisy?'

Daisy shook her head. 'Nope. Those retracting steps and the pictures on the walls were pretty clear, as well as the Jacuzzi thing that miraculously healed us. Oh, and let's not forget that I can hear lightning forming and can see stuff you can't. But then again, you ran up two hundred and twenty-two steep twisting steps in the time it took me to travel twenty.'

Isabella's features darkened. She'd been dreading this conversation. 'Those freaky things,' she said, as her arms whirled in their direction, 'can be explained by science. I'll grant you, there may be some scientific wonders we experienced that aren't documented as yet, but it's only a matter of time. Very soon, everything that happened to us will be seen as perfectly normal.'

'Bull,' Daisy said.

'Daisy!' Isabella scolded. 'No, it isn't.'

'But Isabella,' Archie said, 'look outside at the wreckage. The whole country has been utterly mangled. And we dreamt about it—'

'Listen, Archie,' she snapped. 'We experienced a once-in-a-lifetime storm. They happen. Globally, big destructive floods do occur: America, Pakistan, Australia, China; they have massive meteorological activity just like this. It's quite possible that we somehow picked it up in our dreams. Dreams signal things that you fear, so therefore it was perfectly natural for me, as a scientist, to make that connection, albeit in my subconscious.' She smiled at their confused faces, but her eyes were hard.

'You've got to understand, kids, that there's every chance this is your subconscious playing games with you, mucking about inside your head, telling you things. And remember, these are only dreams. DREAMS, for goodness—'

'So how come,' Daisy interrupted, 'we dreamed of the same things?'

Isabella sat down and leaned forward. Her eyes sparkled as she explained. 'Because people dream about the same things all the time, Daisy. Dreams repeat themselves time and time again, like songs on the radio, like seasons, like our need for food. Like the process of ageing. Life repeats itself. It just does. Why do you think there are hundreds of books on dream interpretation?' She offered the question to the table. 'It's because people like you and me have the same type of dreams every single night, that's why. There's a kind of uniformity to it.'

Silence descended.

Isabella looked triumphantly from one twin to the other, her eyebrows cocked. She prepared herself to leave.

'The thing is, Isabella,' Daisy said, her voice barely above a whisper, 'no one knows what dreams are actually for. It's unclear what the purpose of dreaming really is.'

Isabella scoffed.

Daisy looked up. 'Dream scientists who map our subconscious and study sleeping patterns and REM come to all sorts of broad conclusions because, hard as they try, they don't actually know why we dream.'

Daisy looked Isabella straight in the eye. 'So, it's entirely possible that our dreams have a purpose.' She slipped her pink glasses on and pursed her lips.

'Oh, how awfully clever, Daisy,' Isabella spat. 'Suddenly you're the authority?'

Daisy fixed her with an icy stare. 'Yes. I looked it up. Do your own research.'

The girls eyeballed each other across the table.

'In any case,' Daisy said, running her hands through her hair, 'I can't understand why you're not able to link the dreams we've had about a storm, finding three tablets, and the murder of an old lady, with the pictures in the cave also showed these exact same sequences.'

Isabella chortled. 'You're referring to those cave paintings?'

'Yup, Einstein.'

Isabella stood and smiled thinly. 'OMG. How cute that you managed to find a story in them. I hardly looked at those stupid pictures—'

'They were NOT stupid—'

'Oh, so you think they had meaning,' Isabella said.

Daisy nodded.

'They were caveman scribbles!' Isabella continued. 'Are you seriously thinking you can derive a story, an entire narrative, from those scribbles?' she chuckled. 'They could be interpreted in any number of ways. Really, how dumb can you get—'

'If you'd actually bothered to study them, Isabella, you would have seen our dreams—everything—drawn out perfectly.'

'Even our weirdo features—' Archie added.

'Plus the Ancient Woman,' Daisy said.

'And the flood,' said Archie.

'And the three tablets we've got to find,' Daisy said. 'You saw that, didn't you, Archie?'

He nodded.

'And instructions on how to get out of a sophisticated cave—'

'Not forgetting,' Archie said, 'what a mess the country is in and the probable death of everyone we know.'

Daisy scratched her nose. 'Caveman scribbles, my arse!'

'Stop it!' Isabella yelled. 'STOP IT!' She put her face behind her hands, her hair hanging over like a veil. 'Stop going on at me,' she sobbed. 'Why are you two always having a dig at me?'

'We're not—'

'Yes, you are! Ganging up like... like Ant and Dec.'

Archie and Daisy exchanged glances. 'Ant and Dec don't gang up on anyone.'

Isabella flapped her arms about. 'Thinking how funny you are all the time.' She wiped her nose with the back of her hand. 'Do you have any idea what it's like picking up the pieces after you two?' she raged. 'Covering your backs all the time? To me, none of this makes any bloody sense.'

In one movement, she stood up, picked up a chair, and hurled it into the corner. Then she turned on Archie. 'Look at you,' she seethed. 'You're a pathetic mess, and you,' she said, pointing at Daisy, 'are a stupid, idiotic, thick tart. You're no better than that oaf, Kemp.'

She picked up a glass, held it out, and crushed it into tiny fragments in her hand.

The twins looked on, mouths open.

Isabella turned, shook the contents over the floor, and stormed out of the room.

Daisy picked up the chair and pushed it under the table top. 'That is one seriously confused chick,' she said. 'And, did you notice, no blood.'

'I saw that, too.' Archie said. 'You think Isabella's wrong?'

'Doh! Yeah, of course she is!' Daisy replied. 'Come on, no one in the world has hair like yours or eyes like mine, or holes through their hands which don't bleed when they crush glass into a billion fragments.'

'True,' he said, sagely. 'Cool specs by the way. They suit you.'

'Thanks,' Daisy grinned. 'Isabella has only to look at her hands to realise that something odd is happening. It's too freaky for her overly-regimented mind.'

Archie grinned. 'So, what next?'

'For starters,' she said, smiling at him, 'you need to start wearing a hat.'

'Really?'

Daisy pulled a black hat out of her pocket and threw it at him. 'Try this, it's one of Dad's. Found it while rummaging around upstairs.'

'Have you been through their entire wardrobe?'

'Yeah, pretty much. Go on, try it.'

Archie put it on and Daisy clapped her hands. 'Fan-tastic!'

'I can't go around with a black beanie on my head. I look like a bad French artist—'

'But it's cool.'

Archie took it off and examined it. 'Really?'

'It's got you written all over it. Seriously,' she said, 'if we think that our dreams actually mean something, then you and me are going to have to figure out the next part, with or without her.'

Archie sighed. 'Great.'

'Let's start with those caveman paintings on the wall,' she said. 'Did you study them?'

'A bit,' Archie said. 'I don't think I saw a fraction of what you did.'

'They were all about finding the tablets. I've been searching already.'

'Found anything?'

'Nope. Just these glasses, your hat, and these cool, fingerless, studded leather gloves for Isabella. What do you think?'

Archie inspected them. 'They're so not her.'

She laughed. 'You think? Well, they might make her look a little less of a nerd.'

'But I still don't get what we have to do,' he said.

Daisy put an arm round him. 'Don't worry. Trust me, it's a piece of cake. As I keep telling you, all we've got to do is get to the next stage.'

'Next stage?'

'Yeah, we've just got to find the tablets depicted on the cave wall,' Daisy said, slapping him on his back. 'No idea where we start, but, as I said, we'll figure it out.'

The door yawned open as they entered the living room.

'What do you think, Old Man Wood?' Daisy said.

The old man was looking particularly pale. The lines on his face were deeper and more ingrained than usual. He sat in his chair and stared straight ahead at the wall. No words came out of his mouth.

'Woo-hoo! Anyone there?' Daisy said, waving a hand in front of his face. 'Anyone home?'

Old Man Wood blinked and rubbed his face.

Daisy shook her head, her hair bouncing in the firelight. 'A right load of zombies tonight,' she said, throwing herself onto the sofa. She opened the Bible, flicked through to the first pages, and started to read.

Archie looked at her with his mouth open. 'You all right, Daisy?'

'What do you mean?'

'You're reading!'

Daisy shrugged. 'Why not?'

'For starters, I didn't know you could read.'

'Ha ha. Hilarious, aren't you?' She turned the page, 'I've got a hunch, Winkle,' she said referring to her personal nickname, which she knew deeply irritated him. 'There's something in here. Something that we're missing.'

Archie looked baffled. 'Missing?' He pulled a face. 'You think so?'

'Yup,' Daisy said. 'Still don't know why it's us, though. Beats me.' Her eyes sparkled. She rather enjoyed Archie looking confused. 'There's a link between our dreams, the storm, and the pictures in the cave. If we don't find the tablets, the images on the walls clearly showed that we die—'

'Great—'

'Unless, of course, we miraculously find them,' Daisy added. 'So, it's not all bad.'

'Yes, it is!' he said, 'It's death. The end of this thing we do called living.'

Daisy pouted and returned to her reading.

Archie studied her. 'You actually think we're going to survive, don't you?'

'Yep.'

'How come?'

'Because we beat the storm, and it can't get any harder than that, can it? I also know that I very nearly died, and that you two got a zapping from lightning bolts, hence your hair and Isabella's hands. But I didn't die, thanks to you two. I'm convinced that if we do this together, we're stronger. Oh, and by the way, if any of us fail, we're screwed. All dead, instantly.'

Archie frowned. 'But Isabella doesn't want to know. She's given up.'

Daisy shrugged. 'Then we're already dead.'

Archie leaned forward in his chair, his chin resting in his hands. 'You think she'll shift?'

'Sure. She's just having a little wobble, that's all.'

Archie shook his head. Daisy didn't sound in the least bit worried. 'Aren't you terrified?'

'Nah,' she replied. 'What's the point? Go with the flow, Arch. Go with the flow.' Daisy nodded at her words of wisdom and returned to her reading.

Archie looked puzzled. 'Any idea how long we've got?'

Daisy lifted her head out of the page. 'What, before we die? I'm working on it right now,' she said. She carried on reading, flicking the pages back and forth.

A moment later, she closed the book. 'There are loads of references to the creation of the world, so I thought I'd count the numbers,' she announced. Archie perked up. 'Perhaps the storm represents a new beginning and is aimed at wiping out the world for some reason. Typically, creation stories from around the world work on seven-day cycle. And there are endless references to seven. Seven deadly sins. Seven cycles of life—'

'Seven days of the week,' Archie added.

Daisy shot him a look. 'I'm pretty sure there was a seven-day reference in the cave. The bottom line is this. I'm pretty sure that from the moment the storm went berserk, I'd stab a guess that we have seven days to do whatever it is we've got to do.'

SUE REMEMBERS HER PHONE

Isabella lay on her bed and stared at her cream-coloured bookshelves. She liked the regimented order, the neatness and simplicity of her book-cataloguing. How odd that one of the books was upside down and yet the only person who'd been in was Daisy. She couldn't have rummaged through her bookcase again, could she? Isabella stood up, picked out the book and studied it. "The Evolution of Man." Goodness, what was happening to her sister? Isabella slotted it in the correct way and sat down on her duvet.

It was time to think. Everything that had happened could be linked scientifically and logically, surely? But her arguments had logic holes the size of France. She sighed and rolled over. She wished Sue was here to talk it through. It would be clearer then, she was sure of it.

Sue had this skill of making complex problems easy to understand, like her explanation of particle physics which Isabella had initially struggled to get her head around. Sue asked her to imagine how it was possible to look inside two cars that have no windows or doors. She replied that it was impossible, but Sue told her that the answer was to smash them together. And that, in a nutshell, Sue explained, was what physicists were doing with particles in an attempt to find out what lay beyond.

Isabella swung her legs off the bed, stood up, and stared at her reflection in the mirror. She looked a fraction thinner, her pointy nose a bit sharper, and her eyes wore a watery sheen. As she brushed her hair, she mulled over the argument with her brother and sister.

She held up her right hand and looked through the neat hole in the middle of her palm.

Perhaps she shouldn't have been quite so hard on them. After all, they were only trying to work it out, and they were a lot younger than her and not nearly so clever.

She'd apologise, especially for the chair-throwing and the glass-crushing episode. She picked up a picture of the family that sat in a simple, silver frame by her bed. So odd our parents not being here, she thought. Not a word, either. She wondered if they had even the smallest inkling of what they'd been through, and if they missed her even a fraction of the amount that she missed them.

It had stopped raining for now, but threatening clouds still hung low over the valley. The evening light had a bitty-dusty texture now that the sun's dappled rays had sneaked under a sheet of grey cloud. She opened a drawer and squinted in the half-light searching for a hair clip when she saw her mobile phone.

As she stared at it, she knew it might give them contact with the outside world but as they had no power, aside from the petrol generator, no communications and no TV, her hopes weren't high.

And anyway, who would she call and what would she say?

Her heartbeat quickened at the possibility of receiving news. Terrible news, she suspected. More importantly, she wondered if there might be a message from Sue or her parents.

She placed the phone back in the drawer, pushed it closed and walked away.

Then she ran back, and opened it again.

She pressed the power button and the phone loaded. First one, then three, signal bars came up and the battery indicator showed that half the charge was available.

Messages bleeped in.

Isabella read the first text and bit her lip. She trembled. Others, it appeared, had experienced the same conditions or worse, and many were still going through a terrible time.

The difference was that while they were alive, most of the messages were about whether anyone had found Jimmy, or Gus, Charlie, Poppy, or Lara. These were heart-breaking messages; families in frantic searches of their loved ones. Most, she knew, would never get replies.

In no time at all, Isabella was downstairs and heading towards the living room. She poked her head around the door.

'Daisy, Archie!' she said, her voice quivering with excitement.

Daisy was reading on the sofa. Archie was sitting in the smaller armchair, opposite Old Man Wood who looked bored.

'Firstly, I'm sorry I had a go at you,' Isabella said. 'I... was wrong to yell and explode the glass.'

Daisy turned her eyes up from her book and smiled. 'It doesn't matter. We'll work it out, you'll see.'

'You're reading?' Isabella said. She couldn't remember ever seeing Daisy read.

Daisy rolled her eyes. 'Yeah, yeah. Thought I'd give it a try.'

Isabella shook her head, moved in to the middle of the room, and sat down on the floor next to Archie's chair. 'The other thing,' she said, her voice quaking, 'is that my phone's working. I've got some reception and there's a bit of battery.'

Daisy and Archie's ears pricked up.

'Any messages?' Archie asked.

'Yes, tons.'

In a flash they were gathered around their elder sister, peering over her shoulder.

'Hey! Wait a mo,' she said, 'probably best if I read them out. I'm warning you though, there's no good news. Seriously.'

Daisy got the message, dashed off, and returned with a roll of kitchen paper.

'Right,' Isabella said, quietly. 'Our weird, bad week has just got officially worse.' She looked them both in the eye. 'Are you sure you want to hear this?'

Daisy and Archie nodded.

'OK.' Isabella took a deep breath and let the air out slowly. 'Here goes. First up, a message from Alice. Mr Beattie's body floated past yesterday—face down, so couldn't be sure—but identical blue and red tracksuit, same build.'

Daisy gasped. 'Coach... dead,' she said under her breath, her eyes welling. 'He can't be.'

'I'm so sorry, Daisy,' Isabella said. 'I know how much he meant to you. And just to think, Archie so nearly went with him after the game.'

For several minutes she read on and, as she read, the others stared into the fire. They were lost in their thoughts, tears rolling down their cheeks.

'Are you sure you want to hear more?' Isabella asked, worried that this might not be helping them.

Archie and Daisy nodded.

'Another from Alice. She doesn't think they'll get through another night. She reckons they've had it.' Her voice began cracking. 'It's the rain that's getting them. There's nothing but wet and cold, and they're starving. There's nothing to eat and there's some sort of poisonous sewage in the water. Disease is beginning to spread.' Isabella dabbed her eyes with a paper towel. 'Here are the people missing or drowned.' She read out Alice's list, choking back her tears until she couldn't go on.

There was a long silence. The only noises were the gentle crackling of the fire,

Old Man Wood's slow, deep snores and the tip-tapping of rain, which had started to fall again. The light from the flames licked the inside of the old room.

Finally, Daisy spoke. 'Any news from Sue?'

'No, nothing, no,' Isabella said.

'What about the football teams?' Archie said. 'They must have been the last ones out of there.' The school football match had been played right to the end, even when others began to disappear due to the lightning and thunder bursting out around them.

Isabella scrolled down. 'Chitbury bus discovered five miles downstream.'

Then she read out another school message. 'Missing: Johnson, Cook, Hill, Allen, and Alexander. Gus Williams missing too. Kemp's coat found, but no body.'

'What about little Jimmy Nugent, Jo, and Cassie?' Daisy cried.

'Sorry, Daisy. No word on them, I'm afraid,' Isabella said, as she scrolled on. 'Here's one from the headmaster.'

'SCHOOL ABANDONED DUE TO FLOOD DISASTER. WILL NOTIFY IN DUE COURSE. GOD BE WITH YOU ALL IN OUR HOUR OF NEED—Solomon.'

'I'll reply that we're safe. At least they'll know.'

'I wonder if the school even exists anymore,' Archie said. 'It happened so fast —the football match was mental—'

Isabella suddenly stood up and began pacing the room. 'That's it!' she exclaimed. 'THAT'S IT!' The others watched her, intrigued. 'OK, it might look like I'm backtracking,' she said, 'but you know Sue and I had been working on a 'worst case storm situation' in the event of this phenomenon?'

'Uh-huh,' Daisy replied. 'The whole storm glass thing.'

'Well, yes. You see, Sue dreamt about the flooding as well, and she... she...'

'What is it?' Archie cried.

'Oh heavens,' Isabella whispered, going pale and stumbling. 'It's... it's so obvious—'

'What is?'

Isabella sat down. 'Sue—' she began before stopping.

'Isabella, are you, all right?'

Isabella scrunched her eyes tight. 'Sue told me she had a nightmare about a flood at the school. She said it was the most real and terrifying dream ever. I told her I'd had a dream like that too, so we looked into it to see what might be happening on a physical level. But, she kept on wanting to tell me something else. I kept avoiding her rantings—I thought it was something to do with a crush—'

'Why was it so important?' Daisy asked.

Isabella stood up and resumed her pacing, talking as she went. 'The thing is, Sue is meticulous about note-taking. And believe you me, she records loads of strange things. She scribbled her nightmare down, instantly, step by step, until the images slipped from her mind. It meant that she had a pretty clear idea of what she'd seen, whereas our recollections were basically a frightening assortment of freaky pictures, weren't they. Ours were confusing and scary and we more or less instantly forgot them, and this stems partially from the fact that none of us wrote them down. Agreed?'

'Absolutely,' Daisy said.

Archie smiled. 'Are you saying now that there might be some purpose to our dreams?'

Isabella flashed him a wry smile. 'No, I'm not there yet, Archie.'

'This would explain,' Daisy said, 'why she yelled at you on the football pitch.'

'How do you know that?'

'I can hear everything, remember,' Daisy reminded her with a knowing smile. 'Just before Archie did his "beat up the referee" act, she ran on after you.'

Isabella stopped still. 'You're right!' she said. 'I heard her too. What did she say? You've got to remember!'

'I wasn't really listening.'

'Look, please try and remember, Daisy,' Isabella said. 'It's important.'

Isabella sat down as Daisy ran through what had happened. 'I'd been hacked to the ground and lay still, trying to keep out of the way when little Jimmy Nugent charged in and everyone started fighting. Archie threw one of their guys about four feet in the air—unbelievably cool—and I was probably the only person who wasn't getting stuck in. Then I heard a voice. Sue's voice—yeah, definitely, now I think of it - screaming something like "the rain—it's all your fault".'

The three of them looked at each other.

'Our fault. OUR fault,' Archie said. 'That's pretty full-on. You sure?'

'No, probs not,' Daisy shrugged. 'Something similar, though.'

Isabella groaned.

'No, wait!' Daisy exclaimed. Her eyes glowed. She kneaded her forehead. 'It was about you. That's it. It's "all about you!" That's what she yelled.'

'Anything else?'

'Yes,' Daisy said, turning to Isabella as the memory flooded back. She said, "you're the only ones who can stop it".'

'Me? Stop it?' Isabella said.

'That's close, but it's not quite right,' Archie said, standing up and clasping Daisy's shoulders. 'What she said was, "only you and your family—the de Lowes—can stop it".'

'Stop the rain?' Isabella asked.

Archie shrugged. 'Yeah, I suppose. The storm, the rain, everything. That must be what she meant.'

Daisy clapped her hands. 'And,' she said, as more memories flooded in, 'that we "must find clues in Eden Cottage".'

'Clues, to what?' Isabella quizzed.

Daisy shrugged. 'I don't know. I thought she'd lost her marbles.'

'Maybe she had,' Isabella said. 'Or, maybe you two are making it up. It's not that convincing—'

'Perhaps,' Archie said, 'she was referring to the clues to finding the tablets that were in the pictures in the cave?'

'You really think so?' Daisy said, winking at Archie.

Isabella sighed. 'Look, forget it. I don't think it's fair to jump to conclusions about Sue's mental health state at that point in time by instantly linking her words with your caveman pictures.'

'But you just said how important it was—'

'Yes, I know I did. But before you two think I'm going to believe you, I require proof, and proper science-based proof at that, not some crazy shouting in the middle of a football match with dubious links to Neolithic art. Sue could have been trying to say any number of things.'

'Yeah, right,' Daisy said, her voice cold. 'We've got seven days to find whatever we've got to find and you being like this really isn't helping.'

ASGARD'S POWDERS

Gaia flashed into view. The caves on Havilah were bigger and more majestic than she'd realised. In the shape of an arc, with water cascading over the top of ochre-coloured cliff edges that were dotted with sweeping fronds of ferns and boughs of fallen trees. From here, water flowed into one great underground river. She was deep in the jungles of Havilah's Southern Lands, a place similar to the hot, equatorial landscapes she'd seen on Earth and she'd come to see the new dream powders many of the dreamspinners had been talking about.

She noticed tiny flashes of light and followed them. There were hundreds of dreamspinners funnelling into the main, vast chamber of the caves through a narrow slit in the rock.

In the middle of the chamber sat a large pile of light green crystals; the new dream powders.

Looking up into the tall roof of the cave she noticed fat, hairy, orange and black arachnids with long shiny legs. They were weaving webs like intricate frost patterns.

Gaia switched modes so that she was invisible to all dreamspinners except those who had done the same as her but they could read her vibrations, should she put any out.

She noticed how dreamspinners were walking through the air amongst the spiders, pulling the webs into their magholes. Dream powders were being manufactured for a purpose, like a factory, she realised, not harvested randomly.

Moments later, a dreamspinners flashed through its maghole next to her. Then three more, in quick succession all in the same mode.

'Asgard. I see you.'

'And I you, Gaia.'

'Who are these others? Are they of your kin?'

'They help me,' Asgard said. 'Times are changing, Gaia. See how my production of dream powders keeps dreamspinners busy. It is a wonder, is it not? Different dream powders can now be made while the planet of the Garden of Eden lies empty. I have plans for more caves like this. I intend to make these dream powders only available to dreamspinners who wish to become my kin.'

Gaia felt mildly threatening vibrations. There is nothing to fear, she thought. They are dreamspinners. 'I have come to see and to learn,' she vibrated, politely. 'There is much talk, Asgard.'

On top of the green mound a mist began to descend, floating right on top of the mound.

Asgard detected Gaia's interest in the vapours. 'For some time, I have studied the powder of arachnids. I have concluded that a fresh dream is a better dream,' he vibrated. 'The mist keeps the powders as I wish, for the webs of these spiders are complex and lose their vivacity too quickly.'

'I have never heard of such a thing,' Gaia said.

'Perhaps you would like to try? Of course, they are free for all to use right now. They may not be in due course.'

Gaia's deep black oval eyes betrayed shock. This was nothing short of a barter for dreamspinners loyalty. A notion utterly unrecognisable in their species.

'I will.' Gaia said, as she flashed into visible mode and inverted next to the green pile where other dreamspinners jostled.

The mist smelt of something familiar. Something she had known of late, but the exact specification eluded her.

'Take however much you like,' Asgard remarked. 'dreamspinners are surprised by the quality and the amount of dreams one is able to deliver. I trust you will be, too.'

Gaia morphed a leg into a small trowel-like end and shovelled a small mound into her blue flaming maghole.

'You see!' Asgard said, vibrating loudly to the room. The other dreamspinners fell silent. 'The great, and long-living Gaia, head of her kin, is here with us. She tries the new powders.'

A general vibration fizzed about.

Gaia glanced at Asgard, and inverted to a spot in the middle of the galaxy. Then, wondering what to do with the powder, she inverted again to a faint vibration she had stored away and now honed in on. She needed to find Genesis.

SOLOMON FINDS THE SECRET LIBRARY

Considering the conditions, the children in the tower had behaved splendidly. The curtains of the windows in the tower had made giant blankets, and a large fire burned in the old fireplace keeping the room warm through the night.

Solomon and the other members of staff had attempted to call the emergency services but the lines were down, or constantly engaged. The headmaster lit a couple of candles and went to his desk. He had an idea that the best person to notify was his cousin, Police Commissioner Charlie Stone. He'd let him know about survivors, who were mainly children, and with luck Stone would pull some strings and get them out. Sooner, he hoped, rather than later.

He punched a text into his mobile phone. When it bleeped into the ether he allowed himself a smile.

Perhaps, Solomon thought, it was time to climb up to the top of the tower to examine some of the ancient books.

When he took over at the school, the previous headmaster had indicated that there was no staircase to the tower because the books therein needed to remain undisturbed. He implied that no-one should venture in and no-one should ever know about it. It was their own little secret.

Solomon soon forgot about it until several years ago, when the tower's electrics required a rewire, the lightning conductor replacing, and the masonry required re-pointing and a fresh coat of paint.

One day a ladder arrived with the builders that stretched up to a hidden trap door in what looked like a false ceiling. And, shortly after, John de Lowe, the children's father had appeared.

Solomon had climbed up after John, who, after checking the low, dingy room for what he needed, declared that he needed to study and archive the library in total secrecy. de Lowe had slipped the foreman a fifty-pound note to leave the ladder where it was and, while the archaeologist was collecting his things, Solomon, for a brief, wonderful hour, had taken a torch and opened some of the great, huge old tomes that lay there. In no time he was back down and that was it. The years had passed but the ladder remained, out of sight, behind a bookcase.

Now that Solomon had pushed the ladder together to the spot he imagined contained the secret room, he climbed the long ladder, prised open the hatch, pulled himself through and stared at the huge, dusty leather-bound books once again, he wondered if this library might hold secrets to this terrible event?

He selected a huge leather bound, lifted it to the oak desk, unclipped the metal buckle, and levered it open. The thick sheets of old vellum felt like animal hide as they fell open.

He found a story, drawn out in neat pictures about three knights, he presumed, even though the writing that accompanied it was in a language he didn't understand. Following this was a story of three wise men. Perhaps he was looking at an original Nativity story? For a moment Solomon noticed his heart fluttering. Were these ancient scriptures he'd stumbled across? Examining the page, he noted how the vellum looked as if it had once been rolled up, how the dimensions appeared to be a little crudely cut.

Ancient scrolls turned into a book?

But why here, of all places?

He closed the book up and replaced it with another. This one seemed to show a battle, as if a whole world was at war.

Intrigued, he was about to reach for another when his phone bleeped.

Solomon sat down and opened the app.

It was from his cousin, Stone!

The message read:

OK received. I'll get assistance to you for tomorrow morning at the tower. Can you access the roof? Charlie.

Solomon smiled. Thank goodness.

But access to the roof? He searched the room. How would they get onto the top?

He picked up a candle and walked around trying to ascertain if there was some kind of staircase to the tower roof.

Then he remembered the words of the former headmaster who had once jokingly referred to a secret stairwell that supposedly connected the main room of the tower to the turret. He'd fleetingly wondered about this, but had never given it any further thought.

Now that he looked around, candlelight flickering into all corners, the tiny room appeared as symmetrical, and without any access points—apart from the hatch.

He'd have to check the stairs lower down, to see if there was some kind of sealed door. But as the flooding had risen all the way up to the height of the school chapel roof adjoining it, it was unlikely he would find anything without diving down into the water. And unless they smashed through the lead-held stained glass and somehow climbed up the exterior walls, they were going precisely nowhere. His spirits sank.

His phone bleeped again.

Solomon wondered if it was Stone hassling him already. But in an instance, his dim mood changed into joy.

'By all the spirits!' he exclaimed, removing his glasses. 'They did it. Those fine de Lowes ruddy well did it! They actually made it home. How the heck did they manage that?'

OLD MAN WOOD'S MOMENT OF CLARITY

After the teenagers had read every message about the tragedy unfolding in the valley beneath them, another message popped onto Isabella's screen.

'WONDERFUL! GR8 U SAFE! THANX FOR LETTING ME KNOW. CAN ONLY APOLOGISE 4 NOT LISTENING TO U ISA. WISH I HAD. TERRIBLE LOSSES. MANAGED TO FIND SHELTER IN THE TOWER. HELP TAKING AGES 2 ARRIVE. SEEMS WE R LUCKY ONES. HEARING THAT DISEASE IS RIFE. A STRANGE POISON IN WATER. BE CAREFUL—SOLOMON.'

Almost immediately, a bleep from the phone meant another new text had arrived. Isabella studied it, her hair falling over her face like a curtain. She squealed in delight and thumped the air.

'Who is it from?' Archie demanded, leaning in.

They all turned around as a deep groan emerged from the armchair. Old Man Wood stirred, yawned, and stretched out his long arms. He blinked, rubbed his eyes and smiled as he saw the children around him. Then without warning, the old man jumped smartly to his feet and exploded into laughter.

The children looked on in complete astonishment while deep guffaws echoed from his big, barrelled chest.

Moments later, a thunderbolt crashed over the cottage rattling the windows.

Isabella ducked, and Archie and Daisy instinctively threw themselves behind the sofa. But all the while, Old Man Wood stood and roared with laughter, as if he hadn't a care in the world.

They stared at the large man with their mouths wide open, their hearts fluttering.

Suddenly, a gust of wind shot down the chimney and extinguished the candles. The children froze as they were plunged into darkness, but as their sight adjusted, the flames in the fire flickered rich and vivid colours into the room. They collected themselves.

'Are you all right, Old Man Wood?' Archie whispered.

'Fine, my boy. Fine,' Old Man Wood replied, returning to his chair and leaning forward towards the flames. 'Something smouldering in the back of my mind suddenly burst into flames,' he said. His weathered, bony features were enhanced by the firelight, and his eyes seemed to shine like the stars. His wrinkles looked deeper, as though filled with experiences. 'Something I remembered from a long time ago, that's all.'

'Right, drama over,' Isabella said, gathering herself. 'Would you like to hear who the text was from?' Daisy and Archie moved in next to her, trying to catch a peek at the screen.

'It's from Sue!' she exclaimed.

'You're kidding!'

'She's alive!' Isabella started dancing in front of the fire. 'In fact,' Isabella continued, 'it's better than that. She's with Gus!'

'No way!'

'Yes, way! Together they made it through the storm.'

'But how?' Archie asked. 'Are they in hospital—'

'No, no, it's incredible,' Isabella said, her voice singing. 'I scribbled on a piece of paper about the boat and shoved it in Sue's pocket. When Sue ran off, she bumped into Gus and persuaded him to join her and she found the note. They looted the shop, Gus built a shelter over the boat, and, because of that, they survived! Apparently, Gus has been nothing short of heroic. They're out at sea and they've just caught a fish!'

'Blimey,' Archie said. 'That really is incredible.'

'It's mega news, sis,' Daisy cried, and she hugged Isabella.

'And there's more.'

'What do you mean, more?'

Isabella could hardly stop giggling. She found herself blushing and pushing her siblings away.

'What is it?'

Tears welled in her eyes. 'They've fallen in love.'

Archie reeled. 'Oh no! Gus—are you sure?'

'Gus, with Sue?' Daisy added. 'Didn't see that happening.'

Isabella shook her head. 'They've kissed!'

Archie reddened just thinking about it.

'They've been snogging?' Daisy laughed. 'Epic!'

'Yup!' squealed Isabella. 'Snogging!' she repeated.

'Ooh-eeee!' The girls squealed in delight.

While the joys of Sue and Gus's love affair dominated the conversation, Old Man Wood picked his way around the room and relit several of the candles. Then he slipped out of the room to do the same in the hallway and kitchen.

For the first time in ages, his whole body fizzed with energy, as if a touch paper had exploded a great big memory rocket right inside his mind. While many vital clues, he feared, still remained locked out, one thing had come to him with clarity. The answers to some of his questions lay with special old friends whom he needed to find, and fast. If he was correct, they would fill in his blanks.

While Isabella put the finishing touches to her text reply, the twins were discussing the revelation of Gus and Sas's kissing.

'Tell me,' Archie said, 'how do you actually, properly snog?'

'OK, listen up bro,' Daisy replied in a very educational manner. 'Push your lips together, shut your eyes, open your mouth a bit, poke out your tongue, and swirl it around.'

'Oh, my!' Archie said. His look of revulsion said it all. 'And that's supposed to be nice?'

'Yeah, I suppose,' Daisy replied.

'What if you start dribbling?' he asked. 'And what if you bash your teeth?'

'You don't—'

'How do you know?'

Daisy pouted her lips. 'Cos, I do.'

'Anyway,' Archie asked, 'if you're swirling away, how are you supposed to breathe? Isn't it all just a bit uncomfortable and awkward and what if the person you're kissing has bad breath, like Kemp?'

'God, Archie, you're so ten, aren't you?'

Archie frowned. How come Daisy knew all this stuff? 'Have you actually done it?' he said.

'Might have,' Daisy replied coyly. 'A couple of times.'

Archie eyed her suspiciously. 'I don't think you have. You're telling me a big fat porky pie.'

Daisy winked at him with a smile on her face. 'That's for me to know, and you to find out.'

Old Man Wood returned and coughed. The children fell quiet. 'Time for bed. I'll put the generator on in the morning,' he said. 'But would any of you like to hear one of my stories?'

'Oh yeah! But only if it's got absolutely nothing to do with snogging,' Archie said.

Old Man Wood's stories were fantastic tales, full of heroes, magicians, witches, evil overlords, and brutal wars. They nearly always contained adventures about tree men, who were the bravest and noblest of creatures. The way he delivered the stories felt like fire and ice blended perfectly together; his face alone, full of wrinkles, seemed to express the meaning in the story.

When the stories were happy his eyes sparkled like the bright North Star. And when they were sad, dark clouds cloaked his eyes and his wrinkles grew deep and long. The shadows from the wavering firelight dramatised the effect so much that the children would ask questions for days after, such as, "What happened to the Warlbist when her husband gave in to the Floak?" or "How did the Spurtle really get its fur?"

Daisy smiled. 'How about the Iso story?'

'We always have the Iso story,' Archie moaned.

'Because it's beautiful and she is so awesome.'

'But it's sooo girly—'

'Iso's story is an excellent choice,' Isabella added. 'Just what we need, so long as it's only the beginning.'

'Ah, yes,' Old Man Wood said, winking at the girls. 'A story of love and friendship and derring-do! But afterwards, no questions, it's straight to bed.'

ARCHIE AND OLD MAN WOOD HEAD OUT

Old Man Wood had always been old; his face deeply lined by the journey of time, his teeth worn to dull stumps, his remaining hair random and straggly, his skin blotched and wrinkled. He stared out of the window at the charcoal colours of early morning that filtered through the dark clouds and turned to study the frame of his rectangular four-poster bed, which jutted out into the room like a big wooden box. He noted the strange patterns and carvings which adorned every upright and crossbeam, and wondered if they offered any clues to finding the tablets Daisy had gone on about.

He examined the three rectangular panels at its foot, showing live pictures of the children. Old Man Wood scratched his chin. If it hadn't been for these panels he had discovered during the storm, he would never have been able to work out the children's location and go to rescue them. Hadn't that been a stroke of luck? But how on earth did the panels work, and why?

It was a simple room. On the floor lay five brown, dirt-ingrained rugs. Behind them stood a large wardrobe, where he stored his few patched-up clothes. In front of the window sat a worn brown leather sofa.

Classical wooden panelling, made from many different tree species, covered the walls and made them glow with an unlikely variety of colour. How unfussy it was, how strangely beautiful, and how well it suited him.

Every night since the rain had begun he'd fallen into a deep sleep and then woken, sweating and yelling, gripping the sheets until his hands hurt and his fingernails digging into his palms. Last night it was the same: blinding flashes, searing heat, followed by intense cold.

Goosebumps appeared as he remembered his dream; the strange alien-like creature with a wispy, ghost-like appearance, spider-like in form with several long legs and a blue ring of fire in its abdomen. He closed his eyes, but the snapshots refused to go away. Why did this creature, more than anything he could think of, fill him with such dread?

Old Man Wood frowned and stretched his arms out wide. Maybe he'd be better off in front of the fire with a strong cup of tea. *Might just fix my head and settle my nerves.*

With his brew in hand, he ambled through, grabbed some kindling and a couple of logs and placed them on the embers. Soon, a small golden flame danced nervously around the wood as it tentatively tried to take hold. Old Man Wood sank into his armchair and stared at the fire, trying as best he might to understand the images in his head.

Perhaps the fire needed a bit of a poke.

As he grabbed the steel fire prong, a tune jumped into his head. But this was no ordinary tune.

'Whooosh, hummmy, sshhhhh, whooosh,' he began humming. He didn't know why, but the song sounded like wind pushing through the leaves of trees and as natural as a ditty spontaneously sung by the children.

As he sang, he reached out and prodded the burning logs, enjoying the way the flames danced and licked yellow and tangerine with greater intensity. He hummed the tune a little louder, with more vigour, liking how it blended with the rhythms of the crackling fire. Now his singing was coming from a place deep within him, the tune filling him with a kind of inner strength that began in his loins, spread to his heart, and radiated to his fingertips and toes.

As he stared an object grew in the middle of the fire and floated towards him. In all the apples, he thought, what is it? A lump of… what? Mesmerised, he found his hand drawn towards it and, moments later, he found his fingers uncurling.

His fingers touched it. Much to his surprise he found that the fire and the stone were cool to touch, and it was solid, as if made of granite. He pulled, but the object would not yield.

'Now then,' Mrs Pye's voice called out, shattering his concentration and the song. 'What the blazing saddles do you think you're doing?' She stared at him from the doorway.

Old Man Wood suddenly felt the heat. 'OUCH! Blasted thing!' he cursed, rubbing his hands.

'You all right?' she said. 'Messing with fire, and at your age too—you should be more careful.'

Confused, Old Man Wood stood up and marched around the room rubbing his chin, humming to himself, trying to think. Then he made his way into the boot room, where he donned his cap, threw on his green waterproof coat, and wrestled his boots onto his large feet.

After he'd seen to the cattle, he thought, he'd seek out the old friends he'd remembered earlier at a place he used to know as The Bubbling Brook.

Archie woke with a start.

He yawned, removed the sleep from his eyes, and looked at his watch. Five o'clock. A bit early, but for the first time in ages he felt refreshed after such a long and nourishing sleep without dreaming.

And anyway, this morning, he'd decided to go and throw his knives in the potting shed. This was something he did whenever he was stressed or upset, and he found it always settled his mind. He dressed quickly and crept out of their attic room.

He wasn't the first up. 'Morning, Old Man Wood,' he said as he poked his head round the kitchen door. 'You're up early. Everything alright?'

Old Man Wood waved a hand in Archie's direction. 'Morning, littlun. Peculiar stuff going on in here.' He pointed to his head and then stretched his arms out to pull down the cuffs on his coat. 'Very, very strange things,' he tapped his head again. 'I've been to see the cattle,' he said, changing the subject, 'give them more feed. My, oh my, they looked utterly terrified, which is hardly surprising, considering. None of them have eaten and I squeezed only drops out of Bernice and Burger, dear things.'

He stopped and stroked his chin. 'It's as if they're trying to tell me something. What are you doing up so early?'

'Might go and throw my knives, take my mind off stuff,' Archie replied, rubbing his temples. 'Are you off out again?'

'Yes, littlun, I also need to clear this old head of mine,' he said as he studied the boy. 'Now, before I go, is there anything I can help you with?'

Archie looked up at Old Man Wood. 'I'm really missing Mum and Dad,' he said.

'Of course you are,' the old man replied. He pulled him in for a hug. 'I've noticed that none of you lot are playing. Lots of arguing and funny conversations. What's up?'

'It's the rain, I think,' Archie said, wishing he could say more. It had been raining since the football match, and Archie wondered when it would end. 'Also being stuck here and feeling utterly helpless and worrying about our friends and... and things like the cave, and those pictures, and my stupid hair.'

'Hmmm,' Old Man Wood said. 'Think I know what you mean.'

'Where are you off to?' Archie asked.

Old Man Wood scratched his chin. 'I'm off to find some old friends—they might be able to help at a time like this.'

'Friends? Where?'

'Well, I don't know. Down there, somewhere.'

'You're, er…, quite sure about this?'

'Oh yes, Archie.'

Archie thought for a while. 'Can I come, too?' he said.

Old Man Wood rubbed his mottled head. Taking Archie to find the Bubbling Brook could be a big mistake, foremost because he had no idea where it was. 'I'm not sure you're ready to come along, little Archie.'

'Yes, I am,' he said instinctively.

'If you come along, you're going to have to swear to me, Archie, that you won't mention it to your sisters. Especially Isabella. I heard what she said, earlier.'

'Why?'

'Because I'm asking you, that's why,' he replied. 'Just for now at any rate.'

'I don't understand,' Archie said.

Old Man Wood felt himself getting tangled up with the words. 'Well, these friends might upset you, that's all,' Old Man Wood said gently. 'Thing is, they would most definitely upset young Isabella.'

'Where do they live?'

Old Man Wood draped an arm round Archie's shoulders. 'Once upon a time, I discovered something at the foot of the ruin.' The ruin stood near to the farmhouse on the top of the Moors with a steep cliff that sheered down to the valley floor on one side. The children had played up there all their lives.

'It struck me that I might find it again.'

'Somewhere near the cave?' Archie looked puzzled.

'There or thereabouts, I suppose,' Old Man Wood said, opening the door, which creaked. 'You can come along, but don't say I didn't warn you.'

SEARCHING FOR THE BUBBLING BROOK

Dawn threaded a soft murky light across the vale. In front of them the floodwaters stretched like a vast flowing silver lake.

After slipping and sliding down the steep track, and squelching through the saturated fields, they were soon at the water's edge. Old Man Wood took a couple of deep breaths, shook some mud from his boots, furrowed his brow, and peered into the rain.

'Now, where are those funny old trees?' he said out loud.

'You're looking for trees?'

Old Man Wood nodded.

'There are thousands,' Archie said, shivering. 'Do you know which type they are?'

'Oh, yes. Willows. Great big clump of 'em.'

Archie studied the expanse of water with trees popping out, like miniature crowns.

'Willows?' he said, avoiding a large puddle. 'The valley's littered with willow clumps. Most are underwater. What if it's one of those?'

Old Man Wood strode off, his boots squelching in the mud. 'Something tells me it's around the headland towards Upsall. Come on, Archie, this way.'

After a couple of unsuccessful attempts at entering the thick brambles surrounding one thicket, and then doing exactly the same thing with another, Old Man Wood began to wonder if he'd gone the right way. He stamped his boot down in the sludge and a shower of sloppy, brown water sprayed over some sodden ferns.

He stopped to think. It wasn't brawn that would lead them to the willows, it was brains, just as he often told the children. The place was known as the Bubbling Brook because the water came from under the ground and bubbled, gently. He found an old tree stump, sat down, closed his eyes, and tried to concentrate.

Old Man Wood stood up and sat down again, all the while mumbling to himself. Then up. Now down. Without warning, he shot off, following the water-line towards Upsall. Archie watched Old Man Wood with a mixture of curiosity and growing anxiety. The old man's excitement bordered on madness, real madness. It was like watching a child at a fairground who couldn't work out where his favourite ride had gone.

Archie hurried to keep up. Most of the thickets that followed the water's edge were identical, with their leaves stripped by the rain. Defeated by the first two, they waded through shin-high water, where at length they met a huge cluster of brambles and fallen trees with twisted, smashed branches.

In front of them, a mudslide blocked their path. They slipped, climbed and squelched back up the hill towards the ruin, reverting down to the water's edge.

Soon, a willow clump consisting of new shoots and whips and three huge, old trees blocked their path.

On one side, several large trees stood half-submerged in the floodwater, on the other a mess of trees, rocks, and brambles had collected where the ground had slipped away.

Archie caught his breath. 'Look, there's no way we'll get through there,' he complained. 'Why don't we head back?'

Old Man Wood groaned. 'Nonsense. I'll use a bit of beef and bludgeon a way through the middle,' he replied.

In no time, the old man had shinned up one of the large outer trees and was balancing on a long, thick branch that leaned from one side of the clump to the other. Archie climbed up after him and watched as the old man moved one foot in front of the other, his arms outstretched as if on a tightrope.

A quarter of the way across, Old Man Wood sat down. 'Blasted water!' the old man cried. He bent his leg round, removed his boot, and poured a stream out into the pool beneath him.

As Old Man Wood wrestled his welly back on, he eyed a route across that would involve a couple of leaps from branch to branch.

The old man took a deep breath and puffed out his chest. He jumped onto a low branch, which swayed ominously, before springing and landing on the next.

Archie couldn't believe his eyes. 'Hey, be careful! You sure you're all right?'

'Never been better,' Old Man Wood replied clapping his hands. 'It's a piece of Mrs Pye's cake.'

But at that moment, for no real reason, he lost his balance. Throwing his arms wildly in the air like errant sails on a windmill, he swayed first one way, then the other, like a pendulum. Then, with a look of total surprise on his face, the old man plunged into the pool.

Archie exploded into laughter.

Old Man Wood resurfaced, coughing and spluttering and looking rather like a drowned rat. Archie heaved him up onto the branch and smacked the old man's back. Then, the old man wiped his face with his sodden clothes and sat down.

He shook his head. 'Getting a bit old for this kind of thing, I reckon,' he said, spitting out a little more water.

His head twitched from one side to the other. He sidled along on his bottom. 'Is someone there?' he turned to Archie. 'Did you hear that, Archie?'

Archie scanned the pond and shook his head.

'Apples alive, there are more,' the old man said. 'Laughing like crazy. All round.' Old Man Wood's head shifted from side to side. 'Laughing like I've never heard.'

Archie frowned. 'I can't hear anything, Old Man Wood. You're sure you're–?'

'There, again! Loud as anything. Loads of them.' Old Man Wood climbed up onto the branch and folded his arms. 'You think that was funny, do you?' he said furiously, to the empty pool. 'Well, when I find you lot, I'll show you—mark my words!'

THE SITUATION IN NORTH YORKSHIRE

'I've got to find Archie,' Daisy said, sitting bolt upright.

'He's fine,' Isabella yawned from behind her curtain. 'Don't worry—'

'No, Isabella, he's not. He left early. I heard him slip off. Something's not right.' She climbed out of bed. 'I can kind of sense it.' She flipped on the light, which much to her surprise, flickered into action. The generator was working.

As she slid into her jeans and shirt she tapped on Isabella's duvet. 'Isabella, put your phone on charge now. There's power, but it won't last.'

'You do it,' Isabella groaned. 'I left it downstairs.'

After Daisy had plugged in the phone she headed into the kitchen where she found Mrs Pye ironing in front of the television. The hum of the generator and the chatter of the morning news filled the room.

'The telly!' Daisy exclaimed. 'When did it come back on?'

Mrs Pye looked up. 'Good morning, Daisy.'

'Oh! Morning, Mrs P.'

Mrs Pye scrunched up her face. 'Now then, about ten.'

Daisy smiled. Mrs Pye never referred to time in its entirety, so it could have been seconds, minutes, hours, or days. Sometimes, even months or years.

Daisy ladled a spoonful of thick porridge into her bowl, added treacle and stirred it in. She pulled up a chair and looked up at the screen.

A banner ran along the bottom, "Yorkshire Disaster" it said. Next to it was "helpline number". Daisy wondered whether it was worth a call. Then again, they were fine, so why bother? By the look of things, others were in a far worse state than they were.

'*Experts are saying that the unprecedented flood in the north of the country is partly due to the effects of global warming. But what is baffling forecasters is that this freak storm did not blow in, it simply mushroomed out at alarming speed from a position just to the west of the North Yorkshire Moors.*'

The camera panned to an almost totally submerged village. Daisy gasped. Was that Kettleby, just down the road? Only the spire of the church and a few rooftops were visible. '*It's a similar picture throughout the whole of Yorkshire, Cleveland and Lincolnshire,*' the commentator continued. '*There is no power, or fresh water and human sewage fills the streets. Disease is now a real threat.*'

The picture returned to the studio and a man stood next to a graphic of the North of England. The presenter looked glum. '*A freak weather depression has settled directly over the northern half of the UK.*' The TV graphics changed. '*The problem, as you can see from our satellite image, is that it doesn't appear to be letting up. Although no torrential rain is forecast like we saw on Friday afternoon which, incidentally, was the hardest rainfall ever recorded anywhere in the world, and for the longest sustained period of time, more rain is due, which will cause further havoc as water levels continue to rise. Add this to an exceptionally high tide at York, with an already saturated water table, and it means the rising water doesn't have anywhere to go.*'

The screen snapped to helicopter footage of the flooding.

'*Early casualty estimates range from 3,000 to 30,000 victims. According to the emergency services, it's impossible to tell. Ten counties are in a state of emergency and people within this huge area are being advise that where possible they should evacuate to higher ground on the North York Moors and the Yorkshire Dales. However, resources are limited and it's a slow process. The death toll looks certain to rise, possibly in greater numbers than originally estimated as news filters in from stricken towns and villages across the country.*'

The picture reverted to the news anchor.

'*We'll have regular updates throughout the day, but right now let's go to our reporter in the submerged North Yorkshire town of Northallerton. Some of these pictures are of a distressing nature.*'

Mrs Pye watched the screen, transfixed, her face even paler than normal.

'*This pregnant woman was saved when a neighbour smashed an upstairs window and was dragged out onto the roof. She was one of the lucky ones.*'

The woman, looking frightened and pale, told her story. The reporter continued.

'*A partial service has resumed for many mobile phone networks and the emergency services are urging people to call the national emergency hotline to let them know of their whereabouts. However, network operators say only a limited service is available, so do keep trying.*'

Daisy was about to go when a "News Flash" item popped onto the screen. The broadcaster cocked his head, listening to his earpiece.

'We're getting news of an extraordinary survival story.'

He smiled into the camera as he focused on his news feed.

'Earlier today, an unknown boy was found hanging to a top branch of a tree in the middle of the vast area of flooding near to the ravaged village of Upsall, which was at the very epicentre of the storm. Remarkable footage of the rescue has come in via the North Yorkshire air ambulance crew.'

The screen reverted to a helicopter cockpit and a man with a jumpsuit and mask. Through the windows, the chopper blades whirred in a blur. Below, lay a huge expanse of water and, as the pilot took the helicopter down, right in the very middle of the picture sat the crown of a huge bare tree. Suddenly, muffled cries from the crew cut across the whorl of the rotors. The footage cut back to those within the helicopter who were gesticulating wildly with their arms.

The camera panned back to the tree as the helicopter banked. The lens zoomed in. For a moment, there was a strange silence as the crew and viewers looked into the bare branches of the tree. Then, as the helicopter swung to the left, there, draped over a bough, was a human figure hugging a thick branch.

Mrs Pye grabbed Daisy's arm and gripped tight. Now, the sound cut out altogether. The camera zoomed in even closer to show the boy, unmoving, his naked white flesh clearly visible against the dark water beneath him.

Daisy gasped. Who could have survived the storm, and the flooding, and then climbed up a huge tree, naked? It didn't seem possible. Daisy could hardly breathe as the camera lens reached in until the only thing on the screen was the head and shoulders of a gaunt, white boy. He was utterly beaten and did not have a hair on his head. Bald, like a big baby.

A shiver raced up Daisy's spine. That jawline, and those fat lips were so familiar. But whose? In a flash it hit her. Kemp! It had to be; she could tell his face from a mile away. But where was his thick shredded-wheat mop of hair?

But, if it was Kemp—and she swore it had to be—then Archie needed to know. He'd confirm it.

Seconds later, the images on the TV died, leaving a blank screen.

Mrs. Pye, tears washing down her ruddy cheeks, waddled over and gave the screen a smack.

But Daisy ran into the boot room and, noting that both Old Man Wood and Archie's boots were missing, donned her oilskin, lifted the hood over her tangled blonde mop, and shot out into the rain.

THE MIRACLE BOY

Dr Adrian Muller instantly struck everyone who met him as a kindly man. His sharp nose, thick mop of dark hair that flopped across his forehead and his jutting jaw that moved from side to side when he talked, gave him a curiously academic air. He took hold of the clipboard and ran his finger down the boy's chart. Without meaning to, he raised his thick, dark, eyebrows, which dislodged his half-moon wire-framed glasses. He nudged them back into place without even noticing.

He studied the data again. The boy's survival didn't make sense. 'Are you sure these are correct?'

The nurse, her mousy hair tied up in a bun, confirmed the data. It had been triple checked, she told him. And, keeping her voice low, she said, 'His condition is unlike any of the other flood victims. Typically, what we're seeing is a combination of hypothermia and signs of viral infection. The boy's condition is nothing like that. The good news is, he's out of his coma and we're hoping to talk to him later today.'

Dr Muller shook his head as he looked through the sheet of glass in front of him. The boy lay, his mouth and nose covered by a plastic mask, his arms pricked with drips that dangled from him like flexible plastic straws. Littering his body were bandages, liberally administered, as if he were part-human, part-Egyptian mummy.

Two other men stood next to the medics in the gallery room. One was Police Commissioner Charlie Stone, the tall, reedy, silver-haired relative of Solomon's, who had been put in charge of the nation's flood relief efforts. The other was the Prime Minister himself, Ed Kingsford.

And the PM was more than a little irritated by the whole thing.

Prime Minister Kingsford found himself wearing an anti-contamination suit. He stared through thick glass at a sick, bald child in the isolation unit, labelled as "The miracle boy" by the media. The images of his being found naked in the top of a tree in the middle of a huge expanse of water had caused a sensation around the world, and represented a glimmer of hope.

As the disaster spiralled out of control, his was a good news story amongst the carnage, and the Prime Minister recognised this. How long could he put off facing the press and their questions? Journalists were baying like hounds for a story, and he needed it to be a positive one.

He knew the boy's tale—and his survival, were now a top priority.

GAIA SEEKS GENESIS

Gaia found herself on the edge of the known universes in a place inhospitable to life. This was a star of burning rocks and gases, of unjust storms, and temperatures ranging from intensely hot to bitter cold.

Here was a planet in the making going through the long process of adaptation; from various collisions and coolings, before, a million years from now, it would be ready for new life forms. Because the energy it produced was so intense, it was a good place for a dreamspinner to become undiscoverable.

Gaia had found the right spot.

'I see you, Gaia,' familiar vibrations said.

'And I you, Genesis.' She dipped a leg in her maghole. 'There is a development.'

'You speak of Asgard?'

'Yes,' she said, feeling the powder tucked inside the blue electrical void. 'Asgard is making dream powders on Havilah.'

'Asgard is too hasty,' Genesis snapped. 'The Heirs of Eden may yet succeed. To pass the trial of the storm means that they are the true Heirs of Eden. Has he forgotten such things? And now the Heirs of Eden will learn about their gifts.'

'Even though,' Gaia answered, 'they are only human children?'

'Yes, but it is not so foolish. Children have less to hold them back. Without knowledge and human conditioning, they have more freedom to explore and to wonder. And although they are inexperienced in life, perhaps the energy of the universe has made a clever choice. Their task is not easy, but innocence and the energies of love will help them.' Genesis shifted. 'You have Asgard's powders?'

'I have,' Gaia said, producing a tiny amount of the powder from her maghole. 'It has been sprayed by a vapour. The dreamspinners I collected it from told me this was to make the powders fresher. In my visible form, I could smell something was not right. Have you heard of such a thing?'

She extended the powder-bundle to Genesis.

The old dreamspinners studied it with her large black eyes. 'I cannot tell. Have you seen how they effect humankind, or animals?'

Gaia had not.

'Try the little beasts who scurry. If this dose is intended for human consumption, you will know soon enough. Look out for signs. Then come back to me when this is done.'

Genesis turned away and faced the bubbling magma. 'I sense you wonder what I am doing out here in the wilds of the ether. I am resting, Gaia. I seek the heat of the furnaces of creation to keep my body energised before I must pass. My time is concluding but there may be one last time where I am required.'

'But none have your knowledge,' Gaia pleaded. 'You cannot depart now. Not until this story has unfolded. Stay close to these energies so you can pass on what you know.'

'If I stay too long,' Genesis vibrated, 'the blue gases of heat and light will make me fade, Gaia. My shadow is coming.'

'We will not know what to do.'

'That is why, soon, I will tell you and Gaia all you need to know. Return to me presently with Luna.'

A flare of blue heat shot through both of them. They let it wash over them. 'There must be balance, Gaia. The universe only tolerates balance.'

'I will return.'

Instantly, Gaia, refreshed by the blue heat, inverted through her maghole back to Earth. She found herself in the middle of the city of Mumbai, and inverted again to a large stinking drain filled with rats.

DAISY'S DISAPPEARANCE

If I was Archie, where would I go? Daisy thought. *Dad's shed in the haunted garden wouldn't be a bad place to start. Quiet. Dark. Horrible.*

The shed near the vegetable patch at the bottom of the garden was where her father and Old Man Wood grew potatoes. But they never stayed there after dark. 'It's as if I'm being watched,' their father said, and Daisy knew exactly what he meant.

It was a miserable place, and rain beat down on Daisy's head as she searched for her brother. 'Archie,' she called out. 'Archie! I think they've found Kemp! Come inside and check it out.'

In the distance, the drone of a helicopter forced her to look up into the thick clouds. *Must be the rescue mission swinging into action, moving people to higher ground. But they'd never come up here, where the forest was impenetrably thick* and littered with broken trees and mudslides. Besides, theirs was the only dwelling for miles around.

Behind the plum trees lay an expanse of thick bushes in the shape of a horse-shoe. Daisy made her way gingerly towards the drooping, skeletal branches, her boots sucking noisily in the mud. Here, a small opening led to an old rusted gate.

She stopped and studied it for a moment. *I don't remember that gate. More importantly, where does it lead?*

She removed a couple of sopping-wet hair strands from her face when suddenly, from the corner of her eye, she glimpsed a shining object hanging in the bushes beyond the gate. Daisy peered at it, intrigued. *A tiny jewel. A diamond?* She moved closer.

She noted how the jewel looked more like a pearl in the shape of a teardrop, but sparkly. She liked the thought of it around her neck, against her pale skin.

Daisy gave the gate a shove but it was jammed solid with creepers and rust. She tried again with the same result. It hardened her resolve.

'Come on, Daisy,' she whispered. 'On the count of three: One, two... THREE!'

She slammed into the gate, but instead of meeting resistance, Daisy hurtled straight through. As she tripped, she reached out for the jewel. Before she knew what was happening, she found herself entirely submerged underwater.

'Phleaux!' Tchuch!' she spat, coughing out a lungful of metallic, coppery-tasting water that hinted of ripe cheese. Now her head swam and dizziness threatened to overcome her as a buzzing noise hummed in her ears.

She dragged herself out and fell to the ground. A terrible thought washed over her. *What if she'd just swallowed the deadly, poisonous sewage water?*

And now she noticing the dry grass and how a gentle, warm wind blew over her.

The buzzing sensation between her ears eased and soon ebbed away entirely. She lay still with her eyes shut and wondered if this was how the poison set about its mortal path.

Maybe, she'd died and gone to Heaven.

THE BUBBLING BROOK

Old Man Wood's eyes darted from one side to the other. He crouched down and coughed the remaining water from his windpipe.

'They're laughing at me, Archie. Masses of them—in hysterics!'

Old Man Wood's ears pricked up. 'There! There it is again!' he boomed. 'Can you hear them?'

'Hear who?' Archie quizzed, trying to find the source of Old Man Wood's outburst.

'Uh? You can't hear it?' Old Man Wood whispered. '...must be able to!'

'No, nothing—'

'Again! There they go, loads of them. Laughing, talking, hum-humming.'

Archie strained his ears, 'Hum-humming? I can't hear anything.'

Old Man Wood scrambled across a branch, his head turning to and fro.

'You know,' Archie said, 'maybe you're hearing things. Is there water in your ears?'

Old Man Wood stared at him indignantly, his eyes bulging. He shook his head. 'Definitely not.'

'Look,' Archie insisted, 'let's go home, get some breakfast.' He scoured the area. 'Really, there's nothing.' He watched Old Man Wood shuffle up another trunk.

But Old Man Wood wasn't listening. 'Oh, yes there is, Archie.'

Archie sighed. 'Let's get back, please? You'll catch pneumonia if you hang around too long.'

But Old Man Wood had abandoned his boots and was now scurrying around the trees and bushes like a man possessed. He dashed around the thicket, waded through the pools and peered around the trees.

'Reveal yourselves!' he cried. 'Where the devils are you?!'

On his third attempt to grab his attention, Archie decided that the old man had lost his mind.

What would Headmaster Solomon say if he saw this? Archie wondered. They'd be whisked from the cottage and taken into care. He snapped off a wet, dangling tree branch and tossed it in the water and stared at Old Man Wood who was still bouncing around the pool, ducking here and peering there behind the trees.

Archie felt empty inside. Making as little fuss as possible, he scrambled over the fallen tree trunks and exited out of the clump the way they'd entered, back towards Eden Cottage.

To Old Man Wood, the laughter grew and grew. 'Haaahaaahaaaahaaa! Haaaaaaa! Ha! Woah-ha ha!'

'Cor, this is the most hilarious thing I've seen for years.'

Slowly, it dawned on him.

'Is that you?' Old Man Wood said. 'Is it the sound of the old trees?'

This time, the trees collectively agreed. And their laughter was now a laughter of joy at seeing Old Man Wood, rather than roaring at his antics.

'Archie! I've found them,' Old Man Wood yelled out, before turning back to the brook. 'How come I can hear you, old sticks?'

'Well, hello to you, too, Old Man Wood,' was the reply from the willows. 'The water is sooo high, way up, up over those steps, hum-hum.'

'With any luck, we have ourselves several days of the loveliest special water, hum-hum,' said a voice from the largest of the weeping willow trees. There was a general murmur of approval. 'Can you see us yet?'

Old Man Wood strained his eyes.

'Have yourself another good sip, dear old friend. You must have had a lil' taster in the pool to hear us laughing at you, hum-hum. Heavens above, that was one funny sight, you can still make a tree laugh, old man.'

Old Man Wood cupped his large, old, leathery hands and brought the water to his mouth. It tasted metallic and bitter, as though laced with iron and sulphur. The liquid fizzed and made his eyes wobble for a few seconds. Then, a buzzing sensation rolled in and tumbled about in his mind. When he opened his eyes again, he looked out over the brook.

Where before he noted an array of stems and boughs, now, perched on each tree, were tiny elf-like figures no bigger than shoeboxes, with small, pointed ears and sharp noses.

Each tree elf had rough, coarse skin, like bark, and their tiny bodies were shrouded in mini clothes made from willow leaves. Tiny arms, like twigs, protruded from either side of their bodies and each had sharp eyes, like polished wood, that darted from place to place.

'Aha! Apples-alive!' Old Man Wood exclaimed. 'The spirits of the trees. I see you!'

The old man watched as the young ones ran up and down their smaller trees, their little legs disappearing into the wood. Sometimes they vanished into the trunk altogether and reappeared at the end of a branch dangling from their heads, or sitting on a root at its base.

'Crimpers!' Old Man Wood said, as he hugged the biggest tree enthusiastically. A strange elfin creature was standing with one foot attached to the tree and the other on Old Man Wood's head.

'How many are you?' he asked.

'We're sixty-seven,' said a deep voice from behind Old Man Wood. 'Loads of new little whips and a couple of small trees and, hum-hum, us big'uns just keep on going.'

Old Man Wood closed his eyes. 'Let me see if I can remember. Bethedi…?'

'Well, well, well, hum-hum. Isn't that something?' said a wiry, elderly tree elf dangling off a big tree to the side of the brook. 'He remembers me! So, your memory is still intact, huh?'

'There's the thing,' Old Man Wood replied. 'It isn't—'

'You mean,' the tree elf said as he ducked into his tree and reappeared at eye level with Old Man Wood, 'even with this great rain, you don't know what's a-happening?'

Old Man Wood groaned. 'My brain gets all clogged up. And then there are the nightmares that I don't understand, with little bits that are familiar. But otherwise, dear Bethedi, it's a mystery. I've forgotten the lot.'

'But you do know who you are?'

Old Man Wood frowned. 'I'm not sure I do anymore.'

Hum-hums and him-hims erupted around the brook as the tree elves absorbed this information. 'You quite sure?'

'Yes!' Old Man Wood replied.

'Then, hem-hem, you've come to the right place,' said a soft, higher voice from the third large tree on the far side of the brook. 'And in the nick of time, it would appear. Do you remember me? I'm respidistra, hem-hem?'

'Crespidistra,' Old Man Wood repeated, nodding. He propped himself up on the tree and looked over the water at a slender, feminine willow spirit.

'We lost Jonix a few seasons back,' she said. 'He died from a painful canker, but he had time to pass on his knowledge. We miss him dearly... but lately, a whole raft of baby willows sprouted. Let me introduce you to our saplings.' The elegant willow spirit turned to the nursery. 'Well now, say hello to our oldest and dearest friend, Old Man Wood, hem-hem. He is the greatest and, indeed, the only, being of his kind on this planet of ours!'

With that, a huge 'Hello Old Man Wood,' in an assortment of high and low voices called out over the gentle spring waters, followed by um-ums and im-ims.

Old Man Wood suddenly remembered Archie. He searched around and yelled out. 'Archie, over here, they're here!' he repeated. 'I've found them. Come, look—'

'If you're looking for your friend, he left a little while ago while you were, hem-hem... figuring things out,' Crespidistra said gently, before disappeared into the tree and re-emerging higher up. She gazed out towards the hill.

Old Man Wood followed her eyes and glimpsed Archie looking down. He waved enthusiastically but Archie shook his head. *Oh well,* the old man thought. *It's probably just as well.*

'Can I say on behalf of all the willow spirits, what a magnificent entrance that was, my old friend. You certainly haven't lost your style. Welcome to The Bubbling Brook, where all things speak as one.'

The smaller tree spirits erupted into laughter, pulling their stems one way and then the other so that the noise of twigs snapping and cracking filled The Bubbling Brook like applause.

'Took you a while to find us, though—the water's been high for a couple of days now,' the elf said as she sat at the end of a branch that hung over the water. 'And it's been a long time since we last spoke, hem-hem?'

'I hope you've got some juicy things to tell—?' said another, named Willip. 'It's so boring here. Did you ever manage to find your way into that storeroom?'

'How is that vegetable patch of yours?' said another. 'Some of the birds told us you'd grown star-shaped carrots.'

'And what of that young lady?' asked an elf called Shodwonk who, as his name suggested, was a little lopsided. 'And did you ever hear back from that friend of yours with all those ideas?'

Old Man Wood scratched his head.

'You know, him-him,' Shodwonk continued. 'About five hundred and thirty-two seasons ago. Mr Leonard Vinchi?'

'Oooh yes,' Crespidistra added, 'such a nice young man, hem-hem. And how are your apple trees? The apple-elves rarely get out, claim they're too busy—'

'Now, hum-hum,' said the deeper voice of Bethedi, 'fill us in, won't you. Tell us your news, dear friend.'

Old Man Wood clapped his hands together as a smile spread from one side of his gnarled old face to the other. He beamed at the curious clump with their little tree elves homming and humming. Then, after a bit of a fuss, he sat down respectfully on one half of Jonix's stump, took a deep breath, and began by telling the trees all about the children. He also told them how he'd found Mrs Pye in the woods at the bottom of a gorge, mangled and covered in blood, and that they still didn't know who she really was, or where she'd come from.

He followed this by telling them about his beloved vegetable patch and his trusty cattle. He went into limited detail on his struggle to grow purple spinach, and how the answer to his carrot fly problem was to grow the vegetables in containers on the roof. All the while, the willow spirits listened, asking questions when appropriate, and laughing at exactly the right moments.

Old Man Wood felt as if he was talking to his oldest friends. And, in a way, it wasn't so far off the truth. For no matter how ancient Old Man Wood grew, the willow trees had the ability to remember in astonishing detail each and every word he'd ever told them, from the day they had first met. And this knowledge had been passed on from generation to generation.

These willow elves were information sponges. The perfect living memory bank.

Suddenly, two ducks flashed through the branches and, with a minimum of effort, dropped into the middle of the pool of water. Automatically, they dunked their heads and, moments later, they surfaced, shaking their bills from side to side.

'Hey! You gnarled old pieces of timber,' the first duck said addressing one of the tree elves. 'What do you give a sick bird?'

'Tweetment!' the other duck said, before any of the tree spirits had the chance to respond. 'Hey, and did you see that duck who came in here? He really... quacked me up! Whoaaa! I'm on form today,' the duck continued.

'And what about the owl, huh?' said the second duck. 'He didn't give a hoot!' They both quacked with laughter.

'Haha, oh boy, oh boy, oh boy, we're the best!' The first duck said. 'Anything to liven up you boards. Whoa, geddit? Boards!' the birds sang as they lifted out of the glade.

'Cres,' Bethedi said, 'can't we stop those blasted ducks flying in here, telling their appalling jokes?'

'You know there's nothing we can do, and they're a great deal better than the blackbirds. They simply repeat things over and over again if they like the sound of it.'

Old Man Wood shook his head and laughed. The sound of his rich voice echoed around the brook. He'd forgotten how wonderful the world was when everything could talk—and spell—given the right circumstances.

He was overjoyed. Right now, though, he needed to put the trees' memory to the test and think of some good questions.

Where would he begin? And what questions would be most helpful to them all?

ARCHIE'S KNIVES

Archie squeezed between the old oak upright post and the wooden door that had jammed tight against the cold concrete floor of the garden shed. Once inside, he felt the familiar course fibres of a pile of old empty sacks and fell heavily into them. His cheeks stung with the salt of his tears, and the walk up the slippery hill had made his leg muscles burn. He found the light on his watch. Not yet ten. It felt like lunchtime.

Archie tried to get himself comfortable, to settle his mind. He couldn't think clearly for the noise of the rain, which now drummed hard on the tiles above his head.

He reached behind the sacks, feeling for a cloth bundle.

Archie untied the cloth, pulling out three stunning silver-coloured knives. He ran his hand over the sharp tips and shivered as he thought about his first encounter, three nights ago, with the ghost Cain. He remembered the ruby-encrusted knife Old Man Wood had found the following morning that fell out of the ghost's coat pocket of the coat that Cain had clearly left behind. This was the same knife that Cain had cut him with. He touched the scar on his chin.

What had Cain told him at the time? *'The power of a horse and the courage of a lion'*. It was ridiculous, he thought, even if he couldn't get it out of his head. He smiled as an image of himself, deeply muscled, entered his mind. He wondered if somehow, impossibly, he really had acquired super-strength of some kind. After all, as they escaped from the storm, he'd managed to pull a tree out, carry Daisy to the cave, and push a gigantic boulder out of the way. And yet, here he was, still his reasonably puny self.

He tensed his arms and the muscle bulge wasn't impressive. He patted his hard hair. Maybe it had something to do with being struck by lightning?

Archie's knives were like secret friends. He knew how to hold them, care for them, balance them, and hide them away. It was his one secret, albeit a badly kept one, for Isabella knew and she hated them with a passion.

He remembered the day he found them—two days after his seventh birthday —and they were playing a game of hide and seek in the ruin. He had spied a dark space beneath an outcrop of stone and, without thinking, crammed himself inside, working his body under until he had all but disappeared. As he had scraped the earth furiously to give himself more space, his hand had touched upon a cloth.

His curiosity aroused, Archie reached in and dug faster. Soon, he realised that inside this cloth lay hard objects. Treasure? He remembered the burst of excitement that had fizzled through him. Just then, Isabella had rounded the corner, saw one of his feet, and dragged him out. He had left the bundle there, but even now he wondered why he hadn't brought them out and shared his excitement with the others. Somehow, this treasure was his very own little secret. His—and no one else's.

A few days later, he returned. His fingers touched the bundle again, and the same thrill passed through him. Using a trowel from Old Man Wood's potting shed, he'd teased the package from the hard earth. And as he had scraped, he found that the cloth was bound deep in the chasm, holding the treasure within it. Archie pulled until eventually the bundle popped out like a cork from a bottle. With the evening drawing in, he'd run home and hidden the bundle under the bed. Archie could hardly talk through supper that evening. The following day, with the girls in town, he opened the package.

The cloth itself had felt unusual, certainly like nothing he'd seen before. Wound neatly round and round the fabric, which was as soft as velvet but strong as chainmail, housed three knives, each one about ten inches in length, made from slender sticks of metal. The knives, he recalled, had shimmered as he touched them.

The tips were slender, with sharpened edges leading to a point, like leaves of a plum tree. The handles were flat, like a wide kitchen knife and he noted that as no water had penetrated the metal, no rust or discolouration showed so either no air had got in, or the metal wasn't steel. As he had inspected them, right in the middle of each one, he had found a pattern, a circle of lines swirling—mirrored— top and bottom.

It had taken him several days to work out how they should be used. As hunting knives, they were all wrong; the blades weren't long enough or sharp enough and the handles ungainly. In the woods, as he ambled along, he held one in his hand and rounded a tree. There, beside the carcass of a rabbit, was a rat.

Without thinking, Archie had cocked his arm back and let the knife go. The knife flew through the air and landed with a thud, killing the rat instantly. Archie stared in shock. How had he managed to do that?

From that moment on, Archie wanted to be the best knife thrower in the world. At first, when the house was empty, he threw the knives into an old cork notice board that he kept hidden under his bed.

What he had discovered, by a process of elimination and frustration, and with the help of Old Man Wood, who he'd secretly confided in, was that each knife had a special weight. He figured each one had to rotate through the air at either its own unique speed, or at the same speed but from a different distance.

Archie spent hours trying to work it out. Slowly, it came and, before long, he could automatically judge the weight and the throwing speed of each knife. Then one day, much to his surprise, he rubbed the emblem in the middle and, as if by magic, a smaller knife unfurled itself from the body of the big knife. The same thing had happened on each, and now he had had six knives to play with.

Archie had practiced with the larger knives on an old wooden log in the forest. He hadn't wanted anyone to know because he sensed that all hell would break loose, and in the end, it had.

One day in the woods, while Archie thought the others were fooling around in the house, he'd set up a target which consisted of a woolly mop head and one of Daisy's old shirts which he had pinned against a tree. Archie had mastered his throw from ten feet, and now was attempting a new distance; thirteen feet, which meant holding the knife the other way around. The first two had clattered into the bark and fallen to the ground. Archie weighed up the final one, his heaviest knife. He pulled his arm back and, throwing a little harder, let go. But at that exact moment, Isabella's head had suddenly appeared beside the tree.

The knife flashed through the air and, to his enormous relief, with a gentle thud, the blade had nestled into the wood. For a fraction of a second, Archie wondered whether Isabella knew what he was doing. She had looked at him curiously. Then her eyes followed his, to where he'd been looking. She moved around the tree and saw the end of the knife, straight through the breast pocket of Daisy's old shirt.

Archie grinned at the memory. Isabella had gone berserk, screaming at him for being reckless and stupid and for plotting to kill them. He'd protested but Isabella gathered the knives and ran inside.

From that moment on, his knives would not be tolerated in, or around, the house. On his tenth birthday he'd been allowed to have them back on condition that he always told a grown up when and where he was throwing them. And never, ever, anywhere near Isabella.

❄

In the dimness of the musty, rickety shed, Archie focused on the large log. He balanced the first knife in the palm of his hand, a sparkle of gleaming metal catching a ray of light that had crept nervously under the gap in the door.

Thud.

The knife flew into the thick wood. Archie wanted to throw it quicker, venting this curious anger that kept welling up inside him.

He rubbed his hair, the front cluster of which stood hard as iron.

Thud.

The next kicked out a splinter of wood. Nice one he thought, much better. Exactly in the right spot.

And while he did this, he tried to work out what on earth was going on.

Who was this ghost called Cain, the weird spirit who had visited him, the ghost he'd run away from? How did Cain fit the puzzle? After all, Cain knew all about them, the Ancient Woman, and this crazy Prophecy of the Garden of Eden. But if Cain truly existed where was he from?

It didn't add up.

Archie twisted the knife in his hand, flicking the dull blade around his fingers. To Archie, these confusing thoughts filled his soul with darkness.

And now, to top it off, Old Man Wood had gone totally stark-raving bonkers. Sure, it wasn't illegal to talk to trees, but at 8:30 in the morning—to a clump of willows?

The unfamiliar anger brewed in his veins again. His neck throbbed as a pain shot into his head. 'Why?' he said out loud to the dank air in the shed. 'Why me? What is happening to us?'

Annoyed that there were simply no answers, he weighed up his last knife. He summoned every ounce of strength in his body and, with a cry, threw it as hard as he could at the old stump.

Archie walked across the floor and ran his hands over the two-foot-thick log which now lay on the ground, split clean in half.

He smiled, picked the knife off the floor and, for a reason he couldn't explain, rubbed the centre over his jeans. He looked at it again and, just as he was returning it to the cloth, he realised he'd seen it before.

In the centre of the knife lay the circular emblem of a tree, with branches arching out above, and roots mirrored identically below.

He'd seen the exact same symbol in the cave. His heartbeat quickened. It was the motif at the beginning of the mural that bore fruit, in the middle panel that had depicted death, and finally it had been by the images of rebirth.

For some reason he thought of Kemp. Did his friend die? Had he run to high ground, or, and his pulse raced at the thought, did he actually join with Cain—instead of him? Poor Kemp. Whatever happened, it must have been a nightmare.

If only he could remember the gist of Cain's speech to Kemp in the alleyway moments before the storm broke. The more he pondered this, the more he realised that not only had everything he'd remembered come true, but, importantly, what he'd forgotten could be absolutely pivotal to their outcome.

GAIA FACES ASGARD

Gaia didn't have to wait for long.

A nest of sleeping rats had sucked in the powder, their little bodies digesting tiny amounts Gaia had skilfully administered from a slender needle-like contraption at the end of her long, invisible leg.

Almost immediately, the rats began to react.

Animals were always a joy to give dreams to. The way they snuffled and clawed the air. The way their legs often paddled upside down or when they whined or whinnied or barked or squeaked. The way they shook or vibrated as if in fear.

Moments later, one of the dreamers awoke. Gaia, invisible, silent in the air above, was able to look closely upon the creature.

Puffy, red eyes. A sign of an ailment perhaps, but nothing unusual.

She almost missed it. Yellow pustules, spots, beside the rat's rear leg, more festering in the animal's creases.

The rat scuttled along the drain and stopped, quite suddenly. Then, as if made from stone, the rat fell over, convulsing momentarily before death took it.

Disease, just as she suspected, with an almost instant reaction.

The dusts had pestilence within them. And then she realised the odour she'd smelt was the same stench as the floodwaters on Earth.

In no time, Gaia flashed through her maghole to the jungles of Havilah's rainforest.

Large numbers of dreamspinners hovered outside the cave entrance, marshalled by one of the larger dreamspinners, all waiting for their turn to load up with the new dream powders.

She flashed to the top of the waterfall. Suspended above the chamber, she changed to her visibility status so that the majority would not see her.

Below her, there lay a small, white, fluffy cloud stained in the middle by a mustard-yellow smear. The cloud began to rain, ever so lightly, directly over the green powders below.

Gaia watched, fascinated.

'You are admiring my sprinkler,' said a voice said next to her.

'I see you, Asgard,' she said, flustered by his lack of a formal greeting.

'A neat use of heat and water,' he said.

'What is the meaning of this, Asgard. Why do you do it?'

'Do what?'

'Spread disease with your poisonous powders. There is no balance to your methods. And with no balance, you will be punished by the energies of the universes.'

Asgard drew himself up. 'As I have already expressed to you, Gaia, I do it for the survival of dreamspinners. Life on Earth will soon move on, but dreams still need to be spun. I intend that we dreamspinners are not replaced, that we retain our purpose.'

Gaia vibrated back quickly. 'You are wrong, Asgard. You cannot meddle with such things. We follow the path we have been given, or we die. It is the same with all living entities.'

'We are not any ordinary beings,' Asgard vibrated sharply. 'We are dream-spinners.'

'The notion of right and wrong is not ours to determine, Asgard. We are conduits of energy. We channel energy to life forms. The moment we choose a different fate, we are finished. Besides, what good will this mass of death do?'

Asgard stretched out a long arm towards Gaia, his hand curled in a ball. His other fingers moved together, vibrating again. 'I am speeding up the inevitable, that is all. I am putting the living on Earth out of their misery early. I am helping us to evolve. They should thank me.'

'You are playing as if you are a form of deity and not its messenger, Asgard. Why do you do as Cain bids?'

'Because Cain's people will rise. And if we are to remain as a species with meaning, we must attach ourselves to him.'

Gaia floated close to the pile of powder. 'And what if the Heirs of Eden succeed? Then all you have accomplished is murder. This is not our way. What you have done is against the principles of universal order. The order of life we obey.'

'The Heirs of Eden will not succeed,' Asgard vibrated angrily. 'I grant you they are worthy, but they are human infants. They are weak.'

'Your meddling is your undoing,' Gaia said. 'Other dreamspinners must be aware of your scheme.'

'Now that you know,' he vibrated, calmly, moving closer, 'stay, a while longer.'

'Come no further, Asgard,' she warned. 'Do not taunt me. I do not wish to stay here among your poisons.'

'As the Earth moves,' Asgard said, 'there is nothing you can do to stop it.'

DAISY'S STRANGE GLADE

After several minutes, Daisy placed her hand over her chest and realised the noise she could hear was her own heart thumping. She sat up and opened her eyes.

Stretched out directly in front of her was a glade. It was in the shape of a long triangle, about twenty paces long by twenty wide, tapering to a point further away. Three curiously gnarled, stocky old trees, their trunks the width of large beer barrels with nodules, were showered in showy petals.

On the ground, thick, dark green grass, strewn with daisies and buttercups, made it look as if the garden had been transported from the estate of grand house.

Daisy scratched her chin as she took it all in. The air smelt of early summer, she thought, with the heady perfumes of newly formed flowers. But autumn, she reminded herself, had been and, with the storm, gone.

She stood up and wandered carefully about, looking for signs of danger, but it seemed to be one of the most pleasing places she'd ever been. Bees buzzed and the sun shone on thick, lush grasses.

Looking at the sides, thick, impenetrable blackthorn and holly bushes grew above head height. Examining the lower reaches she realised no one could see in and she definitely couldn't see out.

She moved farther along the triangle to the far end, where, adjoining the space, sat an old dilapidated greenhouse. It was bereft of glass, but within the skeletal supports of a frame lay a most peculiar object.

Daisy squinted at the machine, which, to her untrained eye, looked like a big Victorian garden roller, but without the weighty cylindrical roller section. It had a curiously large handle adorned with scrolls, and this led to a platform that reminded her of a small, square junior trampoline.

She turned over, and stared up at the clear blue sky, bright rays of sunshine warming her.

Daisy took herself back to the soft grass in between the three trees and sat down. Scooping up a handful of recently fallen petals, she threw them into the air, where they caught on the breeze and fluttered to the ground nearby.

Maybe she was hallucinating.

'Am I dead?' she yelled out.

She tried again. 'Hellooo. Is this Heaven?'

Still there was no answer.

All around her blossom began to fall from the trees, like thick snowflakes. Daisy giggled and dived to catch them and then, on hands and knees, she piled them up into mounds.

Soon, she had made a heady scented pile of pink blossom, a sweeter perfumed bed of white, and a softer pile of yellow petals. For a moment, she had a great urge to run around and kick them so that the snow effect was recreated. Instead, she made a bed. Pink for her head, all the rest for her body.

She removed her wet coat and took off her trousers and shirt, hanging them over the branches of one of the old trees. She lay back on the bed of petals in her underwear. Taking a couple of deep breaths, she stretched out her arms, enjoying the sunshine and the sweet fragrances of the blossom that almost overwhelmed her senses. She basked contentedly. After a while, she began to consider her fate.

If this is Heaven she thought, I'm sure it'll be fine to lie here a little longer. She wondered if Archie and the others would miss her as a lump grew in her throat. I never said goodbye... to anyone.

Would Mum and Dad even notice? Old Man Wood might. Just.

I hope they play football in Heaven.

Daisy wiped a tear from her eye.

Perhaps being dead is just like being alive, but with one's energy in a different place... Maybe that's what Heaven really is.

Daisy smiled, happy with her conclusion. But it's a bit boring.

After a short while, she pulled herself up and scanned the charming glade. She re-studied the bushes that fenced her in; thick hawthorn and blackthorn, bearing inch-long needles, and interwoven with brambles and nettles.

She groaned. Trying to get through that would tear her apart, with or without clothes. The only other way out—and even then, she wasn't certain of it—was to follow the line of the ditch under the bushes that resembled barbed wire.

'So,' she asked out loud, having completely forgotten that she was searching for Archie, 'what happens next?'

'You're after the Atrium, right?' a voice from the side answered back.

Daisy shrieked and covered her body with her arms and hands. She looked around. There wasn't anyone there. 'Hey... who's that? Who's there?'

The same voice spoke out again. It wasn't a nasty voice but a kindly old voice, rich in resonance. 'You're here for the Atrium?'

'Holy smoke! I mean, pardon. I mean...' Daisy started burying herself under the petals, 'I don't understand, your Godliness.'

This time, another higher pitched voice joined in from the other side. 'You're here for the Atrium, are you dear? That's all we need to know.'

Daisy tiptoed towards the tree where she'd left her clothes. 'What... what Aytreehum?' she said.

Daisy thought she could hear laughter, certainly sniggering. Her face reddened. She grabbed her jeans and slipped them on in record time.

'Are you angelic?' she asked the voice. 'Like the, um, invisible host?' She was starting to wish she'd concentrated a bit more in church.

'This creature hasn't a clue,' said the higher pitched voice.

'Typical,' said the first, low, kindly voice. 'The first person who comes along for an age, and it's by mistake. Our typical luck!'

'What do you mean?' Daisy said, a little exasperated. 'Mistake? What creature?'

Then a lower voice from right beside her said, 'Don't be alarmed, dear.'

Daisy nearly jumped out of her skin. 'Alarmed!' Daisy shot back. 'Of course, I'm alarmed! Who are you? And, where are you?'

'Poor thing,' the kindly first voice said. 'I believe she's lost.'

There was a pause. Daisy listened. She could hear a kind of whispering.

'Now, a quick introduction,' said the voice that had come from next to her. 'We are the Cherubim of the Rivers of the Worlds. We guard the entrance.'

'Good Lord,' Daisy said, crossing herself. I'm actually dead.'

'My dear,' said the higher pitched voice. 'I don't think you look dead. Do you think you're dead?'

Daisy's eyes darted about. 'Now you mention it, no, not really—'

'Well, there you have it—'

The strange voices laughed again.

Daisy was confused. 'Hang on. You were saying about an entrance? What entrance?'

'Why, just look right in front of you!'

'All I can see is three gnarled, old, fat trees and a kind of knackered greenhouse—'

'We're time-worn, NOT fat!' the second, higher voice shrilled.

Daisy felt as if her head might explode.

Either it's one hell of a dream she thought, or a wicked hallucination. Side effects to Old Man Wood's amazing Resplendix Mix potion? It had to be.

Dead or alive, what did it matter? She lay down in the scented petals, stuffed fingers in her ears to block out the noises that continued to babble on, and basked in the sunshine.

Shortly, thinking that the sun had disappeared behind a cloud, Daisy opened her eyes to find the tree with pink blossom leaning directly above her.

'OMG. You've moved!' she said out loud to the tree.

The tree straightened, a flurry of petals swamping Daisy. 'Oh yes indeedy! I haven't done that for a few thousand years. Apples it feels gooood.'

Certain that the tree had been talking to her, Daisy sat up and brushed herself off. She shut her eyes. 'Hello, my name is Daisy de Lowe, from Eden Cottage, which I think is somewhere over there.' She found herself pointing randomly.

'I have absolutely no idea what's going on, or how I got here, but I'm looking for my brother Archie. He's about my height with strange spiky hard hair, as if someone poured a pot of glue over his head. Oh, and he's a little bit shy. You haven't seen him, have you?'

THE SCALE OF THE DISASTER UNFURLS

'The boy's been looked over by the pathologists,' the doctor said.

'Good,' Commissioner Stone nodded. 'When will their findings be available?'

Dr Muller cocked his head. 'In roughly two to four hours,' he replied. 'They're working on it now.'

'And is this the same illness the others have?' the Prime Minister asked.

'We don't know, Sir,' the doctor replied, his jaw jutting one way and then the other. 'At the moment, it appears not. The symptoms common to the majority of victims are not evident, at least not yet. That's what makes him intriguing. We have the world's leading scientists evaluating this type of influenza, yet the boy here has none of the rashes, skin discolouration, acute vomiting, or bowel dysfunction seen in the others. This fella's main problem is malnutrition, poisoning and burns.'

'Burns?' Commissioner Stone quizzed.

'Indeed,' Dr Muller replied. The news of this had surprised him too. 'Small burns covering all four limbs, front and back and around the neck up to the ears. We think his hair has been singed off. Not a single follicle can be found on his body. In his mouth, we discovered traces of soot and burn-blisters.'

'But how would someone receive something like this?'

'It's as if this boy has been in a fire or been sprayed with a flammable substance.' The doctor raised his eyebrows. 'Were any fires reported?'

Commissioner Stone thought for a minute. 'Further south from where the boy was found there were two big blazes. But the boy would've had to swim or row a raft several miles against the water flow to get to where he was found. And remember, he was found naked. Are there signs of hypothermia?'

Dr Muller shook his head.

'And no major flesh injuries,' the nurse added. 'Not even minor scratches or bruises, just burns.'

The doctor strummed the glass with his fingernails. 'When his samples come back, we'll know if he's a carrier. If he is, then we might be able to monitor the effect of the virus through his body. We'll try and trace the viral elements and isolate it. At the moment, he's our mystery boy and our only hope for a cure.'

'What if he came from somewhere else?' the nurse asked.

'Are you suggesting he fell out of the sky, like an alien, and dropped into the tree?' the Prime Minister said with sarcastic bite.

The nurse blushed.

The Prime Minister noticed and immediately regretted his sharp tongue. 'Oh, forgive me, I'm sorry,' he said. He smiled badly. 'Doctor,' he said, 'how many patients have symptoms of this... disease, and how quickly does it affect them?'

The doctor stared at the floor. 'It acts fast. Ten, to thirty-hours at most from incubation to death, depending on the severity of the strain and the constitution of the patient. There are two-hundred and sixty-two dead at the moment, each victim pulled from the water, all with the tell-tale skin rash and signs of vomiting and diarrhoea. In truth, Prime Minister, we have no idea how many are infected.'

'Is there any way of finding out?'

'None, I'm afraid. We don't know if it's waterborne or airborne, or both. We don't know where it originates, but our guess is somewhere near to the epicentre of the storm, possibly the village of Upsall.' He raised his eyebrows and looked over the top of his spectacles. 'At the moment, we can't tell whether it's an animal-based virus, but we can't rule out if this has something to do with a toxic chemical released into the floodwater.'

The Prime Minister sucked in a breath. 'What about a deliberate form of chemical or biological agent?'

'Unlikely,' the doctor replied. 'Though there are similarities to the untrained eye.'

'Have the early life-savers, doctors and nurses shown any of the symptoms?'

'No, not yet, but many are in the containment zone, just in case,' Dr Muller continued. 'The common factor is that it appears to tie-in with those who have been in continual contact with the floodwater—'

'Which is being analysed as we speak,' the Commissioner added. 'And the boy has obviously spent time in the floodwater, which makes him unique.'

A nervous quiet fell over the gathering. Then the PM asked, 'Do you know where he comes from?'

'No, I'm afraid not, Prime Minister,' Dr Muller said. 'No distinguishing marks, no clothes, no nothing. We can't even tell what colour his hair is, though, from the paleness of his skin, we suspect he's a redhead.'

'And strangely,' the Commissioner said, 'no one has come forward to claim him, even though footage of the boy has been shown repeatedly on every single TV channel around the world.'

The team continued to stare at the boy, working out the next move.

'All right, hear me out,' the Prime Minister began. 'The boy's story has captured the imagination of audiences around the globe... and you think he might start talking in a few hours? Is there any way we can use this as a media event so we can buy some time until we have a clearer idea what this disease is? I mean, if it is contagious, we'll need to work around the clock to start the process of containment, correct?'

'Indeed, Prime Minister,' the doctor said. 'Can I suggest that before the scientists divulge their reports tonight, we start the process of sealing off the wider infected area. If we take into account the movement of people during this time, the cordon needs to cover a significantly larger mileage than just the flood zone.'

Commissioner Stone nodded. 'With the known geographical spread of the flooding stretching for such a vast distance, this operation will be bigger than the evacuation of Dunkirk during the war.'

The Prime Minister coughed, a frown covering his face. 'Let's not run before we can walk, eh? Shouldn't we wait until the scientists report back? What if this thing is imminently curable?'

The doctor twiddled his thumbs. 'Prime Minister, I urge you to start the process as soon as possible. This outbreak is from an unknown pathogen and more cases are being reported every minute. We are fighting a battle with an unfamiliar enemy and time is against us. The flooding is spreading and therefore the disease is spreading. It is not going to get any easier.'

Prime Minister Kingsford had gone pale. The calamity of the situation was sinking in fast.

Commissioner Stone noticed, and coughed. 'We have already begun it... quietly,' he said. 'I know the last thing we need is a media-led panic so I have taken the liberty of putting in place a "containment zone" around Yorkshire. This includes an immediate travel ban for everyone, and I've cancelled leave for all civil servants, doctors, nurses and emergency crews. I realise this goes above my jurisdiction, but as the flood disaster Tsar I had to trust my judgement.'

A murmur of agreement.

The Prime Minister's mood lifted a little now that Stone had had the sense to implement a plan. 'Good thinking. Well done, Stone. Use whatever powers you feel necessary to get to the bottom of this mess. I'll make sure all the relevant authorities are aware.' One of the Prime Minister's personal private secretaries scribbled on his pad and slipped out of the room.

'So, first things first,' the Prime Minister continued. 'We invite selected media in and show them the child,' he turned to the doctor. 'You happy with that, Dr Muller?'

The doctor moved his jaw and nodded slowly. 'Sure. We can try to get the boy talking. It's a long shot but worth a go—'

'Don't you think it might appear a little bit see through, a touch desperate?' the Commissioner asked.

The Prime Minister turned on him. 'Look, Stone, we've got the world's press outside clamouring to know what the hell's going on. Many are already jumping to conclusions. If the word gets out before we have any evidence, think of the consequences. Think of the panic. Imagine the morning's headlines. *"Britain in Quarantine".'* The Prime Minister paused for effect. 'In the rush to leave the disaster zone, the disease will go with it, and that, my friends, will lead to an even worse catastrophe. We need to buy time.'

The Prime Minister kneaded his temples. 'The fact is this. It's our very own biblical mess and we're going to have to deal with it. It's as simple as that.'

'You're correct,' the doctor said. At last the officials were now taking the situation with the deadly seriousness it deserved. 'Good to hear you're right behind us.'

'Call a press conference for midday,' the Prime Minister ordered. 'You'll have the boy's blood results by then. Try and add a positive spin. Expand on the fact that the boy was found against all odds, burnt and naked up a tree—a miracle among the carnage—to give us added time. Update the press team. Commissioner Stone, you've got a day—more if we're lucky—to find out as much as you can and continue the "quiet" work you've started. After that—and when there's a fuller picture—the COBRA team will action a wider containment plan.'

Dr Muller nodded and nudged the Prime Minister gently to the side. 'If this is the start of an epidemic, Prime Minister, you are aware that you have been in an infected area and you must go through a decontamination programme? For safety's sake, I urge you to do this at once and leave immediately after the press conference.'

The Prime Minister cocked his head. Years of being in the firing line of politics had given him a nose for judging people. 'Is there something you haven't told me, doctor?'

Dr Muller shifted and drew the PM out of earshot. 'So far, we've only been able to reach a small number of people, namely from Northallerton. We have no knowledge of the situation in the smaller villages which have been all but eradi-cated.' He frowned as his voice fell to a whisper. 'Early reports indicate that animals too have been found with plague-like symptoms almost identical to the human condition.'

'What is the relevance of this in relation to the outbreak?'

'Well—'

The Prime Minister stared at him open-mouthed as the truth hit him. 'You're saying that the disease, or whatever this is, is wiping out every creature in its path?'

'Perhaps... but we can't rule it out,' the doctor replied. 'As I mentioned, these are unconfirmed reports. Of course, we don't know how the virus spreads, who is likely to catch it, or the conditions of infection. It could be—'

'Why was I not briefed about this?' the Prime Minister snapped. 'Have COBRA been notified?' He turned to the Commissioner. 'Stone, you'd better listen to this.'

Stone joined them as the doctor continued. 'There's a medical unit heading towards the village of Upsall. They left this morning and are due to report back this afternoon.'

'God have mercy upon us!' The Prime Minister spoke under his breath. 'Isn't this the place where the storm started?'

'Indeed. Satellite recordings show that the weather system came from directly above the village—'

'Yes, I heard it was unlike any other storm formation ever recorded. So far, what do we know?'

'It's the location of a well-known local school that inhabits a medieval monastery,' Stone began. 'The village is a popular tourist attraction for walkers in the summer. My cousin happens to be headmaster there. He's called Solomon. He saved a number of his pupils in the old tower.'

The PM pursed his lips. 'We need a thorough investigation of this place, and I mean thorough. Anything suspicious—police records, hospital records—must be analysed and re-analysed. We'll need details of farms, cattle stocks, any previous outbreaks of disease, bird populations... anything and everything.'

'I have a team working on it already,' Stone said.

'Good. All survivors must be moved into the containment zone and analysed. We need answers, and quickly. Like, yesterday.'

The Commissioner nodded.

'And pardon the pun, Stone, but leave no Stone unturned. If this Godforsaken crisis cannot be explained by usual methodology, we need to work on something outside the box. Understand? And if the storm and the disease have both spilled out of Upsall, then I want to know why. Is this perfectly clear?'

Stone smiled. 'Yes, sir. I understand completely.'

The Prime Minister nodded. 'Call on anyone, and I mean anyone, you need in order to assist you. Let nothing get in your way. As far as I'm concerned, Stone, you have whatever power you need to get the bottom of this.'

ISABELLA MAKES A DISCOVERY

For a considerable time, Isabella remained under her bed covers as she woke up. She sat up and rubbed her eyes before stretching her arms out and yawning.

I'll work it out logically, starting with Sue's dream and, when I'm done, I'll present a rational, scientific report to the others.

She grabbed a notebook and pen, and began to think hard about the chain of events that led up to where they were now. She took the lid off her pen and began to write.

A LIST, OF WHO IS / ISN'T IN MY DREAM(S).
Parents:
Not involved. Definitely remember seeing them, but can't place them anywhere and why aren't they here to help!!!
Daisy and Archie haven't mentioned them.
Sue:

- Hasn't appeared in my dreams. WHY NOT… because she's a friend, or is there something else? cousin… or?
- Is she relevant? Probably. Don't know why.
- She predicted the rain and knows about something we have to do. According to her, it's our fault! UH? Why are we to blame for the rain? Don't think so. But, IF SO, HOW?

- Something else about clues...? In Eden Cottage. Have to find something, but what? Tablets? Paintings?
- Is Gus (kiss, kiss) involved—NO. (Don't think so.)

Old Man Wood:
VERY important.

- Crops up all the time. Seems to be more than one of him, but why, oh why, is he in my dreams?
- Resplendix Mix is weird (but amazing). From an apothecary, apparently (they don't exist). Need to get a sample. His funny apples are weird, too.
- Somehow found us in the rain. HOW WAS THAT POSSIBLE??
- Looks freaked out by what's going on. But not particularly bothered by the ridiculous cave pool and Resplendix Mix.
- How old IS he?

Mrs P:
Comes into it at some point (I think) though is it actually her? There's something not quite right about her. Don't know what it is.

Ancient Woman person

- Vital to the whole thing. Daisy's common dominator (Haha!!) but keeps on being killed. Mainly by Archie. UH? No idea why. She seems lost, desperately ill and frail.
- Where is she from??

The cave: (According to the twins)

- Paintings on the wall similar to Sue's comments about finding something. Tablets (again, according to Archie).
- V Odd healing water.
- Gears on stairs and boulder at top. Brilliant engineering so must have been designed. But WHO designed it and WHY... and when?

Daisy:

- Can hear acute things like lightning bolts forming and see astonishing detail, (though is she making it up?)
- Scientific explanation: Electrical charge from lightning bolt altered

nerve motors in these areas. Eyes and ears suffered semi-permanent damage?
- Also, utterly convinced that cave paintings are relevant... hmm
- She died? Resplendix Mix didn't work on her, only me. All V. odd.

Archie:

- Shifted the boulder—though would it have gone anyway?
- Hair stiff and wiry like a mace club. Scientific explanation: A reaction between the particles of the football's material and the lightning strips we gave him when the lighting struck.
- Very freaked out by murder of Ancient Woman.
- Knew about sunset and rain ceasing. HOW? Did he dream this or…?
- Defo seems to know something else but what is it. Something with Kemp??
- Looks a bit lost and has doubts. (Not the only one!)

Isabella read her list and realised she still had no clear idea. Maybe the solution was to interrogate Old Man Wood and quiz him relentlessly until he gave proper, reasonable answers; like *exactly* how old he was.

She'd then grill him about Resplendix Mix, which was both real and yet totally extraordinary… and perhaps she could run a couple of tests on the potion to see if she could identify any of its properties? But then she realised she'd need a lab, and light, and heat, and test tubes, and all manner of things.

She thumped the table and threw her notepad across the room in frustration. How could she prove beyond doubt that these events were part of a natural, albeit freaky course of events?

And then she remembered how the old man said he'd been dreaming too. Perhaps she'd ask him about that as well.

Isabella took off up the main wooden stairs towards his room and knocked on the solid oak door. 'Old Man Wood, are you there?' she began. 'I need to talk.'

There was no reply. Isabella knew he wasn't in. When he was at home, either huge snores would reverberate through the door, or he'd be padding about, or rustling a newspaper, or the curiously reassuring pine-scented aroma from his homemade pipe would drift into the corridor from under the door.

Isabella waited a moment longer, peeked behind her and entered. In the middle sat Old Man Wood's great bed. She tiptoed over the musty little carpets and jumped high in the air, landing in the soft pile of the feather-down duvet and cushions.

With her head propped up by the large, soft pillows she lost herself in thought, and stared at the rain tracing its way down the windowpanes. Her attention turned to the beautiful wooden carvings that depicted strange scenes and images of animals and creatures. These adorned every upright and joint on the old four-poster bed. She smiled as she remembered how, as younger children, they had spent hours creating outrageous stories with the wooden characters and, now that she thought about it, the carvings were never quite the same from one day to the next. *Probably*, she thought, *just their childish imaginations running wild.*

Isabella studied the three wooden panels at the foot of the bed, each one the size of a large, rectangular table mat. She couldn't remember seeing them before but the harder she looked, the deeper the array of colours; light and dark reds, pale and deep blues, and browns, and a mixture of creams and yellows. But over-all, when she looked quickly, the wood was light brown.

Isabella pulled herself up, herself to a sip of water and lay back re-focusing on the panels.

Hang on! A figure in the first panel moved! Oh. No, she thought, giggling nervously at her reaction. *It hadn't.*

But as she stared at it again she noticed she really could see a girl sitting in a bed. She laughed. It looked quite like her, but probably prettier and thinner. *Weird or what?*

She turned her attention to the second panel and realised she could see a girl lying down, sunbathing, between three fat, knobbly trees.

How nice to feel the sun, Isabella thought, but how odd that this semi naked girl was lying in snow. Just as Isabella lifted her head to see what else was on the bed-head, she detected a movement.

It changed! The panel definitely changed. She laughed uneasily. *Come on, Isabella, don't be an idiot. Bed panels don't move.* She shut her eyes and lay back, but a part of her brain wouldn't let the imagery go.

She looked again and, to her relief, it remained motionless.

Then the image moved.

Isabella felt her head going numb. She stared, her bottom lip hanging, forgetting to breathe.

At length she exhaled. 'It's moving. It's really moving... like a...' she muttered. Isabella sat bolt upright, shut her eyes and swung her legs off the bed. 'Like a... telly.'

She walked past the wooden panels and over to the window, where she sat down in Old Man Wood's armchair and shook her head. Was she seeing things?

If it's a kind of wooden telly, she thought, *then it must have power going to it*. She began searching for wires, or a transmitter, or anything that might make a bit of sense. But again, she drew a blank.

After a few minutes, she reaffirmed that she was normal by giving herself some mental arithmetic tests and took herself back to the bed.

She lay back, closed her eyes and then slowly opened them, hoping like mad that she'd been seeing things. But, to Isabella's horror, the girl in the wooden relief stood up, walked first one way and then the other before heading towards the frame of something that looked like a large, dilapidated greenhouse.

Isabella's stomach leapt. However much she didn't want to believe it, she simply couldn't tear her eyes away.

The girl, now clothed, walked into a strange-looking area. Across the floor was an object that looked rather like Old Man Wood's old-fashioned garden roller, but it had a flat ledge like a table. If it wasn't a roller, what was it?

Isabella rubbed her eyes, swung her legs off the bed again, and this time faced the mirror above the fireplace. She looked deeply at her reflection, particularly at her eyes. Then she pulled her hands up to her face and slapped each cheek as hard as she dared.

'OW!' she cried, surprised by the force. 'Wow, that hurt,' she said, rubbing her cheeks and feeling a little foolish.

'OK. I'm real, and this is real, and that slap was definitely real,' she said to her reflection. 'How has Old Man Wood managed to do this?' she continued. 'Is he a secret agent, a spy? Does he work for a space agency or something?' Isabella laughed. Old Man Wood as a spy, hilarious! A spaceman! Even more hilarious. She walked across the room and lowered herself into his armchair.

A frown filled her face and her eyes narrowed. What if he's a wizard, or a witch doctor, or an ALIEN?

A thrill swept through her. It would explain Resplendix Mix.

Isabella returned to the bed, full of trepidation, and settled back in the cushions. She closed her eyes and then half opened them, hoping the images had gone. They hadn't.

This time, she sat up and examined the subtle movement of the panels and the more she studied it, the more enchanted she became.

For some time, the girl in the middle panel sat on the roller-object and nothing happened. Every now and then, her arms were thrown in the air in a familiar gesture that Isabella recognised from somewhere. Then the girl stood up and, with considerable effort, began to pull the roller-object's handle. As she did so, a hole opened up where the table had been.

This is more like it, Isabella thought, pleased to see some action. The girl in the panel returned to the space where the table had been and appeared to look at it. Then she knelt down, and swivelled as if she was talking to someone.

I'm sure I know that bottom, Isabella thought, and the way that body bends forward so easily, like a doll.

Isabella moved her attention to the third panel at the end of the bed, which, up until then, had remained lifeless. But, now that her eyes were accustomed to the colours, she could make out the outline of a body curled up in the corner of a darkened room.

Suddenly she saw a movement. An arm cocked back and then slammed quickly forward.

'Whoa!' she cried. 'What's that all about?' She watched again and shuffled closer to the screen. Moments later, the exact same motion happened. She suddenly realised what she was looking at.

'It's Archie!' she whispered, her heart racing, 'with his stupid throwing knives. I knew he hadn't got rid of them.' She watched closer. The figure stood up and there, on the top of his head, were his extraordinary hair spikes.

Isabella put her head in her hands. If that's Archie, then the middle one... she looked at the picture of the girl in the sunshine again.

That rear! Of course! It was... Daisy's butt! Isabella clapped her hands together.

The third panel is Archie. The middle panel with the roller-object and that bottom is Daisy's, so the last panel is... Isabella threw her hand in the air and the image on the relief copied her.

It was her!

A strange dizziness started to rush in.

Me, here, in Old Man Wood's bed!

Isabella stared back at herself, hardly daring to move. A dull ache jammed her brain.

Keep calm, need to think. Come on, brain; what... OK... who was Old Man Wood, really? And why this bed? For spying on them?

Perhaps it was a kind of child-monitor while the parents were away? No—way too expensive and ridiculous and impossible.

But why did he have it and what did it mean? Why did it exist?

Her heart thumping, Isabella turned back to the wooden screens. Archie's arm flashed forward, throwing another stupid knife. By the dinginess of the scene, she guessed he was probably in that horrible old woodshed.

But where was Daisy? On the panel, it appeared to be sunny, whereas outside —and she looked out of the window—it was dank, rainy, and horrible. In her mind's eye, she ran through every place on the farm but no place came close.

She took a deep breath and, totally absorbed by the spectacle, viewed her sister. But a moment later, Daisy disappeared.

Where is she?

A lump grew in Isabella's throat and her heartbeat quickened. Was the panel faulty?

Suddenly the wooden screen came back to life.

Isabella breathed a sigh of relief as she watched Daisy scuttle about on her hands and knees, trying to move the roller thing.

She's talking again.

Then Isabella watched as Daisy stood up like a sentry and pointed towards the ground. Her mouth was wide open as if... screaming.

Slowly, her body lowered into the ground; first her legs, then her chest, until all that remained was her head. Moments later she vanished entirely.

The screen went blank.

Isabella stared at the panel for several minutes, transfixed, until her large eyes filled with tears. But there was no mistaking it; while she and Archie remained on their panels, Daisy's wooden panel lay empty, lifeless, and dull, like an ordinary section of their dining room table.

Daisy, she realised, had quite literally melted away.

EBORA - THE YORKSHIRE STRAIN

Commissioner Stone was proud of his accomplishments on the Force, proud that he had the respect of his team and proud that, at the age of fifty-two he could still fit into the suit he had bought with his first pay cheque aged nineteen. He prided himself on his fitness, his well-being, and his full head of hair. He liked the fact that others complimented him on his sense of fair play and his ability to under-stand and uphold the rule of law in an uncomplicated manner. He liked the way ladies half his age stole admiring glances at him.

But *this*, this silent and deadly enemy, which was multiplying at an alarming rate, terrified him. No training manual or charm offensive could combat it, even if operations for this kind of "natural event" had been planned for years in advance.

Biblical happenings here in God's own county of Yorkshire. Storms! Plague! It was unbelievable.

Ironically, he'd been looking forward to the day for some time. His older cousin, known by his surname, Solomon, was headmaster at Upsall school and had sent him an invitation to a banquet in celebration of his twentieth anniversary in charge. Rumour had it that it was to be quite an occasion.

In any event, he'd only got as far as his local town of Masham, on the edge of the Yorkshire Dales. Less than half an hour after the rains began, he found himself stranded. Fortunately, he'd come to a halt outside the drive of the Swinton Park Hotel.

It was a huge stroke of luck.

Geographically, the hotel was perfect. Directly across the Vale of York from the village of Upsall, the hotel was isolated enough to prevent unwarranted intrusion and perched high enough in the dales to be out of danger from the flooding. Furthermore, the hotel was big and comfortable; able to house the army of experts summoned at short notice from around the UK.

Over the following day, as the hotel guests were airlifted out, his team and their equipment moved in. The luxurious facilities were turning into the head-quarters of the largest police and medical operation ever seen in the country.

He stroked his moustache as he drew himself up, patted his pressed uniform and addressed the team in front of him.

'Right. I need a speech analyst to fathom what the boy was trying to say. If the word was "Algae", maybe the boy was referring to the state of the water, so I want the water samples back here today, please. I need to know what the "Dunno" is—if it's a thing, a person, a piece of rock or if the boy simply cannot speak clearly. I want teams to work on his family, figure out where he's from: blood samples, DNA screening—whatever it takes. Understand so far?

'I need an up-to-date on the boy's burns—who or what could have given them and how. And I need to understand if this is a terrorist attack on the country—a form of international sabotage or simply a freak, biblical phenomenon. Find out what you can—even if there's a possibility it's an alien attack—is this all perfectly clear?'

The officers nodded. Two ran out of the room.

'OK. Has everyone arrived for the briefing?'

'Yes, sir. They've been flying in all morning. The last guest put down ten minutes ago.'

'Good.' Stone made his way out of the reception area and into the grand hallway where a large, white sheet hung neatly over the paintings of the past owners of the once-grand ancestral home. Crammed in the hallway were a mix of scientists, the military and civil servants. Top brass. The commissioner made his way up the wide staircase.

'Ladies and Gentlemen—Doctors, Generals, I appreciate your coming here at such short notice. I trust you saw the scale of devastation from your helicopters. You'll appreciate we don't have much time.'

Stone paused as he caught the eyes of the people spread out below him. 'The situation, in regard to the viral infection, is far worse than anticipated. In fact, it is worse than our biggest nightmare. Not only is the contagion rate astonishing, but I'm afraid we have no idea how it is spreading. I'm handing you over to Chief Medical Officer Harris. He'll give you the latest update.'

Harris was one of the thinnest, leanest men you could imagine, with a pointed nose and a large, ill-fitting pair of spectacles on his nose. His thinning, scraggly hair made him appear way older than his forty-seven years, and his almost permanent frown didn't help matters. But he was the leading authority on viral strains in the country, if not the world. He made his way to the front, a bundle of files tucked under his arm, and nodded to the projectionist. The lights dimmed and the white screen above them burst into life.

'This plague, named the Yorkshire strain, or Ebora, from the Latin Ebor meaning York—and I do believe that this will become the common name—is a most curious one,' he said, as the first slide came up. 'Here,' he said pointing up, 'are the strains, the mutations, of this virus that we've been able to map so far. You will notice how many there are.' A new image slid into place. 'I'm going to compare it with the legendary viruses of *Plague of Athens*, *Spanish flu* and our most recent scaremonger, *Ebola*. What you'll instantly see is how complex it is.

'Those pandemics spread through touch or via carriers—the virus moving from one organism to the next. The difference of Ebora is multi-fold, and our Ebora strain is not only smaller but considerably more aggressive. Moreover, it appears to mutate randomly and rapidly. Although we have identified several varieties of the strain we believe there are many others out there.' The graphic changed. 'What this means, is that until we crack it, it is almost impossible to contain.

'Here's a graph showing the effect of the African Ebola virus on a victim in twenty-four hours. Now compare it with ours.'

A collective gasp ascended from the onlookers.

'Yes, indeed, the Yorkshire strain is significantly deadlier. Worse still, we've found animals—cattle, foxes, and birds—bearing similar symptoms. It would appear that this outbreak doesn't just stop with humans. It has the ability to attack every living thing.'

A fresh slide showed on the screen. Harris straightened. He looked pale and drawn. 'The next slides will try and explain our current understanding of how the virus spreads.'

Displayed on the screen was a multi-coloured geographical map of the area between the Yorkshire Dales on the left and the North York Moors on the right, reaching all the way up to Teesside and down to Nottingham at the bottom.

He pointed his cane at the newest image. 'The known area of infection is coloured in blue. Two-hundred miles, and counting. This inner red ring, here, is a five-mile radius around the likely source of the outbreak at Upsall, the exact same place as the epicentre of the storm. We don't know if there's a connection, but we're working on it. Now, here's the worrying part.'

On his signal, a translucent sheet was placed over the map. 'This sheet,' he continued, 'shows us the known victims as of early this morning. The lighter green circles around the dots indicates the victims' approximate movements.'

Several marks dotted the map randomly from north to south.

A voice rang out. 'Sir, what does it all mean?'

'I was getting to that,' Harris barked. He smiled thinly. 'In simple terms, it means that the virus is spreading arbitrarily.'

A murmur spread around the room. Harries raised a hand in the air. 'The virus is spreading in a way we haven't seen before. By contact, by wind or by water. Perhaps, it's a combination of all these. The incubation period is like nothing we have ever come across which means there are thousands of people with the symptoms already. I am afraid, until we know more about it, they are at its mercy.'

An explosion of questions shot out. Harris absorbed them and then raised his arms for silence. 'We can only work with what we know,' he said. 'Scientists from all around the world are battling night and day to try and understand how this virus works so that a vaccination can be hurried through. But, as I mentioned, the Ebora mutates fast and the sequences are enormously complex.'

'How long have we got?' yelled a female voice.

'In two days,' Harris said, 'the virus has spread uncontrollably. I'm afraid I don't have an answer.'

'Do you have any leads, any positive news?'

Harris looked glum. 'Even with the best scientific minds working flat out, we're unable to pinpoint the cause and effect of this strain. The common denominator is the fact that the outbreak appears to have started at the storm's epicentre. And that, my friends, is the small moorside village of Upsall.'

DAISY'S DISCOVERY

Daisy squeezed her eyes shut and sucked in a lungful of air as if it were her last.

Suddenly, her legs were dragged from under her as she was swept away. A combination of whizz-zooming at breakneck speed, and being thrown around in a tumble dryer.

Moments later she found herself lying on a soft, dusty floor, her heart thumping.

Those ridiculous trees, she thought, as she gathered her wits. *I took their advice like an idiot!*

With her eyes clamped tightly shut and her head spinning, she spread her fingers and collected a thin, velvety substance. Dust. Fine dust. She pushed her hand in. A lot of dust. How long had this place been empty? She sniffed a combination of decayed cheese and old newspapers.

Slowly, she opened her eyes. 'Where am I?' she whispered.

Her voice echoed back to her several times, eerie and ghost-like. She shivered now that the heat of the warm glade had gone.

A deathly silence surrounded her.

Daisy picked herself off the dusty floor, noticing how the dust cloud she'd made sat almost statically in the air, as if toying with gravity by almost refusing to come down. Not a breath of wind, not a hint of a draft. When she placed her hand into the silky dust it sank down two inches, more perhaps. And when she pulled it out, the imprint in the flat surface was perfect.

Isabella's handprint would look awesome, she thought, as she splayed her fingers and pressed into the dust again.

She coughed, and her ears pricked up as the tiny noise stretched into the distance and then came back. Even the air had a dank, unused feel to it, like a vast, unloved cellar.

It didn't take her long to figure out that there was no one around. Just a flat, slate-like surface of thick dust that went on and on like a vast expanse of fresh sand. Standing up, she saw no indentations or paw prints or drip marks in the thick layer of grey dust.

Daisy looked up and squinted, her eyes slowly adjusting to the dim light. She was in a vast, cathedral-like room, bigger than anything she'd ever seen. It was so big that even when she concentrated it was hard to make out where the sheer sides ended and the roof began, if there even was a roof.

It seemed that, about ten football pitches away, a wall shot up from the floor, intersected by vast pillars. The pillars were like giant ribs, that soared high into the air supporting the structure, and below, a series of arches with dark mouths ran around the base.

If I'm really dead, and this time I absolutely must be, she thought, I don't think this is Heaven, or Hell for that matter. Perhaps I'm in between; in purgatory.

Some way off, near to what she suspected was the middle of this vast, dull construction, stood a strange-looking, dust-laden grey tree. Spindly branches poked out rather sadly, as if they were dead like a skeleton.

She stood up and walked towards the side, conscious of leaving indelible foot-marks behind her. Conscious, too, that although her feet padded silently in the dust, there was a strange, thudding echo which accompanied each step in the deep quiet. After several minutes, she noticed how varied the arches were; some were wide enough for an ocean liner to fit through and these openings and these took minutes to walk by, the chill of their unfriendly, black space shooting up her spine, others had openings like fox-holes nestled on top of each other.

She walked gingerly down a tunnel that could have easily accommodated a pair of African elephants but, after a short distance, as the darkness became over-whelming, she stumbled into a dead end barrier of rock and earth.

She tried another, and another, but they too were sealed. After five tunnels, Daisy felt lost, frightened, and very, very small.

'Hello,' she called out, her voice echoing back. 'Anyone… here?'

Her teeth chattered. *How do I leave?*

She took off towards the strange grey tree, but halfway there something snapped underfoot. She jumped in the air and squealed. Her heart raced. Under-neath the dust, partially buried, lay a skeleton. She worked the dust away from the bones, with legs, ribcage arms, and a human skull. Daisy winced; someone was here a long, long time ago. Someone who never made it out.

'Sorry, mate,' she said. 'Didn't see you there.'

As she studied the bones, her senses on high alert, she heard a strange wheezing noise.

Was it the ghost of the skeleton? She listened again, putting all her concentration into it. The more intently she listened, the clearer the rasping sound was, like old bellows. Now there was a grating—a kind of breathing—getting closer.

Fear grabbed her. Looking down at the skeleton again, she knew she needed to find a way out as fast as she could.

FOOTSTEPS IN THE ATRIUM

The Ancient Woman heard an unusual and distinctive sound. She had first heard it while the dreamspinners were playing a game she had made up many centuries ago. With a faint clap of her old hands or a wheezy cough, the little dreamspinners flicked mini balls of spider web silks towards each other's magholes. If they hit the target, a small puff of smoke burst on a very surprised little dreamspinners. The best effect, therefore, was when a multitude of pellets exploded on one maghole and as such, a sophisticated game had developed, which smaller dreamspinners rarely tired of.

After the Great Closing of the Garden of Eden, the dreamspinners had discovered the Ancient Woman in the small rooms below the vast storage area of spider web dream powders. As her eyes had been gouged out and she could never leave, she was part of their family now, and they provided her with food and water to prevent her body withering to dust, and a degree of comfort from the solitude and darkness, while she waited and waited for the arrival of the Heirs of Eden.

But, many thousands of years in solitude had left her physically wretched. Her skeletal frame was overhung with coarse, over-sized skin, her bony skull had but a few wisps of hair, her empty eye sockets were like dark holes, and the nails on her fingers curled like spiders' legs.

As the trust between them grew, and as the great passage of time crept by, she understood the immense influence of these strange, unknown, dream-giving spiders. And slowly she learnt about dreams.

She discovered how dreamspinners blended old and new spider web silks into all sorts of powerful and exotic concoctions. She was amazed to learn how these strange creatures were only interested in the extraordinary process of dream-making and had no desire to manipulate their power.

She begged them to allow her to try out new dream powder combinations to understand what effects they might have. Aeons later and she became skilled enough to use their dream powders so she could give herself dreams that lasted for days; dreams where she could free her imagination to wander and forget the perpetual darkness, the anguish, and her desperate boredom. In this state, she could fall in love again, dance in the fields of the Garden of Eden, ride the giant horses on the glorious pink Tombalacker Plains. She could talk to her children, kiss them, hug them, teach them all the things she knew, and do it again and again and again.

And she did, until her heart ached like a balloon at bursting point.

Yet ever at the back of her mind was the knowledge that even if the Garden of Eden were to open, she would never see its beauty and splendour.

She heard the noise again.

A padding sound from the other side, in the chamber above.

She listened harder.

Footsteps? Were these the gentle thuds of a human's footsteps? The thought thrilled her and injected her with unimaginable dread.

Her mind sparked into life. Instantly, she pulled her tiny, bony frame off the ground and crept to the curving staircase. Her body, so ancient and pathetic, made it hard for her to move and with every step up, her wasted muscles screamed out.

She forced herself on, her heart pumping, energy flowing through each and every vein as she struggled up the worn treads.

At about the halfway mark, she paused for breath, exhausted. All she could hear was her thumping heart and the grating sound of air trying to squeeze into her withered lungs.

After recovering her poise, she listened again. Yes, she could clearly hear foot-steps walking in the dust above.

An Heirs of Eden, perhaps? But why only one? Had they failed already?

She urged herself on, each step conducting pain through her joints like strands of heated metal. At the top, she searched for her wooden cane. With this she could guide herself up and into her half of the great chamber. She leaned hard on her stick, her body begging for a rest. She shuffled a few paces and stopped to listen, her lungs wheezing like wind through dry leaves.

But now, to her horror, she sensed the person was moving away.

The Ancient Woman headed towards the invisible, glass-like barrier that divided the Atrium in two. It was the barrier the Heirs of Eden would have to open, if they found their way back here.

'Come on! MOVE legs, MOVE body,' she cackled, shuffling as fast as she dared.

Then she heard a sound she hadn't expected. A loud—

CRACK!

She crashed to the ground.

The stick, which had supported her for so long, had snapped clean in two. She couldn't move.

She ran a hand down her side and touched something sharp and fragmented. It wasn't just the stick that had cracked in two, her thighbone had shattered and bone now speared through her flesh.

As her brain realised the extent of the injury, pain coursed through her and she screamed a cry of agony.

ISABELLA RUSHES OUT

Isabella hoped like mad that, when she looked again, the panels wouldn't be there. She opened her eyes.

They were.

She groaned. She could see her outline in the first panel, and Archie's in the last, but the middle panel showed only a blank, empty space. She waved her feet in the air and the panel reflected her movements. If the panels were a true reflection of them at this exact point in time, she concluded, then where had Daisy gone?

She leapt off Old Man Wood's bed, and raced down the stairs three at a time into the hallway. Then she dashed along the corridor, through the door to the kitchen, and all but crashed into the table. 'Have you seen Archie or Daisy?' she demanded, as her eyes searched the room.

Mrs Pye was not impressed. 'Good day to you, too, Isabella,' she said.

'Well? Have you?'

Mrs Pye puffed out her chest and faced her. 'Good afternoon, Isabella.'

'Oh. Hi Mrs P. Well–?'

'Why, Archie went out early...'

Isabella didn't need to hear the rest. In a flash, she pulled on her boots and donned her coat. She found her leather, wide-brimmed hat, and as she drew the toggle under her chin she flew towards the door, inadvertently slamming it behind her. As she turned the corner she narrowly avoided smashing into Archie.

'Oi! Watch out!' he said.

'There you are!' she said, clasping his shoulders. 'Great! Good! Fantastic!'

Archie reeled. 'What's going on, Bells?'

'Quick question, honest answer,' she said. 'And I'm not going to be cross, I promise.'

Archie didn't know what to say.

'You've been throwing your knives, haven't you?'

Archie bowed his head. 'Er, well—'

'You have. Great!' she said. 'Really, it's fine, excellent. Next question. Have you seen Daisy? She went off looking for you ages ago.'

Archie shook his head.

'OK. Didn't think so,' she said. Isabella knew that, if what she'd seen was correct, Daisy wouldn't be found anywhere. But she had to be sure.

'Where are you going?' Archie asked.

'Up to the ruin and then round the farm. I'll meet you in our cupboard, in twenty minutes... I've got to find Daisy. It's important.'

The cupboard was a small room, used by Mrs Pye as a walk-in airing cupboard, for drying and storing towels, sheets and linen. The children used it as their own personal snug, for chatting and for warming themselves up on a cold winter's day.

Archie was confused. 'Right round the farm? It'll take you an hour at least. If you want Old Man Wood, he's in a bunch of willow trees at the water's edge. He's gone mad.'

But Isabella wasn't listening and, in a flash, she shot off towards the ruin.

Gritting her teeth, Isabella ran as fast as she could through the mud and spitting rain, jumping and hurdling branches and boulders with ease. She was amazed at how little time it took her to get there, how her feet seemed to take on a life of their own. She knew the distance was about five-hundred metres. And she reckoned it took less than a minute. *Was that right?* She did a quick calculation: thirty miles an hour. *Impossible: That was faster that Usain Bolt!*

She stood by an old wall, with jagged edges here and there, its grey stones covered in ferns and creepers and stubborn shrubs that had tucked their roots deep into the crevices. The ruin's battlements jutted out before disappeared into the grass below, then rose up like dark shadows until they ran along at twice her height for several metres.

Isabella searched for footprints. *Had only two days passed since they'd limped home from the cave?* It felt like a lifetime; so many confusing, bewildering events crowding her brain. She stopped by a section of masonry, half-submerged in the ground, layered with moss and lichen. *Was this the entrance into the old body of the castle? A kind of gateway?*

Large, tyre-track markings weaved in and out of the scattered boulders. Maybe, these were the residual patterns made by the movement of water finding its natural path, she wondered as she walked towards the gnarled battlements on the far side calling out Daisy's name, the sound of her voice rebounding off the walls.

She hurried on. It was hauntingly silent. Too silent, apart from rain pitter-pattering on the leather rim of her hat.

What if the terrible experiences they'd had had made them imagine things? What if they had some kind of post-traumatic stress disorder? What if some parts were real and other bits... made up, invented?

She'd read about this kind of thing in her textbooks. The brain was a powerful tool, a living computer with an unlimited ability for imagination. Perhaps this theory explained their dreams, and things like the bed, and Daisy's disappearance.

She took a deep breath, put her hands out on the rock, and leaned on them. As she did, a strange noise interrupted her thoughts. She gasped as a terrible chill ran up the very marrow of her spine. Her skin prickled and a nauseous feeling washed right through her. The eyes of a serpent flickered in her head.

She started walking.

It's in your mind, she told herself, *a figment of your imagination.* She stood tall, stretched her arms out wide, and then swung them round and round like a wind-mill as if to swish it away.

It didn't work. She still felt sick and the chill remained. Identical green eyes exactly as she'd dreamt before the storm, every bit the same, if not worse. The beast with the same green eyes that had latched-on to her mind, and made her head swim.

She shivered. *Had the light dimmed or was another storm cloud brewing overhead? How come this once happy place now had such a deep aura of evil, of darkness?*

A rustling noise further along reminded her to check Old Man Wood's cattle. She followed the strange tyre-track markings a short distance, until they ran under a large boulder. She thought briefly about her theory of how channels of water made the marks. *But if this was the case, then wouldn't the tracks run downhill?*

She hurried on and, before long, came to the other section of the ruin, a large, rectangular courtyard dotted with crude rocks and the occasional scraggly bush and tree. At the far end, in the corner, was a shelter for the herd, crudely constructed by Old Man Wood from large rocks and tree trunks and covered by a moss-covered roof of jumbled slates and tiles.

As Isabella approached, a terrible noise spewed out; frantic mooing and bleat-ing. She crept forward, wondering what had unsettled the cows, only to hear a stampede of hooves as the cattle bolted, scattering in different directions, sending mud flying.

Isabella knew the animals well; they were never afraid of her. But now they looked terrified, their eyes wide and shining more than she could ever remember. She talked to them in a soothing voice, and slowly they calmed down. As they moved back under the shelter, she counted them.

Two missing. She counted them again. *Perhaps they had bolted in the storm?*

Isabella tried to work out which ones were missing and, holding her nose, she entered the corral to see if they were at the back. No luck. She made a mental note to tell Old Man Wood.

And still, she could see no sign of Daisy.

DAISY BELIEVES

The beginnings of a panic attack grew. It was a combination of hopelessness and fear, the same kind of feeling she'd had in her nightmares.

She jogged towards the wall.

In the next moment, the sound of a terrible crack cut through the air like a huge branch snapping in two. This was followed by a scream, and its shrill echoed around the huge room like deathly, wailing spirits.

Every hair on Daisy's body stood to attention. Her eyes bulged.

'The devil's coming to get me!' she whispered.

She ran.

Daisy shot towards the large holes to the side of the enclosure and then, running blindly, she searched for a glimmer of light, a way out, or a place to hide. After a few minutes, she drew up in front of a distinctive tunnel with worn markings surrounding it.

She caught her breath, wiped her forehead, and listened. Wailing, or screaming, filled her eardrums.

She readied herself to go when she noticed the stonework. This was a real arch constructed in stone as opposed to a crudely excavated cave-hole. Under the brow of the arch was the outline of a gate and, below this, she looked at a familiar motif, like a crest you might see on a shield, with the exact same circular tree emblem she'd seen in the cave.

Below the circular tree were two distinct icons. She studied them. One bore a leaf, like an oak's, and the other, the picture of a bee.

As she looked around she heard a terrific shrill.

The oak leaf and the bee, she thought. She realised she'd seen it before, but where? *Where?*

She stared hard, her heart thumping. *What did a bee and a leaf mean?*

She concentrated on the images knowing she had to work fast. Then it struck her like a bolt of lightning—it was a clue from her dream. She remembered it now. She had to join the images! That was it!

"BEE-LEAF."

'Bee... leaf,' she said out loud. It struck her. 'It's about BEE-LIEF! That's it!'

All I have to do is believe!

As the piercing, high-pitched noise filled her ears, and without looking back, she took a deep breath, shut her eyes, and walked straight towards the doorway, thinking only of Eden Cottage.

The next thing she knew, she was back in a ditch, but this time she was on the other side of the gate. She shrieked, and jumped, and punched the air as if she'd scored the best goal of her life.

She didn't care that she was drenched through. She laughed and splashed the water, crying with joy.

Daisy de Lowe, she thought, *had just escaped from Hell.*

She had to tell the others. But, as she went, doubt filled her.

What if they don't believe me? After all, the whole thing was... a bit nuts. In fact, she thought, even attempting to explain it will sound utterly bonkers. But they must know, they have to.

And then they could begin the search for the stone tablet things.

Daisy took off, slipping and sliding, up the hill towards home.

ISABELLA EXPLAINS

When Isabella returned to an empty kitchen, she reckoned Archie had sought the warmth of the cupboard, which drew heat from the flue-pipe of the range cooker directly below in the kitchen.

Isabella approached, knocked on the door five times and rattled off last week's password, 'Carrots, cauliflowers and courgettes.'

Archie clicked open the latch.

'Any luck finding Daisy?' he said.

Isabella settled on a soft beanbag and stretched her legs out. She shook her head. 'But I know where you've been.'

Archie reddened. He knew this was coming. 'Me?'

'Yes, Archie. I saw you curled up in the shed, throwing your knives.'

Archie frowned and felt his hair starting to wire up. 'Isabella, there's no way you could have seen me in the potting shed.'

'You were in there, though, weren't you?'

'So what?'

Isabella didn't want to upset him. 'Look I'm not going to go mental on you, OK.' Her eyes widened. 'But aren't you curious to know how I know?'

'A wild guess?'

'Nope. You could have been with Old Man Wood for all I knew.'

'Well, I was, until he went crazy. Have you seen him—'

'No. And it's him we need to have a talk about. I'm afraid there's properly bad news.'

'You're telling me. He needs putting in a geriatric home.'

Isabella smiled. 'Spot on.'

Archie cringed. 'Isabella, you're not making sense,' he said. 'First you say that you've seen me throwing knives and then we need to talk about Old Man Wood. What's up?'

'Well, I actually don't know how to explain it,' she started, her voice barely controllable. 'Old Man Wood's been tracking us... spying on us, and I've found out how he does it—'

'What are you talking about?' Archie said. 'That's ridiculous. He'd never do such a thing. He's our best friend, and he wouldn't harm a bug.'

Isabella leaned in. 'You may think so, Archie, but I have evidence.'

'Get real!' he replied. 'Why would Old Man Wood do anything like that?'

'Listen. Trust me, every single word of what I'm about to tell you is true.'

Archie's hair had now achieved full hard-wire status. He was agitated. It didn't feel right.

Isabella went on. 'I wanted to ask him a few questions, so I popped down to his room. He wasn't there, so I let myself in and jumped onto his bed. At the end of his bed are three screens that show every move we make. Every single move, Archie. One for each of us, like CCTV. Go and look for yourself.'

'But how do you know it was us?'

'You were bundled up in the corner of the potting shed feeling sorry for yourself, throwing your stupid knives and I knew it was Daisy by the way she moves and by the distinctive shape of her bottom. And me, well I was there all along, sitting on the bed.'

Silence filled the small cupboard, only broken by the faint sounds of the range cooker drifting up to them and the hum of the generator.

'You've gone mad,' Archie whispered after a while. 'Just like Old Man Wood.'

'No, I haven't, Archie. I couldn't make this up. I don't have any imagination, you know that.'

Archie groaned. 'Well, if you must know, I think we're missing an important link to Old Man Wood.'

'What do you mean?'

'We all saw that Old Man Wood is connected to us, so there has to be some basis for his odd behaviour.'

'Archie, if Old Man Wood's spying on us then he might not be who we think he is—'

'But really—'

'Look, I'm serious, deadly serious,' she said, her voice quivering.

'This is Old Man Wood you're talking about. Come on.' Archie chuckled, his memory fresh from Old Man Wood's fiasco with the trees.

'Yes! Maybe our loving old man is part of a wider sort of conspiracy—'

'Then why not ask him?' Archie said. 'I mean, he's hardly likely to deny it.'

'That's exactly what I was going to do when I found the screens,' Isabella fired back. 'I mean, think about it. That medicine of his, the way he blunders about looking like he's lost at sea—'

'But he used the medicine to help us, didn't he? He found us at death's door and put us in the cave! Look, I just can't believe he would do anything that would in any way be harmful—'

'But there's more,' Isabella interrupted. 'You know I told you about these panels with each of us on.'

'Yeah. So?'

'Well, this is not great but it's absolutely true—'

'Really–?'

'Yes. Just listen,' Isabella demanded. 'One minute Daisy looked as if she was sunbathing—'

'Sunbathing? Blimey Bells, she couldn't have been.'

'No, she was. It's one-hundred percent the truth. And please stop interrupting me.' Isabella crunched her eyes tight, refocusing. 'Then Daisy talked to someone or something and then she totally disappeared.'

Archie stared at Isabella. 'You've lost the sodding plot—'

'No, I have not, Archie. Her screen went blank. I'll show you. That's why I tore off round the farm. She wasn't anywhere. I checked the place over.'

'But why would she disappear—'

'Ssshh!' Isabella said. 'What's that noise?'

Below them they could hear the sound of the door shutting followed by voices, as though the telly had been turned on. They listened.

'It's Mrs P,' Archie said.

'No, it isn't. Mrs P headed off ages ago. Old Man Wood doesn't watch telly and Daisy's missing—as I told you.'

Archie frowned. 'Then we'd better see who's come to visit.'

Isabella nodded, flicked the latch and quietly, they slipped down the stairs.

STRANGE HOPE

Moments later, as she regained consciousness, the Ancient Woman heard another sound. A reverberation so haunting that it chilled her to the core. It was the unmistakable noise of whirring air, a sound she had heard before she was abandoned, a noise that had troubled, haunted, and eluded her ever since. It was the distinct whirr of the Great Gate, the sound that accompanied those leaving the Atrium to planets elsewhere.

The long wail that followed spoke of utter misery; of torment on a different scale and intensity. 'When will this wretchedness... this cruelty end?' she cried out. 'Finish this. End this. PLEASE... please!' she implored.

Her sobs trailed off, unheard along the empty tunnels. 'Haven't I suffered enough?'

Lying at the top of the stairs, her thoughts tumbled back to happier times here on the Garden of Eden. She recalled how, in a time long gone, her family had once known great joy together in the Garden of Eden making creatures, and plant-life, and all life forms to meet the requirements for all the worlds.

Then came the knowledge of immortality. They hadn't realised it. Age had had no meaning; death had never crossed their paths. Expiry was a concept they had given to life they had created, a containing process so that life forms might be replaced, or altered or, mainly, improved.

But Cain had grown tired of them all. He'd grown restless and played constantly with a beast of his own design. This was the great reptilian beast, a creation of brilliance, a monster that had the ability to morph into any cold-blooded creature instantly; from a tiny tortoise, to a chameleon, to a cobra, to a snarling, fire-blowing, flying dragon, in any order at any time. The beast had become Cain's lethal cohort. Deadly, powerful, and loyal in its own right. Together they had begun to cause havoc across the worlds.

Cain's genius, like his father's, lay in manipulating the creative processes.

She sighed, the memories as clear now as they were back in the depths of time.

Soon, the great elder, Adam, Cain's father, had decreed that it was time for Cain, and his brothers and sister, to inhabit planets of their own. Cain was sent to the planet of Havilah, a planet of astonishing beauty, a planet with the finest of all Adam's creations, given as a gift.

The others settled on various different planets in the multi universal sphere. Rarely did they see one another again.

Only Earth had remained. A planet that had waited for new species made in the cauldrons of life in the Garden of Eden.

That was the beginning of the end, she supposed. She remembered the emptiness after Cain had gone. And then, much later the shock at his betrayal, and his lust for control.

Then stories had filtered back. Cain raising an army, Cain's determination to destroy the foundry of life itself: the Garden of Eden. And the stories had become reality.

Cain's desire to displace his father had led to war and muddle and chaos. He had stopped at nothing.

And then came her capture, and her torture by her own son. The agony of the ultimate betrayal. And then her eyes had been ripped out of their sockets to balance Cain losing his too. Their ability to make magic, to make creations had been purged from them forever.

In the end, the energies of the universe closed the Garden of Eden to stop the war. All that was left was a cold, desperate, endless emptiness. And ruin for everyone.

Why? Why had she offered herself as the ultimate sacrifice? Because no other solution could end the hatred, the greed, and the fighting.

She had spent her days of darkness so that one day there might be a fresh start for life in a new the Garden of Eden, which, in turn would lead to a new beginning for all the worlds.

While she mulled over these thoughts, several dreamspinners moved silently around her, binding her leg with strong spider-like silks and they gave her dream powders to soothe the pain. Soon she would spiral off to a comforting, painless place. The dreamspinners would take good care of her.

She realised that if the Garden of Eden could not be woken, she would be stuck in this Atrium forever, disappearing into dust, her heart the last organ to survive in this empty, lifeless world.

But as she began to drift off, a curious feeling of hope washed over her: whoever had worked out how to get in to the Atrium of the Garden of Eden had worked out how to get out. And no one had done this since the Great Closing of the Garden of Eden.

Calm swept over her like a gentle breeze.

The person who came—and went—must possess she thought, great qualities —magical qualities that would solve the riddles to opening the Garden of Eden. Perhaps he, or she, would return with the other Heirs of Eden? Her brain filled with renewed energy that brimmed with confidence, hope and desire; sensations that she hadn't felt in eons. Her heart began to blaze like an orb of fire, blood pumping around her veins like molten lava.

Next time, she would be better prepared. She would be ready for them.

It wouldn't be long now, she was sure of it. Perhaps, she thought, her story would be told after all.

NEWS UPDATE

Splashes of neon lit the otherwise dark room as the latest news bulletin beamed into the kitchen.

Archie and Isabella sneaked in.

Archie crept past the oak table and chairs, past the island, and looked beyond it.

Nothing. He moved farther forward, turned to Isabella, and shrugged.

Then they heard a sniff. Archie took a pace forward as Isabella went for the light.

In a wet heap on the floor beneath the island sat Daisy, watching the pictures of the disaster.

She looked terrible.

Her head turned briefly, but she quickly refocused on the news.

Archie didn't know what to think. She was drenched from head to toe, and shivering, but she wouldn't take her gaze off the screen .

'You all right?' he said softly.

'Sssshhh,' she replied, pointing a shaking hand towards the screen.

Archie's eyes followed.

On the screen was the image of a room inside a hospital showed a patient lying in a bed. The patient's eyes were half open. A caption ran along the bottom:

NEWS UPDATE: MIRACLE BOY OUT OF COMA

Archie sat down next to Daisy, offering her a couple of drying-up cloths. Daisy grabbed them without taking her eyes from the screen.

Why was Daisy so preoccupied with a bald, sick-looking boy covered in drips and bandages?

The news continued:

'Earlier today,' the commentator said, *'the miracle boy nicknamed Jonah by the medical staff, emerged from his coma. The boy, whose identity is still unknown, was found by the air ambulance team clinging on to a branch at the top of a tall tree surrounded by the floodwaters. Jonah, thought to be a local boy, was suffering from serious malnutrition and mysterious burn marks. Police and medical staff are urging anyone who might know him to ring this number.'*

The camera panned in on the boy who happened, at that moment, to blink, quite slowly.

Archie reached in a little. *That movement.*

Then the boy smiled faintly, his lips parting a fraction. Archie gasped and peered in even more. He turned to see the reaction of his sister. She was doing the exact same thing.

The camera zoomed in even closer. The screen filled with the lips and eyes of the child, who had no hair, eyebrows, nor eyelashes, and who bore a curious red mark on his head as if he had squeezed into a tight hat.

The boy closed his eyes. He was trying to speak. He swallowed, struggling to form a word. After a great effort, a sound emerged.

It was barely audible, but sounded something like "Arljii".

Archie and Daisy knelt forward, watching keenly.

A voice from one of the medical team, her face covered by a white medical mask, gently said, 'Hello. Can you hear me?'

'Algae,' the boy repeated. His eyes opened wider, the struggle to talk seemingly beyond him. But the boy wasn't to be beaten. He swallowed again, the camera highlighting the considerable effort.

'Dunno,' the boy repeated, this time with more urgency. Then the boy collapsed back on his bed as a machine above him started to bleep and a team of medics rushed in, surrounding him.

Immediately, the TV pictures cut out and shot back to the studio, where, emblazoned in big writing along the bottom of the screen were the words:

BREAKING NEWS: THE PRIME MINISTER WILL ADDRESS THE NATION AT 18:00hrs.

SOLOMON'S PUZZLE

Solomon simply couldn't work it out.

On the one hand, the process of finding a hidden stairwell had become deeply irritating. On the other, it made him feel like a private investigator on the telly. And this idea spurred him on.

For two hours, he tried every inch of the hidden room. He'd pushed books, felt for levers on the floor, and run his hand over ever surface at least two times hoping to feel some kind of notch or bump.

When he came down the ladder, he kept his counsel. He didn't want the children or adults to get overexcited with thoughts of escaping the tower if they were only going to be discover they were trapped.

He needed to concentrate.

Solomon took himself over to the architecture section of the library and picked out an old book on stained glass. Then, he lay flat on his back and stared up at the tower above him.

A thought dawned on him. If the architects of the tower had wanted the hidden library to remain a secret, then wouldn't they have built a secret staircase up to it?

It had to be someplace else. To the side?

He examined the white paint. *Was there any secret looking holes or a discoloured area where a staircase, or a hatch may have been filled up?*

No.

He walked around, talking to the children as he passed amongst them, his eyes still on the structure of the building his brain trying to imagine an architectural plan.

The tower, he realised, had a small protruding outcrop, like a hip. He wondered if this was it. He passed the chef.

'How are we for meals?' he asked.

'Should be all right for another two days. After that, boss, it's going to be a struggle.'

Solomon noticed the armour. 'How is our cooking Knight?' he joked.

'I hate to admit it, but it's superb. Finest steel I've ever had the pleasure of working with. Bit tricky to handle though. I'll give the old fella a bit of a clean-up when we're out of here though.' His tone changed. 'If we get out of here.'

'The authorities do know we're here,' the headmaster replied quietly. 'But I don't want to raise anyone's hopes too much until the time comes. There is an almighty operation going on outside of these walls and besides, we have a little bit of a problem. Perhaps you might help me come up with a solution.'

Solomon explained.

When he'd finished, chef looked rather startled. Soon, all the adults knew about the plan. And very soon, they were walking around the two floors of the tower like zombies, running their hands over the surfaces and gently knocking to see if any hollow sounds echoed in reply.

Solomon nipped downstairs far enough so that he could see inside the top of the stained-glass windows peeking above the flooding in the chapel.

He stared at the image coming back at him. *What a difference in colour! How dynamic! The storm waters must have cleaned the glass.*

Instantly, it reminded him of the images in the ancient book.

He took a picture with his phone and then ran up the stairs and straight to the ladder.

Inside the secret library, the book lay open on the desk. He turned the page back and moved his head from the image on his phone to the drawing in the book. There wasn't a great deal to work with. But going on what he had, they were indeed, remarkably similar.

As he examined the images, the stained glass didn't marry it exactly. There was something he couldn't quite work out.

He removed his half-moon glasses and rubbed his eyes. Looking down again, the image now blurry, he caught the briefest outline.

Some kind of figure was missing?

He replaced his spectacles and stared at it again.

His phone bleeped; another text.

Have you found a way to the tower? I need to know. Lack of resources. Too many others to rescue. Let me know in half an hour—or you face a three-day delay. S

Goodness me, Solomon thought. *In two days, we will be eating books,* cookery books *no doubt.*

He searched again for the outline. *Yes. There it was. Like a ghost. Feint. Just like...* An idea shot into his mind.

In no time, he was clambering down the ladder. This time, he made his way past the chef to where the armour had stood.

'Chef,' he began, 'do you remember exactly where the cooking Knight stood?' 'Just there?'

'Where *exactly*? The exact position.'

Chef reluctantly stood up and pointed in the general area.

'Show me precisely how it was standing,' Solomon demanded.

With a puzzled expression plastered on his brow, the chef stood and mimicked the steel plating.

Solomon knelt down beside him and nodded. 'Tell me, where is Sir Guilherme's left hand?'

'The left hand of the armour?' chef queried.

'Yes, chef. It might be a vital part. Do you still have it?'

Chef pointed to the fire. 'I've got a sausage cooking in each finger,' he said.

Solomon frowned. 'I very badly need that hand, chef. Please transplant the bangers to another body part.'

Chef reached in with his makeshift tongs and wrestled the hand off the fire. 'It's very hot, boss,' he said as the sausages fell onto the inside of the breastplate.

'Run downstairs and quench the metal straight away. Then rush back here.'

The chef did as he was told. A few minutes later he handed a steaming, metal hand to Solomon.

Solomon took a deep breath. If this didn't work, he was going to look like an idiot to the crowd that had now gathered round.

He slipped the metal hand over his own and moved into the suit of armours original position. Running his fingertips up the stone edge he waited for something to happen.

A fingertip traced over a small indent. A hole! He worked a fingertip in, finding a perfect fit to his knuckle, but still nothing happened.

Solomon reddened. Why didn't something open?

He felt his phone vibrate in his pocket. Stone wanted an answer.

'Sir. Look, over here,' said a little girl, who was pointing at the grate in front of the fire.

Solomon left the hand dangling and moved to what looked like an air vent. The headmaster studied it for a while. 'Chef, could I have the right foot,' he said.

'Seriously, boss. Can't you have something else?'

'Why. Whatever is the matter now?'

'The right one's got the rest of the bleedin' sausages in it.'

STONE'S BRIEFING

Commissioner Stone slipped his phone into his pocket and stood to address the throng of anxious faces.

'Thank you, Chief Medical Officer, Harris,' he said. 'You now have a sense of this situation. Further information in regard to likely outcomes are being distributed, along with an outline of the strategic operation that is about to come into place. None of it makes for easy reading. All of you have been assigned roles in relation to your skill set. When this meeting is over, please collect your briefing papers from the drawing room along the corridor.' He raised a hand to signal he hadn't finished.

'These papers,' he continued, 'contain sensitive information including links and passwords to Government archives and the main COBRA operations portal on the web. In order for this to remain out of the public domain, you will sign official secrecy documents before you depart, or you will not leave Swinton Park. Is this quite clear?'

A hubbub of noise and nodding heads indicated that it was.

He studied the room. 'Parliament went into an emergency session early this morning and the Prime Minister is chairing a cross-party emergency cabinet. Right now, other heads of state are being briefed, particularly our neighbours in Europe and in the United States. Smart-phones that run on a special-service connection will keep you up to date. Ministers and civil servants are being briefed as we speak,' he continued. 'The main headquarters for the operation will be here and at Downing Street, London. As the virus spreads, which we believe is highly likely, operational headquarters will be situated in rural locations like this outside

Cardiff, Exeter, Manchester, Oxford, Cambridge, Durham, and Edinburgh. The heads of all the emergency services are meeting shortly. Across the country, reserve stores are being stockpiled in aircraft hangers and distribution systems are being organised. In our hospitals, isolation units are being prepared and only dire emergencies will be accepted. Non-life-threatening operations have been cancelled. Every town and village will run their own health centres manned by local doctors, nurses and volunteers.

'Later this afternoon,' he continued, 'the media will be thoroughly briefed by the Prime Minister, who will then address the nation. You will not talk to the media from this moment on. All press and any interviews in regard to the virus and operations will be made through official channels.

'Most of you will be flown out of here to help. You will be given smart-phones that run on a special-service connection so you're kept up to date.

He paused and inspected his notes. Stone cleared his throat.

'From eleven o'clock this evening, all airports, ferry crossings, railway stations, waterways and motorways will be closed. Travel in or out of Great Britain will be prohibited unless authorised by one of you. As of midnight tonight, there will be a total media blackout. The Internet will be temporarily suspended, with access at specific times to be announced. Television and radio stations will play films and repeats and will be the source of news updates. Supermarkets will come under state supervision and armed military units are already moving in to areas where civil unrest is likely. And yes, we do envisage serious panic in towns and cities as people rush for supplies. To that end, a curfew will come into play in every town and city across the country and a zero tolerance approach will be forced upon the citizens of the country.'

The commissioner felt sweaty. 'Be assured, every available expert is working on a solution right now and not just here, but globally. We believe that so long as the virus is confined to the north of the country, these drastic measures might just contain the spread, both south and farther north. But you will need to work fast. The security of the country is at stake.'

He pushed his glasses along his nose. 'As Britain goes into lockdown, the eyes of the world are watching. Let us hope it is not too late.'

The commissioner drew in a deep breath and mopped his brow. The stunned crowd in front of him began to disperse, heads buried in folders.

'Is a chopper available?' he said to the smart young officer next to him.

The officer, Dickinson, made a quick call. 'Ten minutes and it's yours,' he said as he hung up. 'Can I brief the pilot where it's headed?'

'A short trip to Upsall. I want to take a look for myself. Apparently, there are fifty-seven school kids stuck in a tower we need to get out. We can make this one of the good news stories. First off, there's someone I need to speak to—the head-master at the school, name of Solomon. He's in there.'

'It's bang in the middle of the zone, sir,' Dickinson said. 'The area suffered badly. Are you sure it's sensible—'

'I don't care,' the Commissioner snapped back. 'I need that man out of there, dead or alive! With any luck they will have figured out how to get on to the tower roof. Make sure there's a rescue plan for the kids, and don't forget the film crew. '

Dickinson raced off. Stone glanced at his watch and dusted down his jacket. He studied his mobile. Still no word from the scientists. *When would they come back with something, anything?*

He spotted Dickinson returning.

'Are we ready?'

Dickinson nodded and, knowing that the Commissioner liked to stride more than walk, marched quickly ahead.

WHAT HAPPENED TO KEMP?

After showing the footage of the hairless boy in his hospital bed, the TV screen started to flicker, and soon blacked out altogether.

Isabella flipped the light switch, but it wasn't working either, and she noticed how the buzz of the generator no longer droned in the background. She shot out of the house to see if she could restart the motor.

Silence filled the kitchen. 'Was that who I think it was?' Daisy said quietly.

Archie had gone pale. 'What do you mean?' he stammered, trying to hide his face.

'That boy!' Daisy said.

Archie didn't know what to say.

'It's Kemp!' she said. 'It has to be.'

'You think so?'

'Yes, of course. But without hair. It's Kemp, your horrible friend. Bald and burnt.'

For a moment, Archie wasn't capable of uttering a word. 'But how could it be Kemp? He'd been in the alley—'

'Where?' Daisy cut in.

Archie hesitated. 'Well, you know...'

'No, I don't know what you're talking about,' Daisy said, as she started to remove her wet clothes. 'What alley?'

Archie wondered if he should come clean about his meeting with Cain, and Cain's offer. Just before the storm had broken, Archie had met Cain in an alleyway behind his school, and Cain had offered Archie eternal life if he would join forces with him. Kemp, Archie realised, must have taken up the offer instead: Archie hadn't found the right time to tell Daisy and Isabella about this.

'No, it's nothing,' he heard himself say. 'He just said he was going shopping in town, *down the alley*, that's all.'

'Strange, isn't it?' Daisy said as she removed her top. 'I saw the rescue on telly this morning and at the time I thought those big lips could only belong to one person. Do you think his burn marks are from a lightning strike or a burning building?'

'Dunno,' Archie said.

'Does "dunno" mean you really don't know, or are you just repeating what dimwit Kemp said?'

'Eh? Oh, sorry, just trying to work out what he was saying.' Archie said as his brain raced.

Was this Cain's doing? Even so, how on earth did he end up in a tree? Kemp could hardly swim.

Daisy felt like smacking Archie round the head but realised it might damage her hand. Talking to him was like chatting to a goalpost. 'Come on, Archie, his words were a desperate cry for help. Shouldn't we phone the helpline and tell them we know who it is? Don't you think that's, like, our duty?'

Isabella came back into the room. 'Can't seem to get it going. Archie, why don't you have a try? You're good at that kind of thing.'

'We're going to phone the number,' Daisy said, addressing her sister.

'Phone who, about what?'

'Call the emergency number and let them know we think the boy is Kemp.'

Isabella turned on her. 'Why? Why should we do that?'

Daisy hesitated. Isabella sounded unnecessarily sharp. 'Well, he's Archie's friend—'

'And my enemy,' Isabella snapped. Isabella and Kemp had been feuding for years, Isabella often ending up the butt of his schoolboy pranks and jokes. 'If anyone wants to claim him,' she continued, 'let them.' She turned away. 'Come on, Archie, the sooner we get the generator going, the better.'

SOLOMON UNDER PRESSURE

'Good heavens,' Stone muttered as he viewed the distant, brown smear of water and debris that was once the fertile green fields of the Vale of York.

He addressed his team. 'Now, pay attention,' he began. 'I want names and addresses of everyone in this area, starting with Upsall. I want to know who is in the school; pupils, teachers, caterers; who runs the newsagents, who blows the candles out in the church, the postmen, holiday lets, recent tourists, and those who walk their dogs on the left-hand side of the road.'

'But not the right-hand side?'

Stone glowered back. 'I want medical records, health records, birth records, and I need a history of the place from as far back as you can get, including death records, architectural information, Doomsday records. I want to know occupations, I want contractor details.' He paused as he waited for the team to catch up with their note taking. 'We need to find a pattern—or an anomaly. Have you got that?'

'Sir,' one of the officers nearby said, 'this kind of investigation sounds like it would take months.'

Stone fixed him an icy stare. 'Understand this. Money is no object, but time is. Hire everyone and anyone. Use students from the universities of Leeds, Durham, Newcastle—Timbuktu for all I care. We need results. We need to find something that connects Upsall to this plague, do you understand?'

The chopper wheeled to the right. 'And I want everyone, and I mean everyone, who was found in Upsall village to be put in quarantine. Are the military in there yet? Good. Make arrangements for the evacuation of all the survivors up into the moors.' He rubbed his chin. 'Use the castle at Crayke.' He fixed each of the people with eyes that told them to trust him implicitly. 'Your status as part of my team means you can access anyone. *Anyone*,' he emphasised. 'Get on your phones and get about your business. NOW.'

In no time the crew were relaying messages from their communications devices.

A message came through from the pilot. 'We're approaching Upsall, sir.'

'Can you get near the tower?'

The helicopter whirred and levelled out. Beneath them lay murky water where once the pretty village stood. Sticking out like a lighthouse was the old tower of the school and the top half of the tall chapel.

Before long, a marine climbed onto the parapet. A couple of people were there to welcome him. One was the familiar figure of the Upsall headmaster, his cousin, Solomon

Commissioner Stone noticed how weight had dropped off him, and his face, rotund at their last meeting, was more angular than he's seen him in decades and coated with a grey, stubbly beard.

'You have to get the others out,' the headmaster said. 'You can't leave them there. You don't know what it's like.'

Stone patted his shoulder reassuringly. 'We'll get everyone out, trust me,' he said. 'I'm sorry about your party. I know how much it meant.' The chopper soared into the rain. 'Was rather looking forward to it myself.'

The headmaster shrugged. Tears welled in his eyes as he stared out of the window.

'I'm going to come straight to the point, Headmaster,' Stone said. 'We've got a pandemic on our hands and our evidence suggests that it stems from your quaint little village.' He stared out of the window as if sharing the older man's grief. 'You need to tell me everything you know about Upsall.'

'Of course,' Solomon said, gathering himself. 'I'll tell you all I know but I don't know how it'll help.'

The chopper climbed high and from here the devastation was truly remarkable. Water stretched from Teesside in the north, as far as the eye could see to the south. Dotted at various points were outcrops, islands, full of tents and makeshift dwellings, like mini shantytowns.

'Were there any unusual circumstances prior to the storm?' Stone asked.

Solomon thought for a while. 'None. We thought the storm was, for all intents and purposes, just localised. That's what the Met Bureau said.'

'You called the Met Bureau?'

Solomon remembered the incident with Isabella. 'No. Not exactly. I watched the forecast on the television, but there was a girl—one of my brightest students—'

'She thought otherwise?'

Solomon admired the way his young cousin had the knack of picking up little leads like this. 'Yes, probably nothing,' he said. 'A smart kid. You know, just interested—'

Stone lent in. 'And she said what, exactly?'

'Well, she'd made a barometer and insisted there was going to be a terrible storm. Why, I don't know. But she did it on three occasions.'

'Her name?'

'Isabella de Lowe,' he replied without flinching.

Stone scratched her name in his pad and handed it to the officer next to him. 'Get this checked out,' he said. 'Find out if she's alive, what family she has.'

'Oh, I wouldn't worry about her,' Solomon said. 'Her parents are stuck in the Middle East—archaeologists—'

'Look, I need answers and, at the moment, there are none,' Stone said bluntly. 'Everyone, and I mean everyone, is being checked out.'

An alarm bell rang in Solomon's mind. 'But she's only a child—'

'I don't care if she's a bloody donkey. I need to know about everyone.' His tone was tough and unapologetic. 'Where is she from? Upsall or—'

'All I'm saying,' Solomon said, in his most head-masterly way, 'is that this girl came to me wanting to talk about a storm, which she said was going to be bigger than everyone thought.'

'Why?' Stone pressed. 'Do all your students do this?'

'I have no idea,' Solomon replied racking his brain. 'Perhaps she was being intuitive. Some children are remarkable in that respect. She's a bright child, one of our best.'

'Do you know where she lives?'

Solomon didn't like the way this was going. 'In the hills,' he said, waving a hand roughly in the air. 'Extraordinary family, very eccentric.'

'In what way?'

Solomon had forgotten what a persevering human being Stone could be. It was, he realised, one of the reasons he'd climbed to the top. 'Look,' he said. 'I'm tired, exhausted, and hungry, and I don't think this is helping.' He exaggerated a yawn. 'I simply think you're barking up the wrong tree,' he added. The head-master needed to think, to run the conversations through his mind before he'd give his cousin anything else to work on. He certainly wasn't going to allow Stone to hound his students.

Stone surveyed his haggard cousin. 'de Lowe. Is that the name?'

Solomon grunted disapprovingly.

Stone turned to the officer. 'Find out everything about the de Lowe family. History, academic records, family records—the whole damn lot. Understand?'

Solomon was too tired to respond. In his heart there was something about Isabella and her ranting that struck a chord with everything that had happened—as if she knew. But what, and why her?

He slumped into his seat and shut his eyes. He'd think about it once he'd slept, washed, and eaten.

Stone had a fearsome reputation for extracting information and Solomon wasn't comfortable handing over his students, or his friends.

Not yet, at any rate.

LOCKDOWN

When Daisy walked in, Archie was washing oil off his hands, and Isabella sat with her arms folded tight across her chest, staring at the floor.

Oh well, she thought, *better now than never.*

'Right,' she said, pulling up a chair. 'We need to talk.'

Archie joined her. 'The Prime Minister's on in ten minutes,' he said. 'We should watch.'

'We'll do that after I've explained what happened to me earlier,' Daisy said. 'This is important.'

Isabella yawned. 'Fire away, twinkle toes.'

'OK, it's going to sound gigantically bonkers,' Daisy said, pulling off her pink glasses. 'I went to look for you this morning, Archie, and, when I reached Dad's old potato patch, I found a gate with a kind of jewel hanging from a bush.'

Isabella tutted.

'I tried to grab it and, as I reached out, I somehow fell into a ditch. When I'd dragged myself out, I was in sunshine on a small glade with three really old trees totally covered in blossom. I know it sounds impossible but the trees asked me questions—'

Isabella groaned theatrically.

'Please, Isabella, let me finish,' Daisy said, shooting her a look. 'At first, I thought I'd died, you know, swallowed some infected water or something, and I ignored them; but the trees insisted and eventually pointed me towards a strange platform. After a bit of hesitation, I went on to the platform and then flew off to a... a new kind of place.'

Isabella guffawed. 'Yes, yes, I know how you vanished, Daisy. I saw it all. Nice story, by the way.'

'Eh? What...?'

'You disappeared, right? Do you know how I know?'

Daisy shook her head.

'Because I watched as you moved an object on this platform of yours and then... gone.'

Daisy was flummoxed. 'How... how do you know all this?'

'I found some magic panels on Old Man Wood's bed—'

'Magic—'

'Yes. Panels, like TV monitors, which showed that you'd slipped away.'

Daisy's face had turned puce. 'What panels, Isabella? You're talking bull,' she said. 'It's not possible.'

'I'm afraid it is. Happy to show you if you like.'

The children sat silently round the table. Isabella smiled.

'It's a joke, right?' Daisy fumed. 'You're making fun, right?'

But Isabella's face didn't change.

Daisy was seething. 'I knew you wouldn't believe me, but it's all true. One-hundred percent.' She stood up and paced around the table. 'My dreams—our dreams—are really, really happening, right now. Everything we've seen, Isabella, is real. It's not imaginary. And we're running out of time—'

'Daisy, shut up!' Isabella snapped. 'I told you, I saw you, OK? There's really nothing more to say on the matter.'

'Anyone fancy,' Archie began diplomatically, 'a slice of Old Man Wood's starlight apple crumble? I don't know about you, but I'm starving. Nothing like a good pig-out to calm the nerves.'

Archie stood up, pulled some milk from the fridge and pushed a cake tin onto the table. Then he pressed the button that turned on the TV.

Much to everyone's surprise, it flickered into life.

Prime Minister Kingsford looked tired. No amount of make-up could disguise this. He was flanked by senior government ministers and his COBRA team as he stood in front of an oak lectern.

'People of the United Kingdom,' he began, *'Never, in the annals of our history, has this country seen a crisis as grave as the situation that squares up to us now. This evening, I speak to you as your leader. I also speak to you as a husband and a father — an ordinary man. I don't doubt that the words and actions that are about to follow will be met with shock. But I ask you all, before I say any more, to understand that these measures*

have been driven upon us as a very last resort. And, therefore, I urge you to hear what I have to say with level-headed understanding so that, together, we may face the threat in front of us with the decency and common spirit that I know resides within the marrow of each and every one of you.'

He shuffled nervously and glanced back quickly at his team before continuing.

'Following the devastating floods in the Yorkshire area, a virus known as Ebora has emerged. It is a strain that has never been seen before. It is a freak. There is no rhyme nor reason as to Ebora's aggressive nature. It is a silent enemy that we do not, as yet, understand, but rest assured, we will. As I speak to you now, top scientists from around the world are trying to identify Ebora's complex properties in order to find a vaccine. But they require more time.'

The camera zoomed in on his face. *'Earlier today I met with the COBRA team who have been working non-stop to provide the necessary framework that we hope will protect as many lives as possible in the foreseeable future. Their work is being actioned as I speak. This is the result of top-level consultations and has the agreement of all sides of the houses of Parliament.*

'In order to give ourselves the best opportunity to limit Ebora's destructive path, our first step is to restrict the movement of people in and around the country. For the foreseeable future, until we are free from this threat, it is with a very heavy heart that I must announce the following.'

The Prime Minister shuffled his notes and held a long pause. A global audience of billions reached into their TV sets.

'From midnight tomorrow, a net will be pulled over our land and zipped up around our borders. Every airport in Britain, every railway and waterway will be vacated. Motorway traffic will be limited to emergency use only, local travel will be possible, but ill-advised. For safety reasons, internet use will be limited. Supermarkets, power companies, media organisations and their distribution partners will fall under the temporary control of Government departments.

'These drastic measures are to ensure that food and necessary supplies can be provided to everyone, at the right time, without panic and without preference, so that the fundamental elements of our existence may continue.'

The Prime Minister paused to sip some water and then continued.

'While we learn how to tackle Ebora, life must, and will go on. This evening, do not rush to your local stores, do not go outside for unnecessary errands or for social occasions. Consider everything closed. Many of you will have noticed the presence of the military in our cities and in our towns and villages. I urge you not to be alarmed. They are there for no other reason but to protect you, to organise the relief effort and to enforce law and order.'

Kingsford now used all his theatrical skills, and slowly addressed the camera.

'Let me be absolutely clear,' he resumed, *'civil unrest, in any form, will not be toler-*

ated while such great suffering and disruption fills our lives. The penalties for such acts will not only be swift, but severe. I cannot emphasise how important it is that you heed this warning.' Kingsford smiled thinly. *'We will keep you notified as to the progress of the virus and the status of the curfew. Updates will be posted regularly on local radio stations, the BBC website and on terrestrial television channels. But, until a vaccine is found, I cannot tell you how long these measures will be in place.'*

He paused again, peered at his notes before looking directly into the camera. *'In this great country of ours we have overcome many things. Together, we shall persevere. Together, we will defeat this silent and destructive beast.'*

Tears welled in his eyes. *'Go now to your loved ones. Be safe, responsible and ever mindful. And may God bless you all. Thank you.'*

For a minute or two, the children stared open-mouthed at the screen.

It was Daisy who broke the silence. 'Bollocks!' she said.

Isabella turned on her. 'Daisy, there's absolutely no need to swear.'

Daisy was shaking. 'Yes, there bloody well is!'

'No,' Isabella replied icily. 'There isn't!'

'Yes, there rotten, fricking well is!' Daisy yelled.

'Daisy! Stop it!' Isabella cried. 'There's nothing we can do about it, you heard what the PM said.'

'Isabella, how unbelievably thick are you?' Daisy roared. 'Don't you understand? Don't you get it yet?' She stood up and stamped her feet. 'This is our problem, you idiot,' she growled. 'This is our damn problem!'

'No, it isn't,' Isabella replied calmly, 'and for God's sake, stop swearing. Didn't you listen to anything, anything on the telly? It's a national problem—'

'Yes, but it started here! Right here in Upsall. Don't you see?'

Archie moved in. 'Whoa! Cool it, you two,' he said.

'Cool it!' she fumed. 'What's got into you both? Have you lost your minds? Which bits don't you understand? You think you get freaky hair like that or bloody great holes in your hands or glaring red eyes every bleeding day? *Really?* You think these strange things happening to us are normal? Do you?'

Isabella wasn't having any of it. 'Well, it looks like I'm not the only one who's lost my mind,' she snapped back. 'This virus has nothing to do with us. '

'Dur! It has everything to do with us,' Daisy spat. 'If you'd bothered to look at the cave paintings you'd have realised it is exactly what was shown. It showed a plague, like in biblical times, and three stone tablets like... like books, and they needed to be found or everyone dies.'

'Oh dear, Daisy. Now you're completely overreacting.'

'Me, overreacting?' Daisy said, as she stood and swept a mass of curls off her face. She faced her sister, her face puce with anger, her red eyes burning. 'Take a hard look at yourself, Isabella, and think of everything we've been through. Over-reacting? Jeez, I really don't think so.' She gave both of her siblings a piercing look. 'Seems like you two are suffering from total memory failure and a pathetic case of denial—'

'Stop being so irrational and stupid—'

'Stupid? You're the daft ones, not me!' There was no reaction. 'This is about finding those tablet things that were painted on the walls. This is about the three of us. It's about all of us doing whatever we've got to do, together. Which bit don't you get?'

Daisy stormed out and slammed the door. Then she opened the door again and marched back in. 'And there's one more thing.'

Isabella tutted.

'Yeah,' Daisy said, 'I've worked it out.'

'Worked what out?' Archie said.

'What Kemp meant. You know, when he said those words, "Dunno" and "Algae". I know what he was trying to say.'

'What are you talking about?' Isabella said.

'Kemp—in the hospital bed, your holy thickness.'

'Most likely he was simply trying to alert them about the water,' Isabella said coolly.

Daisy shook her head.

Isabella smirked. 'Go on then, spit it out, Professor Stephen Daisy Hawking.'

'Why should I?'

'Or is it another thing that's sprung out of your increasingly fertile imagina-tion,' Isabella said, smiling thinly.

'No. I know, all right,' Daisy fired back. 'But why should I tell you when you will not open your eyes?'

'Try me?'

'Sod you, Isabella. Where the hell is Old Man—?'

The door opened. Old Man Wood's head popped round the doorframe.

'Have I missed something?' he said, as he went over to the range and put the kettle on. 'Everything all right?'

'No, everything is not OK!' Daisy roared, fixing him with a glowing stare. 'An epidemic is about to sweep the country following the worst flooding ever and, LA-DI-DAH, we're the only ones who seem to know anything about it. You're a part of this, Old Man Wood, so it's time you started telling us what is going on!'

SUE GETS A MESSAGE

Gus was relieving himself off the end of the boat, when, all of a sudden, a shriek and a wobble very nearly made him topple overboard.

'Hey!' he shouted. 'Give me a break!'

Sue was yelling. At first Gus thought she was in trouble, but it quickly dawned on him that these were howls of joy. He zipped up and looked under the canopy. Sue was holding her phone, the back-light illuminating her face, tears rolling down her cheeks.

'They're fine,' she said. 'Look!' She handed him the phone.

Sue!!! U did it. Dancing at news! Gus> wow ;-) We survived. No idea how! scary + mad—not sure how real. At cottage. Phone works every now n then. Weird stuff happening. Any idea where u r? National catastrophe here. Thrilled 4 U!!!! Hugs, I D A. xxx

Gus whistled. 'I knew they'd do it.'

'You did not,' Sue replied, hitting him.

'Course I did. They're tougher than you think, cleverer than you think and a lot madder than you think. Not sure which goes with who, though. Must be a few stories about how they got back. No word on the other message you sent them?'

'Nah. They probably think I'm a bit cuckoo.' She wiped a tear from her eye. 'Time for sleep, Mr Williams. It's knackering doing nothing.'

Gus looked up at the night sky which, for the first time since they had been at sea, showed a wide range of stars occasionally blotted out by a woolly cloud. 'Bit chillier tonight, and windier,' he said. He put his hand out. 'I reckon the wind's changed. Can you seal up the other end if I do this one?' He pulled the sail about and jammed it into place. The boat sped forward in perfect union with the wind. He bent down under the canopy and tied off the makeshift end sections.

As they lay shivering on the planks Gus studied the compass on Sue's phone. Set fair, south west. He sighed and turned the power off, noting the two bars remaining.

'I could do with a warm fire,' Sue said, 'wrapped up in my furry onesie watching a good movie—'

'Drinking a cup of hot chocolate,' Gus added, 'with a pile of cream frothing on top.'

'And marshmallows,' Sue added.

Gus wriggled closer. 'Move over. You're the worst bed hog ever—'

'Me?' Sue cried. 'Yeah, right! Your snores keep fish awake.'

Gus chuckled. 'At least I don't fart in my sleep!'

She hit him on the chest. 'Don't be vulgar. That smell is the skanky fish guts at the bottom of the boat.'

Gus yawned. 'Oh, sure!'

Sue pulled the two, thick dust blankets up and rolled over so they were facing each other. They'd given up trying to do the lookout; it was simply too cold, and for two nights not a light or another boat had been spotted. Their body warmth was a necessary comfort.

In the pitch black, Sue put her arms around Gus and very slowly moved her head towards his. Their noses bumped and a soft snicker came out. A moment later their lips met and this time, now that he'd relaxed, it was a far more pleasant experience. Shortly, Sue broke off and rolled over. 'Night, Gus,' she whispered. 'Hey, and Gus, if we don't make it through the night, thank you. Thanks for everything.'

He groaned.

'Sweet dreams,' she said.

DAISY'S TELLS OF HER ADVENTURE

'Mrs P, did you watch the speech?' Archie asked.

Mrs Pye snivelled. 'Aye. Worrying, I reckon,' she sniffed, pulling out a white handkerchief and dabbing her eyes. 'It's... it's that poor boy I feel for. Makes me come over all queer every time I see him, everyone waiting for him to wake up.'

Archie went in for a big hug and was rewarded by a squashing from Mrs Pye's ample bosom. 'Thing is, Mrs P,' he said, as he resurfaced, 'we reckon that boy might be my friend Kemp. What do you think?'

Mrs Pye released him, rubbed her eyes, and burst out crying. 'Well, now, that be something,' she said, between sobs.

'Yeah, amazing if it is,' Archie continued, 'I thought he'd be dead, like all the others.'

She erupted into tears again.

'Oh, I'm sorry,' Archie said. 'I didn't mean to upset you.'

'Never you mind,' she said, wiping her tears on her sleeve. 'Every time I see his dear little face I get an upsetting feeling in me bones, that's all.' She dusted herself off and pulled herself as upright as possible. 'I think,' she declared, 'that a special Mrs Pye sandwich is what you lot need tonight, followed by a thick slice of starlight apple crumble. Might have one myself too, you know. Help get over this terribleness.'

As she always did, Mrs Pye shooed everyone out of the kitchen. 'Come back in fourteen,' she said, as she ushered them out of the door, and the children dispersed to different parts of the house.

✻

Mrs Pye took her meal over the road, leaving the three children and Old Man Wood eating their MPS sandwiches in virtual silence, aside from an occasional slurp or clatter of cutlery.

An MPS was the abbreviation for "Mrs Pye Special". It was a slice of French bread with layers of melted cheese, ham, tomato, and crowned with a poached egg. Mrs Pye insisted that it should be washed down with Old Man Wood's apple juice, which the old man had spent a lifetime perfecting, and which contained no less than nine different varieties from his very old, very gnarled, and beautifully maintained apple orchard.

Afterwards, a sense of calm filled the room. Archie broke the silence, 'So, Daisy, what did happen to you yesterday?'

Daisy took a deep breath, closed her eyes, and began to tell her story.

'It was like twenty Wembley Football Stadiums wide and it just went on and on forever. In the middle, I saw a tree with no leaves, and, thinking I might be dead, I walked off only to tread on a skeleton... the bones crunched under my feet like a pile of sticks,' she said, trying and failing not to laugh.

'Moments later, I heard this truly terrible crack followed by a noise piercing my eardrums. I ran, trying to find a way out. All around were tunnels, thousands of them, some mega, some small, but all blocked. I ran and ran until I found a gateway and I realised I'd seen the gate before—in my dreams—and I figured that all I had to do was believe I could walk through it.' She stopped and tried to gauge the reactions of her brother and sister.

Isabella, Archie, and Old Man Wood stared at her in silence.

'That's what I did,' Daisy croaked. 'And I found myself in a wet ditch.'

Old Man Wood turned on her. 'Daisy, you are a right daft fool!' he said, the colour draining from his face. 'What did you think you were doing?'

The children looked at Old Man Wood, astonished. He had never, ever, raised his voice at any of them. He was clearly as startled as they were, if not more so.

There was an awkward silence.

'Er... well, it was very exciting,' Daisy replied, trying not to cry. 'I rushed back and found the news about Kemp and the plague...'

'Daisy, don't you get it?' Old Man Wood interrupted, moving by her side and draping an arm gently around her shoulders. 'You see, that person never saw the motif. He never worked out the way home. He died a horrible death all alone. That could have been you, my littlun. And you're not ready for that, not yet.'

'But I saw the clues,' she argued, feeling a bit confused, 'so I know my dreams are true. I know it really exists... doesn't it? It all adds up.'

For once, Isabella was quite moved. 'Right!' she said. 'I think we need answers.

Home from *where*, Old Man Wood? And how do you know it was a he who died?' she demanded.

Old Man Wood looked rattled. 'Oh, apples-alive! I can't remember,' he answered, his face scrunched up and his deep wrinkles more pronounced than usual.

Isabella eyed him suspiciously and turned to her sister. 'Daisy, first off, I owe you an apology.' She met her eye and sighed. 'There are some strange wooden panels on the end of Old Man Wood's bed that follow our movements, like TV security monitors, I'll show them to you later. That's how I knew you'd disappeared.'

'But how?'

'I have absolutely no idea,' she said, turning to Old Man Wood who waved a hand in acknowledgement. 'He doesn't know how they work either. But it's how I saw you sucked into the ground and, when you didn't return, I ran off looking for you. And I'm sorry I yelled at you earlier but there is a part of me that simply will not accept that these strange goings on are in any way real. Do you understand?'

Daisy nodded as Isabella continued. 'You see, part of me cannot, and will not, believe all these peculiar things that are happening. That's me, Daisy. It's how I'm made, and there's nothing you or Archie can do about it. My whole life has been built around reason and fact, cause and effect, and it's very difficult for me to believe in anything else.' She smiled at her sister, noting her disappointment. 'But if we're to explore your fantasies, then so be it.'

Daisy half-smiled.

Isabella turned abruptly to Old Man Wood. 'So, here goes. First off, Old Man Wood, we need answers because otherwise we're going to end up in a Genesistic asylum. I guarantee that you will be the first one in.' She tapped the table with her fingertips. 'What is the story of your bed, are the images in the cave anything to do with us, and why did Sue insist the rain is all our fault? We need explanations, we need answers, and we need them now!'

The children gazed at the gnarled old face expecting a spectacular response. But all Old Man Wood said was:

'Mmm... perhaps. Oh dear, my little favourites.'

'Old Man Wood, this is not helping.'

'The bed is a bit of a mystery,' he said. 'But perhaps it's time we found the riddles.'

'Riddles! WHAT riddles?' the children chorused.

'The riddles to finding a place called the Garden of Eden.'

'Like the riddles Sue was yelling at us about?' Archie said. 'And what the pictures in the cave were trying to show us?'

'Hmmm.'

'I knew this plague has something to do with us,' Daisy said, her eyes glowing like lasers.

'Well, now,' the old man said, staring at the floor, 'it's been an awfully long time.' He opened his eyes wide, as if attempting to welcome the world into his mind.

'That's the problem, my dear littluns.' And he rapped his knuckles on his head. 'There's nothing in here anymore. I just don't remember.'

LEO AND KATE

A murmuring spilled out of Gus' mouth. He rolled one way, then the other, knocking Sue. Then Sue heard a noise. Was it Gus, or the wind on the canopy?

Sue woke with a start. 'Gus?' she said, listening to the strange noises coming from him. His head rolled one way and then the other. 'You all right?'

The boat wobbled and pitched, and Sue was hit by a sense of being terribly small and insignificant, of being a tiny speck of life in a vast ocean. She reached across him for the torch, her fingers dabbing at the heavy cloth of the dust sheet. As she did so, her hair brushed across Gus's face.

A moment later, he sneezed violently, waking himself up.

Sue flicked on the torch. 'Hey,' she said, 'you were having a nightmare.' She yawned and rested her head on his chest.

Gus blinked. 'What's going on?' He said, trying to get his bearings.

Sue raised herself up and smiled. 'I think my hair tickled your nose. You sneezed yourself awake.'

The boat pitched as it rode a larger wave and then rounded the crest and headed down again. For the first time, Sue detected a look of anxiety in Gus' eyes.

The wind thudded into the side canopy as the boat plunged into the next wave, water colliding with the helm, water filling their small cabin.

'A storm's coming,' Gus said. His blue eyes were now wide open and, in place of his usual, happy demeanour with his big toothy smile, he wore a frown. The boat lurched and spray showered the canopy. 'It could be pretty unpleasant.'

Sue spoke very calmly, trying not to betray her nerves. 'We've had it, haven't we?' she said.

'Oh, I don't know about that,' he said, regaining his bravado. 'The Joan of' survived the worst storm since Noah, so there's no reason it can't withstand a wee North Sea gale.'

Sue shivered. 'That's Gus-speak for we're totally stuffed.'

Gus took too long to reply. Finally, he sighed and smiling boldly said, 'Nah, not really. We beat the odds last time, who says we can't do it again. And anyway, after all we've been through, a bit of wind will be a walk in the park.'

He shook his legs out, encouraging blood back into his toes and shuffled down the boat. 'I'm going to see what's happening out there, and then we'll need to batten down the hatches.'

He opened up the makeshift canvas door and slipped outside.

Gus's over-confidence simply confirmed Sas's worst suspicions. The boat lurched into a bigger wave and water thudded onto the canopy. Sue grabbed her phone and pressed the power button. The phone display lit up.

Moments later she was tapping away furiously.

Her first was to Isabella. A thought had been niggling away at her.

Me here. Not looking good. G being v brave me less so. Have you found clues? In your house—like pictures. You MUST find them. Sounds mad but think important. If don't speak, love you very much. Sue—n Gus. xxx

Send. *Bleep.*

Sue noted the bars of the battery sinking to red. Two more.

Mum, I love you so much. If you get this, I'm stuck out at sea. Don't worry—never been happier. Thanks for all you have done. I love you xxx

Send. *Bleep.*

Her final message was to her entire address book:

SOS. Sue Lowden here with Gus Williams from Upsall. We're in a small rowing boat in the North Sea. Sucked out after storm. Gale coming. No idea where we are. Please forward. WE NEED HELP!

Send.

'The Joan of' jolted viciously and Sue, thrown off balance, dropped the phone. It landed in the water at the bottom of the boat with a splash.

Gus put his head back under the canopy, his head soaked. 'Do you want the good news or the bad news?'

'Uh,' Sue said as she picked up her phone.

'I said, good news, or bad news?'

Gus sat on the end of the bench and waited for her response. Tears trailed down her cheeks.

Sue wiped the handset and then her eyes. 'Bad news first,' Sue croaked.

Gus smiled his big toothy smile. 'Ace. Right, the bad news is that it's quite a big one.'

'Big what?'

'Bag of bananas, you monkey! Storm! What do you think?'

Sue shivered. 'And the good?'

'Lights! I can see lights!' He was shouting. 'Look... there, can you see it? It's a bleeding lighthouse.'

Sue crawled down the boat and, for a moment, as she popped her head out, she caught the blink of a light way off in the distance. Her muscles tensed and her eyes widened. Was it a mile off, or ten miles away? 'How far?' she shouted.

'I don't know,' he yelled back. 'I'd have a better idea if the waves weren't so big.'

For the first time, now that her eyes had fully adjusted to the murky gloom, she could see wild seas frothing and chopping nearby. A huge, dark wave loomed up. Before she had a chance to move, it broke. She dived inside. The canopy sagged for a moment and then sprang back.

Gus immediately pulled the sail, the umbrella they used as a water holder, and other odds and ends into the boat. He secured their food package with a rope, tying it against the bottom of the seat. 'Here,' he said, 'have some.' He threw her a bag of crisps and a water bottle. 'Drink.'

Sue did as she was told.

'Now,' he said, handing her an assortment of chocolates. 'Tuck these in your pockets. Just in case.'

She grabbed them and pushed two into her jeans and another lot into her jacket.

'I'm scared, Gus,' she said.

'Have no fear, we'll be fine,' he replied, as another wave assaulted the canopy. Quick as a flash, Gus was bailing water. Sue joined in, and, for the time being at least, the water in the boat took their mind off the storm.

Some while later, exhausted by their endeavour, Gus lay down, Sue next to him, gulping in air. Sue was shaking. Gus draped an arm round her. 'Sue', he said reassuringly, 'believe me, everything will work out fine and dandy.'

She trembled. Gus knew it wasn't from the cold. He needed her to be strong. 'Look, it's like at the end of the film, *Titanic*,' he said. 'Remember? When Leonardo DiCaprio holds Kate and they're in the freezing North Atlantic water but they keep going until they get rescued—'

'But HE dies!' Sue shot back.

'Yeah, but he kept her alive, somehow, right to the bitter end. And you know what, I'm going to keep you alive too. Anyway, in our version, it isn't that cold, we're very close to land and you've put out an SOS.' He held her tighter and turned, his eyes wide. 'You have, haven't you?'

'Yes.'

'Good,' he said. 'So, there you go. And we're not in a hulking, metal ship in the North Atlantic miles from anywhere, we're in a tiny rowing boat, somewhere off the coast of... somewhere. Safety, is pretty much guaranteed. And, there's another thing,' he said, his grin returning, 'you're way prettier than Leo's Kate.' He kissed her forehead.

Sue snuggled into his chest as the boat groaned, bashed first one way and then the other, lurching wretchedly, like a ride at the fair.

A churning, all-encompassing feeling of illness swept through her.

Gus' eyes sparkled and he started laughing. He stumbled to the end of the boat, grabbed the fresh water container, took a deep draught and topped up his water bottle. He turned. 'You want some?'

Sue hardly dared move but she reckoned a bit of water might make her feel less queasy. She nodded and slid along the bench, not daring for a minute to let go. Sue gulped, instantly regretting it.

Gus tied the rope around his wrist, pulling the plastic barrel after him. He began pouring the drinking water into the sea.

'What the hell are you doing?' Sue screamed.

'Buoyancy aid,' he grinned. 'If we go down, and of course it's a massive "if" it would be a shame if we drowned.'

'But we need water, Gus!'

'We've got enough,' he shrugged and tapped the water bottle as a wave threw him against the canopy. His grin grew and his eyes shone.

'We'll freeze!'

'Nah! Course we won't. It's October, the sea's at it warmest.'

A roller smashed the canopy and Sue cowered down, trembling.

Gus stumbled over. 'The fact is,' he said, 'we're near the coast. I can sense it. Either it's a short swim, or 'The Joan of' gets wrecked, and a boat comes along and picks us up. Or a helicopter, wouldn't that be cool?'

'No, it would not be!'

'Aw, come on, liven up a bit. I've never been in a helicopter. We're on the verge of getting out of here.'

'You're insane, Gus Williams. Totally bonkers.'

Gus mocked a pained look.

Sue thumped him on the arm. 'OK—gorgeous, but still bleeding bonkers,' she added.

Gus tied a section of wood onto the handle of the barrel with some rope and settled into construction mode.

Sue watched, admiring his speed and concentration, aware that her stomach was rumbling.

'I'm going to be sick,' she said, her hand moving to her mouth. Holding tightly onto the seat and using the rocking motion of the boat, she slipped towards the canopy entrance. As she leaned out a wave smashed her in the face. She reeled and put her head back in and shrieked, shaking the water out of her hair.

Gus laughed.

'Oh, shut up,' she said, as she put her head back outside and let fly.

In no time, her body felt green and deathly. When she opened her eyes, she tried to figure out what she was staring at. A large, black, towering hulk right in front of her. And then it was lost behind a wall of water. Was it a boat, a cliff or something else?

She scrambled in as Gus was tying the other end of the plank onto one of the buoyancy containers. 'What is it?' she said pointing down the boat.

'What's what?'

'The big—thing—out there.'

Gus smiled. 'Cliffs, probably.'

'Cliffs? Is that good or bad?' her attention turned to his contraption. 'What are you doing?'

Gus' eyes sparkled in the torchlight. 'This, my little vomit comet, is our life raft.'

'That!'

Gus looked taken aback. 'Yeah. It's brilliant. You got any better ideas?' His eyes darted to the bottom of the boat where, for the first time, she noted ankle-high water swishing around.

'Bail!' she cried. Immediately, Sue reached for the bailing bucket, her arms flailing in the darkness. She found it, but, as she bent to scoop, she was thrown to the other side of the vessel. A strong hand pulled her up. Gus looked deep into her eyes.

'Sue. The boat is leaking. There's a hole and no amount of bailing can save 'The Joan of'. Not now, not in this.'

After all they'd been through, she could hardly believe it. 'We're going to sink?'

Gus pushed on the torch. 'Nah,' he said, shining the torch up his face in a mock-spooky way. 'This is simply the part where we disembark. You just have to hold on, you understand?' His voice turned more serious. 'Do exactly as I say.'

Sue summoned her strength and nodded through her tears.

'Now, you're Kate, like in Titanic, and I'm Leo.' He kissed her. 'Whatever you do, don't let go. Promise me, Kate, you won't let go.'

Sue threw herself at him and hugged him tight. Somehow, deep down, she trusted him with her whole soul. If Gus said they'd survive, they would. Everything else had worked. Why not this?

Gus noted the water was up to his knees. He slipped out of their embrace, opened his penknife and thrust it through the canvas, tearing the canopy in a neat line.

In no time, the full force of the gale was upon them, blowing hard, and the vessel was filling with water. In the dim light they could see into the night beyond. On one side loomed a cliff and on the other... a boat. Sas's heart soared. Did the boat even know they were there?

'Look!' she screamed.

His face was bursting with a smile and his eyes dancing like stars in the dull night sky. 'Hold on, my Kate,' he said. 'That's all you've got to do.'

Sue smiled back. She'd hold on for Gus this day and every day henceforth.

And, before she had the chance to dwell on it, a huge wave engulfed 'The Joan of".

Gus' big smile was the last thing she remembered as her world was suddenly churned upside down and inside out.

NEW POWDERS

Prime Minister Kingsford ached with tiredness and his head hurt with all the with information he'd had to digest over the last couple of days. He studied the clock. Three in the morning. Damn. He was up at six. Three hours sleep was not nearly enough. He needed to be on top of his game tomorrow. He had an audience to update the Queen, followed by a meeting the American Secretary of State, then a briefing from Stone and the medical team in Yorkshire, followed by endless media sessions and then a long list of calls that had to made to pacify and cajole top brass from around the world.

His head hit the pillow hard as his mind toyed with the huge death toll of storm and plague victims. And he remembered what the kindly Dr Muller had said about being decontaminated following his visit to see the strange boy in Yorkshire. He certainly felt lucky that he had spared. He tried to think of his family holiday as he fell asleep, the images of feet splashing in calm, clear Mediterranean waters.

A short while later, a dreamspinner hovered invisibly above the snoring Prime Minister, its long, opaque legs anchored beside the man's face. The dreamspinner extracted tiny powders from its maghole and filtered a dream which the man sucked in with long, slow breaths.

The dreamspinner wondered how this man, and other humans, would react to their new dream powders. She'd been told that this spider web powder had come from the webs of an arachnid found deep in the caves beneath the mountains in Havilah. And these powders, she'd been told on good authority, gave dreams not too dissimilar to the wonderful spider web powders of the Garden of Eden. Stimulating and enriching, with a twist, Asgard had claimed—an extraordinary twist.

She had loved *knitting and spinning* dreams from the Garden of Eden, knowing what joy they'd give. Perhaps these powders would do the same? Even if they didn't, at least they had a decent dream to offer—and the excitement had been catching on. In milliseconds she was by a child, a little boy, and when she'd *knitted and spun* his dream she sensed a dog sleeping nearby. She checked her powder stock and calculated that there was easily enough for another thousand dreams. This dream powder stretched a long way.

She inverted herself back to the man, excited to see if his dream had begun.

He groaned and turned in his sleep. Then he laughed. Now, he flailed his arms.

Excellent, thought the dreamspinners. *These dreams are rich, exactly as Asgard promised.*

She checked for signs of life in the area. Soon she flashed here and there, *knitting and spinning* dreams until her new dream powders ran out.

As usual, many sleepers were not ready to dream on this night. Maybe sleeping patterns were too erratic, or their sleep was too shallow, or, often, a dream had already been given. She would return soon, but right now her stocks needed replenishing from this new powder-source on Havilah.

And then, as planet Earth rotated on its axis and one side slipped into darkness, she would give new dreams on the other side of the world.

CLUES

Isabella sat in bed, running through her conversation with Old Man Wood the previous night. Her phone bleeped. She read the message and re-read it before rushing downstairs. She found Daisy and Archie curled up on the sofa in front of the fire.

'Look! Another message from Sue! What do you think?' She handed Archie her phone.

He read it out loud:

Gus total hero. Now lost at sea. Have put out SOS. Supplies OK for few days. Boat holding together, just. Fish vile. U saw Kemp on TV? R saw K acting weird b4 storm with old man. Tablets = v good, I think. Clues in pictures? Hurry. Phone dodgy. Think wr near coast. Love u all S xxx

Archie's heart skipped a beat. *Kemp acting weird with old man? That had to be Cain. So maybe they had joined...*

Daisy interrupted his thoughts. 'Sue thinks the clues are in the pictures.'

Archie read the text again. 'Clues in pictures? It's not a great deal to go on. Do you think she means in the actual image of the picture itself—or within the frame of the picture, like a piece of paper stuck behind it?'

Daisy shrugged. 'I guess we'll have to study every picture in the house. Come on, Archie, no time to lose.'

Isabella stepped in front of her. 'If you're going to do this, you need a process. If there's no method it'll be chaos.'

'You're in?' Archie quizzed.

'Only because I've got nothing better to do,' she replied. 'If you really think there's something in this madness, I might as well organise you.'

'Great, thanks, Isabella.'

'I'll do upstairs, you two do the rest,' Isabella ordered. 'Bring all the pictures into the sitting room and line them around the walls, starting from the door and working round the room. I'll go the other way. Then at least I can catalogue them and return them to their correct position later.'

'What do you think we're looking for?' Archie asked Old Man Wood.

The old man stroked his chin. 'It must be old, appley-old,' he said. 'And perhaps with writing you won't understand, so look for a strange script or peculiar scribblings.'

Isabella groaned. 'Are you sure it's not on the wooden panels in your bedroom?'

'I don't believe so,' Old Man Wood replied. 'Those look like stories, not instructions.'

'And are you sure there's not a mural behind your wooden panels —'

He shook his head.

'What about a ceiling painting?' Daisy added, 'like the Michael-what's-his-face one?'

Isabella laughed, although Daisy felt it sounded more like a scoff. 'Michelangelo? Here in Yorkshire, on the moors?'

'Yeah, even here on the moors, Isabella. Why not?'

'I'll tell you what, Daisy,' Isabella sneered, imitating her voice, 'why don't you search out with your eyes, dude. Or are they not working?'

Daisy fixed her sister with a stare. 'Why don't you go feel for it, holey-hands?'

'Will you two shut up and start looking?' Archie said. 'Come on, Daisy!'

Before long, an amazing assortment of oil paintings and watercolours lined the walls of the sitting room. Isabella dashed around upstairs and emerged with several older-looking canvases, and, more importantly, they thought, antique-looking oil paintings on wood. They were so old the paint had cracked like a mosaic.

'I found them in the spare room.' Isabella said, as she studied the paintings. 'Old Man Wood... over here! Do these images trigger *anything*?'

Together they leaned over them, trying to see if there were markings that might be clues, or if the backs had writing on them.

The majority of the paintings were of ancestors who bore an uncanny resemblance, Daisy thought, to a younger Old Man Wood. The rest were landscapes or seascapes.

For over an hour, they studied the pictures. Isabella, having catalogued the entire collection in record time, decided that they ought to be divided into groups: pictures with water and trees in one corner, abstract pictures in another, still-life oils—by the sofa, portraits with people—near the window, and those with animals on the adjacent wall. But even when they'd studied them twice, there wasn't a single distinctive element that they recollected.

'What about the carvings in Old Man Wood's room?' Archie said, his voice betraying his frustration. 'Would you mind if we have a look? You know, a fresh pair of eyes.'

'Be my guests,' Old Man Wood said, and as a group they headed up to his room.

'Look!' Archie said, jumping on the bed. 'The screens!'

It was the first time the twins had seen themselves on the curious panels.

'How very, very cool,' Daisy said, as she pouted and tossed her hair. 'These are super-awesome. Archie, babes, basically we've got our own TV channel,' Daisy said. 'Can we record stuff?'

'Oh, grow up!' Isabella scolded. 'And stop admiring yourselves. Daisy, you start over there.'

The twins slipped reluctantly off the bed and started to inspect the carved panelling. Although the gnarled wood with odd-looking animals and curious faces was intriguing, there was nothing distinctly different.

Isabella slumped to the floor. 'This is ridiculous. How can we find what we're looking for, when we don't even have a single clue?'

'I bet you,' Daisy said, as she scratched the carpet with her fingernails, 'whatever we're looking for will be right under our bums.'

'The expression,' Isabella sighed, 'is right under your nose—not your bottom.'

Archie's dark eyes sparkled mischievously at Daisy, and he whispered. 'She'll know that, cos she's such a big arse!'

Daisy giggled and nudged him in the ribs.

'Hilarious,' Isabella replied, screwing a face at him. 'Come on kiddie-winks, no good hanging around here.' She ushered them to the door. 'More searching required downstairs.'

But as Archie scoured the room one last time, something caught his eye. 'You know,' he said, 'What if Daisy's right?' He pointed at the floor.

'Where? What do you mean?' Isabella said.

'There. The rugs.'

'Rugs?'

'Yeah... look at them. They're old, patterned... Persian or something, aren't they, Old Man Wood?'

The old man squinted at them, a look of surprise on his face.

'Big deal,' Isabella scoffed. 'We're looking for a picture not old, mangy carpets.'

Archie reddened a little. 'But look carefully,' Archie said, kneeling down where they'd been sitting. 'There are marks on them. We shouldn't write them off just because they're not on a wall.'

Isabella sighed. 'Those marks are stains, right, Old Man Wood? Utterly vile. I'll ask Mrs P to throw them away.'

Old Man Wood shrugged and turned for the door.

But now it was Daisy's turn to stare at the rugs. 'Surely, it's worth a look, isn't it, Isabella?'

Isabella tutted. 'Seriously? They probably haven't been washed for—'

'Ooh, I say,' Daisy said. 'There's something on this one, it's got a kind of tree in the middle. Wow, maybe you're right, Archie! What if *these* are the pictures?'

'Oh! for goodness' sakes. Fat chance,' Isabella said. 'You know as well as I do that those marks are years of ground-in mud and grime.'

Daisy picked up one of the rugs and Archie copied her. In no time, the five little rugs were folded over the end of the wooden bed.

The children stood back, only to find themselves admiring five grey-brown mats. But the faintest outline of a pattern where Daisy had been picking at the fibres with her fingernails had begun to show.

'They are disgusting little things,' Isabella declared.

'I'm not so sure,' Archie piped up. 'But I do know that the best way to clean a rug is to give it a massive whack.' He grabbed one, threw it over his shoulder and slung it down hard on the bed end.

A plume of dust filled the room. They ran for the door, coughing and spluttering.

'Genius,' Isabella said scathingly. She smacked Archie on top of his head, only to find a hair spike going straight through the hole in her palm. 'This is ridiculous,' she said, ignoring Daisy's laughter as she struggled to extract her hand.

'Oh, stop it,' she said, turning on her. 'Come on, guys. Isn't this a little bit desperate? I mean we haven't even analysed all the picture frames yet.'

Isabella shook out her hand and found her hand-hole shrinking back to its original size. 'Sometimes, you two really don't possess a single particle of intelligence. We clearly need to look harder.'

Old Man Wood gathered the five filthy little rugs. 'I'll beat them outside and hang them out on the line,' he said. 'These little things could do with a bit of freshening up.'

A MESSAGE

A little while later, Mrs Pye waddled across the courtyard, her feet splashing in the puddles. She hummed to herself, and then stopped and stared at the washing line. Five rugs hung like wet towels, muddy water dripping from each one. Had she forgotten them?

She racked her brain. Filthy though they were, she was sure she'd replaced them on Old Man Wood's floor. She tutted to herself, bustled over, removed them at arm's length and placed them in a washing basket. She couldn't imagine the old man suddenly wanting to clean them, so had one of the children...?

But those children weren't exactly forthcoming in the laundry department.

Before long, she found herself scrubbing each rug in the old stone sink in the washhouse. She was amazed at the steady flow of filthy, dark water coming out but, realising the time, and without really giving it too much thought now that the generator was on, she gave up and threw all five rugs in the washing machine.

When the wash came to its juddering conclusion, she hung them out to dry in two neat rows on the Sheila's Maid above the range in the kitchen.

Mrs Pye was delighted with their spectacular colour. Each one shone radiantly and felt soft and clean. She smacked her hands together in a moment of washing triumph and, feeling rather pleased with herself, picked up her bag and returned to her flat across the courtyard.

❄

'This is hopeless,' Archie said. 'We've been doing this for hours.' He picked up a modern landscape painting, which had hung in their parents' bedroom.

'I love this picture,' he said quietly to Old Man Wood. 'A house set by a vineyard, the sun going down. A distant fire, the colours of the vines. Somehow,' he said, 'it reminds me of Mum—lovely, calm and pretty, just like her.' His bottom lip quivered. 'And what I'd do for some sunshine right now.' He sniffed and shut his eyes. 'Do you know where they bought it?'

'Hmmm,' Old Man Wood said, placing a comforting hand on Archie's shoulder. 'I'm certain that it came back from a holiday some years ago,' he said softly. 'It won't be long before they're home.'

Archie turned it round so he was now looking at the back. There, much to his surprise, he found a picture postcard stuck with tape to the top and bottom corners. The picture showed a deep, crimson-red rose set on a white background. That was all. Archie gently removed the tape and turned it over.

A typical red rose from the vineyards of Tuscany, was the description, and below it, in his mother's neat handwriting, was the following:

My darling,
I want you to know that we love you very much, and our hearts and dreams will always be with you.
Best of luck, whichever flight you choose.
Your loving —
Mother and Father

What a weird message, he thought. 'Best of luck in whichever flight you choose'. *What was that supposed to mean? And why was it addressed to just 'My darling' and not 'My darlings'?*

It was as though it was addressed to him and him alone.

Quietly and with his back turned to the girls he closed his eyes, kissed the postcard and slipped it into the back pocket of his jeans.

OLD MAN WOOD TAKES THE BLAME

Old Man Wood slumped into his chair. He ought to return to the Bubbling Brook. The trees would know the answers, but what would the children think? Then again, did it really matter?

The willow trees had told him that he himself had hidden the eggs a long time ago using complex magic. More importantly, Old Man Wood discovered that the eggs were a link to the rain and that the children were the Heirs of Eden, as he suspected.

But because the trees made the process sound so obvious and straightforward, he hadn't deepened his questioning and now he regretted it. He wondered if he shouldn't go back and talk to them again. But doing that meant he would have to think of the right questions and he didn't know what those questions were.

In the meantime, he had to try something, so he pulled himself together and, with Archie and Daisy in tow, headed upstairs to his room and began searching the large assortment of carvings hoping that something—anything—might jolt his memory.

In due course, he announced to the disappointed faces of Archie and Daisy, who had followed his every move, that he didn't know.

He lifted himself out of his chair, when he caught the familiar sound of pots rattling from the kitchen. No doubt Mrs Pye was fishing out saucepans, preparing tea. Was it so late already? A bit of nourishment to get his brain in gear was just what he needed to help him think of the right questions for those funny old willows.

❄

Mrs Pye sauntered into the kitchen and released the rope on the Sheila's Maid. She folded each rug in half, and then in half again. She piled one on top of the other and placed them in the washing basket. She noted the unusually fine fabric, the lightweight, silk-like textures with delicate stitching and neat embroidery. Why, oh why, had they sat disregarded on Old Man Wood's floor?

She filled a saucepan and placed it on the hot plate. Then she picked up the basket and headed out of the kitchen towards the cupboard. As she walked past the living room, she peeked through a gap in the door and gasped.

'What in Heaven's name above have you lot been doing?' she cried.

The children stood up, a sure admission of guilt, and looked around them. Frames of oil paintings and portraits and sketches and watercolours lay scattered over the room.

'We are trying, dear Mrs Pye,' Isabella said, in her smartest voice, 'to find something in a picture. The problem is, we're not sure what it is, but we do know it is vitally important.'

Archie and Daisy nodded in agreement.

Mrs Pye turned from one to the next and back, her already ruddy face reddening.

Isabella, oblivious to the housekeeper's glare, added quietly, 'Sue said so.'

'Sue said so!' Mrs Pye exploded. 'Sue said so!' Her face was now bright red, as if someone had turned up a heat dial. 'Your friend Sue, who lives in Northallerton, said you should gather all the pictures in this house and deposit them in one room. Because you're looking for something AND YOU DON'T KNOW WHAT?' she tutted in disbelief. 'Now come on, Isabella, you can do better than that.'

The children instinctively turned towards Old Man Wood.

'The thing is,' the old man hesitated as he pulled himself up, 'Isabella's right. I'll... er... tell you about it later. This,' and he gestured around the room, 'is all my doing, Mrs Pye. Don't worry, each and every picture will be put back in its proper place, I promise.'

'I should hope so,' she replied, her eyes boring into each of them. 'You ought to know better, the lot of you. If you're missing something, ask me. I'd be surprised if I don't know its whereabouts. I want this room and all these pictures back where they belong by tomorrow night even if you haven't found what you're looking for. I'm responsible for the domestics while your parents are away and, believe you me, they would not be happy.'

A long, embarrassing silence hung over the room. Eventually, Archie piped up and said sweetly, 'What we're trying to find is a picture with some sort of old writing or marks on it, something that might be connected with this rain? Maybe you could help?'

Mrs Pye's face instantly melted into a smile. 'I'll keep my eyes open,' she said, and exited out of the room carrying the basket. But something in the back of her mind made her stop. She opened the door. 'Any of you lot know anything about some filthy ruggy things left out in the rain?' She looked at the blank faces of the children, '...on the washing line?'

'Ah, yes! Those are mine,' Old Man Wood said. 'Thought they could do with a clean.'

'By leaving them out there? Tuh. Typical!' Her small eyes lit up. 'Well, I've had a right proper go at them. You should see the difference. Beautiful things. Come alive they have. I'll put them in the cupboard.' She turned smartly and marched off along the corridor, humming to herself.

And if he doesn't want them, she thought, I'll have 'em for myself.

She stroked the top one and it seemed to reciprocate her touch, like the warmth of a sleeping cat.

'What was that all about?' Archie asked as he prised open the back of an old wooden portrait with a screwdriver.

Old Man Wood walked over and held the frame. 'She gave my old rugs a clean,' he said. 'Tickled blue about it too. She said they'd all come alive. Don't you listen to anything she says?'

'Not really,' Archie said, staring at the next family portrait. 'How long have you had them?'

'Had what?'

'Those grimy old rugs!'

'Apples-alive! I can't remember,' Old Man Wood scratched the back of his neck. 'It's a long time, though.'

Archie moved on to the next portrait. 'How old are these?'

Old Man Wood walked over. 'I've no idea—'

'The date on these portraits,' Daisy shouted from across the room, 'is on the back or, generally, in the bottom right corner. It's the same with quite a few of them for some reason. This one is from 1638... and here's one from 1702.'

Archie joined in by holding up a very delicate portrait. 'Oh, I see. Look... 1595!'

Isabella, who was in the hallway listening in, said, 'I can beat that. This shield goes back to 1382, I think that's right? It's Roman numerals.'

A sense of excitement and expectation filled the room. The notion of being surrounded by such antiquity built up a sense of awe, as if the people in the portraits had somehow gathered into the room and joined them in their search.

'Isn't it funny,' Archie said, as he studied a series of individual portraits, 'how each of these have the same kind of creamy, rectangular backgrounds with pale little swirls on, while the actual images on the paintings are only slightly different?'

Daisy stared at the pictures, her concentration intense. 'My God,' she whispered. The others leaned in.

'What is it, Daisy?'

Daisy's eyes were glowing. 'The backgrounds are the same, like five... panels.'

'Panels?' Archie said. 'I can't see anything like that, just sort of... blurs.'

'I knew it!' Isabella said. 'I told you there were wall panels somewhere in the house.'

Old Man Wood sighed. 'Isabella, wall paintings would never last, young'un. They simply wouldn't survive—'

'What else could they be?'

Daisy looked up. 'If they're not panels and they're not pictures, then we're missing something. What else hangs on a wall, has colour and could last the test of time?'

The children sat down in a circle, their brains working hard.

Archie began fidgeting as an idea noodled into his brain. Slowly, a smile filled his face. 'Idiots!' he said.

'What?' Isabella said.

'The only other thing that last are tapestries, wall hangings—'

'Like those massive old carpets on church walls?' Isabella said. 'Don't be ridiculous—'

'I'm not.' Archie stood up. 'I think I've got it,' he said. And before anyone could blink, he flew off down the corridor and then up the stairs, the floorboards creaking at every footstep.

'Where's he gone?' Daisy said.

'I believe,' Isabella said, 'Archie thinks the drape above his bed might be the thing we're looking for.'

'Really?'

Isabella sighed. 'Stranger things have happened, I suppose.'

STONE SPEAKS WITH SOLOMON

Solomon was grateful for the shower and change of clothes. He ate a lamb chop with mashed potatoes, remembering to chew every morsel, otherwise his hungry stomach would hurt him later.

'I'm going to be honest with you, Charlie,' Solomon said to his cousin, 'the school has nothing to do with this.'

'That's all very well, but the evidence suggests that the storm's epicentre was directly overhead. And it's from here that this blasted pathogen started.' Stone pulled out a graphic. 'Have a look at these satellite images. The reason the meteorological geeks didn't pick it up was that it appeared like a localised weather event. In a matter of hours, it built and built while combining with the humid weather in the area to generate its own peculiar entity, and then "boosh". Look, here.'

On the screen, Solomon viewed the graphic. The storm was coloured in red, its centre a much darker hue, which ballooned out until a massive area was swathed in black. There was no mistaking that it stemmed from Upsall.

'Nobody's ever seen anything like it.'

'But why Upsall, Charlie?' Solomon began. 'We're a small community with an old school built on the foundations of a monastery just like the abbeys at Fountains, Rievaulx and Byland nearby. Have you checked them out?'

The Commissioner nodded. 'They're underwater—like Upsall—but the difference is, those others are ruins, Upsall isn't.' Stone picked his nails. 'Something makes me think this disaster begins here and ends here. I don't know what it is, but I'm going to find out.'

Solomon wiped his lips with a paper towel. 'I'll help you all you want, my old friend. You know I will. But, as I said earlier, if you think it's got anything to do with the school, I think you're barking up the wrong tree.'

'You mentioned the girl coming to you,' Stone said, his eyes boring into the older man. 'Tell me more about this de Lowe family?'

Solomon shifted. 'Well, the mother and father are archaeologists, currently out in the Middle East on a dig. The children are popular and gifted. There's not much more to it than that.'

Charlie rubbed his chin. 'Why did that girl come to you knowing the storm was about to happen?'

'I have no idea.'

'I do,' Stone replied. 'She knew something. Something about all of this, and she wanted to let you in on it.' Stone rubbed his hands. 'What else did she tell you?'

Solomon smiled thinly. 'We've been over this before,' he said, leaning back in his chair. 'She simply bustled in saying that her homemade barometer was indicating extreme pressure. She's a scientist, and a good one. We encourage pupils to act on their instincts and she did just that.'

'But don't you think it's uncanny?'

'No, I do not,' Solomon bristled. 'We want our students to be decent, responsible citizens, and reacting to her findings is a part of that. It isn't complicated, you know.'

Stone sensed unease in the headmaster. 'When their parents are away on their archaeological trips, who looks after them?'

Solomon tensed. He'd hoped Stone wouldn't bring this up. 'There's an elderly uncle and a housekeeper. I saw them myself only the night before. In their circumstances, they do a splendid job.'

Stone opened up the folder in front of him, pushed on his reading glasses, and scanned the document. 'There's no mention of an uncle.' He thumbed through another couple of pages. 'Ah-a, but it does mention a woman, named here as Mrs Pye, who was taken in by the family thirteen years ago. It says here she was found with terrible injuries in the forest beneath the moors.' He looked up and said slowly, 'And has possible brain damage.'

'That's ludicrous,' Solomon snapped. 'I don't see what this has to do with your enquiries.'

Stone's lip curled. 'I'm just doing my job, trying to find out what the hell is going on.' He smiled. 'Who is this old uncle? Why no record?' Stone pulled out some historical documents. 'After all, they're an old, distinguished family in the area, right?'

Solomon stared out of the window. 'Yes, I suppose they are.'

'Says here there's a whole stained-glass window in the church dedicated to the de Lowe family. Seems they go back a long, long way. So, I repeat my question. Who is their uncle?'

'I don't know how this is relevant,' Solomon replied, feeling the heat. 'He's a loner, a hermit who lives with them. There's probably no record of him because he's never been on record for anything.'

'He was born, though,' Stone fired back. 'There's been a legal duty to record all births for more than two hundred years. Why is he not mentioned?'

'Perhaps,' said Solomon, 'you should ask the parents. I am the children's headmaster, I do not study the historical records of every child's family in my care.'

'But it says here that the school has given a bursary to the de Lowes for centuries,' Stone countered. 'And in fairness, the school was started by the family, was it not?'

Solomon couldn't deny it. He shrugged and scratched his head.

Stone hadn't finished. 'Strange, isn't it,' he said, 'the name *de Lowe*. Where did that come from? I mean, it's not exactly common.'

Solomon pursed his lips. 'I'd say it's almost certainly of French origin. Probably a knight from the Norman conquest, given land here by William of Normandy.'

'French, huh,' Stone said, leaning back in his chair. 'I thought it might be Flemish, or Breton.'

Solomon suddenly sat bolt upright. A thought struck him like an arrow through the eye.

Stone noticed. 'Is there something you want to tell me?'

Solomon regained his composure. 'Oh, dear. No. I was just reminded of the last time I saw those poor children. They were walking home. They wouldn't have stood a chance.'

'How come?'

'They were on the playing field when the storm broke. Little Archie had been struck down by a lightning bolt. That was the moment when I realised I had to get as many people to safety as possible. I gathered up a whole bunch of children—anyone really—and we ran to the relative safety of the tower.'

Actually, now that he remembered, *it was Sue and Isabella yelling on the football field that had given him the creeps. They were screaming about the storm as if there was something they knew.*

Stone eyed him curiously. 'To be clear, you're saying a lightning bolt struck Archie de Lowe, and he survived? I'm intrigued.'

'I can only suppose he didn't receive a direct hit.'

Solomon's thoughts were elsewhere. *Why hadn't he thought of it before? Their name! Stone clearly didn't know his French; de Lowe, or perhaps, de l'eau—French for water — the essential ingredient of life. Was this a coincidence — part of some ancient code?*

And how could he forget! The stained-glass window in the chapel! It had been staring him in the face for twenty-five years. A beautiful, but grubby artwork with three panels showing three figures bearing gifts. And filling the background; water, or, de l'eau! de Lowe!

His heartbeat quickened. He had to get back to Upsall as fast as he could.

'Charlie,' Solomon said. 'I'm exhausted and it has been a shattering few days. Would you mind if I slipped off to bed? You know where I am, if you wish to question me further.'

Stone clasped some papers together. 'Very well. It's late and there's a hell of a day coming.' He stood up smartly. 'If there's anything you need, shout.'

Solomon knew this was his chance. 'I'd be happy to do some research into some of the school books if you like. Being high up in the tower, the library was unscathed, and there are several large old tomes which may shed some light on the history of the area. Perhaps there are plague records from the Black Death.'

Stone eyed him suspiciously before his face lightened. 'Yes. Great. Thank you. That's exactly what I need; an academic with local knowledge. I'll get you back there first thing in the morning.' He pressed his phone. 'See to it that Headmaster Solomon is returned to Upsall at first light. Give him a linked phone and full access to the site.'

The order was confirmed.

A rap at the door made both men turn. The young officer Solomon had noticed before came in. 'Sir,' he said, 'there's been a development with the boy in intensive care. He's awake.'

Solomon raised an eyebrow. 'A boy?'

'Yes,' the officer said. 'Most unusual. He was discovered in the top of a huge tree, of all things. He's making a remarkable recovery. We might be able to talk to him in the morning, after all.'

Stone checked his watch. Nearly midnight. 'Reports are due in for the next few hours and I've got to brief the PM at seven tomorrow morning. I'll get an hour or two of sleep if I'm lucky.' He yawned and addressed the officer.

'Let's talk to the boy at nine. Make sure he has everything he needs. It'll give him more time to recover before the scientists get their hands on him.'

The officer nodded and left the room.

'You haven't heard about the boy they found in the middle of the flooding?' Stone said. 'Been headline news around the world. Bloody miracle-boy! Burnt all over. We've been waiting for him to come around so we can talk to him.'

'Yes, I did hear a rumour,' Solomon said. 'Was he one of mine?'

'I doubt it,' the commissioner replied. 'Found too far downstream. The strange thing is, there's no sign of the virus on him which, given his position, is quite frankly astonishing. In fact, his whole survival, in line with the injuries he sustained, doesn't really add up.'

Solomon breathed a sigh of relief and stood up. 'Well, good luck, Charlie. I don't envy you, but I'll do my best and let you know if I uncover anything of note.' He headed for the door.

'Excellent, thank you.'

Stone stretched his arms behind his head out as the door closed.

He re-ran Solomon's reaction through his mind, especially the bit when he'd mentioned the de Lowe family.

Something didn't stack up.

He pressed the intercom. 'Dickinson.'

Shortly, the officer strode in.

'The headmaster leaves at dawn for Upsall. Do something for me, will you? Fit him with video surveillance. From the moment he lands, I want a handpicked member of your team to monitor exactly what he's studying. You know the score.'

Dickinson nodded. 'And mike enabled?'

'If done without a trace.'

Dickinson straightened. This kind of work was his speciality. 'Does the school-master wear glasses?'

'Is there a headmaster who doesn't?'

Dickinson feigned a smile. 'Then I'll add a microgram lens to one of them. Consider it done.'

'Good. And keep this to yourself, Dickinson. Report back to me at lunchtime. We'll run over his initial findings then.'

ONE HUNDRED FORTY-SIX

INTERROGATION

Over breakfast, reports bombarded Stone's office. His early link-up with the Prime Minister had been a dreadful ordeal not least because the PM was in a foul mood, complaining about his, his son's and his dog's, ill-health. By nine o'clock, an early morning fatigue swept over him. He needed at least five hours sleep, not two.

And the news coming in was awful, astonishingly awful. The plague, even at this early hour, appeared to have spread randomly across the country. Thank God the media had been tempered, or the pandemonium and unrest would be unthinkable. But, conversely, unless they found answers soon, panic across the world was a real possibility.

His entourage swept into the confines of the hospital unit. Surgical masks and gloves were donned following a spray-down with a fine decontamination mist. It reminded him of the outbreak of foot and mouth disease on cattle. He pulled in a secretary. 'Is there a report on livestock? No? Then I want one in an hour.' The secretary scurried away, phone at the ear.

Kemp lay in the same bed, in the same room behind the glass. This time he was sitting up, with all manner of medical equipment plugged into him: drips connected with his arms and, for his burns, dressings covered his head and upper torso.

Commissioner Stone turned to Doctor Muller. 'What progress? Is he ready to talk?'

The doctor contemplated his answer. 'He's doing fine in a medical sense, but we've got nothing out of him so far. Not a pip. He just stares into space. Whatever he's been through has scarred him terribly.'

Stone clenched his fist. Interrogating people was a skill he prided himself on. From a young age he had had the knack of prising information out of people, whether by charm, force, or by verbal intimidation. But a sick boy? He contemplated his approach.

'Can he speak?' Stone asked.

'Oh yes. He's been repeating the words "Go away" in his sleep, and various other short, garbled sentences. To be honest, nothing he says makes any real sense.'

Minutes later, Stone, looking like a plastic yeti, entered the room. He walked round the bed, nurse and doctor flanking him, and noticed that the boy's eyes were wide open and, exactly as the doctor said, staring at a point on the wall.

Stone didn't feel sorry for many people. In truth, he despised those who portrayed any form of weakness and that's why, as a rule, he disliked children. But, as he took a seat next to this boy, a sense of sadness filled him. Here was a boy who no one knew—who no one had claimed—but who had clung onto life so bravely.

'Hello, my name is Commissioner Stone,' he began. 'We're thrilled you've woken up at last.'

The boy didn't move a muscle.

'You've been on quite a journey by the looks of things,' he went on, noticing a strange shift in the boy's eyes—a small sign of worry, perhaps. 'But we're here to make you better, get you back on your feet, with the best medical staff looking after you. And you're safe here, we'll make quite sure of that.' Stone glanced up at the doctor and nurse for encouragement. They nodded.

'We would very much like you to tell us what happened. As much as you can remember, OK?'

Still the boy stared into space.

'I'm going to tell you some pretty scary stuff about what's been going on, so it'll really help if you can answer some of my questions. Then we'll try and find family and friends to come and get you. How does that sound?'

The boy remained impassive, but licked his lips.

Stone noticed. 'Can you tell me your name?' he asked.

Stone waited.

The boy closed his eyes.

'Can you tell me where you live?'

The boy opened his eyes, and briefly they met the commissioner's.

That's a start.

'What do you remember about the storm?' he said. 'Can you tell me anything about it?'

The boy stared into the distance again, his eyes unwavering.

Stone sighed. *This boy wasn't going to give anything away. He was wasting his time. Perhaps he needed a different approach.*

'Look, buddy,' he began, quietening his voice. 'There's a disaster happening outside these walls which might affect the whole world. Somehow, and Lord only knows how, you survived with inexplicable burns all over your body. We're here to help you, but we need to find out what you know.'

The boy shut his eyes again and swallowed as if to speak.

The doctor, nurse and commissioner waited with bated breath for some words. The doctor made as if to speak but Stone shot him a glare. Aside from the bleeping of the monitors, silence filled the room.

'All right, I get it,' Stone said. 'Look, I understand what you've been through. But we know you can speak. You see, you've been sleep-talking.'

The boy's eyes narrowed.

'And the longer you refuse to cooperate,' Commissioner Stone added, 'the more I think you're hiding something. Because experience tells me that people who don't talk have nasty little secrets. What do you think, fella?'

The boy swallowed again but continued to stare at the wall. Again, they waited.

'You're scared. I can tell,' Stone said, just above a whisper. 'But I don't have time for this, lad. Are you going to play ball or not?'

Silence.

'If you don't, I'm going to fill your veins with a truth serum and you'll be singing like a bird before you know it.'

'You'll do no such thing!' Doctor Muller spat.

It was precisely the response Stone had hoped for.

'Yes, I damn well will!' he yelled. 'I have the authority to do anything to get to the bottom of this mess, so back off.'

The doctor and nurse both wore shocked expressions.

The boy moved his eyes from the doctor to the Commissioner and back again.

An indication of fear; Good, Stone thought. He leaned in. 'And the other thing you need to know, is that we've found your friends,' he lied.

The patient's eyes widened but still he uttered not a word.

Stone was just getting going. 'So, let's start again,' he began, his tone full of persuasive menace. 'Your name, your school and how you ended up at the top of a tree when everyone else was swept away. You've got till the count of five to answer me or I'm throwing you out of this hospital.'

The nurse gasped.

Stone turned on her. 'You, out!' he commanded. 'Get out! Both of you.'

'Never!' the doctor replied. 'You have no right. We have a duty of care to the boy.'

'Oh, really,' Stone said sarcastically. 'How frightfully honourable. For your information, I have a duty of care to the rest of the bleeding world.' His eyes were cold. 'Security! Get them out, now!'

Within seconds, the doctor and nurse were man-handled from the room.

Now, it was just him and the boy.

For the first time, the boy's face betrayed fear.

Stone leaned over the boy. 'Five... Four.'

'Three,'

'Two.'

'One.'

'Kemp,' the boy croaked.

The Commissioner thought he'd misheard. 'What was that?'

The monitor by the boy's bed started bleeping. 'My name is Kemp.'

Stone smiled. 'What else?'

The boy's face was contorting. Was he in pain? If so, he deserved it. 'What else?' he demanded.

'If,' Kemp began, as he tried to work up enough saliva to speak.

'If what, Kemp?'

'If you want to know,' the boy whispered, 'find Archie de Lowe... if he isn't dead.' Kemp's head fell back limply on the pillow.

Stone turned and stormed out of the door, ripping at his overalls as he went.

'Damn that Solomon!' he cursed. 'He knew. He bloody well knew. It's been Archie de Lowe all the bleeding time!'

RIDDLES ON THE RUGS

Archie appeared with the basket of rugs.

'Where did she say these had come from?' Isabella asked. 'They're beautiful.'

As Mrs Pye had also noticed, the rugs seemed to purr with pleasure. Isabella's heart was beating with excitement. 'Let's hang them up. Perhaps there's a map on them.'

Archie found a box of tacks and climbed up the stepladder with the first one. He pushed the tack into the corner of the rug and, as he started to push it in, a sudden heaviness forced him to drop it. Archie frowned. He tried it again, with exactly the same result. On his third attempt, as he pushed the tack into the corner, he felt it almost wriggle free from his grip.

Archie shook his head. 'We're going to have to come up with another plan,' he said. 'I can't get these in.'

Daisy moved beside him. 'Come on, Archie. You're normally pretty good at this kind of thing.'

'I've a much better idea,' Isabella said. 'Lay them out in the hallway. Then we can examine them from the stairs. Old Man Wood, is there any chance of a bit of light? Can you make the generator run a little longer?'

Old Man Wood strode off to find a lamp in his store and check the fuel in the generator. Isabella, Archie, and Daisy laid out the five carpets neatly below the stairwell.

Isabella climbed a quarter of the way up the staircase, directing Archie at the bottom. 'Move that one along a bit. That's it. And make sure that one isn't overlapping. Good. Where's Old Man Wood? It's way too dim under the stairs? I can't see them clearly ... or maybe they're blurred.'

Old Man Wood returned with two lamps, which he lit, illuminating the area. Archie and Daisy moved the lights into the optimal place, and then the twins joined Isabella.

All of them peered over the banisters. From here, the colours reflecting back were bright and sharp.

A renewed sense of excitement filled the hall.

Daisy ran up a couple more steps, peered over, and then climbed up three more steps. She then climbed a further four, until she was almost at the top. Then down one, her head jigging backwards and forwards.

Likewise, Archie moved up two steps, then down four and up five. Old Man Wood, who was much taller, stayed on the third step, but then decided to copy the children.

Isabella moved a couple of steps down and stayed there staring at the five rugs, her lips moving but no sound coming out. It was a most peculiar sight; the four of them shuffling up and down the staircase and, apart from a bit of polite barging and the occasional muffled gasps, there wasn't a sound from any of them.

Finally, Daisy broke the silence with tremendous excitement in her voice. 'There's writing all over them,' she announced, 'which changes at varying distances.' She climbed to the top of the stairs. 'Archie, grab a pen and write this down.'

Archie found a sheet of A4 and a pen.

'Right,' Daisy began. 'This is a bit complicated. It appears to work on different levels so I'm going to scoot up and down, OK?'

She skipped down a couple of risers and then up to the top as if double-checking. 'We'll start with this one; the second rug along.'

Archie moved next to it.

'From up here,' she began, 'this is what it says:-

'The first you hid in the heart of the house.'

'And now, if I move down here, the same writing changes to:

That warms you night and day.'

Daisy daintily skipped down another four stairs.

'Get it out by poking me —'

'And singing your favourite song along the way!'

'How did you read that?' Archie quizzed, staring at Daisy's blazing eyes. 'I can see that each rug seems to change like a kaleidoscope as we move nearer and farther away. But in pictures, not words.'

'Same,' Isabella said. 'I see tablets and scrolls and fire but...'

Daisy smiled. 'You know, magic eyes, remember! Did you write it down, Archie?'

He nodded.

Daisy ran up the steps again.

'Right Archie, let's try that one. Yup, there.' She pointed at the rug adjacent to the first and he moved beside it. 'Are you ready for number-two?'

'*For the second one you find,*' she read, before skipping down a couple of steps.

'*Burp it from the family belly.*'

'Are you sure?' Archie quizzed.

'Yeah! That's exactly what it says. Just write it down.'

'*To do just this,*' Old Man Wood continued from the bottom step.

'*You have to eat—*'

'*…Blab… ister… berry jelly!*' Daisy said.

'Blabisterberry Jelly?' Archie repeated, pulling a face as he wrote it down. 'What's that? Something like strawberry jelly? Read it again.'

Daisy did, and she even spelt it out.

'Blimey,' Archie said, scratching a hair spike. 'How are you supposed to burp jelly without it coming back through your nose?'

'Maybe the people who set this up had an awesome sense of humour,' Daisy said. 'Bells, we're going to have to do a nose trick—'

'I'm pretty sure ancient riddles didn't have nose tricks in mind when this was created,' Isabella said.

Daisy shrugged. 'Then again, maybe they did.' She ran upstairs again and nodded down to Old Man Wood.

'Are you ready for the next one?' she called out. 'It's that one over there.'

Archie signalled with a thumbs-up.

'Right, here we go:

The third you search,' she began,

'*Is underneath your nose. It is clear, pure and cold.*'

She waved at Old Man Wood.

'*In order to draw it out,*' his deep, rich voice boomed,

'*You need to send a rose.*'

'Send a rose?' Archie repeated as he scribbled on the pad. 'What the—'

'Gibberish,' Isabella said, running her hands through her hair, 'written by someone with absolutely no aptitude for poetry. It has to be… *must* be, a red-herring.'

Daisy scampered up the stairs once again. 'OK, next one coming up. Ready?'

She leant over the banister and stared hard, her red eyes glowing.

'*Put them all together, then get out of the way…*' she ran down a couple of stairs,

'*What you will find will prove a guide—*'

Old Man Wood joined in,

'*For all the other worlds.*'

'Got it Archie?' Daisy asked.

'Yeah, yeah. All down. Pretty weird, though.'

'Final one coming up. Ready?' Daisy said. 'Hang on a mo, this one's a bit faded.'

'I can't believe you can see anything,' Isabella said. 'You're making it up.'

Daisy shot her a look, which, with her red eyes, wasn't something you could ignore.

'*You have but seven days and seven nights, as Earth moves in its cycle, from first lightning strike and thunderclap,*' she began, '*the world awaits your arrival.*'

Old Man Wood sat down heavily on the step next to Archie and very quietly read the poem from Archie's sheet of paper:

'*The first you hid in the heart of the house*
'*That warms you night and day*
'*Get it out by poking me,*
'*And singing your favourite song along the way!*

'*For the second one you have to find*
'*You burp it from the family belly.*
'*To do this, you have to eat*
'*Corbucca Jalea!*

'*The third you search for is underneath your nose.*
'*It's clear, pure and cold.*
'*In order to draw it out*
'*You'll need to send a rose.*

'*Put them all together,*
'*Then get out of the way*
'*What you find will prove a guide*
'*For all the other worlds.*

'*You have but seven days and seven nights*
'*As Earth moves in its cycle*
'*From first lightning strike, and thunderclap*
'*The world awaits your arrival.*'

'Apples alive!' the old man exclaimed after the first verse. 'Blast!' after the second and, when Archie had finished, 'extra apple double blast!' His face was ashen and twisted. He put his head in his hands and started to sob.

The children looked at each other, their eyes wide.

'What's the matter?' Isabella asked, taking hold of a hand. 'Is it bad...?'

'Bad? Oh yes, my dear,' the old man replied, his lips trembling. 'It is extremely bad.'

He looked at them earnestly, tears forming in his eyes. 'It appears that so great is the stretch of time that has passed since I wrote it,' he pointed at the rugs. 'The greatest length of time you can ever imagine, that I have already failed in the task that was given to me.'

There was an uncomfortable silence. The children looked at one other, and then at Old Man Wood, as if he had completely lost his marbles.

Isabella patted his arm. 'I know the poems are pretty awful, but they aren't that bad,' she said gently, playing along with him. 'Dear Old Man Wood, the rhymes are actually quite sweet.'

Old Man Wood shook uncontrollably. 'I suppose I just never thought that this... would ever happen. I'm so sorry. I'm afraid I may be to blame for the greatest catastrophe to befall the worlds.'

Old Man Wood tried to pull himself together by blowing his nose extremely loudly.

'Why don't you start,' Isabella began softly, 'by telling us everything that you know? Perhaps it will make things easier.' She exchanged nervous glances with the others.

'Hmmm... yes,' the old man sniffed. 'That's a good idea.'

He lifted his head and stared deeply into the children's eyes. 'As you may have worked out by now, I am not who... who... er... who you think I am.'

'Then, who are you?' Daisy squeaked.

'Oh! Goodness me,' Old Man Wood replied. 'It's almost impossible for you to understand, my littluns. And it's going to sound a bit barmy. Well, utterly, appley-barmy. You must promise you won't be afraid.'

The children nodded nervously.

'Very well,' he said, picking himself up off the stairs. 'I'll tell you what I can remember, and fast, for if I'm not mistaken, the sands of time have been moving against us for far too long.' He glanced at the rugs. 'This goes back an awfully long time. Oh, deary me, how do I even begin?'

'Try,' Isabella said.

Old Man Wood cleared his throat. 'There's a whole history, lost and forgotten... until now. It was my role, I think, to help when the time came.' He began sobbing again.

The children guided him to his armchair, where he sat slumped in a sad heap with tears rolling down his cheeks.

'And this history relates to the floods and the plague?' Daisy asked.

This was met with more groaning. 'Apples, yes!'

'And we're the link, aren't we?' she said.

Old Man Wood turned his wrinkled face and bloodshot eyes to them. 'Oh yes. Yes indeed, my littluns. You three, my favourites, are the key to the whole thing.'

SOLOMON'S SWIM

Solomon pulled another heavy, leather-bound book from the library shelves. Translated from Latin, the book was called *"Stained Glass in the Churches of Northern England"*.

He carried it to the desk where it thudded down. He pushed his glasses up his nose and flicked through plates of stunning, intricate drawings, page after page. Finally, he came to the end where he found one last entry:

Upsall Abbey, Date: Medieval. Designer: unknown. Fabricator: Local.

He read the description, translating the Latin out loud as best as he could:

'...an unusual triptych, in the medieval style with adaptations of ancient symbolism, possibly pagan. It is recognised for the strong use of natural elements in its design and of curious, detailed, seated figures. One figure is similar to that of Christ, with hands showing holes from the cross, another holds a mace above his head and the third bears eyes like fire. Embracing all three is a large, disjointed emblem of the Tree of Life. Below each figure, smaller scenes tell of an apocalypse, namely flooding, disease and famine.

'Positioned in the laps of these figures are three stone tablets, each one bearing the motif of the Tree of Life. Above, angels feed the figures from the clouds.'

Solomon's heart nearly stopped.

He stared at the dark images of flooding and disease. *Wasn't that uncanny? Why, and what exactly were they being fed?*

His first impression was that these were pretty rotten images drawn from memory by someone not in the least bit interested. He decided, now that he was on his own, to see it for himself, even if this meant he'd have to get wet.

Solomon located a swimming mask in the lost property bin and made his way down the stairs until he reached the foul-smelling water that licked the walls and stairs of the tower and chapel.

He removed his clothes, bar his and vest underpants, adjusted the mask on his head to its maximum setting, took a deep breath, and plunged into the water.

He swam easily on the surface, the noise reverberating off the vaulted ceiling only a few metres above him. Then, he kicked off to the side and hoisted himself up onto a stone ledge.

From here, he realised that he had to climb up over the stone screen that separated the aisle from the nave. He spied a circular opening above which he figured he could climb up to. But halfway through, Solomon realised this gallant approach was a tactic for a younger man. He tried to pull himself back but found himself wedged in. There was no alternative but to go headfirst.

He puffed out his cheeks, wiggled his bottom, wobbled his belly, and slipped forward.

A moment later, with a cry, Solomon plunged through the air, belly-flopping into the water below.

'Sir, I think you'd better take a look at this.'

Stone looked up to see Dickinson walking towards him.

'What is it now?' he snapped.

'Your headmaster friend, sir... I'll put the video feed through.'

Stone ushered him in. 'It'd better be worth it, Dickinson.'

'You won't be disappointed.' A smile crossed the officer's face.

Stone stared at the screen, trying to work out where he was.

Dickinson filled him in. 'He's swimming, sir, in the chapel. He's climbed the wall aisle and now it looks as if he's a bit stuck.'

'Stuck. Jammed in? What on earth is he doing?'

'He spent some time flicking through a load of old books on stained glass windows and I'm not sure he's found what he wanted, so he's taken the plunge. Literally. Knows his Latin, though.'

'Of course, he does! He's a ruddy teacher—'

Suddenly, the image moved fast towards the water. For a minute all they could make out were dark stains and bubbles of watery activity.

Dickinson could hardly suppress his laughter.

'Is the feed–?'

'Waterproof? Yes, it's watertight, sir. Not sure about the mike.'

They watched as Solomon swam to the side and climbed a jutting beam. He looked around. In front of him was the top of the tall stained-glass windows with its colourful spray of light.

From the office, the two men followed his eyes. 'There!' Dickinson said. 'It's definitely the windows he's after.'

And as Solomon stared at the top of the ancient glass pictures, trying to deduce their meaning, so too did Stone.

Then, Solomon took a deep breath and they watched as he plunged into the cold water.

Solomon stared through his mask in disbelief. The deluge had cleaned the panes!

These weren't the grimy windows he'd seen in the book, nor the ones he'd seen every day for years, but vibrant, shining, coloured glass, bursting with life.

He surfaced, pulled himself onto the beam, removed his glasses, folded them, and tucked them under the elastic of his pants.

While submerged, the window told a story like a comic-book. Three people, a flood, a plague, and even the old de Lowe castle, now a ruin. All common factors. *Perhaps these three figures were ancestors of the three de Lowe children? But who,* he thought, *were the curious angelic creatures sitting above them, giving them a substance that resembled dust?*

It reminded him of Isabella's dream about the storm. A premonition perhaps?

Solomon reached for his specs, fixed his mask over his face, and dropped in again. This time, as the outdoor light brightened, it illuminated the window further and another layer of detail shone through.

Solomon-stayed down as long as his lungs would allow before surfacing. On the beam, he popped the glasses back in his pants. *Gifts,* he thought, *and challenges that must be accomplished or else, it appears, the world fails.*

'Curious,' he said out loud between shivers. 'And a snake-like beast with a dragon's head lies in wait.' He wiped his forehead. *Could this be the de Lowe myth that one of their ancestors had slain a dragon... or was it something else?*

He remembered the circles. Six circles all intersecting with one circle around. Seven in all. He'd seen it before. 'Seven days?' he said, 'Of creation?' the words echoed back at him.

Or did it stand for seven days of de-creation.

He stiffened. *Was this a coincidence?* After all, the nucleus of the storm and plague had begun right here.

Then he realised the symbol was the seven seeds of life.

In his bones Solomon knew this terrible event had something to do with the de Lowe children, and this window was most likely part of an ancient mystery that concerned their family.

Temporarily, Stone's picture went blank and then, just as Stone thought about giving up, the image returned.

The microphone picked up every word.

Stone listened and looked. Then he leant back in his chair with his arms folded behind his head.

'You know what, Dickinson,' he said, as he stared out of the window. 'This is the only thing we've got. The only damn thing we've managed to trawl up is a mad old headmaster swimming in sewage and staring at an old stained-glass window while banging on about the seven days of creation.'

Stone stood up and grabbed his jacket. 'You know what, Dickinson? I need to see that boy again. The boy who calls himself Kemp. I need to find out what he really knows about young Archie de Lowe.'

CAIN RETURNS

Kemp stared at the ceiling, bored. Now that his drips had been taken away he could move about, but to where? And why, oh why, had he told that weaselly man about Archie? What would happen to his friend if they found him? Would he be paraded in front of the TV cameras, subjected to interviews, get put on drips and given endless blood tests?

Kemp rolled off the bed. 'I need the toilet,' he yelled through the glass. 'And not in the piss-pot.'

The nurse came through. 'You're feeling perkier, young man,' she said.

'Yeah. I certainly am,' he replied with a smile. 'Any chance I can stretch my legs?'

The pretty nurse smiled back, and shuffled out. She rang a number, talked for less than a minute, and returned. 'There's a toilet just around the corner. Why don't you pop along there? I'm sure no one will mind.'

As he walked slowly along the corridor, Kemp noted guards at every door. *Were they all for him? Was he seen as a threat?*

He found the toilet and opened the door. It was a large cubicle with a loo, basin, mirror, and a bath with a shower. He locked the door and stared at his reflection.

'Boy,' came a soft voice.

Kemp froze, his eyes widening.

'Take off your gown, so you can see me.'

Kemp removed his dressing gown and let it fall to the floor. But before it hit the ground, it was scooped up.

'It is you!' Kemp snarled. 'What are you doing here, Cain?'

The ghost put the gown on. 'I wanted to apologise,' Cain said, his voice just above a whisper.

'Too bloody right. Now get out of here—'

'In my excitement, I cared for you poorly, despicably. But I realised my mistake just in time. I managed to save you.'

'Save me? Yeah, right,' he spat. 'So why are you back?'

'Because I need you,' Cain implored, his voice silky.

Kemp guffawed. 'Why do you think I would ever go back to you after the way you treated me?'

'I made a terrible, terrible error, boy.'

Kemp sat down on the loo seat. 'That's not nearly enough.'

'Because, together, we can be powerful.'

'Still no! No way!'

'Because I will give you food and water. I will let you sleep. Because I know we can do this together.'

'No!' Kemp hissed. 'Piss off!'

Cain sighed. 'Then you will remain here as a medical phenomenon, getting poked and prodded and having things pushed into you. And you too will get the disease. Everyone will. And you will suffer a horrible, painful death—'

'It'd be better than living in you, in your hell.'

Their conversation was interrupted. 'Is everything all right in there?' a voice called out from the corridor.

'Yeah, got a bit of constipation,' Kemp replied, thinking quickly. 'I'm going to have a quick shower in a mo. I won't be long.'

'Jolly good. Shout out if you need a hand, and if you're really struggling, just pull the red emergency cord.'

Cain tried again. He had one last card. 'Join me, boy. This time it will be different. I swear it. I have made arrangements—'

'Yeah, right. You said that before.'

'This time, I swear it... on your mother's life.'

Kemp flinched. 'My *mother's* life?'

'Yes,' Cain said slowly. 'Your mother lives. I have found her.'

'It can't be true,' Kemp squealed. 'She died when I was young. What are you saying?'

'It's a long story, boy,' Cain said, sensing his moment. 'But every single word is true. I spoke with your father's spirit. He told me everything.'

'Then why did she not come for me?'

'Because, young man, after their accident, she lost her mind. Now, she is better, but she does not know of you. I swear, on all the spirits of the universe that this is the truth.'

Kemp stared dumbfounded.

'Come with me and together we will see to it that she lives with you for the rest of your life. Is this not what you truly wish?'

Kemp placed his hands over his bald head. There was nothing, *nothing* he wanted more in the world.

Cain pressed. 'You need to come with me now,' he urged. 'This time, I will not fail you. You know what you must do. Put on the robe.'

Cain hovered to the door and grabbed a see-through bath-cap from the shelf. He put it on. 'Do it willingly, just as you did before the storm.'

Kemp switched on the shower and removed his nightshirt. 'My mother, huh?'

'You have only a few moments to decide.'

Kemp moved under the cold water. When he was fully drenched, he stepped out, shivering.

'Have you made your choice?'

'I have,' Kemp said and he grinned through his shivers. 'But this time, Cain, cold water will ease the pain.'

Stone marched in.

'The boy's having a shower,' the nurse said, smiling at him. 'He's feeling an awful lot better. A remarkable recovery, so says Dr Muller.'

'Excellent,' Stone replied.

The nurse nervously examined her watch. 'I'll hurry him along.'

Several minutes later, she returned. 'I can't get a reply, maybe you could try?'

Stone sensed worry in her tone and moved in front of the toilet door. 'Kemp, it's Commissioner Stone here. You OK in there, young man?'

They listened. Only the running of the shower could be heard.

'How long?' he said to the nurse.

'About ten minutes.'

'Ten minutes! Rats! Dickinson, open that door.'

The officer ran to the fire extinguisher and pulled it off the wall. Moments later, he smashed it against the lock like a battering ram.

The door swung open.

Stone ran in and searched the small cubicle. On the floor was the boy's medical gown.

'Oh, Christ alive!' Stone said as he slumped against the wall. 'He's gone.'

'What do you mean, gone?' the nurse said. 'It's impossible. I've been here the whole time.'

But they could all see it was empty.

'What the hell is going on?' Stone yelled. 'Where is that damned boy?'

Stone leant down and picked up the flimsy garment. As he did, a pile of fine, grey ash fluttered to the floor.

THE SONG OF THE TREES

However hard he tried, Old Man Wood simply couldn't speak properly. Words stuck in his throat and twisted in his mind.

The children looked at him with an equal combination of awe and concern.

'Would you like a cup of tea?' Archie asked. Wasn't that what grownups had when they needed comforting? That, or alcohol; perhaps he needed both.

The old man smiled and Archie took himself off to the kitchen. He pulled out the largest cup he could find and brewed a strong cup of tea. For good measure, he added a large dash of Old Man Wood's homemade spirits, knowing that every now and then Old Man Wood enjoyed a tipple. Archie took a small sip, grimaced, and spat it out in the sink. A bitter taste filled his mouth.

He found the sugar bowl, stirred in a couple of heaped teaspoons, sniffed the brew, then dipped a finger in and licked it.

He returned to the sitting room where he handed it to Old Man Wood who was sitting in his chair being comforted by the girls.

The old man beamed as he took the cup and blew on it until it was cool enough. Then he took a large gulp. 'Interesting tea, Archie,' he said, as his few remaining head hairs began to curl. He winked at Archie. 'Touch of my special brew…?'

Archie nodded.

'Clever boy!' he said, and in no time, Old Man Wood's face had returned to its familiar woody, ruddy complexion.

'If you're feeling ready to chat,' Isabella began softly, 'why don't you tell me about the bed, and why you're spying on us.'

'Hang on!' Daisy butted in, irritated that Isabella had sneaked in first. 'What about the Glade and Atrium thing-a-me?' Her questions were far more important. 'I mean it's another world, isn't it?'

'What about the poems and the rugs?' Archie said. 'And what and where are the tablets?'

Their questions got louder and louder as Old Man Wood listened patiently to their increasingly hysterical arguing while sipping his tea.

When he spoke, his words came out very softly but with an authority they hadn't heard before. 'First off, young'uns,' he said, as the children instantly quietened, 'we must find these tablets, as a matter of urgency.'

Archie pulled a face at the others.

'I'll try and piece things together for you,' the old man continued, 'because this goes back one heck of a long time, and it will not be easy.' He looked each one of them in the eye. 'Do you understand?'

They nodded.

He took a deep breath. 'Right, then. As you may have suspected, I am not exactly your "Uncle". You see, I have been here since the dawn of humankind—'

'Don't be silly,' Daisy laughed. She patted him playfully on the back. 'Heard it all now—'

'You can't be, you'd be long gone,' Archie added.

'That's impossible! Stop being so dramatic, Old Man Wood,' Isabella said. 'Archie, how much booze did you add—?'

'Ahhh. Hmmm, now then, my dear children. This is a great problem,' he continued. 'What can I say?' he regarded them lovingly. 'Thing is, I have lived in this house through the age of humans for an awfully long time, since way before your records even began. As a family, we moved several times to look around and see places and there have been many adventures. But it would not be inaccurate to say that I've been here on this hill for thousands of years... waiting, I believe, for this very moment.' Old Man Wood paused and his crinkly face lightened.

The children stared at him, not certain they'd heard him correctly.

'I've had the very greatest pleasure in bringing up generation after generation of my family and you three are the last in the line. You are... how can I put it... a little bit special.' Old Man Wood cupped his mug between his large, weathered hands, took another large sip. He beamed at each one in turn.

'And this house alone has seen a lot of rebuilding. Spent a great deal of time doing it, all by myself,' he chuckled. 'And you know what, most of them are pretty similar to the original, I suppose. It's been all manner of things from a forge, a school, a public house and a shop to name but a few. And, once upon a time, there used to be houses nearby. Now, what else? Well, not a lot at the moment, but I reckon it's coming back slowly.'

He held Isabella and Daisy's hands. 'You must have realised by now that all of these strange events, like your hair, and eyes, and hands, are connected to the rain and the rising water. I found it out from the trees at the Bubbling Brook; the ones I took you to see, Archie,' he said, turning to the boy who stared back with his mouth open.

'I did find them, you know, but I'm not sure I asked the right questions. You see, they memorised everything I ever told them and they'll tell it back, if you ask the right questions. But as I couldn't remember what was going to happen, or what I'm supposed to do, or… who I am... well...'

Isabella had had enough. 'This is utter madness!' she yelled. 'You're insane or sick, or blind drunk. I can't bear it.' Tears welled in her eyes as she pleaded with the others.

'Can't you see, he's deluded. He needs urgent medical attention.'

Archie pushed her down firmly. 'Wait, Isabella. Let him finish.' He'd noticed how Old Man Wood's eyes widened as he sipped the strong tea and how he hiccupped as if it were doing something to his brain.

'Madness or not, Bells,' he whispered, 'we need to hear this.'

'You see,' Old Man Wood continued, 'when I read those passages in Genesis in your Bible and laughed my head off, well, it's just that whoever wrote it must have had more than a couple of drinks in 'em and I know that for sure.' He flicked a glance at Archie.

'Pl-eeee-ase,' Daisy squeaked, 'what are you talking about?'

'The bit about how the world was created and all that, Daisy. I'm quite sure you know the one. The thing is, it doesn't say that much. In fact it doesn't really say anything at all. It is, I suppose, a story to start humankind off at a not-too-embarrassing-point.'

'Embarrassing point?' Daisy quizzed. 'I don't understand.'

'Oh, littluns. You'd think the greatest event of humankind, your creation and the creation of every other living thing here on Earth, would be given a few more believable lines. But, *hic*, as it happens, it was a story I told to some strange man sitting round a campfire as a bit of a joke, ha, ha.' He grinned and wiped his mouth with his sleeve.

'You see, life was a little complicated before all that—oh yes—*hic*. A tricky and bad time. It was after a few too many jars of Walterbrew as it happens. Now, there's a drink.'

He slurped on his tea, which had the effect of sending his hair curling outwards and his eyes bulging even more. 'Can't believe I remembered that.'

'Old Man Wood, I don't think you're well,' Isabella said, before addressing her siblings. She pointed at her head and twirled a finger. 'Seriously, we need to do something. He's totally lost it.'

The old man ignored her and carried on rambling. 'This bloke, you see, quite a clever fellow, terribly serious and, hmmm... well, it just seemed a good idea at the time. Couldn't resist it, I suppose, appley-entertaining.' He hiccupped again.

'There's truth in that passage, though. There really is another place full of treasure and things beyond one's wildest imagination. And Cain and his beast,' he spat, 'are hmmm... and the other thing is the flood...'

On the word "flood" he slurred badly, and Old Man Wood checked himself before belching. But he was on a roll and this wasn't going to stop him.

'Oh yes, I do feel a little guilty,' he continued, 'if you know what I mean. Well, you may say it's not possible, but I tell you it's true. I was there... amazing isn't it? I wrote those poems... did I say that? Such a long... what actually happened is quite different because, well... hmmm... all those places exist, or used to, rather like here, once. Otherwise you might get... now what the apples was I talking about?' he continued, forgetting himself.

A blink of lightning, followed by a ripple of thunder, sent a message that another storm was close by. It seemed to intensify the situation.

'Stop this rambling!' Isabella demanded. 'Just tell us, in plain English, what on earth it is you're talking about!'

Daisy, however, giggled and leaned in on him. 'Go on. Tell us, Old Man Wood. Tell us more.'

But now Old Man Wood, whose few head-hairs were standing erect on his head like the threads of a worn, wire brush, began humming a strange tune. And, as the rhythm built, it sounded as if wind was rushing through trees.

He clambered out of his chair and stood tall in the room. His big trunk filling the space in front of the fire, as a strange whooooshing and swissssshing sound came out of his mouth and vibrated round the room.

Moments later, his hands and body moved in a slow, graceful way, as the children looked on astonished.

After a short while, Old Man Wood fell heavily back in his chair.

Daisy perched on the arm. 'Tell us more about your song,' she began. 'It's beautiful.'

Old Man Wood smiled a little drunkenly and sipped his tea. 'I think it is the song of the trees,' he said. 'Reminds me of this whole other place from a time long ago. Feels apple-marvellous, though, doesn't it?'

'Teach it to us,' said Daisy, who was sitting on his other side.

Isabella gasped and shook her head violently in Daisy's direction.

'Really?'

'Oh, yes,' Daisy said at once, smiling sweetly.

'Liked it, did you?'

'Absolutely loved it,' Daisy said, beaming.

Old Man Wood couldn't refuse a smile like that. After taking another large swallow of tea, he climbed out of his chair.

'Whoooosh, swissshshhh, swissshy, swoosh,' he began, his eyes closed in concentration, his arms pulling slowly around like a gentle breaststroke motion.

Daisy stood up and copied him and was immediately right on track with Old Man Wood, as if she absolutely understood him.

Isabella, on the other hand, found it dreadfully embarrassing. The song and the movements didn't register one iota.

The pace built up.

As before, the deep vibrations of Old Man Wood's voice made the whole room tremble. And when the music reached its climax, a curious wind curled around them, and up their spines.

The children looked from one to the other and then back again.

'Encore, encore, more, more!' Daisy said, enraptured.

'Please, not again!' Isabella complained, just as the lights failed and the noise of the generator departed.

Now they heard only the sounds of their breathing, and the distant cracks and rumbles of a storm overhead. Archie ran off and found the lamps they'd used to highlight the rugs in the hallway. He positioned them on either side of the room, where they cast a deep orange glow.

Old Man Wood's face, now greatly accentuated by the soft rays, beamed from ear to ear.

Daisy clapped encouragingly. 'That was apple-tastic,' she said.

Old Man Wood drained the rest of his tea, and put the mug on the mantelpiece with a clatter.

He breathed in deeply and smacked his chest. 'This time,' he said, 'go a wee bit higher. Feel the tune in your blood. The song will take you there, if you believe in it.'

'Can I start?' Daisy said. 'It's really beautiful and moving, like being in paradise.'

Old Man Wood's booming laugh rebounded off the walls. 'That's exactly what it is! Clever littlun! Well, of course you can. I'll take it up as soon as you begin.'

Daisy began. She closed her eyes and extended her arms. 'Whoooosh, swishes, swiffy swissh whoooosh,' she hummed.

Old Man Wood smiled. Even if the Daisy didn't have a clue what the song meant, it thrilled him that the song resonated with her. He couldn't think how it had come to him, but it reminded him of a time when things in his head weren't quite so foggy and the song seemed to unlock a door into a room full of secrets.

He joined in, this time even more enthusiastically, whirring the strange noises in and out of his mouth. He gesticulated, slowly at first, with his strong arms and hands, building up his movements as the song increased in tempo. Before long, it sounded exactly like wind rushing through leaves in a big tree.

Suddenly, Archie had an idea.

He slipped out of his chair. While Isabella listened, shocked by Old Man Wood and Daisy's extraordinary movements and their swishing, whooshing noises, he crawled on all fours behind the back of the armchair to the fireplace. He located the poker and thrust it into the fire, shifting the logs in the embers. For a brief moment, he felt rather foolish.

Under his breath he recited the words of the poem.

'The first you hid in the heart of the house
'That warms you night and day
'Get it out by poking me,
'And singing your favourite song along the way!'

Archie looked up to see Daisy standing, copying Old Man Wood, humming and moving her arms in slow, controlled waves. She wore a huge smile on her face.

Isabella, on the other hand, lay on the sofa, her knees up to her chest with her head buried in her hands.

Archie picked up the rhythm and began to hum along. As he got the hang of it, he decided to bolster the fire up anyway, and thrust the poker in once again.

With a tiny flash, a strange flicker came out at him. Archie's heart skipped a beat.

He poked with a little more urgency. The light intensified.

He looked about. *Had anyone else seen it?* Daisy and Old Man Wood were singing as if in a trance. Isabella?

He turned his eyes back to the fire and found that, right before his eyes, an object very slowly approached. He could hardly breathe.

But Old Man Wood had come to the end of his song and, the moment he finished, whatever he had seen receded back into the orange glow.

CAIN'S DELIGHT

The boy was back! Ha! I knew he'd come—I was right! It had gone exactly to plan.

Cain wanted to thump the air in joy, or at least kick something. But he knew he needed to keep his energy levels in check this time around.

He hadn't worked out how they might communicate with each other, but he thought it was worth giving it a try.

'Boy, can you hear me?' he said, repeatedly, booming the words out.

Cain listened. Nothing. Perhaps this was the wrong approach.

In his head, he thought of a question very precisely.

I would like to know your name, boy! A tingle of noise returned and although it sounded like gibberish, he thought it might be worth developing.

He listened again. *There it …was again, a type of communication, though a bit echoey.*

Suddenly, another absolutely brilliant idea struck him. It was risky, but the boy had nowhere to go, and in the spirit of being honest with the child it had to be worth a try.

Cain ushered their ashen body onto the floor. Then, in the same way as he'd left the boy in a tree, Cain pushed out of the body, as though plying himself out of a thick, tight, rubber mould, only this time not doing it too fast or with quite as much force.

Now removed, Cain wrung his hands and looked down at the boy's naked torso sprinkled in ash.

Kemp stared back, spitting ash from his mouth. He sat up. 'You let me out?'

Cain audibly sighed from beside him. 'As I said, this time it will be different. This time, I need to look after you, I have to earn your trust, boy.'

Kemp realised the ghost genuinely meant it. 'My name, by the way, is Kemp,' Kemp said.

'Ah, so you heard?'

'Yeah. And please don't yell. I can hear you quite easily when you speak. Were you trying to think it, too? Felt like there was a filter in the way.'

Cain smiled. 'How interesting. Just as I suspected.'

Kemp began to dust himself down. 'Any chance of some clothes?'

'Of course, you may have whatever you wish,' Cain said and he picked up the bath cap which hovered nearby. 'Schmerger!' Cain yelled.

Shortly, his tidy manservant appeared with a long, neat, pointed black beard. He wore a strange black hat that muddled between a skullcap and a beret.

Kemp covered his privates.

'Find a robe for your new master, Schmerger. Quick, quick!'

Schmerger's almost expressionless face hinted of a frown, and his long nose bent down as he bowed. 'Sire.'

He returned with a burgundy robe adorned with golden snakes. Kemp slipped it on admiring the warm, light fabric and the patterns.

'Now for your welcome home surprise!' Cain said.

'Surprise?'

'Yes, yes. Come along, boy. Come along. Follow the strange hat!'

Kemp strode through an extraordinary building that looked somewhere between a vast cave and a palace. On one side, he saw jagged mountain rocks inlaid with jewels and gold. On the other, a vast chimney breast was flanked by huge windows and, at the very end was a wall filled with shelves filled with drawers. Everything, the furniture, the rocks, the windows and the floor were covered in dust.

Kemp ran his finger along a table top. 'Don't you have a cleaner?' he asked.

'I'm sorry?'

'The whole place is filthy!' Kemp said, brushing away more dust to reveal the surface underneath. 'Blimey, is that gold?'

'Oh, probably,' the hat replied. 'Gold is a bit common here. Wait till you see the jewel tables. I'm sure they're kicking about somewhere. They were particular favourites of mine.'

'Jewel-tables? What do you mean?'

'In the room I'm taking you to,' Cain said, 'there is a banqueting table made entirely from a seam of green emerald that would sit fifty of my guests. In the feasting chamber, there was a table top made entirely from one ruby. When I had eyes I used to enjoy the rich varieties of the reds, especially under a bright moon. Though, I remember that daylight made the whole experience a little overbearing. Terrific for masking blood of a good murder. In all the reception rooms we have table tops made entirely from diamonds, sapphires, and various other glittering stones.

'Well, nothing glitters anymore,' Kemp said. 'This place, is disgusting.'

The hat stopped. 'My dear boy, there has been very little I could do about it. But now that you're here, it's the perfect opportunity to get my— I mean, *our*— palace back into shape.'

The hat continued on into the great chamber until they arrived at a two huge, dark wooden doors.

'Go on, open it.'

Kemp pushed the door. As he did, the smell of roast chicken, fried bacon, and all sorts of other delights wafted over him. 'Food!' he cried. 'Real food. Tons of it!'

The glowing green table top was crammed with an assortment of chocolates, fruit, cake, and meats of all sorts. Kemp made his way over, his eyes wide. 'All this, for me?'

'Indeed. You now have a kitchen and Schmerger has found chefs, to use as you wish.'

Without hesitation, he tucked in.

Cain listened to the sounds of his eating, intrigued. 'You know, boy, I think our relationship is going to be quite splendid. Why don't you tell me your preferred hours of sleeping, your meal times, and other things you like doing. That way, when you're not with me, you can do as you wish unless I require you for, say, important business, or emergencies.'

Kemp reckoned this beat hospital a million times over. 'As long as there's a cold shower nearby before I join you.'

'Yes, good thinking. Was it easier?'

'Oh, yeah. Miles. I hardly felt a thing.'

'Any other demands?'

Kemp licked his lips. 'The deal with my mother, Cain. She must be saved. I'm sure she'd love it here.'

'Of course,' Cain said. 'I will do what I can to honour this.'

'And I'd like to see my mate, Archie,' he said.

'That would be Archie de Lowe?'

'Yes.'

Cain grinned. He liked this boy more and more. 'Who knows, Kemp, if we play our cards right, perhaps we could get him to come here permanently.'

'That would be utterly brilliant!' Kemp enthused. 'I can just imagine it. We'd have a blast.'

'You certainly would,' Cain said. 'But all in good time, Kemp. All in good time.

After my terrible treatment of you, I feared you would shun me for death. Now, I could not imagine a better way in which we have patched up our differences.'

The ghost was ecstatic. He had the boy back, his virus was breaking out all over planet Earth as humans slept, and the Heirs of Eden were not even close to finding the tablets. But there was one thing that would make this day even more perfect.

He remembered the poison, the lethal Havilarian Toadstool Powder that he had poured into the sugar bowl at Eden Cottage on the night he'd first met Archie.

Cain had nipped into the kitchen and, using his heightened senses, located sweet sugar granules—the perfect mask for such a deadly poison.

Havilarian Toadstool Powder was a substance made from tiny, microscopic, squealing little toadstools which sucked the life out of anyone who imbibed it. And although it was useless to humans, the powder was lethal to those who came from the Garden of Eden, those who, in other circumstances, could not die.

He rubbed his invisible hands together. *What were the chances,* he wondered, *that the old man had already helped himself to a nice, sweet drink?*

What were the chances, he thought, *that the old man was already writhing in agony, with tiny toadstools helping themselves to his flesh and blood, eating him away so that he would end up as helpless as he had been?*

Cain even imagined the scene of the old man supping a hot drink, steam rising from his mug, just like the humans used to do in the tea caverns of Havilaria, while the Heirs of Eden looked on at his painful demise in horror.

He tilted his head back and roared into the high ceiling.

Life, was getting better and better.

SUE'S MESSAGE

Seeing Old Man Wood like this made Isabella as unhappy as she could ever remember. As his song ended, she slipped off to the kitchen where she heard the gentle drone of the generator and worked out that it might run for another fifteen minutes or so if they were lucky.

For a while, she thought she might slope off to bed and leave them to it but instead, she flicked on the telly with the remote control and opened the fridge to see if Mrs Pye had left anything worth snacking on. She peered inside. Nothing she fancied, so she grabbed an apple, sat down and took a large bite.

For a while she watched news repeats going round and round in a loop.

She bit in hard again, wiping juice off her chin as a message announced itself in bold red letters.

"AN IMPORTANT ANNOUNCEMENT."

Daisy and Archie came in just as the picture changed. It showed a live feed from a press office filled with weary-looking officials.

A tall, grey haired man, with a moustache and a pointed nose, made his way to the lectern. An elegant, lady, the new Deputy Prime Minister, introduced him as the chief coordinator of the flood crisis, Commissioner Stone.

'First of all,' he began, 'I speak on behalf of the COBRA unit to offer my thanks to all those who have dug deep in keeping the citizens of our island safe at this terrible time. The help and resolve given by so many continues to touch the lives of millions.

'I will be frank,' he said, looking directly into the camera, 'this epidemic, the so called Yorkshire Plague or Ebora, reached all parts of the country overnight. There is no *logic to its method nor is there a cure. Not yet at any rate. Medical centres are overwhelmed as doctors, who do not have symptoms themselves, struggle to keep up. If you think you may have the symptoms, please ring our helpline number at the bottom of the screen. Our advice is to be patient, drink plenty of fresh water and keep warm. And please, stay at home.'*

He shifted and smiled. *'While many suffer, we have heard stories of immense bravery and heroism. We're going to share some real-life situations from the flooding. These are tales of dogged British resilience. And above all,'* he said, his voice quivering, *'they are stories of hope.'*

The screen cut from the press conference to a beach, where waves crashed someway behind the sand. On it, a reporter waited for the link-up.

'Here I am, near the beautiful Suffolk coastal town of Southwold,' he said. The camera panned to a lighthouse and then to the colourful beach huts. *'Famous for its beer, and as an upmarket holiday resort, last night it was the scene of an extraordinary rescue. I'm handing you over to Serena Strutt who continues the story.'*

'Thank you, Bill,' said Serena, her perfect smile beaming at the camera. *'On the day of the storm, two children from the village of Upsall in North Yorkshire found a rickety old rowing boat in a run-down boathouse. They built a canopy over the vessel from odds and ends, and survived what is now understood to be one of the most vicious storm ever recorded.*

'Against incredible odds, they were spotted by the local coastguard during a fierce gale off this very coast. These remarkable children were subsequently saved.'

The children watched in silence, mesmerised. They were huddled together, their arms locked around one another.

'I have with me here, one of the survivors, Sue Lowden.'

The moment the words were out of the reporter's mouth the kitchen erupted. Daisy and Archie leapt up and down, screaming their heads off. Isabella sank to the floor, tears free-falling down her cheeks.

'Sue,' Serena said, *'what an amazing story. I know you're still quite numb from your experience, especially as Gus Williams, your partner on the boat, has gone to hospital, but please tell us more.'*

The camera moved and Sue came into shot. She'd lost weight but her eyes sparkled. *'I just want to thank Gus,'* her eyes began welling up, *'he was amazing.'*

'At snogging,' Archie quipped.

'Oh, shut up,' the girls said together.

Back on the screen, Sue recalled some of their adventures, such as how they'd escaped the boathouse, made a sail, and caught a fish.

Serena Strutt shook her head. *'Sue, what a truly astonishing story. Of course, our thoughts are with Gus. Is there anything else you'd like to say?'*

Sue looked down at her feet as if trying to rein in her emotions. Then, very slowly, and as the camera zoomed in on her face, she looked directly into the lens. *'Infected now,'* she said sadly, before adding, *'lush.'*

For a second, Serena looked confused, but undeterred, she draped an arm around the girl. *'Thank you, Sue. I know this is a very emotional time, and we wish Gus a speedy recovery. From Southwold, back to you in the studio.'*

The sense of joy in the kitchen was extraordinary. But, while Archie and Daisy danced around, Isabella sat down at the kitchen table with a pen and paper. She was instantly struck by the oddness of Sue's remark. Sue never, ever, used words like "lush". That was a Daisy kind-of-a-word, not a Sue word.

Daisy pulled a chair up. 'What's up, sis? Thought you be jumping over the moon.'

Isabella shook her head. 'Inside, I am, believe me. But something's wrong. That sentence at the end—it wasn't what Sue would ordinarily say in any circumstances.' She pushed the pencil through the hole in her hand and spun it round making a strange starry shadow on the paper.

'Doesn't "lush" mean, "cool".'

'Yeah, that's right. Gorgeous, lush, peng, whatevs. You're right, though. It was as if she'd worked something out.'

'Maybe you're right. What if she planned this, for us?' Isabella wrote down the sentence on the paper and looked at it.

She rearranged the letters in a circle and tried to see if there was a pattern or some obvious code. As she pondered the letters she asked: 'Archie, why don't you check on Old Man Wood.'

Archie slipped out of the kitchen and returned a couple of minutes later. 'He's wandering around with his hair sticking out on end. I think he's, sort of, OK.' He hesitated. 'Look, while you were singing that hummy song, a weird object came out of—'

'Sweet mothers!' Isabella exclaimed. 'I think I've got it!'

Daisy and Archie crowded round.

'Take the word, "*Infected*",' she began. 'In it is the word, "*find*". She crossed out the letters. Now, what's left? "*The*". She crossed that out as well.

They stared at the paper. Daisy clapped her hands. 'Look! The word "uncle".'

'Excellent,' Isabella said, surprised by her sister's quick grasp of anagrams. 'Which leaves', she continued, '"S, O, W".'

'Find the uncle sow,' Archie said, 'or, wos. You think she meant Old Man Wood?'

'Possibly,' Isabella replied, pulling the pen in and out of her hand-hole. 'But it's not like her to make a glaring error like that. She knows perfectly well what his name is. Hang on, what if it's *"clown"*. Then you've got, *"E, U, S"*.'

'Sue?' Daisy said. 'That's it! *"Find the clown, Sue"*.'

Isabella shook her head. 'It doesn't stack up.' She stood up and, like Archie, began pacing the room. 'I mean what could she possibly be referring to?'

Daisy sat down in her place, and played with the letters again, her eyes casting a gentle pink light over the paper.

She rearranged the final letters and clapped her hands.

Isabella ran over, studied the paper, and squeezed Daisy's shoulders.

'Archie,' she ordered, 'make another cup of that tea for Old Man Wood, exactly the same as before.'

'You sure?' he said. 'With a dash of his special brew? You realise it might kill him.'

'Yes! Add more sugar if you think it's too vile. Just do it, now!'

'God. OK, but why? You saw what happened to him—'

'Archie, it's Sue's message. Daisy's cracked it.'

He skipped over and read it out loud.

'FIND THE CLUES, NOW.'

From the sitting room, they heard a deep groan. The children turned towards the door.

'He was fine a minute ago.'

'He's probably crashed out on your tea, Archie,' Daisy said, grinning.

'The least we can do is make sure he's comfortable,' Isabella said.

They trooped back into the living room, a room they barely recognised as paper, canvas, and pictures littered every inch of floor.

'Lord above!' Isabella whispered. 'If Mrs Pye sees this, she's going to go utterly mental.'

'It's a warzone—'

'Chill, guys,' Daisy cut in.

Archie re-lit a couple of candles and joined the girls next to Old Man Wood on the sofa.

'He's fast asleep,' Isabella said.

Daisy wasn't so sure. 'Yoo-hoo. Old Man Wood, you there?'

He groaned.

'Hi,' she said, resting a hand on his forehead. 'You should go to bed. There's a busy day coming up.'

A flicker at the corner of his mouth. 'I... I think—' he whispered before slumping back.

Daisy smiled. 'You think you're a bit worse for wear, eh, Old Man Wood?'

The old man suddenly looked ashen-grey and withered and old. He tried to sit up, his eyes bloodshot.

The children gasped.

'Poison,' he spat. 'You've got to—'

'Poison?' Isabella exclaimed. 'What poison?'

Old Man Wood tried to speak but the words wouldn't form. His bony hand grabbed Isabella's wrist. She squealed as he gripped it hard and levered his head off the pillow. He stared at her with watery, scared eyes, 'Y-o-u... y-o-u-r... p-o-w-errrr...'

And then his grip loosened and his head fell back slowly onto the pillow like a stone falling through water. His eyes shut.

A look of peace descended over him.

The stillness in the room was deafening.

Stunned, the children instinctively stepped back as a huge rumble of thunder rolled over the cottage, rattling the glass in the windows.

'Holy smoke!' Archie said, trembling. He fell to his knees and wiped a tear from his eye. 'I think we've just killed Old Man Wood.'

WATER TREATMENT

Lying on the sofa opposite the fire, Old Man Wood was as still and as white as a stone sculpture. The gentle embers from the fire glowed red and orange, lighting the hearth and accentuating the old man's pale, drawn features.

The children peered over him in shock, their lips trembling.

Tears rolled freely down Archie's cheeks. 'I killed him,' he said. 'The only person who had a hope in hell of figuring out what's going on, and I think I murdered him with a cup of tea.' His lip wobbled. 'I only added sugar and a shot of homemade liquor...'

Daisy shook her head. 'He's not dead.'

'Yes, he is! He hasn't moved or breathed for ages—'

'Don't you listen to a word? He told us he can't die,' Daisy said. 'He said he was our great, great, you-know, loads of great grandfathers, or whatever. Therefore, Archie, it's impossible he's dead, isn't it?'

Archie looked at her, confused. 'But he's not breathing and what if he made that stuff up.'

Isabella reached in and placed two fingers on his neck. 'There is a pulse, Archie. It's weak but it's definitely there. Have a feel.'

Archie replaced her fingers with his, scrunched his face but shook his head. 'I can't feel anything.'

For some time, there was an awkward silence.

Finally, Daisy couldn't bear it any longer. 'What do you think we should do?' she said. 'Let him sleep it off? We have to do *something*.'

'If he doesn't wake up,' Archie replied, 'how will we find the other tablets.' He sat down on the arm of the armchair and gently slapped the old man's face trying to rouse him. Then he pinched his cheek.

'Come on, Old Man Wood. Wakey-wakey,' he said gently. 'Please, Old Man Wood, you've got to wake up—'

'Water!' Daisy said. 'Let's shock him with a bucket of ice-cold water. That's what they do in films. Or we could give him a shot of whisky.'

'NOT alcohol,' Archie said. 'He's had far, far too much of that—'

Without listening, Daisy whizzed off and returned with a bucket half-full of cold water. She thrust it in Archie's direction. 'You killed him, so you do it.'

Archie took the bucket but stood still, appalled by the prospect. 'I only did it because Isabella told me to and she wanted me to make another one. It was Isabella's idea, so she should do it.'

They turned to their elder sister.

'Absolutely no way,' Isabella said firmly. 'If you think a water shock is the best idea, then I suggest you both do it.'

The twins looked at one another.

'And anyway, what if he wakes up and properly freaks out?' Archie said.

'Old Man Wood would never do such a thing—'

'Daisy, didn't you notice what happened before? He's unhinged. What if he's now permanently crackers?'

'Unhinged?'

'Well, yeah, he's damaged, possibly beyond repair. You know, like a crazed lunatic psychopath, or worse.'

'Archie, if you haven't cottoned on by now, the whole world has gone crazy, and we're right in the middle of it.' Daisy said. 'Here, give it to me.'

In one movement, Daisy grabbed the bucket and emptied the contents in a long stream directly over Old Man Wood's head, the water flowing over his nose, down the deep lines of his face, and onto his chest.

Instinctively, the twins took a step or two backwards, in case Old Man Wood suddenly stood up and flailed his thick arms.

But Old Man Wood's deathly mask didn't budge.

The twins turned to each other, laughing nervously, and slightly in awe of the volume of water soaking the sofa and carpet.

Daisy's eyes were wide open. 'Still nothing?'

'I told you he was dead,' Archie said, his face crumpling.

Daisy shook her head. 'But why would Old Man Wood lie about death like that? He would never, ever do such a thing. It just doesn't add up.'

❄

Daisy's acute hearing tuned into the TV. Commissioner Stone, she heard, was thanking the various officers around him and trying to placate viewers that the nation shouldn't be too worried. He sounded confident. *'One final thing,'* he said, a crooked smile crossing his face, *'we now know that the epicentre of the storm centred on the small moor-side village of Upsall…'*

In a flash, she ran back in the kitchen.

'Archie, Isabella!' Daisy called out. 'You dudes should watch this.'

'We'd particularly like to speak to anyone who was in the area of Upsall the day the storm broke,' the Commissioner continued, as Archie and Isabella came in. *'We know many were tragically lost and almost certainly swept away, like the brave Gus Williams and Sue Smith, who we heard from earlier.'*

Another camera honed in on the lean, moustachioed face of Commissioner Stone. Clumsily, Stone turned towards it.

'But there is one family we know whose three children were on the football pitch at that time. There's no doubt the floodwater took them, but if anyone has seen or heard from any of them, particularly this young man on your screen now, Archie de Lowe, then please get in touch with your local authority representative.'

A picture of Archie, a couple of years younger, filled the screen.

Archie could feel his hair hardening. 'Jeez,' he said. 'Why me?'

'Who is the only person,' Isabella asked, 'who they know, who knows you?'

Archie squinted trying to work out what she meant.

'Kemp. That's who,' Isabella said, as she wheeled away. 'You're a fool, Archie. I told you not to trust him.'

'Oh!' Daisy exclaimed. 'I forgot to tell you guys something. You know when he said those words in the hospital—'

'"Algae", and, er "Dunno"… wasn't it?' Archie said.

'Those exactly. Well, I reckon he was trying to contact you.'

'What do you mean?'

'For "Algae" read, "Archie",' Daisy said. 'And for "Dunno", read—'

'"de Lowe",' Archie finished.

They looked at each other. 'Do you think he was trying to warn me?'

'Almost certainly,' Daisy said.

Isabella shrugged. 'Looks like we'll never know. But what we do know is that, because of him, they're now hot on our trail.'

A QUESTION OF BALANCE

Gaia appeared in a tiny flash.

'I see you.'

'And I you,' Genesis replied.

'Our species is ill, Genesis. Asgard has taken the dreamspinners in a direction I am deeply uncomfortable with.'

The old dreamspinners dipped two legs into her maghole, pulled them out, and inspected them for wear.

'It is the way of the universe, Gaia. Do you understand how this works? Are you aware of what is going on?'

'I do not comprehend what you mean,' Gaia replied.

'Great changes are coming to the universes, changes which affect us all. These great events are not just selected for humankind, or elven kind, or for the great trees in all the worlds. These changes are sent to challenge the great Elders, the ones who have been here since the beginning.'

'Like Adam?'

'Exactly. And the changes will also test dreamspinners, too. We have been here, forged from gas and dust and light, right from the very beginning. Our role has always been to show life in a different way. That way is being questioned.'

'Are you suggesting the rules by which we have stuck are broken?'

'I am suggesting, dear Gaia, that our story is about to be written again. If we are not smart, then we will, as Asgard suggested, die, because we have not forged a new path.'

'You agree with that rogue, Asgard?' said Gaia.

'I do not. But I do believe in balance.'

'How?'

'Simple, Gaia. We must always seek balance. If it cannot be found, we make it.'

'We change?'

'Yes. Now, you understand. We too must evolve,' the dreamspinners said, flashing his long arms. 'Asgard has a head start on us. It is time for us to catch him up.'

A FINAL SONG

'We're going to have to sing this song again,' Archie said. 'Like it or not.'

'How are we going to do it without Old Man Wood?'

'Easy. I think I've got the rhythm and the sounds,' Daisy said.

Isabella bowed her head. 'Then why don't you start us off?' she said.

'Thing is, darling, it's important we all join in,' Daisy said. 'Can I suggest we draw straws to see who's going to lead?'

They did.

'Isabella, it's you. Take it away!'

'But I was hopeless at it.'

'Try!'

Isabella stood up and closed her eyes. She tried to get the first words out, but for some reason, and however hard she tried, the words stuck in her throat.

Daisy simply hadn't registered Isabella's discomfort from earlier. She had an idea.

'Let's start together. Archie, all we need is one lamp for cool atmospherics, and then we'll hold hands.'

'Really? We're not at kindergarten, or a bunch of hippies.'

'We're just holding hands, dudes. Listen, Bells, it won't hurt, I promise,' Daisy said. 'Then, I think we should think hard about Old Man Wood and the fire and mum and dad, and Sue and Gus, and think about everything in our dreams, everything that's happened. Think of all the things we really love. You know, quietly. A kind of inner moment—'

'Why?' Archie asked.

'Because, you numpty, if we don't do this properly we're going to be stuck here without any tablets and with a dead old man and then everyone will die from the disease, horribly, including you. And besides, it'll get us in the mood to sing our socks off.'

In the dim light, Daisy sat next to the sofa and held Old Man Wood's cold hand in one and Isabella's in her other. Soon they were all linked.

Rumbling sounds of a nearby storm peppered the sky overhead.

'On the count of three,' Daisy whispered, 'then, just go with the flow.'

With their eyes shut the countdown commenced.

Archie began swaying. Before long, a soft hum emanated from him. Isabella, her eyes shut as well, also began to move from side to side.

Daisy was a little surprised. She shut her eyes and thought of Old Man Wood. She tried to imagine him as a young man, full of hope singing the song of the trees on the strange planet he'd mentioned.

She began swaying and let her mind empty. Much to her surprise, an image of Kemp drifted in, refusing to budge. She shook her head, but decided to run with it anyway to see where it would lead.

A large roll of thunder boomed around the house, the noise shuddering through them.

'Sssshhh, woohshhhh,' Isabella began, her voice no more than a whisper.

Daisy joined in, Kemp's image gone, her mind blank.

'Hummm, swiff, swishy, wwoooosh,' Daisy sang, as the vibration of the words moved up through her body, feeling their way through her tendons and into her capillaries.

Now Archie joined in, this time more enthusiastically, whirring the strange noises in and out of his mouth. He started slowly at first, building up as the song increased in tempo, so that before long he'd made it sound like the wind rushing through leaves.

Another cackle of thunder.

'Swiffy, swoooosh, swissh, hummmy, whooo, whoooosh.'

Isabella, her eyes tight, let go of Old Man Wood's hands and, instinctively, Daisy, and then Archie joined her.

Together the children stood in front of the embers of the fire and joined hands again.

Goosebumps ran up their backs.

The tempo increased, the song getting louder and louder.

'Swwooosh, swiiishshhhhi, swisshshhh, woooosh.'

Archie, sensing the moment, took the song up an octave, and in no time was consumed by the mesmeric, chanting tones.

Suddenly, from rather sad embers, the fire exploded into life.

Isabella and Daisy, without even realising, raised the tune up even further with louder hummy, swishy, and whooshy noises.

The momentum grew and grew. They unlocked their hands and whirled their arms in the air.

Rain battered the farmhouse, lightning flashed and thunder crashed.

'Swiffy, hummm swish sshshh. Swiffy swissh whoooosh, swissshshhh hmmm...'

Louder and louder.

Daisy suddenly took the piece to a whole new level, roaring the song out. Isabella climbed an octave higher, and as they did, wind flew around the room, sweeping over them.

Archie opened his eyes. Daisy's hair stood fully erect on her head and her face had the look of a wild, sea-worn pirate. Her ruddy eyes set off her smooth skin, her face flickered in the firelight, and her concentration was absolute.

Isabella, by contrast, had tears spilling from of the corners of her eyes.

The storm outside crashed about, rain lashing violently down onto the tiles of the old building. Flashes of lightning illuminated the room as a massive crack of thunder shook the building.

A whirring noise, as if a thousand ghosts had swept into the room at once snapped every hair on the children's bodies to attention.

Now they flailed their arms around wildly as an extended gust of wind picked up a bundle of papers and littered them around the room like confetti.

'Did anyone open a window?' Daisy shouted over the din, trembling a little in awe as the wind whirled around her. But her voice was drowned out by the music and the bangs and cracks of thunder.

The song mellowed. Bits of paper floated gently to floor.

Daisy and Isabella, soaked in sweat, looked over to Archie, lost amidst the muddle of paper and debris.

From out of nowhere they saw a fabulous smile spread across his face. And they could hardly believe what they saw, for in his hand was an ancient, stone tablet. On the top, etched in gold, was the emblem of the Tree of Life, a tree with roots that joined with the branches forming a globe.

'Oh, my... oh, my,' Daisy cried. 'Look! Isabella! It's true! The tablet!'

They said it together:

'The first you hid in the heart of the house
'That warms you night and day
'Get it out by poking me
'And singing your favourite song along the way.'

Archie thumped the air as they jumped up and down. 'One down, two to go!' he said.

And then he turned to the sleeping figure on the sofa and knelt down in front of him. 'Hey, Old Man Wood, you weren't so hopeless after all!'

GOODY BAG

Golden brown in colour, hard as steel and inlaid with beautiful scrollwork, the tablet from the fire was roughly the size and weight of a paperback book. As Archie touched it, a cosy tingle, like the warmth of love, burst over him.

He traced the engraved surfaces, running his fingers along the lines of the symbol of the Tree of Life. Its characteristic swirls mirrored up and down, and he noted that it was the same artwork they had seen on the walls of the cave, and on his knives.

They passed it round, marvelling at its beauty.

'Look,' Isabella said, as she handed it carefully over to Archie. 'I don't know what to say.'

'Well, you should be thrilled to bits that Sue's alive—'

'And Gus too,' Daisy added. 'He's such a hero.'

'Yes, of course,' Isabella said, beaming. 'What I meant,' and she stuttered, trying to find the right words, 'what I really meant to say, was, thanks.'

'Thanks? For what?' Daisy replied.

'For not believing a word I was talking about,' Isabella said.

'We never do, anyway,' Daisy responded, raising her eyebrows. 'Here, you have it again, Isabella.' Daisy said, handing her the tablet and rising from the kitchen table.

Isabella momentarily looked furious but quickly pulled the tablet to her lips. Just as with Archie, a glow, a rush, a joyful sensation shot into her. It was like a fizz of confidence that pushed her fears and worries sideways.

Isabella smiled and pulled it to her chest. 'Look, I'm so sorry I didn't believe you, I just couldn't. Now, I can see how massively wrong I've been. By the way, where's the paper you wrote the poems on?'

Archie pulled it out of his pocket and handed it over.

Isabella read it and frowned as Daisy returned to the table.

'Looks like there's a problem?' Daisy said.

'Just a bit,' Isabella said, and she proceeded to read the last poem:

'You have but seven days and nights
'As Earth moves in its cycle.
'From first lightning strike and thunderclap
'The world waits your arrival.'

'I was right,' Daisy said. 'Remember, Archie? I told you I thought we had seven days—'

Isabella put her hands up. 'I've been holding this whole thing up, haven't I?' She bit her lip. 'And we've got to find two more of these little beauties in three days.'

'So?' Daisy said.

'It took us three days just to find this one.'

'Only because you were poncing about, being all sciencey and dull.' Daisy said.

On any other occasion, Isabella would have torn into her. 'I know, and I'm sorry,' she said. 'Truly sorry.'

Daisy smiled and pulled out a bag. 'We'll find the next one in the morning. The one about searching for Blabisterberry Jelly, or whatever it's called. Right now, it's about time we started to look the part.'

Daisy reached in and slipped on her metal-rimmed, pink-lens spectacles.

She tossed the bag to Archie who pulled out a hat and he passed it on to Isabella.

'What is it?' Isabella asked.

'Just put it on. You too, Archie.'

'Seriously?' he said. 'Do I have to?'

Isabella opened the bag, her face full of questions, and removed the contents.

'Go on,' Daisy insisted.

'Studded, fingerless, black leather gloves?'

'Absolutely!' Daisy clapped. 'Mrs Pye and I have made some adjustments. Same with yours, Archie. Hope they fit.'

Isabella slipped them on and was amazed to find how comfortable they were. 'What's with the stud popper thing in the middle?'

'Oh, that's a trouser popper. Mrs P's idea, so your gloves don't slip off.'

Isabella didn't know whether to laugh or cry. 'Oh, Daisy, I don't know—'

Daisy leaned over the table and put a finger to her sister's lips. 'Sshh. No more excuses, Bells. If we're going to save the world, we might as well try and look the part. In any case, it's time, sister, that you had a bit more bling.'

Mrs Pye had reinforced Archie's beret with leather patches for his spike-ends, and added three studs around the rim.

'Oh, you do look handsome, my dear Archie,' Daisy joked. 'In a rugged, French-peasant kind of way.'

Isabella was impressed. 'That, Daisy, is a very good idea.'

'Yup,' she agreed. 'No more getting poked by his hair, right?' Daisy shot off and returned holding Isabella's phone.

Isabella knew exactly what she was thinking and burst out laughing.

Archie protested, 'Please, Daisy. What now?'

'I think,' Daisy said, mischievously, 'that it's time for a very special selfie!'

Moments later as the shutter clicked on the camera, they heard a deep groan. The children turned towards the door.

'Old Man Wood!' Isabella said.

They rushed back into the living room, a room they now barely recognised. Paper, canvas, and pictures littered every inch of the floor.

'If Mrs Pye comes in,' Isabella whispered, 'she's going to have a heart attack. It's a war zone—'

'If we don't find the remaining tablets, Bells,' Archie said, 'then there won't be a world left in which she can offload her tidiness anger. We'll deal with it later. Hey, he's under there—'

'And fast asleep,' Isabella said.

Daisy wasn't so sure. 'Old Man Wood, are you there?'

He groaned, and they looked at one another nervously.

'Please, Old Man Wood! Wake up,' Archie said, his heart thumping in his chest. 'Please don't be dead…'

The old man twisted his head slightly.

'Old Man Wood?' Archie cried, relief flooding his voice. 'Thank goodness! You're back!'

'Careful Arch,' Daisy said. 'He's so drunk on your alcoholic tea he might well spew all over you!'

'Thank you for those lovely, sweet words, Daisy,' Isabella said, nudging her sister in the ribs. 'Typically thoughtful, and timely.'

She moved beside Old Man Wood. 'Let's make you comfortable, shall we,' Isabella said, resting a hand on his forehead. 'He's terribly hot. Too hot, almost as if his skin's prickling,' she said to the others.

'We should get you to bed, Old Man Wood. Busy day ahead tomorrow. More tablets to find.'

A flicker crumpled the corner of his mouth. 'I... I think—' he whispered before slumping back.

'What?' Daisy said. 'You think you're still a bit—'

'No, Daisy!' Isabella cut in. 'He's been poisoned. Just look at him.'

The old man's face was withered and grey and he groaned as he tried to sit up.

'What were you saying?' Isabella asked, sweetly.

'...you found it,' Old Man Wood croaked. 'I knew you would.'

They smiled widely, delighted, and relieved to hear him speak.

'You must move on to the next task without me. Please, hurry.'

'You're coming too,' Archie said. 'Not sure we can do it on our own.'

The old man, washed saliva into his mouth and prepared to talk again. 'Maybe. Maybe not,' was all he said, closing his eyes.

Isabella leant down and kissed him on his forehead. Daisy followed.

'Sleep well, Old Man Wood,' Archie said.

'Let's see if we can get him up to his bed,' Isabella said.

'How?' Archie replied. 'He's a very large, heavy man.'

Daisy nudged him. 'Oh, come on, Archie. You're the world's strongest boy. It's time you proved it.'

To be continued...

Want to find out what happens?
Go straight to your store.

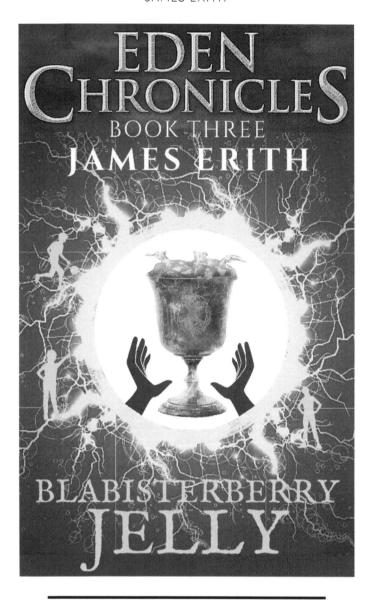

Read Book Three, Blabisterberry Jelly, NOW!

<<<<>>>>

BOOK THREE - BLABISTERBERRY JELLY

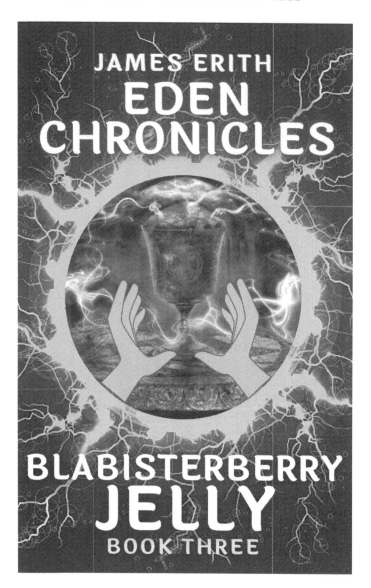

The Riddles

'The first you hid in the heart of the house
'That warms you night and day
'Get it out by poking me,
'And singing your favourite song along the way!

'For the second one you have to find
'You burp it from the family belly.
'To do this, you have to eat
'Blabisterberry jelly!

'The third you search for is underneath your nose.
'It's clear, pure and cold.
'In order to draw it out
'You need to send a rose.

'Put them all together,
'Then get out of the way
'What you find will prove a guide
'For all the other worlds.

'You have but seven days and seven nights
'As Earth moves in its cycle
'From first lightning strike and thunderclap
'The world awaits your arrival.'

DEAD, OR ALIVE

'He weighs a ton,' Archie complained.

'For crying out loud, Archie, you pulled that tree out and carried me miles, and pushed an enormous ten-ton boulder out of a cave.' She rolled her eyes. 'Come on, get with the programme.'

Archie shook his head and turned red. He groaned. 'But I can't do it *all* the time, Daisy. I'm not super-strong now. It's only when I'm angry or really need it.'

'Then I'm going to make you angry, Winkle,' she said using his detested nickname very slowly and deliberately. 'Very, very angry indeed.'

'Don't, I'm not in the mood.'

Daisy ignored him. 'Winkle, Winkle, Winkle—'

'Stop it!'

Daisy grinned maliciously. 'Where's Isabella? She's usually pretty good at helping me with this kind of thing.'

Isabella yawned and stood up. 'Here, watching you both.' She kicked at a bundle of debris on the floor. 'I hate to be the bearer of obvious news, but if Mrs. Pye walks in here, she's going to have a heart attack.'

'Big deal,' Daisy said. 'She could help us move Old Man Wood if superman-boy here refuses to co-operate.'

Isabella laughed. '"Superman-boy"? That has to be the worst hero-label of all time,' she crowed. 'Logically, shouldn't it be "Super-boy"?'

'Oh, Bells. Really?' Daisy said. 'That is so, so... lame.' She studied her watch. 'Anyway, Mrs. Pye won't be over until supper. So either we go to her now and explain what's been going on and how Old Man Wood ended up dead—or comatose—or we have an hour to get Old Man Wood into his bed and back to normal.'

The children looked at one another.

'Well, come on brain-box,' Daisy said to Isabella. 'Stop thinking and give us a hand.'

Isabella grabbed some matches and lit several candles en-route to Old Man Wood's bedroom.

Then, with a terrible struggle, the children managed, huffing and puffing, to drag the huge figure of Old Man Wood to the foot of the stairs.

'Archie, it is incredibly inconsiderate of you not to find this strength of yours when we could really do with it,' Isabella stormed.

'Yeah, isn't it just,' Archie said, struggling under the dead-weight of the old man's shoulders. 'Can you please grab him—I can't hold him here forever.'

'No.'

Archie summoned his strength. 'Look, guys, I don't know how my muscle thing works, OK?'

Daisy marched up to him and slapped him hard around the face, the noise cracking like a whip.

'What was that for?'

'Because you need to focus and start controlling this gift of yours—'

'But there's no need to hit me.'

'Yes, of course there is! Get a grip.'

Archie reddened and his mace-like hair visibly tightened. 'Daisy, I'll get you back for this.' He took a deep breath. 'You two hold a leg each.'

Archie lifted and, almost as if he wasn't trying, he started up the stairs bearing almost the entire weight of Old Man Wood.

In no time, Old Man Wood lay in his bed. The flicker of light from a lone candle emphasised the deep wooden carvings on his bed, and the soft glow of the panels at the foot of his bed highlighted the lines on his face.

'I hope he'll be all right,' Isabella said as she pulled the duvet up over his body. 'It can't be good for a man his age to be ill like this.' She laid a hand on his forehead.

'What if he really has been poisoned? I mean, that's what *he* thought it was— he definitely said something about poison,' she said. 'But where would it have come from? And why aren't we all infected?'

'Maybe he caught the virus we heard about on the telly?' Daisy said, as she also rested a hand on Old Man Wood's brow. 'What if he caught it from visiting those trees he told us about—you know the ones, Archie.'

'You're right,' he said. 'He went right underwater—whereas I didn't.'

'But *I* did,' Daisy said.

'Did what?'

'Got drenched when I fell in the ditch on the way to that weird atrium place. And I'm all right, I think.' She randomly sniffed her armpit as if that was an indicator of health.

Isabella squeezed her shoulder. 'I'm afraid there's not much we can do about it —but pray,' she said softly. 'He needs to rest, that's all—there's nothing more we can do.' She moved a pillow out of the way so that the old man's head lay flat.

'Archie,' Daisy asked, cocking her head, 'what did you put in his tea?'

He raised an eyebrow. 'Two measures of rum and a spoonful of sugar. I dipped my finger in it and licked it—utterly disgusting.'

'But there was also something really odd about it,' Daisy said. 'Like toadstools and squealing.'

Archie shook his head. 'Daisy, you do come up with some rubbish.'

'No, I don't.'

'Well, it did the trick; we found the first tablet, didn't we?' he said.

'All I'm saying,' Daisy said, 'is that I definitely thought there was something in it.'

'Uh-oh, here we go—another magic eyes moment coming up, eh?' Isabella quipped. 'Well, I won't be having any tea from you, Archie. Poor, dear Old Man Wood.'

'If you ask me, that tea had magic mushrooms in it,' Daisy said. 'Don't they kill you?'

Isabella shrugged. 'What gets me is this: we only found the tablet because of the song which came from the clues on the five ancient rugs, so does this mean Old Man Wood has been around for as long as he claimed? You know, since the beginning...'

'But the beginning of what?' Daisy added.

'I don't know,' she said. 'But how would he know about the song and the storm and everything else if he wasn't telling the truth?'

Archie nodded. 'And remember his despair that *he* was somehow to blame—'

'And, of course, there's this weird bed with its wooden telly panels,' Daisy added.

'And spying on us too,' Archie said, taking off his beanie and stroking his foremost hair spike.

'The one thing we do know is that we have to solve the riddles—so we might as well try and figure out where the next tablet is as fast as possible. Something about jelly—'

'Blab—' Archie tried. 'Or blisters—'

'Heck,' Isabella blurted out.

'What is it?'

'Oh, nothing,' Isabella said, but her face told a different story. 'Really, it's nothing important,' she said.

'You sure?' Daisy said, sensing her discomfort.

Isabella groaned. 'I forgot to tell Old Man Wood about his cattle.'

Archie and Daisy looked confused. 'What about them?' Daisy said.

'When I ran off to find you, I went up to the corral in the ruin and counted the cows and the sheep—two were missing. I was going to say something but we got caught up in all... this.'

'He'll be gutted if it's true,' Archie said. 'Especially his cows. But they can't exactly go anywhere—'

'Unless they're stuck in all this mud,' Daisy said. 'Or struck by lightning and gone A.W.O.L.'

'Or washed away in a mudslide,' Archie added.

'We'd better check—it's the least we can do.'

'You two go,' Isabella said, a little too quickly, 'while I look after Old Man Wood.'

'Why?' Daisy snapped back. 'Are you afraid of the dark?'

'No, of course not,' she said. 'It's just that I've already been, and you haven't.' But Isabella wasn't telling the half of it. She'd been scared out of her wits by a strong sensation that invisible eyes had bored into her and connected with her brain.

Archie grabbed her arm and pulled her up. 'Come on. We could do with some fresh air, and that includes you, Bells,' he said. 'We won't be long and besides, he needs quiet and rest.'

Old Man Wood's chest moved slightly and the briefest sigh passed his lips. The children looked at one another and smiled.

Archie studied Old Man Wood's unmoving face. 'By the looks of things, he'll be out for hours. With any luck, in the morning he'll be able to help us with the next riddle. And anyway,' he said, as another thought struck him, 'if any of the animals are stuck it'll take all three of us to pull them free,' and he smiled at his sisters, 'Superman-boy or not.'

Above them, a large moon emerged low in the young night sky, chasing away the remnants of the storm. It cast a thin light over the sodden ground, the starlit sky mirrored in large, overflowing puddles. The children picked their way carefully up the hill towards the cattle, avoiding fallen trees and deeper pools, using torch and moonlight to guide them.

By the edge of the ruin they stopped and sat down on a low stone wall—part of the old escarpment—and looked out across the valley at the immense, grey, moving mass of water reflecting the crisp moonlight.

The whirl of helicopter blades in the distance cut across the silent night.

'I hope the Talbots are OK. Their house has probably been submerged,' Isabella said, brushing away a strand of hair with her gloved hand.

'What about old Granny Baker?' Daisy added. 'She's not moved in years. I wonder if anyone managed to get her onto a rooftop.'

'What, in her wheelchair?' Isabella scoffed. 'Poor thing, she's probably floating towards York with all the rest of them.'

'You are unbelievable sometimes,' Daisy remonstrated. 'There's suffering down there in the valley on a scale we simply can't appreciate. People are hurting, their loved ones are missing and, just because we survived and Sue and Gus survived, it doesn't make it OK. Think of those messages on your phone, Bells! Houses ruined, possessions gone. Death, everywhere. Don't you get it?'

'Of course I do,' she fired back.

They looked forlornly over the mass of water until Archie broke the silence. 'They're looking for us, you know. We're wanted like... like murderers, like escaped convicts. Maybe we should turn ourselves in and tell the authorities everything we know—'

'Seriously?' Daisy said, appalled.

'Yeah?! Why not?'

'Because they simply won't believe us, that's why.'

Isabella nodded. 'The mere fact that Sue was telling us to get on with finding these tablets and went so far as to stand in front of TV cameras and come up with an appalling anagram means that she has to be deadly serious. If she thought it was a better idea for us to come in, she'd have probably turned to the camera and said, simply, "Come on in, de Lowes, you have nothing to fear". The fact that she didn't, and then had to shroud it behind some dodgy word-play, means, in my humble opinion, that we have *everything* to fear.'

Isabella grabbed hold of Archie's hand and looked into his eyes, as though in reassurance. 'Archie, whatever Kemp may have told them, it's more than likely that we are presumed dead. I mean, just look at the destruction out there and the list of lost and missing people on the texts on my phone.' She swept her hand over the wreck of the Vale of York in front of them. 'Sue won't have told them anything. Solomon might have, but there's every chance he's been struck down with this disease. After all, he was bang in the middle of it. So the mere fact that they had to put out a wanted notice on national telly after a monumental announcement means that they're grasping at thin air.'

Archie wasn't so sure. 'Do you think they'll come after us?'

'I'm afraid I don't know what to think, bro,' Isabella replied. 'But don't you think they'll have other things to worry about? There must be over a million people displaced, or dead—and that alone is going to keep them pretty preoccupied.'

'Yeah, of course,' Archie agreed. 'But what if they've figured it out?'

They fell silent again, none of them volunteering a response.

Archie thought it might be the right time to bring up the extraordinary revelations of Old Man Wood. 'Where do you think Old Man Wood comes from? He... he's... he's... do you think he's an alien?'

'Alien!' Daisy said. 'What deranged alien planet would have an old bodger like him? Planet "Apple"?'

Archie chuckled. 'So you think he's human; human-ish, like us?'

'Yeah, of course he is,' Daisy said. 'He's just a bit of a stir-fry, slightly bonkers, kinda random, super-old, wizardy-person.'

Archie and Isabella exchanged sideways looks.

'Then how do you explain how he fits in?' he said.

'Some deep, ancient magic he knows about—or it's a bloody good illusion,' Daisy replied. 'He's probably been practising since he was a little boy—'

Isabella guffawed. 'The only thing Old Man Wood practises is making apple juice and growing weird-shaped carrots,' she said. 'Of course he's an alien,' she said. 'As everybody knows, producing apple juice from sixteen varieties of apple tree is a well-known alien trait.' She smiled at her sarcasm. 'Seriously, if his bed and the rugs are not of this Earth, what other conclusion can there be?'

Daisy took off her pink glasses and rubbed her eyes. 'What if,' she started, 'an alien took over Old Man Wood's form—?'

Isabella spluttered.

'No, really. I mean, how else can we explain his weird songs and strange rugs with moving poems? He might be part of an advanced alien race from space—'

'Advanced?'

'OK, maybe not so advanced—'

'Daisy,' Isabella said, 'if you were an alien, would you really choose Old Man Wood as your representative on Earth over five billion other possible candidates?'

Daisy looked offended. 'Why not?' she said. 'He's the kindest, sweetest man in the universe and he wouldn't harm a fly. If you were an alien wouldn't you go for the kindest, nicest person?'

'I don't know,' she said, frowning. 'Probably not—'

'Well, I would. It's stereotypical nonsense stirred up by Hollywood that aliens are always bad, apart from, of course, ET.'

Isabella shook her head. 'There's a perfectly logical reason for this though: bad people are generally manipulative and don't care about anyone or anything aside from their own circle. Therefore, they crush good people and win—'

'No, they don't. Good people have a habit of coming out on top. That's why the human race has been so successful—'

'Nonsense,' Isabella said. 'Humans are only winners because their brains are more advanced than anything else's. We can think things through—unlike someone sitting pretty close to me. It doesn't make a spot of difference if people are nice or decent or—'

'Stop it, Bells,' Archie interjected. 'Daisy was only offering a theory on the back of inexplicable evidence. Have you got a better explanation?'

Isabella poked at the see-through hole in her hand, her hair over her face like a veil, and held her silence.

Archie rubbed a hair spike through the cloth of his beanie. 'What if he's actually telling the truth?' he said. 'What if he really has been around for all this time and he simply forgot everything—like he said?'

Isabella guffawed again.

'I mean, they used to live to a great age in the Bible didn't they—so maybe he's from Old Testament times and got stuck in a time-warp ...?'

'Oh, shut up, Archie,' the two girls said in unison.

'No, no,' he countered, refusing to give in. 'I'm betting Old Man Wood was the exact same person he is today when Dad was a little boy. And I bet you he's the same person in all those oil paintings we collected from around the house.'

'Thank you, Winkle—'

'I just don't believe he's capable of making up such a tall story.'

Archie paused, allowing the girls a moment to respond. They didn't. 'So, maybe he's a wizard. We've seen the moving bed panels, so we know he's full of magic tricks, and he's full of pain about forgetting his "life mission" which, as far as I can tell, involves saving this place called the Garden of Eden. And we all know Eden existed in biblical times, either as a real place or as part of the creation story.

'Maybe,' he continued, 'it's not only an allegory for early man, but a story about an entirely different planet? Maybe the whole story at the beginning of Genesis is a kind of code, a cleverly plotted fable full of clues, before it delves into the history of the early Israelites?'

Isabella flicked the hair off her face, her eyes glowing with wonder. 'I'm quite amazed,' she said, 'that you were actually paying attention to my lecture.'

Archie grinned. 'Yes, of course I was. The thing is, there are too many oddities. He talks to trees and grows star shaped carrots and is fixated by apples. And the tablet only came out after we all sang his weird song which blew the house apart and in so doing proves that the riddles on the rugs are true.'

The girls nodded in agreement.

'More importantly, he featured vividly in our dreams as a great, old, wise, mystical man who may well be part of time eternal and who is actually trying to help us.'

They sat silently on the cold stone. A chill grey wind blew gently across them, smelling of damp, matching the girls' mood. What he'd said rang true; they just didn't want to believe it.

'OK, Mr. Know-it-all,' Isabella said. 'Explain why it happens to be us and not anyone else.'

Archie shrugged. 'Perhaps it's because we just happen to be the poor sods who live in Eden Cottage, who he looks after,' he said. 'Think about it. The cottage is full of curiosities, like the rugs and your atrium-y place, Daisy—'

'But why can't he remember anything?' Isabella said bluntly. 'He's no help whatsoever. Every time we want to know something, he dithers, or goes off on one of his walks, or gets giddy, or drunk or... or he dies.'

'Isabella!'

She put her hands in the air. 'What I'm trying to say is that he hasn't actually helped us with anything—'

'Don't you think there's a reason for that?' Archie said.

'What do you mean?'

'The reason he can't tell us is because he doesn't know. He sort of knew it once but doesn't anymore.' Archie removed his beanie and scratched first one, and then another hair spike. 'Anyway, if he is as old as he says he is, no wonder he's forgotten everything.'

'What are you talking about?'

Archie shook his head. 'Seriously, can you remember things from when you were three or four years old?'

Both girls shook their heads.

'Exactly! You can't. If Old Man Wood's as old as he says he is, it's going to be a pretty big struggle to get him to recall detail from hundreds, if not thousands, of years ago. When the tablet came out of the fire, he knew about it in a vague, roundabout way—like with the song—and he needed us to prompt him and vice versa—'

'Problem is, Archie,' Daisy said, 'we still have to solve the riddles.'

Isabella nodded.

'And we're running out of time.'

Isabella looked sheepish. 'I know, and it's my fault,' she said quietly.

'That's irrelevant now,' Archie said, warmly. 'Deep down, Old Man Wood knows everything—we need to coax it out of him, show us how to do it.'

'Certainly won't be easy if he's dead,' Daisy added.

'Even if he's alive,' Isabella added, 'he's going to slow us down.'

Spitting rain now fell. They screwed up their faces as larger drops began to fall. The children stood up ready to move.

'Tomorrow we have to find the remaining tablets,' Archie continued, adjusting his beanie. 'They hold the key to finding this 'Eden' world—whatever it is—even if we don't know why it involves us.'

Daisy draped her arms around Isabella and Archie's shoulders. 'Don't get me wrong, guys, but let's be honest. Without Old Man Wood, I don't think we've got a chance of finding anything.'

PRESSURE MOUNTS

Commissioner Stone yawned. He stared at himself in the mirror, noting dark purple bags under his eyes—even darker than the last time he'd looked. As he dragged a razor across his face, even his stubble felt harder than usual.

Another fitful sleep—four hours tops. He needed twice that.

'Good morning, sir,' came a muffled cry from outside the hotel suite door. 'We have the deputy PM and the Head of the European Commission waiting for you.'

Stone nicked his narrow, bony chin and a bubble of blood dropped into the basin. He swore. 'Tell them I'll call back—give me ten minutes.' He cupped his hands and splashed cold water on his face, the shock running through his body. Exactly what he needed.

He towelled his face, hoping the cut would start to congeal, and applied a generous splash of cologne. The liquid stung. *But it was nothing*, he thought, *to what lay ahead.*

He opened the bathroom door, his dressing gown fastened around his midriff, to find his room packed with people. On seeing him, they all spoke simultaneously.

Stone stared open-mouthed.

'Sir, you need to see this,' said a large lady with short red hair, thrusting a file at him. He brushed it aside.

'We need to speak, urgently,' a small, squat, dark haired man with a bushy beard demanded.

Stone ignored all of them and cut his way through the throng to the bed. 'What the hell is going on?' he yelled, as he spotted Dickinson remonstrating with a man in a white coat. 'Dickinson,' he roared. 'What is the meaning of all this?'

The officer extracted himself. 'Bedlam, sir,' Dickinson said, calmly. 'I've kept them at bay for the last half an hour but couldn't keep them out. We've got trouble from just about every department in this country. Actually, more like the world.' He cocked his head. 'Best if we head back to the bathroom.'

Stone grabbed his trousers and looked around at faces he'd previously noted from the newspapers or television.

'Why in hell are they in here?'

'All the Government facilities are overwhelmed, sir, or unobtainable. The PM has vanished.' He locked the door and a hollow silence filled the cubicle.

Commissioner Stone dressed, then closed the lid and sat down on the toilet. Dickinson settled on the edge of the bath.

'The Ebora virus has spread overnight, massively,' Dickinson began. 'Apparently, you're the only person with any real authority—that's what they're saying —and this comes from the PM's office as well. Most of that lot arrived in the last hour—it's like a helicopter park out there. One hundred and five at the last count. It's amazing no one's been killed if I'm honest.'

Stone swore under his breath. 'Right, here's the plan. Set three secretaries up with desks in the hall and we'll process this lot like a post office queue. While they're doing this, I want you to go and find Doctor Muller and my cousin, the headmaster, Solomon. Bring them in straightaway.'

Dickinson unlocked the door, fought his way across the room and stood up on the bed. 'Your attention!' he shouted. The noise level abated. 'Commissioner Stone will come out and address you if you give him some room. So please, let's have a little decency and order in here.'

He slipped off the bed and wormed his way out of the room.

Stone made his way over, clambered onto the bed and addressed the room.

'Thank you for barging your way in,' he said, his Yorkshire accent heavy with sarcasm. 'Having woken up barely fifteen minutes ago, I must inform you that I am not as yet up to speed with developments. As you can see, I am not even fully dressed.'

He smiled and scoured the room, reading their faces. *They're on edge, scared witless,* he thought, *the whole damn lot. Time to be friendly, reassuring. If they want leadership, they're going to have to wait for it, not swamp me.*

Dickinson poked his head around the door and nodded.

Stone cleared his throat. 'Quiet, please. In order that we can deal which each one of your important queries, I would like you to give your details to my secretaries who are waiting in the main hall. I will then be able to see you as soon as I can, in an orderly, civilised manner.' He sounded like a customer relations officer.

'And if your query cannot be met by me, then you will be referred to the correct department—'

'But this is urgent, it cannot wait—' a suited gentleman with a foreign accent shouted.

Stone's pale blue eyes bored into him. 'I don't care who the hell you are, sir. Understand? We'll do this my way or I'll toss you back out into the flooding. Get it?'

The tall man's dark eyes met Stone's, before turning away.

Stone grabbed his jacket and made his way into the bathroom while the melee departed.

In just five hours, the world has gone mad, he thought. *And I'm the one expected to supply the answers.* He swore.

Stone adjusted his tie and studied his reflection in the mirror. *I don't even know the bleeding questions,* he thought, *let alone the answers.*

❉

Dr. Muller moved his jaw from side to side and nestled his spectacles on the arch of his nose. 'We have a pandemic, as I suspected.'

'You're suggesting the disease is out of control?'

'I'm not suggesting, sir—'

Stone swallowed. 'Has anyone reported in—the geneticists, the scientific fraternity—has Dr. Harries called?'

The doctor shook his head. 'There's been too little time. The spread is unprecedented—'

'What of the boy? Has he been found?'

Dickinson stared at the floor. 'We've searched everywhere. Not a trace, I'm afraid, aside from the ash we found in the toilet.'

'Have forensics tested it, carbon tested or whatever they do?'

'It is just ash, sir.'

Stone thumped the desk. 'I don't care if it's shit! Is there any good news? What the hell are we going to tell everyone? They're clamouring for information. What do you suggest? Tell them we don't know a bloody thing? Tell them that our one hope—our one pinprick of light—has simply vanished into thin air? How's that going to sound?'

The others shifted nervously.

'Does the Prime Minister know?'

The doctor took a deep breath. 'Half of the cabinet have the Ebora virus. The rest are involved with the containment process along with military chiefs and others.'

Stone gathered himself. 'Doctor, what other cheery news?' he began sarcastically. 'Has it spread out of the containment zone? Out of Yorkshire? Don't tell me it's reached Manchester and Leeds?'

The silence said it all.

'Oh, Christ,' Stone said. 'It has, hasn't it?'

Dr. Muller's face remained impassive. 'I'm not sure how to tell you this, but reports are coming in from across the pond. As people are waking up, they're reporting the same signs. And we know how fast it incubates—'

Stone eyed him curiously. 'The pond? What—the English Channel? It's reached Europe?!'

'Plenty of cases in Europe have also been reported, Commissioner. But I meant America. Across *that* pond—the Atlantic.'

Stone's eyes nearly popped out of his head. '*America! America... are you bleedin' sure?!*'

Dickinson marched in. 'The US Secretary of State would like to speak to you.'

Stone uncurled his fingers, pulled out a handkerchief and dabbed his brow. 'Can't he speak to the PM—or one of the Cabinet?'

'Here's the problem. The PM is indisposed—'

'Indisposed?'

'Yes, unavailable, sir—'

'Yes, I know what indisposed means.'

Dickinson whispered in his ear. 'According to the Prime Minister's wife, he has Ebora symptoms.'

'Christ alive!' roared Stone, kneading his temples. 'What next?'

'Well, I was coming to it, but the Home Secretary instructed me to let you know that as of 07:00 hours this morning, you have been granted full powers to do whatever is necessary and with any means known to humankind to get to the bottom of this, sir. She's waiting for your call.' Dickinson raised his eyebrows. 'May I suggest you call her directly before you talk to our American cousins?'

Solomon bustled in, shutting the door firmly. He exhaled. 'Who on earth are all those people in the hall?'

Stone lifted his eyes at the sound of Solomon's voice and removed his glasses. 'A spokesman for the President of the European Union, the Secretaries of State for four of our near neighbours, the First Minister of Scotland, the head of OPEC, a couple of major global industrialists, a supermarket chief executive or two, the supreme commander of European forces, Field Marshall Allen and the Chairman of the London Stock Exchange. And that's just the ones I recognise. Even Lord "bleedin'" Sugar and Sir Richard "blast-off" Branson are apparently en-route. And Bono's on the phone every fifteen minutes. Anything else you want to know?'

Solomon wiped his brow. 'Good Lord. I'm sorry, cousin, I had no idea—'

Stone leaned back in his chair and clenched his hands. 'What did you discover at Upsall, headmaster?'

Solomon knew this wasn't an informal chat.

'Plenty—I'd like to think—though a little more time would be beneficial—if at all possible.'

Deep down, Solomon knew a lot more time was needed. He'd looked upon the stained glass windows in a totally new light and in it he'd recognised the de Lowe children, the flooding, the pestilence and he'd touched on something—a message maybe, that he felt the de Lowe's understood.

The question was, how much should he tell Stone on the basis that this "feeling" was entirely conjecture?

Stone raised his eyebrows and smiled back, but his eyes were hard. He'd recorded Solomon's movements on a hidden camera. He knew Solomon's every move. 'Tell me,' he said, 'what you discovered.'

Taking a deep breath, the Headmaster began. 'As you know there is an extensive hidden library in the tower at Upsall. I tried to find some connection to this plague and, given the shortness of time and the large selection of tomes therein, I struggled to come up with anything of note. However, I was drawn to the stained glass that fronts the chapel. You know of it?'

Stone flicked his eyes at Dickinson. *So far, so good. Exactly right.* 'Yes, a murky thing—'

'It is a triptych,' Solomon continued. 'Three stained glass paintings as one that show the Father, Son and Holy Ghost. On them are references to water, pestilence and one other curious-looking event. The first two are, of course, relevant to the situation we have at present.'

Solomon wiped his lips. 'Before you jump to any conclusions this is standard imagery commonly found in medieval artworks. However, if you're searching for an easy connection, a soft target if you like, it's right there on the glass.'

'What about the de Lowes? Is the stained glass related to their ancestry in any way?'

Solomon nudged his glasses. 'Almost certainly,' he began. 'I believe the family would have been involved in the building of the monastery and, thereafter, in the formation of the window. Records I unearthed tell of a family here under the name of "De L'eau" at Domesday. Then, I discovered one even earlier name.'

He paused and looked at his cousin. '"Aquataine".'

Solomon smiled in his head-masterly way as he noted the confused look on Stone's face. 'The link? Well, clearly it's in the commonality of the word for water:

De l'eau is the French for "water" and, the Latin for "water" is Aqua—as in this name of, Aquataine—'

'Shouldn't it be Aquitaine,' Stone said, 'you know, with an "I"?'

'My thoughts exactly,' Solomon said. 'But I've seen the name spelt this way on several parchments, so I don't think so. Perhaps it is trying to tell us that there is some connection between the water of the surnames and the water that surrounds us.'

The Commissioner rubbed his face, touching the shaving cut on his chin. This was exactly what he'd hoped for, just the sort of information he needed. 'So, we have a flood that begins in Upsall. And we have a pandemic that begins in Upsall. We have a girl who predicted the flooding and whose ancient family name means "water", and we have an eccentric old man — a hermit — who lives with them, who is of unknown origin. We have a stained glass window in Upsall with three figures surrounded by flood and disease. *Uncanny, isn't it?*' he said, cocking his head to the side. 'So what, or perhaps, *who* connects these things?'

Solomon smiled back his most practiced teacherly-smile. 'Am I getting a sniff, Charlie, that you're attempting to link the de Lowe family to the disaster?' He raised his eyebrows. 'If you are, then my question is this: what could those three possibly know? They're school children, how can they possibly be involved?'

Stone smirked. 'There! Isn't this the conundrum in a nutshell. You tell me?' he said, throwing the question back. 'What dirty little secrets might an old family like the de Lowes harbour, huh?'

The headmaster shrugged. *Whatever happens, don't rise to his taunts*, he told himself. 'I'm not sure I quite understand.'

Stone's manner changed. For a brief moment he trailed a finger over some papers and then looked up. 'By the way, I thought you might like to know that we've found two more of your pupils.'

'Goodness me, who?'

'A girl by the name of...' Stone looked over at Dickinson.

'Sue Lowden,' Dickinson added, reading a clipboard. 'And, a chap by the name of Gus Williams. He's in hospital.'

Solomon peered over his glasses. 'That's terrific news! Yes, they're mine all right. Lovely kids,' he said, enthusiastically. 'So much anguish and darkness and now two survivors. Amazing isn't it?'

Stone cocked his head. 'She was interviewed on the telly. Said she owed it all to Williams—saved her life by making a canopy over a small rowing boat. A right hero.'

'She's a fine student and he's a decent lad.'

Stone drummed his fingers on the desk. 'The thing is, when my man interviewed her she mentioned she was a very close friend of Isabella de Lowe,' he said, his voice barely above a whisper and soaked with irony. 'Now, isn't that a surprise?'

Solomon didn't like the way this was going. 'Not at all,' he said, trying hard not to show any feelings. 'Those two were almost inseparable.'

'Is that so?' Stone said, glaring at the headmaster. 'Apparently, Isabella de Lowe gave her the idea to find the boat. Now that's pretty sharp thinking, don't you reckon?'

'Yes, as I said, they're smart kids.'

'So smart that she even managed to tell her about it before the storm struck.'

Solomon's face dropped. 'She's no fool, Charlie. She's a brilliant student—'

'As you keep telling me. Let's go again. This is the same student who went out of her way to ask you to call off the match and your celebrations, because she knew that vast storm was heading your way? And the same girl who made a "storm glass" to prove it.'

Solomon didn't know what to say. 'I've told you all I know,' he said examining his watch. 'I take it you're getting Sue and Gus transferred back here.'

'Yes, of course,' Stone said, rubbing his hands. 'For some proper interrogation.'

Solomon's eyes hardened. 'You'll do no such thing.'

Stone slammed his palms on the table. 'I'll do whatever it takes. And I don't care if it's the Pope, the President or Her Majesty the Queen. My job is to find out what the hell is going on here—'

'But duress, Charlie? She's a child—'

'*I need her to talk,*' Stone said coldly, his eyes boring into Solomon. 'And I'm running out of time.'

'I will not let you do that with my pupils,' Solomon said, standing up.

Stone grinned. '*Especially* with your pupils, it seems.'

'You were always hard, Charlie, and I don't begrudge you your situation, but these children are in my care. You'll interrogate her over my dead body—'

'That can be arranged,' Stone said. 'Sit down old man.' He nodded at Dickinson who pushed the Headmaster down. 'Count yourself lucky you're not going to feel a few volts up your arse as well. And one more thing, before I discuss our progress with the Deputy Prime Minister and the US Secretary of State. That boy, you know, the one found up a tree, burnt like he'd been sprayed by some flammable liquid. We found out his name. A bit of a tip off.'

Solomon tensed. 'Who was it?'

'Kemp. The boy's name was Kemp.'

'Kemp? My goodness—'

'Yeah. Ring any bells?'

'Yes, golly-gosh. Indeed. Well, well. How remarkable.'

'Isn't it? Funny how your pupils keep popping up from the dead in the most unexpected places.'

Solomon shook his head. *It was impossible. Kemp's coat had been found. Besides, Kemp was renowned for being a poor swimmer.*

'Do you want to know who Kemp called for?' Stone said. 'The one and only person he named—the person who he implied might have the tiniest inkling about what's going on out there?'

Stone stood up and moved in close to his older, portlier cousin and whispered in his ear. *'Archie de Lowe.'*

Solomon's jaw dropped.

Stone walked round to his chair behind the desk, sat down and leaned in. 'I thought you were here to help me headmaster, not get in my way. So, do you now understand why I need to know what these kids know? *Comprenez-vous?*'

'Yes, of course. Very well,' Solomon croaked. 'But let me do it, Charlie. All you'll do is scare them. They trust me.' Solomon raised his eyebrows, his heart thumping wildly as he mopped his brow. 'Let *me* ask the questions, my way. I know how these children work. I'll get the results you need.'

Stone eyed him for a while. 'Fine,' he said. 'A helicopter with thermal imaging is on its way to their cottage as we speak. If any of the kids are there, we're going to pick them up. Believe me, headmaster, if you don't get everything I need—full co-operation—I'm going to be hot on their heels and no-one's going to like it. I can absolutely assure you of that.'

AT THE RUIN

The courtyard by the ruin was surrounded by the last few remains of a wall which had, over time, disappeared under mud and moss and bushes and the odd straggly tree. As they approached, a thick silence filled the air, broken only by an occasional grunt or gloop of feet swilling about in the mud near the old corrugated iron-roofed corral.

On hearing footsteps, the livestock groaned and mooed and baaed before tentatively emerging from the tin shelter. For several minutes Isabella, Archie and Daisy counted and then re-counted the animals while speaking in soothing, calming voices.

Archie shook his head. 'Three out of nine cattle and one sheep missing. Bella, is that right? Have you guys checked right at the back?'

The children walked slowly into the body of the metal-roofed shelter, their boots sticking in the ankle-high sludge, slurping at every movement, making sure each step counted so they wouldn't slip or slide, occasionally leaning on animals that refused to budge.

Suddenly, a terrible whirring noise rattled overhead, making the structure rumble. The children automatically folded their torches in their tummies and held their breath, and Daisy plugged her ears too. In no time, the helicopter had passed.

'Let's go!' Isabella cried, turning. 'We can be saved!'

Archie grabbed her arm. '*From what, Bells? Saved from what, exactly?* It's just like Sue said. They're onto us—best if we stay hidden until we've found these tablets.'

Whirring sounds filled the night sky as the helicopter appeared to linger over the cottage before flying off.

By the time they'd waded out of the corral the helicopter was a distant speck in the night sky.

'Do you think they knew we were in there?' Daisy said breathlessly.

Archie shook his head. 'It shot up from under the cliff face, so I doubt it. Anyone find the missing animals?'

'No, and I counted twice,' Daisy said, her voice muffled as she held her nose.

Isabella groaned. 'That means that two more have gone since I was last here—although I could have been wrong with the sheep. They looked terrified enough at the time. Did you notice how their eyes are glazed over. Three look sick, diseased, even.'

The thought that somehow the disease had spread to the animals was not welcome.

'Let's go home,' said Daisy, shivering.

'Right away,' Isabella agreed, but almost immediately, a strange, slithering noise could be heard from nearby. She looked around, her eyes bulging, her face as white as snow.

Out on the grassed area of the old ruin they shone their torches over the rocks and bushes and, as they did, a cold chill crawled over the three children—as if they were being watched.

Daisy's teeth began to chatter. 'We need to get out of here,' she said, flinching. 'I think there's some weird thing hanging about.'

'What is it?' Archie asked.

'I dunno,' she whispered.

With their senses now on high alert, the children started through the rock-dotted courtyard towards the track, hairs erect on the backs of their necks. A low rumble rolled out through the evening sky. Collectively, their pace quickened.

Soon they were running.

Without knowing how it had happened, Isabella found herself sprinting, skimming over fallen trees and dashing past piles of rock, hurdling huge puddles and suddenly she was at the end of the field near the cottage.

She turned to check on the other two, but saw nothing except the night gloom. *Perhaps,* she thought, *they'd gone another way.* But where? They weren't that stupid. She smiled. *It's these feet again, making me run like the wind. They'll be back soon enough,* she thought, and she let herself in, conscious that she was barely out of breath.

❆

Daisy and Archie watched Isabella accelerate away from them into the murky darkness. They stopped to catch their breath and looked at each other quizzically.

'When did Bells learn to run like that?' Daisy panted.

Archie shrugged. 'Don't know. But that was utterly ludicrous,' he said, leaning on a smooth, grey boulder. 'Actually, if you think about it, she tore around the property in about twenty minutes yesterday—'

'And she must have bounded up the two hundred and twenty-two stairs to escape the collapsing cave like some kind of super-leopard,' Daisy said.

'Did you notice another thing?' Archie said, as he rubbed his chin. 'She hates it up here. She was shaking like a jelly.'

'Yup. I noticed that too. Sweating too, and as white as a sheet.'

Archie peered into the gloom. 'Daisy, I think we owe it to Old Man Wood to find the other animals. What do you think?'

'We can try.'

'Cool. Let's check if there's anyone or anything about who shouldn't be.'

Daisy moved her head from side to side as though examining the area. 'Something is hanging about. I can't tell what it is though. Sounds a bit like... do you think it might be a bloke stealing them? Making creepy noises to scare us off?'

'I don't know,' he said quietly. 'But it isn't right. I think we should find out.'

'What if it's a lunatic, with a gun?'

Archie frowned. 'Then we should find out.'

'Can't we wait till morning?'

'We won't have time. Come on.'

Daisy eyed him curiously. 'Very well, brave brother—ye with the spiky hair. Lead on.'

Archie smiled. 'Do you want to go first?'

'Oh, get a move on,' she said, taking the lead and marching back the way they'd come. 'Let's see what's lurking yonder, huh?'

In silence, the only noise being the squelching and squishing of their boots in the mud, they doubled back to their original position and then headed further in towards the fallen-down castle keep, strewn with boulders.

'To be honest with you, Archie,' Daisy said as she went, 'I could hear something moving about after we'd counted the animals. But the thing is, it wasn't a sound I've ever heard before.'

Daisy picked her way through the old walls and slabs of stone of the ruin with ease, despite the thick cloud that obscured the moonbeams. The harder she concentrated the easier it became.

Soon she was manoeuvring as if it were light, skipping over rocks and jumping across gullies as though it were daytime, her senses on high alert.

Carefully, she crept up to a shaft of rock and leaned into it, remaining quite still, listening. There—again, the exact same noise as before; a curious mix of heavy, syrupy breathing, like large, wheezy bellows. 'You must be able to hear it now?' she whispered.

There was no response.

'Archie?' she whispered into the cold night air. She turned. 'Archie! Where are you?'

She hadn't registered that Archie wasn't right behind her. She retraced her steps, weaving back through the low ruins, her eyes following her footprints.

Without warning, her legs disappeared from under her and a heavy, hard object struck her sharply on the back of her head. Disorientated she fell forward, her arms pulled hard behind her back. She tried to wriggle free.

'REVEAL YOURSELF,' said a familiar voice.

'Let go of me!'

'Who are you?!' he hissed.

Daisy couldn't believe it. 'Your sister, you bloody numpty!'

'Whoever you are, YOU are not my sister.'

'Unfortunately, I am, Archie, you stupid, spiky, knob-end.'

There was a pause while Archie, baffled by the response, wondered what to do next.

'OK! What's my nickname?'

'Winkle. I alone call you Winkle. I don't know why, but it just suited you when you were little and it stuck because it really, really irritated the hell out of you.'

Archie loosened his grip. "Winkle" was her private name for him. Slowly he turned her round to face him, not loosening his grip on her too much.

'What the hell was that all about—?'

'Your... your eyes, Daise!' he said, 'what's happened to your eyes? Are you... all right?'

Daisy pushed him away. 'What *are* you talking about, there's nothing wrong with my eyes,' she said crossly, 'apart from being red, like a traffic light on stop.'

She rubbed her skull, more concerned with the blow to the back of her head. 'That really hurt, Archie—what's up with you?'

'No seriously, Daisy. You're lucky I didn't smack you harder. Look, are you sure you're OK? I mean... look, I don't know how to tell you this but they're glowing, like dishes. It's like you're an alien! Your eyes are burning like torches. I thought YOU were the monster.'

A chilly wind blew over them. They shivered.

'I'm really sorry, Daisy. I didn't realise—'

Daisy hoped Archie couldn't see her tears. 'I don't know what's happening to me, Arch,' she whispered. 'I've got these weirdo eyes which kind of go into overdrive when I concentrate. You won't believe what I can see—things in incredible detail—like individual particles in the storm glass—or objects miles away, or seeing stuff in the dark. And every time I use them, it gets stronger and I discover more. It's like a game, going up levels all the time.'

She wiped her cheek and continued. 'Remember when we came up here and looked out over the flooding? I got a bit caught up wondering if I could actually see people sitting on their rooftops waiting for help. Well, I could! I really could see water flowing through the streets. And running up here tonight—it was as clear as it would be on a sunny day, apart from... well, it wasn't, was it?'

Archie couldn't think of anything to say.

'Archie, it's not the only thing; I can hear amazing stuff, too. When the rain stopped at home, all you lot could hear was the sudden quiet but I heard drips of water splashing directly under the house.'

'What do you think it is?'

Daisy rubbed her eyes. 'If I'm right, I think it's got something to do with the water in the third poem. The "clear" and "pure" bit.'

Archie repeated as much as he could remember.

> 'The third you search is under your nose.
> 'It's clear, pure and warm (I think).
> 'In order to ... something or other
> 'You need to send... hmm, can't quite remember.'

'At first I thought it was to do with bogeys—you know, being underneath your nose,' she said smiling again. 'Do you think there's a stream under the house?'

Archie looked at her with renewed wonder and, instinctively, even though Daisy's eyes were still glowing, but not as brightly, he moved in and hugged her.

'Does it hurt?' he asked, his voice hushed.

'What? My head?'

'No, you daft cow. Your eyes.'

Daisy shook her head. 'No. Just goes a bit tingly, that's all.'

They both sat quietly. 'Can I ask,' Archie said cautiously, 'what was it *really* like in this atrium place you went to? Did you use your mega-eyes in there? Did you hear anything else apart from a great blood-curdling scream? And did you really get out just by looking at a door—?'

'Simmer down,' she whispered. 'The atrium was terrifying... it's hard to remember anything in detail. I was lucky—'

Suddenly, a snorting sound, like a wave blasting through a blow-hole, burst out from the other side of the rock.

Archie crouched down.

Hooves clattered on the flattened rocks nearby and pounded the wet ground.

Cattle and sheep ran quickly. A crisp bark, cracked the air, slicing through the silence followed by a low, hissing sound.

'What the—'

Daisy pushed a finger over his lips. She could hear his heart thumping.

'What is it?' Archie whispered, as they slipped down the cold slab of rock.

'Sshh. Let me listen.'

Shortly, another strange bark was followed by a hiss, this time much closer.

'It isn't a fox, or any kind of dog,' Daisy said, under her breath, her brow furrowed in concentration. 'It definitely isn't a bird call, or a ferret and it's not a cow, or a goat, or anything from the deer family. I don't think it's a cat—you know, like a lion or leopard or panther. It's certainly not a chicken, or a sheep, or any of the rodent family. It's not a hyena because they laugh... and I doubt it's a crocodile, because I've never heard one, and they go "snap", but it could be a bison or rhino from Africa, so —'

'Daisy!' Archie hissed, 'stop! You don't have to go through the entire animal kingdom.'

'Oh. Sorry,' she said.

'So, what is it?'

'I don't know! But it's definitely not an elephant or a bear or a llama ...'

Archie glared at her.

For a few moments they sat stone-still behind the large, weathered slab of rock. Smeared across the dark sky ran the wavy form of a rain cloud.

'What are we going to do?' Daisy whispered, trying not to appear too cowardly. 'We can't stay here shivering all night only to get eaten.'

Archie nodded. 'Any ideas?'

'How should I know? What do *you* think we should do?'

'*I don't know.*'

'Well, it was your idea!'

'Sshhhhh,' Archie squealed, 'it's really close!'

The slither of something snake-like moved just out of eye-shot. The twins hugged the rock. Then it grunted loudly, and barked.

Daisy squirmed and her ears filled with pain. Tears ran down her cheeks. She smothered her ears.

'Daisy!' Archie whispered. 'What is it?'

'A noise! Incredibly high-pitched. It's killing me.'

For some strange reason he couldn't quite understand, Archie stood up, ricked his neck from side to side and jumped out onto the grass to the side of the rock ready to face whatever it was head on.

'... NO!' Daisy cried.

But almost immediately the farm bell rang, its toll echoing eerily up the hillside.

In a flash and with a slither, whatever had been there, vanished and the painful, shrilling noise had evaporated, like the strange beast.

Daisy shook her head and stepped out to join Archie.

Holding their breath, the twins moved around to the other side of the rock. Nothing. Just the same, curious, track-marks.

They listened and waited, exchanging looks, wondering if it was safe to run for their lives. With Daisy's eyes on full beam, they simultaneously sprang off and sprinted through the mud and over branches and rocks towards the track.

As they stopped to catch their breath by the old rutted path, a voice came out of the dark below.

Instinctively they crouched down.

'Yoo-hoo!'

'Who... who's there?' Daisy called out.

'Only me!'

Archie and Daisy exhaled audibly and smiled.

'What are you doing up here, Mrs P, scaring us to death?'

'Well, little ones, I came to find you. And I thought I might see a helidoctor, rescuing all them poor folk and that. But I might ask you the same; what you doing, you two, out here in the dark at this time?'

Archie caught Daisy's now back-to-normal eyes. 'We were looking for, er, for... for Blabisterberry Jelly,' he said, at which they both burst out laughing.

'For, eh... what?!' Mrs. Pye shrieked, her voice sounding a little more shrill than normal. 'Jelly? At this time of night?'

'No, Mrs P—it's a kind of joke,' Archie said. 'It's something we've got to find —apparently. But don't worry—it's not important right now.'

'Did you find any "helidoctors"?' Daisy asked.

'I didn't, no. Got a little waylaid I'm afraid to say. But I heard one right bang overhead while I was lying in me bath. Stayed there some time, too, till me water went all chilly and I ended up with granny-fingers.'

For the rest of the walk they moved in silence, their boots squelching in the mud. When they arrived near the cottage, Mrs. Pye coughed, very lightly, but just enough to send a shiver down their spines.

Mrs. Pye, aware that she was being looked at, started coughing more until Archie felt compelled to give her a pat on her back.

Could Mrs. Pye's cough be linked with the bark they'd heard at the ruin? No, not Mrs. Pye.

Perhaps the strange events of the past day had stretched his mind so that he was over-alert to every squeak, splutter and cough.

CAIN AND KEMP

For Kemp, the euphoria of being alive, and not in hospital, remained. No interrogations by that dreadful man, Stone; no being stuffed full of tubes and wires; no nurses covered in protective clothing padding and prodding him and filling him with disgusting medicines or sharp needles. No worries about anything.

Much to his astonishment, Cain had delivered on all his promises—food coming out of his ears, a palace to run about in, servants at his disposal, and jewels and treasure everywhere. The place was smothered in riches and Kemp was dazzled by it all.

Cain's demands on him were minimal. Schmerger, the strange, bearded, unsmiling servant, had given him a salve for his burns which healed in record time and Kemp soon felt better than he had for an awfully long time.

For the moment at least, Cain's mood bordered on delirious. He sang and laughed and showed Kemp around the palace, telling stories—all of which sounded ludicrous—and repeatedly told Kemp that it was all his. Not only that, but it was his to do with as he wished.

His to enjoy, his to destroy—if he so wished.

Overshadowing this, Kemp wondered whether Cain would deliver his mother as he had sworn he would.

Festering at the back of his mind, he wondered if Cain had fabricated the truth about his mother. After all, evidence suggested that she had died a long time ago.

It didn't help that he didn't entirely trust Cain. Cain was dangerous, he sensed, and Kemp couldn't help asking himself why Cain wanted him so badly? *What, exactly, was the ghost's grand plan?* he thought.

Cain hadn't avoided the subject, since Kemp hadn't asked, but Cain's demeanour compelled him to require some answers.

That time came at supper.

Kemp grabbed a spoon and helped himself to a bowl of beef stew. He couldn't remember eating anything quite so tasty in years. Cain's overcoat floated across and parked up next to him.

'Why?' Kemp asked.

'Why, *what*, boy?'

'Why do you need me?' Kemp asked bluntly. 'What's this Prophecy of Eden thing-a-me-jig you told me and Arch about? What's it got to do with you?'

'I wondered when you'd ask,' the gap between Cain's hat and collar said. 'The universe is exceedingly old, boy. Every now and then there's a shift, a repositioning in how it aligns itself.' He appeared to sniff the air. 'It is doing so right at this precise moment and your friends the de Lowes, by way of a long, ancient and rather tedious selection process, have received dreams in which they have been given instructions on how to open the Garden of Eden. If you must, it is the ultimate test for your entire species. If they fail, then mankind will be seen to have failed and life on Earth will be erased. Earth will begin afresh, with different, new beings.'

Kemp looked incredulous. 'Archie has to save the world. Ha-ha, that is bloody hilarious.'

He grabbed a chicken leg and licked it before biting deep into the flesh. 'Fat chance he's got. In any case,' he said with his mouth full again, 'it doesn't make sense. Humans are doing all right, aren't they? We're civilised and all that—we've got TV and the internet, satellites, fast-food, nuclear stuff and massive football stadiums. What's not to have?'

The ghost sighed. 'Running a planet is far more than those things, my dear fellow. I know it'll be difficult, but you're going to have to stop thinking like a ridiculous Earth human. There's really no use for it here. You see, the energy of the universe is made by zillions of things and, when something happens in one area of the universe, it almost certainly has a knock-on effect elsewhere. Humans were given a time in charge but, in all honesty, they haven't really cared for the others particularly well, have they? I've heard that it's gone a little lop-sided.'

'Others? Lop-sided? *What others?*'

Cain coughed gently. 'The other animals, plants, soils and living things that they were meant to care for. All organisms have a purpose and neglecting one puts tremendous pressure on the others. The knock-on effect, if you will.'

Kemp sneered, but nodded almost knowingly.

Cain interpreted this as a green light to continue. 'If your friends succeed then there is hope for the planet that the present incumbents might turn it around, though it is highly unlikely. If not, then new inhabitants will be made in the Garden of Eden and filtered in to what will essentially be a brand new Earth. With any luck, we should be able to control that filter.'

Kemp crammed a parcel of cheese wrapped in bacon into his mouth and chewed it thoughtfully. 'So what you're saying is that humans have massively screwed it up, right?'

'The long and the short of it is this: if mankind hasn't evolved and matured enough to survive a few simple tasks, then it simply doesn't deserve stewardship of the blue planet—Earth. Your type of mankind will come to an end. Another will begin. It's happened before and it will happen again.'

'Blimey. And everything you've just said,' Kemp said in between wiping his mouth on his sleeve, 'was given in dreams to those de Lowes.'

'Indeed. This shift in the universe sparked a series of dreams sent out by the dreamspinners. That's the name for the ugly spidery things we travel through.'

'I wondered how they fitted in.'

'They are the most ancient of all creatures that belong to the universe—if they are creatures.'

'Those things with the electricity-filled abdomens belong to the universe?'

'Absolutely.'

Kemp cupped the back of his head in his hands and leaned back. 'You know what, Cain, I think that is the biggest loads of bollocks I've ever heard.'

Cain eyed him curiously. 'I don't understand.'

'What I mean,' Kemp said, 'is that it doesn't make any sense.'

'It makes perfect sense,' Cain said. 'Nothing could be clearer.'

Kemp scrunched his face up. 'You're saying that Archie, Isabella and Daisy have been chosen to survive some massive challenges and if they don't, several billions of humans and everything else on the planet will get trashed.'

Cain sounded undeterred. 'Some trees will probably survive and much of the sea-life made it through last time. But yes, everything else will be destroyed.'

Kemp helped himself to a large slice of chocolate cake. 'It's not very fair, is it?' he said. 'I mean, what kind of universe comes up with stupid stuff like that? For school kids?' A drizzle of chocolate slipped out from between his large, plump lips. 'Anyway, you don't reckon they'll do it, do you?'

'That, my boy, is why I wanted to save you. The challenges were designed for strong, wise men, versed in nature and in magic and in war. You're right, they were never designed for children.'

'But, you didn't want me, you wanted Archie,' Kemp said, his voice hardening.

'Of course. But Archie's folly is your opportunity,' Cain replied, his deep voice smooth and syrupy. 'Archie is an Heir of Eden who has been given a strong ancient gift—why shouldn't I have desired a union with him?'

Kemp felt slighted, but it was true. 'What are these gift things that make them so important, then?'

'Physical attributes mainly,' Cain said, 'extended uses of the senses; heightened vision, hearing, smell and increased strength—that sort of thing. Nothing too dramatic.'

'Wow. Cool,' Kemp said thickly. 'And this Garden of Eden—what's that all about? Why does it have to be opened? Why doesn't everything stay the same?'

'You really are full of questions. Perhaps it is all this food.' Cain smiled. 'The answer, my boy, is many-fold. You see, the Garden of Eden is where new species were created and developed. If a species proved successful it was placed upon a planet to develop and evolve and primarily have some sort of useful function.'

Cain paused and wondered how much he should tell. 'For a long while, the Garden was closed. You see, there was a... how should I put it... a disagreement about how it functioned, about the legitimacy of what was being created.'

'Sounds like a right load of tosh.'

'Indeed,' Cain said, 'whatever tosh means. But it was certainly complicated.'

Kemp bit into an apple. 'But if the Garden of Eden is miraculously opened, won't everyone survive?'

Cain chuckled throatily. 'The chances of Eden opening is so utterly remote that it is almost not worth considering, but I have in place my own safety net of sorts, just in case.

'You see, after the flooding, comes pestilence, which is out there causing bedlam. All the clues are written down at the beginning of those old historical books you Earth humans seem to get so much pleasure from. Anyway, I thought I might speed the process up.'

'Don't tell me,' Kemp said, 'you've given the disease to the de Lowes?'

Cain suddenly realised the boy was smarter than he looked. 'Not a bad idea, but unfortunately, the Heirs are protected. Now, here's a clue. Those ugly dreamspinners came to me with the news that there are no more dream powders remaining from their main stores. So, in return for a bit of help from them, I have allowed them to create some dream powders here, subject to a few modifications. Do you understand?'

Kemp rubbed his greasy chin thoughtfully. 'Yeah, I think so.'

'Very well. Try again.'

'OK,' Kemp grinned and rubbed his chin. 'How about you've given the disease to all the world leaders through your dreamspinner mates, and as they get ill, each country blames it on the other and then they blow the shit out of each other.'

'Bravo. Another fine suggestion, but no, I'll tell you. All I've done, my friend, is slip a little of the disease into my brand new store of dream powders.'

Kemp smiled. 'And these dreamspinners dish out dreams every night—around the world?'

'Precisely.'

Kemp wiped his mouth with his sleeve. 'You're spreading this disease as people sleep. That, my ghostly buddy, is blooming genius.'

Cain was delighted. 'You see, I'm not just a pretty face.'

Kemp banged the table as he laughed. 'They won't know what's hit them. And so fast and un-warned and utterly brilliant—they'll never work it out because no one really knows how dreams work, right?'

'Absolutely. My thoughts too,' Cain said. 'Superb little plan, isn't it?'

However, a thought struck Kemp and his face darkened. 'You promised to bring my mother here, didn't you? That was our deal.'

'And I will,' the ghost said, purring. 'I'm glad you mentioned this because I wanted to talk to you about your mother. It's important that our relationship is based on the truth. Don't you think?'

'Truth?' Kemp said, nervously. 'What is it—is she dead? She is, isn't she?'

Cain remained silent.

'Or... she's in a mad-house or something?' Kemp's voice creaked.

Closer than you think, Cain thought. 'Do you know how your parents died?'

Kemp nodded. 'Car crash, in the hills.'

'Correct. Before I returned you to Earth, I met up with your father's ghost.'

Kemp looked astonished. 'You can do that?'

'Why, of course. After all, I too am a kind of spirit, though I have considerably more substance than the truly dead. Spirits are easy to find if you know how, but frightfully airy and irritable. Your father told me about your mother, about the accident when you were just a babe. He told me many things.' His voice dropped. 'But the most fascinating thing is that your mother never died. She was found. She survived.'

Kemp's brain slowed to a halt as he computed Cain's story. The apple in his hand dropped to the floor.

'She lives, truly. Your mother is as alive as the next person.'

Kemp swallowed. 'You're having me on,' he said very quietly.

The ghost made a sound as if it were sucking in a mouthful of air. 'No, boy.' The ghost removed the hat and placed it on the table.

Kemp shook his head. 'I thought you'd bring her to me as, you know, as a ghost, a spirit or something.'

'My thoughts exactly. I too am most surprised by this turn of events—'

Kemp eyed the top of the coat curiously. 'You're sure this isn't a joke, right?'

'I swear, on my death, that I am telling you the truth. However, the news isn't as good as you might wish. You must be prepared that, if I bring her to you, she will reject you. There is a strong chance that she will not want to know you.'

Kemp looked confused. 'That's not true, Cain. Of course she would. I'm her son.'

'I understand how you feel,' Cain said, sighing. 'However, she remembers nothing of you. She suffered damage to the brain—'

'Brain damage?' Kemp looked wounded. 'But mothers always, always know their children,' Kemp said defensively, 'no matter what. She'd know me, I'm sure of it. What's her name?'

Cain's overcoat stood up so that he was standing in front of the boy. 'I didn't think you'd believe me, but I do not lie. And the terrible part of this is that there is a strong likelihood that you too will reject the woman.'

'As if I would do such a thing,' Kemp stormed. 'Never! Who is she?'

'Very well,' Cain said. 'But don't tell me I didn't warn you.'

Kemp levelled with the ghost. 'Tell me who she is.'

'Your mother,' Cain said slowly, 'is the exact same woman who looks after the de Lowe children—'

Kemp's eyes hardened as he worked out exactly who the ghost was talking about. Then he burst out laughing. 'You're having me on, aren't you? Mrs. Pye... Mrs. bleeding Pye? Is that the best you can do? Mrs. Pye, that big, ugly, old hag.' Kemp slapped his thighs and bent over double, great guffaws spilling out of him. After a while, he straightened and then sat down. Only now, his eyes watered.

The overcoat sat down beside him. 'I told you this wouldn't be easy. Often, young man, things are best left exactly as they are.'

Kemp's mood changed fast. In no time his face raged with anger. 'Listen here, Cain,' he roared, 'I'm telling you, Mrs. Pye is NOT and *cannot be* my mother. Do you understand?' Kemp stood up, tears flowing. 'She can't be. It's impossible.'

Cain hovered next to him and whispered in his ear, 'Thing is, boy, it is the truth. She really is.'

HAVILARIAN TOADSTOOL POWDER

Isabella let herself in, stripped off her waterproofs and entered the kitchen. She added a couple of logs to the belly of the stove, grabbed a clean tea towel and dried herself off.

She popped the kettle on the range and, while she waited for it to boil, she shook as she remembered the sensation that had entered her mind and filled her with dread. *Those eyes,* she thought, *and that noise,* which had washed through her head like a mass of incomprehensible, jumbled words and sentences.

She poured the boiling water. A cup of tea for herself and an apple tea for Old Man Wood, in case he was feeling better.

On the table were two candles and she searched around for a match. She looked in all the obvious places but either they'd run out or they'd been taken next door. She felt heat building in the tips of her fingers and, thinking of a flame, she clicked the end of her thumb and forefinger. To her amazement, a tiny spark flew out. She laughed, nervously, and inspected the end of her thumb and her digit. *Static?*

She tried again and this time another spark fizzed out, fading in the air. *But it doesn't make sense.* Something had to make it spark. She clicked her fingers again and this time a tiny flame shot out of the end of her thumb. Isabella didn't know whether to jump for joy or scream in terror.

But the strange thing was that it didn't hurt and, if anything, felt entirely natural. She sat down and studied her fingers in more detail, a surge of euphoria rushing through her. She placed a flame below her fingers, but they didn't discolour or burn or singe. It was as if her hands had become impervious to heat and pain.

Isabella lit the candles, knocked on Old Man Wood's door and entered, placing the candles on the tables. Then, she went back for the tea, which she set beside the still outline of the old man lying in his bed.

'We heard noises at the ruin!' she said softly as she busied herself about the room. 'I left Daisy and Archie out there,' she said, leaning briefly over him, his face obscured by the dim light and the folds of a blanket. 'I'm afraid there's bad news with the cattle: three cows missing and one sheep. Too dark to tell which ones though.'

She lit another candle on his table then returned and jumped up onto the bed, which wobbled and creaked a little. Then she lay back on the soft downy pillows at the side of the old man.

Old Man Wood lay perfectly still and she very carefully reached over and read his pulse. She squinted. Faint, but definitely something. She propped herself up and turned her gaze towards the wooden panels at the foot of the bed.

'You'd have seen us, if you'd watched the panels,' she said.

No response at all.

Isabella sighed, 'There's some tea for you—apple tea, to make you strong,' she said, remembering his tea-mantra.

As she sipped hers, she turned her attention to the images on the wooden panels.

There was Archie, crouching down as if waiting for something. In Daisy's panel she could make out a running human figure, similar to her sister, but with glowing eyes, like car headlamps.

Why was Daisy's panel doing strange things?

A strange slurping sound emanated from Old Man Wood. 'I think her panel's gone a bit funny, Old Man Wood,' she said, nudging his arm. 'There's tea on your bedside table,' she repeated, 'if you'd like it.'

Suddenly Archie attacked the figure with the bright eyes and threw it violently to the ground.

Isabella sat bolt upright. 'Archie's beating it up! He's pinning it down!' she cried, leaning towards the panels. 'Go Archie! No one messes with Superman-boy!'

She chuckled at the thought, and stared at Daisy's panel. 'Oh! Hang on!'

Archie's beating Daisy up? she thought. *Are they messing about?* 'Hey, Old Man Wood, did you see what led up to this?'

For a moment she wondered if she should dash up there and sort them out but, as she viewed, they seemed to slump down behind a rock, chatting.

She checked her watch. Typically, delicious smells would drift out of the kitchen at this time, at which point Old Man Wood would nearly always comment on what it might be and rub his tummy in anticipation. But there were no fabulous smells and still he didn't stir a muscle. 'I wonder where Mrs. Pye is?' she said. 'I'm starving.'

Isabella leant over to his side of the bed and called out, sweetly, 'Old Man Wood?'

No reaction.

'Can I get you anything?'

His face, in the dim candlelight, looked milky-white and a terrible fear swept through her that he might have passed away while she was talking to him.

She slid off, grabbed a candle and walked around the large bed to the other side and set it down on the bedside table. Old Man Wood's face was mostly hidden by the folds of a thick pillow and his body was covered by a duvet. She perched on the edge of the bed and gently levered the pillow out of the way.

Isabella's heart began to race. Something about him didn't look right.

'Come on, Old Man Wood, wakey-wakey,' she teased. Nothing, again. A terrible panic began building in her mind. 'Please. Wake up. Please.'

She moved in to inspect his face, lifting the candle up to offer more light.

She cupped a hand over her mouth as her stomach lurched. 'OH-MY-GOD!' she said standing up quickly but with the presence of mind to put the candle down first.

Old Man Wood lay motionless, his eyes shut, his skin as white as snow. Dotted over his face in tiny clusters were tiny white toadstools which she traced all the way down his neck.

She folded back the duvet and unbuttoned the top three of his shirt buttons. As she folded back the lapels, she stepped back from the bed stunned.

Before she could help herself, she retched.

WHAT ARE THEY?

In the candlelight tiny, pulsing, toadstools poked out of his chest like minute pins holding weenie umbrellas.

Instinctively, Isabella reached for his wrist and held it, counting. A murmur, the faintest, faintest dimmest of beats, that's all.

Get an ambulance. No, it won't get here—the air ambulance—they're rescuing people from the flooding. What about phoning the hospital, they'd know what to do?

She clenched her fist. With no power, they had nothing. No phone, no communication.

In any case, she thought, *the hospital probably didn't even exist anymore.*

COME ON. Think! THINK!

She slapped her forehead as if it might trigger an idea; there must be some way of making him better! Resplendix Mix! Old Man Wood's potion he'd used on them. *But where was it?*

She tore round the room searching for the strange bottle without a lid.

She rummaged through his coat and trouser pockets, through his chest of drawers and then ran downstairs and scoured the sitting room.

She returned up the stairs, entered Old Man Wood's room and leaned against the wall. Reality was hitting her hard. *We're lost if he doesn't survive*, she thought.

Then, without knowing why, she moved towards him and placed a hand on his brow. Pinpricks of heat, like mini, red-hot needles emanated from the toadstools. She kept her hand there, her palms crossed on his forehead.

Now the temperature built. Her hands were tingling, sucking out heat. The longer she did it the more disgusted and furious she became until a rage began to bubble up inside. And the angrier she became, the hotter the heat pouring into her hands. Soon the heat was almost too much to bear.

She removed her hands and quickly turned down the duvet covering his body. Suddenly a large, vile green toadstool the size of a hammer sprouted out of his belly and sliced through his shirt. Isabella squealed.

She rocked backwards, holding her mouth. '*NO!*' she cried. '*NO!*'

Now that his shirt had slipped off his chest, she could see hundreds of multi-coloured fungi littering his body, like bits of confetti, *eating* him.

Old Man Wood's last words, she realised, weren't about the poison *in the water* —they were concerning the poison *he'd taken.*

Isabella backed away towards the door. *Someone, give me the strength to do something. Anything.*

She stared and the longer she did the more frustrated and cross she became. Fury filled her growing like a furnace.

Another large, green and red toadstool sliced out of his chest, the noise like tearing metal foil.

Without warning, her whole body burned as though on fire. The surge consumed her, the heat inside her body roaring until her blood boiled and her temples throbbed as if her arteries might burst.

Her eyes blazed as if they were made of lava. She clenched her teeth, but the intensity deepened, hotter, faster—until her entire body was set to explode.

She extended her hands and pointed them at the two main, menacing toadstools, thriving, it seemed, with each flashing pulse, growing taller and fatter.

A strand of hair blew over her face as a wind picked up around her. From her hands an orangey-pink mist radiated, wrapping Old Man Wood in a wispy pink cocoon. Soon, it looked as though he was surrounded by fire.

Isabella let out a long piercing cry of anger and pain.

A second later, the body of Old Man Wood rose above the bed, the pink glow encircling and rotating like candy floss.

A high-pitched whirring noise built up and up until the intensity was almost unbearable, the cocoon swirling faster and faster.

The toadstools on the old man's body began to quiver, like birthday candles on a bowl of jelly.

All of a sudden a toadstool exploded off Old Man Wood's body, smashing into the ceiling. Then another—shattering the mirror—and another through the windows.

Toadstools from every part of his body rapidly discharged, peppering the walls, ceiling and bed. The noise was like a gun fight, fires starting on the wooden panelling surrounding the room.

All the while Isabella stood still, her hands extended, her concentration absolute as the swirling glow over Old Man Wood forced the toadstools out.

Soon, her energy wavered and the cocoon around the old man weakened. Only one remained. The large, lime green toadstool on his chest.

Exhausted, her strength gone, her body spent, Isabella had nothing more to give. She dropped her hands. The pink energy fizzling away.

Dizzy, her head as heavy as lead, Isabella stumbled into the wall and fell to her knees.

'I can't,' she cried. 'I'm so, so sorry, Old Man Wood... I'm so terribly sorry.'

And she collapsed on to the floor.

THE RING OF BABYLON

Gaia reached out a long, silvery claw. So, Asgard had sided with Cain and the news coming back through the ether painted a bleak picture.

Cain had added the plague to their dream powders to make lethal dreams. The spread was unimagined, unaccountable, swift and devastating. *It was the perfect mass-murder weapon.*

'How many dreamspinners are using Cain's spider web powders?'

'Hundreds,' a smaller dreamspinner vibrated, 'maybe thousands. More go every minute.'

'And each one uses his powder?' She already knew the answer.

I need Genesis, she thought. *She'll know what to do.*

She reached out for the vibration of the old dreamspinner, channelling her energy into the universe. A wavy, strange vibration tickle returned—slight and distant.

In a flash, Gaia inverted through the electric middle of her body, flashing through the universe to the spot where she desperately hoped Genesis would be.

She arrived moments later in a cave. A cave as tall as a mountain and half as wide. Was there such a place on Earth, or Havilah?

Gaia's opaque, silvery legs walked on the air towards the middle as though on an invisible grid.

Genesis would not be invisible here, Gaia thought, and she altered herself so she might also be seen. By doing so, she would see any dreamspinners that had themselves turned visible.

As she suspected, Genesis was waiting for her. 'You have come. Good. At least there is one of the ancient order still in possession of their faculties.'

Gaia had almost forgotten what a large, intimidating dreamspinner Genesis could be. Around her neck, and down the length of her shimmering silvery body, grey hoops gave her a formidable appearance. And far from the broken creature that had departed to die after giving the boy his Gifts, she looked menacing.

Her three black eyes pierced into Gaia. 'You know?'

'I do, mother. Our order, our traditions, are being dismantled, our purpose lost, dreamspinners corrupted. Asgard has aligned with Cain. Disease spreads from powders made from the spider webs in Havilah. As the sun goes down while Earth rotates, he spreads dreams of fear and failure. Death extends across the planet.'

Genesis tilted her head. 'Cain should *never* be trusted. Asgard showed him our secret and he has grasped it in his ghostly hands. Dreamspinners have been led to believe that the Heirs of Eden cannot open the Garden of Eden, so Asgard makes it his business to determine our future. He sees no hope in the Heirs of Eden.'

Genesis raised herself up. 'But the Heirs have *every* chance. That is why the universe selected them. Furthermore, there are ancient mysticisms that Asgard does not know.'

The great dreamspinner's posture fell a little and her vibrations quietened. 'I should have shared these with you many suns and moons ago, Gaia. And when I do, I will make a calling to stop this madness.'

'A calling, mother?'

'Yes. You will see. I alone know of it. There is a power to recall dreamspinners from every corner of the universe. But first, let me inform you of the ancient ways, for my time is not long now, and you, Gaia, will take my place. One mother of the universe to another.'

Genesis rose up again. 'The prophecy is far from failing. Even now, as the old man suffers from Cain's poison, there is hope. For he is protected by a charm the Heirs possess and which Cain long ago abandoned. It is the magic of love. Besides, these Heirs are not so weak or so frail as Asgard imagines, nor are they so stupid or so slow. It is a clever choice to use children as the Heirs; they are neither too cowardly nor too proud, as Asgard assumes. And they learn fast. And, moreover, it contains the element of surprise. Cain and the Mother Serpent will underestimate them.'

Genesis dipped one long, bony leg after another into the electric blue fire of her maghole, which raged harder than Gaia had seen for some time.

'You helped the old man find his Resplendix Mix, did you not?'

Gaia was astonished. 'Indeed. I wanted balance—'

'Balance. Good,' Genesis hummed. 'Now you will need to go further. The old man once possessed a branchwand. Find it and deliver it before the third tablet is found. Discover the dreams for informing him of its purpose. I will show you how to do this.

'And know this: Cain's twin, Abel, is not so crazed anymore. Time has banished his anger and he seeks his revenge. Like Cain, his shadow grows. And even though he will not come out of his place of hiding, Abel has promised a great gift.'

'But what of us?' Gaia asked. 'Is Asgard truthful? Is our time at an end?'

Genesis flicked her legs into her maghole. 'Tell me, Gaia, what do you know of the Prophecy?'

'Three tablets lead the way to the Key of Eden,' Gaia replied. 'The lock must be released to open the Garden and then life will begin anew, the Garden reborn. New species will come unto Earth and Havilah. But one failure will prove mankind's failing, and the Earth will be cleansed.'

'And, tell me, what if the Heirs have the three Tablets but do not find the key? Do you know what happens then?' Genesis asked.

'They die—?'

'Not necessarily. Opening the Garden requires that a great power be unleashed. We dreamspinners have the means to create, when there is no more. These things have been long forgotten.'

'Create? Create what, mother?'

'Here.' Genesis passed over a polished, sparkling white ring made of a glass-like stone.

'What is it? I know of no such things.'

Genesis' dark eyes sparkled. 'This is the Ring of Babylon, hidden on the walls of the cave and shrouded from common knowledge.'

Genesis ruffled her body so that she appeared, for a moment, larger, like a huge angel, her silvery, almost see-through body cloaking her strange spidery frame. 'If the Heirs succeed in finding the tablets, there is a choice if they still cannot release the lock.'

'I do not know of it, mother.'

'If the children survive, there are still options for their survival thing the Heirs can do. Point the ring at the red planet. One of the Heirs must push their breath through it. That is all. But it must be done before the sun goes down on the eighth day. This is a measure of absolute last resort and Adam will not be reminded until there is no hope.'

'How does it work?'

'One breath of life through the Ring of Babylon will create holes in space through which will be sucked life-givers.'

'For life-giver, you talk of comets?'

Genesis confirmed it. 'When one life-giver collides with Earth and another with Havilah and The Garden of Eden and Assyria and Cush, five new places of habitation will be formed. This will signal the end of the ancient order and the beginning of the new.'

'Eve and the old man, Cain, Abel and Seth will die?' Gaia said. 'I had no idea. Then a new time really will begin. A new time for us all, even dreamspinners...' Gaia flickered her legs out. 'Then Cain cannot prevail. He fails.'

Genesis dipped a couple of legs in her maghole. 'After a great sleep, the Heirs of Eden shall be the stewards.'

'The Heirs? But there are only three. How are they to reproduce and populate?'

'There are others, Gaia. When the time is right, the process of populating the worlds will begin. And when they are of a great age they will die, as it always should have been. The mistake of endless life will never be repeated. Remember, Gaia, this may only happen if they are alive at the end of the seven days and if they have all the tablets.'

'After defeating Gorialla Yingarna, the mother serpent—'

'And if they overcome Blabisterberry Jelly and find their way to Eden.'

Gaia shuffled and cleaned two legs in her maghole simultaneously. 'One failure—'

'Is all it takes,' Genesis interrupted.

'I understand.'

'Good. Remember it well. And Gaia.'

'Yes, mother?'

'Cain and Asgard must never know of the Ring of Babylon and neither must the heirs. Return to me in due course, there are other things I will show you, but now is not the time.' Genesis held the white ring up, and it glittered as if it were made of one piece of elasticised diamond.

'The other purpose of the Ring of Babylon is to summon dreamspinners so I can attempt to halt the error of their ways. While they come to me, they cannot spin dreams filled with poison.'

She tapped on it quickly as if it were a drum, creating reverberations that hummed high and low, deep and soft, loud and searching.

'Stand with me, my daughter of the universe, and watch.'

Back in their invisible state, the two dreamspinners waited as the humming continued wailing, its sound at once both harmonious and haunting, singing into the expansive universes.

It didn't take long.

Moments later, as if by magic, dreamspinners started popping out of the sky into the huge cavern in tiny flashes, pinpricks of light, until the huge chamber was packed with thousands of opaque, spidery-looking creatures with fiery, blue middles.

SOLOMON'S INTERROGATION

'Headmaster!' Sue rushed up to him and gave him a hug.

The headmaster hadn't anticipated it and only after a moment reciprocated.

'You survived!' she said, 'I can't believe how lucky we are.'

The words filled Solomon with a pang of guilt; *how had he lived, when so many had died?* he thought. 'And you are well?' he asked. 'How is our hero, Gus?'

'Oh, he's doing really well, thanks,' she said, smiling back at the familiar, yet slightly less rotund face of the headmaster. 'In fact, he's bored and itching to get out of his bed. Seems like all he had was a sort of mini-flu.'

'What a great relief,' Solomon said, and he meant it.

Sue looked around. 'Cool place, isn't it? What's it called, Swinton Park? I heard it was once a beautiful hotel.' Another helicopter buzzed overhead and settled down just behind a large cluster of bare trees just out of sight through the windows. 'I've never seen so many helicopters in one place,' Sue said, almost in awe. 'Have you met the Commissioner? He's a bit of a creep if you ask me. I've got a "debriefing" with him in half an hour.'

The headmaster had forgotten what a lively, pretty girl she was—and clearly desperate to talk. 'Sue, I wouldn't mind a brief catch up before you see him. Find out all about your extraordinary adventure. Can you spare a moment—outside? Have you got a coat?'

Sue caught his eye. 'Sure.'

They pushed open the double doors that led from the reception and rounded the thick stone walls heading up the path in the darkness. Solomon continued on around the lake towards the gardens.

'Headmaster, where are we going?'

'Please, call me Solomon, won't you, Sue? We're not at school now so you can leave the airs and graces behind, don't you think?' He smiled his head-masterly smile, his small, tea-stained teeth a little too evident. 'A little bit further, if you don't mind stretching your legs.'

He stopped for a minute and turned to face the vale behind them. 'Such a beautiful place isn't it, perched here on the Daleside of the Vale? Did you realise that Upsall is almost exactly opposite on the edge of the Moors, right over there?' he said, pointing into the distance. 'And have you seen the lake? It's well worth a visit in the morning. Dug by hand, so I'm told, and now overflowing like a mini Niagara Falls. A most impressive sight.'

Sue thought this commentary was rather odd but, as they walked around a clump of dense yew trees, she spotted a bench lit by an old street light. Solomon beckoned her to sit down.

He pulled out a notepad and a pen.

We're being monitored, he wrote. *You are in terrible danger.*

'Can you hear the geese over there?' he said. 'They're Canadian, you can tell by their distinct call.'

I'm bugged. You are too.

'Er ... Gosh—wow!' she said, the colour draining from her face. She shook her head and felt a hard nodule on her lapel. 'You're very knowledgeable,' she stuttered, her brain fizzing. 'Are they, er, related to Iberian Geese?' she said, racking her brain about birds.

He nodded encouragement.

Why? she wrote.

'Perhaps,' he said peering at the pad. 'You may well be right, I'm no expert. There used to be a famous deer herd here, but I believe all the animals have been put down,' he continued. 'A very ancient breed, by all accounts.'

They're on to the de Lowes.

'Oh! I like deer,' she said, rather thickly.

Crap, she wrote, before scribbling it out.

Solomon was a little taken aback and gave her one of his most knowing looks. 'I can't begin to tell you how thrilled I am to see you again,' he said. 'Tell me, how did you find that old rowing boat? I'm rather astonished it held together. Was that Isabella's idea?'

He scribbled fast. *I have to ask.* He pointed at her lapel again and gave her an encouraging look.

She grabbed the notebook and coughed as she turned the page. 'Well, yes! I suppose it was. Isabella realised the huge storm cloud might blow at any time. It was pretty obvious really. I mean, there was lightning shooting out everywhere, and all they had to do was run up the track home. She probably reckoned I wouldn't get home so, just in case, she suggested the boat. In hindsight, it was totally inspired. Then, luckily, I bumped into Gus.'

Sorry, don't normally swear.

'Sue, can I ask? What made Isabella so infatuated with the storm cloud? I know you both came to see me with a home-made barometer, was it something to do with this—were you just playing "scientists"?'

Sue shot him a curious look, trying to ascertain what sort of reply he was fishing for. 'Yeah, I suppose so. Isabella went a bit crazy on weather forecasting and...'

She stalled and stared at the ground.

'My dear,' Solomon said. 'Is there something you'd like to tell me?'

'Well, yeah, there is one more thing—but it's a bit weird. Actually no, don't worry about it—it's probably irrelevant.'

Solomon pressed her. 'Tell me everything,' he encouraged. 'I'm intrigued that Isabella knew enough to think of getting you a boat, but why didn't you simply head up into the tower—like many of the children and me?'

'We did calculations, sir.'

'Calculations? Whatever for?' Solomon raised his eyebrows in anticipation.

'OK—this will sound ridiculous.' Sue took a deep breath. 'I'd had a dream about a storm. Actually, it was more like a nightmare. Thing is, it felt so clear I thought it might be a premonition, you know, when you see something before it actually happens.'

Solomon nodded.

'Anyway, I told Isabella about it. You see, I always try and write my dreams down the moment I wake up. Amazingly, she believed me.'

'So it's happened before?'

'Yes. A couple of times. Anyway she then got all excited about it—in a scientific, meteorological way, you understand—'

Solomon smiled encouragement and mouthed: '*good*'.

'—and then she started looking at storm data on websites and she got more and more carried away until she made a barometer which kept bottoming out and all the while, much to our astonishment, the cloud kept growing until she came to the conclusion that this one was going to be the biggest of the lot. From her calculations, I don't think she thought the school tower would make it.'

'And all this came from a dream?' Solomon said, almost to himself. 'Fascinating.'

He handed Sue a note, with a finger over his lips.

No more!

Sue smiled back at the headmaster. It was nice to have someone to talk to.

There's more, she wrote, *much more.*

'Getting a bit chilly, isn't it?' Solomon said, rubbing his hands together. 'Let's go back inside shall we?' They linked arms. 'I am so terribly sorry about your losses. I am afraid our whole community has suffered dreadful personal tragedy. We are very much the lucky ones— I doubt if the populace will ever really recover. Life has a habit of bouncing back, though, so let's hope that maybe one day things will return to something near normal.'

Sue looked pensive. 'Why are there so many people rushing around with protective kit on?'

'You mean you don't know?'

Sue shook her head. 'I've heard there's some kind of virus out there. Is it true?'

Solomon pushed his glasses back on. 'My dear, absolutely. The country is in quarantine, everything—and I mean *everything*—has ground to a halt. According to a military chap I sat next to at lunch, half the towns and cities are up in flames. Mass looting—general pandemonium. By a total fluke, Swinton Park is possibly the safest place in the world, right now.

'You look a little pale, Sue, let's sit down by the fire. I thought they might have told you.' They walked inside, took off their coats, nodded at a couple of uniformed men who rushed by and sat down by the fire. 'But I guess there have been other things to worry about.'

Sue's face had gone white. 'Seriously? Is it the truth?'

'Indeed. Never more so. Why do you think Gus is in his little room? I believe it has been named *Ebora*, a rather crude blend of the Roman word for *York*—Ebor, and the *Ebola* outbreak in Africa. The problem is, these scientists have absolutely no idea how to contain it.'

'None at all?'

'Not only does it spread by touch and by bodily fluids, but it appears to fly through the air. And the strange thing is that, quite suddenly, it turned up the length of America, as though it flew west with the night. Maybe it did, who knows?'

'America?' Sue said. 'That's impossible.'

'Yes, both sides of North America and South America too, apparently.' He exhaled loudly and smiled. 'In a way it's a miracle neither of us has caught it. But, since they have no idea how it operates, there's no preventative advice that they can give to those who haven't been affected.'

Sue screwed her eyes shut and clenched her hands as the magnitude of what he was saying sunk in.

Solomon noticed, reached over and patted her arm lightly. 'As you know, it all began right here in Yorkshire. Upsall is the epicentre, they say. On the meteorological charts, the storm mushroomed out of Upsall and covered a good part of the

United Kingdom. The animations are most impressive. We're here because we're about the only people known to have survived. Our dear friend, the Commissioner, seems to think that there is something, or someone, in Upsall that can tell us more.'

Sue scribbled on the pad. *There is.*

'Sue,' the headmaster continued, alarm in his face, 'do you know of anything that might somehow link this storm or the Ebora with Upsall School or with any of your friends?'

Sue's eyes met the headmaster's. *Do I trust him? I have to — who else is there?*

She pulled her pen out.

It's the de Lowes, she wrote, allowing him to read the page.

She carried on writing and very calmly said, 'No, not that I'm aware of.'

The headmaster smiled and gave her a very faint wink out of his right eye. 'And does Gus know of anything, anything at all, Sue?'

'I don't think so,' she said handing over the notebook.

He read it.

They have to find three tablets. Then kill an old woman — I think.

'—Murder?' he coughed, before realising his mistake. 'In the village?' he added, too late. He passed the notebook back as he waffled on about a rather curious death claim in the village, hoping to mask his slip-up.

Sue cringed. She scribbled again.

If they fail, we die. They're running out of time

Solomon looked up, his face red from his gaff. 'Exactly as I thought,' he said. 'I never suspected anything else from you other than complete honesty.'

How do you know? he wrote.

She took back the pad. *I dreamt about it. So far, everything true.*

She handed the book back to the headmaster. He smiled at her and tossed it onto the fire. 'Thank you, my dear. Now, I think it's time we'd paid a visit to the dear Commissioner. He's been looking forward to meeting you.'

As they stood up, a crowd of people arguing loudly walked into the room. Solomon leant in very quickly and whispered into her ear. 'Sue, whatever happens, you absolutely *must* trust me.'

Solomon and Sue waited for half an hour in the ante-room outside his office as a stream of people filed in and out. Every so often they caught a few words or exclamations from Stone as the door opened and closed.

Dickinson, smart as usual, his hair neatly combed to one side, ushered them in and remained with them, sitting to the side of the desk, his tablet switched on ready for note-taking.

Stone rubbed his eyes, leaned back in his chair and drew a hand through his thick silver hair. He fixed Sue with a crooked smile. 'So, I'll tell you what we know,' he began, talking directly to her. 'And as I go, why don't you fill in the blanks. And please, don't muck me about, girl. We're fighting a losing battle here and if I don't think you're co-operating, I have the means and the methods to make you talk, understand?'

Sue gulped and nodded.

'Firstly, this storm and Ebora have both got something to do with Upsall.' He lifted his eyes to meet hers. 'Secondly, there's a connection with the de Lowe family.'

Sue gasped. 'How do you know that?'

'So you agree, do you?' Stone shot back.

'No, I... er, I never said that.' She flashed a look at Solomon.

Stone knew he'd struck gold. 'We know—don't we, headmaster—that there's something a bit quirky with this family? You see, your friend Kemp told us.' Stone said, going straight for the jugular.

'Kemp? He's alive?' she stammered before controlling herself. 'What would Kemp know?'

Stone smiled shiftily. 'Oh, he appeared to know all about it.'

'About what?'

'You tell me.'

For a moment there was silence. Stone leaned forward. 'Tell me about your dream, Sue?'

'Dream?'

'Yes, those things you have at night, you know, while you sleep—I'm told you had one all about the de Lowes. A kind of premonition? Am I right?'

Sue nodded.

'Why do you think that was?'

'I don't know. I dream quite a bit and I write them down. I like trying to work out their meanings.'

'How very interesting. I used to write a diary at night when I was your age until my mother found ink smudges all over my pillow.'

Sue smiled. 'Oh, I use a Biro or a pencil so it doesn't make such a mess.'

Stone pressed his intercom. 'Has it arrived yet? Good. Send it up when you're ready.' He turned back to her. 'Excellent. That means your diary won't have deteriorated in the floodwaters too much.'

'You can't do that,' Solomon stormed. 'They're a girl's private thoughts—'

Stone slammed his hand down on the desk. 'Screw her thoughts, Headmaster.

I can do what I damn well like.' They glared at one another. 'Where are the de Lowes, Sue? Where are they right now?'

'I have no idea,' Sue stammered. 'We last made contact on the rowing boat a couple of days ago. I think they were at home, although the text didn't say.'

'You're lying again,' Stone said. He turned. 'Dickinson. Was anyone at the property when you flew over?'

'Our thermal-imaging camera found the outline of one female adult. More than likely that of their housekeeper, Mrs. Pye. No others, sir. We circled the remains of the house twice, sir. No other bodies in sight.'

Sue felt sick. 'I don't know. Really I don't.' She fought back her tears.

'First Kemp vanishes, now the entire de Lowe family go absent,' he yelled. 'Dickinson, has anyone found the parents yet?'

'Negative, sir. We have a team scouring their last known locations.'

'Tomorrow, at the crack of dawn, I'm sending in a little expeditionary team to check out their little hovel on top of the hill. You better be certain they're not there, Miss Lowden.'

A knuckle rapped at the door. A man with a protective facial mask entered and handed a plastic bag to Dickinson. 'I've given it a bit of a dry, but it was pretty well protected by the bag,' he said, before exiting.

Sue recognised it immediately. 'That's mine—'

'Actually, I think you'll find it's Government property,' Stone smiled as he opened up the pink hardback diary. 'Tell me, what date did you say you had this epiphany?'

Sue face turned to thunder. 'About two weeks ago.'

Stone flicked through, eyebrow raised. 'Gosh. What drivel, all these feeble girlie thoughts. Ah. Here we are. Entry for Tuesday 28th October.

'*Another nightmare,*' he read.

Stone looked up, his face puce with anger. 'Is that it?' He flicked through several other pages. '*Another nightmare*? Is that all you wrote? What about all this "recording your bleeding dreams"?'

'I did,' Sue exclaimed. 'It's all there.'

Stone hurled the book at her. 'Find it! NOW!'

Sue nervously flicked through.

Next to her, Solomon burst out laughing, stood up and reached into his pocket. 'What's so damned funny?'

'It's just that, oh dear,' Solomon mopped his eyes with a handkerchief. 'Are you, my dear cousin, trying to ascertain what her dreams were all about?'

'Of course I ruddy well am.'

'Well, why don't you simply ask? Sue told me and I have to say that, when she told me, they were so ludicrous I didn't feel it was worth mentioning.'

Stone puckered his mouth. 'So tell me what she told you, Solomon. I'll be the judge of that.'

Sue shot the headmaster a worried look. *I have to trust him*, she thought.

'Sue's dreams were about the de Lowes finding three tablets that had code or whatever it is on them to save the world.'

Her heart sank.

'Tablets?' the commissioner said. 'What kind of tablets?'

'Computer tablets, I imagine—you know, iPads or the like—such as Dickinson's holding. Isn't that right, Sue?'

Sue's eyes almost popped out of her head. She laughed nervously. 'Er, yeah. I told you it was a bit weird.'

Stone eyed them both. 'Well, why isn't it on the recordings then?'

'Because, my dear old fellow, Sue was so embarrassed about telling me that I asked her if it might be easier to write it all down. So she did, on condition that I burned it afterwards. If you seriously believe there is anything worth following up concerning Sue's dream you'll probably find that the de Lowes have long departed Eden Cottage in search of these electronic devices. They're probably looting the High Street as we speak. Otherwise I think you might have to consider that Sue simply had a premonition about a very great storm. People do, you know.'

Stone swivelled on his chair and clenched his fists. It didn't add up.

'You dreamt about a storm, Sue, and in particular its violent nature. You also dreamt of the de Lowes, correct? So what's to say there isn't some fragment of truth to all of it?'

He stood and paced the room, shaking his head. 'Let's consider what we have. One ancient family who live by a ruin next to an ancient monastery, a biblical storm and a biblical plague, and you think electronic iPad tablet devices are involved?'

'That's what I saw,' Sue lied.

Stone moved right up to her, almost sniffing her. 'We'll find out tomorrow then, won't we?' he whispered quietly into her ear. 'If the de Lowes are home then I'm going to squeeze them until they squeak—for a bloody month if need be. If they're not, then believe me, I'll track them down.'

Stone returned to his seat and took a deliberately deep breath. 'Now, where do you think they would they go for these things? York? Leeds?'

Sue thought quickly. 'Perhaps, if there's any truth in the matter, you might be looking at this the wrong way. In my experience, Commissioner, dreams often highlight things that hint of something else. Dreams detect signals of worry or stress in the brain. So if you look at it like that, the key question isn't *where do you find the tablets*, but, perhaps *what you might use them for*. In which case, sir, there's every likelihood they may already have them.'

Stone stared at her and then the headmaster. 'Do you get this kind of shit all the time, Solomon?'

He turned his gaze to Sue. 'So, what you're suggesting is that they're after some kind of digital... code?'

Sue shrugged. 'I don't know. A code or a sequence or something.'

'Do they own iPads or similar tablets?'

'Not as far as I'm aware.'

Stone nodded and checked his watch. 'Right. Thank you, both. Sue you may go.'

A rush of relief swept over her. 'I'm here to help, sir,' she said. 'Please—if there's anything I can do to assist—'

'Thank you, I'll bear it in mind,' he said, smiling badly. 'Right now, Miss Lowden, I have other business to attend to. I've noted your offer and I'll let you know.'

SOLOMON'S THEORY

Stone sat down heavily and yawned. 'Still getting bloody nowhere,' he said to Solomon, irritably.

'I've had everyone screaming at me all day. Do you have the faintest idea what kind of huge turd is hitting this continent-sized fan? Well, I'll tell you. This place should be called Turdistan. No one has a bleedin' clue how this Ebora is getting around. It's a total bloody mystery.'

He rubbed his eyes as a wave of fatigue swept over him. 'And now the scientists say they need at least six weeks before they can crack it. Current estimates tell us we don't have six days, let alone six weeks!'

Solomon frowned as an idea popped into his head. He looked up as he accepted a cup of tea from Dickinson.

'Charlie. Something has struck me. Do you have a world map—even better, do you have a world map where the known outbreaks are marked?'

Dickinson nodded. 'Yes, it's on the global updater, sophisticated software developed in Estonia—I can hook it up to the projector if that's of any help.'

'Yes, it would be. And Dickinson, would you be able to play the recording back of me and Sue? There's something I said which may have a little more truth in it than I realised. About a third of the way through, I'd say.'

He sipped his tea while Dickinson played with his gadgets.

'This better be good, Solomon,' Stone said, eyeing him cautiously.

'It's a ruse, Charlie. And you may well throw it back in my face, but I think we're going to need to search a little more 'out of the box' as those young management fellows say.'

Dickinson pressed play. Their voices came across remarkably clearly.

Solomon perked up. 'A little further along. Not much. Yes—here.' They listened.

'… *not only does it spread by touch and by bodily fluids, but it would appear to fly through the air* …'

'*And the strange thing is that, quite suddenly, it turned up the length of America, as though it flew west with the night. Maybe it did, who knows?*'

'*America? That's impossible.*'

'*Yes, both sides of North America and South America too, apparently. In a way it's a miracle neither of us has caught it* —'

'Stop,' Solomon said and bit his lip. 'Play it again.'

When the passage finished for the second time, Stone piped-up. 'Headmaster, are you suggesting that this virus can fly?'

'No, not exactly.' He turned to Dickinson again. 'Can you spark your projector into life? Jolly good. Now, is there a kind of electronic gizmo which displays a time-line for when these occurrences took place?'

'By "occurrences",' Dickinson said, 'I take it you mean the approximate recorded times of Ebora infection?'

'Absolutely, I'm keen to see if there's a link to the disease being reported in relation to the time of day.'

'OK,' Dickinson said, 'I think I know what you mean.' Dickinson tapped away for a little while.

Soon, a large map of Yorkshire and the Northern half of England filled the screen covering the white wall. At the top was the date and time.

'Right, with any luck, this graphic should play the sequence from the very first engagement with the disease right up to the current minute.'

Dickinson dimmed the lights. 'The map should zoom out as the virus' spread increases,' he said, as he hit a key and the sequence began.

They stared in silence as the map stayed put while the time-clock flickered through the motions. 'OK, now it's midday on Friday—this is when the storm struck,' Dickinson said. 'Would you like me to super-impose the meteorological map as well?' He tapped away, reversed the time and then pressed play.

On the screen, a huge storm-cloud in purple, yellow and red colouring mush-roomed out of Upsall moving at an amazing speed until it covered a circular area reaching from Northumberland to Nottingham to the north and south and Scarborough to Manchester on the east and west axis.

'As you can see,' Dickinson said, 'at about five p.m. the bulk of the storm suddenly dissolves into ordinary rain clouds.'

'Dickinson. Pause it there, if you will,' Solomon said. 'Thank you. Is there any way you can overlay a night and day shadow map on top—'

'Showing the sun's passage around the globe? No problem.'

Solomon shook his head. 'Amazing what these little tablet things can do, isn't it?'

The adjustment took a little longer. 'Right,' Dickinson said. 'By the way, just an observation, but notice how the torrential rain cloud dissipates at the exact moment the sun goes down?' He returned to the current graphic. 'Anyway, let's see how this works.'

The map continued on its time-led journey. As the clock ticked through Saturday, a few specks in red, denoting the virus, began to appear, growing in number but generally spanning out only across the immediate area of the Vale of York.

The map then went darker, showing night.

The red dots began increasing in number though the night and the map zoomed out a little to include reports of infection from London and the South of England. Through Sunday, the red on the map widened a little but mainly intensified in Yorkshire, the north and midlands. As Sunday night came around this pattern was repeated.

On Monday, three days after the event, the general increase continued overnight when suddenly the map zoomed out. As morning extended, a vertical line of red dotted the atlas, spanning an area in the northern hemisphere from Reykjavik in Iceland to Lisbon in Portugal and Marrakesh in Morocco.

Then, quite unexpectedly, the globe spun on its head, showing a less orderly but unmistakable colouring of red dots weaving through the heart of Africa all the way down to South Africa.

Now the globe spun again as day broke across the Eastern shore of America.

All three men stood up.

'Pause it there!' Solomon said, his voice quivering. 'Thank you, Dickinson.' He faced his cousin. 'Now, if my theory is correct and the infection has spread at night, as we sleep,' he said, his brow furrowed, 'the next bit should be rather interesting.'

As the line of darkness gave in to the light of morning, following behind, like a red wave, came thousands of tiny dots. And as they watched, Ebora quietly swept across the Americas, North and South, quite literally as day follows night.

When the animation finished the three men remained in silence for a considerable time.

'So, Ebora comes at night?' Stone said.

'In waves,' Solomon agreed, mopping his brow.

'Maybe it's a biological agent, triggered by the dark?' Dickinson added.

Solomon hummed. 'I see where you're coming from, but does it really add up? Ebora originates from Upsall, spreads around as you'd expect with no particular order to it and then, two days later, it follows a strict pattern. As though something has taken it on—'

'Maybe there's a night particle—?' Dickinson added.

'A night particle?' Stone coughed. 'Come on, lad. Even I know there is no such a thing. More likely, someone's taken a flight from here to New York and it's spread hand to mouth—'

'In a day? It's impossible, Charlie. You know that.' The headmaster said, sitting down. He removed his glasses and dabbed his eyes.

'Now, who would like to hear my theory?' he asked.

'I'm all ears,' Stone replied with a heavy drip of sarcasm.

'You're going to find it hard to believe, Charlie, but hear me out. First of all though, here's a riddle for both of you. *What goes by night, has many forms and is given to all people?'*

'This is no time for riddles, Solomon.'

'Actually, yes, I think it jolly well is.'

'Ghosts, spirits?' Dickinson volunteered.

'No. Nice idea. You're in the right kind of area.'

'This is ridiculous—'

'Rain!' Dickinson said.

'Wrong!... although in one sense you are, I suppose, absolutely spot on. Here's a clue. What does the riddle have in common with Sue?'

'Are all your classes like this?' Stone said, flatly.

'She had a dream about the storm?' Dickinson said.

Solomon clapped his hands. 'Now we're getting somewhere. Yes, she *dreamt* about the storm. The answer to the riddle is, *"Dreams".'*

Stone clapped slowly. 'Bravo. Where the hell is this going, Solomon?'

The headmaster was on a roll. 'We know that Sue had a premonition. And it was so clear and so frightening that it even made her friend scared out of her wits —scared enough to chart weather sequences from around the world. And then, lo and behold, her dream came true. In fact, everything about it came true! So what I'm saying is this: either she has some kind of psychic powers or, perhaps, she was given that dream.'

'Oh, bloody hell,' Stone tutted. 'What—by freaking aliens?'

Solomon shrugged. 'I don't know! But what I do know is that throughout the world, come nightfall, the one common factor irrespective of creed and gender and race and animal type... and anything else that sets us apart from one another, is that we sleep and therefore we... dream.'

Stone took his feet off his desk, stood up and paced around the room, scratching his chin. 'Am I right in thinking that you're saying little alien bugs are flying about dishing out dreams?'

Solomon shrugged. 'I don't know. It is simply a theory. But we haven't got anything else, have we? And Ebora isn't caused by a lack of hygiene or spread by vermin. It is something else, Charlie. We may have to contemplate running with some distinctly unsettling propositions if we're to get to the bottom of this.'

Stone harrumphed. 'Dickinson, what do you think?'

The young officer had gone a little pale. 'I think it's utterly brilliant, sir.'

Stone rolled his eyes. 'Brilliant? Bollocks to that. Brilliant? So, what do you think I should do? Ring up the President of the United States of America and tell him to order his people not to go to sleep, in case they bloody well dream?'

He stood up. 'I can just imagine the scene at the White House. *The Brits have a plan for the Ebora,* he'll say, *this deadly virus they've unleashed on the world. It's called "Stay Awake". Gee, why didn't we think of that?'*

Stone's cold eyes bore into the headmaster. 'In my humble opinion, Solomon, that has to be the most unhelpful crappy piece of advice I've ever heard.'

Solomon eyed him curiously for a while and pushed his glasses up the bridge of his nose. 'Charlie, you're an excellent police officer with outstanding qualities, but sometimes I do think you really are one of the stupidest people I have ever had the misfortune of stumbling upon.'

Stone glared at him.

Solomon continued. 'You must realise that if what I'm saying is anywhere close to the mark, then what we're witnessing, right now, is some kind of alien or extra-terrestrial threat to us as a race. We may well be being led into extermination.'

Stone chortled. 'Wiped out? Don't be silly. Humans always find a way.'

'Hear me out, Charlie. You just said we haven't got an answer. Face it, our brain functionality does not allow us to think of anything outside of our general programming. If you ask me, my dear chap, something sinister and world threatening was opened up in Upsall. This power—or whatever you want to call it—is not only lethal, but without precedent. And, like it or not, it would appear to me that there are only three people in the world who know anything about it. My guess is that those three just happen to be the de Lowe children.'

Stone shook his head. 'They're bloody kids. Kids causing trouble with something they don't understand. That's my guess.'

'But so what if they're kids, Charlie? It makes perfect sense. Their minds are open and not closed—like yours, mine and most of the human race. Take a look at the boy, Kemp. What happened to him wasn't an accident of the storm: those burns, his malnutrition. They weren't the result of Ebora. And then, quite suddenly, he disappears off the face of the planet, leaving a puff of ash. In my opinion, he's a part of this too, Charlie. And it's something we cannot fathom.'

Solomon paced the room like a lecturer. 'Remember the stained glass windows of Upsall church? They clearly showed that after rain, comes pestilence. And Dickinson neatly pointed out that the terrifying storm cloud evaporated at the exact moment the sun went down. The question is, why didn't it continue on to pulverise the rest of the country? Something made it stop, which is why it moved on to the disease. We are being beaten and battered by something brilliantly clever, Charlie. And, it is utterly ruthless.' Solomon sat down. He needed a drink.

'Have you quite finished?' Stone said, as he chewed a fingernail and spat it out over the floor. 'Thank you for that huge load of complete shite. Let me remind you of a couple of things. Firstly, that I run the show round here, and secondly, I do not need any jumped-up loony theories about aliens and dreams. Do you understand, headmaster? What I need is proper, logical solutions and I need them now.'

The headmaster smiled at him wearily. 'As I said, it is a theory, that's all. Please don't forget that all I am trying to do is help you. I lost most of my students in this disaster and I, too, intend to get to the bottom of this one way or another.'

Stone acknowledged him with a wave of his hand. 'Dickinson, did you get the results of the ash from Kemp's disappearance?'

Dickinson sorted through some emails on his computer. 'Ah, here. Inconclusive, I'm afraid,' he said, looking up. 'The carbon dating machine appears to have broken down.'

Stone swore. 'What does it say?'

Dickinson read on. 'Well, the results that came back said that the ash was over a million years old. That the boy somehow—combusted—'

'Kemp burnt himself to death?' Stone spat. 'Incinerated into a small pile of ash in the toilet?'

Dickinson smiled. 'Hence why they think the machine is faulty.'

Solomon sensed his moment. 'Look, if I can get into that house of theirs, maybe I can find out if there's anything that might match what I found in the church. Surely it's worth a try?'

Stone eyed him curiously. 'Yeah, alright. Take the girl with you. She knows them well enough. But on one condition: you only go if they're not there. I don't want you interfering if and when we find them. Is that clear? Our team will be there shortly after dawn. They'll be back by midday. You'll know by then.'

'Good,' Solomon said. He stood up, thanked Stone and Dickinson, and let himself out.

Outside the door, he exhaled loudly.

If the children were there, as Stone suspected, then there was no way he could get the de Lowe's away from the cottage before the soldiers arrived at dawn. And if his theory had any weight, well, then what?

❄

Dickinson sat down. 'Persuasive—your cousin. I like him. I wish my teachers had had his charisma.'

'But not very useful on a practical level, I'm afraid,' Stone said. 'Bloody lunatic if you ask me.' He scratched his creased brow. 'Play that recording again. There's a bit towards the end that I didn't quite understand—it's been nagging at me. Something he says doesn't add up.'

Two can play at this game, Stone thought.

Dickinson clicked back towards the end. Then back a little.

'Yes. That's probably about right. OK, let it roll.'

The recording came to life, filling the room.

'Sue, do you know of anything that might somehow link this storm or the Ebora with Upsall School or with any of your friends?'

'No, not that I'm aware of.'

'And does Gus know of anything, anything at all, Sue?'

'I don't think so.'

- long pause -

Then, not so loudly:

'Murder?... In the village ...?'

Stone leant in. 'What's going on there, Dickinson? Did she mouth something to him?'

Dickinson ran it back and they listened again. 'It's like they're sort of having another conversation, separately.'

Stone put his hands behind his head and exhaled. 'Is there a chance, Dickinson, that Solomon and Sue are taking us for one BLOODY great big ride? Why do I have a very deep suspicion that underneath this Ebora disaster lies some kind of murky secret?'

'What do you want me to do, sir?'

'Go with the crew at dawn. Watch, listen—find out all you can. And believe you me, when we get those kids I'm going to shove so much electricity up Archie-bleeding-de Lowe's backside that his hair will be standing erect for the rest of his life.'

His COBRA hotline buzzed.

'Mark my words,' he continued. 'Sometime soon they're going to have to come running out of their burrow and when they do, I'll be there.'

Dickinson strode towards the door.

'One more thing, Dickinson: I want you to personally radio me when you get to that cottage at first light, understand? I want you to be my eyes and ears.'

Stone picked up the receiver. 'Stone,' he said. He listened for a minute, cringing at the sharp tones cutting down the phone.

'Secretary of State,' he said, trying not to express his irritation. 'No, I didn't realise you've had the Americans demanding to send in their troops, nor coming here to find the cause of Ebora. Please remind them that the best help they can give us is in areas such as forensics and molecular science—'

He listened to the shrill voice on the other end.

'Then it seems to me,' he said, 'that we could do with them helping to keep the peace, not in threatening to blow the hell out of Yorkshire, or any place else they suspect.'

The Secretary of State spoke at length again.

Stone responded. 'On that matter,' he said, 'I have a lead in regard to Archie de Lowe and his sisters. Nothing certain, but I'll know more in the morning when my team have swept through their cottage. I'll call you at eleven with an update.'

Stone replaced the phone and mopped his brow.

It was out of control. The world was in crisis. The Americans now blamed Middle Eastern terrorist groups for planting Ebora and destroying the west, the Chinese were blaming the Russians and the Europeans were blaming the Americans who were ready to decimate the North of England with a very, very big bomb in order to stop its spread at source.

Stone shook his head. *It was already too late for all that.*

He thumped the table. Everything would be a good deal easier if they could just find Archie de Lowe.

ISABELLA'S POWER

The twins were by the track, near to the courtyard, when they heard Isabella screaming.

Daisy and Archie looked at each other, then Mrs. Pye.

'It's Bells,' Daisy said. 'Something has happened.' They rushed inside following the noise up the stairs. As they turned into Old Man Wood's room their eyes met a quite extraordinary sight.

For from the crack in the door they saw Old Man Wood's mushroom-littered body levitating in a cocoon of swirling pink light coming from Isabella's hands.

As they stepped inside, the fungi began to detonate. Daisy and Archie threw themselves behind the door as toadstools thudded into the panels and wall and door like rifle bullets. As the noise died down they poked their heads inside. Isabella, on her last reserves, stumbled and fell against the wall.

Archie rushed to her, holding her up.

Daisy followed. 'What is it?'

Archie glanced at Old Man Wood's chest, where the last remaining toadstool glowed from green to white. 'I think he's dying,' he said.

Suddenly, it grew.

Archie ran forward and attempted to rip it off but only succeeded in burning his hands.

Then, without knowing why, he moved behind his sister, extended his arms around her body and directed her wrists aloft. Daisy instinctively did the same so that Archie was sandwiched in the middle, their arms pushed forwards.

He shut his eyes.

'Be strong, Bells,' he said. 'Reach inside and draw out every sinew and fibre—and then go a little bit further.'

The lagging pink cocoon suddenly fizzled into life.

With one last, deep breath she screamed:

'OUT... **OUT!**'

She thrust her hands at the fungi and slammed everything she had at it. Archie and Daisy shut their eyes.

The toadstool quivered and swayed, but stuck.

'More, everyone,' Archie yelled, 'Together, all of us. Bells, ONCE MORE... on the count of three.

'One, two...

NOW!'

A huge volley of power rocketed out from the children's extended arms, the recoil throwing them against the wall. The toadstool flinched, then swayed and shook, before blasting off Old Man Wood's chest, circling the room twice like an out of control firework and smashing into the bed panels at the foot of his bed, spraying the room with wood and splinters.

As the pink cocoon faded, Old Man Wood's body floated down.

Archie and Daisy untangled themselves and picked themselves up off the floor.

Darkness filled the room save for the crackle of fire on the panelling spreading quickly towards Old Man Wood's bed.

Isabella lay on the floor, motionless.

Archie acted fast. 'Daisy, get Isabella out of here!'

He ran to the bed and, in two deft movements, lifted the torso of the old man and then hoisted him effortlessly over his shoulder, his body swamping him like a bear.

Outside, Archie laid Old Man Wood next to Isabella. He looked over her pale sweaty face, brushed her hair away and gently kissed her forehead. Soft breaths came out over long intervals, her face ashen and her eyes closed but ringed with dark patches, like a panda.

'Hey, Bells,' he whispered. 'You did it. You saved him, I'm sure of it.' He detected the faintest glimmer of a smile. A tear rolled down her cheek. He smiled back and wiped it off. 'Back in a minute.' Without hesitating, Archie rushed back in and, wielding a carpet, smothered the flames.

He ran down the corridor to the bathroom, emptied the contents of the bin on the floor, filled it with water and returned to extinguish the glowing embers. Finally, coughing lightly, he rejoined Daisy, who was dabbing Isabella's brow with a wet cloth.

'What were those things?' Daisy whispered.

'No idea,' he replied. 'What she did was... astonishing, utterly amazing! She's got wicked powers!' Archie said, staring proudly at his big sister. 'Awesome.'

Isabella stirred.

Daisy offered her a cup of water. 'Did you know you could do that, Bells?' she asked.

Isabella smiled.

The twins grinned but a groan moved their attention to Old Man Wood.

Archie felt for the old man's pulse.

'Nothing,' he said. 'It's like it's vanished.'

Archie wiped his nose, holding back his tears. 'We're too late.'

Daisy reached out and took the old man's hand. 'I'm so, so sorry, Old Man Wood.'

For several minutes, Archie and Daisy sat by the old man's still body.

Finally Archie spoke. 'What happens now?' he whispered. 'How do we find the tablets without Old Man Wood?'

Daisy shook her head. 'I don't know. We've had it, haven't we?'

A strange groan came from the floor, like a whiny floorboard. Archie and Daisy looked at one another, then moved their gazes downwards.

'Well, I'm not bloomin' dead yet,' a deep, croaky voice said.

'Old Man Wood!' Daisy cried, giving him a hug.

'Aw, ow! Gently now,' he said, as he opened his eyes.

His accentuated wrinkles formed a smile and his eyes shone like jewels in the candlelight. 'Apple juice,' he said. 'And a little bit of Resplendix Mix, if you don't mind.'

'Yes! Of course,' Archie said. 'Where is it?'

Old Man Wood forced saliva into his mouth. 'Coat,' he said. 'In the bootroom.'

Archie switched on his torch and tore off downstairs, returning with the strange medicine and a bottle of Old Man Wood's apple juice.

'Here,' he said, offering the golden liquid of the Resplendix Mix to Old Man Wood's lips. The moment it touched them, colour began to return to his cheeks. Old Man Wood blinked and sighed and then ooh-ed and ah-ed and grimaced as the healing medicine went to work.

Archie took it over to Isabella and did the same. Just a drop, like Old Man Wood said. The bottle opened for her and, before long, Isabella's eyes were wide open.

Then Old Man Wood smiled, a look of intense happiness on his face. But, as footsteps creaked up the stairs his expression quickly turned to alarm.

The children froze. Then slowly they turned to face whatever was coming up.

A voice rang out from the dark beyond them. 'What, in the Devil's name is going on?' it said. 'I don't know what's got into you lot. Making every effort to totally destroy the house, huh! What a terrible din, the likes of which I can't remember.'

Mrs. Pye peered into the dark. 'Been lighting fires have you? Well I hope there's a good reason for all this queer behaviour.' She shook her head. 'Your tea's on the table, or had you forgotten?'

She trudged slowly back down the stairs, tutting.

The four of them sat on the landing, chuckling like naughty schoolchildren.

Archie was the first to speak. 'What happened? What were those toadstool things?'

The old man sat up and slowly stretched his arms out wide. 'All I can say is that it's not every day you get poisoned with Havilarian Toadstool Powder. It's the most deadly powder known to... well... certain things. If I am in fact alive, which I suppose I must be, then I'm probably one of the few that has ever survived. So how did that happen? Who or what do I have to thank for saving my flesh?'

'You'd better thank Isabella,' Daisy said, clapping her hands. 'She did it and I have to say, it was wicked!'

'Well, I never,' Old Man Wood croaked. 'And how—?'

'Using a cocoon of pink light and energy,' Archie said. 'But your cool wooden TV panels got smashed to bits.'

Old Man Wood seemed unconcerned. 'We needn't worry about that now. What's important is that we're here and I reckon we'll be a good deal stronger for it.'

He shuffled over to Isabella and helped her up into a sitting position, and then wrapped his arms around her. 'Thank you, littlun,' he said into her ear. 'I owe you.' Then he picked himself up off the floor, stood up and ran his arms high above his head. 'Right, as Mrs. Pye said, tea is on the table and I for one am *famished.*'

Old Man Wood's body tingled as though it had been crammed full of electric-tipped feathers and his head fizzed with excitement.

Right now, his secrets, his magic and even his purpose were pouring back to him as though a chain had broken and unlocked the gates of his mind.

The time had arrived, no doubt about it. The opportunity to help the Heirs of Eden plot a return to the Garden of Eden had come at last. Finally, just as he'd quietly suspected, the chance had come to re-ignite the sparks of creation.

The children *had* been given the Great Dream and, it appeared, the legendary Gifts of Eden. Old Man Wood shut his eyes and smiled; that was enough thinking for now.

First, he needed nourishment. Then he would let the memories fill his head.

A LESSON FROM THE PAST

'Why did those toadstools make you so nearly die Old Man Wood?' Daisy asked as she scraped her fork around her plate. 'You said something about Havilarian Toadstool Powder but we've never heard of it before. Did you poison yourself?'

Old Man Wood chuckled, his chest heaving up and down. 'It is no mystery, my littluns,' he said, 'and, no I didn't. You see—'

'But what exactly was it?'

'A terrible substance, no doubting it,' he said, studying their blank faces. 'Must be something close by, but *how it got there* is indeed a mystery. In any case, whoever did it must have tried to put us off—to stop you lot making it to the other worlds—'

Archie dropped his fork and it clattered over his plate. 'What other worlds?' he said. 'I didn't know there were other worlds. I thought all we had to do was find three tablets. How many worlds are there?'

'Three,' Old Man Wood replied calmly and without pausing. 'There were five, but two of them blew themselves to pieces. Now, if I remember rightly, those ones were called Cush and Assyria—though I don't reckon there's much there any longer. They got a little too clever for their own good and forgot what Nature was all about.'

He leaned back in his chair and rubbed his chin. 'Without sounding too miserable, it might be that Earth is heading the same way. But anyway, where was I? Ah, yes. The other two planets are Earth and Havilah. Yes,' he said, thoughtfully, 'those two are the last remaining ones. Of course, there's also the Garden of Eden, but no one knows what's happened there. It's been closed an awful long time, since the great flood—'

'*The Garden of Eden?*' Isabella interrupted, suddenly wide-awake. '*The Garden of Eden,*' she repeated, '*with the flood? That* Garden of Eden?' she leaned across the table. 'You're talking about the Biblical place, with Adam and Eve, the serpent, Cain and Abel, Noah... you know, Genesis... animals going in two by two?' She fixed the old man with her hardest stare. 'It isn't a real place, you know. Everyone knows that!'

Old Man Wood frowned. 'Well, er... no. I mean, yes. Oh appley-deary me. In the books, it's not quite the same thing... only a smidgen of it—'

'Look,' Isabella said. 'Those Bible stories succinctly explain life before the records that come after it. If you carry on like this, Old Man Wood, we're going to have to think again about putting you in an old people's home.'

Daisy rolled her eyes. 'Bells, I thought you'd left all that behind?'

'There's no way in the world that Genesis and Creation could have physically happened.'

'It's *worlds*,' Archie corrected her.

Isabella glowered at him. 'Life on this planet *evolved*, everyone knows that.'

'Ah,' Old Man Wood said. 'I was getting to that bit—'

'There's more?' she said.

'Oh yes, littlun. You see, once upon a time, there really was a great flood on the Earth—like the one we've got now I suppose—'

Isabella slumped back in her chair. 'And now, it's a nursery story.'

'Back then,' the old man continued, 'the "Rivers" flooded and remained flooded so nothing could travel from one world to another—'

'Rivers?'

'Oh yes. The Garden of Eden and Havilah are like Earth in a geographical, roundabout kind of way.'

Isabella massaged her temples. 'This is completely and utterly crackers,' she said. 'No known life forms in the universe have ever been found. And, furthermore, you're damning a whole civilisation of believers.'

Old Man Wood laughed, 'Bella, this isn't going to be easy—'

'Easy—?! The Bible and those other religious texts are sacred books, worshipped globally—'

'But the beginning holds the clues to what's going on NOW,' Old Man Wood argued. 'How else were they going to pass on the knowledge, the special secrets—?'

She glared at him. 'Entire cultures begin with this story!'

Old Man Wood shrugged. 'Well, no-one knew it'd be quite such a popular story at the time. And, anyway, it seemed like a good place to start—'

'Oh my God,' Isabella said, slowly. 'This is deeply, deeply flawed,' she said, shaking her head.

'What are *Rivers*?' Archie interrupted. 'I take it these aren't *real* rivers are they? And anyway, isn't Assyria somewhere in Africa? I'm sure Mum and Dad mentioned it last time they were back.'

Mentioning their parents made the children suddenly a little reflective and an uneasy silence hung in the air.

Old Man Wood turned to Archie. 'I haven't explained it properly, have I?' he said, relieved to move away from Isabella's grilling. 'But you're absolutely appley-right about one thing! *Rivers* are the connections between worlds—'

'Like wormholes?' Daisy said, as though a little spark had burst into a flame. 'Portals that transcend space, and all that stuff.'

The old man clapped his big hands together. 'Why, that exactly!' he said. 'Wormholes, portals, *Rivers*—they're one and the same thing. And yes, those places here on earth, Assyria, the Garden of Eden, Cush and Havilah, many others—were named in memory of their own worlds far, far away in other universes a long, long time ago.'

Daisy continued, intrigued. 'So, you said that people stopped travelling from planet to planet through these "Rivers". Why did these worm-holey things close down?'

'Hmm. Now, that's a good question,' Old Man Wood said, his face deeply lined in thought. 'War and a difference of opinion, I suppose. You see, those stories, like that Genesis one, were nearly right,' he said, his face darkening. 'But, oh, what a terrible time, even if it did save Earth and Havilah.'

'I don't understand. How could a massive flood *save* Earth?' Daisy asked, confused. 'Didn't everyone die apart from Noah? And anyway, what happened to this Garden of Eden place?'

Old Man Wood hummed as he thought about his answer. 'As far as I can remember, hordes of bad folk found a way of going back through the *Rivers* and into the Garden of Eden because, up until then, you could only go out of the Garden and not in. As a result, the Garden found itself being poisoned; its structure eroded and destroyed, and then ... war.'

Old Man Wood's eyes filled with tears, his brow deep and furrowed. 'A terrible war. People tried to make a claim on the Garden of Eden, and when the fighting finally stopped, blood covered the worlds, rivers ran red, flames singed the land, bitterness ran through veins, treachery mastered minds. Hatred and anger everywhere. A horrible time.'

Old Man Wood wiped his eyes and pulled himself together a little. 'To put it to an end, there was a moment of extraordinary sacrifice, one moment that alone is worth the Garden of Eden coming back to life.'

For a while, silence reigned as Old Man Wood stared into the distance. The children hardly dared to breathe.

Isabella took a deep breath. 'OK—so if what you're saying has some truth to it, what made this Garden of Eden so special?' she asked quietly. 'Why did it matter?'

Old Man Wood regarded her, his face deadly serious. 'Because, my dear little Bells,' he said, 'it's where everything began. That's why—'

'Everything?'

'Yes, everything. How do you think all these billions of things that make up the world around you actually started?' He studied their puzzled faces. 'Everything—dinosaurs, people, trees, fish, bugs, flowers, bacteria, clouds, particles, atoms, matter, energy—even your dreams—were all started in the Garden of Eden. From there, each creation began to grow and mature or die, or, as you lot say, evolve.'

Isabella shook her head. 'But I thought life began on Earth from a collision involving a meteor or a comet?'

The old man leant back in his chair and roared with laughter. 'Big-bangs, lumps of rock in space colliding with each other,' the old man said. 'Oh, yes, those life-givers did happen, but a long time before the living things came about. And it took an awful lot of knocking and banging them together to make the right kind of place. And who says they won't come again?'

Isabella's face had turned the colour of milk, Archie glumly stroked his foremost hair spike and Daisy massaged her temples.

Old Man Wood clapped his hands. 'But enough of all that. It's complicated—and anyway, weren't we talking about Havilarian Toadstool Powder?'

The children nodded.

'Well, young 'un's,' he continued, 'Havilarian Toadstool Powder is a very rare powder that blends itself to look like anything it's mixed with: liquid or solid—so it's hard to know how I digested it. It's so deadly that it's the only thing that can nearly kill me ...'

'What do you mean?' Isabella queried, her voice barely above a whisper. 'Nearly kill you. Does that make you... I mean... are you... please, don't tell me you can't... actually... die?'

'I'll die if I return to the Garden of Eden, one day,' Old Man Wood said slowly. 'But if I don't, then I suppose I'll carry on like I have done, indefinitely.'

Isabella coughed and looked as if she were about to vomit all over the floor.

Daisy, on the other hand, shut one eye and ruffled her hair deep in thought. 'You're saying you've been alive... forever?'

Old Man Wood smiled back a little warily. 'Yes, littlun.'

'Blimey,' and then she swore, '... sorry, WOW!' Daisy squealed. 'You've really lived... that long? Forever, and ever, amen?'

Old Man Wood shifted, turning pink.

'Then, that makes you... you're... you're immoral?' Daisy squealed.

'It's *immortal*, not immoral, you numpty,' Isabella snapped.

'Yeah, yeah. Whatever,' Daisy said, nodding. 'Pretty awesome.'

Archie was visibly trembling. 'But you can't be—'

'Look carefully,' Old Man Wood said. 'That's me in all those pictures you've pulled off the walls.'

'I told you so, I told you so,' Daisy said, squealing with delight. 'Does that make you, like... God?' she asked. 'Please say yes!'

Old Man Wood smiled. 'I promise you,' he said 'my situation is nothing more than a terrible curse. A burden that is heavier than you can possibly imagine. I was telling you about the poison...'

But now that he studied the children's expressions, Old Man Wood realised they deserved more of an explanation. 'If you must know, I've watched you humans develop for an awfully long time.'

The children looked at each other and then at Old Man Wood with their mouths ajar, the enormity of these words not lost on them in spite of their young years.

After a long and very awkward silence, Isabella spoke. 'Look, this is a bit of a head-fry, and I'm still not sure I really, truly grasp what you're saying. So let me recap: You're saying that *Rivers* are connections between worlds? Yes?'

'Indeed,' Old Man Wood replied. 'They are the routes between Earth and other planets. Daisy has already experienced one when she visited the atrium.' He smiled warmly at Daisy.

'And you're saying that the Garden of Eden really did exist, right, like a huge laboratory?'

Old Man Wood agreed.

'And the Garden of Eden is a planet, and not actually a garden—with flowers and berries and veg?'

'That's right.'

'And that every living thing came from there?'

He raised his eyebrows.

'And then these other places went to war, and in so doing shut it down. And you've been around for the whole time since?'

The old man nodded.

'And now, we've got to discover three tablets by way of five random poems on five mangy old rugs to get to these other worlds—particularly the Garden of Eden?'

'Hmm, well, yes, I suppose.'

Isabella screwed up her face as though she was on the verge of bursting into tears. 'You've got to agree it is utterly irrational,' she muttered. 'Why?'

'To open the Garden of Eden, of course,' Old Man Wood said. 'It's a source of incredible power. The power of creation is something you here on Earth can barely imagine.'

'But why *now* and, more importantly, *why us*?'

Old Man Wood stretched his arms out wide. 'Something has shifted in the universe and, as a result, you have been given the Great Dream. And it's you lot, because your direct family line happens to have been under my care for thousands of years. It is a test, I believe, like those examinations you have at school, only a little bit more important.'

He rubbed his chin, thinking. 'Not all my brains have returned inside here,' and he pointed at his skull, 'but as far as I remember, this test was put in place to see whether those chosen on the planet were ready.'

'Ready for what?'

'To survive and move mankind on to its next stage.'

Isabella didn't like the sound of this. 'And if they aren't ready and fail, then what?'

'Hmm, good question,' Old Man Wood said. 'Let me think. I believe the species on the planet will be done away with.'

'Done away with?' Isabella said. 'You mean killed?'

Old Man Wood shrugged.

'Like the dinosaurs?'

The old man hummed. 'Yes, I suppose you're right. Those horrid scaly things were a terrible nuisance. But you see, when the universe had something better planned it got rid of almost all of them except crocodiles and birds and a few others. The universe changes—it just does that, you know. A new time is upon us and it's going to try and do it again.'

'Didn't an asteroid hit the earth and wipe them out?' Daisy said, quietly. Her bones ached, and her head throbbed. She remembered the cave paintings, and the final panel. Now, the puzzle was coming together.

Old Man Wood continued. 'It's not the first time, and it certainly won't be the last. There have been all sorts of new types of mankind—'

Isabella butted in: 'Homo habilis, homo erectus, Neolithic man and now us, homo sapiens,' she rattled out. 'Dad taught me. But I thought they came one after the other, in some kind of order?'

'Clever of you to know all that,' Old Man Wood said, encouragingly. 'Then, perhaps it's time for another one—'

'If we don't fail,' Archie added.

'Yes. Something like that,' Old Man Wood said. He stood up and piled the plates together, the candlelight accentuating the grim reality and faces of the siblings. Then he opened the door to the range cooker where the embers sat like small duvets of ash over glowing bodies and added a couple of logs. The children's eyes followed him as he went about his business as though he were a kind of pet alien; freaky, yet all theirs.

'Well now,' the old man said as he sat down again and looked up at the kitchen clock. 'Best get off to bed. There's a busy day ahead finding these tablets and it's already near enough eleven.'

'Shouldn't we be searching for them right now? Archie said. 'If it's so important, we don't have a moment to lose. Daisy, you thought there were seven days in which to do this... I think I can remember the poem:

'*You have but seven days and seven nights*
  '*As Earth moves in its cycle*
  '*From first lightning strike and thunderclap*
  '*A world awaits your arrival.*

'How long is it since that first lightning bolt?' He rubbed his strange hair in recollection of the event which birthed his spikes. 'Three days... four?'

Daisy screwed up her face as she attempted to recall the days and nights, counting them off on her fingers. 'After tonight, I reckon there are three days left.'

'Over half way already,' Archie said, flatly. 'And, so far, all we've managed to do is pretty much destroy the house, get on the "international missing persons" list, start a Biblical storm, lose three of the animals and set off a global plague—'

'And we only have one tablet.'

'Yes. Is that good, or bad?'

'Shocking,' Daisy said. 'And we don't even know what the other riddles mean.'

Old Man Wood pointed towards Isabella whose forehead lay neatly perched on the table, her hair folding down in front. 'You won't be getting much joy from clever-clogs over there.'

As he said it, Isabella stirred, yawned and moved her head so that it lay on her forearm. 'I'm still awake,' she murmured, 'listening to your incredibly interesting conversation.' She yawned. 'And by the way, if there are any tablets that need finding up by the ruin, count me out. I would rather the world slips to a miserable end than scout around up there again.'

'Thanks for your huge support, as always, Bells,' Daisy said, yawning. 'I'm going to bed. Coming?'

The other two stood up.

Daisy hugged Old Man Wood. 'Are you going to bed too?'

'No, my dear littluns.' he said, 'there are a few things I still need to find out.'

'Like what?' Archie said.

'Like what the poems on the rugs are all about. Since I have no idea what Blabisterberry Jelly means, or where we'll find it, I guess I'm going to have to do some rooting around.' He smiled broadly. 'Before you head upstairs, does anyone know what happened to those poems Archie wrote down?'

Archie sighed. 'They're somewhere next door, probably ripped to bits when we found the tablet. I'll go and find them.'

Daisy laughed, thinking what a terrible state the room was in. 'Wait for me, Arch,' she said. 'I'll lend you a hand, they could be anywhere.'

MEMORIES RETURN

Isabella reluctantly stood up and, with leaden feet, followed Archie, Daisy and Old Man Wood into the dark living room where the embers of the fire glowed like dulled molten gold. After watching them poke and prod at the debris in the candlelight, turning over bits of paper here, shuffling others there, Isabella's impatience got the better of her. 'Oh, come on! You're all being completely hopeless,' she roared. 'Stand back, please, and leave it to the pro.'

They backed away and in a matter of moments Isabella's body flashed from one side to the other, up and down the room, her hands shooting here and there collecting up sheets of paper, her feet moving like a blur, her fingers shuffling through the slips of torn paper. When she slowed, she held a large, stacked pile of paper with, at the very top, the sections that made up the strange poems.

'How-the-hell-did-you-do-that?!' Archie said, wide-eyed in shock.

'Easy,' she replied.

Daisy shook her head. 'You know, Isabella, you're really taking organisation to a scary level.'

Isabella cuffed her on the arm. 'On the day of the storm,' she began, 'when I woke up, my feet and hands ached for hours.' She held them up. 'I know I can heal and protect with my hands, like I did with Old Man Wood, but sometimes my feet move as if they're jet-propelled, I've been zooming about—when I ran back from the ruin I wasn't even out of breath.'

'We noticed,' Archie said drolly. 'Daisy has always been faster than you.'

'Well, not anymore!' Isabella said, her eyes twinkling. 'And the rest you know about.' She drew in a large, satisfied breath. 'It does seem to work better when I concentrate—'

'Same with mine,' Daisy said. 'Though my things are not only seeing kind of weird stuff but hearing it too. You won't believe the odd sounds I hear.'

She caught Archie's eye. 'For example, there's some kind of watercourse underneath the house. I bet you didn't know there's a noise dripping away, did you? And mice all over the place nattering away all the time. They are sooo dull—'

Isabella, Archie and Old Man Wood looked at Daisy with increased fascination.

Archie looked her hard in the eye. 'You mentioned it at the ruin. Read the poem, Bells!' he demanded. 'It's the third one, I think.'

Isabella obliged.

'The third you search is underneath your nose.
'It's clear, pure and cold.
'In order to draw it out
'You need to send a rose.'

'I thought it was: *clear, pure and warm,* like snot,' Archie said. *'Clear, pure and cold* has to be water.'

'It's coming from under the house,' Daisy said. 'Drip, drip, dripping-away.'

Old Man Wood suddenly became agitated. 'By all the apples!' he said springing out of his chair.

DOFF!

Old Man Wood's bald head walloped a low beam and the noise echoed around the room.

'**OW!**' Old Man Wood howled. 'OW, damnable beams!' he rubbed his bald, moon-scaped pate. 'Always thought I'd built the bleedin' house too low!'

He sank down cautiously into the armchair, blinking and screwing up his face and rubbing his head like mad.

'I hope it won't muddle him up again,' Isabella whispered to Archie.

'Hmmm,' Old Man Wood eventually muttered and the children collectively breathed a sigh of relief. 'I'm sure there was once a well in the middle of the house, and if I'm not mistaken there was also, secretly, a tunnel connecting the ruin to this house, which many, many moons ago was a popular inn. You wouldn't believe how different it was...'

'Do you have architectural plans tucked away in your cellar?' Archie asked. 'I mean, you said you'd rebuilt it about thirty times. You must know the layouts like the back of your hand.'

Old Man Wood thought for a while. 'I can't remember... oooh... no. It's been so long, you can't conceive how long, that I've been waiting for all this to happen. So even though I now remember where I come from, which, I suppose, is soldered into my brain, there's an awful lot in-between which is a blur.'

He noted their disappointed faces.

'There was a time, several hundred years ago, when I thought it was time to return to the Garden, but it was a false alarm—even the Universe gets it wrong from time to time,' he smiled at the thought. 'Thinking that my reason for being had passed, memories started to ebb away, like the tide, I suppose. There's a massive amount that I don't think I'll ever get back, but the tide is rushing in again, faster than a galloping horse.'

Old Man Wood smiled kindly. 'We're just going to have to work it out together. If it's any help, I'm sure there was a network of cellar rooms underneath the ruin —like a labyrinth, I suppose. I got lost there for a couple of weeks once upon a time. Most unpleasant it was too, so I haven't been there much recently.'

'When was that?' Archie asked.

'Oooh now. Let me think. Probably a few centuries ago. Back in the ...' He counted several hundred on his hand. 'About the mid seventeen-hundreds.'

The children looked at each other, dumbfounded, trying to get their heads around this vast stretch of time. A couple of days with Auntie Spoon felt like a few hundred years, so goodness knows how it must feel to be so old.

'Before Australia was discovered?' Isabella pressed.

'Hmmm, well, yes I suppose it is rather a long time for you little things to contemplate. Now, you must have heard about them Aboriginal peoples. Most interesting bunch and they've been there a long time—'

'I know we need to find the well and the tablets and all that stuff,' Daisy interrupted, 'but is the Q'ash Warshbit a real thing, did it *actually* exist?' she asked. 'Were those stories about Iso that you told us in front of the fire, actually true?'

'Oh yes! Most definitely, all those stories really happened. One day you might actually meet Iso—she's out there somewhere, I'm sure of it. You never know—'

'Please!' Isabella roared, giving Daisy a hard stare. 'Would you two be quiet for a moment! How are we going to find the dripping water?'

Old Man Wood paced around the room for a few minutes, alternatively rubbing his chin and his head, and humming to himself. Finally he sat down in his armchair and sighed.

'I think, my little ones, we may have to go up to the ruin and find those old cellars.'

Isabella groaned. 'But what about the "thing" we heard at the ruin?'

'Well, you and your MAGIC powers should be able to sort it out,' Archie said, sarcastically. He appeared disappointed that he seemed to have missed out on the wider, perhaps cooler, distribution of gifts.

The girls looked away, embarrassed.

Old Man Wood leaned in, his brow deeply ridged. 'What kind of *thing* are you talking about?' he asked.

Daisy started to recall how they had heard a strange cough and an evil bark and how, just as the bell had rung, Archie had idiotically jumped out and found nothing there. 'And on the way back we bumped into Mrs. Pye.'

'Are you quite sure the noise wasn't Mrs. Pye?' Isabella said.

Archie burst out laughing. 'Mrs. Pye it definitely wasn't. She's more like a strange looking angel than a monster—isn't that right, Old Man Wood?'

Old Man Wood looked shaken, his face pale and withdrawn. He waved a hand in the air.

Isabella rolled her eyes. 'You know perfectly well that monsters don't exist here in Yorkshire.'

'Are you absolutely sure about that, sis?' Archie said. 'Coz the panels on the bed didn't really exist, did they?'

Daisy caught his eye. 'Nor the exploding toadstools,' Daisy added, 'and the tablet coming out of the fire was pretty imaginary.'

Archie clapped her on the back. 'Come on Bells! *Anything* is possible. Don't you understand; our dreams—these strange events—are leading us to this Garden of Eden place. We're inexplicably linked to it, and nothing can stop it.'

Isabella looked crestfallen. 'Look, I know, alright. But if we have to find one of the tablets at the ruin, I'm not going.'

Old Man Wood noticed her anxiety and draped an arm around her shoulders. 'Bells, together we'll be fine, I'm reckoning. Nothing like a good night's sleep to stamp out your worries.'

'Are you sure we shouldn't start right away?' Archie said, persisting.

'No. We have to find Blabisterberry Jelly next,' Old Man Wood began. 'My friends, the willows, may just have the information we need. I'll head down there shortly. Tomorrow will be quite a day so I suggest you grab every moment of sleep you can.'

Archie nodded. 'So that's it then,' he said firmly. 'Tomorrow, at dawn, we find Blabisterberry Jelly,' he said, looking at the poem as though it would be dead easy. 'Let's meet at six for breakfast.'

ONE HUNDRED SIXTY-EIGHT

THE TRUTH OF KEMP'S MOTHER

'As I said,' Cain began, 'I am simply telling you the truth. That woman is your mother.'

'Then take me to her,' Kemp demanded, 'this minute. We'll settle it once and for all.'

Cain was beginning to regret ever having mentioned the boy's mother. The ghost hovered away and let the overcoat slip to the floor. A body of dust puffed up and the specks played briefly in the light as tiny particles of glitter.

'What benefit will it be for anyone?' Cain said. 'The woman will not see you as her son as much as you do not wish to take her as your mother. Why complicate? Why muddy the waters? What can you possibly gain?'

'If you're saying Mrs. Pye's my mother, fine, let's go and ask her. If she denies it then I know you've been lying,' Kemp said. 'If she says that she is, then so be it. But if you're telling me lies, I will never go with you again.'

'You are not listening,' Cain responded, angrily. 'Of course she will deny it. She will deny ever knowing you because she doesn't know you exist, boy. Then what? Would you like me to present a fake, to make you *feel* better? So you can live out your fantasy of having a mother?'

Kemp didn't have an answer, but something troubled him. 'Why won't she remember me?' he said, staring at the floor.

'When your father died,' Cain said, as a brilliant idea popped into his mind, 'your mother escaped the accident, but not without terrible injuries. Because of them, she has no recollection of anything before that time. What I am about to tell you may be hard to stomach.'

'Go on,' Kemp said.

'You might think this is not possible, but it is,' Cain began earnestly, 'the old de Lowe helper—'

'Old Man Wood?'

Invisible to the boy, Cain beamed. 'Yes, I believe that is what they call him. He found her and seeing her broken took her back to the de Lowe cottage to care for her. But as he attempted to heal her, that old man did a terrible thing. I'm afraid, boy, that what you're about to hear won't be easy to digest.'

'How do you know this?'

'Your father's ghost told me this, so it must be true.' Cain grinned and thumped the air.

Kemp prickled. 'What did my father tell you?' he said, quietly.

'That Old Man Wood, for reasons I expect of pure bloodiness, cut into her head with a large, sharp knife and removed a section of her brain, a piece of her memory.'

Kemp's eyes bulged. Then a shadow of doubt passed over his face. 'I never thought the old man was the blood-thirsty type,' he said. 'Always seemed as soft as putty to me.'

Cain responded swiftly. 'One of the biggest lessons I can give you is that there's always, always, more to people than meets the eye. Take me, for example. At first you found me reprehensible and vile, didn't you? And with good reason.'

Kemp nodded, slowly.

'And now we're quite the best of friends, aren't we? You're learning fast, boy. I've heard stories about that old man from various ghostly friends of mine and I'm told that he harbours a terrible past—'

'Really?'

'Absolutely! Of bloodletting and gore. Unmentionable cruelty. There's little doubt that the old man thinks nothing of cold-blooded murder.'

'Old man whatshisface? Are you sure?'

'When I heard he was in charge of the Heirs of Eden, I wondered for the safety of those poor de Lowe children.' Cain wondered if he'd gone too far.

'Have no fear though, boy. You are with me now, and safe enough. I will take you to your mother. But do not say later that you did not heed my warnings.'

Kemp sat deep in thought, twisting a knife around his fingers. 'I think I need to get it over with,' he said at length. 'I need to know, one way or another.'

'Very well,' Cain said. 'In the morning, at first light on Earth, I will summon Asgard. He must sacrifice two of his dreamspinners for us to travel there and back. They will need forewarning.'

Cain called into the air, 'Dreamspinner, dreamspinner, dreamspinner.'

Seconds later a tiny flash was followed by an opaque, white, almost arachnid creature, standing in mid air.

'Asgard, tomorrow at first light I must honour my promise to the boy. We go to find his mother at Eden Cottage. Can you give us transport within your brethren?'

Asgard tapped the air beneath him. 'There are many who are old and would rather die than see the demise of the dreamspinners. They are yours, for now. But be warned, Cain. Genesis, our mother, has returned from her self-imposed exile. She draws many dreamspinners to her. Even those who are old.'

Cain smiled. 'But as we know, Asgard, there are but three days left to open the Garden of Eden. The Heirs have but one tablet. The task is beyond them and all the while the Earth cries out of its own accord.'

Asgard stared at Cain, the dreamspinner's three black eyes boring into the ghost. 'I will be here just before dawn for your trip to Earth.' And in the next moment, he had vanished.

Cain turned to Kemp, who was cramming a chocolate-coated strawberry tartlet into his mouth. 'Now, rest, boy. Tomorrow you will discover the truth and it may not taste quite as sweet.'

GUS ESCAPES

Gus beamed his biggest, toothiest grin at Sue as she walked through the door, a big suit covering her from head to foot like a spaceman. She ran over and, without thinking, jumped up into his arms.

'Missed you,' she said, as tears formed in her eyes.

'Me, same,' he replied. 'Though it's not quite the same kissing a plastic helmet.' He put her down and stepped back. 'Cor! I'm digging the sexy outfit,' he joked.

Sue hit him playfully on the arm.

'I'll leave you two to it, then,' said the nurse who'd accompanied Sue in. 'To be perfectly honest with you, there's nothing wrong with you, is there, Gus?' The nurse looked her up and down. 'I have a strong feeling, young lady, that you'll survive without the suit,' she added, winking.

The door snapped shut.

'When are they letting you out?' Sue said through the protective helmet.

'Don't know. No one knows anything round here. They're all shit scared, apart from that nurse. She's totally chilled, but if I go "BOO" to the others they shriek and run away!'

Sue held his hand.

'Thing is, I'm fine, one hundred percent. All I had was a twenty-four hour bug, nothing serious. Certainly not this Ebora, otherwise, by the sounds of it, I'd already be dead.'

'Thing is,' she said, 'you're a survivor. So they'll want to know what makes you so special.'

'You don't know?'

'Course *I* do,' she smiled. 'Just the other numpties round here.'

Even though her surveillance bug was pinned to her clothes in the changing room she knew she should keep her voice down. 'Gus. Do guards watch over you?'

'Not really,' he shrugged.

'What about doctors?'

'Nah. The nurses are alright. There's a camera over there and someone outside, but I'm pretty sure they're asleep half the time. Last night whoever it was slipped off at about ten o'clock. When I popped off to the toilet there was no one around. But they do the rounds in roughly four-hour cycles. Yesterday they came in to take blood three times, urine twice and... it's a wonder there's anything left. Do I look a bit pale?'

Sue laughed. 'Very—'

'Anyway, for the last twelve hours I've been the last thing on their minds. They're trying to make a serum or something. They're really not interested in me.'

'Good,' Sue replied, moving close. 'That creepy Commissioner is close to finding out about Archie and the others. We've got to help them. So I'm getting you out.'

'Cool,' Gus said. 'How?'

'I don't know.'

'What you've come here without a plan?' Gus said feigning shock. 'How very un-Sue like.'

'Actually,' she said as an idea rocketed into her head, 'I have. Where are your clothes?' He pointed at the cupboard. Sue marched across, took them out and, as subtly as possible, placed them on the bed.

Sue searched the small room and pulled up a privacy screen at the far end spreading it around the bed as far as it would go. She sat down on the bed and beckoned Gus to do the same. She unzipped her headpiece, detached the poppers and pulled it over her head. Her hair tumbled out.

In the confines of the small bed, she began to slip the remaining part of the protective suit down her body. 'Give me a hand, please.' Her eyes twinkled.

Gus' smile spread across his face, a mix of glee and nervousness. In a short while, Sue lay naked on the bed save for her underwear. She looked up at Gus beside her who was painfully trying not to look.

She giggled. 'Kiss me.'

Gus hesitated, stunned by Sue's directness. 'You're kidding!'

'Go on,' she whispered.

Gus hesitated.

'Don't worry—it's all part of the plan.'

'This is your plan?'

'Yes, and you're on camera, so it had better be good!'

Gus didn't need to be asked again.

In the corridor outside, the nurse hurried down to the desk outside Gus Williams' door and checked the clipboard.

Time to get the girl out. She looked up at the screen and for a moment couldn't think what she was looking at. Then it dawned on her.

She readied herself to march in but then she remembered being fourteen and the feeling of being kissed. She smiled. If the news was as bad as everyone said, how many more youths would miss out on this simple pleasure?

Better to gently warn them.

The nurse knocked on the door. 'Miss Lowden. Time to go! And don't think I don't know what you two are up to!'

From behind the door she could hear giggling followed by hysterical laughter.

Oh, to be young and in love, the nurse thought. 'I'll be back in five minutes,' she said and then called out. 'And when I come back, I want you out of there.'

The nurse smiled. There's absolutely nothing wrong with that boy. Cheeky lad and all. She'd give them their last few minutes alone. She sighed. There were more important things to be getting on with than peeping at them on the monitor.

Sue listened as the nurse's footsteps tapered off down the corridor. 'Right, Gus. Get in the protective suit.'

Gus leaned in again. She moved away.

'Uh?'

'Get in that suit, NOW!'

Gus looked confused.

'It's your way out, silly,' she said, her eyes sparkling. 'People round here know who I am, but we can't have you just wandering about. If you put the suit on, no one will know any better.' She pulled his t-shirt on. It smelt entirely of him and it felt strangely reassuring.

'I'm going to make a run for the toilet while you get changed. You'll need to make a dummy in the bed with the pillows—make it look as realistic as you can. As soon as you hear the nurse return, open the door in your protective suit, turn to the bed and blow a kiss, switch off the light, pretend to snivel like a girl and head down the corridor.' Sue smiled at the thought of it.

'Go directly outside and walk to the right. I'll join you. There are loads of people milling about and tents dotted here and there. Just walk like you mean it.'

'You're mad!' he said.

'I'm not, Gus. We need to help Archie and his sisters and I need you. And besides,' Sue said with a sparkle in her eye. 'If you ever want to see me nearly naked again, you'd better do exactly as I say.'

OLD MAN WOOD'S PROBLEM

The willows, Old Man Wood thought, *may not know about the water under the house but they are sure to know how to eat Blabisterberry Jelly.*

As the children headed up the stairs to their attic room, the old man donned his coat and boots and slipped quietly out of the back door, down the path to the potting shed, selected a clean, plastic, water-tight bucket and, using his torch to help him find his way, he trudged down the steep, treacherous terrain past the decimated remains of vegetables and ruined fruit trees. When he found the brown water line, he followed it, just as he had with Archie, until he came to the impenetrable willow barrier—the Bubbling Brook.

'Bethedi,' he whispered. 'You awake?'

'Uh! Eh! What time d'you call this?'

'Who's there?' said another voice. More voices joined in and shortly Old Man Wood found he could see the figures of sleepy elf-like tree-spirits rubbing sleep out of their tiny eyes and leaning out from their respective boughs or dangling from branches like bats.

'It's me,' Old Man Wood said, shining his torch around. 'I need to ask about a few things.'

Bethedi's gnarly old tree spirit bounded down the tree and perched near his head. The tree-elf stretched his arms wide and yawned. 'For sure, my old friend. We've all got good memories, hum-hum. Ask away.'

'I've discovered many things,' Old Man Wood began, 'like those little rugs with verses written on them. And you're right, time is running out on us.'

The wind picked up and blew heavy drops of water off the branches where they sprinkled down into the pool. In the torch light, Old Man Wood watched the water rings spreading out and beyond. In the corner of his eye, he noted that, attached to each tree, little elves moved along branches and stems to listen.

'Now before you start, hum-hum, make yourself comfortable,' Bethedi said. The old man wiggled his bottom onto a stump and leaned back on a tree trunk. 'You have questions? Well, good. I am pleased to hear it.'

'Tell me,' the old man said, 'what in the apples is Blabisterberry Jelly? Where would I find it and what do we do with the three tablets if we find them?'

Bethedi roared with laughter.

'Oi—you—cut it out!' sang a thrush from higher up. 'We're sleeping. You know the rules: no talking after nightfall.'

'Hum-hum. You are a right one,' whispered Bethedi. 'It's lucky that in the deep roots and folds of our bark we hold your secrets close. You told us Willows about three tablets and a very cunning plan, hum-hum. Well, do not be a-worrying; we remember. Your secrets are safe, even from those a-blasted birds, hum-hum. You want to know about Blabisterberry Jelly.' Bethedi took a deep breath.

'Blabisterberry Jelly, my old friend, is the most amazing, cunning, hilarious and terrifying potion ever created. Made from about three hundred ingredients— each one doused in magic—so that even the great wizard, Merlin, your old friend, didn't like to use it, hum-hum. Remember how you told us that he never really understood it, or how to control it?'

For some time, Bethedi told a few stories about Blabisterberry Jelly and, as he spoke, the nature of the mixture began to come back to Old Man Wood.

'But why is it dangerous?' he asked. 'And how does one of the stone tablets come from it?'

Bethedi hum-hummed. 'Now here's the thing, hum-hum,' the little elf began. 'If used in the wrong way, Blabisterberry Jelly is lethal. Too many grew frightened of it because they couldn't trust it. This was the reason you used it to protect the stone tablet. The riddle you found will reveal the tablet, but only to those who truly believe, hum-hum.'

And so, as the night drew on and the rain came and went, Old Man Wood rediscovered some of the mysteries of Blabisterberry Jelly, and bits and pieces of his long life and adventures. Finally, he asked about the water source under the house that Daisy had mentioned. 'Did I ever tell you of a well under the house?'

Bethedi thought for a while and hum-hummed, knowing what to say, but not quite knowing how to say it. 'Yes, dear old friend,' the tree-elf said at long last, rubbing his tiny, long beard. 'Once you talked of a well, deep in the hillside. The only route to it was through a labyrinth beneath the old castle. It was guarded by a fearsome beast you saved from execution when the Garden of Eden closed.'

'Why would I do a thing like this?'

'When the tablets and their riddles were put in place for the new time, the beast would have suffered an eon of sleep and, on awakening, either it would die or the new Heirs of Eden would prevail. Never was there a better test of bravery and cunning than to outmatch and outwit the monster.'

'Apples-alive!' Old Man Wood said, shocked.

'Oh yes, hum-hum,' Bethedi said, leaning back and gauging Old Man Wood's reaction. Then he continued, selecting his words carefully.

'When you put these spells in place many thousands of years ago, you did it to deter impostors who might stumble upon the secrets, but no one wanted you to go so far, hum-hum. The clues were too difficult and we knew you would never be the same person as the energetic youth you were then.' Bethedi's voice was deep and sincere.

'And now, my dear friend, you are old, humanised and soft. You have lost your magic and your youth. You fooled yourself that you would be young forever. You see, we trees understand the ageing process better than most things borne of Mother Nature. With great age comes wisdom and understanding, but also a loss of skill, courage and clarity.' Bethedi ducked behind a leaf and momentarily rubbed the corner of his mouth with it.

'I know the water is up and you have to find the tablets and try and get into the Garden of Eden—everything is talking about it—but you will struggle, if indeed your Heirs conquer Blabisterberry Jelly. You told us it was your finest riddle—and your hardest. And you were quick to tell us Willows how clever you'd been, but, hum-hum, unfortunately you kept it from us. Sorry, dear friend, but we cannot help you further. For this, you are on your own.'

Old Man Wood slumped further down the trunk. He, more than anyone, should have known better. Living things never remain the same, they change and evolve. Why would he be any different?

Old Man Wood thanked them and, feeling quite stiff from leaning so long on the tree, bade them goodnight.

He lowered the plastic bucket into the Bubbling Brook and watched as the water filled it. And with his mood as dark as the night surrounding him, the old man started home, slipping up the wet, muddy slope careful to keep as much water in the bucket as possible.

Deep, troubling thoughts filled his mind. From what he'd heard, he was almost certainly leading them to a violent, terrible death. He needed his wits, and a bit of magic wouldn't go amiss, he thought. But *where the apples would that come from?*

He heaved the bucket up, feeling the weight in his arms. And how would he explain the secrets of the Beast—or whatever it was—when he didn't have a clue?

KEMP GOES HOME

'Now when we arrive with the woman,' Cain said, 'her reaction may be one of profound shock. She will not understand what she sees and nor should she. Together, our appearance is that of an ash-covered human, as if we have climbed out from a foul, sooty chimney.'

Cain mused on his description and wondered whether this was the right approach. 'Perhaps I should let you talk to her alone,' he mused. 'Seeing an ashen man will almost certainly make her nervy.'

Cain lunged athletically and jogged up and down on the spot as if to remind the boy who was in control. 'If I do this, under no circumstances must you make her scream or wake the others. Understand? We do not want to be found. Furthermore, these dreamspinners are a cautious breed, my friend, and we would not want to be accused of being caught meddling with the prophecy. Goodness knows what might happen. I would be stranded and you, dear child, would more than likely lose your life.'

"Yes, yes, yes,' Kemp said impatiently and he pushed his wet arms up and through the arm-holes of the overcoat that hovered in front of him. Then, as before, he donned the trilby hat that the ghost preferred. Pain prickled through him but, in comparison with the first time, it was like a mild case of pins and needles.

Cain sensed the boy had settled and called out into the dark sky. 'Dreamspinner, dreamspinner, dreamspinner.'

Seconds later, two tiny flashes appeared. Asgard, along with another, even more grey-ringed dreamspinner hovered above them, their flashing magholes reflecting blue light on Cain's ashen body.

Cain clapped his hands and a puff of ash exploded into the sky. 'Excellent. As quick as ever, Asgard. Good, good.'

Asgard floated upon the air as though standing on an invisible cloud. 'This is Avantis. She travels one last time.'

An ashen Cain bowed low in front of the dreamspinner. 'We are humbled by your sacrifice,' the ghost crowed.

'My sacrifice is nothing in comparison to yours, Master of Havilah.'

'Time to go. Light breaks on Earth shortly,' Asgard said.

Avantis moved in front of Cain. 'I am ready, when you are.'

'Good,' Cain replied. And without further ado he dived through the extended maghole.

In the blink of an eye, Cain and Kemp lay on a cream carpeted floor.

Slowly they picked themselves up and Cain looked around, noting how the woman slept soundly in her bed.

The room, Kemp noticed, was simple, uncluttered and painted in a soft pink. Photo frames of the de Lowe children in various holders and old wedding pictures of their parents crowded the table and dresser tops. A scrap book on her desk stuffed with local newspaper mentions of the children, and a recent picture of Daisy and Archie in the football team lay on an open page ready to be glued in. On another table sat a couple of trinkets, a small silver cup, a necklace and a glass jar with an ornate silver top.

At the far end of the room, in the corner, was the television facing a comfortable armchair with floral pink cushions and a matching blue cover-throw.

Cain stood up as the woman stirred—this was his chance. He moved towards her and sat down almost weightlessly on the bed, close enough to place a hand over her mouth if she were to scream.

Then, true to his word, Cain removed himself from Kemp, his spirit flying freely into the room. 'Take your hat off, boy. It doesn't really suit you. And the coat. I'll hang them up outside the room and wait there for you when the hand on that timepiece moves to here,' he said, pointing at the clock.

'Good luck, boy. And if it's any help,' he whispered, 'you are the son of Tobias and Lucy Kemp.'

'Forty minutes?' Kemp said.

'You are on your own now. I need to pay someone a visit.'

❄

Dickinson killed the engine and let the RIB drift in towards the makeshift shore-line. A huge beam of light scoured the scrub for a suitable landing area and within a few moments one of the men, a compact, shaven-headed man with a crooked nose, named Geddis, thrust an oar in so that the boat swung round and beached perfectly. Four of the five jumped out and, water up to their knees, pulled the boat until it slid noiselessly onto the bank.

'It's mud, sir,' Geddis announced. 'Damn hellish amount.' He sniffed the air. 'And fog closing in fast. Might take some while to get up that hillside, sir.'

Dickinson stared through the misty early morning darkness, a hint of light growing in the east across the hills. 'You two head right. Two left. Back here in five minutes,' Dickinson said. 'Look for tracks—signs of anyone coming or going. And if you spot anyone, take them. Under no circumstances maim or kill. I need these people alive.' He clicked his radio, snapped his headphones open and pushed them over his ears. 'Dickinson reporting in. We have touched land.'

Dickinson listened, then replied. 'Thick fog, sir. Visibility approximately ten metres. Not sure how much use the camera will be until we get close to the house. Scouting the perimeter area at this moment.'

Shortly, Dickinson's radio burst into life. 'Sir,' came the metallic tone of one of the soldiers through the radio. 'Footprints. One, two days old. Hard to tell—prints saturated by mud and water.'

'What sizes?'

'Some big, some small, sir.'

'Can you tell where they lead?'

'No, sir. Looks like they lead into the flooding. Impossible to tell, sir.'

Dickinson rubbed his chin. *Maybe they've already gone,* he thought, *exactly as that girl Sue said.* Perhaps they really had gone to find an electronic tablet. There was only one way to find out.

Dickinson buzzed his radio. 'I'm coming over. We'll wait for more light before we begin the ascent. No-one will see us in this stew.' He paused and pressed the button again. 'Reconvene at the boat in five minutes.'

Archie woke up sweating.

He'd dreamt of Cain. Cain laughing from under a cloak with such bitterness that his blood boiled and pulsed in waves around his body. Then, Cain merged into Kemp, becoming a monster before spitting ash in his face like a fire-breathing dragon. Archie's head throbbed. He sat up and wiped his brow, then opened his eyes and stared out from under the huge drape at the dark, silent room. His chin stung, from where the ghost had nicked him with the dagger only three nights before.

He rubbed the newest cut, a thin clear liquid moistening his fingers.

Archie checked his watch, then climbed out of bed and, treading lightly on the creaking floorboards, found his way to the table where he lit a candle and slipped down the stairs. In the bathroom, he held the candle up to the mirror and inspected the cuts. There they were—not more than a centimetre long, open, hot, angry and sore, and in exactly the same position either side of his chin. Cain's doing—to remind him, perhaps?

And anyway, why, hadn't Resplendix Mix cleaned it up, like it had with everything else?

Archie tried to forget about Cain but this was easier said than done. Those haunting words of his kept reverberating round his brain. *'Courage, young man, so you are feared and respected,'* and *'Your strength will be without doubt. I assure you these rewards will be genuine.'*

The iciness in that cold, deep voice swished around his head. Archie needed to wake up. He splashed cool tap water over his face and looked back at his curious reflection. His crazy hair, gelled into wire-like points, was tight and strong and he realised that his follicles somehow reflected his mood. When he relaxed, a softness came to his spikes which might, in a very tiny way, be shaped or sculpted.

He prised open the most recent cut with his fingers, and then picking up a nail brush on the side of the bath, scrubbed the gash hard, as if it were an ink mark. He winced as the wound opened and blood dripped out, decorating the white ceramic basin with deep crimson drops, each one splashing over such a large area, fixating him.

He was snapped out of his daze by Daisy calling down the passageway. 'Winkle, get a move on! I need to go!'

Archie grabbed a handful of toilet roll and pressed it firmly to the cut, hoping the wound would congeal. Daisy walked in, her hair stuck to her face in a gigantic mess.

'What are you doing?' she said, moving a clump of curly blonde strands from her forehead.

'Random cut that needed a bit of a clean,' he said.

Daisy screwed her face up and grunted. 'Your hair's still crap,' she said, as she stared at her face in the mirror, moving closer and closer so that in the candlelight her eyes looked particularly ruddy.

'Awesome. Wonder what else they'll do today?' she said, as she opened her eyes as wide as possible and pretended she was a vampire, snarling and clawing randomly at her reflection.

Archie laughed. 'Don't be a fool. And hurry up. We've got Blabisterberry Jelly to find—or had you forgotten?'

'Forgotten? Nah. I can hardly wait,' she said. 'Off you go.'

A cold chill hung about them in the dark kitchen. Isabella lit three further candles to offer a bit more light and Archie scrambled around for some newspaper and kindling which smouldered before igniting on the old embers of the fire in the belly of the old range cooker.

Daisy sat in a heap next to the table. 'What do you reckon it is?' she said.

'What is?'

'Blab-ista-stuff, or whatever it's called?'

'Blabisterberry Jelly?' Isabella said smartly. She turned her head skyward as if deep in thought. 'By the sound of it, it may well be some kind of fungus or tree-growth or pus-filled plant. Or perhaps the "jelly" refers to a kind of gelatine mineral deposit, like oil.'

Archie lowered four plates onto the table. 'What if it's some kind of jelly fish? A weird creature from out there in the flooding.'

Daisy looked horrified. 'Oh God, I hope not. I hate jelly fish. It'll be full of disease and dead stuff. Bells, can I have an extra helping of cheese on my Mrs Pye Special sandwich and a double egg? I'm starving.'

'Give me a chance,' Isabella shot back. 'The oven's not hot enough. Anyway, stop being a slob—get some apple juice out and lay up,' she ordered. 'Has anyone seen Old Man Wood?'

'I heard him snoring from Mum and Dad's room earlier,' Archie said. 'He's moved in.'

Isabella sliced the thin loaf of crusty bread that Mrs. Pye had left out, added ham and several slices of cheese to each, followed by a chunky wedge of tomato on top. 'You'd better go and get him. Make sure he hasn't gone mad or died again.' She dripped three drops of sauce on top. 'Anyone know where Mrs P is? Very odd that she's not put in an appearance.'

Daisy smiled wickedly. 'I'll go and kick a ball around in the courtyard. If that doesn't wake her up, nothing will.'

Archie tore off up the stairs in one direction as Daisy shot out of the back of the house and on to the courtyard where she found a ball and began to kick it against the wall right beneath Mrs. Pye's apartment.

As the water boiled, Isabella turned into the kitchen where she realised the quiet wasn't in her imagination. She was on her own, so she opened the oven door and slipped the first of the Mrs. Pye Specials onto the top shelf, and soon the smell of melting cheese made her mouth water like crazy.

Beneath them, in the courtyard, Kemp could hear a ball being kicked; its thudding reverberating annoyingly through the window panes.

Kemp stared at the plump woman waking in front of him. She tossed from side to side and groaned. Could this odd looking woman really be his mother? He didn't know whether to laugh or cry, to scream with annoyance or with delight, as a horrible doubt lingered. No—impossible. She couldn't be. Suddenly Kemp wanted to be as far away as possible, not in this room, not even within a hundred miles of here. Kemp stood up and gingerly crept towards the door.

He turned his head back to the woman, just as she stretched her hands out, drew them together and fanned them out, flexing her pink digits in front of her face. A snapping, cracking, popping sound came out of each little joint, but one thing caught Kemp's eye.

He stared hard at Mrs. Pye's hands. There, again. As she did it, now he did the same.

One odd, strange movement.

He pushed his arms out and flexed his fingers and then pushed his thumbs together, which, just like Mrs. Pye's, bent back at a quite extraordinary angle.

He'd never met anyone who could get even close to this level of dexterity, this bendiness, the way the thumbs pushed flat on their pads at ninety degrees.

Mrs. Pye opened her eyes, stared at his thumbs, then at her hands, doing the same motion. Slowly, she fixed her gaze at him, her initial reaction betraying shock and fear and now curiosity.

Kemp stared back, mid stretch, his thumbs bent back and for what seemed like an eternity, the room filled with silence.

'Please, don't scream,' Kemp implored.

Mrs. Pye scrunched up her face and eyed him curiously.

Kemp stood stone still, not sure what to do next.

'What do you want?' Mrs. Pye forced out.

'I just wanted to see you.'

'You're Archie's friend, now, aren't you?' Mrs. Pye finally said, and she shifted up the bed to see him better.

Kemp nodded.

Mrs. Pye tutted. 'And you've lost your lovely hair. If I remember, it was bright—'

'Ginger,' Kemp butted in. 'Just like—'

'Mine,' she said and, as she did, she smiled, although it looked every bit like a scowl to Kemp.

'Yeah,' he said.

The long silence returned. Kemp stared at the woman, her funny scars, her fat lips and her slightly long nose and, in particular, those sharp, light blue eyes. It was like looking at a distorted mirror.

Maybe Cain was right.

'I need to get up, young man,' Mrs. Pye said. 'So unless you've other business ...'

Kemp hesitated. 'Yes. I mean, no. I mean—'

'What's the matter? You got a problem with one of my lot?' She shot a look towards the desk with the scrapbook and photos of the de Lowe children.

'No, no. Not them,' Kemp said.

'Well then, be off with you. Don't know what you're thinking, creeping into people's houses. I've a good mind to telephone them police.'

But Kemp's feet remained glued to the floor. 'Mrs. Pye,' Kemp stuttered, trying to find the right words and then, summoning every ounce from a place deep within him, he said: 'How did you, er, how did you get those scars?'

Mrs. Pye shot him her most dastardly look. 'None of your business.'

'The thing is,' he replied, as tears filled his eyes. 'I do believe it is.'

ONE HUNDRED SEVENTY-TWO

A SIP OF WATER

If his theory was correct, and the virus was being spread by something in dreams, Solomon thought his chances of survival were probably greater than most. After all, he'd been a light sleeper for years and he rarely, if ever, dreamt.

He woke before dawn, dressed and headed outside to find Dickinson with his team preparing to take a Land Rover down to the water. From there they would motor across the Vale of York to the edge of the Yorkshire Moors and then climb up to Eden Cottage.

They exchanged pleasantries.

'Dickinson,' Solomon began. 'Please keep me updated. If they're not around, I'd like to drop in as soon as I can to tie up some of my research.'

The officer nodded. 'We should be in and out in no time. With any luck we'll be back at lunchtime.'

'I've been given a radio. What frequency are you on?'

Dickinson gave him the information and gathered his protective helmet.

Solomon smiled. 'Good luck. Let's hope they haven't caught the Ebora virus, huh?'

As they departed, Solomon went back to his lodgings and then on to find Sue in the room above his. He knocked on the door. When he knocked again, the noise told him a good deal of scrambling was going on. Sue wasn't alone.

'It's Solomon, Sue. Can you let me in?'

More scrambling from inside. Finally the door opened. Sue's head peeped round the door. 'Morning, sir,' she said gaily, a twinkle in her eye.

Solomon moved in and shut the door behind him. 'Stone's obedient dog has gone to sniff out Eden Cottage,' he began. 'He reckons he'll be back by lunchtime, so we'll need to be ready to go.'

Sue looked up from her perch on the bed. 'OK,' she said. 'What do we need to do?'

'First get your hands on some of the protective suits. Three of them.'

'Three?'

'Yes. One for you, one for me and one for Gus.'

'Gus?'

'Yes. Gus who is hiding in the cupboard.'

Sue reddened. 'Sir?'

Solomon smiled at her. 'You must think I was born yesterday,' he said. 'Besides, I'm a schoolmaster. Come on out of there, Mr. Williams.'

The door swung open and the large figure of Gus tumbled out over the floor in a muddle of arms and legs.

Solomon helped pick him up. 'Right now, I am your friend, not your headmaster,' Solomon said. 'So let's be grown up about this.' Gus sat down beside Sue and stared, red-faced, at the floor. Solomon moved over to the radio and turned up the volume. Then he sat down next to them on the bed.

'We know,' he began quietly as the song crashed into the chorus, 'that the de Lowes are on to something quite astonishingly important. There are clues littered everywhere; in the old books in the library, the stained glass and, I'm sure, in their house, but what it is they have to find, I don't know.'

Solomon rubbed his hands. 'However, the world is falling apart at an alarming pace and until they get hold of this thing, I have a terrible feeling that this deterioration will continue swiftly and without mercy.' Solomon looked from Sue to Gus and back again. 'From the chaos out there, they may already be running out of time.'

The headmaster raised his eyebrows. 'I am increasingly certain that we must keep Archie and his sisters away from Commissioner Stone and his cronies. Officialdom will only hinder the children, and my instinct tells me is that it is up to the de Lowes, and only the de Lowes to find what they have to find. If not, then I am quite sure Isabella would somehow have managed to bring this to the authorities' attention.' The headmaster removed his spectacles and rubbed his eyes.

'I cannot begin to tell you how much pressure Stone is under. I'm talking pressure on a massive, global, governmental scale. And the problem is that he thinks finding Archie de Lowe is the answer to all his woes. As such, that man will stop at nothing to find them. He will want to extract every grain of information out of Archie and indeed his sisters.'

The music went quiet as the song ended, and Solomon did the same.

'Here's what I think,' he said as the next song burst into life. 'We need to be ready for two situations.'

'Two?' Gus queried.

'Indeed. The first is the eventuality that the children are at the cottage and are brought back here, in which case we'll need to set them free, at all costs. The second option applies if they are not at home. If that is the case, then we need to get into Eden Cottage and find out whatever we can in order to protect them. But it is vital that we keep this from Stone and send him and his boys on a wild goose chase.' He smiled at Gus and Sue. 'And to that effect, to get you both to Eden Cottage with me, I have a plan.'

Old Man Wood came downstairs holding a large bucket filled with water. He placed it in the hallway and made his way into the kitchen. '*Stop eating*!' he shouted, waving his arms in the air. '*Please! STOP, NOW!*'

'Why?' Isabella said. 'Is it the Havilarian Toadstool Powder?'

'No, no. You must be ravenously hungry for Blabisterberry Jelly—'

'You *eat* Blabisterberry Jelly?' Archie said as he chewed on a combination of ham, egg and cheese. 'Are you sure?'

'*YES!*'

'I hope it's as good as this,' Daisy said, forking in a huge mouthful.

'*NO!*' the old man begged. 'Daisy... please don't.'

Daisy lowered her fork and fixed him with her red eyes. 'So what does this jelly look like?'

'That's the thing. I don't know,' he began, 'but you'll find out, I can assure you. Believe me—but it really is vital you're starving.'

'I'm always starving!' Archie said, as he made to help himself to more.

'*NO!*' the old man roared and he reached onto the table and tossed Archie's plate into the corner of the room where it smashed into fragments.

'Archie,' the old man said firmly, 'I am deadly serious. This is no game, it is not a joke. Blabisterberry Jelly is lethal, it will kill you.' He turned towards the plate in the corner. 'I am sorry about your wasted Mrs. Pye Special, though.'

Daisy stared at her plate, desperate for another mouthful, but instead she stood up and tossed her plate across the room where it too smashed into little pieces.

'Daisy!' Isabella cried.

Daisy shrugged.

'Why couldn't you put it in the bin like an ordinary human being?'

'Bells,' Daisy said, flipping her pink glasses from her forehead to the brow of her nose, 'this is no time for rubbish bins. And besides, we aren't ordinary human beings.'

'Clear it up,' Isabella demanded.

Daisy snarled. 'Don't you ever listen? We are about to go and eat Blabister-berry Jam or whatever it's called and we may well die and you want me to clear up a plate?'

She grabbed Isabella's plate and threw it like a Frisbee across the room, where it too smashed into tiny pieces.

Isabella's face turned puce and she stamped her foot.

'*Enough*,' Old Man Wood roared.

The girls sat down, a little bit in awe of his raised voice.

'I learnt about Blabisterberry Jelly from the Willows at the Bubbling Brook last night. It's a good deal easier if you're hungry, but impossible if you're not.'

The children looked at him with concerned faces. 'Now, my littluns, first things first, we need to find it.'

'Find it?' Isabella said. 'Where? In the house, outside the house, by the ruin?'

'Why,' the old man began with a smile, 'somewhere round here I'm reckoning. But first,' and his face grew into a smile, 'follow me. I've got a little something you'll all be needing.'

They followed him out of the kitchen and into the hallway.

Old Man Wood produced a mug, bent down and filled it with the not entirely clean water from the plastic bucket. 'Now, drink some of this. It's a wee bit special.'

Isabella knelt down and sniffed it. 'Smells funny. Slightly sulphuric. Are you sure it hasn't been infected? If it comes from the flooding, you do realise it's almost certain to kill us.'

'My dear Bells,' the old man said, 'it's from the Bubbling Brook—'

'But your Bubbling Brook place is within the vicinity of the flooding, is it not?' Isabella said, knowingly. She stood up. 'This sample needs testing and at the very least boiling before anyone touches it—'

'It is *special water*, Isabella,' Old Man Wood said, his tone exasperated.

'But why is it so special that it doesn't require treating?' Isabella insisted.

Old Man Wood looked at her stunned. Then he turned to the other two for support.

Isabella noticed. 'All I'm trying to say is, why should this sample be absolutely fine in contrast to a sample taken from anywhere else in the floodwater because, to all intents and purposes, they must be from the same source and therefore infected?'

He shook his head. 'Because this water will enable you to speak, read and write in any language,' the old man said. 'Don't ask me how it works. It's an appley-funny-peculiar sensation at first, but you'll get used to it.'

Daisy shrieked. 'Ooh! I get it. I had some when I went into the glade—remember?' she said. 'I've had the coolest conversations with things. Did you know, this house is full of little notes from lovey-dovey mice?'

'Those are droppings, Daisy,' Isabella said.

'Depends on how you read them, Isabella,' Daisy said. 'All they go on about is food and sex. They're at it all the time and they go on and on and on ...'

'Like someone else we know?' Archie said.

Daisy hit him. 'Here, give it to me.' She grabbed the glass of water from out of Old Man Wood's hand, raised it to her lips, sniffed it and then, as she stared Isabella in the eye, downed it in one. 'Ah,' she said, and she belched and sat down with her eyes shut tight.

'You are quite disgusting,' Isabella said, wafting her hand in front of her.

Old Man Wood passed the mug to Archie. 'A couple of mouthfuls should do it,' he said, his eyes raised in earnest. Archie did as the old man recommended and passed it on to Isabella, who very reluctantly and only after popping in a finger and licking it, took a couple of small sips.

'Come on, Bells,' Daisy said. 'That's hardly going to work.'

'Just because I'm not as greedy as you,' Isabella said. She fixed her sister's eye and drained the glass. 'Urrrggh!' she cried, pulling a face as Daisy laughed.

'Disgusting... pheteucx!' Her eyes watered and instantly it felt as if her eyeballs were walloping about her head like pinballs.

As their brains fizzed and their ears crackled and eyes spun, Old Man Wood explained how it worked. 'When you concentrate on something you'll find there's a difference. But when you concentrate *an awful lot,* that's when it starts happening; you'll see and hear things... well, you'll find out soon enough. Don't worry,' he reassured them, 'you won't whoosh up into the air or grow a moustache or anything like that.'

He led them out into the courtyard where sunlight was attempting, rather sadly, to break through the thick white fog coming up from the valley. 'Now, littluns,' he said, smiling, 'somewhere around this courtyard, according to my old friend, Bethedi, there's a sign on a wall or a stone on the floor. It'll tell us what to do.'

'What sort of sign?' Archie asked.

Old Man Wood shook his head. 'If I knew, young man, I reckon I would tell you. Perhaps it's like peculiar writing you find on walls in the towns ...?'

'Graffiti?'

Old Man Wood appeared confused. 'I suppose,' he said, 'it could be graff...

whatever that is. But you'll need to look carefully—it could be anywhere. Now, for apples' sake concentrate, the lot of you.'

DAISY'S DISCOVERY

Daisy's search faltered immediately. Instead of looking for the writing or the sign outside, she had been distracted by a peculiar, strange, high-pitched squeaking sound coming from somewhere inside the house, which had been bothering her for a couple of days. She went back in to the house to investigate and ended up back in the kitchen, rooting through the condiment jars and flour pots and herbs. Eventually she honed it down to one particular area and, now concentrating at her utmost, she could see the offenders through the cupboard door.

She ran back outside. 'Old Man Wood, you'd better come and check this out.'

Soon the others joined her. And even though Daisy's hearing was a hundred times greater than theirs, Archie and Isabella also heard a strange noise coming from within the cupboard.

'It's a trapped mouse,' Archie volunteered.

Daisy shook her head. 'Nah. Too many. Sounds like a whole load of them—'

'An infestation?' Archie said.

Daisy nodded knowingly as Isabella took two steps back. 'Actually, by that scurrying noise, I wouldn't be surprised if it's a whole load of rats trapped behind the door waiting to rush out.' She caught Archie's eye and winked, trying not to laugh.

'Yeah, definitely rats,' Archie said, waiting for the explosion. 'I hope they don't bite too much.'

'Oh, shut up, you two,' Isabella said from behind the door. 'Stop it! Stop being so childish. You know I hate them.'

The twins thought this was brilliantly funny. Daisy opened the door and both of them started shrieking, and then they howled with laughter at Isabella's terrified reaction. 'Oh chill your pants, Bells,' Daisy said, pulling the sugar bowl out. 'The noise is coming from here. I promise you there are no rats.'

Now that they were concentrating on the bowl, the high-pitched commotion grew. Daisy placed the bowl on the work surface as four pairs of eyes peered into it, baffled. For a while, all they could see were the granules of sugar. But it quickly became clear to Daisy that this wasn't entirely sugar. She found herself looking at a mixture of microscopic toadstools that kept on morphing into granules like miniature Christmas lights in a random flashing sequence.

She stood up and took a step backwards. 'These are microscopic mushrooms,' she said.

'Are you sure?' Isabella said. 'Not sugar?'

'Definitely not. Try one. I dare you.'

Isabella shook her head. 'Fungi? Here?' Isabella's expression dropped. 'What if this is the Havilarian Toadstool Powder?!' she cried.

'The stuff that nearly killed you, Old Man Wood.' Daisy added. 'What do you think?'

Old Man Wood studied it, but it was hard to tell from his expression if he could even see the fungi let alone hear them. 'If it is,' he began, 'it's lethal stuff, especially to me.' The children backed away as Old Man Wood shot off out of the room.

'What's it doing here?' Daisy said. 'It's a very odd place to live—'

'No, it isn't,' Archie cried. 'It makes total sense.'

Daisy looked confused. 'Go on, Sherlock. Reveal all.'

'I added a spoon of sugar into the tea full of rum that sent Old Man Wood bonkers,' he said. 'At the time you two thought it was a bit funny.'

Old Man Wood returned wearing a pair of rubber gloves and holding a small glass jar.

'Havilarian Toadstool Powder can't escape from this old thing,' Old Man Wood said. 'Would one of you mind pouring it in? If it touches me, I might end up a bit like last time.'

Isabella carefully jigged the sugar and slowly the powder emptied from one container to the other. As Old Man Wood sealed the latch, the screeching howls from the tiny toadstools ceased.

The children exchanged glances. 'But why only you, Old Man Wood?' Archie asked.

'Because the toadstools only poison those from the Garden of Eden, that's why,' the old man replied. 'Which reminds me—if we ever get there, the only way to dispose of these horrible things is in the River of Life.'

Old Man Wood slipped the jar into his coat pocket.

'You sure you don't want me to take it?' Archie said. 'What if you fall and it breaks?'

Old Man Wood smiled. 'Need to be some strength for this to break. In any case, it'll remind me to be a little bit more careful.' He ushered the children out. 'Come on, come on. We have the urgent matter of finding Blabisterberry Jelly.'

After a few minutes, it became clear that what they were searching for was akin to finding a needle in a haystack. Hundreds of stones from the cobbles on the floor to those in the walls, and even the roof, bore some kind of writing or message. And worse still, many had messages on that were so old and scuffed that they took considerable deciphering.

"... NOT HERE. SORRY," said a weathered grey stone that Daisy found. And then, as she neared Mrs. Pye's flat, she found another three similar messages. Irritated, she opened the door of one of the shed doors beneath Mrs. Pye's flat, let herself in and lay on the floor.

This old stable, used mainly by Old Man Wood, was crammed full of things to mend. Dotted on the floor and hanging off the walls were an assortment of old chairs and picture frames and lamps and parts of old bicycles and even an old piano, its ivories removed. To Daisy's left sat a colourful carpet with a big hole in the middle and, to her right, a doll she recognised from her childhood that was missing an arm, a leg, and an eye.

Daisy rather liked it in here and sat down among the odds and ends as the dappled daylight filtered in through the dirty, cobweb-filled windows. For a minute the quiet allowed her to empty her mind. She closed her eyes, oblivious to the cacophony of new sounds and images around her. She breathed deeply and for a while sleep called her.

Suddenly she heard a familiar kind of noise, which was neither a squeak nor anything unusual. She roused herself. Perhaps the wind had pushed the door, making it groan. But as she thought about it, she realised there was no wind only the gently swirling cloud down in the valley swamping the vale.

She listened again and heard a voice. A boy's voice talking slowly, whispering and... weeping. It wasn't Archie and it certainly wasn't Old Man Wood. She listened harder and realised the words were coming from Mrs. Pye's flat directly above her.

Then she heard, unmistakably, Mrs. Pye's distinctive tones.

Who the heck was it?

Quietly, Daisy slipped out of the mending room, ran down the courtyard and bounded up the stone stairs on her toes, barely making a sound. At the top, she prised open the door to Mrs. Pye's apartment, slipped inside, tiptoed down the narrow, dark corridor and stopped outside Mrs. Pye's bedroom door.

She caught her breath, her senses on high alert. She listened. Nothing. Just muffled sounds, like... sobs, crying. Daisy desperately wanted to look inside but something told her not to. She stared hard at the door as if willing it to move aside. Then, much to her astonishment, she found herself seeing right through the wooden door, as though she had somehow opened up a large porthole of glass. And the harder she stared, the clearer the image.

There, in front of her, was the large figure of Mrs. Pye sitting on the bed with her eyes closed and a wide grimacey-smile traced across her face, a smaller figure folded into her bosom.

Astonished, yet intrigued, and nervous that she was seeing things, Daisy tip-toed down the passageway and, as her concentration moved from seeing to keeping quiet, she found herself staring at the dark magnolia-coloured wall. When she regained her concentration, the see-through portal reappeared and she found herself looking at a boy. A boy she'd definitely seen before. But who was it?

Suddenly it came to her, though it made no sense. It looked like the boy from the TV, the boy who survived the storm, the miracle child, the boy otherwise known as... Kemp.

KEMP!

She swore, under her breath. What was he doing here! Isabella's greatest enemy... here... with Mrs. Pye... how? Had the world ended already? Was she in a parallel universe or something?

She watched. For ages, they didn't say anything, just held each other as though *they had just found each other and didn't want to ever let go,* she thought. Daisy noticed tears streaming down Kemp's face and then she began to see the similarities.

The hair, the lips, the piggy blue eyes.

Daisy was filled with a strange prickly sensation. She shuddered as she remembered what Archie had told her about Kemp losing his mother when he was a baby. And she recalled Old Man Wood's story of how he had found Mrs. Pye in the hills, as near to dead as you could get, mangled and scarred with no memory.

The whole truth of the matter came to her: Kemp and Kemp's mother, Mrs. Pye. And at that moment, as she watched the boy through the wall, her heart pinched and ached for him.

And for the first time in her life, Daisy de Lowe felt ashamed of her behaviour towards Kemp. This sad boy, who hadn't had the best of luck in life, a boy who'd never known his mother or father, a boy they'd pushed aside and turned into a monster.

Daisy shook her head and moved down the corridor. How did Kemp get here? After all Eden Cottage was stuck out in the middle of nowhere. Furthermore, wasn't Kemp in hospital? He had to be, unless the TV interview had been pre-recorded. Maybe he found out and escaped? But it was miles and miles over terrible flooding.

It didn't make sense. But, then again, nothing made sense any more.

Daisy crept along, deep in thought. A shiver worked up her spine, a feeling as if something was watching her. She shook it out.

At the top of the stone staircase she noticed a strange overcoat hanging on the wall.

She looked back down the corridor. Kemp's coat? No, too big, but then again, too small for the voluptuous figure of Mrs. Pye. Perhaps it had been there all along, for years? Perhaps, Mrs. Pye had left it there as a reminder that she might one day find a man in her life?

Daisy lent in and smelled the fabric. Old, like moths and soot and peat combined, she thought. She sniffed again. More like the ash that drifted about when Dad cleaned the fires. She fingered the fabric, noting how intricately the patterns ran together, and as she did she heard a soft, deep voice, almost purring. Her arms freckled with goose bumps.

Daisy wondered if she should put it on, to warm her up. All she had to do was reverse into it.

She turned around and put her right arm behind her, searching for the hole that led down the arm of the coat. There. She thrust her arm quickly down into the coat and, as she did, she gasped.

An intense, cold rush sped into her arm, like icy treacle. She moaned. It felt so cold, but yet so warm and electrifying.

She twisted her body around as if to push her other arm in when the door flew open.

In front of her stood Kemp. His mouth open.

Daisy, in shock, let the left arm of the coat swing.

'Daisy,' he said, moving quickly towards her. 'I know you generally do the opposite of anything I say, but I absolutely urge you, in fact I'm begging you, not to put that coat on.'

Daisy shrugged and looked him up and down. Kemp had lost weight and his baldness made him different; less childish, she thought, as a curious tingle ran through her. 'Give me two good reasons,' she said.

'Please don't,' Kemp said. 'For once in your life, just believe me,' he said. 'You really don't want to do it.'

Daisy felt for the other arm-hole. 'That's not even one reason,' she said, as she slid her arm into the coat. She closed her eyes as the freezing syrupy feeling swam through her arms and into her chest.

'Don't do it,' Kemp said, his voice betraying his worry. 'Get out of there, Daisy. *Get out of there NOW!*'

But already Daisy's eyes were shutting, and the sound of a man's laughter filled her ears.

BAD NEWS FROM AMERICA

'It's impossible, sir,' Dickinson said. 'Visibility is down to no more than a couple of metres.'

The radio crackled back. 'I don't bleedin' care if you can't see your effing noses, you're going to get up there and then back here, with or without those children.' Stone's voice calmed down. 'Dickinson, I need to know. And fast. We can't risk the helicopters. You're on your own. Do you copy?'

Dickinson shrugged. 'All I was saying, sir, is that we will not be able to proceed at the speed we anticipated.'

'What the hell do they train you for?' Stone yelled down the radio. 'Sunning yourselves? It's not a bloody holiday.'

Dickinson turned to the unit. 'You heard the man.' He pulled out some instruments from his rucksack. 'We need to move.' He delved into his bag. 'Compass, map, heat sensors. Everyone should have the same, if you haven't, I need to know. Understand? It's like semolina out there and if you get lost don't expect us to come looking for you.'

Dickinson had served in four tours: Afghanistan, Syria, the Balkans and Iraq. But never had he encountered conditions like this. A white-out as thick as custard spread out over a wasted, destroyed landscape. It gave him the collywobbles just thinking about it. Going in blind. Utterly devoid of sight. At least, he reasoned, there wouldn't be land-mines or IEDs or sniper fire to worry about, only bogs and brambles and random pools.

He never imagined he'd be plucking three children out of a remote hillside cottage in the midst of a global meltdown.

The country was already out of control. In places, reports said that the army were shooting anyone suspected of having Ebora. Elsewhere, the dead were being laid out on the doorsteps, exactly as they'd done at the time of the Black Death.

The difference being that this was viral, and back then it was bacterial. Both were horrible, nasty, silent killers. Both terrifying, unknown enemies.

They'd had the best of it tucked away at Swinton Park, trying to hold things together. But that would change and Dickinson knew it wouldn't take long. And he had half a mind to see if he could engineer a way of staying.

He shone his torch into the white wall of cloud and the light bounced back. The bottom line, according to Stone, was that they were doomed unless these kids came up with the answer.

That's how Stone operated, he supposed. As a predator sniffs out a weakness or a flaw, he'd chase and chase until he pulled his prey down, extracting whatever information he needed. And nearly always he was proven correct. He'd done it time after time, over and over again.

But, Dickinson thought, *kids on the search for tablets—electronic or otherwise—to stop the world's greatest catastrophe?* It just didn't stack up.

Unless you added in the Headmaster's idea that the disease was being spread by dream-giving aliens, then they had nothing to work on. Nothing whatsoever aside from the suspicions of every nation that it was some kind of hideous biological weapon attack.

Maybe they should bomb the hell out of Upsall and be done with it, he thought.

They had barely started before Simonet, operating the tracking system, came bustling over. 'Bad news, sir.'

Dickinson halted. 'What now?'

'The tracking device has frozen, sir. Satellite down. We can wait for them to come on-line again, but no guarantees.'

Dickinson kneaded his temple. 'No. We need to keep moving. Let's get up this hill and work it out from there.' He turned to the four others. 'Keep tight and don't wander off. If you do, you'll get lost. If by a miracle you manage to spot a significant feature, like a waterfall or cliff face, call a halt and we'll see if we can locate it on the map.' Dickinson stared at the Ordnance Survey map.

'If we head directly up from our landing point, we should be there in twenty to thirty minutes. Any deviation by the smallest degree and it'll take significantly longer.'

Dickinson's radio buzzed into life.

'Corporal,' crackled Stone's voice from the command centre. 'You may have noticed a satellite failure.'

'Affirmative, Commissioner. The imagery disappeared less than a minute ago.'

Dickinson could have sworn he heard the Commissioner sigh. 'Good. Well, you should know where you are.' The crackle of the radio cut out and then came on again. 'I, er, have news just in.'

'I take it this is not good news, Commissioner.'

The radio went silent for a while.

Dickinson didn't like the sound of this one bit.

Stone's voice was softer. 'I mentioned before,' he began, 'that various nation states believe that this area of Yorkshire is the originator of this global catastrophe. Well, the United States tabled an emergency proposal to destroy the entire area.' The radio went silent. 'I'm talking pretty much the entire northern half of the country in what they are calling, *a global action of absolute last resort.'*

'When?' Dickinson said.

Stone's voice betrayed his emotion. 'They wanted to detonate at midnight tonight, leaving a chance for the top brass to get out. But we told them our situation and, to my surprise, we managed to get an extension. So, gentlemen, we have approximately three days to find out what the hell is going on. I need you in and out of there, like yesterday, fog or no fog. If the children aren't there, let me know... in fact I think I'm going to send the headmaster towards you as fast as possible to see if any of his findings from the church at Upsall match up. Might be worth having you lot about to help him up to the cottage. Then I need you back. There's trouble kicking off everywhere. I think the news leaked.'

The soldiers stared at one another, stunned.

'For Queen and country,' Dickinson said quietly, 'and for this entire planet. Lads, you're now on the world's most important mission: to find these kids. Fail, gents, and we've all had it.' He patted a couple on their backs. 'Time to get a move on.'

A STRANGE NEW LANGUAGE

To the common eye the insignificant scratches or scuffs littering the walls were scribbles of one sort or another; love notes, bits of information, travel updates, even stories. Some had been added years and years ago and said things like: 'PLAGUE, KEEP OUT!'

Other inscriptions had been painstakingly crafted. Many were recent, and where it was dry, like under the extensively wide eaves, considerable bird scribblings made for compulsive reading.

Archie felt faint, and starving. He climbed the stepladder and sat reading the graffiti, mesmerised and slightly forgetting that he was looking for clues as to how to find Blabisterberry Jelly. A small part of him wished that his eyes and brain would stop and, when that happened, his concentration withdrew so he saw nothing bar scuffs and scratches.

Old Man Wood had been searching the house around the front and came back to see how they were getting along. 'Any luck, Archie?'

Archie buried his face in his hands. 'I never knew other THINGS could write!'

The old man chuckled. 'You lot don't know much, I suppose,' Old Man Wood said. 'It's a secret that's been kept back from human types. You see, humans have one way of communicating, everything else another. That's just the way of it.' He clapped Archie on the back. 'It happened a long time ago, part of the Great Deal. I'm sure you'll learn about it one day.'

Archie's eyes rested on a message on the dry windowsill which otherwise would have looked like a series of distorted birds' messes. He concentrated hard and shortly a message came out. He read it out to Old Man Wood.

WANTED: SINGLE GEESE FOR LOVING HOLIDAY CRUISE TO SOUTHERN HEMISPHERE. SEE ORAVIO AT THE GRAVEL PITS—TWENTY FLAPS SOUTH-WEST WITH THE WIND. IF IT TAKES YOU MORE THAN THIRTY, I'M TOTALLY NOT INTERESTED.

Archie rubbed his foremost hair spike whose texture was comfortingly smooth. 'That wouldn't be the fat goose that waddles around out here looking a little bit pleased with himself?' he asked.

Old Man Wood shrugged. 'Suppose it could well be.'

'That Goose calls himself Oravio?' Archie said.

Old Man Wood nodded.

'And he comes up here, to... to find a date?' Archie sounded put-out. 'Like all the other animals in the area. Our house is like an enormous dating magazine. It's animal "Tinder",' he laughed, 'a giant community notice board.'

'What did you expect?' Old Man Wood said, putting a comforting arm around his shoulders, 'that other living things don't communicate?'

'But what do you mean by *communicate?*' Archie said. 'Animals don't talk like we do—all they do is sniff each other's bums or twitter or quack or baa or moo. They aren't smart, like us.'

Old Man Wood's deep laugh boomed out. 'Ooh, you're right there, they're not clever—like humans! Clever at putting themselves first at the expense of everyone else and all that, but it doesn't mean other living things can't and don't talk.'

The old man scratched his chin as he gathered his thoughts. 'You see, Archie, one of the flaws of the human race was to fail to recognise that living things do actually converse with one another. All these animals, these creatures and trees and insects and plants, *they know*. It's just that, after a while, the humans couldn't be bothered. Which is hardly surprising, I suppose, because the population of man grew and grew and there were other things to worry about, I'm sure. But it's a shame, nonetheless. Some of those birds are mightily entertaining. Look at those pigeons ducking out the way of cars. To them, it's a mighty fine entertainment—'

'Except when they get hit.' Archie added.

Isabella had wandered over and was listening intently to the old man. 'Don't tell me that trees actually talk?' she scoffed. 'Creatures, TREES actually chatting away to each other. You'll be telling me they watch TV next. You are joking, right?' Isabella said.

Old Man Wood raised his wrinkly brow and shook his head.

'See, Archie?' she said. 'He's making it up.'

'No I am not, Bells,' Old Man Wood said. 'Take your cat, Psycho-cat. Look at the way he moves, swishes his tail, paws his face, rubs against you and opens his eyes when he's cross. He's talking away to you—but you have no idea what he's really saying. You call it "body language" and that's what creatures do to give you clues. The next time you see Psycho-cat, just remember that.' The old man raised his dark eyes to the sky as if remembering things from a long time ago. Then he exhaled slowly. 'The great divide in communication is something that took me hundreds of years to get used to, especially with trees—'

'With trees?' Archie said.

'Yes, Archie, like those Willows which I wanted to show you.'

'But they don't *really* talk, do they?' Isabella said.

'Of course they do,' Old Man Wood replied, his tone a little more upset than usual. 'Trees are the greatest living things on the planet. They are way older than humans and far cleverer. Their roots stretch deep into the earth, their branches high into the sky. They listen out for every season; they play with the winds, with the air and the birds. They clean the waters and filter the air and they sing songs when they swish and they sway and they are funny and sad and beautiful.'

The children listened silently as Old Man Wood continued. 'Each living thing has energy and this is otherwise known as *spirit*. It's strong in some and dim in others and it is this spirit, this energy, which binds us all together. It is the energy we get when we love and when we care and when we feel. It is this energy that allows us to be.'

The old man sighed as he remembered. 'But the trees had a terrible time, especially after everything they had given up.'

'You're talking in riddles again, Old Man Wood,' Isabella said. 'What do you mean, "given up"?'

'Now let me think,' he said as he rubbed his chin. 'In the Garden of Eden, most of the trees moved, some faster than others. But when they came to Earth they had to give up their mobility. There wasn't really room for them all to be running around. So they found a suitable place and dug in their roots—like anchors I suppose—to support the planet, hold it together, help us breathe.'

Isabella shook her head. Her belief system was being mightily challenged. Unless she remained calm, she could see herself slipping into madness.

'So you're saying humans are rubbish?' Archie quizzed.

Old Man Wood laughed his booming laugh. 'No. Humans are wonderful. Smart, clever, resourceful. But they look after themselves first at the sake of every other thing, even though they tell themselves they don't. They always have and that, my boy, is why they've been so successful. And it's why you must succeed,' he said turning to them.

Old Man Wood noticed their perplexed looks.

'I'm afraid the water from the Bubbling Brook will shock you,' he said sweetly. 'But from now on, it is essential that you open your eyes, your ears—and your minds!'

DAISY AND CAIN

Daisy closed her eyes and groaned as an immense feeling of power grew inside her.

She could trace where the sensations of the cold, an almost painful icy flow, ran through her sinews like thick oil. A powerful, strange, exotic feeling began to build as a wave slowly swept over her, through every little vein, down every artery, into her hands, teasing the nerves in her elbows, her breasts, her genitals and into her knees and then to the end of each toe. The sensation tingled parts of her she never knew even existed. She gasped and cried out.

She could hear a low, silky voice talking directly into her brain. 'There is so much more,' was all it said.

Daisy moaned, but something wasn't right. She forced her eyes open and saw Kemp. 'What... what's happening to me?'

Now the voice came back at her and the feelings intensified. 'Come with me,' it said, 'willingly, like the boy and you will have everything. Say "Yes" and it will be done.'

Daisy almost gave in then and there as a slither of cold ran through her body and circled her midriff before plunging into her groin. A blinding flash blew through her brain and the feeling grew and grew before rocketing through her body.

She breathed deeply, trying to regain control. *Too much.* She opened her eyes. Kemp, again, a look of deep concern plastered on his face, pulling at her arm, pleading, yelling. Had he noticed?

Daisy gathered herself but her arm was stuck. Something in the coat held it.

She thrashed one way, then the next, but the more she did so, the more a curious sensation built in the fingers of the trapped arm. At first it felt like pricks from small, sharp pins but soon these joined together until collectively they hurt more and more as if thousands of pins were thrust in. Soon it burned. She gritted her teeth. Her hair was singeing.

'Let go of me!' she seethed.

She tugged, but it stuck, as if caught in a vice. 'Let go of me, now!' she cried.

'Let her go!' Kemp said, his voice firm. 'She does not go willingly.'

The pain receded.

'Let her go now, or I will never go with you again.'

Suddenly, Daisy lay on the floor, her arm red and tender halfway to her elbow. The delicate hairs on the backs of her fingers were singed.

Instantly, she knew that Kemp had suffered the same fate.

'Please, go... now,' said a soft voice above her—Kemp's voice. A voice so gentle, she'd never have believed him possible of uttering it.

In a millisecond, Kemp had taken her place and his arms pushed into the sleeves of the grey coat. From out of the coat pocket he pulled out a curious-looking trilby hat. He boxed it out and, with a tiny smile on his face, slipped it over his head. As he did this, not once did he take his eyes off her. Not once did his expression alter.

Then, as if by magic, underneath the long coat, Kemp suddenly morphed into a human figure of ash. But the person the ashen features revealed was an older-looking human with sweptback hair and scabbed skin marks. Daisy scampered backwards as the figure loomed over her and then pounced towards her face, ash falling from it.

'Come with me,' it demanded. 'Come. You know you want to.' Ash fizzed out of its mouth showering her like a fountain. And then, with a windy chuckle, the grey-coated ash-man stood up and dived headfirst down the stairwell, vanishing in a tiny blue flash.

Daisy's heartbeat raced and she looked down at nothing but a tiny pile of ash on the stone stairs below.

DECIPHERING THE CODE

Daisy sat in stunned silence. Her red eyes shone brightly, like the depressed brake lights of a car. Her heart thumped. That, she thought, was weirder than when she'd landed in the Atrium or whatever place that was.

What sort of monster lived in a coat? Was it a ghost? She shook as she thought about it, her whole body resonating at the memory. Those feelings—so cold and painful and yet hot and exhilarating—at the same time. Like her dreams.

And how come Kemp was with it? In fact, was Kemp actually dead, or alive, or now some kind of spirit? But she'd felt the flesh and blood of his arm pulling at her, trying to release her from the creature and thinking of that, she'd sniffed the sharp smell, the distinctive pungent tang of his burned hair.

Kemp had warned her, so why didn't she listen? Was she simply so bloody against him she wasn't prepared to give him a chance? And then she thought of Kemp talking to Mrs. Pye. His tears and their soft, loving words. Inside, Daisy felt terrible and her heart wanted to reach out and tell him that he was OK, and that she understood.

'Mrs. Pye,' she said as she leapt up and ran along the corridor. She stood outside Mrs. Pye's bedroom door and swallowed. *What should she say? What words would be comforting enough for Mrs. Pye or... simply, right?*

She knocked on the door and, with a deep breath, walked in. Mrs. Pye sat on the bed, her body swaying from side to side, tears rolling down her cheeks.

Daisy ran up and threw her arms around her. But although Mrs. Pye reacted by closing her eyes, she continued swaying, murmuring incoherently.

When Daisy pulled out of her embrace and took a step back, Mrs. Pye carried on doing the same thing, her eyes staring, lost across the room, her voice like a slow chant, her body rocking back and forth, to and fro.

Daisy waved her arms in front of her face.

Oh no, she thought. *Mrs. Pye has slipped into a mental state of shock.*

For a little while, Daisy did everything she could think of to try and snap Mrs. Pye out of her state. She tried yelling 'BOO' suddenly and very loudly in her ear, she pinched her cheek and gave her a mild Chinese burn, but Mrs. Pye was immovable. Daisy then did a dance right in front of her, which in normal circumstances would have had Mrs. Pye chortling and telling her to "stop it, you daft brush".

Finally, Archie appeared. 'What are you doing?' he said, as he popped his head around the door.

Daisy shrugged. 'It's Mrs. Pye. She's away with the with the bleeding fairies. Watch this.' Daisy then proceeded to swirl like a Spanish dancer right in front of Mrs. Pye before clapping her hands loudly right in front of her face.

'I see what you mean,' Archie said, a frown ridging his forehead. 'Any idea what's set her off? Something must have happened.' He frowned. 'Maybe she saw that the authorities were looking for us on TV, that we're wanted. Or maybe it's because we've smashed up the house—'

"Nah. I found her like this. And we do look a bit weird,' Daisy said.

Right now, she needed to get her head together about what had happened with Kemp, and how he'd discovered that Mrs. Pye was Kemp's mother, and how she'd been manhandled by a ghost let alone explain it all to Archie. She shook her head.

Archie put a hand on her shoulder. 'Sorry to drag you away, Daisy, but we could do with a hand out there... it's a bit complicated and we're getting nowhere. We'll check up on Mrs. P later, OK?'

Archie first of all gave Mrs. Pye a hug and then Daisy moved over to Mrs. Pye and, looking into her eyes, planted a small kiss on her forehead and said, 'we'll be back shortly to make sure you're alright, I promise.'

'So, here's the problem,' Archie said. 'When you concentrate the whole place turns into of a nightmare of notes and letters.'

'I know. Irritating, isn't it?'

They met up with Isabella and Old Man Wood in the middle of the courtyard.

'You know something,' Daisy said dreamily as she stared at the wall next to the front door, 'it's probably a good thing that humans don't understand any of this. Listen to this classic.' She moved in and pointed to the windowsill.

'*NEST VACANT,*' she read raising her eyebrows.

'*FAMILY EATEN. NEST WILL ROT IF NOT OCCUPIED. LOOK IN THE HAWTHORN BY THE BUBBLING BROOK. ASK FOR SPRINKLE THE THRUSH.*'

Daisy shook her head. 'And there's more. Listen to this one.

'*PREDATOR EVASION COURSES: PROTECT YOURSELF AND YOUR FAMILY. BASED ON GROUND BREAKING RESEARCH BY DR. ROB ROBIN, GUARANTEED 35 PERCENT SURVIVAL INCREASE.*

'And then, in smaller writing, it says; *Conditions apply.*'

Isabella burst out laughing. 'They're adverts!'

Archie kicked a loose stone, which flew out of the courtyard towards the path. 'But it isn't helping us find Blaster-whatever-it-is Jelly. And I'm starving. Are you sure we can't eat something?'

'Certainly not,' Old Man Wood replied, groaning as he attempted to move some loose stone slabs from the corner of the yard.

Daisy shook her head. 'What did the willow trees say? Are you sure they meant this courtyard, not the ruin?'

'Oh yes, this is the right place alright.'

Daisy sat down. 'Have we checked everywhere?'

'Twice,' Archie said, settling beside her. 'Can't your eyes find it?'

Daisy looked incredulous. 'No, Archie, apparently they can't,' she said flatly.

Archie's stomach rumbled. It he wasn't allowed to eat any food at least he could look at it. He decided to nip inside and sneak a peek inside the fridge.

He stood up, walked across the steps and, just as he opened the front door, he looked down at the metal foot-grate. Bending down, he moved it aside and there, in large letters, were the words:

'BLABISTERBERRY JELLY'

'Over here! I think I've found it!' he said. In no time four faces were peering over the stone.

'There's small writing beneath it,' Daisy said. 'Bit worn out—looks like instructions.'

Archie sniffed. 'I'll pull up the slab? It'll be underneath.'

'I don't think so—' she said, but already Archie was on his hands and knees trying to squeeze his fingers into the gap on one side. He groaned and pulled and heaved until his face started to sweat.

Daisy watched Archie straining. 'You haven't lost your strength, have you?'

Archie bristled and he made an even greater effort.

Eventually he relented.

Daisy smiled. 'Now, let me read the instructions to you,' she said, in a very irritating kind of school-mistressey manner. She adjusted the pink glasses on the bridge of her nose and cleared her throat.

'*TO OPEN ME,*' she read, '*KNOCK THREE TIMES* AND *PRESS ON EDEN'S...* and the final word is scuffed. It goes something like, blank, blank, blank, maybe blank, then a P, blank, blank. I think.'

_ _ _ ? P _ _

They all looked at each other quizzically.

'Gatepost?' Isabella said, getting excited. 'It could be a... gatepost?'

'We don't have a gatepost, we have a rock,' Daisy said.

Archie rubbed a hair spike. 'The rock does look like a gatepost,' he said hopefully. 'But it's missing a "T".'

'It's a massive grey rock, or obelisk, with *"Eden Cottage"* etched into it.' Daisy said. She ran to the top of the yard and concentrated hard on the gate-rock and just as before all sorts of writing started to appear.

A fresh one, not yet blurred from the rain read:

"NOPPY LOVES SCROPPY. BUNNY KISSES."

Further up were watered down names from a deer called Lush, a fox called Sand and a badger called Leaf. Perhaps they lived here too. Then one caught her eye, nestled under the dry overhang of the stone.

"RED TO THE RABBITY FAMILY. SORRY ABOUT FLOPPY BUT I AM A FOX. THE FLOODS HAVE MADE IT VERY DIFFICULT TO EAT ANYWHERE ELSE. DON'T HOLD IT AGAINST ME."

'Wow!' Daisy said under her breath. 'Incredible.' And then she just made out a very recent addition beneath it:

"BEWARE. EVIL SURROUNDS THE OLD RUIN FOR ALL."

Daisy swallowed. 'There's nothing!' she shouted.

'Nothing?' said Archie. 'Are you sure? I mean magic eyes or not, were you concentrating hard enough?' he said sarcastically.

'Shut up, Arch—what's got into you?' Isabella said. 'You're getting really nauseating.'

'If it's that irritating, zap me with your hands?'

'I'm very tempted, Archie.'

Archie didn't react. He stood dead still. A brilliant idea had suddenly leapt into his head.

'I think I've got it!' he cried. 'Listen. It's got nothing to do with the gatepost. It's *carpet*—you know: blank, blank, blank, P, blank, blank.'

'*The hand-mark on one of the rugs,*' Isabella cried. 'Archie's right!' She ran inside and, moments later, returned with the carpet rolled under her arm.

She re-read the riddle: 'TO OPEN ME, KNOCK THREE TIMES AND PRESS ON EDEN'S CARPET.' Isabella looked delightedly at her siblings. 'Well, there's only one way to find out. Who's going to press and who's going to knock?'

'I'll press on the hand mark. Archie knocks,' Daisy said. 'Are you ready? On the count of three.'

'One, two, THREE'

Daisy moved her hand in alignment with the smaller outline of the hand on the carpet.

KNOCK, KNOCK, KNOCK.

They held their breath.

Then, ever so slowly, the paving slab with 'Blabisterberry Jelly' written on it started to fade away and in its place appeared a stone stairway.

The children and Old Man Wood exchanged glances. 'We did it,' Isabella said, nervously.

From the bottom of the steps a sweet perfume wafted up to them. They stared down. Then a lovely, sweet voice came up to them.

'Hello there!' it said. 'Well, now, there's no time to dally. Come along, come along.'

Isabella cringed, her body filled with trepidation. 'Oh hells-bells,' she whispered. 'We've really got to go down there, haven't we?'

TROOPS ARRIVE AT EDEN COTTAGE

'Look, sir, buildings,' Geddis said, relieved. 'The fog's a little thinner up here.'

The stony corner of a building, like a ship, quickly emerged out of the white, creamy soup.

'OK, quiet. Protective clothing on, please.' Dickinson said.

Without hesitating, the troops donned the white protective helmets and gloves.

'Call in on your MICs please.' The troops responded. 'Geddis, anything on the sensors?'

Geddis shook his head. 'Nothing, here, sir.'

Dickinson waved them forward. 'Remember, if you see them, do not shoot—is that perfectly clear? Shoot as a very last resort and not to kill. Did you get that, Talbot?'

The four soldiers responded to their commander in the affirmative. At least there were no problems with the microphones and earpieces.

By now the fog had caught them up and, in order not to get swamped by the huge blanket of white cloud, the troops moved silently, hugging the wall, moving in a line of five.

Dickinson stopped near the front door. 'Geddis, do you read anything?'

'Negative. Nothing in the courtyard area. And as far as I can tell nothing through these three windows on this side of the house.'

'Inside,' Dickinson commanded, tipping his head.

The men moved fast, opened the door and entered the hallway.

'Looks like someone's been in here already, sir,' said Pearce, the tall, wiry commando, as he inspected the mess of frames, canvasses and pictures lying in heaps all over the floor. 'Someone's given the place a good going over. I reckon they've already been and gone.'

Dickinson sucked in a breath as he inspected the pictures. 'Maybe they searched the house and took the kids.' *After all*, he thought, *the helicopter hadn't reported any sign of life during its reconnaissance mission.*

His earpiece crackled. Geddis' voice came through, breathing hard. 'Better make your way upstairs, sir. There's been one hell of a struggle up here. It's riddled with bullet holes.'

Dickinson instructed Talbot to come with him, leaving Pearce and Mills downstairs to search the remainder of the downstairs.

At the top of the stairs, signs of a battle could be seen on the landing where a burned rug lay on the floor.

Dickinson inspected it. 'Over a day old, maybe they've been gone longer than we thought.'

'In here, sir.'

Dickinson moved in and looked around. The room, as Geddis said, was a wreck. Small holes littered the wooden panels on the walls; the four-poster bed lay in a heap, the bottom end in bits, splinters scattered over the floor. 'Jeez, what happened here?'

'First impressions would be a gunfight. By the look of it, a hell of a lot of rounds. Machine gun, possibly a grenade or two.'

Dickinson ran his hand over the carvings on the bed. 'Any ideas who was involved?'

The pair searched the room.

'Have you noticed something?' Dickinson remarked. 'It doesn't really stack up. Masses of bullet holes but no—'

'Shells.'

'Precisely.'

Geddis whistled. 'You're right. There are no shells, sir, anywhere,' he said, scouring the floor. 'And, if I'm not mistaken, looking at the holes, they've used one helluva strange gun.'

Dickinson took out a tiny camera and began filming.

The headphones in his helmet crackled. 'Sir, Pearce here. We're going across to the other buildings. No sign of life in the main building. A few smashed plates, but the oven is warm. Did you say there was a housekeeper, sir?'

'Affirmative. Apparently she lives on site, in one of the outbuildings. Call me when you find her.'

Dickinson checked his phone and wondered whether to call Stone. No, perhaps he'd do it when he had a proper feel for what had gone on.

He shook his head. Clearly there had been a terrible struggle, but there had to be a clue—something—that gave them a chance to find out where they may have gone. Surely, they would have left a message somewhere?

'Commander,' the radio blared.

'Dickinson here.'

'You'd better come over. We've found someone. I think it's the woman you were talking about.'

Dickinson clenched his fist. 'Excellent. Coming over.'

'Follow the building. You'll eventually bump into Mills. Doesn't look as if she's got plans to go anywhere,' Pearce replied.

Dickinson reeled. 'What do you mean? Is she dead?'

'Negative, sir. You'll have to see for yourself. Looks like shock.'

Dickinson left Geddis to check out the other rooms, slipped out of the front door, and was immediately swallowed up by the dense fog. He moved around the courtyard until he saw Mills standing beside a stone flight of stairs.

Pearce met him at the top. 'I don't think she knows we're here,' he said.

When the commander walked into the bedroom, there, sitting on the bed and staring at the wall, was a large woman dressed in a pink, woollen dressing gown. Her piggy eyes were red from crying, and red hair hung loosely across her face and down her neck. Her forehead bore the deep traces of scarring and her plump, full lips were parted as a strange humming noise emanated from her. She rocked to and fro every so often, her arms across her chest as though protecting herself from cold.

Dickinson stepped in front of her and, when her reaction didn't alter, he squatted down and moved his palm a couple of inches from her face as though cleaning an invisible window.

'Hello?'

Not a flicker. He tried again with the same result before rejoining the other commandos outside the room.

'You're right. It's shock,' he said.

Mills agreed. 'I've seen this type of behaviour before. Might be best, sir, if you take off your protective garments and go in and start talking normally. She doesn't appear to have any Ebora symptoms.'

Dickinson nodded, removed his gear and re-entered the room. He knelt down before Mrs. Pye.

'Hello,' he said, awkwardly. 'I'm from the national rescue centre which is currently based at Swinton Park, near Masham. Do you know where that is? We're trying to find the cause of all this misery,' he said softly. 'You know, the storm and the rainwater and now there's been an outbreak of a terrible disease which is spreading.

We have a feeling that Archie and Isabella and Daisy might know something that could really help us get to the bottom of it. That's why we're here, so please don't be alarmed.' He ran a hand through his sandy hair, turned towards Mills and shrugged.

Mills gestured for him to keep going.

'Can you tell me where they are—the children?'

Mrs. Pye remained staring at the wall.

'Can you tell me your name?' he tried. 'Do you know what happened in the house?'

The woman continued to stare at the wall.

Dickinson waited patiently, before standing up and heading outside. This wasn't going to be easy. She needed medical help, and it wasn't going to be forthcoming from them. Perhaps he should call Stone, see if he had any ideas.

Dickinson unclipped his phone.

Stone picked up straight away. 'Well? Any luck?'

'It looks like someone's beaten us to it,' Dickinson said.

'Hell!' Stone swore. 'Any sign of the children?'

'Nowhere to be seen, sir. The place is a mess. There's been some kind of battle upstairs, odd gunfire marks in the wooden panelling, and a couple of fires have started.'

Stone sucked in a breath. 'Weapons? That's not good. What kind of shells?'

'That's the strange bit. There aren't any. It's as if they cleared up after themselves.'

Stone's silence spoke volumes. 'Are you quite sure?' he said at length.

'Affirmative. I've taken footage,' Dickinson said. 'And it would appear that someone has rifled through all the pictures—'

'Pictures?'

'Yes, sir. Framed pictures, canvasses, oils. They litter the downstairs rooms.'

'Anything else?'

'We've found the housekeeper, sir.'

Stone's tone lightened. 'What did she have to say?'

'Nothing yet, sir. She's in shock—scared out of her mind. Mills said he'd seen something like it before, in the Middle East—a girl who'd seen her entire family tortured to death in front of her.'

'Can you get *anything* out of her?'

'We're trying but it's negative at the moment. She hums and stares at the wall, shaking.'

'Try again, Dickinson,' Stone ordered. 'Use electricity to jar her or water-board if necessary... we need answers—'

'But torture, on a woman?'

'It's called *interrogation*, Dickinson,' Stone snapped, 'and I don't care how you do it. I just need results.' He slammed down the phone.

Dickinson went back into the room and knelt down in front of Mrs. Pye.

'Hello,' he said. 'It's me again. We really need to know what's happened and you're the only person we can find. You see, if we don't find the answers, the whole area around here will be destroyed by a very big bomb. So in order to prevent this, and the loss of hundreds of thousands of lives, we could do with your help.'

Still the woman rocked and stared at the wall.

Dickinson's patience began to desert him. 'Please,' he begged. 'Everyone is going die if we don't get some answers.'

A tiny flicker flashed in Mrs. Pye's eye and Dickinson wondered if she could hear him after all.

'All we need are a few simple answers,' he urged.

The woman resumed her staring and humming.

Dickinson hated this. He didn't have Stone's cold-hearted approach to interrogation, the iciness needed to extract answers. Maybe they should take her back with them so Stone could work on her? Then again, perhaps he should try a different approach. If he wasn't mistaken, she cared for the children. She must have feelings for them.

'Archie and the girls will die if you don't help them,' he began. 'Do you understand? Your children will be killed by this terrible thing if you don't help us find them.'

The woman suddenly turned to him. Her eyes moist again and tears ran down her cheeks as her shoulders heaved. 'Taken,' she said, her vocal chords straining. 'From me.'

And then she resumed her rocking and staring at the wall.

CAIN'S NEW IDEA

'Who cares what I did?' the ghost crowed.

'I do,' Kemp said angrily.

'You? But, my boy, you loathe them. That's what I rather liked about you. And now, suddenly because I, a mere spirit, go and give Daisy de Lowe a little tickle, you get all upset.'

'Tickle? That wasn't a tickle, you violated her—'

'Oh come now. I wasn't harming her, quite the opposite,' Cain said, 'and she is rather exquisite, if you ask me.'

Kemp's face looked ready to explode.

'You're not jealous, are you?' Cain asked. 'Or worried that I'd take her instead of you?'

Kemp shook his head. 'Of course not,' he said thickly. 'What you did was plain stupid.'

'Why? Surely you must see by now that the de Lowes are going to die. Those pathetic Heirs of Eden still haven't got a clue what's going on, although I'll grant you, by the amount of debris downstairs, they are trying.'

'But now Daisy knows I'm alive,' Kemp said.

'So what, boy?' Cain snapped. 'It doesn't matter. Why not have a bit of fun with them? If I was allowed to kill her, I would.' He paused. 'Then all of this would be over.'

'So why didn't you?'

'Because if I, or anyone else for that matter, interferes directly with the Heirs of Eden's quest, they will have succeeded.'

'Then you nearly gave it to them on a plate,' he said. 'How stupid can you get?' Kemp scratched his head; he needed to change the subject. 'Anyway, thanks for taking me to my mother,' he said. 'You were right.'

Cain drifted closer. 'My pleasure, boy. How did it go?'

'She knew,' Kemp said. 'We share the same thumbs; they bend right back like this.' He manipulated his digits.

'Fascinating,' Cain said, drily.

'When I looked closer, I was just like her. You know, hair, lips, even our noses are the same. She's bloody ugly though, unlike me.'

Cain laughed. 'So now we share our secrets.'

'Yeah,' Kemp said. 'And mum's coming here when the world gets destroyed, just as you promised, right? And please, don't do what you did with Daisy again, OK. It's freaky and a little bit pervy.'

Cain smiled. 'Ah, yes, yes. Of course,' Cain replied. Cain wondered if having the boy's mother around wouldn't be such a bad thing. Keep him under control; guide him in other ways, someone to play him off against.

Another thought had been niggling away at him. If Earth was to finish, as was increasingly likely, and Kemp was the sole survivor, then the boy would need a companion or two. Ghosts were hardly ideal playmates.

In due course, the boy would wish to reproduce and raise a family. But Havilah's human population were stuck, frozen in time like small, glass, upside down dishes littered upon the ground.

'You rather like her, don't you?'

'What?' Kemp said. 'My mum? Yeah, of course—'

'I meant the girl.'

'Daisy?' Kemp immediately went defensive. 'She's annoying and a show off and stupid, but she is pretty—'

'So you do like her!'

Kemp smiled. 'You're a horrible ghost, aren't you?'

'Perhaps,' he whispered into Kemp's ear.

'Stop doing that,' Kemp said, swishing at the air with his hand.

Cain moved through Kemp to the other ear. 'Or is there another girl?' he said.

'Stop that!'

Cain laughed with the boy. 'Come on, tell me.'

'No! Go away. Who I fancy is none of your business.'

'It's every bit my business,' Cain said, pretending to sound a little offended. 'Anyway, to find out all I have to do is look into your mind.'

'You wouldn't—'

'I already have.'

Kemp smiled and tried to think if there really was anyone else. 'Well if you must know, before you go rummaging through my head, there's a girl called Sue who is pretty hot.'

'Hot?' Cain chuckled. 'You don't mean that in a literal sense, do you? She doesn't actually feel hot, does she?'

'No! It means she's a bit of a babe, like Daisy, but with brains.'

'How interesting,' Cain mused.

Kemp sighed. 'Thing is, Daisy *hates* me. Sue, on the other hand, is properly gorgeous, and *really* hates me. The crap thing is she's the best friend of Isabella and Isabella hates me more than anyone or anything in the world, so basically it would never happen.'

'Why not? Strange things happen all the time,' said Cain, who hummed a strange, wispy tune, a trait which Kemp knew as his way of thinking. 'Why does Isabella detest you so, boy?'

'Well it started when I put a dead rat in her gym bag, which rotted and filled with maggots. When she found it, it made her so ill she ended up in hospital.' Kemp grinned. 'She's never forgiven me.'

Cain laughed. 'I tell you what,' he said at length, 'why don't we go and find her?'

'Isabella?'

'No, you fool. The girl who you say is the "hot" one?'

'Sue? She's probably dead like all the others—'

'I'll ask her spirits to find out, or better still, let me have a word with Asgard. The dreamspinner will find out in no time. Ghosts can get a little touchy, especially those related to the recently deceased—'

Kemp felt a little uneasy. 'Look, it's very nice of you to help me, but I'll save you the hassle. I promise you, she'll never, ever go with me, dead or alive. And anyway, what would I say to her? She's like, really clever and smart.'

'And you're not, boy?' Cain sighed. 'You're switched on enough to have joined me. In any case, you can give her a choice. Tell her it's you, or death.'

'That's not a great chat up line.'

'It worked for me.'

'Well, you're a ghost—'

'Indeed, but I wasn't always like this, you know. A long time ago I was extremely powerful and I intend, with your help, to reacquaint myself with that position.'

'So, why are you so interested in my love life, or lack of it?'

Cain appeared to sigh. 'As you know, I live forever,' he said wearily. 'You, however, will not. When Earth is no more, I can assure you that at some point you will wish to raise children.'

Kemp looked repulsed. 'OMG!'

'Whatever "OMG" means, I note the horror on your face. Don't be naive, boy. It is a perfectly natural development in the cycle of a living thing to procreate, to keep the wheels of life turning. For some species it is their sole purpose. It is said that with the failure of the Heirs of Eden, the humans on Havilah will awaken.' He shrugged, invisibly. 'But who knows if and when this will happen. With my help, you and your offspring will rule Havilah and Earth and the Garden of Eden. If this is to happen, you will need a woman with whom you can procreate.'

Kemp looked blank.

Cain spelt out. 'You'll need to make babies.'

It took Kemp a while to register. 'Blimey,' he said as the penny dropped. 'I'll be like the first guy in the world. Everyone will be based... on me!' he said at length.

Cain agreed. 'Lucky worlds, huh?'

'Blimey. Like Adam and Eve... you're a bloomin' genius.'

'Yes, I know,' Cain said, sounding rather smug. 'So, tell me,' he added, 'who is the superior, Daisy or Sue?'

Kemp weighed it up. 'Daisy is bottom of the lowest class, but she's smarter than she makes out and she's an athletic goddess. Sue, on the other hand is top of everything but shocking at games.'

'Then we must entice Sue into our little family, to complement your strength and athleticism.'

Kemp beamed. 'You'll do that for me? How?'

Cain, though completely invisible to Kemp, sat down and thought.

'We'll steal her,' he said at length.

'Steal?'

'Indeed. Though you must ask her first, so that we can gauge her reaction. Then, if she won't come willingly, we'll simply take her.'

'You can't do that!'

'My dear boy, of course I can. I'm Cain, and in a couple of days we'll be the most powerful person in the universe. Your Earth is about to end. Everything will die.'

'I still don't think she'll come. You haven't met her.'

'She'll come,' Cain croaked. 'There's one thing that divides living things from dead things. Living things will do anything in their power to actually live, boy, and not die. You're a testament to that, aren't you?'

Kemp nodded thoughtfully. 'She's pretty stubborn though.'

'Tell me, truthfully. Will she really refuse life for death?' Cain sighed. 'Never. Humans always say honourable, noble things like that, but they don't mean it. Sue will not get a better option. And when she understands the situation and her frankly perilous position she'll come over to us boy, with reluctance. Then time will do its healing. It will be significantly easier if she comes without making a fuss.'

BLABISTERBERRY JELLY

Daisy heard a mechanical buzz, then a muffled voice. 'Someone's here!' she said, as the sound reached her again. She froze at the top of the steps.

'What is it?' Isabella said.

Daisy concentrated hard. 'Footsteps, boots.'

'The army?' Isabella replied.

'Two people with walkie-talkies. Men's voices, I think. They're close. I think the fog has heightened the sound.'

Isabella ushered Old Man Wood down the stairs. 'Come on, Daisy.'

Daisy peered into the fog at the direction of the noise. Then she took off into the thick cloud and disappeared into the yard.

Isabella swore. *That idiotic, stupid girl.*

Moments later, Daisy reappeared and raced down the steps. 'Come on!' she said. 'Quick.'

'What do you mean, *quick*?' Isabella hissed. 'I've been waiting for *you*.'

'Either of you have any idea how to shut the stairwell?' Daisy said, urgently.

'Who is it?' said Archie, eagerly.

'Soldiers,' Daisy said, 'in protective helmets. They've got guns.'

'Oh terrific,' Isabella whispered.

Voices and the sound of boots scuffing the flagstones could be heard near the corner of the courtyard.

The children stared at each other and then, with a curious *whoosh*, air swept around them and sealed the trapdoor at the top of the stairs shut, leaving a small echo reverberating around the room.

Now, no exterior sounds could be heard and the three children and Old Man Wood collectively exhaled and turned towards a simple, round, stone table and four stone stools. On the walls were torchlights, which, much to Isabella's annoyance appeared to run brightly, but off neither electricity nor any type of fossil fuel she'd ever seen.

In the middle of the stone slab sat a large, shining, golden goblet containing a substance rising above its rim, like ice-cream above a cone.

'So this is Blabisterberry Jelly,' Old Man Wood said, expressing the general look of surprise on their faces as they stared at the cup filled of golden brown, toffee-looking, apricot-coloured goo.

A whooshing, rushing, firework sound came from the goblet, and while Daisy and Archie leaned in, Isabella instinctively ducked under the table and then pretended she hadn't.

'OOOh! Hello, my dears! Who do we have here today?' the voice was that of a sweet old woman, not too dissimilar to their great-grandmother, and certainly in no way menacing or frightening. Her words were delivered as though it was an everyday occurrence to have visitors.

The children looked at one another.

'Is it a ghost?' Archie whispered.

'I don't know. I can't see it.' Daisy stared back at him, her eyes wide.

They scanned the room.

'Now, don't be shy,' the sweet, elderly voice continued. 'I want to hear all about you.'

The children stared at one another and then at Old Man Wood, who simply shrugged.

'Well, my darlings,' it continued, 'let me see if we can break the ice on this fine little gathering.'

Daisy pointed towards the goo. 'I think it's coming from there,' she whispered.

The goblet of goo continued. 'I see that we have two beautiful girls, a lovely, handsome, young man, and, aha, you've brought along Grandpa. Now, let's have a look at all of you. Goodness, so very fit and healthy and may I say how terribly youthful you three are. Isn't that a surprise?' The tone sounded almost mocking.

'If you don't mind, I need to do a bit of an inspection, to make sure I know *exactly* who you are.'

Before any of them had the chance to react, a vapour drifted up from out of the bowl, and began to swirl around them like the tendrils of a climbing plant encircling a tree-trunk, each member of the family ensnared within, as if bound by a rope.

Then the smoke disappeared into their ear, mouth and nose cavities and, as it rushed inside, more followed until the children could feel it inside them, tickling their minds, chilling their lungs and freezing their guts.

Just as they were getting used to it, smoke drifted back out of their orifices and back into the goo once more.

All four breathed deeply as if their internal organs had received a smart little tidy-up.

'Bless you all, my dears,' the voice said. 'So you've found me at long last. Goodness, you've taken your time though, haven't you? Well, not to worry. I believe your search for the tablets is well under way. How do you think you're doing?'

The children scuffed their shoes over the floor awkwardly.

'Er... not too bad,' Daisy said, reddening.

'You're talking to pot of marmalade, Daisy,' Isabella whispered.

'I don't care,' Daisy said from out of the corner of her mouth. 'At least it's polite marmalade.'

The strange, pleasant, old woman's voice piped up again. 'I can't begin to tell you how excited I am. I'd offer you a cup of tea or the like but, my sweets, that isn't possible... so, tell me, what are your names? You look like a right little lamb. Yes, you with the lovely blonde locks.'

'Er... Daisy,' Daisy said, looking straight at the goblet of goo.

'So,' the sweet voice said, 'Daisy, my darling, do *you* think you can do it? You look plucky enough to me.'

Daisy's face contorted. 'Do what?'

'Eat me,' the voice said.

Daisy laughed awkwardly. 'Ah-ha... *eat... you?* What exactly do you mean—if you don't mind me asking?'

'As I said. You must eat me, my dear.'

Daisy snorted and a small bogey blew out of her nose and landed on the rim of the cup where it immediately burned up.

'Seriously?' she said, a little embarrassed.

From the silence that filled the small chamber, Daisy realised the goo was being deadly serious. 'Oh, right. Well, yeah, of course... I knew that,' she said, cringing, and staring wide-eyed at her siblings.

The voice from the goo sensed her discomfort. 'I do not wish to be disrespectful sweetheart, but you *did* find the riddles?'

'Yup, of course we did.'

'Then, tell me, little darlings, that you studied them?'

Daisy's face had turned from pink to red and Archie noted Daisy's unease. He coughed and recited the second verse of the riddle.

'For the second one you have to find
'You burp it from the family belly.
'To do this, you have to eat
'Blabisterberry Jelly!'

'Very good,' said the voice, displaying a hint of sarcasm. 'You see, *I* am Blabis-terberry Jelly and all you have to do is eat me. Clear, so far?'

The children nodded, dumbly.

'Well, come on then,' Archie said as he made a lunge for the goblet.

'Not so fast, young man,' the voice said, as a small cloud of smoke puffed out of the goblet in his general direction.

Archie reeled and fanned the billow with his arm.

The sweet voice turned a little sterner. 'It isn't quite as simple as that. In order to succeed, you have to believe that I am, quite simply, the most delicious food you have ever tasted. It really is incredibly easy.'

Old Man Wood groaned. 'And what if we can't?' he asked.

'If you don't *believe,* you don't belch. And if you don't belch, you don't get the tablet, and if you don't get the tablet... you die.' The voice softened. 'Isn't that right, young man?'

Archie smiled as the cogs of the puzzle slipped into place. 'My name is Archie, ma'am,' he said politely. He licked his lips ready to tuck in.

'Know this, handsome Archie,' the kindly voice of Blabisterberry Jelly contin-ued. 'If you think about my form and eat me as you see me, you will taste the thing you see, and not the food you desire. Do you all understand?'

Archie nodded. *What a doddle,* he thought.

Daisy was feeling increasingly thankful that she'd hardly touched her breakfast.

'It is important you are clear about this,' said the voice.

'What a result,' Archie whispered. 'I hope it's gonna be good, 'cos I am starving.'

But Isabella's hands trembled. 'I don't like the sound of this,' she whispered. 'Not one little bit.'

The goblet heard her. 'My dear, which bit in particular do you not like?'

Isabella hesitated. 'Well, what if it isn't possible to eat whatever it is? What if it's so disgusting—I mean, does it matter?' she asked, her voice cracking.

'Aha! A very good question pretty young lady, whose name is...?'

'Isabella.'

'Isabella, such a pretty name for such a delicate face. I will be honest with you, if you don't eat your platefuls you will never leave. Is that perfectly clear?'

Isabella swallowed.

'And, another word of advice,' the voice continued, 'the longer it takes, the larger the portion sizes become?'

The children nodded, not entirely clear about where this was leading.

'Good,' the Blabisterberry Jelly said. 'You're a smart bunch, aren't you? Grandpa must be so proud.'

'But what if I really can't eat—'

'Then, my dear, you'll get a little... overwhelmed.' A high-pitched cackle echoed around them, and then, as before, the sweet tones resumed. 'This is why my portions always start so small. It's terribly easy. Just believe what you want to believe. You have only yourself to fear.'

Isabella's stomach churned. *Portions? Portions of what, exactly?*

In the marrow of her bones something told her that this absolutely, definitely, wasn't going to be a piece of Mrs. Pye's cake.

TO THE COTTAGE

Dickinson had seen enough.

Taken from her. That's all she'd said—three times. When pressed about where they had gone, she'd stared at him with sadness in her eyes and returned to staring at the wall.

He waited for Stone to pick up.

'Sir,' Dickinson said, as his phone clicked. 'We've searched everywhere. The woman told us the children have been taken and I'm afraid we can't get any more out of her. To be honest, I doubt if she knows any more –she's in a terrible state.'

'Did you use other methods?' Stone asked.

'Absolutely,' Dickinson lied. 'If anything, it made her worse.'

For a moment the line remained quiet as Stone thought it through. 'You reckon the house has been ransacked and the children abducted?'

'That's one theory,' Dickinson replied. 'We've been round the house and buildings twice and not a squeak of life. All I can tell you is one hell of a struggle took place upstairs and downstairs. Some of the children's clothes we found were covered with bloodstains and torn to bits. Even the generator hasn't been on for a while. I hate to say it, sir, but there's a strong chance they're already dead.'

Stone cussed into the radio. 'I've got Solomon and Sue here. Is there anything they can salvage?'

Dickinson rubbed his chin. 'Whoever it is must be a step ahead of us. If Solomon can find any links to the chapel that'll be something. You've got nothing to lose, and it might not be a bad idea to have Sue look after the woman. She might loosen-up if she sees a friendly face. I'll fix up a camera in her room so we can see if she's faking it or not.'

'Nice idea,' Stone replied. 'When you've done that, get down to where you left your boat. Meet the RIB coming over from our side with the headmaster and girl. You'll need to guide them in.'

'Heading down now, sir. Thickest fog you've ever seen.'

'Fine, but I need you back here. We had a perimeter break last night. This place must be secure while we begin the evacuation. I think word about the Americans' intention has sneaked out.'

'OK, Roger that,' Dickinson said. 'We'll be there as soon as we can.'

Stone turned to Solomon. 'Eden Cottage is empty. From what Dickinson said, the children have been abducted, so you're on, cousin. Find out all you can. Take Sue, she can look after that caretaker woman and we'll ask her to see if she can figure out what happened. The RIB leaves as soon as you've got your things together. You'll find supplies for several days and I'm giving you a radio. Touch base the moment you're in the house, and then at four hourly intervals during daylight hours. Is that clear? I'll also give you some fuel—see if you can't start up that generator.'

'Good, thank you,' Solomon said. 'What if there's nothing after a day or so?'

Stone understood what he meant. 'I'll do what I can to get you out of there,' he said. He stood up and looked his elder cousin in the eye. 'If we've not got you out after three days, take provisions and seal yourselves in the cellar. Understand? Go deep and you should be alright.'

Solomon nodded.

'The clock is ticking and we need results.'

'Indeed, Charlie. You know I'll do my utmost to get to the bottom of this.'

Sue strode down the path, hoping like mad Gus had managed to get down there before her. In no time, she was swallowed up by a blanket of fog and, had it not been for the familiarity of where to go and the hard tarmac beneath her feet, she wondered if she would have got lost. Her fears were short lived. Despite the protective suite, she recognised Gus before he noticed her for, even though Gus was tall for his age, he was undoubtedly smaller in build than the other men and women who scurried around the small RIB.

Sue slipped on the protective helmet. She moved in closer.

'Hi,' she said, winking at Gus through the plastic mask. 'I'm Sue. Is Mr. Solomon here yet?'

Gus raised his hand. 'He's over there,' he said, his voice a little lower than usual.

Sue followed his gaze and just managed to make out the headmaster heading towards them.

'Hello, sir,' Sue said, as he approached.

'Ah. There you are Sue. Jolly good. Have you got everything you need?' He turned to the man next to him. 'These two are with me.'

The man, squat, with jet black hair and a matching bushy beard, eyed them up. 'I was told only one.' He checked his pad.

'No, both are coming,' Solomon said. 'Top level researchers. And we need to get a move on.'

The man scratched his beard. 'Better check with security,' he said, and he reached wearily into his pocket.

'Can I ask your name?' Solomon asked directly.

'Corporal Lambert.'

'You are aware, Corporal, that I have been given *carte blanche* on this operation by Commissioner Stone? I also happen to be his cousin and head of this investigation.'

Lambert stiffened. Solomon noted his hollow eyes and scarred face. He probably wasn't someone to mess with. 'Perhaps I can persuade you otherwise—we're in such a terrible hurry. Perhaps this might help a little...'

He reached into his pocket and withdrew a few notes. They shook, Lambert accepting the money with a sly smile.

'Alright,' Lambert said, slipping the cash into his back pocket, 'you've paid the ferryman, but I'll still need names. There were two incidents last night, one involving people breaking out, the other with people breaking in. One of them was the kid who survived in a boat. Apparently he's got the disease—that's what they're saying. If security's breached apparently we've 'ad it.'

'Very good, Corporal,' Solomon said, hardly daring to catch Sue or Gus' eye. 'Can I suggest we get going—I'll fill you in as we go? It's quite a distance in these conditions and Dickinson is needed back here pronto.'

Lambert weighed up the suggestion before helping each of them into the twelve-foot RIB and pointing to where he wanted them to perch on the thick, air-filled sides.

Solomon sat on one side, Sue and Gus, the other.

After balancing out the additional weight of fuel and provisions, Lambert gave the boat a shove and hoisted himself up and over the side.

Moments later the engine throbbed into life.

'How can you tell where to go?' Sue asked, looking around. 'It's a total white-out.'

Lambert smiled, showing off a silver capped tooth. He then produced a small electronic device from the inside pocket of his coat. 'This clever navigation system, darlin',' he said. 'Links up to a tracer on the other side. That's them—the red dot.' He showed her, clearly pleased with himself. 'We're the green flashing one. All we've got to do is aim for it. So long as we don't smash into anything too chunky or the light disappears, we'll be there in a couple of hours. Slow goin' in this stuff.'

Sue shivered as the cold, damp, fog leached into her. Apart from the mechanical throb of the engine and the gentle thump of water on the prow, the eeriness and quiet of the water filled her with unease.

Every so often the boat clunked or biffed on something and, holding on extra tight to the safety rope around the edge, she peeked out into the endless, still, white veil. Before long, she slid down the inflated rubber edge and leant on Gus' leg. More than anything, all she wanted to do was snuggle up next to him, just as they had done on "The Joan Of".

Soon, every hair on her body stood to attention. She imagined hands reaching out and grappling at the boat, grotesque, zombie-like bodies hauling themselves in, or pulling them overboard. They were in a corridor of death, and a dark, terror filled her.

Eventually, she shrank down and lowered her head to her chest so that she couldn't see, grateful for the throbbing heartbeat of the engine. The fog's stench was a heady combination of stale water and devastation and it permeated every particle of air.

Lambert peered into the gloom, adjusting the rudder every once in a while and slowing if he saw larger objects looming out of the fog at them. 'Who's the lad then?' he said at long last, pulling out a pad and pen.

Solomon coughed, relieved someone had broken the silence. 'My technical assistant, you mean?'

'Don't he speak?'

Solomon flashed a look towards Gus. 'His name, if that's what you mean, is—'

'Kemp,' Gus answered.

'Absolutely,' Solomon added, raising his eyebrows at the boy. 'Kemp,' he repeated.

'University of Durham, PhD student studying religious artefacts,' Gus continued. 'Specialising in the stained glass windows of the churches of Northern Britain.'

It took all her concentration for Sue not to explode with laughter. Was his voice lower *and slightly posher*?

Lambert nodded, impressed. 'You reckon there's some kinda link then, do ya? That's what I've been hearing, Kemp. Some spooky thing from hundreds of years back, come back to punish us. You know, like in them old times, when the Gods sent plagues and stuff to kill everyone.'

Gus turned towards Sue, his huge, toothy smile evident through the clear plastic hood. 'Um ...'

'That's exactly the sort of thing we're going to see if we can find out, Sergeant,' Solomon butted in. 'You see, Kemp has an almost unique perspective on these matters. He was born in a house bang next to York Minster, where he was fortunate to have access to some of the rarest forms of ecclesiastical artworks in the world, weren't you, Kemp?'

Gus stared at the headmaster for a while. 'Indeed,' he said coolly. 'A very unique... childhood.'

Solomon was enjoying himself. 'Didn't you write a thesis on it?'

Gus spluttered. 'Yeah. Er... about triptych stained glass window arrangements and other things,' he said hurriedly.

'Gothic?' Solomon said.

'Absolutely,' Gus replied, wondering what had got into the man. '90's Gothic-revival kind-of-thing.'

'90's Gothic revival?' Lambert said. 'You're pulling my leg.'

Solomon chuckled. 'My dear old thing we're talking about the Thirteenth century—'

'1290's, to be precise,' Gus added. 'An important time in—'

Sue shrieked, 'How long before we arrive?'

Lambert looked down at the screen. 'About fifteen minutes. You lot had better keep look out. I'm told there's loads of stuff lying round the edges—you know, cars, trees—maybe a rotting cat or two.' He smiled. 'Maybe a few human corpses.'

When the RIB brushed on the bare tops of willow tree clumps submerged beneath the water, they knew they must be close. Lambert negotiated through piles of metal, plastic and wooden debris until, eventually, Gus spotted a faint circular ring of bright light glowing out of the fog not too far away.

Lambert aimed for it, cut the engine, and let the boat drift in.

Shortly, instructions came from the bank, and while Lambert guided the rudder, Gus grabbed the nylon painter and tossed it to one of the talking figures on the side of the water who pulled the boat further in. Then he jumped off the prow into the mud, where a blond-haired man helped him regain his legs.

As Sue did the same, Gus moved to the fringes, tested the weight of a rucksack and hauled it up onto his back. With his head kept low, he waited while the others gathered their provisions and, in no time, they began the tricky, slippery climb up the hillside towards Eden Cottage.

STARLIGHT APPLE CRUMBLE

Without warning, a fountain of sparkling dust blew out of the goblet of goo, like a firework. Streams of bright, vibrant colours creating a dazzling, glittery cloud that soon hovered over the table.

The children and Old Man Wood smiled at one other, wide-eyed in amazement. Then, the dust parted and formed swirling circles above them, like coloured halos.

These halos descended down over their heads, spinning in front of their eyes and over their ears, a noise tingling like miniature bells.

The children instinctively shut their eyes, as the strange particles swept into their heads through all available holes and tickled their brains.

When the noise reappeared, they opened their eyes to find the halos in front of them, each one moving towards the middle of the table like fat bagels flying in slow-motion.

As they met, another explosion of glitter spewed into the air with the sound of broken glass.

In front of the children's astonished eyes the dust divided and descended in equal parts onto their plates.

When the children and Old Man Wood looked down, the colourful glitter had gone. They stared at their stone plates with mouths open, their eyes on stalks.

A second later, screams of horror and shouts of absolute disgust erupted in the small chamber.

❄

Old Man Wood reeled.

On his plate a miniature dreamspinner crawled on long, opaque legs around the rim of the stone platter, it's translucent, jellyfish-like body with a hole where its abdomen should have been, pulsating with mini forks of blue lightning.

Old Man Wood sat quite still with his mouth open, staring at the creature, while all around him the children screamed and hollered and wailed and gagged at the sights in front of them.

Apples alive, I did this, he thought. *These things are our worst fears. It is a trial of will.* At least that's what the Willows said. It had to be true, but how in all the apples on all the planets in all the universes had he done it?

Shocked, he stared at the creature moving around the plate, trying to think. But the longer he stared and the children screamed, the larger the strange, spidery creature grew.

When Daisy came over and threw her arm round him wailing, he snapped out of it, and remembered where he was and what he had to do.

'SILENCE!' he roared. 'Listen to me, and listen hard. Look at me, Isabella— you too Daisy. Look me right in the eye.' The children did as he asked. 'Whatever you do, DO NOT look at your plates until I tell you. Right, good.'

Old Man Wood took a deep breath. 'All of this is not real, my littluns,' he said, his tone softer. 'What you have to imagine is that this plateful is your favourite food, your most favourite meal in the world.'

'That's impossible—'

'No, little Bells, it is not,' he said. 'WE HAVE TO DO THIS or Blabisterberry Jelly will overwhelm us. Keep looking at me, girls, and you, Archie.' He held each pair of the children's terrified eyes.

'You have to believe me,' he said, as he picked up a spoon and fork.

'Keep looking at me. Good. Now, I'm going to prove how easy this is. I'm imagining, with all my heart and soul, that this is my favourite food...'

'Starlight apple crumble?' Archie said.

'Exactly!' Old Man Wood said. 'It's a thick slice of warm, yumptious, starlight apple crumble on my plate where the apple is sweet and juicy and the crumble crunches. How it melts in the mouth.'

The Old Man shut his eyes and concentrated hard on a mouthful of starlight apple crumble helped along with a huge dollop of thick, creamy custard.

He opened his eyes and looked down. For him, the strange, thin, spidery creature began to recede into apple crumble covered in yummy custard. The others looked on, riveted by the repulsive scene of Old Man Wood about to eat an alien-like spider.

'You see,' he said, cutting into the dreamspinner, 'you have to believe that what you are about to eat is what you *truly* want to eat. It doesn't have to be big or clever, but Blabisterberry Jelly will know if you mean it. I promise you this, my littluns, you must not be found wanting.'

Old Man Wood shut his eyes and helped himself to the mouthful, pushing the pulsating spoonful with a long leg hanging out into his open mouth.

All the children could see was the quivering electrical abdomen of the dream-spinner flashing, electrifying his stubby teeth as he bit down.

'Cor! That is utterly fan-tab-ulistic!' Old Man Wood spluttered, helping himself to another spoonful. 'This has... mmm... to be the greatest... yummiest... sweetest, starlight apple crumble I've ever had in all my life.'

He piled in again. 'And I should know,' he enthused as he chewed, electric blue crackles of lightning washing round his mouth, 'Coz I've been making it for an awfully long time.'

A DISGUSTING WAY TO DIE

Daisy shook with fear.

She simply couldn't believe Old Man Wood was eating the most horrific, weird, spidery-alien-thing she'd ever seen. The sight filled her with dread and she noted how Isabella and Archie's faces were pale and green.

No books, no schooling, *nothing* could prepare them for this kind of experience. Daisy shut her eyes and took a deep breath. Holding onto her nose she sucked in a huge lungful of air, exhaling slowly before repeating the process two or three times.

How did the goo know?

The *incident* had happened three years ago. They'd been playing football and some of the boys started getting rough, kicking her and tripping and making dangerous tackles. She smiled now she thought about it, how similar it had been to the match against Chitbury.

She'd tried hard, desperately hard not to cry. But her legs hurt and it was so unfair! When the tears rolled, the boys made it worse, calling her names—one even spat on her. And, even worse was the way they enjoyed her discomfort.

On their way home, Daisy hardly spoke. When she did, she'd told Archie that she'd never cry again. No one had a right to make her so upset and, from that day forward, she vowed she would never shed another tear.

Instantly, Archie turned to her and offered her a bet, partially as a bit of fun, and partially because he argued that crying wasn't a bad thing to do. Three weeks' worth of school sweet-tuck if he made her cry within a week.

She'd laughed at him.

Three days went by and Daisy had all but forgotten the incident of Archie's bet. But then, after school one day, they passed a young man walking down the lane from the ruin with a large black Labrador. He was a rambling type often seen walking from village to village across the moors.

As they played in the ruin, Archie spotted it. That evening just before supper, Archie ran up with a garden trowel, found the juicy dog mess, cut it in two, and carefully placed a dollop in each of her woolly boot slippers, before leaving them out by the back door.

They played football until the sun down went down and as an evening chill came over the moors they'd warmed up by the fire. Daisy asked if anyone knew where her woolly boot slippers were. When Archie told her they were by the back door, she marched off and found them.

Without thinking, she pushed her feet in.

Seconds later, the entire family rushed out to find Daisy shrieking hysterically then screaming. Then vomiting and retching. The tears flowed.

She remembered that turgid smell and the way it stuck like glue between her toes, got under her toenails and then, amazingly, transported itself all over her during her tragic attempt to remove it.

She lay in bed for a whole day, and for several weeks spent hours cleaning her feet, scrubbing them almost obsessively.

Now that she thought of it, she'd never paid out the bet. He'd been in way too much trouble.

Daisy took a deep breath.

Sitting proudly on Daisy's plate lay a well-formed steaming, brown dog-turd, gleaming with a sheen as though freshly laid. Daisy prodded it in stunned amazement and for a second wondered if it could be fake, or a type of joke chocolate. But when she caught a whiff of its distinctive odour, she instinctively retched.

Then, holding her mouth and stomach, she vomited behind her.

Daisy returned to stare at the smelly, sweating, stinking turd. 'Dog shit!' she whispered. 'And I've got to eat it.'

Her guts contorted involuntarily and looked up at Isabella, who had climbed on her stool, petrified. Things were clearly not going well for her either.

They all screamed again and, as they did, the turd grew a little larger.

'NO!' she yelled, but on that, it expanded a fraction more. She closed her eyes and tried to calm down.

Why? Every time she'd seen a dog poo from that moment on, she'd given it a wide berth and if anyone trod in one and her nose caught that certain whiff, her stomach twisted and her face turned white, then green, and she had to lie down or throw-up.

And now, somehow, like it or not she was going to have to tuck into it with a knife and fork. She wanted to retch but, instead, she stretched her arms out wide to allow for more oxygen. She clenched her eyes tight.

Old Man Wood had to be right. He'd done it—right in front of their eyes and if he could, so could she.

Daisy thought hard. If the turd was an illusion she had to replace the grotesque with something totally amazing. But what? Thank God she'd missed out on breakfast.

OK, she thought, *which meal stood out head and shoulders above any other she'd ever had?* Nothing sprang to mind until the aroma of the Chinese meal they'd had for her last birthday treat in Southallerton tickled the sensors in her brain. Yes! That Peking crispy duck all flaked and rolled up in pancakes with cucumber, spring onions and a dab of plum sauce. Nothing had ever tasted quite so wonderful.

But ever present, in a corner of her mind, she could sense it; stinking, vile, slimy. She opened her eyes and stared and, as if the turd understood, it grew. Daisy's stomach leapt again.

She shut her eyes again. *Crispy, shredded, aromatic duck,* she thought, *with extra plum sauce, wrapped up in a pancake.*

Come on, Daisy, she urged, *it is utterly delicious—and it has to work.*

Archie stared at Old Man Wood.

Why did the creature creeping around the plate make him feel so uneasy? Why was it so familiar? Archie racked his brain. Then suddenly it hit him: this was the same creature that had sat above Daisy while she slept—the night he'd woken, the night of their final nightmare—before it started, before everything went mad and the rain came down and before the destruction and the plague and the riddles. Before they had any inkling that they were linked to these strange goings on.

His pulse quickened. This spidery-creature looked like a smaller version of that one and, now that the memories returned, he remembered how, at first, he thought the creature might be taking something from Daisy but soon came to the conclusion that it was actually *giving her something.* Yes, that was it. Giving her a powder from the ends of its long legs. And he'd wondered then if this strange creature had been supplying them with their weird dreams.

He scratched his hard front hair spike. The objects on their plates represented their worst fears—he could see that: Daisy with her terror of dog poo, Isabella with her revulsion to dead rats.

On his plate, four round, human eyeballs like marbles twitched, their muscles and tendons attached to each side like the ectoplasm of a bloody jellyfish.

As he inspected them, he noticed how much larger were the ones which bore pale-blue irises in comparison to the other two that had dark, nutty-brown colouring.

Each eye dripped with blood and stared back at him as if they were watching him—*staring madly at him—following him*, Archie thought.

A strand of a nerve twitched, rolling one of the eyeballs over. Then another did the same.

Isabella screamed again, so too, Daisy.

He joined in.

Who could do such a totally horrendous thing? This wasn't a trial, it was torture.

He shuddered. Were these the eyes of the Ancient Woman, sucked out and now for his consumption? They had to be. That horrific dream-image never went far away: the extreme violence of his actions, the peculiar sensation of murdering someone and how it had felt so natural, so right.

Every time he'd woken up, he'd been consumed by guilt until he found this feeling replaced by an anger that he found hard to control.

He examined his plate. *Two sets of eyes? Why? The ancient woman... who else?*

A terrible chill swept through him, as the realization hit him. The other set must belong to Cain. Cain the ghost, who'd told him his eyes had been removed when he'd sat in his room, scaring him witless.

On his plate lay the missing body parts of the two people he feared the most; a spook and an imaginary figure from his dream?

Jeez, his head must be screwed.

But if Old Man Wood's strange spider was real, then maybe the Ancient Woman was also real? And maybe, if he was going to kill her—perhaps his dreams stood as a warning?

Archie liked this thought. It made some sort of sense.

He remembered what Cain had said about protecting this Ancient Woman— Cain's mother –against those that might harm her.

So, perhaps his job was to shield her.

Thinking about Cain's concern for his mother, he thought of his own. Why wasn't she here, helping them? Did they have any idea what had happened to them, what they were going through? There hadn't been a word, nothing.

Maybe, he thought, *they had been abandoned*. Left to get on with it.

Archie's gloom was punctured by the scraping of a fork on the stone platter in front of Old Man Wood. He looked up to see a portion of electricity-filled jellyfish with thin, almost translucent bones heading towards the old man's mouth.

Archie watched, dumbfounded, as Old Man Wood devoured the curious ghost-like spider.

So why, Archie thought, *do spidery-alien creatures give Old Man Wood such fear?* If the creature had been dishing out dreams, as he suspected, then what did it say about Old Man Wood?

Maybe, it showed an uncertain future, or was Old Man Wood in denial about something... something about this Ancient Woman and Cain?

Watching the old man tackling his plateful with relish, his eyes shut in bliss, loaded Archie with courage.

If Old Man Wood can do it, he thought, *then so can I.*

Without knowing why, Archie shut his eyes as he imagined the eyes to be everlasting gob-stoppers. He felt for his plate, picked one of the eyeballs up in his fingers and popped it straight into his mouth. A moment of bliss swept over his face.

'Wow, this is the bes' gosoppa I've eva ha,' he said, as he swirled it round his mouth.

'Keep going, Arch,' Daisy said, clapping wildly.

'Those eyes will soon disappear from your plate...' Old Man Wood said, egging him on.

Only, this comment made Archie open his eyes and look down at his plate to see the vile assortment of eyes and their tendrils. He lost his concentration and went very pale.

Uh oh, he thought, as he felt a movement from the eyeball tickling the roof of his mouth and the trail of nerves flickered the back of his throat. Worst of all he was sure he could feel the eye growing. It felt the size of a ping-pong ball.

He wretched violently and the eyeball popped out bouncing rather dramatically a couple of times on the table.

Archie shook his head. 'Idiot,' he mumbled.

'Sorry about that, Arch,' Old Man Wood said, wincing. 'For a moment, I thought you had it.'

Archie head-butted the table. '*I'm* the idiot, not you! I thought of an everlasting gob-stopper. By its very nature, it's an incredibly dumb thing to do.'

Archie wracked his brain. There had to be an easier way of doing this. He stared at the eyeballs on his plate, which stared straight back, as though testing him. Then they grew a fraction. *Oh please,* Archie thought. They were about the size of normal eyes now. Any larger and this was going to get messy.

Not eating their platefuls was going to be a horrible way to die.

GUS IN THE ATTIC

Sue found it strange being de-briefed by Dickinson in the de Lowes' house with Gus, the headmaster and not a de Lowe in sight.

She sighed. A week ago, who could have possibly imagined that they were on the cusp of Armageddon? And a week ago, she would never have believed she could be so madly in love with anyone, let alone odd, hilarious, brilliant, gorgeous Gus.

The dense fog that lay over the fields and forests in the great Vale of York made for a quiet, empty, alien atmosphere. And an expectation lingered that something unpleasant might be about to interrupt it.

Dickinson had stopped the group to rest three times and Sue had been grateful for the breaks. On the first, Dickinson instructed the party to thread rope between them so that no one might wander off in the wrong direction.

When the stone walls came into view, they had collectively breathed a sigh a relief. Inside the building, where she'd spent so much time playing, it felt cold and uninviting. Even the normally toasty sitting room with its warming flames and low beams struck them as being mysteriously empty and unwelcoming. Sue feared the worst.

Solomon set to work laying a fire as Dickinson began. 'Sue, in a moment I'm going to take you over to the woman we found—'

'Mrs. Pye?'

'Yes,' he said. 'You know her, don't you?'

'She's lovely.'

'Good,' Dickinson said. 'She's suffering from shock. You're to look after her, make sure she's fed and watered and if she lets on about anything, names, where the children might have gone, that sort of thing, let us know immediately. Write it down so you don't forget.' He winked at her.

His radio crackled. 'I'm going to leave you both one of these,' he said, putting a handset on the arm of the sofa. 'Call in if and when you get a sniff of progress. I'm guessing Stone briefed you.' He looked knowingly at the headmaster who nodded and turned away.

Dickinson addressed the noise. 'I've just got to introduce the woman to Sue, and then we'll be off.'

'Still no signs?' Stone's voice crackled back.

'Dead as a dodo, sir.'

'I've sent units in to the local town centres—anywhere where electrical tablets and the devices are sold. Though I'll be surprised if there are any left. Looting like you'd never believe.'

'OK, Roger that. Anything else you need from here, sir?'

'Just a quick word with Solomon, if he's about.'

Dickinson handed over the radio.

The headmaster pressed the button. 'Solomon here.'

'Good. You know what the score is. Don't sleep until you've combed through everything, understand? We don't have time. And remember what I said.'

Solomon handed back the radio.

'Right, Sue,' Dickinson said. 'Let's find Mrs. Pye, then I'll leave her in your hands.' Dickinson looked around. 'Anyone seen that understudy of yours?'

Solomon picked a matchbox up from the top of the wooden mantelpiece, opened it, and struck a match. 'I've sent him upstairs to begin logging everything up there. As the Commissioner said, there's no time to waste, is there.'

Dickinson smiled back. 'Yes. Quite.' He turned for the door. 'Good luck—keep us posted.' And with that their boots scuffed on the floor as they headed out of the front door, across the paving slabs and into the fog.

While Sue nursed Mrs. Pye, the headmaster and Gus listened from the edge of the building to the sludging and slurping sounds of boots and the chatter of the men as they departed down the slope. When the noise petered out, they made their way back to the living room.

'Gus, I really do think you ought to remove that helmet and the rest of that gear,' Solomon said. 'I must say, I very nearly laughed out loud when you said you were Kemp.'

Gus smiled toothily back at him. 'Anything to liven things up a little. Strange how his name popped into my head.' Gus began looking at the clutter, made up predominantly of pictures dotted around the room. 'What *have* they been up to?'

'That's what we need to work out, my boy.'

'It's as though they were looking for something in the pictures and then left in a bit of a hurry—'

'You're telling me,' Solomon said, picking up one of the old portraits. 'I'll inspect the kitchen. If they left in the middle of the night there may be traces of a meal. After that we need to try and figure out what on earth they've been looking for with all of these.'

'It's quite a mess,' Gus said. 'I'll go and check their room, see if there's anything that might give us some idea of timing.'

Solomon smiled. 'Well, at least I know where Archie gets it from. All of this could very well be his doing.'

Gus headed up the stairs. When he reached Old Man Wood's room he called for Solomon and together they inspected the remnants of the room in silence.

Gus whistled. 'It's like a nail bomb's been detonated in here—'

'Yes, but without the nails,' Solomon said as he inspected the strange, irregularly-sized holes dotted around the wooden panelled walls. 'And no shell cases or cartridges—that's what the soldiers were saying. There's no metal here at all.'

'Are you suggesting,' Gus said, 'that something organic made this mess?'

Solomon stroked his chin. 'I don't know. But it is most unusual.'

Gus took off up to the attic room where he searched each of the children's areas. He tried to see if there was a tell-tale article of clothing that might give away their whereabouts or a book or a slip of paper or a note. He searched Archie's mess first, then Daisy's area and finally, Isabella's immaculate section: bed made, books put away, everything in its place. He turned to go when he noted a drawer below her bedside table. Gus stared at it and tried to pull it open, but found it jammed tight. There wasn't a keyhole, so how could it be locked? He traced his fingers around the bedside table, feeling only solid sides. Then he placed his hand underneath and rocked the base one way, then another. Gus smiled. The drawer slid open the other way. A hidden drawer, *neat*. He peered inside. Her diary lay there with a pen clamped underneath an elastic strap.

Gus picked it out and opened the thick, pink, bound book. He noted the dates and flicked through, catching snippets of familiar names as he went until he reached more recent entries. He skimmed the extract of her trying to work out who and what the people in her dreams meant. He turned the page over and read about their adventures, their odd magical gifts, about Old Man Wood being the oldest man ever and how much she missed Sue.

A terrible thought hit him. Sue and Isabella were close, like twins. How would Sue react if Isabella had been killed? Nervously he turned another page. Now the entry was smaller, and here he saw a five-verse poem. Nothing more, no explanation, but it appeared to be about finding three tablets and another world called Eden. Was this what it was all about?

He heard the groan of a floorboard. Instinctively he froze and crammed the diary into his pocket.

The noise deepened. Footsteps. He noted that while the tread was silent the creak of the floorboards gave whoever it was away.

It had to be Sue coming to sneak up on him. He smiled. He could pretend he hadn't heard her and surprise her with a kiss. OK, she might get really cross or pretend to be annoyed—but only for a moment, then she'd melt and laugh, and then kiss him.

Why not give her a happy surprise?

Gus grinned as he waited by the drawn curtain, until he could almost hear her breath through the other side of the velvet. Then, in one sharp movement, Gus whipped the curtain to the side.

'TA-DAH!' he said, moving in for the kiss.

'Hello, Williams,' said a curiously familiar voice.

Gus stopped just in the nick of time, his lips still puckered.

Then he stumbled and collapsed down on the bed.

'Y... YOU? HOW?!'

THE ILLUSION CRUMBLES

Every time Daisy stared at her plateful her stomach churned. 'It's the smell, Old Man Wood, I can't do the stink, you know that!' she looked exasperated. 'We don't have a dog, because I can't handle the whiff! *I don't do it!*' Her lips quivered and her eyes began to water. 'I can't—'

'Look at me, Daisy. Now,' Old Man Wood ordered. 'You must overcome your fears. That's what this is about. Push fear out of your mind and draw in the things you love.' He looked deep into her eyes. 'You can do this, no sweats, but you *must* concentrate, littlun. So, close your eyes, sweet Daisy—there, that's it—and imagine something apple-tastically delicious. Imagine it exactly, imagine every last little piece. Imagine how yummy that first bite is—the texture, the aroma, that apple-crunchiness, the smoothness. And remember, that thing in front of you is only an illusion.

'You saw me do it, didn't you?' Old Man Wood continued, 'so you must believe me when I tell you that the reward is well worth the trouble.' An idea popped into his head. 'Daisy, I want you to keep your eyes shut, understand?'

She nodded.

'Would you like me to give you a spoonful of your... your...'

'Duck. Crispy, aromatic, Peking duck,' Daisy said, quickly.

'Yes. A great choice,' he said. 'With cucumbers, spring onions and a blob of plum sauce?'

'Ooh yeah. Exactly,' she said and a flicker of a smile briefly turned up the corners of her mouth.

Daisy took a deep breath, clenched her eyes tight and licked her lips.

'Good. Now imagine the scene. It's your birthday party at that Chinese restaurant,' Old Man Wood said. 'Everyone is smiling, laughing—there's music and the waiters show you over to an immaculate white tablecloth where you take a seat. You're wearing your new red dress. Mum and Dad are squabbling over the wine list. Mrs. Pye is tidying Archie. Then it arrives; your fabulous crispy duck on a large platter. Everyone stops and stares, jealous of your excellent choice... and it's all yours. Your face lights up when you see it. Doesn't it smell wonderful?'

'Yes. Oh yes!' Daisy said. 'That's lush. Keep going, please.'

'Now, concentrate on the smells of the aromatic duck. It's been stripped off the bone and you've added a spoonful of plum sauce and sprinkled spring onions and cucumber on top. Now I'm rolling one up for you.'

Old Man Wood cut off a portion of the steaming dog turd from Daisy's plate.

'By goodness this is the finest pancake I've ever seen,' he said. 'Would you like to try it?'

Daisy nodded, her eyes closed tight.

'Open your mouth. I'll pop in your first delicious mouthful.'

Archie's eyes were bulging out of his head as he watched Daisy and his cheeks began puffing in and out. He pulled his hands up over his eyes and stared through the cracks of his fingers. A small squeal escaped from his lips but Old Man Wood flashed him an icy stare.

Daisy opened her mouth and took in the first mouthful, and it really was the most delicious mouthful of crispy aromatic duck she had ever tasted.

'Another bite, Daisy?' asked Old Man Wood gently.

'Oh my God, YES! It's AMAZING!'

Old Man Wood sliced another chunk off the large pile of canine excrement and raised it to her lips.

She opened her mouth wide as a tiny maggot crawled out of the poo. 'Mmm mmmmm. Guys, this is absolutely, divinely, scrumptilious,' she said. She took the whole mouthful in one go, licking her lips.

But suddenly, from the other side of the table came a loud

GA-DONK!

Followed by a crash.

Isabella lay motionless on the filthy floor. A thin trail of blood extended from the side of her head where she had clipped the stone table.

'Ah! No. Deary me,' Old Man Wood said, as he rushed over to her side. 'Are you there, littlun? Come along, wakey-uppy.'

He dabbed the cut with a handkerchief. She stirred and groaned and then wretched loudly, the noise reverberating around the room.

With Old Man Wood's help, she sat upright and felt for her head. 'OW!'

He kissed her forehead. 'Apples alive! Oh my! Oh my!' he said solemnly. 'This is harder than I ever would have thought, my specials,' he said, as if in private to Isabella.

'I don't think I can do this, Old Man Wood,' she said groggily.

'OH GOD! Get it off! GET IT OFF!' Isabella screamed. 'NO! NO! NOOO!'

She jumped off her stool and pointed at it accusingly, all the while backing away. 'I CAN'T EAT THAT,' she yelled. 'NO WAY!'

On Isabella's plate lay a decaying rat. Its inners crawled with hundreds of maggots that seemed to move as one body. Suddenly the rat with the maggots crawling inside it grew.

Isabella screamed and she shut her eyes, trembling. Then she curled up in a ball on the floor.

'But I think you can,' Old Man Wood said firmly. 'It's about what's going on in here.' He tapped his head.

'But it's impossible. You don't understand.'

Old Man Wood sighed and, while making a fuss of her and checking there were no obvious signs of concussion, he helped her up.

He turned to the table. For a moment he wondered if his eyes had deceived him.

'What in all the apples?! How... how did you manage that?'

Daisy's plate sat empty. Archie's too.

'Daisy licked her plate clean,' Archie said, squirming. 'It was quite easily the most repulsive thing I have ever seen. Anyway, everlasting gobstoppers are the dumbest things to choose, so I thought I'd shut my eyes and swallow them whole. They actually weren't that bad. Could have done with a glass of water to wash them down.'

Without warning, much to his and the others' surprise, Archie belched long and loud, the sound reverberating around the stone chamber rather eerily like a huge frog-croak.

In any other circumstance, it would have propelled the twins into uncontrollable hysterics, but this burp carried on and on and, as it did, a peculiar balloon grew from his mouth, expanding as he expelled the air. When he'd finished, he peeled it off his face, and left it to hang in mid-air, as if it were a helium balloon on a string.

'Bloody hell,' Daisy whispered.

'Fab-tab-e-dozey!' Archie cried, delighted with himself. 'It's the *belching from the family belly*! If we all do one—and join them up, then surely that's the way to get the second tablet!'

Daisy turned to Archie rather seriously. 'Archie. Girls like Isabella do not go round burping, and certainly not blowing out sticky bubbles,' she looked at him rather seriously. 'And for your information, neither do I.'

Unfortunately for Daisy a long, trumpet-like noise blasted out of her throat for the best part of several seconds. Out popped out a similar, sticky, golden balloon.

Stunned, she peeled hers off and joined the balloon to Archie's.

Almost immediately, an enormous deep croak, like a tree crashing down, grumbled out of Old Man Wood's mouth that went on and on and ended with another bubble. He instantly turned red and apologised profusely.

Archie could barely control himself. He convulsed until tears rolled down his cheeks. But his laughter ceased when they turned towards Isabella, who sat shaking in her chair, her face pale and sweaty.

Then their stares turned towards her plateful and collectively they gasped.

The size of the dead rat crawling with white maggots had now quadrupled to the size of a small cat.

Since all three of the children had, at various times, vomited in the tiny chamber, the aroma in the room was akin to a lavatory on a ferry boat full of sea-sick passengers.

But Isabella in particular had other things to concentrate on. For every minute that went by, the pressure was mounting. She curled her fingers up so that her nails dug into the palm of her hand to stop herself blacking out and, helped by Old Man Wood began some calming breathing measures.

'Your sister and brother have done it. And me, too—and utterly fan-tab-ulicious it was too. So you can do it. You know it's all about that smart head of yours, littlun.'

Isabella's lips began quivering. 'But I had months of therapy because of this.' She sobbed. 'Months... and now this... this... torture.'

'Come on, Bells,' Daisy said, moving in beside her and giving her a sisterly hug. 'It's simple—you know, mind over matter.'

She flashed a smile at Archie. 'If it's any help, mine was the most delicious dog poo I've ever had—'

'Don't be disgusting—'

'I'm not. It was perfectly cooked.'

'Firm on the outside with a nice soft centre,' Archie said.

'If I had half a brain,' Daisy said, 'I should have chosen a chocolate log.'

'Or lemon turd.'

'Or a big brownie.'

The twins howled with laughter.

Isabella's face, however, was set like thunder. Daisy noticed.

'Oh, come on Bells. I'm only joking. Look, all you have to do is concentrate on something you really, really want.'

'Why not try the Old Man Wood method? It was brilliant on Daisy,' Archie said, nudging the old man. 'Want to give it a go?'

Isabella nodded.

'Great.' Archie took a deep breath. 'Come on, you can do this. Now, shut your eyes. I'm sure your maggoty... er...

Daisy fired him a look.

'...your plateful, will be as delicious as, um, as, er...'

'...as mum's banoffee pie...' Daisy said, quickly.

'With an extra helping of my special thick cream,' Old Man Wood added. 'I know how much you love it.'

'With a couple of jelly babies on top?' Daisy said, licking her lips.

For the first time Isabella's lips crinkled into something that resembled a smile. Her face had more of a controlled look upon it. 'Yes. That sounds good.'

'Now, really, really believe it,' Old Man Wood said, his voice soft, deep and mellow. 'The sweet smells, how it feels in your mouth, how fabulous it looks...'

She forced herself to utterly concentrate until all she could think about was the sweet, textured, chocolaty toffee, and the dollops of cream and the squishiness of the bananas.

Old Man Wood cut out a slice off the rat and filled her spoon with a few stray maggots.

'The first amazingly scrumptious helping of thick banoffee pie coming up,' Archie said, as the old man offered up a heaped spoonful, complete with decaying dark fur, sinews and claws, to Isabella's mouth.

'With a few assorted jelly babies,' Daisy added, noticing the maggots.

The twins could hardly bear to watch.

As the spoon rose, silence filled the little room.

As Isabella's mouth closed over the spoon, Daisy let out a tiny gasp.

Then Archie emitted a kind of high-pitched squeak, a noise made not in horror, more in shock.

Isabella's mouth closed over the spoon, but she'd lost her concentration and instead of banoffee pie, the foul things she saw, rather than the toffee treat that had filled her mind, swamped her mouth.

She screamed, phleaux-ing and retching and hysterically flapping her arms, spitting endlessly.

As fast as he could, Old Man Wood draped his arms around her and held her tight, saying gentle things.

When the sobbing and moaning ceased, he released her.

Isabella looked at her plate and then across to the pale faces of her siblings.

On her plate was the maggoty rat, now the size of a fully-grown badger, dead and stinking and writhing with not hundreds, but thousands of maggots.

For the second time in only a short while, Isabella passed out.

Daisy shook her head, her expression betraying deep worry.

'She's out cold and that thing on her plate is... huge. She'll never do it on her own.'

'And it's beginning to stink.'

'Just like that trapped-under-the-floorboards-Archie-shoe-pong,' Daisy added, unhelpfully.

'Shut it, Daisy,' Archie fired back. He stroked a hair spike. 'Can't we just eat it?' he said. 'I mean, I'm game if you are.'

Daisy shrugged. It was a good idea considering the choices. 'OK. Nice one. What's it going to be?'

'Well, I was quite getting into the idea of banoffee pie. Those eyeballs didn't really fill me up. I think I can still feel them moving around.'

Daisy closed her eyes for a minute, imagining the Italian desert. 'Yup. Banoffee pie it is,' she said. 'Old Man Wood, you look after Bells, we're going to finish this off for her.'

The twins leaned over the table and stared at the vast meal of a deteriorating rat filled with maggots. They each picked up a fork and glanced at one another for reassurance.

'Right,' Daisy said. 'On the count of three, the most delicious banoffee pie, in the universe.'

'In the universe,' Archie agreed.

'One, two ...' and before they even got to three, the twins plunged their forks into the sticky mess.

A millisecond later, a massive electric charge shot through their forks.

Their bodies zinged and catapulted backwards. They thudded into the wall and collapsed to the floor.

Archie groaned. 'So,' he said, as he rubbed himself down, 'no sharing. That's nice and clear.'

He looked over towards Daisy who lay motionless in a puddle of vomit.

'Oh! Great! Looks like she's out too,' and then he looked at the rat which was now the size of a medium-sized dog.

'What do you suggest, Old Man Wood?' he asked. 'Because if we don't come up with some way of getting Isabella to eat this, pretty soon we're going to die in the remains of a decaying rat. And maggots are going to eat us alive. If you've got an idea, now is the time to say something.'

But Old Man Wood stared back, his face as white as chalk, shaking his head. 'I... I don't know. It may already be too late.'

SOLOMON AND SUE

Sue made quite a fuss of Mrs. Pye.

After several minutes where Mrs. Pye stared at the wall, her body moving back and forth, Sue finally managed to get Mrs. Pye to look at her.

'It's me—Sue,' she said. 'I'm here with the headmaster and my boyfriend, Gus Williams.' It was the first time she'd ever said *my boyfriend* to anyone and the words slipped out with ease, and filled her with pleasure.

In fact she had a good mind to run around the courtyard singing: 'I've got a boyfriend and he's amazing and he loves me too-oo-ooo', adding in things like 'he's clever, he's cool, he's sweet but also hunky, la-la, in a kinda geeky way!' and then she'd whoop and scream in a stupidly high pitch fashion. And then she'd look about hope no-one was watching.

'We—Gus and me, survived the storm,' she said, barely controlling herself. 'I got a text from Bells. Amazing isn't it? Old Man Wood found them, didn't he?' she said, admiring herself in the mirror. Her skin exuded radiance. Was this from the spell of love?

'It was Bells' idea,' she continued, 'and Gus' genius at woodworking that saved us, I suppose. A, what would Old Man Wood say, "apple-tastic" miracle, Mrs. Pye, that's what it was.'

Sue sat down on the bed and took one of Mrs. Pye's hands in hers. 'The world's gone crazy since I saw you last, and that wasn't even ten days ago. I hope those men weren't nasty to you? I don't think they meant to be. I guess they're just as confused as everyone else. A horrible man interrogated me. He had stinky breath and hard, calculating eyes that gave me the shivers. Anyway, it's a bit of a fluke that we managed to get away.'

Sue stood up and wandered around the room, picking up little pictures of the smiling, often toothless, de Lowe children growing up in the assorted frames on her mantelpiece.

'You don't know where they are, do you? We reckon they left in a bit of a hurry, probably in the night or early this morning. There's a terrible mess every-where. Have you seen it? It looks like they've been in some kind of fight. Were there other people involved?'

Sue spotted a flash of alarm in Mrs. Pye's eyes. Did it relate to the missing chil-dren or the messy house?

'Let me get you a nice cup of tea,' she said. 'You look like you could use one. If I find a crumpet, I'll bring one over. Bit of jam—would that be alright?' Sue smiled sweetly. 'Now, don't you be going anywhere. I'll be back in a bit.'

Sue headed out of the door and, as she turned back to Mrs. Pye, for the first time, Mrs. Pye looked at her and smiled in her very odd way. 'Thank you,' she croaked, her voice shallow and troubled.

Sue smiled back. 'You really don't have to thank me, Mrs P. You're the one who needs thanking—for looking after them so beautifully.' Sue went over to her and planted a big kiss on her cheek. 'Back shortly.'

She turned and slipped away with a spring in her step, down the wooden stairs, around the rim of the foggy courtyard and back into the picture-filled mess of the cottage.

Solomon looked up as she walked in. He was studying a selection of older portraits on which the figure of an old-looking man with a strong family resem-blance stared back. Each bore a similar, subtle-patterned background with date-marks a century or more apart. 'Any luck with Mrs. Pye?'

'She spoke two words: *Thank you*,' Sue said. 'Amazing, isn't it, the power of a cup of tea? Do you want one?' she asked.

'Yes, please. That would be lovely. Horrible tea at the hotel—a little too fancy for me,' Solomon said, returning his gaze to the pictures. 'It's really most strange.'

'Strange?'

'Well, yes. How the children and that old man have vanished without a trace. But I spotted a half-eaten toasted-sandwich lying on the floor of the kitchen. It didn't look old, if you ask me. I reckon it was discarded quite recently. Bread like that has a habit of hardening overnight and this slice seemed quite edible.'

'They call those sandwiches *empses*,' Sue said. 'Stands for *Mrs. Pye's Specials*.

It's the de Lowe staple food when they're hungry—more often than not at breakfast. They're delicious—stuffed with cheese, ham, tomatoes and a poached egg. I'll try and make one if you're hungry, but Mrs. Pye's really are sensational. Have you seen Gus?'

'I believe he's somewhere upstairs, rooting around, seeing if he can come up with anything. A few odd noises coming from there. Scrapes and bashes, as if he's taken to moving furniture around. You might want to go and see how he's doing.'

Sue carried on through to the corridor that led into the kitchen. She added paper and kindling and then a couple of smaller logs into the belly of the range-cooker and, much to her joy, the fire spat into life.

Shortly, she opened the door, tossed in two larger logs, shut off the lighting vent, filled the kettle and set it on top of the range hob.

Wouldn't Gus be impressed?

She had half a mind to run upstairs and find him, but her thoughts turned back to strange old Mrs. Pye. She'd drop off a cup of tea for her and then go and find him.

She smiled at the thought. Alone with Gus at last. Sue plaited a section of hair as she let her imagination wander. *Was he,* she wondered, *at that very moment thinking the same thing?* Thinking of her? She smiled. *Of course he was.*

Sue inserted the whistle in the kettle spout and headed out of the door to rejoin the headmaster in the living room. When she saw him, she found he was comparing the portraits with the images he'd taken of the stained glass windows in Upsall church.

'Mr. Solomon,' she began, 'do you think there's something... you know, happening?'

The headmaster took off his glasses 'What kind of *happening* are you thinking of, Sue?'

'Some sort of end-of-the-world situation, you know, like Armageddon or something catastrophic from out of the Bible.'

Solomon sighed. 'There's no doubt our flooding and plague has remarkable parallels with ancient myths and legends. The question we need to ask, I suppose, is whether these things are in any way, normal. Events that come round as part of the general cycle of life—'

'Like a freak-of-nature? You think it might be a one-off?'

Solomon raised an eyebrow. 'Actually, Sue. No. No, I don't think it is,' he said, putting on his spectacles. 'There are too many strange occurrences, too many situations that boil down to something inexplicable and very sinister indeed.'

'Then, do you think the de Lowes are pivotal? After all, I dreamt of them, and I know Isabella had nightmares about all this stuff and Stone seems to think they're important.'

'That's what I mean,' Solomon said. 'Don't get me wrong, Stone can be a nasty piece of work, but he's jolly good at his job. He has a nose for sniffing out this kind of thing, an uncanny habit of finding the truth. He's going nearly mad with the overall confusion and his desperate lack of progress. The clock is ticking ever faster. Untold pressure is building on him in a big way.'

Solomon sat down heavily in Old Man Wood's chair, removed his spectacles and sighed. 'Look, I may as well tell you, Sue. The whole situation with the flooding and Ebora is steamrollering out of control. The Americans are going to drop a rather large bomb on North Yorkshire.'

Sue gasped. 'They're going to nuke us? Why?'

'The Ebora virus reached their shores a couple of days ago. It swept across the continent as night follows day. As our American cousins woke up, boof—there it was. Ebora had already made its mark. Don't you think that's a little strange?'

The headmaster stretched his arms out and rubbed his eyes. 'The pattern is continuing like this across the globe. An pandemic of global proportions. But I did hear just before we left that the rates of infection had somewhat decreased.'

'So, you're suggesting,' Sue said, 'that the virus *moved in the dark*?'

'Yes and no.'

'Now *you're* being cryptic.'

Solomon smiled. 'I think that it has something to do with sleep. My own hunch is that it may be about dreams.'

Sue's ears twitched. 'You really think so?'

'I know it may sound ridiculous, my dear, but I'm pretty sure we have to think outside our normal areas of understanding. I hardly dare say it, but our human mind is so programmed for a certain way of thinking that "out of the box" ideas are simply shuffled out of the way as if they are entirely insignificant. As a teacher I am, I fear, partly to blame. Our role is to bring children up to speed with the world we live in—to cope with the hustle and bustle of life on our planet. Anything out of the ordinary and we learn to siphon it off. We leave it to be discarded as irrelevant or slam it as nonsense. Do you have any idea of what I'm talking about, Sue, or does it sound like meaningless clap-trap?'

'No, I think I'm running with you,' she said. 'Just about.'

'Jolly good. Because I believe there are signs just about... everywhere. Tiny, abstract clues, so remote to our way of thinking that we cannot possibly begin to understand them.' He leaned down and picked up the portraits.

'Take these pictures. They date hundreds of years apart and yet I suspect they're one and the same thing, repeated over and over, as if they are a reminder—'

'Of what?'

'I wish I knew, dear girl,' Solomon said, examining the first and then the second. 'Now I'm struck by these rather interesting portraits. As you know, fashions change. Art, from the seventeenth century, has a totally different look and feel to art from the nineteenth century. And yet, looking at these, we find the same posture and the same background. It almost appears to be the same person. My guess is that these portraits are trying to tell us something.'

Sue peered at the pictures. 'I know it couldn't possibly be him, but you know, the nose, eyes, the kindly way he looks at everything. Don't those pictures remind you of Old Man Wood.'

Solomon leaned in and together they studied them. 'Sue, my dear, perhaps you're right, impossible as it seems. The problem is, we've got two days to figure this out and unless the de Lowes suddenly reappear and tell us what's going on, I'm not sure we've got the necessary skills or equipment—or time—to make a proper go of it. We're plucking at straws.'

'Do you think we're going to die?'

The headmaster smiled in a reassuringly head-masterly way. 'Yes, I'm afraid to say that I rather think we are,' he said. 'At the moment it looks very much like we're on a path of no return.' He sighed. 'Dying is nothing to worry about, my dear, because it is the one certainty in life—aside, of course, from taxation.' He chuckled inwardly.

'Our time may be coming a little sooner than we might have liked.' He shook his head. 'It is such a shame considering you and your friend's great abundance of talent. But enough of this depressing talk. May I suggest, that from this moment on, we absolutely believe that anything is possible. Agree?'

'Yes!'

'Good. With immediate effect we must throw away the shackles of everything we've ever been taught. Let's give our last few days our absolute all. Treat it like a fight to death!'

Sue felt better hearing a more positive tone. 'I agree,' she said. 'Where do we start?'

Solomon stood up purposefully and rubbed his chin. 'My suspicion is that this has something to do with a history that goes so far back in time that records don't exist—at least not for anyone to make sense of them. First off, let's try and find out if Mrs. Pye has noticed anything unusual—'

He was interrupted by the whistle on the kettle screeching loudly. Sue rushed off and returned with a pot of tea and several steaming crumpets. She poured a mug for the headmaster and another for Mrs. Pye. Armed with this, and a hot crumpet, she nipped out of the front door and around the foggy courtyard to see her patient.

A JOKE GONE WRONG

'Here, Mrs. Pye,' Sue said, putting the tray down on the table, 'a nice mug of tea for you and a crumpet, you must be starving. I found one of Old Man Wood's blue-coloured jams, bit of an odd colour for a jam, if you ask me, but I hope you like it.'

She removed the lid and sniffed it. 'Does he add colouring to it for a bit of fun, or is it some sort of weird blue fruit he uses?'

She handed Mrs. Pye the tea.

Mrs. Pye sipped as Sue continued to talk and soon nibbled on a crumpet.

'How's that going down?' Sue said, sitting next to her.

Mrs. Pye pulled a handkerchief out of her dressing gown pocket and blew her nose. 'Much better,' she said, before slipping it back in her pocket. 'And all thanks to you, little Sue. You're a kindly one, aren't you?'

Sue smiled. 'Well, it's a great relief to see you looking so much better. For a while I was pretty worried—what would the others say if they'd seen you in such a state, huh? They'd be worried sick.'

Mrs. Pye shook her head. 'They've gone a little in the head, you know?'

'Really?' Sue said, raising her eyebrows.

'Oh aye. I think everyone's gone a bit in the head to be honest. All these comings and goings, you know. One minute here, the next they've shot off. And then strange noises and the children pulling pictures down and making a mess and explosions. I hardly dare go over there. Don't know what I might find.'

'When did you last see them?'

'The children were about this morning. I heard 'em. Don't know how you missed them, unless they was taken—'

'But has anyone been here apart from those soldiers this morning?' Sue asked.

A little cry came from within her as Mrs. Pye turned away.

'What is it?' Sue asked quietly, moving in and holding her hand.

The older woman pulled herself together a little. 'Now then,' she snivelled, 'there was another person.' She shook her head.

'Really?' Sue said softly. 'Who?'

Mrs. Pye burst into tears once again. 'You'd never believe me!'

'Of course I would.'

Mrs. Pye shook her head. 'But he wouldn't have taken them. Couldn't have.'

'Who?'

'That boy... my—'

'Which boy?' Sue said, confused.

'My son,' she squealed. 'My baby.'

Sue's mind raced. 'Are you alright, Mrs. P? Do you... do you want to lie down?'

Mrs. Pye squeezed Sue's hand tight. 'My child came to me, Sue. He did, really. Then he left—but he couldn't have taken the others with him. He didn't mean no harm. Just wanted to see me. Tell me he knew.'

'Knew what?' Sue repeated.

'That I was his ...'

'His, what?' Sue said.

'You know... mother,' Mrs. Pye said through her tears. 'That I was his—'

Sue reeled '... Mother?' she repeated.

'I always thought there might have been a child. But, you know, the accident and all that.'

Sue remained baffled. 'Are you sure? Are you sure it wasn't a ghost or something like that?'

'Don't be silly,' Mrs. Pye said. 'I know perfectly well who it was.'

'You *know* him?'

'Ooh, yes dear. Archie's friend. Don't think you girls like him so much.'

'*Don't like him?*' she said in amazement.

Sue leant back and studied her. Thick hair, fat lips.

Mrs. Pye looked up from her light blue, piggy eyes. 'You call him Kemp?' she said.

But Sue knew Kemp was miles away at Swinton Park. 'Kemp?'

Mrs. Pye nodded. 'That's the one.'

Sue shook her head, baffled, when all of a sudden the mist lifted.

'*Oh, Kemp!*' she laughed. 'But *that* Kemp only arrived by boat an hour or so ago, with me and the headmaster.'

How sweet that Gus had gone to see her first... but then again, how incredibly nuts to tell her he was her son. Why would he do that?

Sue shook her head. 'Look, I'll let you in on a secret. That Kemp is actually called Williams. Gus Williams.' And then she added because she couldn't resist it. 'My boyfriend.'

Mrs. Pye pulled her handkerchief out once more and sobbed into it.

Sue thought the whole thing most peculiar. Was Mrs. Pye confused? Was Gus confused?

Perhaps she should find Gus and ask him if he'd been over here being Kemp. And if so, that his joke had misfired badly.

FIGHT TO THE DEATH

'Surprised? Yeah, I bet you're bloody surprised!' Kemp said.

Gus took a step back. 'What are you doing here... you're not part of this, are you?'

Kemp sighed and sat down at the chair by the desk. 'Well, Williams, you could say I got here... by accident.'

'What happened to your head?' Gus asked.

Kemp ran a hand over his white cranium. 'Burnt off... it's a long story,' Kemp said, and smiled his fake, fat smile. 'Let's just say I had a lucky escape.'

'From what?'

'Death, I suppose,' he said, lifting his eyes to meet Gus'.

Gus suspected something fishy. 'What are you doing... what do you want?'

Kemp wiped his nose with the back of his hand. 'To be honest,' he began, 'it wasn't you I was hoping to find.'

'Who, then?' Gus said, confused. 'Archie?'

'Nah. The de Lowe's are a bit indisposed at the minute. Eating for their very lives.' He grinned. 'It's quite possible they'll never be seen again.'

Gus screwed up his face. 'I don't understand. Have you done something to them?'

'Me? No! Look, there's no way you could possibly understand,' Kemp said. 'It's none of your business.' He puckered his lips. 'Thing is, Williams, what exactly are *you* doing here, rummaging about Isabella de Lowes' bedroom like a perv?'

'I'm with Sue and the headmaster,' he replied coolly. 'We've been sent by the authorities to help find the de Lowes. They're in trouble but no one seems to know what it is. You know where they are?'

'Yeah, 'course I do,' Kemp said, thickly. 'To be honest, there isn't much I don't know.'

'Then tell me!'

'They're locked in a small room, not too far from here,' Kemp volunteered, 'until they work something out.'

Gus looked confused. 'How do you know all this?'

'I have an... associate, who's pretty worldly—'

'Worldly? I thought you were stuck in the hospital, burnt—'

'I was,' Kemp interrupted. 'But my companion had a change of heart.'

'Who is this guy?'

'He's an old man, that's all you need to know—'

Gus looked quizzically at Kemp. 'Hey! I know—I saw you,' he said, jabbing a finger at Kemp. 'You and an old man in the alleyway moments before the storm broke.' He rubbed his hands as he remembered. 'Weren't you? Someone in a long coat and a hat.'

Kemp leaned in and tapped his nose. 'As I was saying, Williams, it's really none of your business.'

An awkward silence fell between them.

'So, if you're not here for Archie,' Gus started, 'and you're not here for the de Lowes, you're here to see the headmaster, right?'

Kemp chuckled. 'Oh yeah. Hilarious. Nope, wrong again. I'm here for more... personal reasons.'

'To see Old Man Wood?'

Kemp shook his head. 'No, you daft, lanky git,' he said. He was enjoying Gus' confusion. 'Not old man whatshisface.'

'Then who?'

'I'm here to get Sue,' he said bluntly. 'You know, sexy Sue, best mate of freak-of-nature, Isabella-de-bleeding-Lowe.'

Gus' jaw dropped, and for a brief moment his brain froze as if he'd eaten a tub of ice-cream. *Had he heard that right?*

'I'm sorry,' he said at long last, 'you said, *get* Sue. What, exactly, are you talking about?' His fingers were shaking.

'Precisely that.' Kemp creased an eyebrow. 'You got a problem with it?'

Gus composed himself. 'What,' he said slowly, trying to mask his growing anger, 'makes you think Sue would be in any way interested in you?'

'Aha. Finally, a decent question, Mr. Williams. You see, this little union I'm going to propose, is based entirely on a lack of rival suitors.'

'Union? Lack of rivals?' Gus felt himself perspiring.

'Yeah.'

'Why?'

'Jeez, Williams. Don't tell me you haven't worked it out?'

Gus shrugged. 'This disease thing?'

Kemp raised an eyebrow. 'You're finally getting there,' he said. 'It's going to kill everyone, except me and Sue.'

Gus shook his head. 'But I still don't think she'll go with you, Kemp. She totally hates your guts—'

'I didn't say she would. That's why I said I'm going to *take* her.'

Gus felt winded. 'But she's going out with me,' he said softly. 'She's not yours to take—'

'Oh dear, oh dear. Is that right?' Kemp leered back. 'Unlucky.'

The curtain swished out of the way.

'The thing is,' said a much deeper and rather croaky voice to the other side of him, 'you're all going to die.'

'Bloody-nora!' Gus said, jumping out of his skin. '*What the ...*'

'Oh,' Kemp said. 'Meet my... associate. He's a ghost.'

Gus glanced around nervously as the voice started again.

'He'll be doing her a favour, you know.' The ghost parted the curtain and reappeared moments later wearing an overcoat and hat.

Gus gasped. 'What... who... are you?'

'I'm a spirit, and this young man has become my flesh and blood. Come on, boy, there's no time to lose.'

Gus tried to compose himself. 'You won't be able to take her with you,' he said. 'She'd rather die than go with you. I know her better than anyone. Trust me, Kemp.'

Kemp tutted. 'Thing is, Williams, you won't be any good to her when you're dead. Because, in a couple of days, everything here will be dead or dying and there's nothing you'll be able to do about it.'

'You don't know her!' he spat.

Kemp smiled his fat, cheesy, smug smile. 'You're missing the point,' he said coolly. 'I don't *have* to!'

'She won't do it!'

'Then I'll quite simply scoop her up, kicking and screaming. Like up a little dolly. It's as simple as that. You see, Gus, I'm going to need a woman to start a family, a very, very big family. Have loads of kids and all that.' He smiled, delighted by the agony it must be giving Williams.

'You'll do it over my dead body,' Gus roared.

'Very well. That's easily arranged. Look, I hate to break it to you, Williams, but like it or not, Sue's going to be, like, my very own *Eve*. After the annihilation of the planet, together, we're going to repopulate the world.'

Gus looked on in astonishment as Kemp casually walked over to the ghost and pushed an arm down the coat. First his legs and then his left hand morphed into a curious material.

Dust fell to the floor. Ash?

A terrible fury tore through Gus. Before he knew what he was doing, he hurled himself at Kemp, his hands going directly for his throat, crushing Kemp's windpipe.

Kemp gargled and tried to fight back but, being made of ash, his punches to Gus' midriff came to nothing more than puffs of dust.

Gus squeezed harder, gritting his teeth.

Kemp's face reddened and he fell to his knees.

'*Let go of him,*' the ghost's voice ordered.

'NO,' Gus roared, 'unless he promises not to touch Sue.'

As the ash leached up Kemp's body towards his neck, Gus was finding it increasingly difficult for his hands to stay attached. Ash flew about as though scattered by an electric fan.

Kemp floundered and Cain could feel his suffering.

'HALT!' the ghost cried out. 'This helps no one.'

Gus snarled. 'As I said, NO!'

'I will make you an offer—'

'Not good enough. Promise me—'

'Promises do not exist. I will make you the very best next thing: an offer,' Cain said. 'But only if you release him now.'

'Help!' Kemp croaked, his head puce.

Gus released Kemp and, as he did, Kemp's body crashed to the floor. Moments later, the ghost stood next to Gus watching Kemp fighting for breath.

The ghost's hat tilted upwards. 'You have no idea what you've just got yourself into.'

The tense figure of Gus stood shaking, staring alternately at Kemp and then at the ghost.

'What is your name?' the ghost barked.

'Gus.'

'Gus,' the ghost repeated. 'Good. I cannot be doing with a weakling as my companion. You have given yourself a chance to save yourself. And you may be a better match than this boy, although he does have certain qualities I admire.'

'Tell me your offer,' Gus panted. 'But before that, tell me who you are!'

'I am the ghost of Cain. I cannot die but my power was removed and my flesh stripped from me. I exist as a spirit and I am the Master of Havilah and soon to be ruler of the universe. Is that sufficient?'

Gus said nothing.

'Here's my offer—'

'Let me kill him,' Kemp said, hoarsely.

'No. In matters like this,' Cain said, 'it is important to keep one's word. However, only one of you can come along.' He addressed Kemp. 'The boy bested you. He deserves a chance.'

'A chance?'

'To survive, boy.'

'What sort of chance?' Kemp's voice hinted on nerves.

'One of you must die.'

'*Die?*' both boys repeated.

'Indeed. You will fight each other in a fight to the death. The winner comes with me and brings the "hot" girl named Sue.'

'To the death?' Gus said, shaken.

'There is no room for another.'

Gus whimpered.

'Just one winner,' Cain said. 'But you must willingly, with all your heart, and with all your soul, agree to come with me—or the deal's off. You agree?'

Kemp sat on the floor, caressing his neck. His face was purple with rage. 'I know this freak, Cain. He'll never do it—he'll never, ever, go with you,' Kemp croaked. 'He doesn't have the balls—'

'Do what?' Gus fired back. 'Go with who?'

Kemp coughed. 'Look, Williams. You have to give yourself freely to the ghost. When you're combined, he's the one in control and, believe me, he's a freaking maniac. My advice to you, Williams, is don't do it. It's one step too far.'

'But it's alright for you is it, Kemp?'

'Listen to what the ghost said: you don't know what you've got yourself in to. I promise you, Williams, for you, death would be better.'

Gus shook. 'Why do you say this?'

'Because it's true. You're giving your soul to the devil, Gus. You'd be better off dying rather than suffer what he has to offer.'

Cain tutted from under his hat. 'Well, well, well, boy. What a dramatic speech. Who knows,' he said drily, 'Gus has earned the choice, and it is a simple one; do nothing and die helplessly in the oncoming destruction of the planet. Or kill you and spend the rest of his life ruling all the known worlds with me, alongside a girl he clearly cares very deeply for.'

Cain paused. 'Personally, I think my offer is rather a good one; I know which one I'd choose. What do you think, Gus? It must be tempting? And, of course there would be so many fewer relationship issues for me to deal with.'

The ghost turned towards Gus. 'Therefore I offer myself to him right now to discover what lies ahead.'

It took a couple of moments before Kemp clicked. 'But... you can't—what about me?'

'Be quiet, boy,' Cain snapped. 'As I said, Gus has earned the right to give our union a try. If he prefers death, then he cannot complain that he never had a fair chance.'

Gus quaked. 'What do I—?'

'Willingly put the coat on,' Kemp said, reluctantly. 'Like I was doing when you went for me. But don't struggle. Then put on the hat. Close your eyes as the feeling moves up into your head. You'll get a wicked burning feeling, so relax and don't fight it. Take a good look at my baldy head if you want proof of what happens when you struggle. Got it?'

'Sure,' Gus said.

'How else do you think I ended up in hospital covered in burns, huh?'

Gus stared at his foe.

Kemp grinned. 'It was by way of this lunatic.'

Gus examined Kemp. He hesitated.

'Look,' the ghost said, sounding a bit bored, 'if you cannot freely join with me then there is no contest. You, my old friend, win. It's as easy as that.'

'Wait,' Gus said. 'I need to think—'

'Sorry, there's no time for any of that,' the ghost crowed. 'It's now or never. Come along, Kemp.'

Kemp stood up and rubbed his neck. 'I didn't think you could,' he jibed. 'Always been just a little too much like a chicken.'

In a flash, Gus moved in front of Kemp.

Then, looking Kemp straight in the eye, he thrust one arm down the coat's sleeve-hole and, without delay, the other. His eyes rolled back and he squeezed out a long groan.

Now, the cold treacle-effect coursed through his body, along every vein and artery and down every sinew and fibre in him, thrilling him.

Kemp closed in.

'Keep away,' the ghost barked. 'We won't be gone long.'

Gus groaned ever more as the cold liquid rounded his brain.

'Dreamspinner, dreamspinner, dreamspinner,' Cain barked into the air.

'You're not going,' Kemp said desperately. 'You can't leave me here.'

'Of course we are. I have to show the boy what he would be missing. It wouldn't be fair otherwise.'

Two dreamspinners appeared out of the sky.

'Back to Havilah, right away,' he barked, and, using Gus' body, Cain bent down.

'You know,' he said to Kemp, 'it might not be a bad idea to be friendly to this "hot" girl. Trust me. You will never have a more opportune time to try.'

And with that, Cain and Gus dived off through the maghole of the dreamspinner and vanished in a tiny flash of light.

Silence filled the room. Kemp scanned the attic, the floor of which lay covered in ash.

He heard footsteps starting up from the bottom of the stairs, creaking lightly at first, then louder, step by step.

'Gu-uss,' a voice called out.

Kemp squirmed. Shit. Sue. What would he tell her? The truth? Make something up?

'Gus, honey, where are you?' she said. 'Are you hiding from me, big fella?'

Kemp looked around for somewhere to hide. In Isabella de Lowe's bed? Hell. The bloody irony.

What was he going to do?

THE DEAL

Kemp thought fast. What should he say? Could he run off to see his mother? *His mother!* Just the thought filled him with such joy that a burst of love, of joy, coursed through his veins.

But what good was that now? He'd accepted an offer of a fight to the death, against Gus Williams. *To the death!* Kemp shook. Could he do it? He had to: if he won, he would have a mother—the one thing he'd yearned for all his life.

Sure, they'd give each other a kicking, a few punches, but... death. That was an entirely different matter. In front of him lay the currency of survival; the price of living, the ledger of life and death.

More importantly, Kemp thought, *did Gus have it in him to kill him?*

Already, in their short time together, Cain had done unspeakable things, but it was always Cain's doing, not his. Never his.

To Cain, every life was expendable and in their new arrangement he was the body, the muscle and he'd learnt that it wasn't worth arguing. Whatever Cain wanted, he obliged, and as such, Kemp didn't care either.

The experience was thrilling and powerful. With this attitude he felt like a king, a god. But this was Cain's hand at work, not his. When it came to his schoolmates, even if they didn't like each other, murder by *his* hands was an entirely different matter.

In two bounds he was in Archie's section, throwing himself on the bed.

The door opened. The floorboards groaned.

He heard her call out, rather sweetly, 'Gus?'

Suddenly the rings of the curtain pulled back. His heart thumped in his chest.

A gasp.

Whatever you do, please don't scream, he thought.

She stared as he moaned. He turned awkwardly in the bed.

She rushed towards him, concerned.

Kemp knew exactly what he had to do. He needed her sympathy.

He needed to fake it.

Make it look like he was a victim.

He rolled and cried out, as though in agony.

Soft hands rested on his forehead.

He groaned.

He smelt her as she sat beside him. A simple, soft, fragrance, like perfumed blossom.

'I'm sorry,' he said, sadness in his tone. He couldn't think of anything else to say. 'Please... please don't hurt me,' he added, for effect.

Her hand moved from his forehead across his bald head. 'I'm not going to hurt you, understand?'

He nodded.

'Is it you, really you?' she said, a puzzled tone to her voice. 'I don't understand. How did you get here?'

Kemp rolled over and faced her, tears in his eyes. 'I don't know... I... I stole a boat... walked ...' he stammered. 'No one was here when I arrived.'

Sue walked around the room. When she opened the curtain to Isabella's section, she stopped and kicked at a pile of ash. 'What happened in here? It's like there's been a fire—but without a fire?' she examined some of the marks in the ash. 'Do you know where Gus is?'

Kemp shook his head. 'Sorry.' He noted the disappointment in her face and pulled himself up. 'You... you survived, you made it.'

Sue came over. 'Ssh,' she said. 'Can I get you something? You must be starving.' She smiled and held his hand briefly. 'Mrs. Pye told me your news.'

Kemp flinched. 'News?' he repeated.

Her eyebrows lifted and she smiled sweetly. 'That she's your mother,' she said. 'I think it's one of the most amazing stories I've ever heard.'

Kemp smiled. He couldn't help it. 'Thanks, Sue,' he said. 'Look, I'm so sorry—'

'Don't—'

'No... I'm sorry about being such a terrible dick-head to you and Isabella. I've learnt my lesson.' For once, he meant it.

'That's really sweet of you,' she said. 'And it's all in the past. Let's forget about it, OK?' She smiled. 'Looks like you've been through enough to last several lifetimes.'

'Yeah,' he said in as affected a way as he could achieve.

Sue remained sitting on the side of Archie's bed. 'You sure you don't know where Gus is?'

'Sorry, I've been asleep... for hours, I think.'

'And that ash. Any ideas? It's like Mrs. Pye filled a bucket from the fire and dumped it over Isabella's floor.' She screwed her face up. 'Weird, isn't it? Thing is, I'm sure he came up here,' she said, scrutinising Kemp's body and the similar, strange-looking, dusty marks on him.

'Oh well. Gus probably sneaked downstairs at some point.' She looked into his eyes. 'Why don't you grab a bite in the kitchen—if you're feeling strong enough— tell us about your adventures? Someone in the hospital told me all about you. They said it was a miracle you survived, said that you were the bravest person they've ever come across. There's a pot of tea just brewed if you want.'

She turned and walked round the room, inspecting it. Then she headed off down the stairs, looking back at him before disappearing out of view.

Kemp forced a smile back, turned over and exhaled. *Oh hell. Little did she know what was about to kick off in this game of survival...*

Sue looked nice enough—exquisite, if he was honest—but the thought sucked on him like a leech that if Sue came with him to Havilah, he'd ruin her, like a group of school kids carving their names on priceless artwork with penknives. Besides, wasn't she just a little too old for him? Daisy would be a better bet, for sure, but how would that happen?

Kemp wanted to cry. He'd survived and found his mother, and he'd been prepared to die for that chance, so what was the point of throwing it all away now? But if he didn't take Sue, then Gus would, because Gus loved her and was prepared to die for her.

And, he suspected, that if it came to a simple choice, Gus would indeed kill him.

So, Kemp thought, if he was to have his mother and a girl, it had to be Sue and therefore, Gus would have to die.

And when that happened, it would break her heart, and it would break his heart too.

'You're staying here,' a voice said, out of the blue.

Kemp sat bolt upright. 'What? Cain? Is that you?'

'I said, you're staying.'

Kemp thought he'd mis-heard. 'No, I am not. I need to get out of here, with you, now.'

'A change of plan, boy,' Cain responded. 'You will stay here until the Heirs of

Eden—your de Lowe chums—either come out of there alive, or do not come out at all. You will prepare for a fight to the death with Gus. I cannot have both. There are fewer dreamspinners than Asgard thought.'

'I want to go with you,' Kemp implored. 'Girl or not—'

Cain sucked in a breath. 'You don't want the "hot" girl?'

'I didn't say that.'

'You implied it, boy.'

'I never—' Kemp thumped the pillow. 'I don't bleeding well know, do I?'

Cain's presence loitered. 'I sense confusion in your mind.' He sniffed the air. 'I sense that maybe you desire another. Perhaps it is the other Heir of Eden, Archie's twin. Hmmm. It is a better choice, but, dear boy, have you forgotten? That the Heirs of Eden are about to die in the chamber of Blabisterberry Jelly in a quite horrible suffocating death.' The ghost sighed. 'You will fight Gus at the ruin and you will win because there is something I know that you do not.'

Kemp drew in a breath. 'What?'

'Even if the children come through, the final tablet of Eden rests within the rocks of the ancient building near this house.'

'At the ruin? On top of the cliff?' Kemp said. 'But there's nothing there—'

'Beneath it,' Cain cut in, 'a structure is carved into its belly. Here, a beast has woken after a long, deep sleep. This beast, Gorialla Yingarna, the mother serpent, is my friend. We go back in time. She knows that the price of her freedom is the death of the Heirs of Eden.'

'What do you propose to do with this monster-mate of yours?'

'I cannot free it from its walls, for the ancient rules of the universe say that meddling directly with the Heirs of Eden and their quest will bring them imme-diate triumph. I do not wish to lose as I, like you, have a mother to save. That is why, secretly, I have chosen you to be with me, not that other boy. He doesn't have the necessary charm nor your warped sense of justice. Furthermore, he is more afraid of killing you than you are of him.'

Kemp buzzed at the thought. But if the idea of battering Gus to death filled him with dread, goodness knows what kind of state of mind Gus must be in.

'What's your plan?'

Cain, though invisible, smiled. Kemp felt it. 'We cheat.'

'Cheat,' Kemp said, 'Really?'

'Of course, you numbskull.'

'How?'

'I will show you,' Cain said. 'This way the pain will be easier for both of you to bear. Moreover, if Gus dies in, let's say, a terrible accident, where perhaps you are trying to save him, eventually Sue may, at length, give you her trust. She never needs to know there was a fight, or that we made an *arrangement*. You will fight

Gus at the ruin where there is a hidden entrance that leads into the structure beneath the ruins. I will point it out to you. Get him close and Gus will fall into the beasts' lair—a little meal for the mother serpent.'

'What if he gets me first?'

'You must avoid him at all costs. I will do the final flourish for, as you know, I do have an element of oomph in my ghostly being.'

Kemp outwardly exhaled. He could live with this plan. Once again, the ghost's scheming felt neat, tight.

Footsteps—a boy's, walking up the stairs.

Gus entered, rubbing his scalp.

'Some of your hair missing?' Kemp said, grinning. He sniffed the air. 'You honk.'

Gus raised his not-so bushy eyebrows. 'All your hair disappeared, so I don't know why you're so pleased with yourself. Or hadn't you noticed?'

Kemp smiled badly. 'Think you can handle it?'

'Yeah. Course I can. No big deal,' Gus said. 'Me and the spirit got on just fine, didn't we?'

'You did well, boy,' Cain said. 'Now you know how to dance with the devil. Are you ready to live with it?'

'Yeah,' Gus said confidently. 'When?'

Cain summoned Asgard and together they spoke in a low voice. Then his trilby turned towards the boys and tilted upwards.

His voice sounded victorious. 'The Heirs of Eden,' he crowed, 'are in serious trouble. Should they not succeed in their task within the next hour, they will die. In this case you will fight at noon tomorrow. If, by some miracle, they succeed and emerge from the cavern, you will engage with one another five hours after midnight at the ruin, as light breaks. It will give you a chance to say your farewells.'

'That's it then?'

'Yes. Time is running out for everyone. The end is fast approaching. One of you will live and the other will die.' Cain's voice lowered. 'Say not a word to anyone. Especially the "hot" one. Do not cross one another and do not be late. I will provide a weapon for each of you at the appointed hour. For my part, I am off to see the stage of your duel and speak with Gorialla Yingarna so she knows what to expect.'

Cain tilted his hat. 'Until tomorrow, boys.' And then he vanished, leaving his coat and hat falling to the floor.

GAIA REVEALS

Gaia, the dreamspinner, flashed from the corner of the cavern, in which Blabisterberry Jelly was causing untold havoc, and arrived in the attic room where Kemp lay in wait for Sue. She hid in a corner, invisible to the human eye.

Right now, the children looked as likely to fail as they ever had. And, with only two and a half days to go, Cain was spinning his web around them using the children's friends as his allies. Even as a spirit, Cain was a smart operator, but how far would he push the parameters of the unwritten rules?

Gaia inverted through her maghole and found Genesis. 'Mother, you seem better,' she said, walking towards her.

'Enough!' Genesis snapped back. 'We must aid the Heirs of Eden. The finding of Blabisterberry Jelly is all in the mind. Use dream powders to stimulate the girl.'

'I have done much already. I dare not meddle again.'

Genesis reared up. 'Gaia! Does Asgard care?'

'But we are different.'

'Huh! Do as you did with the old man. Dreamspinners do not want—will never want—dream-powders from Havilah. It is a nasty, short-term solution. Go now. Let the girl understand the true nature of Blabisterberry Jelly.'

Gaia inverted and flashed to the scene of foodie hell in the small room. In no time she was over Isabella, the dream powders invisibly sucked deep into her lungs with every long, deep breath.

There. It is done.

With any luck, she would dream fast, and then the girl will wake. As long as the girl interpreted the visions correctly, her understanding would be enriched and her choices clearer.

Gaia looked at the table and the foul, rotting beast that now sat upon it.

Blabisterberry Jelly grew in proportion to the time and struggle. She knew that at a certain point of enlargement, there came a tipping point, whereby one person's eating alone would not suffice. For if Blabisterberry Jelly suspected it could not be beaten, it would grow exponentially, quickly suffocating those inside the room.

By the size of the huge, decaying monster pulsing with maggots on the table, that moment had already been and gone.

ISABELLA COMES TO LIFE

Isabella leapt to her feet as though a bolt of lightning had smashed into her. 'I've got it!' she said, pointing a finger in the air.

Archie jumped. 'Bells! You're back! You OK?'

'Couldn't be better,' she said. She turned towards Daisy. 'What happened to her?'

Archie wondered if this was the same Isabella. 'Knocked out,' Archie said, 'just like you.'

Isabella whistled, picked her way across the foul-smelling floor and picked Daisy up. 'Come on, come on, little sis. I'm going to need your help.'

'Help?' Archie said. 'For what?'

'To eat that enormous banoffee pie on the table. I can't do it on my own.'

Archie exchanged looks with Old Man Wood and twirled his finger around his temple as if she were mad. They sat down as Daisy stirred.

'OK,' Isabella said. 'Now, come on. Why don't we all tuck in?'

'Because,' Archie said, 'the last time we tried, Daisy and I were propelled into the wall *and,* believe it or not, the wall won.' He raised his eyebrows. 'Between you, me and these four walls, I'm not sure I'm ready to do it again.'

'I am,' Daisy slurred, as she joined them, nestling her head in her hands. 'Beats death-by-maggot any day.'

'Excellent, Daisy!' Isabella cried. 'Come on then! Let's do it!'

'You cannot be serious?' Archie said, nervously.

'I'm deadly serious, bro. Loosen up,' Isabella said, as she held her spoon in one hand and kissed it in a mildly theatrical way.

Daisy picked hers up and tried to do the same but it went wrong and clattered to the floor.

'Leave that there, Daisy darling,' Isabella said. 'You won't be needing it.'

Archie and Daisy exchanged glances.

'This is how we're going to proceed,' Isabella said. 'I'm going to sing a song.'

'Really? You're going to sing?' Daisy quizzed. 'Do you have to?'

'Of course. I have the finest voice in all the world.'

Archie heard a small guffaw from Old Man Wood. He found himself staring at the floor to hold back the floodgates of nervous hysterics.

Isabella stood up. 'Now, it goes like this,' she began. 'I'll stand here in front of my banoffee pie and, on my command, you lot are going to line up over there.'

'She's gone completely mad,' Archie whispered.

Old Man Wood draped an arm around him. 'She's got a plan, Archie, and no one else has a plan, and we need a plan, and apple-fast. Let's see how it goes, huh?'

Isabella turned on them. 'Be quiet you two!' she said. 'The first spoonful is for me, then, the next one is for you. I can't eat all of that banoffee pie on my own, so you're going to help me. Are you all clear with this?'

Archie and Daisy swapped glances. 'I'm not sure we're allowed to eat yours. It nearly killed us last time we tried.'

'We'll see about that,' Isabella said. 'The difference is that this time, *I'm* going to feed *you* with *my* spoon.'

'You sure this is going to work?'

Isabella looked astonished. 'Of course it is! Do you think I'm crazy, or something?'

Daisy pulled a face that implied they did.

'Anyway,' Isabella continued unabashed, 'I don't think there's another option, do you? Now, mine is delicious banoffee pie. Yours can be whatever you want it to be. But you must say it out loud.'

This time, it was Daisy's turn to question her. 'Sis, are you totally one hundred and a little bit percent sure about this?'

'Of course! The brain works far better with spoken commands rather than concealed inside the grey matter.' She sucked in a massive breath. 'Now I want you to sing with me—are you ready Daisy?'

'Sing?'

'Absolutely. Follow my lead.'

Daisy nodded, slowly.

'Archie?'

'Er, yeah. I suppose.'

'Not good enough. Yes or no?'

'Yes,' Archie said, beads of sweat bubbling on his forehead.

'Old Man Wood?'

'Absolutely. Can't wait.'

'Good. That's the way.' She shut her eyes. *'Banoffee pie, banoffee pie, I need banoffee pie,'* she chanted.

She continued, a little more assuredly, clapping slowly in time with the words encouraging the others to join her. She cut away a spoonful.

'Banoffee pie, banoffee pie, I need banoffee pie,' she popped the spoonful in her mouth. 'Del-i-c-i-ous!'

Isabella pointed at Daisy as she chewed. Daisy came forward and opened her mouth.

'Duck pancake, duck pancake' she said out loud. The others joined in. *'I need a duck pancake.'* Isabella sliced a spoonful off and fed Daisy's open mouth.

'Mmmm.'

'Banoffee pie, banoffee pie, I need banoffee pie,' Isabella said again, quickly popping a spoonful in her mouth.

Now it was Archie's turn, *'Steak and chips, steak and chips,'* everyone joined in. *'I need steak and chips!'* Archie munched it down, a look of blissful surprise on his face.

'Banoffee pie, banoffee pie, I need banoffee pie,' they sang as Isabella scoffed on her latest helping.

Old Man Wood came up to the table.

'Starlight apple crumble with lovely thick cream, starlight apple crumble with lovely thick cream. I need starlight apple crumble with lovely thick cream,' they laughed, as their mouths struggled with the words.

He devoured the spoonful.

'Banoffee pie, banoffee pie, I need banoffee pie,' they sang. Isabella demolished another mouthful.

'Roast chicken dinner,' Daisy tried and repeated clapping her hands. *'She needs a roast chicken dinner.'*

Gulp.

And on it went:

Archie; *'Strawberries and cream.'*

Old Man Wood; *'Fish pie.'*

Daisy; *'Liver and bacon.'* (ugh, from Archie!)

Archie; *'Scrambled eggs.'*

Old Man Wood; *'Beef stew.'*

Daisy; *'Chocolate ice cream.'*

Archie; *'Spaghetti Bolognese.'*

Old Man Wood; *'A juicy apple.'*

Daisy; '*Chicken stir-fry.*'

Archie; '*Seafood paella.*'

Old Man Wood; '*A juicy pear.*'

Daisy; '*Strawberry jelly.*'

Archie; '*Orange jelly.*'

And they looked at one another, wondering if Old Man Wood might say *Blabisterberry Jelly,* but instead he said:

'*Carrot jelly.*'

'You're so weird, Old Man Wood,' Daisy said, and in the same breath, '*lemon sorbet.*'

Archie; '*Veg spring roll.*'

Old Man Wood; '*Starlight apple crumble.*'

After each mouthful, Isabella took a large spoonful of the maggoty-rat-banoffee pie.

After a lull in enthusiasm where the pace lessened, the children and Old Man Wood puffed out their cheeks, their tummies expanding.

'We're nearly there,' Daisy announced. 'A couple more each, that's all. She clapped her hands. 'We can do this!'

The noise level increased.

'*Fillet steak, fillet steak,*' Archie said. '*I need fillet steak,*' they shouted.

Isabella tucked in again. But she was struggling to maintain her concentration.

Archie noticed. When it came round to him again he said, '*Celery, celery. I need celery.*'

'Ugh. *Celery,*' Daisy quipped. 'Everyone knows Celery is disgusting.'

'... But it's mainly water, isn't it?' he said. 'I'm not sure I can fit anything else in.'

'Two more,' Daisy yelled. 'Come on, Old Man Wood.'

The children clapped repetitively. But Old Man Wood's brain had gone blank

'What is your food, Old Man Wood,' Isabella demanded.

'Hmm, there is something—'

'Another apple, perhaps?'

'Not this time,' he said rubbing his chin. 'This one's special,' he said with a big smile on his wrinkly old face. 'Yes, I know! Mammoth testicles!'

The children collectively looked at him.

'Mammoth testicles?' Archie said.

'Mammoth bollocks?' Daisy said, incredulously.

'Oh, it's an apple-tastic delicacy I believe I used to be very fond of.'

Isabella cut out a portion as the others clapped.

'*I need mammoth testicles,*' they howled, laughing.

'Last one, Bells!' Daisy yelled, 'it's all yours.'

Isabella felt so enormous that it would need a crane to move her. She took a deep breath. 'OK. Here we go.'

'What's it going to be?' Archie asked.

'There is one thing,' she said, eyeing up the goblet, 'that has to be the best thing of all—'

'Oh, no.' Archie said. 'I'm not sure that's a good idea.'

'Oh, yes it is,' she said, drawing a deep breath. '*Blabisterberry Jelly*,' she said. '*I need Blabisterberry Jelly.*' Her eyes sparkled as the others looked on with a mixture of amazement and trepidation.

'*I need Blabisterberry Jelly,*' they yelled.

Isabella gathered the last morsels onto her spoon, held it up to the others like a toast, and shoved it in.

'*Eurgh... Revolting...*

'*YUM...*

'*OH NO! ... Urggugh...*

'*... ooooohHHHH*

'*CRIKEY ... OW! ...*

'*INCREDIBLE!*

'*... No! Hang on... good! Oh YES!... no ...*

'*Blimey... Yeeeessss!*

'*WOOOOOWEEE!*'

She tossed her spoon into the corner of the room and wiped her mouth.

Silence filled the room.

'God, I'm full,' Daisy said, swaying on her stool.

'Me too. Don't think I can move,' Archie replied. 'I think I'm going to be sick.'

All four sat for a minute, digesting.

Finally Archie spoke again. 'Well, I'm not sure I can believe it,' Archie said. 'Tell me, Bells, what did Blabisterberry Jelly taste like again?'

Daisy hit him on the arm.

Getting up, smiles spread across their faces. Suddenly all four of them were jumping up and down, as energetically as they could in view of the vast quantities they'd scoffed, like a football crowd enjoying a dramatic win.

Suddenly it happened.

From out of Isabella's mouth the most enormous burp they'd ever heard burst forth, like the long, unwavering note of a French horn, and it continued on and on, producing a balloon out of her mouth that looked like a mini amber-coloured tent.

Archie laughed so hard that he had to hold his sides and for a moment thought his eyeballs might come up. Then he burped again, followed by Daisy and finally Old Man Wood, who looked deeply embarrassed, the noise a cacophony of burpy trumpeting.

Daisy clapped her hands. 'Put them together. Put the burp-bubbles together. Isn't that what we've got to do?'

Carefully they stuck the strange, floating, sticky bubbles together. Nothing happened.

'Are you sure we're doing this right?' Isabella said.

'Well, I don't know,' Archie said. 'It's not like I know anyone who specialises in this kind of thing.'

Immediately, a huge...

"POP"

... as though a massive cork had blown out of a champagne bottle, reverberated around the room, followed by a *"PUFF"* like a firework, with a plume of colourful, showy glitter.

And there, on the table lay a stone tablet, identical to the one that had come from the fire, with matching markings.

The stairwell they'd come down in the first instance reappeared and they dashed up it and into the dark, foggy courtyard. Collectively they drew in a large lungful of fresh air and, when they looked back, the stairs had reverted to a normal, grey-coloured paving slabs as though nothing had happened and the room had never been.

Archie was desperate to know one thing. 'Old Man Wood, we had to overcome our worst fears. Daisy hates dog poo after the slipper episode when she was little, Isabella screams the house down if she sees rats—or maggots for that matter—and those must have been the eyes of the blind Ancient Woman from my dreams. But who, and what, were those weird kind of spiders doing on your plate?'

'Hmmm,' Old Man Wood said, a little taken aback. 'That, littlun, is most observant. That spidery-thing you saw, if I'm not mistaken, was a dreamspinner. These aren't spiders like the ones that busy themselves in the corners of a room. *These dreamspinner creatures give dreams to living things.*'

'Dreams?'

'Oh yes. There's very little known about them—humans don't even know they exist—until now, of course. They're extraordinary, remarkable things.'

'But why do you fear them so much?'

'Anyone as old as I am fears them, for they know the truth of space and time. And if you must know, I had the same nightmare involving a dreamspinner spider night after night. The dream was trying to tell me something.' He scratched his wispy hair as he wondered about it, his frown lines growing deeper on his brow.

'You see, dreamspinners control what goes into your dreams and, in a way, your ability to think, create and discover. Dreamspinners put in the seed, the germ of an idea, or thought into your head, but then it's up to the individual receiver as to how it germinates—how it's interpreted.'

Archie's heartbeat quickened as he thought about the creature he'd seen over Daisy before the storm. 'So these dreamspinner things are responsible for the crazy, mad dreams we had?' he said.

'Certainly. Those dreams were almost certainly given to you by one of those spidery creatures I gobbled up!'

Archie shivered. This explanation was a little more complicated than he felt like understanding right now. He glanced over at Daisy who looked as if she was about to throw up. 'Come on, you lot. Time to get inside. I really need to lie down.'

More than anything though, a tickling in his stomach gave him the feeling he, too, needed to be very sick indeed.

A nagging thought toyed with Old Man Wood's mind: If Archie's "fear" was to eat the eyes of this blind, Ancient Woman he'd spoken about, then who did the other eyeballs belong to? After all, there had been *two* sets of eyes on his plate.

Old Man Wood searched the depths of his mind. Somewhere, somehow, he'd known both. One, a soft, nutty-brown set, with a look of yearning. The other two fractionally larger, with a distinct, icy, pale-blue madness about them.

Why did these warrant his attention? They were familiar—eyes from a long time ago, but whose? And as he wondered, he remembered something vitally important. Wasn't there something utterly crucial about eyes? Something brilliant and possibly sinister? Something magical that he couldn't quite lay his finger on?

Why, oh why, was Archie so desperately frightened of them?

A CURIOUS REUNION

'For goodness' sake, be quiet you two,' Solomon said. What a perfectly awful evening. While he'd tried to continue his investigations, Kemp and Gus Williams had been at each other's throats, their comments towards one another were acidic to put it mildly.

Finally he snapped. 'I'm fed up with you two,' he said. 'You're not helping me, or anyone. I rather hoped it might be a little more jolly.'

The fact that Kemp had turned up out of the blue remained Solomon's biggest shock thus far. Solomon knew that he had escaped from a toilet in the isolation ward in mysterious circumstances, leaving only—so he'd been told—a small pile of ash.

By his own admission, Kemp told them that he'd stolen a boat and rowed through the night across the floodwaters, landing—quite remarkably—at the foot of the cliff by the de Lowes cottage. It had to be balderdash, he thought. The soldiers used tracking devices for the crossing and, although it was do-able, the chances of success were highly improbable.

Aside from the general upset he caused Gus, Kemp appeared different: confident and more caring. The way he'd spent so much time helping Mrs. Pye out in the kitchen after he'd coaxed her out of her apartment. The way he smiled every time he looked at the strange woman who appeared happier than ever before. The way Kemp reached for plates and washed up without having to be asked. And then there was the way he smiled every time he looked over towards Sue. These were the actions of a young man almost... in love. *Perhaps*, he thought, *Kemp was in love with life*.

Solomon shook his head. By the look of things, one would have thought that Kemp, not Gus, was the loved-up partner, for Gus looked pale and withdrawn and, quite frankly, ill.

Was Kemp really flirting with Sue? But why so blatantly in front of Gus? To wind him up?

His thoughts were interrupted by a noise.

'Quiet!' he said, whispering hoarsely.

They stopped and listened.

'Ssshh. There,' he said, pointing his arm. 'Outside.'

The five of them, Mrs. Pye included, listened as the fire crackled in the hearth.

Yes... and now chatter, footsteps. A bang outside the front door.

'Hide!' Solomon whispered. 'Now!'

Sue, Solomon and Mrs. Pye edged behind the sofa, blowing out the candles that dotted the tables until only dim light emanated from the hearth. Gus and Kemp crept up either side of the big oak door, their backs leaning in to the plaster.

Jumbled voices, footsteps, laughter. A cough. A retch. Vomiting. More vomiting. Cheering.

Williams and Kemp exchanged glances, puzzled looks on their faces.

Now a hand on the door latch. It twitched upwards.

Kemp picked out a long wooden stick.

'What are you doing?' Gus whispered.

Kemp hesitated. 'You know—just in case.'

The door swung open. A strange head appeared in the dim light, dotted with weird spikes.

Kemp swore. 'It's a freaking alien!'

'Smack it,' Gus said, as he dived behind an armchair.

In a flash, Kemp swung the thick wooden stick down on top of the spiky head. But instead of incapacitating the intruder, splinters flew in every direction. The head remained quite still and then, with a growl, the body flew up, hands outstretched with such speed and precision that Kemp didn't have a chance. In an instant, Kemp was pinned to the wall, a hand tight around his neck. He gasped for breath.

Archie snapped the remains of the stick with one hand.

'Get off me,' Kemp howled.

'Who are you?' Archie roared, trying to make out who the person was in the dim candlelight.

'P-p-p le... eeese don't hurt me,' Kemp squealed.

'Archie! Let go of him!' Daisy ordered.

Archie ignored her and lifted him up off the floor with his one hand that was glued to his neck.

'Who are you?' Archie repeated.

'Kemp,' he whispered. 'It's... me... Kemp,' he said, struggling, his eyes bulging.

'Let him go!' Daisy shouted.

'Kemp?' Archie repeated. 'It can't be Kemp—he's in hospital. We saw it on the telly.'

Archie threw him to the floor and stood over him.

'Archie? Is that you?' Kemp said, rubbing his neck. 'What happened to your head?'

'Speak for yourself. What happened to yours?'

Kemp moved a hand from his neck to his bald dome. 'Long story, Arch,' he coughed. 'I'll tell you about it one day.'

Daisy marched over and offered Kemp a hand. 'Sorry about Archie throwing you—he doesn't know his own strength.' She scoured the dark room, her eyes lighting up like car headlights.

'Mrs. Pye, you can come out from behind the door... it's OK, it's only us.' She looked down. 'There's a girl facedown behind the sofa and someone behind the armchair. Is that you, Gus Williams? Come out now! I can see you.'

She shook her head. 'And... er... Mr. Solomon. What the hell are you doing here?'

Daisy's eyes started returning to normal as the people emerged, stunned.

Isabella walked over to the candles on the windowsill, clicked her thumb and finger, whereupon a flame, like a gas lighter, shot out of the end of her nail.

Gus, Solomon, Sue and Kemp backed off against the walls.

Candlelight soon filled the room.

'Oh heck,' Archie said, retching. 'Sorry guys, gotta go.' He barged past the bewildered looking headmaster and shot up the stairs, the sounds of his puking echoing through the house.

'What's the matter with him?' Kemp said.

'All that rich food at our... picnic party,' Daisy said, smiling at him.

Kemp smiled back, looking into her eyes. His heart skipped a beat. Her eyes glowed, like beautiful rubies in the fire. Kemp couldn't take his eyes off her. Daisy had turned exotic, almost divine.

The odd thing, though, was that Daisy couldn't stop staring at him and for the first time he could ever remember, it wasn't in a sour, hateful way.

'SUE!' Isabella screamed. 'Is it you?'

'No it's an illusion. *Of course* it's me!'

They both screeched in delight and ran across the room, embracing and crying and giggling with delight.

'And Gus?'

Gus, for the first time in a while, beamed at everyone with his wonderful, toothy smile.

'Oh my god. Our National heroes!' Isabella said, embracing him. 'How... what... how... did... it's impossible...'

'Headmaster Solomon can probably explain it best,' Gus said as Archie slapped him on the back. 'We've all come a long way in the last three days.'

The headmaster coughed and moved across to the children. 'Now, first off, please promise you won't set fire to me, Isabella, or see through me, Daisy, or get Archie to beat me up?'

'Don't worry, I'll try not to vaporize you,' Daisy said. 'But look out for Isabella's burps. I promise you, she has recently done the longest one ever. Definitely a world record.'

Isabella's face, even in the dim light had turned notably puce. Noticing, the headmaster roared with laughter, everyone else joining in.

Sue and Isabella eventually settled down on the sofa, Old Man Wood in his armchair, Gus and Archie on one side of the hearth and Daisy, Mrs. Pye and Kemp on the other.

'So, why are you here?' Isabella asked.

'Do you guys have any idea what's going on?' Sue said. 'Out there, the world is falling to bits and the men in charge seem to think it's got something to do with you lot—'

'You're the most wanted people on the planet,' Solomon interjected. 'It's a stroke of luck the entire valley is shrouded in thick fog, or several battalions of Her Majesty's armed forces would almost certainly be sharing this jolly scene with us.' His voice took on a softer tone. 'Sue is right, though, isn't she?'

Isabella's emotions suddenly got the better of her. 'We're caught up in a nightmare!' she said, wiping away a tear. 'A living hell.'

Sue cradled her. 'You're OK, though, aren't you?'

'Only by the skin of my teeth. I'm not very good at this kind of thing. The twins have been amazing.'

Archie shook his head. 'We have to do this thing together. We all bring different things. You won't believe how fast Isabella can run—'

'Or what she can heal,' Old Man Wood butted in.

'Or eat,' Daisy threw in. 'And burp.'

'There's a plague flying across the world, ' Sue said. 'Your hell isn't very far away.'

Solomon coughed in his most head-masterly way. 'I am supposed to turn you in to the authorities, directly. They want to know what secret you're harbouring. But I take it from what I've seen of you so far that there is something rather important you must do?'

The children looked from one to another.

Isabella piped up. 'We found some riddles which we have to solve. The deeper we delve, the more clues we seem to stumble across—'

'I knew it!' the headmaster said. 'And it is only you three who can do this—and of course you, Mr. Wood?'

They nodded.

Solomon stood up and began pacing the room, thinking. While he did this, Mrs. Pye took it as the perfect opportunity to make an announcement. 'Now then, you children must be starving.'

Isabella caught the others' eyes and together they burst out laughing.

Mrs. Pye ignored them.

Archie piped up. 'I can't speak for you lot, but we're pretty full, so don't worry about us.'

Mrs. Pye looked slightly irritated. 'Have you been eating behind my back then, huh?'

'Only a bite.'

'What?'

'It's a strange thing—you've probably never heard of.'

Mrs. Pye reddened. 'Go on. Try me.'

'Well, it's a funny thing,' he continued, 'called Blabisterberry Jelly!'

'Blabster-whatty-ellie?!'

'All you need to know is that it isn't as good as a Mrs. Pye Special,' Daisy said.

Mrs. Pye smiled, or grimaced. 'You other's want one?' She counted the nods from Sue, Gus and Solomon. 'Four emps coming up.'

'I'll help,' Kemp volunteered, following Mrs. Pye out of the room.

Solomon sat down and looked over the top of his glasses. 'You should know this,' he said rather solemnly. 'Unless there is evidence of progress, and that means finding you, a rather big bomb is due to land on this area.' He searched their faces. 'However, if you're handed over, I take it this would be bad news?'

'Extremely,' Archie said. 'We have less than three days to go.'

Solomon shifted. 'The same time as the bomb is due to go off.' He paced up and back, rubbing his chin. 'Therefore the question is this: how can we help you?'

'By making sure we aren't stopped,' Archie said.

Solomon smiled. 'Just as I thought. By the way, what on earth has happened to your head?'

'Oh! That's from when I got struck by a lightning bolt at the football match—'

'You think that's bad,' Isabella said. 'Look at these.' She removed her half-gloves and held her hands up.

Sue gasped. 'Holes? How come?'

'Another massive lightning strike. But I'm telling you, the science absolutely doesn't add up. Want to see something cool?'

'Sure.'

'Then watch this,' Isabella closed her eyes and pointed her hands at the wood basket. Suddenly a log hovered in the air and moved in mid air across the hearth to the fire where it nestled into the burning embers.

Sue swore out loud. 'Bells, where did you learn to do that? It's like you've discovered *the Force*, from *Star Wars*!'

Isabella laughed and winked at the others. 'You should see what Daisy can do! And anyway, Sue Lowden, where in hell did you learn to swear like that? At sea, perchance, with Captain Williams?'

Sue blushed.

Isabella pulled her to the side, 'Time to tell all, dear friend. And do not omit even the tiniest details!'

ONE HUNDRED NINETY-THREE

A SMALL REFLECTION

Stone thumped the desk.

So much didn't make sense; didn't join up. 'Let's check that camera you planted in the old woman's apartment,' he said to Dickinson.

Dickinson tuned in the receiver. The TV showed the blank wall. Dickinson fast-forwarded the screen, zooming through the footage.

On and on the film continued. 'Nothing, sir.'

Stone scratched his chin. 'Well, if they're not there, any joy from the shopping malls?'

'Most are underwater in the area surrounding Upsall. They'd have had to get out of the flood zone, and that's about a two hundred mile radius.'

Stone examined the screen. 'STOP IT—right there!'

Dickinson paused the recording.

'Back a little.'

'There!' Stone said. 'Forward a couple of frames.' He stood up and moved over to the screen. 'Can you blow this up?' he said pointing at a picture.

'This one?'

'Yes, Dickinson. The one in the frame. Zoom in on it.'

Soon the picture ballooned onto the screen. Stone clapped his hands and swore under his breath. 'I knew it. I bloody knew it.'

'It's a photograph of the de Lowes' parents on their wedding day, sir,' Dickinson said. 'One of the one's on her dresser.'

'Is it really, Dickinson. Look carefully, lad. Look very carefully.'

Dickinson peered in. 'I still can't see what you can, sir.'

'Try the reflection.'

Dickinson adjusted the settings and whistled. 'You know,' he said, 'I've been wondering where he'd got to?'

'Kemp?'

'Yes. He had to turn up somewhere. And if he's there, what's to say the rest of them haven't suddenly decided to make an appearance.'

For the first time in a long while, Stone smiled. 'Dickinson, time to get back there. And damn fast if you ask me.' He checked his watch. 'First light, fog or not. Understand? We've been way too soft on them. I think we've been played for fools.'

He leaned back in his chair and stretched his arms behind his head.

'This time, my friend, they're going to be in for a proper reality check.'

ONE HUNDRED NINETY-FOUR

TO THE DEATH

Gus hadn't wanted to leave Sue's side. When Isabella and Daisy excused themselves for bed, he hovered around until everyone had left. They cuddled.

'You need to go, Gus,' she said softly, stroking his face. 'You'll be alright on the sofa—won't you?'

His dark eyes searched hers longingly. 'Yeah. Look,' he began, hesitantly, 'I just want you to know something.'

'What?' Sue said.

He smiled. 'That I... um... well, I love you, Sue. And that whatever happens, it's been fun, really fun.'

'You too,' she said, her eyes sparkling, a cloud of confusion briefly passing over her face.

'And thank you, for everything,' he said.

'Go. You're turning into a soft little bear, Gus Williams. Away to bed, my Leo. I'll see you later.'

He held her hand and prepared to leave. 'Just don't forget me in the morning, alright?'

Her face glowed like velvet in the soft candlelight and he sucked in every sweet detail, every line, remembering it.

He kissed her on the lips briefly, shutting his eyes as though savouring the moment forever. Then he slipped away, down the creaking staircase, along the corridor, the main stairs and past the rugs lying at the foot of the stairs before collapsing on the sofa.

He wiped his tears and breathed deeply, trying to control himself.

He checked his watch. Midnight. Four hours of sleep, and he'd need every minute—if he could get to sleep.

Gus lay down and pondered the last few days, and the day to come. Destiny is a funny old thing, he thought.

He'd be dead by now if it wasn't for Sue. She'd saved his life. Now, he had the chance to save hers.

He thought of Kemp with her, kissing her, fondling her, and his stomach tightened. Nothing, nothing in the world, the universe, could make him angrier.

Then he closed his eyes and drifted into a fitful sleep.

※

Kemp lay down on Mrs. Pye's large bed.

What a wonderful, perfect, brilliant evening, he thought. He turned to look at his mum lying there beside him, a smile on her funny, snarly, scarred face.

She looked at him, he at her as they held hands. Breathing in unison.

Being with his mother felt as though a hole in his heart had been patched up: when he caught her watching him from a doorway, or staring at his hands or squeezing his shoulder.

Little gestures that spoke of a deeper bond, whose once loose ties had been sewn neatly back together again, gave him a new sense of wholeness.

And then, he'd talked to Daisy for what felt like hours. He'd talked about Archie, and he'd told her about Cain and the agony and the choice he'd had to make and how he'd been left in the hospital full of needles and drips.

They even talked about their animosity but agreed how amazing Mrs. Pye was. And he belly-laughed when she told him about Blabisterberry Jelly. And he had said things and opened up to her like he'd never done to anyone before. Not even Archie.

And she was hilarious and crazy and clever and beautiful and... he couldn't help feeling that she even... liked him. Yeah. She definitely liked him.

It wasn't a sloppy kiss, just a stretched out peck on the cheek that seemed to linger for too long—that kind of kiss. But he'd felt her breath on his cheek, her smell intoxicating, her hair brushing his scalp. A simple, perfect, neat kiss from Daisy de Lowe.

He grinned. It wasn't so long ago that she'd kicked him in the shin and he'd texted his friends to tell them to literally knock her out of the cup final.

He'd laughed about it, nervously at first, but when he reminded her that she'd teased him about fancying her, he felt himself blush. And she smiled at him and shook her head, and her hair fell wildly over her face and then she'd stared deeply into his eyes with eyes that reminded him of an erupting volcano. And, for the first time ever in life, his heart had raced, soaring high into the sky, fluttering like a bird.

And then he'd returned to the comfort of his mother's unquestionable love. Kemp lay back and stared at the dark ceiling.

And all this joy would vanish if he didn't defeat Gus.

He shut his eyes. From intense happiness to terrible despair in one brief moment. Wasn't life a bitch?

He clenched his fist. No way would he lose this feeling. Not in a million years. Not ever.

To keep it, all he had to do was beat the living crap out of Gus, and then follow Cain's plan.

A quick tap on the shoulder was all it took.

Gus woke with a start, opened his eyes to see Kemp staring down at him, his arm raised as though ready to thrust it down.

Gus panicked. 'NO!' he yelled.

'Come on,' Kemp smirked. 'Time to go—and keep the noise down.'

They stole out of the house, the latch clicking into place as the door closed behind them.

'We'll never get to the ruin in this,' Kemp said, waving his arms at the dark, dense, soupy fog around them.

'Then we won't have to try and kill each other like barbarians,' Gus replied. 'Listen, Kemp, can't we be sensible and not do what that creepy spirit wants.'

'Watch your words, young man,' said a familiar, deep voice. Cain's voice.

Gus reddened.

'I know it is hard to believe, but unlike everyone else on this rather dull planet, one of you has the chance to survive and flourish. The other will not.'

'But the de Lowes beat the weird food test,' Gus argued. 'How come you're so sure they'll fail? I mean, what if they do succeed?'

'They can't.'

'Why not?'

Cain sighed. 'Walk with me while I tell you.' Cain hovered forward, as a bright flame flickered into life at head height. 'Follow this, but keep close or the fog will swallow you up.'

The boys walked along, every now and then turning a little to the left or pulling sharply to the right. All the while, Cain spoke.

'To open the Garden of Eden, the Heirs of Eden must do unspeakable things—'

'But so are we,' Kemp argued.

'There's a chance though, for one of you to live,' Cain said. 'For them, success is so very far away.'

'Why?' Kemp said bluntly.

Cain seemed to suck in a mouthful of air. 'We are headed towards a labyrinth, built under the hills where the old castle once stood. In this belly of rock there is a beast that has only recently awoken after a very long sleep. The beast, there since the time of the Great Closing, does not wish to die. Furthermore it is angry and hungry and bitter and desperate.'

'Yeah? Big deal,' said Kemp. 'So what makes it so special?'

The light disappeared and Gus almost clattered into Kemp.

'The beast is the snake of the Tree of Knowledge. The same serpent who tricked humankind, the beast who rules half of every kingdom; the beast who penetrates minds and toys with them, bending them to her will.

'Her skin has never been penetrated and her fangs spray deadly poison, as well as fire and ice. She is both huge and small, and can disappear like a chameleon. This beast has slain entire armies and defeated hordes of ogres and giants, werewolves and ancient beasts.

'Sometimes, she is known as Satan or Beelzebub or the Devil. Her name is Gorialla Yingarna. She is the "mother serpent", the creator of valleys and mountains.' Cain paused, for effect.

'And your dear little friends will have to kill her to get what they need. Be under no illusion, the beast is a perfect creature, an organism above others and a lethal weapon. And to survive, the beast must kill the Heirs of Eden. That is why they cannot succeed.'

Cain moved on. The boys trudged after him silently.

Then he stopped again. 'And, even if these children do, by a miracle, happen to triumph, there is another challenge that they cannot do, no matter how high the stakes, no matter how many billions will die. They must kill one of their own.'

Gus felt like being sick. 'Really?'

'So you see, a new time is coming for mankind. One of you will be there to forge it with me, and one of you won't. Be assured, the one who fails now will suffer a death infinitely less painful and drawn-out than the gruesome death inflicted upon your friends. I almost pity them.'

Soon, Cain had led them to the ruin. 'Stand behind this rock, while the fog is cleared.'

'Who's going do that?' Kemp said.

'Gorialla Yingarna will burn it out. Both of you will have a stick fashioned from the root of a baobab tree. They are hard and light and can inflict terrible damage if used in the right way.'

The ghost left them, heading off alone and, moments later, a great burning, roaring noise like a furnace bellowed into the air around them. The boys ducked as flames licked around the rocks, the heat scorching their faces.

Then the voice called out to them. 'It is time, boys.'

'Are there any rules?' Gus said.

'No. You may do as you please. If there is no clear winner, Gorialla Yingarna will decide.'

The boys grabbed their wooden clubs and moved out into the main part of the ruin, the arena lit by two burning bushes.

They faced each other.

'Good riddance, Kemp,' Gus said. And with those words, he launched a furious assault with a turn of speed that caught Kemp completely off his guard.

DAISY HEARS NOISES

Daisy stirred. Deep in her bones, an ache remained, that would not go away.

She rolled over, then back again.

She sat up and tiptoed around the attic room, glimpsing the early light of dawn that highlighted the foggy cloud like dirty cotton wool.

Inside the room, Sue slept on the sofa, her snores gentle and then petering out as she moved her head.

Daisy crept back to bed and sat up, thinking.

Quiet.

She smiled about Kemp, reddening at the memory. He'd kissed her goodnight, or did she kiss him? OK, so it was only a peck, but her heart had jumped at the sensation. And she'd wanted to... but then … she blushed.

She closed her eyes and listened to the quiet. So still she could hear the beat of her heart.

Then she heard it; a strange talking noise. She shook her head as though something had climbed into her ear.

There, again.

She tuned in. Someone talking and then... Gus. It had to be. And now Kemp.

It couldn't be. She shook her head.

Something about death. Something about a fight.

But they were downstairs, weren't they?

Without hesitating, Daisy shot off and inspected the living room but found an empty sofa, the blankets discarded. She checked the bedrooms.

She opened the door and searched the building opposite. Still nothing. She stood outside in the murky light and listened.

Suddenly a roar, like a dragon, burst out of the fog. She stared up the hill, and now that she thought about it, a fleck of light made the fog brighter.

Goosebumps raced across her skin.

They were at the ruin.

She rushed in and grabbed her boots, coat and hat, closed the door and set off into the fog.

The farther she went, the clearer the noises. She ran and jumped and skidded as fast as she could, burning a hole in the vapour with her eyes.

As she turned off the track she heard it. Sounds of grunts and cries and moans. Fighting. Wood cracking on wood.

She moved further around, where she might see into the courtyard of the ruin and slipped between a tiny gap that separated two sheer boulders, an old hiding place she knew well from games of hide and seek. It gave her a perfect view. And from experience, she knew it was impossible to be seen unless from right up close.

Now that she looked out, in the centre, a small tree burned and the fog fell away like the edges of an arena.

Gus, his dark hair matted to his forehead, teeth gritted, attacked hard, smashing down with his stick on top of Kemp.

Her heart leapt.

Kemp managed to fend off several blows, then swung but without great purpose, turned and limped towards her hiding place.

She could see how his face was smeared with blood. A gash cut angrily across his forehead, reminding her of Mrs. Pye's scar. His lip split, his ear bleeding. He hobbled.

Gus walked behind, teasing him. Ready to smash him again.

Why? She thought. *Why were they beating the living daylights out of each other?*

Kemp rallied and slashed back, catching his upper legs.

Now, they were only ten metres away.

Gus held his stick out and, in a flash, walloped it down on Kemp's shoulder. Then, another blow, this time to the kidneys.

Kemp doubled over and fell. 'Stop!' he cried.

Gus moved over him. 'Sorry, mate,' he said, almost apologetically. 'You know the deal. There's only room for one. Only one can inherit the Earth.' He laughed nervously. 'And just so you know, I would rather have you die than for you to take Sue.'

Daisy pulled herself further into the crevice between the rocks. *Take Sue? What did he mean?* She scoured the area searching for something that might explain all of this.

And there it was.

Sitting on a rock to the side was a lizard the size of a lion, a forked tongue flicking in and out of its mouth. She turned back to the boys and when she looked up again, the lizard had gone. But now, she noticed, on the other side was a huge snake, like a boa constrictor, coiled neatly in a pyramid shape.

A cold, icy feeling swept through her. Was it one and the same thing?

Kemp ran, but Gus was too fast. A sickening thud over Kemp's back made him crash to the floor only yards from her hiding place.

Blood soaked his face, his head streaked with red.

Daisy winced. Tears formed. She wanted to do something but knew that whatever was happening here, it wasn't her fight.

Gus leant on a rock nearby. 'There,' he yelled out into the air as though addressing a crowd. 'What would you have me do? Beat him to a pulp? He's finished. Aren't you, Kemp?' Tears ran from his eyes. 'Aren't you?'

A cold voice answered him. 'Your requirement is to eliminate your opponent. No more and no less.'

Gus roared his disapproval. 'Come on! We're kids! Kids! This is barbarous. Is this what you would have us do, huh? Go round destroying everyone, like maniacs?'

Gus slumped to the ground and sobbed.

'The fittest of the species always survive,' the voice continued with a trace of mockery. 'The defeated never write history, so they never shape history.' And then, almost as an afterthought, the voice added, 'this sort of lack of killer instinct is why the Heirs of Eden will fail. Because they are weak. Because they, like you, are pathetic children. Show me your strength Gus, and you will prevail.'

Gus gritted his teeth in frustration and moved out into the open towards Kemp.

Daisy looked through the slit of stone at the prostrate body of Kemp. She bent her head and noticed a small rock in front of her foot, the size of a tennis ball. She worked it free with her foot.

Gus screamed. 'Come on! Please! Let him go... this is crazy!'

Daisy levered her foot back and kicked the stone ever so gently. It rolled over the stony ground and doffed Kemp on the shoulder.

She watched, wide-eyed, as, very slowly he craned his neck and for a moment stared directly at the gap, certain that his eyes met hers.

Now his hand rested over the stone. He raised his head again.

She could've sworn that he saw her.

Kemp lay still.

Was her action too late? Was he too far gone?

Daisy desperately wanted to rush out and grab him. Wake him up, but in no time Gus returned and stood over him.

'Sorry, Kemp,' he said. 'I really don't want to do this.' He raised his stick in the air.

Daisy couldn't bear to watch and shut her eyes.

And then suddenly there was a crunching noise, like the snapping of twigs.

Gus howled and fell to the ground.

They tore into one another... Kemp rolled on top and pummeled him once, twice, three times with the stone in his hand.

And there was Gus, flailing wildly, aiming for the throat, punching anything.

When she opened her eyes again, the two boys lay on the ground, blood streaming from their wounds.

Kemp was the first to pick himself up.

'Run, Williams,' he croaked. 'Go. Get out of here.'

Kemp eyed up the sticks and picked them up. He tossed one out of the court-yard into the fog.

'Piss off out of here,' he roared. 'Now. Anywhere.'

Gus stirred and dragged himself to his knees.

Daisy noted the damage to his face—a front tooth chipped, swollen lips, his nose flattened and bruised.

Kemp walked away towards the far end.

Gus following. Both limping.

Kemp kept on.

Gus tried to break into a run as if to catch him.

At the far end Kemp stopped.

She heard him pleading.

'Run, Gus. Please, leave me alone.'

'It's too late for that,' Gus said, circling him.

Kemp shook his head. 'No, it isn't. Gus, please.'

Gus smiled his big, toothless grin. 'Then you should go.'

Gus rushed him, but it was slow and clumsy. Kemp had time to step aside and crack him with the stick. Gus reeled, his feet unsteady.

Daisy's tears fell. She looked away and saw, instead of the boa constrictor, a monster, similar to the dragon in the stained glass of Upsall church. The dragon flew close to the boys and disappeared.

She refocused on Kemp, who pushed Gus away, but back he came, staggering like a drunk.

Kemp shrugged. Then, with a huge swipe, he walloped Gus in the midriff, and, as he raised the stick and cracked it over Gus, who toppled one way and then the other, and vanished into thin air.

Daisy shook, her whole body filling with grief.

Nearby, a deep, powerful roar was followed by the strange "bark" that she'd heard with Archie.

Kemp raised his hands to his face, let out a desperate cry and, slowly, sank to his knees.

AN OFFER

Daisy moved out of her hiding place, shaking.

What had she done? Her stomach knotted, her head throbbed with white, empty pain: This was her fault.

HER FAULT!

She thought of Isabella and especially Sue. Could she tell them she had given Kemp a weapon with which he had slain Gus?

Brave Gus who had escaped the storm only to be brutally murdered—and she hadn't lifted a finger to help.

Worse still, *she* was party to his murder.

Cain hovered over to Kemp. 'The deed is done, boy,' he said, quietly. 'You have won.'

Kemp stared numbly at the rock.

Whispering, the spirit continued. 'You have an opportunity to seize the girl, this Heir of Eden you are so fond of.'

Kemp looked confused, but when he turned, he found Daisy looking at him, from the other end of the courtyard.

His heart sank.

'Go to her now,' Cain whispered. 'Go to her and persuade her to come with us. It is the best chance you will ever have.'

'She will despise me,' Kemp said, drawing his sleeve across his face. 'I have done something awful.'

Cain slapped him across the face. 'Wisen up, boy. You can save her. Maybe not now, *but later*. She will go to a dark place where her life will hang in the balance. You have the power to offer her an alternative to death.'

Kemp cocked his head. 'Save her later, how?'

'All she has to remember, boy, are the words used to call the dreamspinner, Asgard. You know what they are. Asgard will know what to do.'

The corners of Kemp's mouth turned up.

He limped towards her.

'Daisy,' he called. 'Stop.'

She wiped her tears. '*Why?*'

'I didn't mean it. You know that... I had to.'

'But... murder?' she cried. She wanted to punch him.

'Because, Daisy, we're all going to die—'

'No, we're not!' she cried, her voice quivering. 'We're going to find the tablets —you'll see.'

'You won't. There's too much for you to do. Deep down you know it's beyond you—'

'Then we'll die trying.' She rubbed her eyes and faced him. 'That's all you need to know.'

'Look,' he said, 'there was only... only room for one of us. Me or Gus.'

'What are you talking about?'

'It's the ghost. He can take only one other, to be a part of him. Soon there won't be anyone left on this planet. Just a spirit, and me, and well, there's an arrange-ment. The winner can take one other. A girl. So it was a choice.'

Daisy glared at him icily. 'You killed him, Kemp. You're a murderer.'

Kemp stared at the ground and wiped his lips. Then he looked her in the eye. 'You helped me, Daisy. That makes you complicit. So you are also a murderer.'

She reeled, stunned that he understood her actions too.

Kemp's blooded face stared at her imploringly. He stepped forward. 'You don't understand. If Gus had won, he'd have taken Sue—'

'But *you* won.'

'Yeah,' Kemp replied. 'Because when I saw your eyes in the darkness of the rock where you were hiding, I realised I wanted *you*. I want *you* to come with me, Daisy—more than anything else. Nothing has ever felt so right.'

He moved in close.

Daisy noted the terrible beating he'd received. The mangled face, the deep burgundy cut across his forehead. She had a terrible urge to smack him and clenched her fists, but when he stretched his arms out to her, she reached out and took his hands.

'Come with me, Daisy de Lowe.'

Daisy stared at him and swallowed.

'Please?' he implored. 'I don't want you to die.'

Her lips flickered and she squeezed his hand. 'I can't,' she said. 'It's impossible.'

His face fell. 'Look, you don't have to come, you know, right away,' he said, bowing his head.

'I must go,' she said, knowing she needed to be back at the cottage. She turned.

He thought quickly. 'Daisy, your next task involves killing a serpent,' he said, stopping her in her tracks. 'By all accounts, it cannot lose—'

She hesitated. 'Why not?'

'Because it can be any reptile, big or small, with every power known to exist.' He shuffled closer as she tried to edge away. 'Listen to me,' he said. 'If you are near to the end, you must shout out for me. Call for me.'

'Call you?'

'Yes! If there's time, I will come, I promise, and then all of this... this craziness will be over. I swear it.'

The strange voice Daisy heard earlier rang out. 'Time to go, boy, with or without her.'

Kemp leaned in quickly so that his breath touched her ear. 'If you're really, truly stuck, if you're on your knees with nowhere else to go, there's one thing you can do—'

'Come on, boy, the light is growing, we must be away.'

Kemp winced and spoke with more urgency. 'Say these three words out loud. You'll feel a force field in front of you. Dive towards it—through it—thinking of me. You've got to trust me, Daisy de Lowe.'

Daisy cringed. 'What words?' she croaked.

He smiled and moved his cheek to hers, so that she could smell him and almost taste the matting blood on his cheek.

He whispered three words:

'Dreamspinner. Dreamspinner. Dreamspinner.'

And then, in a flash, he turned, dived and vanished into thin air.

... to be continued...

Go straight to Book Four, The Dragon's Game or get the Eden Chronicles Books Set - Books 4,5 and 6.

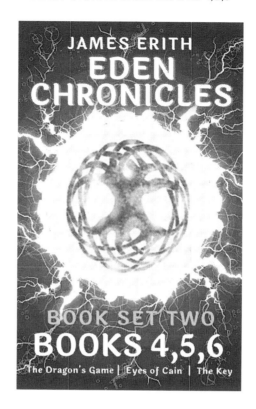

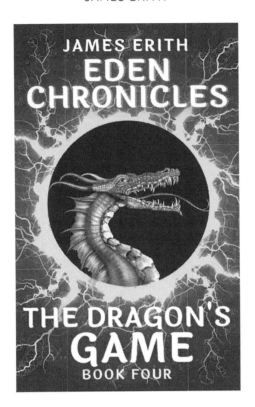

YOUR HELP MATTERS...

Dear reader,

I hope you enjoyed part two of my Eden Chronicles series. If you did, please leave a review! Any review will help me in my measly quest for world domination and, of course, to find new readers!

So please spare a moment to give EDEN CHRONICLES BOOKS SET 1 your REVIEW from the online version of the store where you purchased it. It's taken me ten years to write the series thus far, but two-minutes of your time would make every hour of that time well-spent.

I'm working on several new projects right now. Your words really will spur me on to finish my next words.

In advance, a very big thank you.
Best wishes, as ever,

James

AUDIOBOOKS

Eden Chronicles books are being brought to life by award-nominated voice artist Rory Barnett.

Rory's voices are amazing… check out his extraordinary range by grabbing your copy today.

The Power and The Fury and Spider Web Powder are available at most audio-digital outlets:

The Power and The Fury—audiobook

Spider Web Powder—audiobook

ALSO BY JAMES ERITH

Join my Author list to find out what's coming up…

EDEN CHRONICLES series:

TRUTH—Eden Chronicles Prequel—A novella. (ISBN: 978-1-910134-31-3)

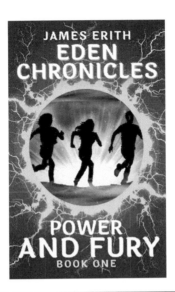

Power & Fury—Eden Chronicles, Book One (ISBN: 978-1-910134-50-4) The Power and The Fury, narrated by Rory Barnett, is now available in audiobook.

Spider Web Powder—Eden Chronicles, Book Two (ISBN: 978-1-910134-39-9) (Now available on Audiobook)

Blabisterberry Jelly—Eden Chronicles, Book Three (ISBN: 978-1-910134-22-1)

The Dragon's Game—Eden Chronicles, Book Four (ISBN: 978-1-910134-27-6)

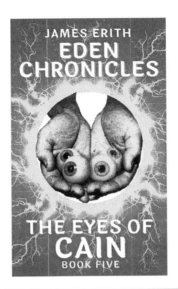

Eyes of Cain—Eden Chronicles, Book Five (ISBN: 978-1-910134-34-4)

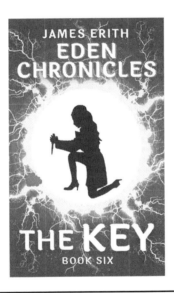

The Key—Eden Chronicles, Book Six (ISBN: 978-1-910134-42-9)

Eden Chronicles Books Set—Books 1, 2 3 (ISBN: 978-1-910134-17-7)

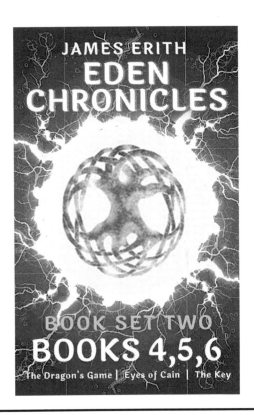

Eden Chronicles Book Set 2—Books 4, 5, 6 (ISBN: 978-1-910134-32-0)

TIME STAMP 2084

Set in 2084, and the world is a very different place; artificial intelligence runs everything; life happens through visual and sensual reality and the world is sanitised, and safe...

But has it gone too far? Are we no longer human?

Have we lost our soul?

When Virtual Reality holiday modeller, Bert Chalmers, discovers the ominous truth of their situation, he must travel back in time to halt the pandemics and the subsequent empowerment of artificial intelligence of the 2020's.

But he's not travelling back to the beginnings of the internet age as he thinks. He's off to the beginning of mass communication...

Welcome to 1840 and the dawn of the Penny Post.

But how will Bert, and his companion, Tor, find a way of immunising the population at the dawn of the Industrial Revolution?

Find out more.

Go to www.jameserith.com and find the Time Stamp header.

Due for release early-mid 2021.

CONTACT ME

There's a pile of good stuff about Eden Chronicles on my website and please sign up to my author newsletter for updates, observations and freebies.
    jameserith.com

..and drop by my Author Facebook page:
    James Erith Author - Give it a like,
    and follow me on Bookbub.

That would be ace.

Thanks for reading my stories. I look forward to meeting you out there...
    James xxx

ABOUT THE AUTHOR

Restless after schooling, James traveled and experienced plenty of adventures. He has been shot at, scaled Pyramids, climbed mountains, been through earthquakes, police detained and even swum with beavers.

James specialized in getting lost quite a bit, for example; in the Canadian wilderness in bear season, as well as experiencing hypothermia, dysentery, muggings, altitude sickness, thefts, a broken neck, desert breakdowns, etc.

Inadvertently these experiences set James to tackle a big writing journey. (If only he'd gone into real adventuring like old school-friend, Bear...)

In the 1990s James worked as a journalist for the financial pages of the Yorkshire Post, scooping the infamous Gerald Ratner; 'Crap' story.

James designed and built gardens for several years in London before upping sticks to a small village between the Dales and the Moors of North Yorkshire.

The inspirational landscape of bleak hills, old monasteries, and expansive views were an ideal choice for the setting of the Eden Chronicles series. James commenced writing the series in 2007.

Following a brief and rather embarrassing appearance on ITV's,"Honeymoons from Hell" TV show (fleeing a psychotic African safari operator), James became an extremely minor celebrity. Fortunately, this happened pre-YouTube!

As a youth, James had his sights on playing the game of cricket for England, but a long list of injuries and a genuine lack of talent forced the issue. However, a notable sporting triumph in 2013 saw James row the English Channel and the 21 tidal miles of the River Thames in aid of MND and Breakthrough Breast cancer.

James is a stay-at-home-Dad, a cub-scout leader and he retains his childhood passion for making dens, pitching fires, and tall stories.

james@jericopress.com

facebook.com/JamesErithAuthor

twitter.com/jameserith

instagram.com/edenchronicles

goodreads.com/jameserith

pinterest.com/jameserith

amazon.com/author/jameserith